RICHARD WRIGHT

RICHARD WRIGHT

LATER WORKS
Black Boy (American Hunger)
The Outsider

THE LIBRARY OF AMERICA

Black Boy, American Hunger, and *The Outsider*
reprinted by arrangement with HarperCollins Publishers, Inc.

The paper used in this publication meets the
minimum requirements of the American National Standard for
Information Sciences—Permanence of Paper for Printed
Library Materials, ANSI Z39.48—1984.

Distributed to the trade in the United States
and Canada by the Viking Press.

Library of Congress Catalog Number: 91-60540
For cataloging information, see end of Notes.
ISBN 0-940450-67-4

First Printing
The Library of America—56

Manufactured in the United States of America

ARNOLD RAMPERSAD
WROTE THE NOTES FOR THIS VOLUME

Grateful acknowledgment is made to the National Endowment for the Humanities, the Ford Foundation, and the Andrew W. Mellon Foundation for their generous support of this series.

Contents

BLACK BOY
(AMERICAN HUNGER)

They meet with darkness in the daytime
And they grope at noonday as in the night . . .

—JOB

For
ELLEN *and* JULIA
who live always in my heart

Part One:

SOUTHERN NIGHT

His strength shall be hunger-bitten,
And destruction shall be ready at his side.

—JOB

Chapter I

ONE WINTER MORNING in the long-ago, four-year-old days of my life I found myself standing before a fireplace, warming my hands over a mound of glowing coals, listening to the wind whistle past the house outside. All morning my mother had been scolding me, telling me to keep still, warning me that I must make no noise. And I was angry, fretful, and impatient. In the next room Granny lay ill and under the day and night care of a doctor and I knew that I would be punished if I did not obey. I crossed restlessly to the window and pushed back the long fluffy white curtains—which I had been forbidden to touch—and looked yearningly out into the empty street. I was dreaming of running and playing and shouting, but the vivid image of Granny's old, white, wrinkled, grim face, framed by a halo of tumbling black hair, lying upon a huge feather pillow, made me afraid.

The house was quiet. Behind me my brother—a year younger than I—was playing placidly upon the floor with a toy. A bird wheeled past the window and I greeted it with a glad shout.

"You better hush," my brother said.

"You shut up," I said.

My mother stepped briskly into the room and closed the door behind her. She came to me and shook her finger in my face.

"You stop that yelling, you hear?" she whispered. "You know Granny's sick and you better keep quiet!"

I hung my head and sulked. She left and I ached with boredom.

"I told you so," my brother gloated.

"You shut up," I told him again.

I wandered listlessly about the room, trying to think of something to do, dreading the return of my mother, resentful of being neglected. The room held nothing of interest except the fire and finally I stood before the shimmering embers, fascinated by the quivering coals. An idea of a new kind of game grew and took root in my mind. Why not throw something

5

into the fire and watch it burn? I looked about. There was only my picture book and my mother would beat me if I burned that. Then what? I hunted around until I saw the broom leaning in a closet. That's it . . . Who would bother about a few straws if I burned them? I pulled out the broom and tore out a batch of straws and tossed them into the fire and watched them smoke, turn black, blaze, and finally become white wisps of ghosts that vanished. Burning straws was a teasing kind of fun and I took more of them from the broom and cast them into the fire. My brother came to my side, his eyes drawn by the blazing straws.

"Don't do that," he said.

"How come?" I asked.

"You'll burn the whole broom," he said.

"You hush," I said.

"I'll tell," he said.

"And I'll hit you," I said.

My idea was growing, blooming. Now I was wondering just how the long fluffy white curtains would look if I lit a bunch of straws and held it under them. Would I try it? Sure. I pulled several straws from the broom and held them to the fire until they blazed; I rushed to the window and brought the flame in touch with the hems of the curtains. My brother shook his head.

"Naw," he said.

He spoke too late. Red circles were eating into the white cloth; then a flare of flames shot out. Startled, I backed away. The fire soared to the ceiling and I trembled with fright. Soon a sheet of yellow lit the room. I was terrified; I wanted to scream but was afraid. I looked around for my brother; he was gone. One half of the room was now ablaze. Smoke was choking me and the fire was licking at my face, making me gasp.

I made for the kitchen; smoke was surging there too. Soon my mother would smell that smoke and see the fire and come and beat me. I had done something wrong, something which I could not hide or deny. Yes, I would run away and never come back. I ran out of the kitchen and into the back yard. Where could I go? Yes, under the house! Nobody would find me there. I crawled under the house and crept into a dark hollow of a brick chimney and balled myself into a tight knot. My mother must not find me and whip me for what I had done. Anyway, it was all an accident; I had not really intended to set the house afire. I had just wanted to see how the curtains would look when they burned. And neither did it occur to me that I was hiding under a burning house.

Presently footsteps pounded on the floor above me. Then I heard screams. Later the gongs of fire wagons and the clopping hoofs of horses came from the direction of the street. Yes, there was really a fire, a fire like the one I had seen one day burn a house down to the ground, leaving only a chimney standing black. I was stiff with terror. The thunder of sound above me shook the chimney to which I clung. The screams came louder. I saw the image of my grandmother lying helplessly upon her bed and there were yellow flames in her black hair. Was my mother afire? Would my brother burn? Perhaps everybody in the house would burn! Why had I not thought of those things before I fired the curtains? I yearned to become invisible, to stop living. The commotion above me increased and I began to cry. It seemed that I had been hiding for ages, and when the stomping and the screaming died down I felt lonely, cast forever out of life. Voices sounded near-by and I shivered.

"Richard!" my mother was calling frantically.

I saw her legs and the hem of her dress moving swiftly about the back yard. Her wails were full of an agony whose intensity told me that my punishment would be measured by its depth. Then I saw her taut face peering under the edge of the house. She had found me! I held my breath and waited to hear her command me to come to her. Her face went away; no, she had not seen me huddled in the dark nook of the chimney. I tucked my head into my arms and my teeth chattered.

"Richard!"

The distress I sensed in her voice was as sharp and painful as the lash of a whip on my flesh.

"Richard! The house is on fire. Oh, find my child!"

Yes, the house was afire, but I was determined not to leave my place of safety. Finally I saw another face peering under the edge of the house; it was my father's. His eyes must have become accustomed to the shadows, for he was now pointing at me.

"There he is!"

"Naw!" I screamed.

"Come here, boy!"

"Naw!"

"The house is on fire!"

"Leave me 'lone!"

He crawled to me and caught hold of one of my legs. I hugged the edge of the brick chimney with all of my strength. My father yanked my leg and I clawed at the chimney harder.

"Come outta there, you little fool!"

"Turn me loose!"

I could not withstand the tugging at my leg and my fingers relaxed. It was over. I would be beaten. I did not care any more. I knew what was coming. He dragged me into the back yard and the instant his hand left me I jumped to my feet and broke into a wild run, trying to elude the people who surrounded me, heading for the street. I was caught before I had gone ten paces.

From that moment on things became tangled for me. Out of the weeping and the shouting and the wild talk, I learned that no one had died in the fire. My brother, it seemed, had finally overcome enough of his panic to warn my mother, but not before more than half the house had been destroyed. Using the mattress as a stretcher, Grandpa and an uncle had lifted Granny from her bed and had rushed her to the safety of a neighbor's house. My long absence and silence had made everyone think, for a while, that I had perished in the blaze.

"You almost scared us to death," my mother muttered as she stripped the leaves from a tree limb to prepare it for my back.

I was lashed so hard and long that I lost consciousness. I was beaten out of my senses and later I found myself in bed, screaming, determined to run away, tussling with my mother and father who were trying to keep me still. I was lost in a fog of fear. A doctor was called—I was afterwards told—and he ordered that I be kept abed, that I be kept quiet, that my very life depended upon it. My body seemed on fire and I could not sleep. Packs of ice were put on my forehead to keep down the fever. Whenever I tried to sleep I would see huge wobbly white bags, like the full udders of cows, suspended from the ceiling above me. Later, as I grew worse, I could see the bags in the daytime with my eyes open and I was gripped by the fear that they were going to fall and drench me with some horrible liquid. Day and night I begged my mother and father to take the bags away, pointing to them, shaking with terror because no one saw them but me. Exhaustion would make me drift toward sleep and then I would scream until I was wide awake again; I was afraid to sleep. Time finally bore me away from the dangerous bags and I got well. But for a long time I was chastened whenever I remembered that my mother had come close to killing me.

Each event spoke with a cryptic tongue. And the moments of living slowly revealed their coded meanings. There was the wonder I felt when I first saw a brace of mountainlike, spotted, black-and-white horses clopping down a dusty road through clouds of powdered clay.

There was the delight I caught in seeing long straight rows of red and green vegetables stretching away in the sun to the bright horizon.

There was the faint, cool kiss of sensuality when dew came on to my cheeks and shins as I ran down the wet green garden paths in the early morning.

There was the vague sense of the infinite as I looked down upon the yellow, dreaming waters of the Mississippi River from the verdant bluffs of Natchez.

There were the echoes of nostalgia I heard in the crying strings of wild geese winging south against a bleak, autumn sky.

There was the tantalizing melancholy in the tingling scent of burning hickory wood.

There was the teasing and impossible desire to imitate the petty pride of sparrows wallowing and flouncing in the red dust of country roads.

There was the yearning for identification loosed in me by the sight of a solitary ant carrying a burden upon a mysterious journey.

There was the disdain that filled me as I tortured a delicate, blue-pink crawfish that huddled fearfully in the mudsill of a rusty tin can.

There was the aching glory in masses of clouds burning gold and purple from an invisible sun.

There was the liquid alarm I saw in the blood-red glare of the sun's afterglow mirrored in the squared panes of white-washed frame houses.

There was the languor I felt when I heard green leaves rustling with a rainlike sound.

There was the incomprehensible secret embodied in a whitish toadstool hiding in the dark shade of a rotting log.

There was the experience of feeling death without dying that came from watching a chicken leap about blindly after its neck had been snapped by a quick twist of my father's wrist.

There was the great joke that I felt God had played on cats and dogs by making them lap their milk and water with their tongues.

There was the thirst I had when I watched clear, sweet juice trickle from sugar cane being crushed.

There was the hot panic that welled up in my throat and swept through my blood when I first saw the lazy, limp coils of a blue-skinned snake sleeping in the sun.

There was the speechless astonishment of seeing a hog stabbed through the heart, dipped into boiling water, scraped, split open, gutted, and strung up gaping and bloody.

There was the love I had for the mute regality of tall, moss-clad oaks.

There was the hint of cosmic cruelty that I felt when I saw the curved timbers of a wooden shack that had been warped in the summer sun.

There was the saliva that formed in my mouth whenever I smelt clay dust potted with fresh rain.

There was the cloudy notion of hunger when I breathed the odor of new-cut, bleeding grass.

And there was the quiet terror that suffused my senses when vast hazes of gold washed earthward from star-heavy skies on silent nights . . . .

One day my mother told me that we were going to Memphis on a boat, the *Kate Adams*, and my eagerness thereafter made the days seem endless. Each night I went to bed hoping that the next morning would be the day of departure.

"How big is the boat?" I asked my mother.

"As big as a mountain," she said.

"Has it got a whistle?"

"Yes."

"Does the whistle blow?"

"Yes."

"When?"

"When the captain wants it to blow."

"Why do they call it the *Kate Adams*?"

"Because that's the boat's name."

"What color is the boat?"

"White."

"How long will we be on the boat?"

"All day and all night."

"Will we sleep on the boat?"

"Yes, when we get sleepy, we'll sleep. Now, hush."

For days I had dreamed about a huge white boat floating on a vast body of water, but when my mother took me down to the levee on the day of leaving, I saw a tiny, dirty boat that was not at all like the boat I had imagined. I was disappointed and when time came to go on board I cried and my mother thought that I did not want to go with her to Memphis, and I could not tell her what the trouble was. Solace came when I wandered about the boat and gazed at Negroes throwing dice, drinking whisky, playing cards, lolling on boxes, eating, talking, and singing. My father took me down into the engine room and the throbbing machines enthralled me for hours.

In Memphis we lived in a one-story brick tenement. The stone buildings and the concrete pavements looked bleak and hostile to me. The absence of green, growing things made the city seem dead. Living space for the four of us—my mother, my brother, my father, and me—was a kitchen and a bedroom. In the front and rear were paved areas in which my brother and I could play, but for days I was afraid to go into the strange city streets alone.

It was in this tenement that the personality of my father first came fully into the orbit of my concern. He worked as a night porter in a Beale Street drugstore and he became important and forbidding to me only when I learned that I could not make noise when he was asleep in the daytime. He was the lawgiver in our family and I never laughed in his presence. I used to lurk timidly in the kitchen doorway and watch his huge body sitting slumped at the table. I stared at him with awe as he gulped his beer from a tin bucket, as he ate long and heavily, sighed, belched, closed his eyes to nod on a stuffed belly. He was quite fat and his bloated stomach always lapped over his belt. He was always a stranger to me, always somehow alien and remote.

One morning my brother and I, while playing in the rear of our flat, found a stray kitten that set up a loud, persistent meowing. We fed it some scraps of food and gave it water, but it still meowed. My father, clad in his underwear, stumbled sleepily to the back door and demanded that we keep quiet. We told him that it was the kitten that was making the noise and he ordered us to drive it away. We tried to make the kitten leave, but it would not budge. My father took a hand.

"Scat!" he shouted.

The scrawny kitten lingered, brushing itself against our legs, and meowing plaintively.

"Kill that damn thing!" my father exploded. "Do anything, but get it away from here!"

He went inside, grumbling. I resented his shouting and it irked me that I could never make him feel my resentment. How could I hit back at him? Oh, yes . . . He had said to kill the kitten and I would kill it! I knew that he had not really meant for me to kill the kitten, but my deep hate of him urged me toward a literal acceptance of his word.

"He said for us to kill the kitten," I told my brother.

"He didn't mean it," my brother said.

"He did, and I'm going to kill 'im."

"Then he *will* howl," my brother said.

"He can't howl if he's dead," I said.

"He didn't really say kill 'im," my brother protested.

"He did!" I said. "And you heard him!"

My brother ran away in fright. I found a piece of rope, made a noose, slipped it about the kitten's neck, pulled it over a nail, then jerked the animal clear of the ground. It gasped, slobbered, spun, doubled, clawed the air frantically; finally its mouth gaped and its pink-white tongue shot out stiffly. I tied the rope to a nail and went to find my brother. He was crouching behind a corner of the building.

"I killed 'im," I whispered.

"You did bad," my brother said.

"Now Papa can sleep," I said, deeply satisfied.

"He didn't mean for you to kill 'im," my brother said.

"Then why did he *tell* me to do it?" I demanded.

My brother could not answer; he stared fearfully at the dangling kitten.

"That kitten's going to get you," he warned me.

"That kitten can't even breathe now," I said.

"I'm going to tell," my brother said, running into the house.

I waited, resolving to defend myself with my father's rash words, anticipating my enjoyment in repeating them to him even though I knew that he had spoken them in anger. My mother hurried toward me, drying her hands upon her apron. She stopped and paled when she saw the kitten suspended from the rope.

"What in God's name have you done?" she asked.

"The kitten was making noise and Papa said to kill it," I explained.

"You little fool!" she said. "Your father's going to beat you for this!"

"But he told me to kill it," I said.

"You shut your mouth!"

She grabbed my hand and dragged me to my father's bedside and told him what I had done.

"You know better than that!" my father stormed.

"You told me to kill 'im," I said.

"I told you to drive him away," he said.

"You told me to kill 'im," I countered positively.

"You get out of my eyes before I smack you down!" my father bellowed in disgust, then turned over in bed.

I had had my first triumph over my father. I had made him believe that I had taken his words literally. He could not punish me now without risking his authority. I was happy because I had at last found a way to throw my criticism of him into his face. I had made him feel that, if he whipped me for killing the kitten, I would never give serious weight to his words again. I had made him know that I felt he was cruel and I had done it without his punishing me.

But my mother, being more imaginative, retaliated with an assault upon my sensibilities that crushed me with the moral horror involved in taking a life. All that afternoon she directed toward me calculated words that spawned in my mind a horde of invisible demons bent upon exacting vengeance for what I had done. As evening drew near, anxiety filled me and I was afraid to go into an empty room alone.

"You owe a debt you can never pay," my mother said.

"I'm sorry," I mumbled.

"Being sorry can't make that kitten live again," she said.

Then, just before I was to go to bed, she uttered a paralyzing injunction: she ordered me to go out into the dark, dig a grave, and bury the kitten.

"No!" I screamed, feeling that if I went out of doors some evil spirit would whisk me away.

"Get out there and bury that poor kitten," she ordered.

"I'm scared!"

"And wasn't that kitten scared when you put that rope around its neck?" she asked.

"But it was only a kitten," I explained.

"But it was alive," she said. "Can you make it live again?"

"But Papa said to kill it," I said, trying to shift the moral blame upon my father.

My mother whacked me across my mouth with the flat palm of her hand.

"You stop that lying! You knew what he meant!"

"I didn't!" I bawled.

She shoved a tiny spade into my hands.

"Go out there and dig a hole and bury that kitten!"

I stumbled out into the black night, sobbing, my legs wobbly from fear. Though I knew that I had killed the kitten, my mother's words had made it live again in my mind. What would that kitten do to me when I touched it? Would it claw at my eyes? As I groped toward the dead kitten, my mother lingered behind me, moving in the dark, her disembodied voice egging me on.

"Mama, come and stand by me," I begged.

"You didn't stand by that kitten, so why should I stand by you?" she asked tauntingly from the menacing darkness.

"I can't touch it," I whimpered, feeling that the kitten was staring at me with reproachful eyes.

"Untie it!" she ordered.

Shuddering, I fumbled at the rope and the kitten dropped to the pavement with a thud that echoed in my mind for many days and nights. Then, obeying my mother's floating voice, I hunted for a spot of earth, dug a shallow hole, and buried the stiff kitten; as I handled its cold body my skin prickled. When I had completed the burial, I sighed and started back to the flat, but my mother caught hold of my hand and led me again to the kitten's grave.

"Shut your eyes and repeat after me," she said.

I closed my eyes tightly, my hand clinging to hers.

"Dear God, our Father, forgive me, for I knew not what I was doing . . ."

"Dear God, our Father, forgive me, for I knew not what I was doing," I repeated.

"And spare my poor life, even though I did not spare the life of the kitten . . ."

"And spare my poor life, even though I did not spare the life of the kitten," I repeated.

"And while I sleep tonight, do not snatch the breath of life from me . . ."

I opened my mouth but no words came. My mind was frozen with horror. I pictured myself gasping for breath and dying in my sleep. I broke away from my mother and ran into the night, crying, shaking with dread.

"No," I sobbed.

My mother called to me many times, but I would not go to her.

"Well, I suppose you've learned your lesson," she said at last.

Contrite, I went to bed, hoping that I would never see another kitten.

Hunger stole upon me so slowly that at first I was not aware of what hunger really meant. Hunger had always been more or less at my elbow when I played, but now I began to wake up at night to find hunger standing at my bedside, staring at me gauntly. The hunger I had known before this had been no grim, hostile stranger; it had been a normal hunger that had made me beg constantly for bread, and when I ate a crust or two I was satisfied. But this new hunger baffled me, scared me, made me angry and insistent. Whenever I begged for food now my mother would pour me a cup of tea which would still the clamor in my stomach for a moment or two; but a little later I would feel hunger nudging my ribs, twisting my empty guts until they ached. I would grow dizzy and my vision would dim. I became less active in my play, and for the first time in my life I had to pause and think of what was happening to me.

"Mama, I'm hungry," I complained one afternoon.

"Jump up and catch a kungry," she said, trying to make me laugh and forget.

"What's a *kungry*?"

"It's what little boys eat when they get hungry," she said.

"What does it taste like?"

"I don't know."

"Then why do you tell me to catch one?"

"Because you said that you were hungry," she said, smiling.

I sensed that she was teasing me and it made me angry.

"But I'm hungry. I want to eat."

"You'll have to wait."

"But I want to eat now."

"But there's nothing to eat," she told me.

"Why?"

"Just because there's none," she explained.

"But I want to eat," I said, beginning to cry.

"You'll just have to wait," she said again.

"But why?"

"For God to send some food."

"When is He going to send it?"

"I don't know."

"But I'm hungry!"

She was ironing and she paused and looked at me with tears in her eyes.

"Where's your father?" she asked me.

I stared in bewilderment. Yes, it was true that my father had not come home to sleep for many days now and I could make as much noise as I wanted. Though I had not known why he was absent, I had been glad that he was not there to shout his restrictions at me. But it had never occurred to me that his absence would mean that there would be no food.

"I don't know," I said.

"Who brings food into the house?" my mother asked me.

"Papa," I said. "He always brought food."

"Well, your father isn't here now," she said.

"Where is he?"

"I don't know," she said.

"But I'm hungry," I whimpered, stomping my feet.

"You'll have to wait until I get a job and buy food," she said.

As the days slid past the image of my father became associated with my pangs of hunger, and whenever I felt hunger I thought of him with a deep biological bitterness.

My mother finally went to work as a cook and left me and my brother alone in the flat each day with a loaf of bread and a pot of tea. When she returned at evening she would be tired and dispirited and would cry a lot. Sometimes, when she was in despair, she would call us to her and talk to us for hours, telling us that we now had no father, that our lives would be different from those of other children, that we must learn as soon as possible to take care of ourselves, to dress ourselves, to prepare our own food; that we must take upon ourselves the responsibility of the flat while she worked. Half frightened, we would promise solemnly. We did not understand what had happened between our father and our mother and the most that these long talks did to us was to make us feel a vague dread. Whenever we asked why father had left, she would tell us that we were too young to know.

One evening my mother told me that thereafter I would have to do the shopping for food. She took me to the corner store to show me the way. I was proud; I felt like a grownup. The next afternoon I looped the basket over my arm and went down the pavement toward the store. When I reached the corner, a gang of boys grabbed me, knocked me down, snatched the basket, took the money, and sent me running home in panic. That evening I told my mother what had happened, but she made no comment; she sat down at once, wrote another note, gave me more money, and sent me out to the grocery again. I crept down the steps and saw the same gang of boys playing down the street. I ran back into the house.

"What's the matter?" my mother asked.

"It's those same boys," I said. "They'll beat me."

"You've got to get over that," she said. "Now, go on."

"I'm scared," I said.

"Go on and don't pay any attention to them," she said.

I went out of the door and walked briskly down the sidewalk, praying that the gang would not molest me. But when I came abreast of them someone shouted.

"There he is!"

They came toward me and I broke into a wild run toward home. They overtook me and flung me to the pavement. I yelled, pleaded, kicked, but they wrenched the money out of my hand. They yanked me to my feet, gave me a few slaps, and sent me home sobbing. My mother met me at the door.

"They b-beat m-me," I gasped. "They t-t-took the m-money."

I started up the steps, seeking the shelter of the house.

"Don't you come in here," my mother warned me.

I froze in my tracks and stared at her.

"But they're coming after me," I said.

"You just stay right where you are," she said in a deadly tone. "I'm going to teach you this night to stand up and fight for yourself."

She went into the house and I waited, terrified, wondering what she was about. Presently she returned with more money and another note; she also had a long heavy stick.

"Take this money, this note, and this stick," she said. "Go to the store and buy those groceries. If those boys bother you, then fight."

I was baffled. My mother was telling me to fight, a thing that she had never done before.

"But I'm scared," I said.

"Don't you come into this house until you've gotten those groceries," she said.

"They'll beat me; they'll beat me," I said.

"Then stay in the streets; don't come back here!"

I ran up the steps and tried to force my way past her into the house. A stinging slap came on my jaw. I stood on the sidewalk, crying.

"Please, let me wait until tomorrow," I begged.

"No," she said. "Go now! If you come back into this house without those groceries, I'll whip you!"

She slammed the door and I heard the key turn in the lock. I shook with fright. I was alone upon the dark, hostile streets and gangs were after me. I had the choice of being beaten at home or away from home. I clutched the stick, crying, trying to reason. If I were beaten at home, there was absolutely nothing that I could do about it; but if I were beaten in the streets, I had a chance to fight and defend myself. I walked slowly down the sidewalk, coming closer to the gang of boys, holding the stick tightly. I was so full of fear that I could scarcely breathe. I was almost upon them now.

"There he is again!" the cry went up.

They surrounded me quickly and began to grab for my hand.

"I'll kill you!" I threatened.

They closed in. In blind fear I let the stick fly, feeling it crack against a boy's skull. I swung again, lamming another skull, then another. Realizing that they would retaliate if I let up for but a second, I fought to lay them low, to knock them cold, to kill them so that they could not strike back at me. I flayed with tears in my eyes, teeth clenched, stark fear making me throw every ounce of my strength behind each blow. I hit again and again, dropping the money and the grocery list. The boys scattered, yelling, nursing their heads, staring at me in utter disbelief. They had never seen such frenzy. I stood panting, egging them on, taunting them to come on and fight. When they refused, I ran after them and they tore out for their homes, screaming. The parents of the boys rushed into the streets and threatened me, and for the first time in my life I shouted at grownups, telling them that I would give them the same if they bothered me. I finally found my grocery list and the money and went to the store. On my way back I

kept my stick poised for instant use, but there was not a single
boy in sight. That night I won the right to the streets of
Memphis.

Of a summer morning, when my mother had gone to
work, I would follow a crowd of black children—abandoned
for the day by their working parents—to the bottom of a
sloping hill whose top held a long row of ramshackle,
wooden outdoor privies whose opened rear ends provided
a raw and startling view. We would crouch at the foot of
the slope and look up—a distance of twenty-five feet or
more—at the secret and fantastic anatomies of black, brown,
yellow, and ivory men and women. For hours we would
laugh, point, whisper, joke, and identify our neighbors by the
signs of their physiological oddities, commenting upon the
difficulty or projectile force of their excretions. Finally some
grownup would see us and drive us away with disgusted
shouts. Occasionally children of two and three years of age
would emerge from behind the hill with their faces smeared
and their breath reeking. At last a white policeman was stationed behind the privies to keep the children away and our
course in human anatomy was postponed.

To keep us out of mischief, my mother often took my
brother and me with her to her cooking job. Standing hun-
grily and silently in a corner of the kitchen, we would watch
her go from the stove to the sink, from the cabinet to the
table. I always loved to stand in the white folks' kitchen when
my mother cooked, for it meant that I got occasional scraps
of bread and meat; but many times I regretted having come,
for my nostrils would be assailed with the scent of food that
did not belong to me and which I was forbidden to eat. Toward evening my mother would take the hot dishes into the
dining room where the white people were seated, and I
would stand as near the dining-room door as possible to get a
quick glimpse of the white faces gathered around the loaded
table, eating, laughing, talking. If the white people left anything, my brother and I would eat well; but if they did not,
we would have our usual bread and tea.

Watching the white people eat would make my empty
stomach churn and I would grow vaguely angry. Why could I
not eat when I was hungry? Why did I always have to wait

until others were through? I could not understand why some people had enough food and others did not.

I now found it irresistible to roam during the day while my mother was cooking in the kitchens of the white folks. A block away from our flat was a saloon in front of which I used to loiter all day long. Its interior was an enchanting place that both lured and frightened me. I would beg for pennies, then peer under the swinging doors to watch the men and women drink. When some neighbor would chase me away from the door, I would follow the drunks about the streets, trying to understand their mysterious mumblings, pointing at them, teasing them, laughing at them, imitating them, jeering, mocking, and taunting them about their lurching antics. For me the most amusing spectacle was a drunken woman stumbling and urinating, the dampness seeping down her stockinged legs. Or I would stare in horror at a man retching. Somebody informed my mother about my fondness for the saloon and she beat me, but it did not keep me from peering under the swinging doors and listening to the wild talk of drunks when she was at work.

One summer afternoon—in my sixth year—while peering under the swinging doors of the neighborhood saloon, a black man caught hold of my arm and dragged me into its smoky and noisy depths. The odor of alcohol stung my nostrils. I yelled and struggled, trying to break free of him, afraid of the staring crowd of men and women, but he would not let me go. He lifted me and sat me upon the counter, put his hat upon my head and ordered a drink for me. The tipsy men and women yelled with delight. Somebody tried to jam a cigar into my mouth, but I twisted out of the way.

"How do you feel, setting there like a man, boy?" a man asked.

"Make 'im drunk and he'll stop peeping in here," somebody said.

"Let's buy 'im drinks," somebody said.

Some of my fright left as I stared about. Whisky was set before me.

"Drink it, boy," somebody said.

I shook my head. The man who had dragged me in urged me to drink it, telling me that it would not hurt me. I refused.

"Drink it; it'll make you feel good," he said.

I took a sip and coughed. The men and women laughed. The entire crowd in the saloon gathered about me now, urging me to drink. I took another sip. Then another. My head spun and I laughed. I was put on the floor and I ran giggling and shouting among the yelling crowd. As I would pass each man, I would take a sip from an offered glass. Soon I was drunk.

A man called me to him and whispered some words into my ear and told me that he would give me a nickel if I went to a woman and repeated them to her. I told him that I would say them; he gave me the nickel and I ran to the woman and shouted the words. A gale of laughter went up in the saloon.

"Don't teach that boy that," someone said.

"He doesn't know what it is," another said.

From then on, for a penny or a nickel, I would repeat to anyone whatever was whispered to me. In my foggy, tipsy state the reaction of the men and women to my mysterious words enthralled me. I ran from person to person, laughing, hiccoughing, spewing out filth that made them bend double with glee.

"Let that boy alone now," someone said.

"It ain't going to hurt 'im," another said.

"It's a shame," a woman said, giggling.

"Go home, boy," somebody yelled at me.

Toward early evening they let me go. I staggered along the pavements, drunk, repeating obscenities to the horror of the women I passed and to the amusement of the men en route to their homes from work.

To beg drinks in the saloon became an obsession. Many evenings my mother would find me wandering in a daze and take me home and beat me; but the next morning, no sooner had she gone to her job than I would run to the saloon and wait for someone to take me in and buy me a drink. My mother protested tearfully to the proprietor of the saloon, who ordered me to keep out of his place. But the men reluctant to surrender their sport would buy me drinks anyway, letting me drink out of their flasks on the streets, urging me to repeat obscenities.

I was a drunkard in my sixth year, before I had begun school. With a gang of children, I roamed the streets, begging pennies from passers-by, haunting the doors of saloons, wandering farther and farther away from home each day. I saw more than I could understand and heard more than I could remember. The point of life became for me the times when I could beg drinks. My mother was in despair. She beat me; then she prayed and wept over me, imploring me to be good, telling me that she had to work, all of which carried no weight to my wayward mind. Finally she placed me and my brother in the keeping of an old black woman who watched me every moment to keep me from running to the doors of the saloons to beg for whisky. The craving for alcohol finally left me and I forgot the taste of it.

In the immediate neighborhood there were many school children who, in the afternoons, would stop and play en route to their homes; they would leave their books upon the sidewalk and I would thumb through the pages and question them about the baffling black print. When I had learned to recognize certain words, I told my mother that I wanted to learn to read and she encouraged me. Soon I was able to pick my way through most of the children's books I ran across. There grew in me a consuming curiosity about what was happening around me and, when my mother came home from a hard day's work, I would question her so relentlessly about what I had heard in the streets that she refused to talk to me.

One cold morning my mother awakened me and told me that, because there was no coal in the house, she was taking my brother to the job with her and that I must remain in bed until the coal she had ordered was delivered. For the payment of the coal, she left a note together with some money under the dresser scarf. I went back to sleep and was awakened by the ringing of the doorbell. I opened the door, let in the coal man, and gave him the money and the note. He brought in a few bushels of coal, then lingered, asking me if I were cold.

"Yes," I said, shivering.

He made a fire, then sat and smoked.

"How much change do I owe you?" he asked me.

"I don't know," I said.

"Shame on you," he said. "Don't you know how to count?"
"No, sir," I said.

"Listen and repeat after me," he said.

He counted to ten and I listened carefully; then he asked
me to count alone and I did. He then made me memorize the
words twenty, thirty, forty, etc., then told me to add one,
two, three, and so on. In about an hour's time I had learned
to count to a hundred and I was overjoyed. Long after the
coal man had gone I danced up and down on the bed in my
nightclothes, counting again and again to a hundred, afraid
that if I did not keep repeating the numbers I would forget
them. When my mother returned from her job that night I
insisted that she stand still and listen while I counted to one
hundred. She was dumfounded. After that she taught me to
read, told me stories. On Sundays I would read the newspapers with my mother guiding me and spelling out the words.

I soon made myself a nuisance by asking far too many questions of everybody. Every happening in the neighborhood, no
matter how trivial, became my business. It was in this manner
that I first stumbled upon the relations between whites and
blacks, and what I learned frightened me. Though I had long
known that there were people called "white" people, it had
never meant anything to me emotionally. I had seen white
men and women upon the streets a thousand times, but they
had never looked particularly "white." To me they were
merely people like other people, yet somehow strangely different because I had never come in close touch with any of
them. For the most part I never thought of them; they simply
existed somewhere in the background of the city as a whole.
It might have been that my tardiness in learning to sense
white people as "white" came from the fact that many
of my relatives were "white"-looking people. My grandmother, who was white as any "white" person, had never
looked "white" to me. And when word circulated among the
black people of the neighborhood that a "black" boy had
been severely beaten by a "white" man, I felt that the "white"
man had had a right to beat the "black" boy, for I naïvely
assumed that the "white" man must have been the "black"
boy's father. And did not all fathers, like my father, have the
right to beat their children? A paternal right was the only

right, to my understanding, that a man had to beat a child. But when my mother told me that the "white" man was not the father of the "black" boy, was no kin to him at all, I was puzzled.

"Then why did the 'white' man whip the 'black' boy?" I asked my mother.

"The 'white' man did not *whip* the 'black' boy," my mother told me. "He *beat* the 'black' boy."

"But why?"

"You're too young to understand."

"I'm not going to let anybody beat me," I said stoutly.

"Then stop running wild in the streets," my mother said.

I brooded for a long time about the seemingly causeless beating of the "black" boy by the "white" man and the more questions I asked the more bewildering it all became. Whenever I saw "white" people now I stared at them, wondering what they were really like.

I began school at Howard Institute at a later age than was usual; my mother had not been able to buy me the necessary clothes to make me presentable. The boys of the neighborhood took me to school the first day and when I reached the edge of the school grounds I became terrified, wanted to return home, wanted to put it off. But the boys simply took my hand and pulled me inside the building. I was frightened speechless and the other children had to identify me, tell the teacher my name and address. I sat listening to pupils recite, knowing and understanding what was being said and done, but utterly incapable of opening my mouth when called upon. The students around me seemed so sure of themselves that I despaired of ever being able to conduct myself as they did.

On the playground at noon I attached myself to a group of older boys and followed them about, listening to their talk, asking countless questions. During that noon hour I learned all the four-letter words describing physiological and sex functions, and discovered that I had known them before—had spoken them in the saloon—although I had not known what they meant. A tall black boy recited a long, funny piece of doggerel, replete with filth, describing the physiological relations between men and women, and I memorized it word for word after having heard it but once. Yet, despite my retentive memory, I found it impossible to recite when I went back into the classroom. The teacher called upon me and I rose, holding my book before my eyes, but I could make no words come from me. I could feel the presence of the strange boys and girls behind me, waiting to hear me read, and fear paralyzed me.

Yet when school let out that first day I ran joyously home with a brain burdened with racy and daring knowledge, but not a single idea from books. I gobbled my cold food that had been left covered on the table, seized a piece of soap and rushed into the streets, eager to display all I had learned in school since morning. I went from window to window and printed in huge soap-letters all my newly acquired four-letter words. I had written on nearly all the windows in the neighborhood when a woman stopped me and drove me home. That night the woman visited my mother and informed her of what I had done, taking her from window to window and pointing out my inspirational scribblings. My mother was horrified. She demanded that I tell her where I had learned the words and she refused to believe me when I told her that I had learned them at school. My mother got a pail of water and a towel and took me by the hand and led me to a smeared window.

"Now, scrub until that word's gone," she ordered.

Neighbors gathered, giggling, muttering words of pity and astonishment, asking my mother how on earth I could have learned so much so quickly. I scrubbed at the four-letter soap-words and grew blind with anger. I sobbed, begging my mother to let me go, telling her that I would never write such words again; but she did not relent until the last soap-word had been cleaned away. Never again did I write words like that; I kept them to myself.

After my father's desertion, my mother's ardently religious disposition dominated the household and I was often taken to Sunday school where I met God's representative in the guise of a tall, black preacher. One Sunday my mother invited the tall, black preacher to a dinner of fried chicken. I was happy, not because the preacher was coming but because of the chicken. One or two neighbors also were invited. But no sooner had the preacher arrived than I began to resent him, for I learned at once that he, like my father, was used to having his own way. The hour for dinner came and I was wedged at the table between talking and laughing adults. In the center of the table was a huge platter of golden-brown fried chicken. I compared the bowl of soup that sat before me with the crispy chicken and decided in favor of the chicken. The others began to eat their soup, but I could not touch mine.

"Eat your soup," my mother said.

"I don't want any," I said.

"You won't get anything else until you've eaten your soup," she said.

The preacher had finished his soup and had asked that the platter of chicken be passed to him. It galled me. He smiled, cocked his head this way and that, picking out choice pieces. I forced a spoonful of soup down my throat and looked to see if my speed matched that of the preacher. It did not. There were already bare chicken bones on his plate, and he was reaching for more. I tried eating my soup faster, but it was no use; the other people were now serving themselves chicken and the platter was more than half empty. I gave up and sat staring in despair at the vanishing pieces of fried chicken.

"Eat your soup or you won't get anything," my mother warned.

I looked at her appealingly and could not answer. As piece after piece of chicken was eaten, I was unable to eat my soup at all. I grew hot with anger. The preacher was laughing and joking and the grownups were hanging on his words. My growing hate of the preacher finally became more important than God or religion and I could no longer contain myself. I leaped up from the table, knowing that I should be ashamed of what I was doing, but unable to stop, and screamed, running blindly from the room.

"That preacher's going to eat *all* the chicken!" I bawled.

The preacher tossed back his head and roared with laughter, but my mother was angry and told me that I was to have no dinner because of my bad manners.

When I awakened one morning my mother told me that we were going to see a judge who would make my father support me and my brother. An hour later all three of us were sitting in a huge crowded room. I was overwhelmed by the many faces and the voices which I could not understand. High above me was a white face which my mother told me was the face of the judge. Across the huge room sat my father, smiling confidently, looking at us. My mother warned me not to be fooled by my father's friendly manner; she told me that the judge might ask me questions, and if he did I must tell him the truth. I agreed, yet I hoped that the judge would not ask me anything.

For some reason the entire thing struck me as being use-less; I felt that if my father were going to feed me, then he would have done so regardless of what a judge said to him. And I did not want my father to feed me; I was hungry, but my thoughts of food did not now center about him. I waited, growing restless, hungry. My mother gave me a dry sandwich and I munched and stared, longing to go home. Finally I heard my mother's name called; she rose and began weeping so copiously that she could not talk for a few moments; at last she managed to say that her husband had deserted her and her two children, that her children were hungry, that they stayed hungry, that she worked, that she was trying to raise them alone. Then my father was called; he came forward jauntily, smiling. He tried to kiss my mother, but she turned away from him. I only heard one sentence of what he said.

"I'm doing all I can, Your Honor," he mumbled, grinning.

It had been painful to sit and watch my mother crying and my father laughing and I was glad when we were outside in the sunny streets. Back at home my mother wept again and talked complainingly about the unfairness of the judge who had accepted my father's word. After the court scene, I tried to forget my father; I did not hate him; I simply did not want to think of him. Often when we were hungry my mother would beg me to go to my father's job and ask him for a dollar, a dime, a nickel . . . But I would never consent to go. I did not want to see him.

My mother fell ill and the problem of food became an acute, daily agony. Hunger was with us always. Sometimes the neighbors would feed us or a dollar bill would come in the mail from my grandmother. It was winter and I would buy a dime's worth of coal each morning from the corner coalyard and lug it home in paper bags. For a time I remained out of school to wait upon my mother, then Granny came to visit us and I returned to school.

At night there were long, halting discussions about our going to live with Granny, but nothing came of it. Perhaps there was not enough money for railroad fare. Angered by having been hauled into court, my father now spurned us completely. I heard long, angrily whispered conversations between my mother and grandmother to the effect that "that woman ought to be killed for breaking up a home." What irked me was the ceaseless talk and no action. If someone had suggested that my father be killed, I would perhaps have become interested; if someone had suggested that his name never be mentioned, I would no doubt have agreed; if someone had suggested that we move to another city, I would have been glad. But there was only endless talk that led nowhere and I began to keep away from home as much as possible, preferring the simplicity of the streets to the worried, futile talk at home.

Finally we could no longer pay the rent for our dingy flat; the few dollars that Granny had left us before she went home were gone. Half sick and in despair, my mother made the rounds of the charitable institutions, seeking help. She found an orphan home that agreed to assume the guidance of me and my brother provided my mother worked and made small payments. My mother hated to be separated from us, but she had no choice.

The orphan home was a two-story frame building set amid trees in a wide, green field. My mother ushered me and my brother one morning into the building and into the presence of a tall, gaunt, mulatto woman who called herself Miss Simon. At once she took a fancy to me and I was frightened speechless; I was afraid of her the moment I saw her and my fear lasted during my entire stay in the home.

The house was crowded with children and there was always a storm of noise. The daily routine was blurred to me and I never quite grasped it. The most abiding feeling I had each day was hunger and fear. The meals were skimpy and there were only two of them. Just before we went to bed each night we were given a slice of bread smeared with molasses. The children were silent, hostile, vindictive, continuously complaining of hunger. There was an over-all atmosphere of nervousness and intrigue, of children telling tales upon others, of children being deprived of food to punish them.

The home did not have the money to check the growth of the wide stretches of grass by having it mown, so it had to be pulled by hand. Each morning after we had eaten a breakfast that seemed like no breakfast at all, an older child would lead a herd of us to the vast lawn and we would get to our knees and wrench the grass loose from the dirt with our fingers. At intervals Miss Simon would make a tour of inspection, examining the pile of pulled grass beside each child, scolding or praising according to the size of the pile. Many mornings I was too weak from hunger to pull the grass; I would grow dizzy and my mind would become blank and I would find myself, after an interval of unconsciousness, upon my hands and knees, my head whirling, my eyes staring in bleak astonishment at the green grass, wondering where I was, feeling that I was emerging from a dream . . .

During the first days my mother came each night to visit me and my brother, then her visits stopped. I began to wonder if she, too, like my father, had disappeared into the unknown. I was rapidly learning to distrust everything and everybody. When my mother did come, I asked her why had she remained away so long and she told me that Miss Simon had forbidden her to visit us, that Miss Simon had said that she was spoiling us with too much attention. I begged my mother to take me away; she wept and told me to wait, that soon she would take us to Arkansas. She left and my heart sank.

Miss Simon tried to win my confidence; she asked me if I would like to be adopted by her if my mother consented and I said no. She would take me into her apartment and talk to me, but her words had no effect. Dread and distrust had already become a daily part of my being and my memory grew sharp, my senses more impressionable; I began to be aware of myself as a distinct personality striving against others. I held myself in, afraid to act or speak until I was sure of my surroundings, feeling most of the time that I was suspended over a void. My imagination soared; I dreamed of running away. Each morning I vowed that I would leave the next morning, but the next morning always found me afraid.

One day Miss Simon told me that thereafter I was to help her in the office. I ate lunch with her and, strangely, when I sat facing her at the table, my hunger vanished. The woman killed something in me. Next she called me to her desk where she sat addressing envelopes.

"Step up close to the desk," she said. "Don't be afraid."

I went and stood at her elbow. There was a wart on her chin and I stared at it.

"Now, take a blotter from over there and blot each envelope after I'm through writing on it," she instructed me, pointing to a blotter that stood about a foot from my hand.

I stared and did not move or answer.

"Take the blotter," she said.

I wanted to reach for the blotter and succeeded only in twitching my arm.

"Here," she said sharply, reaching for the blotter and shoving it into my fingers.

She wrote in ink on an envelope and pushed it toward me. Holding the blotter in my hand, I stared at the envelope and could not move.

"Blot it," she said.

I could not lift my hand. I knew what she had said; I knew what she wanted me to do; and I had heard her correctly. I wanted to look at her and say something, tell her why I could not move; but my eyes were fixed upon the floor. I could not summon enough courage while she sat there looking at me to reach over the yawning space of twelve inches and blot the wet ink on the envelope.

"Blot it!" she spoke sharply.

Still I could not move or answer.

"Look at me!"

I could not lift my eyes. She reached her hand to my face and I twisted away.

"What's wrong with you?" she demanded.

I began to cry and she drove me from the room. I decided that as soon as night came I would run away. The dinner bell rang and I did not go to the table, but hid in a corner of the hallway. When I heard the dishes rattling at the table, I opened the door and ran down the walk to the street. Dusk was falling. Doubt made me stop. Ought I go back? No; hunger was back there, and fear. I went on, coming to concrete sidewalks. People passed me. Where was I going? I did not know. The farther I walked the more frantic I became. In a confused and vague way I knew that I was doing more running *away* from than running *toward* something. I stopped. The streets seemed dangerous. The buildings were massive and dark. The moon shone and the trees loomed frighteningly. No, I could not go on. I would go back. But I had walked so far and had turned too many corners and had not kept track of the direction. Which way led back to the orphan home? I did not know. I was lost.

I stood in the middle of the sidewalk and cried. A "white" policeman came to me and I wondered if he was going to beat me. He asked me what was the matter and I told him that I was trying to find my mother. His "white" face created a new fear in me. I was remembering the tale of the "white" man who had beaten the "black" boy. A crowd gathered and I was urged to tell where I lived. Curiously, I was too full of fear to cry now. I wanted to tell the "white" face that I had run off from an orphan home and that Miss Simon ran it, but I was afraid. Finally I was taken to the police station where I was fed. I felt better. I sat in a big chair where I was surrounded by "white" policemen, but they seemed to ignore me. Through the window I could see that night had completely fallen and that lights now gleamed in the streets. I grew sleepy and dozed. My shoulder was shaken gently and I opened my eyes and looked into a "white" face of another policeman who was sitting beside me. He asked me questions in a quiet, confidential tone, and quite before I knew it he was not "white" any more. I told him that I had run away from an orphan home and that Miss Simon ran it.

It was but a matter of minutes before I was walking alongside a policeman, heading toward the home. The policeman led me to the front gate and I saw Miss Simon waiting for me on the steps. She identified me and I was left in her charge. I begged her not to beat me, but she yanked me upstairs into an empty room and lashed me thoroughly. Sobbing, I slunk off to bed, resolved to run away again. But I was watched closely after that.

My mother was informed upon her next visit that I had tried to run away and she was terribly upset.

"Why did you do it?" she asked.

"I don't want to stay here," I told her.

"But you must," she said. "How can I work if I'm to worry about you? You must remember that you have no father. I'm doing all I can."

"I don't want to stay here," I repeated.

"Then, if I take you to your father . . ."

"I don't want to stay with him either," I said.

"But I want you to ask him for enough money for us to go to my sister's in Arkansas," she said.

Again I was faced with choices I did not like, but I finally agreed. After all, my hate for my father was not so great and urgent as my hate for the orphan home. My mother held to her idea and one night a week or so later I found myself standing in a room in a frame house. My father and a strange woman were sitting before a bright fire that blazed in a grate. My mother and I were standing about six feet away, as though we were afraid to approach them any closer.

"It's not for me," my mother was saying. "It's for your children that I'm asking you for money."

"I ain't got nothing," my father said, laughing.

"Come here, boy," the strange woman called to me.

I looked at her and did not move.

"Give him a nickel," the woman said. "He's cute."

"Come here, Richard," my father said, stretching out his hand.

I backed away, shaking my head, keeping my eyes on the fire.

"He is a cute child," the strange woman said.

"You ought to be ashamed," my mother said to the strange woman. "You're starving my children."

"Now, don't you-all fight," my father said, laughing.

"I'll take that poker and hit you!" I blurted at my father.

He looked at my mother and laughed louder.

"You told him to say that," he said.

"Don't say such things, Richard," my mother said.

"You ought to be dead," I said to the strange woman.

The woman laughed and threw her arms about my father's neck. I grew ashamed and wanted to leave.

"How can you starve your children?" my mother asked.

"Let Richard stay with me," my father said.

"Do you want to stay with your father, Richard?" my mother asked.

"No," I said.

"You'll get plenty to eat," he said.

"I'm hungry now," I told him. "But I won't stay with you."

"Aw, give the boy a nickel," the woman said.

My father ran his hand into his pocket and pulled out a nickel.

"Here, Richard," he said.

"Don't take it," my mother said.

"Don't teach him to be a fool," my father said. "Here, Richard, take it."

I looked at my mother, at the strange woman, at my father, then into the fire. I wanted to take the nickel, but I did not want to take it from my father.

"You ought to be ashamed," my mother said, weeping. "Giving your son a nickel when he's hungry. If there's a God, He'll pay you back."

"That's all I got," my father said, laughing again and returning the nickel to his pocket.

We left. I had the feeling that I had had to do with something unclean. Many times in the years after that the image of my father and the strange woman, their faces lit by the dancing flames, would surge up in my imagination so vivid and strong that I felt I could reach out and touch it; I would stare at it, feeling that it possessed some vital meaning which always eluded me.

A quarter of a century was to elapse between the time when I saw my father sitting with the strange woman and the time when I was to see him again, standing alone upon the red clay of a Mississippi plantation, a sharecropper, clad in ragged overalls, holding a muddy hoe in his gnarled, veined hands —a quarter of a century during which my mind and consciousness had become so greatly and violently altered that when I tried to talk to him I realized that, though ties of blood made us kin, though I could see a shadow of my face in his face, though there was an echo of my voice in his voice, we were forever strangers, speaking a different language, living on vastly distant planes of reality. That day a quarter of a century later when I visited him on the plantation—he was standing against the sky, smiling toothlessly, his hair whitened, his body bent, his eyes glazed with dim recollection, his fearsome aspect of twenty-five years ago gone forever from him—I was overwhelmed to realize that he could never understand me or the scalding experiences that had swept me beyond his life and into an area of living that he could never know. I stood before him, poised, my mind aching as it embraced the simple nakedness of his life, feeling how completely his soul was imprisoned by the slow flow of the seasons, by wind and rain and sun, how fastened were his memories to a crude and raw past, how chained were his actions and emotions to the direct, animalistic impulses of his withering body . . .

From the white landowners above him there had not been handed to him a chance to learn the meaning of loyalty, of sentiment, of tradition. Joy was as unknown to him as was despair. As a creature of the earth, he endured, hearty, whole, seemingly indestructible, with no regrets and no hope. He asked easy, drawling questions about me, his other son, his wife, and he laughed, amused, when I informed him of their destinies. I forgave him and pitied him as my eyes looked past him to the unpainted wooden shack. From far beyond the horizons that bound this bleak plantation there had come to me through my living the knowledge that my father was a black peasant who had gone to the city seeking life, but who had failed in the city; a black peasant whose life had been hopelessly snarled in the city, and who had at last fled the city—that same city which had lifted me in its burning arms and borne me toward alien and undreamed-of shores of knowing.

Chapter II

THE GLAD DAYS that dawned gave me liberty for the free play of impulse and, from anxiety and restraint, I leaped to license and thoughtless action. My mother arrived one afternoon with the news that we were going to live with her sister in Elaine, Arkansas, and that en route we would visit Granny, who had moved from Natchez to Jackson, Mississippi. As the words fell from my mother's lips, a long and heavy anxiety lifted from me. Excited, I rushed about and gathered my ragged clothes. I was leaving the hated home, hunger, fear, leaving days that had been as dark and lonely as death.

While I was packing, a playmate came to tell me that one of my shirts was hanging damp upon the clothesline. Filled more with the sense of coming freedom than with generosity, I told him that he could have it. What was a shirt to me now? The children stood about and watched me with envious eyes as I crammed my things into a suitcase, but I did not notice them. The moment I had learned that I was to leave, my feelings had recoiled so sharply and quickly from the home that the children simply did not exist for me any more. Their faces possessed the power of evoking in me a million memories that I longed to forget, and instead of my leaving drawing me to them in communion, it had flung me forever beyond them.

I was so eager to be gone that when I stood in the front hallway, packed and ready, I did not even think of saying good-bye to the boys and girls with whom I had eaten and slept and lived for so many weeks. My mother scolded me for my thoughtlessness and bade me say good-bye to them. Reluctantly I obeyed her, wishing that I did not have to do so. As I shook the dingy palms extended to me I kept my eyes averted, not wanting to look again into faces that hurt me because they had become so thoroughly associated in my feelings with hunger and fear. In shaking hands I was doing something that I was to do countless times in the years to come: acting in conformity with what others expected of me even though, by the very nature and form of my life, I did not and could not share their spirit.

(After I had outlived the shocks of childhood, after the habit of reflection had been born in me, I used to mull over the strange absence of real kindness in Negroes, how unstable was our tenderness, how lacking in genuine passion we were, how void of great hope, how timid our joy, how bare our traditions, how hollow our memories, how lacking we were in those intangible sentiments that bind man to man, and how shallow was even our despair. After I had learned other ways of life I used to brood upon the unconscious irony of those who felt that Negroes led so passional an existence! I saw that what had been taken for our emotional strength was our negative confusions, our flights, our fears, our frenzy under pressure.

(Whenever I thought of the essential bleakness of black life in America, I knew that Negroes had never been allowed to catch the full spirit of Western civilization, that they lived somehow in it but not of it. And when I brooded upon the cultural barrenness of black life, I wondered if clean, positive tenderness, love, honor, loyalty, and the capacity to remember were native with man. I asked myself if these human qualities were not fostered, won, struggled and suffered for, preserved in ritual from one generation to another.)

Granny's home in Jackson was an enchanting place to explore. It was a two-story frame structure of seven rooms. My brother and I used to play hide and seek in the long, narrow hallways, and on and under the stairs. Granny's son, Uncle Clark, had bought her this home, and its white plastered walls, its front and back porches, its round columns and banisters, made me feel that surely there was no finer house in all the round world.

There were wide green fields in which my brother and I roamed and played and shouted. And there were the timid children of the neighbors, boys and girls to whom my brother and I felt superior in worldly knowledge. We took pride in telling them what it was like to ride on a train, what the yellow, sleepy Mississippi River looked like, how it felt to sail on the *Kate Adams*, what Memphis looked like, and how I had run off from the orphan home. And we would hint that we

were pausing for but a few days and then would be off to
even more fabulous places and marvelous experiences.

To help support the household my grandmother boarded a
colored schoolteacher, Ella, a young woman with so remote
and dreamy and silent a manner that I was as much afraid of
her as I was attracted to her. I had long wanted to ask her to
tell me about the books that she was always reading, but I
could never quite summon enough courage to do so. One
afternoon I found her sitting alone upon the front porch,
reading.

"Ella," I begged, "please tell me what you are reading."

"It's just a book," she said evasively, looking about with
apprehension.

"But what's it about?" I asked.

"Your grandmother wouldn't like it if I talked to you about
novels," she told me.

I detected a note of sympathy in her voice.

"I don't care," I said loudly and bravely.

"Shhh— You mustn't say things like that," she said.

"But I want to know."

"When you grow up, you'll read books and know what's in
them," she explained.

"But I want to know now."

She thought a while, then closed the book.

"Come here," she said.

I sat at her feet and lifted my face to hers.

"Once upon a time there was an old, old man named Bluebeard," she began in a low voice.

She whispered to me the story of *Bluebeard and His Seven
Wives* and I ceased to see the porch, the sunshine, her face,
everything. As her words fell upon my new ears, I endowed
them with a reality that welled up from somewhere within
me. She told how Bluebeard had duped and married his seven
wives, how he had loved and slain them, how he had hanged
them up by their hair in a dark closet. The tale made the
world around me be, throb, live. As she spoke, reality
changed, the look of things altered, and the world became
peopled with magical presences. My sense of life deepened
and the feel of things was different, somehow. Enchanted and
enthralled, I stopped her constantly to ask for details. My

imagination blazed. The sensations the story aroused in me were never to leave me. When she was about to finish, when my interest was keenest, when I was lost to the world around me, Granny stepped briskly onto the porch.

"You stop that, you evil gal!" she shouted. "I want none of that Devil stuff in my house!"

Her voice jarred me so that I gasped. For a moment I did not know what was happening.

"I'm sorry, Mrs. Wilson," Ella stammered, rising. "But he asked me—"

"He's just a foolish child and you know it!" Granny blazed. Ella bowed her head and went into the house.

"But, granny, she didn't finish," I protested, knowing that I should have kept quiet.

She bared her teeth and slapped me across my mouth with the back of her hand.

"You shut your mouth," she hissed. "You don't know what you're talking about!"

"But I want to hear what happened!" I wailed, dodging another blow that I thought was coming.

"That's the Devil's work!" she shouted.

My grandmother was as nearly white as a Negro can get without being white, which means that she was white. The sagging flesh of her face quivered; her eyes, large, dark, deep-set, wide apart, glared at me. Her lips narrowed to a line. Her high forehead wrinkled. When she was angry her eyelids drooped halfway down over her pupils, giving her a baleful aspect.

"But I liked the story," I told her.

"You're going to burn in hell," she said with such furious conviction that for a moment I believed her.

Not to know the end of the tale filled me with a sense of emptiness, loss. I hungered for the sharp, frightening, breathtaking, almost painful excitement that the story had given me, and I vowed that as soon as I was old enough I would buy all the novels there were and read them to feed that thirst for violence that was in me, for intrigue, for plotting, for secrecy, for bloody murders. So profoundly responsive a chord had the tale struck in me that the threats of my mother and grandmother had no effect whatsoever. They read my insistence as mere obstinacy, as foolishness, something that would quickly pass; and they had no notion how desperately serious the tale had made me. They could not have known that Ella's whispered story of deception and murder had been the first experience in my life that had elicited from me a total emotional response. No words or punishment could have possibly made me doubt. I had tasted what to me was life, and I would have more of it, somehow, someway. I realized that they could not understand what I was feeling and I kept quiet. But when no one was looking I would slip into Ella's room and steal a book and take it back of the barn and try to read it. Usually I could not decipher enough words to make the story have meaning. I burned to learn to read novels and I tortured my mother into telling me the meaning of every strange word I saw, not because the word itself had any value, but because it was the gateway to a forbidden and enchanting land.

One afternoon my mother became so ill that she had to go to bed. When night fell Granny assumed the task of seeing that my brother and I bathed. She set two tubs of water in our room and ordered us to pull off our clothes, which we did. She sat at one end of the room, knitting, lifting her eyes now and then from the wool to watch us and direct us. My brother and I splashed in the water, playing, laughing, trying our utmost to fling suds into each other's eyes. The floor was getting so sloppy that Granny scolded us.

"Stop that foolishness and wash yourselves!"

"Yes, ma'am," we answered automatically and proceeded with our playing.

I scooped up a double handful of suds and called to my brother. He looked and I flung the suds, but he ducked and the white foam spattered on to the floor.

"Richard, stop that playing and bathe!"

"Yes, ma'am," I said, watching my brother to catch him unawares so that I could fling more suds at him.

"Come here, you Richard!" Granny said, putting her knitting aside.

I went to her, walking sheepishly and nakedly across the floor. She snatched the towel from my hand and began to scrub my ears, my face, my neck.

"Bend over," she ordered.

I stooped and she scrubbed my anus. My mind was in a sort of daze, midway between daydreaming and thinking. Then, before I knew it, words—words whose meaning I did not fully know—had slipped out of my mouth.

"When you get through, kiss back there," I said, the words rolling softly but unpremeditatedly.

My first indication that something was wrong was that Granny became terribly still, then she pushed me violently from her. I turned around and saw that her white face was frozen, that her black, deep-set eyes were blazing at me unblinkingly. Taking my cue from her queer expression, I knew that I had said something awful, but I had no notion at that moment just how awful it was. Granny rose slowly and lifted the wet towel high above her head and brought it down across my naked back with all the outraged fury of her sixty-odd-year-old body, leaving an aching streak of fire burning and quivering on my skin. I gasped and held my breath, fighting against the pain; then I howled and cringed. I had not realized the meaning of what I had said; its moral horror was unfelt by me, and her attack seemed without cause. She lifted the wet towel and struck me again with such force that I dropped to my knees. I knew that if I did not get out of her reach she would kill me. Naked, I rose and ran out of the room, screaming. My mother hurried from her bed.

"What's the matter, mama?" she asked Granny.

I lingered in the hallway, trembling, looking at Granny, trying to speak but only moving my lips. Granny seemed to have gone out of her mind, for she stood like stone, her eyes dead upon me, not saying a word.

"Richard, what have you done?" my mother asked.

Poised to run again, I shook my head.

"What's the matter, for God's sake?" my mother asked of me, of Granny, of my brother, turning her face from one to another.

Granny wilted, half turned, flung the towel to the floor, then burst into tears.

"He . . . I was trying to wash him," Granny whimpered, "here," she continued, pointing, "and . . . that black little Devil . . ." Her body was shaking with insult and rage. "He told me to kiss him there when I was through."

Now my mother stared without speaking.

"No!" my mother exclaimed.

"He did," Granny whimpered.

"He didn't say *that*," my mother protested.

"He did," Granny sighed.

I listened, vaguely knowing now that I had committed some awful wrong that I could not undo, that I had uttered words I could not recall even though I ached to nullify them, kill them, turn back time to the moment before I had talked so that I could have another chance to save myself. My mother picked up the wet towel and came toward me. I ran into the kitchen, naked, yelling. She came hard upon my heels and I scuttled into the back yard, running blindly in the dark, butting my head against the fence, the tree, bruising my toes on sticks of wood, still screaming. I had no way of measuring the gravity of my wrong and I assumed that I had done something for which I would never be forgiven. Had I known just how my words had struck them, I would have remained still and taken my punishment, but it was the feeling that anything could or would happen to me that made me wild with fear.

"Come here, you little filthy fool!" my mother called.

I dodged her and ran back into the house, then again into the hallway, my naked body flashing frantically through the air. I crouched in a dark corner. My mother rushed upon me, breathing hard. I ducked, crawled, stood, and ran again.

"You may as well stand still," my mother said. "I'm going to beat you tonight if it is the last thing I do on this earth!"

Again she charged me and I dodged, just missing the stinging swish of the wet towel, and scooted into the room where my brother stood.

"What's the matter?" he asked, for he had not heard what I had said.

A blow fell on my mouth. I whirled. Granny was upon me. She struck me another blow on my head with the back of her hand. Then my mother came into the room. I fell to the floor and crawled under the bed.

"You come out of there," my mother called.

"Naw," I cried.

"Come out or I'll beat you to within an inch of your life," she said.

"Naw," I said.

"Call Papa," Granny said.

I trembled. Granny was sending my brother to fetch Grandpa, of whom I was mortally afraid. He was a tall, skinny, silent, grim, black man who had fought in the Civil War with the Union Army. When he was angry he gritted his teeth with a terrifying, grating sound. He kept his army gun in his room, standing in a corner, loaded. He was under the delusion that the war between the states would be resumed. I heard my brother rush out of the room and I knew it was but a matter of minutes before Grandpa would come. I balled myself into a knot and moaned:

"Naw, naw, naw . . ."

Grandpa came and ordered me from under the bed. I refused to move.

"Come out of there, little man," he said.

"Naw."

"Do you want me to get my gun?"

"Naw, sir. Please don't shoot me!" I cried.

"Then come out!"

I remained still. Grandpa took hold of the bed and pulled it. I clung to a bedpost and was dragged over the floor. Grandpa ran at me and tried to grab my leg, but I crawled out of reach. I rested on all fours and kept in the center of the bed and each time the bed moved, I moved, following it.

"Come out and get your whipping!" my mother called.

I remained still. The bed moved and I moved. I did not think; I did not plan; I did not plot. Instinct told me what to do. There was painful danger and I had to avoid it. Grandpa finally gave up and went back to his room.

"When you come out, you'll get your whipping," my mother said. "No matter how long you stay under there, you're going to get it. And no food for you tonight."

"What did he do?" my brother asked.

"Something he ought to be killed for," Granny said.

"But what?" my brother asked.

"Shut you up and get to bed," my mother said.

I stayed under the bed far into the night. The household went to sleep. Finally hunger and thirst drove me out; when I stood up I found my mother lurking in the doorway, waiting for me.

"Come into the kitchen," she said.

I followed her and she beat me, but she did not use the wet towel; Grandpa had forbade that. Between strokes of the switch she would ask me where had I learned the dirty words and I could not tell her; and my inability to tell her made her furious.

"I'm going to beat you until you tell me," she declared.

And I could not tell her because I did not know. None of the obscene words I had learned at school in Memphis had dealt with perversions of any sort, although I might have learned the words while loitering drunkenly in saloons. The next day Granny said emphatically that she knew who had ruined me, that she knew I had learned about "foul practices" from reading Ella's books, and when I asked what "foul practices" were, my mother beat me afresh. No matter how hard I tried to convince them that I had not read the words in a book or that I could not remember having heard anyone say them, they would not believe me. Granny finally charged Ella with telling me things that I should not know and Ella, weeping and distraught, packed her things and moved. The tremendous upheaval that my words had caused made me know that there lay back of them much more than I could figure out, and I resolved that in the future I would learn the meaning of why they had beat and denounced me.

The days and hours began to speak now with a clearer tongue. Each experience had a sharp meaning of its own.

There was the breathlessly anxious fun of chasing and catching flitting fireflies on drowsy summer nights.

There was the drenching hospitality in the pervading smell of sweet magnolias.

There was the aura of limitless freedom distilled from the rolling sweep of tall green grass swaying and glinting in the wind and sun.

There was the feeling of impersonal plenty when I saw a boll of cotton whose cup had spilt over and straggled its white fleece toward the earth.

There was the playing chuckle that bubbled in my throat when I watched a fat duck waddle across the back yard.

There was the suspense I felt when I heard the taut, sharp song of a yellow-black bee hovering nervously but patiently above a white rose.

There was the drugged, sleepy feeling that came from sipping glasses of milk, drinking them slowly so that they would last a long time, and drinking enough for the first time in my life.

There was the bitter amusement of going into town with Granny and watching the baffled stares of white folks who saw an old white woman leading two undeniably Negro boys in and out of stores on Capitol Street.

There was the slow, fresh, saliva-stimulating smell of cooking cotton seeds.

There was the excitement of fishing in muddy country creeks with my grandpa on cloudy days.

There was the fear and awe I felt when Grandpa took me to a sawmill to watch the giant whirring steel blades whine and scream as they bit into wet green logs.

There was the puckery taste that almost made me cry when I ate my first half-ripe persimmon.

There was the greedy joy in the tangy taste of wild hickory nuts.

There was the dry hot summer morning when I scratched my bare arms on briers while picking blackberries and came home with my fingers and lips stained black with sweet berry juice.

There was the relish of eating my first fried fish sandwich, nibbling at it slowly and hoping that I would never eat it up.

There was the all-night ache in my stomach after I had climbed a neighbor's tree and eaten stolen, unripe peaches.

There was the morning when I thought I would fall dead from fear after I had stepped with my bare feet upon a bright little green garden snake.

And there were the long, slow, drowsy days and nights of drizzling rain . . .

At last we were at the railroad station with our bags, waiting for the train that would take us to Arkansas; and for the first time I noticed that there were two lines of people at the ticket window, a "white" line and a "black" line. During my visit at Granny's a sense of the two races had been born in me with a sharp concreteness that would never die until I died. When I boarded the train I was aware that we Negroes were in one part of the train and that the whites were in another. Naïvely I wanted to go and see how the whites looked while sitting in their part of the train.

"Can I go and peep at the white folks?" I asked my mother.

"You keep quiet," she said.

"But that wouldn't be wrong, would it?"

"Will you keep still?"

"But why can't I?"

"Quit talking foolishness!"

I had begun to notice that my mother became irritated when I questioned her about whites and blacks, and I could not quite understand it. I wanted to understand these two sets of people who lived side by side and never touched, it seemed, except in violence. Now, there was my grandmother . . . Was she white? Just how white was she? What did the whites think of her whiteness?

"Mama, is Granny white?" I asked as the train rolled through the darkness.

"If you've got eyes, you can see what color she is," my mother said.

"I mean, do the white folks think she's white?"

"Why don't you ask the white folks that?" she countered.

"But you know," I insisted.

"Why should I know?" she asked. "I'm not white."

"Granny looks white," I said, hoping to establish one fact, at least. "Then why is she living with us colored folks?"

"Don't you want Granny to live with us?" she asked, blunting my question.

"Yes."

"Then why are you asking?"

"I want to *know*."

"Doesn't Granny live with us?"

"Yes."

"Isn't that enough?"

"But does she *want* to live with us?"

"Why didn't you ask Granny that?" my mother evaded me again in a taunting voice.

"Did Granny become colored when she married Grandpa?"

"Will you stop asking silly questions!"

"But did she?"

"Granny didn't *become* colored," my mother said angrily. "She was *born* the color she is now."

Again I was being shut out of the secret, the thing, the reality I felt somewhere beneath all the words and silences.

"Why didn't Granny marry a white man?" I asked.

"Because she didn't want to," my mother said peevishly.

"Why don't you want to talk to me?" I asked.

She slapped me and I cried. Later, grudgingly, she told me that Granny came of Irish, Scotch, and French stock in which Negro blood had somewhere and somehow been infused. She explained it all in a matter-of-fact, offhand, neutral way; her emotions were not involved at all.

"What was Granny's name before she married Grandpa?"

"Bolden."

"Who gave her that name?"

"The white man who owned her."

"She was a slave?"

"Yes."

"And Bolden was the name of Granny's father?"

"Granny doesn't know who her father was."

"So they just gave her any name?"

"They gave her a name; that's all I know."

"Couldn't Granny find out who her father was?"

"For what, silly?"

"So she could know."

"Know for what?"

"Just to know."

"But for *what*?"

I could not say. I could not get anywhere.

"Mama, where did Father get his name?"

"From his father."

"And where did the father of my father get his name?"

"Like Granny got hers. From a white man."

"Do they know who he is?"

"I don't know."

"Why don't they find out?"

"For what?" my mother demanded harshly.

And I could think of no rational or practical reason why my father should try to find out who his father's father was.

"What has Papa got in him?" I asked.

"Some white and some red and some black," she said.

"Indian, white, and Negro?"

"Yes."

"Then what am I?"

"They'll call you a colored man when you grow up," she said. Then she turned to me and smiled mockingly and asked: "Do you mind, Mr. Wright?"

I was angry and I did not answer. I did not object to being called colored, but I knew that there was something my mother was holding back. She was not concealing facts, but feelings, attitudes, convictions which she did not want me to know; and she became angry when I prodded her. All right, I would find out someday. Just wait. All right, I was colored. It was fine. I did not know enough to be afraid or to anticipate in a concrete manner. True, I had heard that colored people were killed and beaten, but so far it all had seemed remote. There was, of course, a vague uneasiness about it all, but I would be able to handle that when I came to it. It would be simple. If anybody tried to kill me, then I would kill them first.

When we arrived in Elaine I saw that Aunt Maggie lived in a bungalow that had a fence around it. It looked like home and I was glad. I had no suspicion that I was to live here for but a short time and that the manner of my leaving would be my first baptism of racial emotion.

A wide dusty road ran past the house and on each side of the road wild flowers grew. It was summer and the smell of clay dust was everywhere, day and night. I would get up early every morning to wade with my bare feet through the dust of the road, reveling in the strange mixture of the cold dew-wet crust on top of the road and the warm, sun-baked dust beneath.

After sunrise the bees would come out and I discovered that by slapping my two palms together smartly I could kill a bee. My mother warned me to stop, telling me that bees made honey, that it was not good to kill things that made food, that I would eventually be stung. But I felt confident of outwitting any bee. One morning I slapped an enormous bee between my hands just as it had lit upon a flower and it stung me in the tender center of my left palm. I ran home screaming.

"Good enough for you," my mother commented dryly.

I never crushed any more bees.

Aunt Maggie's husband, Uncle Hoskins, owned a saloon that catered to the hundreds of Negroes who worked in the surrounding sawmills. Remembering the saloon of my Memphis days, I begged Uncle Hoskins to take me to see it and he promised; but my mother said no; she was afraid that I would grow up to be a drunkard if I went inside of a saloon again while still a child. Well, if I could not see the saloon, at least I could eat. And at mealtime Aunt Maggie's table was so loaded with food that I could scarcely believe it was real. It took me some time to get used to the idea of there being enough to eat; I felt that if I ate enough there would not be anything left for another time. When I first sat down at Aunt Maggie's table, I could not eat until I had asked:

"Can I eat all I want?"

"Eat as much as you like," Uncle Hoskins said.

I did not believe him. I ate until my stomach hurt, but even then I did not want to get up from the table.

"Your eyes are bigger than your stomach," my mother said.

"Let him eat all he wants to and get used to food," Uncle Hoskins said.

When supper was over I saw that there were many biscuits piled high upon the bread platter, an astonishing and unbelievable sight to me. Though the biscuits were right before my eyes, and though there was more flour in the kitchen, I was apprehensive lest there be no bread for breakfast in the morning. I was afraid that somehow the biscuits might disappear during the night, while I was sleeping. I did not want to wake up in the morning, as I had so often in the past, feeling hungry and knowing that there was no food in the house. So, surreptitiously, I took some of the biscuits from the platter and slipped them into my pocket, not to eat, but to keep as a bulwark against any possible attack of hunger. Even after I had got used to seeing the table loaded with food at each meal, I still stole bread and put it into my pockets. In washing my clothes my mother found the gummy wads and scolded me to break me of the habit; I stopped hiding the bread in my pockets and hid it about the house, in corners, behind dressers. I did not break the habit of stealing and hoarding bread until my faith that food would be forthcoming at each meal had been somewhat established.

Uncle Hoskins had a horse and buggy and sometimes he used to take me with him to Helena, where he traded. One day when I was riding with him he said:

"Richard, would you like to see this horse drink water out of the middle of the river?"

"Yes," I said, laughing. "But this horse can't do that."

"Yes, he can," Uncle Hoskins said. "Just wait and see."

He lashed the horse and headed the buggy straight for the Mississippi River.

"Where're you going?" I asked, alarm mounting in me.

"We're going to the middle of the river so the horse can drink," he said.

He drove over the levee and down the long slope of cobblestones to the river's edge and the horse plunged wildly in. I looked at the mile stretch of water that lay ahead and leaped up in terror.

"Naw!" I screamed.

"This horse has to drink," Uncle Hoskins said grimly.

"The river's deep!" I shouted.

"The horse can't drink here," Uncle Hoskins said, lashing the back of the struggling animal.

The buggy went farther. The horse slowed a little and tossed his head above the current. I grabbed the sides of the buggy, ready to jump, even though I could not swim.

"Sit down or you'll fall out!" Uncle Hoskins shouted.

"Let me out!" I screamed.

The water now came up to the hubs of the wheels of the buggy. I tried to leap into the river and he caught hold of my leg. We were now surrounded by water.

"Let me out!" I continued to scream.

The buggy rolled on and the water rose higher. The horse wagged his head, arched his neck, flung his tail about, walled his eyes, and snorted. I gripped the sides of the buggy with all the strength I had, ready to wrench free and leap if the buggy slipped deeper into the river. Uncle Hoskins and I tussled.

"Whoa!" he yelled at last to the horse.

The horse stopped and neighed. The swirling yellow water was so close that I could have touched the surface of the river. Uncle Hoskins looked at me and laughed.

"Did you really think that I was going to drive this buggy into the middle of the river?" he asked.

I was too scared to answer; my muscles were so taut that they ached.

"It's all right," he said soothingly.

He turned the buggy around and started back toward the levee. I was still clutching the sides of the buggy so tightly that I could not turn them loose.

"We're safe now," he said.

The buggy rolled onto dry land and, as my fear ebbed, I felt that I was dropping from a great height. It seemed that I could smell a sharp, fresh odor. My forehead was damp and my heart thumped heavily.

"I want to get out," I said.

"What's the matter?" he asked.

"I want to get out!"

"We're back on land now, boy."

"Naw! Stop! I want to get out!"

He did not stop the buggy; he did not even turn his head to look at me; he did not understand. I wrenched my leg free with a lunge and leaped headlong out of the buggy, landing in the dust of the road, unhurt. He stopped the buggy.

"Are you really that scared?" he asked softly.

I did not answer; I could not speak. My fear was gone now and he loomed before me like a stranger, like a man I had never seen before, a man with whom I could never share a moment of intimate living.

"Come on, Richard, and get back into the buggy," he said. "I'll take you home now."

I shook my head and began to cry.

"Listen, son, don't you trust me?" he asked. "I was born on that old river. I know that river. There's stone and brick way down under that water. You could wade out for half a mile and it would not come over your head."

His words meant nothing and I would not re-enter the buggy.

"I'd better take you home," he said soberly.

I started down the dusty road. He got out of the buggy and walked beside me. He did not do his shopping that day and when he tried to explain to me what he had been trying to do in frightening me I would not listen or speak to him. I never trusted him after that. Whenever I saw his face the memory of my terror upon the river would come back, vivid and strong, and it stood as a barrier between us.

Each day Uncle Hoskins went to his saloon in the evening and did not return home until the early hours of the morning. Like my father, he slept in the daytime, but noise never seemed to bother Uncle Hoskins. My brother and I shouted and banged as much as we liked. Often I would creep into his room while he slept and stare at the big shining revolver that lay near his head, within quick reach of his hand. I asked Aunt Maggie why he kept the gun so close to him and she told me that men had threatened to kill him, white men . . .

One morning I awakened to learn that Uncle Hoskins had not come home from the saloon. Aunt Maggie fretted and worried. She wanted to visit the saloon and find out what had happened, but Uncle Hoskins had forbidden her to come to the place. The day wore on and dinnertime came.

"I'm going to find out if anything's happened," Aunt Maggie said.

"Maybe you oughtn't," my mother said. "Maybe it's dangerous."

The food was kept hot on the stove and Aunt Maggie stood on the front porch staring into the deepening dusk. Again she declared that she was going to the saloon, but my mother dissuaded her once more. It grew dark and still he had not come. Aunt Maggie was silent and restless.

"I hope to God the white people didn't bother him," she said.

Later she went into the bedroom and when she came out she whimpered:

"He didn't take his gun. I wonder what could have happened?"

We ate in silence. An hour later there was the sound of heavy footsteps on the front porch and a loud knock came. Aunt Maggie ran to the door and flung it open. A tall black boy stood sweating, panting, and shaking his head. He pulled off his cap.

"Mr. Hoskins . . . he done been shot. Done been shot by a white man," the boy gasped. "Mrs. Hoskins, he dead."

Aunt Maggie screamed and rushed off the porch and down the dusty road into the night.

"Maggie!" my mother screamed.

"Don't you all go to that saloon," the boy called.

"Maggie!" my mother called, running after Aunt Maggie.

"They'll kill you if you go there!" the boy yelled. "White folks say they'll kill all his kinfolks!"

My mother pulled Aunt Maggie back to the house. Fear drowned out grief and that night we packed clothes and dishes and loaded them into a farmer's wagon. Before dawn we were rolling away, fleeing for our lives. I learned afterwards that Uncle Hoskins had been killed by whites who had long coveted his flourishing liquor business. He had been threatened with death and warned many times to leave, but he had wanted to hold on a while longer to amass more money. We got rooms in West Helena, and Aunt Maggie and my mother kept huddled in the house all day and night, afraid to be seen on the streets. Finally Aunt Maggie defied her fear and made frequent trips back to Elaine, but she went in secret and at night and would tell no one save my mother when she was going.

There was no funeral. There was no music. There was no period of mourning. There were no flowers. There were only silence, quiet weeping, whispers, and fear. I did not know when or where Uncle Hoskins was buried. Aunt Maggie was not even allowed to see his body nor was she able to claim any of his assets. Uncle Hoskins had simply been plucked from our midst and we, figuratively, had fallen on our faces to avoid looking into that white-hot face of terror that we knew loomed somewhere above us. This was as close as white terror had ever come to me and my mind reeled. Why had we not fought back, I asked my mother, and the fear that was in her made her slap me into silence.

Shocked, frightened, alone without their husbands or friends, my mother and Aunt Maggie lost faith in themselves and, after much debate and hesitation, they decided to return

home to Granny and rest, think, map out new plans for living. I had grown used to moving suddenly and the prospects
of another trip did not excite me. I had learned to leave old
places without regret and to accept new ones for what they
looked like. Though I was nearly nine years of age, I had not
had a single, unbroken year of school, and I was not conscious of it. I could read and count and that was about as
much as most of the people I met could do, grownups or
children. Again our household was torn apart; belongings
were sold, given away, or simply left behind, and we were off
for another long train ride.

A few days later—after we had arrived at Granny's—I was
playing alone in a wild field, digging in the ground with an
old knife. Suddenly a strange rhythmic sound made me turn
my head. Flowing threateningly toward me over the crest of a
hill was a wave of black men draped in weird mustard-colored
clothing. Unconsciously I jumped to my feet, my heart
pounding. What was this? Were these men coming after me?
Line by line, row by row, the fantastic men in their wild colors were descending straight at me, trotting, their feet pounding the earth like someone beating a vast drum. I wanted to
fly home but, as in a dream, I could not move. I cast about
wildly for a clue to tell me what this was, but I could find
nothing. The wall of men was drawing closer. My heart was
beating so strongly that it shook my body. Again I tried to
run, but I could not budge. My mother's name was on the tip
of my tongue and I opened my mouth to scream, but no
words came, for now the surging men, each looking exactly
like the other, parted and poured around me, jarring the
earth, their feet stomping in unison. As they flooded past I
saw that their black faces were looking at me and that some of
them were smiling. Then I noticed that each man was holding
a long, dark, heavy, sticklike object upon his shoulder. One of
the men yelled something at me which I did not understand.
They were past me now, disappearing in a great cloud of
brown dust that looked like a part of their clothing, that made
them seem akin to the elemental earth itself. As soon as they
were far enough away for me to conquer my fear, I dashed
home and babbled to my mother what I had seen, asking her
who the strange men were.

"Those were soldiers," she said.

"What are soldiers?" I asked.

"Men who fight in wars."

"Why do they fight?"

"Because their country tells them to."

"And what are those long black sticks they have on their shoulders?"

"Rifles."

"What's a rifle?"

"It's a gun that shoots a bullet."

"Like a pistol?"

"Yes."

"Would the bullet kill you?"

"Yes, if it hits you in the right place."

"Who are they going to shoot?"

"Germans."

"Who are Germans?"

"They are the enemy."

"What's an enemy?"

"The people who want to kill you and take your country away from you."

"Where do they live?"

" 'Way across the sea," my mother explained. "Don't you remember that I told you that war has been declared?"

I remembered; but when she had told me, it had not seemed at all important. I asked my mother what the war was about and she spoke of England, France, Russia, Germany, of men dying, but the reality of it was too vast and alien for me to be moved or further interested.

Upon another day I was playing out of doors in front of the house and I accidentally looked down the road and saw what seemed to me to be a herd of elephants coming slowly toward me. There was in me this time none of that naked terror I had felt when I had seen the soldiers, for these strange creatures were moving slowly, silently, with no suggestion of threat. Yet I edged cautiously toward the steps of the house, holding myself ready to run if they should prove to be more violent than they appeared. The strange elephants were a few feet from me now and I saw that their faces were like the faces of men! I stared, my mind trying to adjust memory to reality.

What kind of men were these? I saw that there were two lines of creatures that looked like men on either side of the road; that there were a few white faces and a great many black faces. I saw that the white faces were the faces of white men and they were dressed in ordinary clothing; but the black faces were men wearing what seemed to me to be elephant's clothing. As the strange animals came abreast of me I saw that the legs of the black animals were held together by irons and that their arms were linked with heavy chains that clanked softly and musically as they moved. The black creatures were digging a shallow ditch on each side of the road, working silently, grunting as they lifted spades of earth and flung them into the middle of the roadway. One of the strange, striped animals turned a black face upon me.

"What are you doing?" I asked in a whisper, not knowing if one actually spoke to elephants.

He shook his head and cast his eyes guardedly back at a white man, then dug on again. Suddenly I noticed that the white men were holding the long, heavy black sticks — rifles! — on their shoulders. After they had passed I ran breathlessly into the house.

"Mama!" I yelled.

"What?" she answered from the kitchen.

"There are elephants in the street!"

She came to the kitchen door and stared at me.

"Elephants?" she asked.

"Yes. Come and see them. They're digging in the street."

My mother dried her hands on her apron and rushed to the front door. I followed, wanting her to interpret the baffling spectacle I had seen. She looked out of the door and shook her head.

"Those are not elephants," she said.

"What are they?"

"That's a chain gang."

"What's a chain gang?"

"It's just what you see," she said. "A gang of men chained together and made to work."

"Why?"

"Because they've done something wrong and they're being punished.

"What did they do?"

"I don't know."

"But why do they look like that?"

"That's to keep them from running away," she said. "You see, everybody'll know that they're convicts because of their stripes."

"Why don't the white men wear stripes?"

"They're the guards."

"Do white men ever wear stripes?"

"Sometimes."

"Did you ever see any?"

"No."

"Why are there so many black men wearing stripes?"

"It's because . . . Well, they're harder on black people."

"The white people?"

"Yes."

"Then why don't all the black men fight all the white men out there? There are more black men than white men . . ."

"But the white men have guns and the black men don't," my mother said. She looked at me and asked: "What made you call them elephants?"

I could not answer her at the moment. But later, brooding over the black-and-white striped clothing of the black men, I remembered that in Elaine I had had a book that carried the gaudy pictures and names of jungle beasts. What had struck me most vividly were the striped zebras that looked as if someone had painted them. The other animals that had gripped my imagination were the elephants, and by association the zebras and the elephants had become linked and identified in my mind to such an extent that when I had seen the convicts dressed in the white and black stripes of zebras, I had thought they were elephants, beasts of the jungle.

Again, after an undetermined stretch of time, my mother announced that we were going to move, that we were going back to West Helena. She had grown tired of the strict religious routine of Granny's home; of the half dozen or more daily family prayers that Granny insisted upon; her fiat that the day began at sunrise and that night commenced at sundown; the long, rambling Bible readings; the individual invocations muttered at each meal; and her declaration that Saturday was the Lord's Sabbath and that no one who lived in her house could work upon that day. In West Helena we could have a home of our own, a condition that now loomed desirable after a few months of Granny's anxiety about the state of our souls. Naturally a trip was agreeable to me. Again we packed. Again we said good-bye. Again we rode the train. Again we were in West Helena.

We rented one half of a double corner house in front of which ran a stagnant ditch carrying sewage. The neighborhood swarmed with rats, cats, dogs, fortunetellers, cripples, blind men, whores, salesmen, rent collectors, and children. In front of our flat was a huge roundhouse where locomotives were cleaned and repaired. There was an eternal hissing of steam, the deep grunting of steel engines, and the tolling of bells. Smoke obscured the vision and cinders drifted into the house, into our beds, into our kitchen, into our food; and a tarlike smell was always in the air.

Bareheaded and barefooted, my brother and I, along with nameless and countless other black children, used to stand and watch the men crawl in, out, over, and under the huge black metal engines. When the men were not looking, we would climb into the engineer's cab and pull our small bodies to the window and look out, imagining that we were grown and had got a job as an engineer running a train and that it was night and there was a storm and we had a long string of passenger cars behind us, trying to get them safely home.

"Whooooooooeeeeeeeee!" we would say.

"Dong! Dong! Dong!"

"Huff-huff! Huff-huff-huff! Huff-huff-huff-huff!" we would say.

But our greatest fun came from wading in the sewage ditch where we found old bottles, tin cans that held tiny crawfish, rusty spoons, bits of metal, old toothbrushes, dead cats and dogs, and occasional pennies. We made wooden boats out of cigar boxes, devised wooden paddles to which we twisted pieces of rubber and sent the cigar-box boats sailing down the ditch under their own power. Many evenings the fathers of the children would come out, take off their shoes, and make and sail the boats themselves.

My mother and Aunt Maggie cooked in the kitchens of white folks and my brother and I were free to wander where we pleased during their working hours. Each day we were left a dime apiece to spend for lunch and all morning we would dream and discuss what we would buy. At ten or eleven o'clock we would go to the corner grocery—owned by a Jew—and buy a nickel's worth of ginger snaps and a bottle of Coca-Cola; that was lunch as we understood it.

I had never seen a Jew before and the proprietor of the corner grocery was a strange thing in my life. Until that time I had never heard a foreign language spoken and I used to linger at the door of the corner grocery to hear the odd sounds that Jews made when they talked. All of us black people who lived in the neighborhood hated Jews, not because they exploited us, but because we had been taught at home and in Sunday school that Jews were "Christ killers." With the Jews thus singled out for us, we made them fair game for ridicule.

We black children—seven, eight, and nine years of age— used to run to the Jew's store and shout:

> *Jew, Jew, Jew*
> *What do you chew?*

Or we would form a long line and weave back and forth in front of the door, singing:

> *Jew, Jew,*
> *Two for five*
> *That's what keeps*
> *Jew alive.*

Or we would chant:

> *Bloody Christ killers*
> *Never trust a Jew*
> *Bloody Christ killers*
> *What won't a Jew do?*

To one of the redheaded Jewish boys we sang:

> *Red head*
> *Jewish bread*
> *Five cents*
> *A Jewish head.*

To the fat Jewish woman we sneered:

> *Red, white, and blue*
> *Your pa was a Jew*
> *Your ma a dirty Dago*
> *What the hell is you?*

And when the baldheaded proprietor would pass by, we black children, poor, half-starved, ignorant, victims of racial prejudice, would sing with a proud lilt:

> *A rotten egg*
> *Never fries*
> *A cheating dog*
> *Never thrives.*

There were many more folk ditties, some mean, others filthy, all of them cruel. No one ever thought of questioning our right to do this; our mothers and parents generally approved, either actively or passively. To hold an attitude of antagonism or distrust toward Jews was bred in us from childhood; it was not merely racial prejudice, it was a part of our cultural heritage.

One afternoon a group of black boys and girls were standing about outside playing, laughing, talking. A black man dressed in overalls went up the steps and into the flat adjoining the one in which I lived.

"This is Saturday," a black girl said to me.

"Yeah. But why you say it?" I asked.

"They gonna make a lotta money in there today," she said, pointing to the door through which the man had disappeared.

"How?"

Another black man went up the steps and into the flat.

"Don't you know?" the girl asked, incredulous.

"Know what?"

"What they selling . . . !"

"Where?"

"In there where them men went," she said.

"Nobody sells things in there," I said.

"You kidding?" the girl said in honest disbelief.

"I ain't. What they selling? Tell me."

"You know what they selling," she said, looking at me with a teasing smile.

"They don't sell nothing in there," I said.

"Aw, you just a baby," she said, slapping her dingy palm through the air at me in a contemptuous gesture.

I was puzzled. Was there something happening next door to where I lived that I did not know? I thought I had poked my nose into every bit of conceivable business in the neighborhood; if something was being sold next door, then I certainly wanted to know about it. The building in which I lived was a double frame house of one story; the building originally had been a one-dwelling unit and had been converted into two flats, for there were doors in our flat that led into the flat adjoining. These doors had been locked, bolted, and nailed securely. The family next door seemed quiet; men came and went, but that did not seem odd to me. But now the girl's hints made me want to know what was happening over there. I entered our house and locked the door, then put my ear to the thin wall that divided the two flats and listened. I heard faint sounds, but could make nothing of them. I listened at a bolted door and the sounds came a little louder, but I still could understand nothing.

Quietly I pulled up a chair, placed a box upon it, and climbed up and peered through a crack at the top of the door. I saw, in the dim shadows of the room beyond, a naked man and a naked woman upon a bed, the man on top of the woman. I lost my balance and toppled backwards to the floor. I lay still, wondering if the man and woman next door had heard me. But all seemed quiet and my curiosity returned. Just as I had climbed up again to look, a sharp rapping came on the windowpane behind me; I turned my head and saw the landlady from next door looking at me. My heart thumped and I scrambled down. The landlady's black face was pressed hard against the windowpane; her mouth was moving violently and her eyes were glaring. I was afraid to stay in the house or go out. Why had I not thought of lowering the shade? Evidently I had done something terrible, if the wild anger written on the woman's face was any indication. Her face went from the window and a moment later a loud pounding came at the front door.

"Open this door, you boy!"

I trembled and did not answer.

"Open this door or I'll have to break it!"

"My mama ain't here," I said vaguely.

"This is my house and you open this door!" she shouted.

Her voice overpowered me and I opened the door. She rushed in, then stopped and stared at the clumsy scaffolding I had rigged up to look into her flat. Why hadn't I taken it down before I opened the door?

"Boy, what do you mean?" she asked.

I could not answer.

"You scared my customers," she said.

"Customers?" I repeated vaguely.

"You little snot!" she blazed. "I got a good mind to beat you!"

"Naw, you won't!" I said.

"I'm gonna make your folks move outta here," she railed. "I got to make a living and you go and spoil my Saturday for me!"

"I . . . I was just looking . . ."

"Looking . . . ?" She smiled suddenly, relenting a little. "Why don't you come on over like the rest and spend a quarter?"

"I don't want to go to your old house," I told her with my nine-year-old indignation.

"You're a plague," she said, deciding that I would not be a customer. "I'm gonna get you outta here!"

When my mother and Aunt Maggie came home that night, there was a scalding argument. The women shouted at each other over the wooden railings on the front porch and their voices could be heard for half a mile. Neighbors listened. Children gathered and gaped. The argument boiled down to one issue: the landlady demanded that my mother beat me and, for once, my mother refused.

"You oughtn't have *that* in your house," my mother told her

"It's my house and I'll have in it what I damn please," the landlady said.

"I wouldn't've moved in here if I had thought you were running *that* kind of business," my mother said.

"Don't talk to me like that, you high-toned bitch!" the landlady shouted.

"What do you expect children to do when you do *that*?" my mother asked.

"Them bastard brats of yours ain't no angels!" the landlady said.

"You're just a common prostitute!" Aunt Maggie pitched in.

"And what kind of whore is you?" the landlady shouted.

"Don't you talk to my sister like that!" my mother warned.

"Pack up your rags, you black bastards, and get!" the landlady ordered.

It ended with our packing and moving that night into another frame house on the same street, a few doors away. I still had only a hazy notion of what the landlady was selling. The boys later told me the name of it, but I had no exact conception of it in my mind. Though I knew that others felt it was something terribly bad, I was still curious. In time I would find out what it was.

Something secret was happening in our house and it had reached a serious stage before I knew it. Each night, just as I was dozing off to sleep, I would hear a light tapping on Aunt Maggie's windowpane, a door creaking open, whispers, then long silences. Once I got out of bed and crept to the door of the front room and stole a look. There was a well-dressed black man sitting on the sofa talking in a soft voice to Aunt Maggie. Why was it that I could not meet the man? I crept back to bed, but was awakened later by low voices saying goodbye. The next morning I asked my mother who had been in the house, and she told me that no one had been there.

"But I heard a man talking," I said.

"You didn't," she said. "You were sleeping."

"But I saw a man. He was in the front room."

"You were dreaming," my mother said.

I learned a part of the secret of the night visits one Sunday morning when Aunt Maggie called me and my brother to her room and introduced us to the man who was going to be our new "uncle," a Professor Matthews. He wore a high, snow-white collar and rimless eyeglasses. His lips were thin and his eyelids seemed never to blink. I felt something cold and remote in him and when he called me I would not go to him. He sensed my distrust and softened me up with the gift of a dime, then knelt and prayed for us two "poor fatherless young men," as he called us. After prayer Aunt Maggie told us that she and Professor Matthews were leaving soon for the North. I was saddened, for I had grown to feel that Aunt Maggie was another mother to me.

I did not meet the new "uncle" again, though each morning I saw evidences of his having been in the house. My brother and I were puzzled and we speculated as to what our new "uncle" could be doing. Why did he always come at night? Why did he always speak in so subdued a voice, hardly above a whisper? And how did he get the money to buy such white collars and such nice blue suits? To add to our bewilderment, our mother called us to her one day and cautioned us against telling anyone that "uncle" ever visited us, that people were looking for "uncle."

"What people?" I asked.

"White people," my mother said.

Anxiety entered my body. Somewhere in the unknown the white threat was hovering near again.

"What do they want with him?" I asked.

"You never mind," my mother said.

"What did he do?"

"You keep your mouth shut or the white folks'll get you too," she warned me.

Knowing that we were frightened and baffled about our new "uncle," my mother—I guess—urged Aunt Maggie to tell "uncle" to bribe us into silence and trust. Every morning now was like Christmas; we would climb out of bed and race to the kitchen and look on the table to see what "uncle" had left for us. One morning I found that he had brought me a little female poodle, upon which I bestowed the name of Betsy and she became my pet and companion.

Strangely, "uncle" began visiting us in the daytime now, but when he came all the shades in the house were drawn and we were forbidden to go out of doors until he left. I asked my mother a thousand whispered questions about the silent, black, educated "uncle" and she always replied:

"It's something you can't know. Now keep quiet and go play."

One night the sound of sobbing awakened me. I got up and went softly to the front room and peeped around the jamb of the door; there was "uncle" sitting on the floor by the window, peering into the night from under the lifted curtain. My mother was bent over a small trunk, packing hurriedly. Fear gripped me. Was my mother leaving? Why was Aunt Maggie crying? Were the white people coming after us?

"Hurry up," "uncle" said. "We must get out of here."

"Oh, Maggie," my mother said. "I don't know if you ought to go."

"You keep out of this," "uncle" said, still peering into the dark street.

"But what did you do?" Aunt Maggie asked.

"I'll tell you later," "uncle" said. "We got to get out of here before they come!"

"But you've done something terrible," Aunt Maggie said. "Or you wouldn't be running like this."

"The house is on fire," "uncle" said. "And when they see it, they'll know who did it."

"Did you set the house afire?" my mother asked.

"There was nothing else to do," "uncle" said impatiently. "I took the money. I had hit her. She was unconscious. If they found her, she'd tell. I'd be lost. So I set the fire."

"But she'll burn up," Aunt Maggie said, crying into her hands.

"What could I do?" "uncle" asked. "I had to do it. I couldn't just leave her there and let somebody find her. They'd know somebody hit her. But if she burns, nobody'll ever know."

Fear filled me. What was happening? Were white people coming after all of us? Was my mother going to leave me?

"Mama!" I wailed, running into the room.

"Uncle" leaped to his feet; a gun was in his hand and he was pointing it at me. I stared at the gun, feeling that I was going to die at any moment.

"Richard!" my mother whispered fiercely.

" You're going away!" I yelled.

My mother rushed to me and clapped her hand over my mouth.

"Do you want us all to be killed?" she asked, shaking me.

I quieted.

"Now you go back to sleep," she said.

"You're leaving," I said.

"I'm not."

"You are leaving. I see the trunk!" I wailed.

"You stop that noise," my mother said; and she caught my arms in so tight a grip of fury that my crying ceased because of the pain. "Now you get back in bed."

She led me back to bed and I lay awake, listening to whispers, footsteps, doors creaking in the dark, and the sobs of Aunt Maggie. Finally I heard the sound of a horse and buggy rolling up to the house; I heard the scraping of a trunk being dragged across the floor. Aunt Maggie came into my room, crying softly; she kissed me and whispered good-bye. She kissed my brother, who did not even waken. Then she was gone.

The next morning my mother called me into the kitchen and talked to me for a long time, cautioning me that I must never mention what I had seen and heard, that white people would kill me if they even thought I knew.

"Know what?" I could not help but ask.

"Never you mind, now," she said. "Forget what you saw last night."

"But what did 'uncle' do?"

"I can't tell you."

"He killed somebody," I ventured timidly.

"If anybody heard you say that, you'll die," my mother said.

That settled it for me; I would never mention it. A few days later a tall white man with a gleaming star on his chest and a gun on his hip came to the house. He talked with my mother a long time and all I could hear was my mother's voice:

"I don't know what you're talking about. Search the house if you like."

The tall white man looked at me and my brother, but he

said nothing to us. For weeks I wondered what it was that "uncle" had done, but I was destined never to know, not even in all the years that followed.

With Aunt Maggie gone, my mother could not earn enough to feed us and my stomach kept so consistently empty that my head ached most of the day. One afternoon hunger haunted me so acutely that I decided to try to sell my dog Betsy and buy some food. Betsy was a tiny, white, fluffy poodle and when I had washed, dried, and combed her, she looked like a toy. I tucked her under my arm and went for the first time alone into a white neighborhood where there were wide clean streets and big white houses. I went from door to door, ringing the bells. Some white people slammed the door in my face. Others told me to come to the rear of the house, but pride would never let me do that. Finally a young white woman came to the door and smiled.

"What do you want?" she asked.

"Do you want to buy a pretty dog?" I asked.

"Let me see it."

She took the dog into her arms and fondled and kissed it.

"What's its name?"

"Betsy."

"She is cute," she said. "What do you want for her?"

"A dollar," I said.

"Wait a moment," she said. "Let me see if I have a dollar."

She took Betsy into the house with her and I waited on the porch, marveling at the cleanliness, the quietness of the white world. How orderly everything was! Yet I felt out of place. I had no desire to live here. Then I remembered that these houses were the homes in which lived those white people who made Negroes leave their homes and flee into the night. I grew tense. Would someone say that I was a bad nigger and try to kill me here? What was keeping the woman so long? Would she tell other people that a nigger boy had said something wrong to her? Perhaps she was getting a mob? Maybe I ought to leave now and forget about Betsy? My mounting anxieties drowned out my hunger. I wanted to rush back to the safety of the black faces I knew.

The door opened and the woman came out, smiling, still

hugging Betsy in her arms. But I could not see her smile now; my eyes were full of the fears I had conjured up.

"I just love this dog," she said, "and I'm going to buy her. I haven't got a dollar. All I have is ninety-seven cents."

Though she did not know it, she was now giving me my opportunity to ask for my dog without saying that I did not want to sell her to white people.

"No, ma'am," I said softly. "I want a dollar."

"But I haven't got a dollar in the house," she said.

"Then I can't sell the dog," I said.

"I'll give you the other three cents when my mother comes home tonight," she said.

"No, ma'am," I said, looking stonily at the floor.

"But, listen, you said you wanted a dollar . . ."

"Yes, ma'am. A dollar."

"Then here is ninety-seven cents," she said, extending a handful of change to me, still holding on to Betsy.

"No, ma'am," I said, shaking my head. "I want a dollar."

"But I'll give you the other three cents!"

"My mama told me to sell her for a dollar," I said, feeling that I was being too aggressive and trying to switch the moral blame for my aggressiveness to my absent mother.

"You'll get a dollar. You'll get the three cents tonight."

"No, ma'am."

"Then leave the dog and come back tonight."

"No, ma'am."

"But what could you want with a dollar *now*?" she asked.

"I want to buy something to eat," I said.

"Then ninety-seven cents will buy you a lot of food," she said.

"No, ma'am. I want my dog."

She stared at me for a moment and her face grew red.

"Here's your dog," she snapped, thrusting Betsy into my arms. "Now, get away from here! You're just about the craziest nigger boy I ever did see!"

I took Betsy and ran all the way home, glad that I had not sold her. But my hunger returned. Maybe I ought to have taken the ninety-seven cents? But it was too late now. I hugged Betsy in my arms and waited. When my mother came home that night, I told her what had happened.

"And you didn't take the money?" she asked.

"No, ma'am."

"Why?"

"I don't know," I said uneasily.

"Don't you know that ninety-seven cents is *almost* a dollar?" she asked.

"Yes, ma'am," I said, counting on my fingers. "Ninety-eight, ninety-nine, one hundred. But I didn't want to sell Betsy to white people."

"Why?"

"Because they're white," I said.

"You're foolish," my mother said.

A week later Betsy was crushed to death beneath the wheels of a coal wagon. I cried and buried her in the back yard and drove a barrel staving into the ground at the head of her grave. My mother's sole comment was:

"You could have had a dollar. But you can't eat a dead dog, can you?"

I did not answer.

Up or down the wet or dusty streets, indoors or out, the days and nights began to spell out magic possibilities.

If I pulled a hair from a horse's tail and sealed it in a jar of my own urine, the hair would turn overnight into a snake.

If I passed a Catholic sister or mother dressed in black and smiled and allowed her to see my teeth, I would surely die.

If I walked under a leaning ladder, I would certainly have bad luck.

If I kissed my elbow, I would turn into a girl.

If my right ear itched, then something good was being said about me by somebody.

If I touched a hunchback's hump, then I would never be sick.

If I placed a safety pin on a steel railroad track and let a train run over it, the safety pin would turn into a pair of bright brand-new scissors.

If I heard a voice and no human being was near, then either God or the Devil was trying to talk to me.

Whenever I made urine, I should spit into it for good luck.

If my nose itched, somebody was going to visit me.

If I mocked a crippled man, then God would make me crippled.

If I used the name of God in vain, then God would strike me dead.

If it rained while the sun was shining, then the Devil was beating his wife.

If the stars twinkled more than usual on any given night, it meant that the angels in heaven were happy and were flitting across the doors of heaven; and since stars were merely holes ventilating heaven, the twinkling came from the angels flitting past the holes that admitted air into the holy home of God.

If I broke a mirror, I would have seven years of bad luck.

If I was good to my mother, I would grow old and rich.

If I had a cold and tied a worn, dirty sock about my throat before I went to bed, the cold would be gone the next morning.

If I wore a bit of asafetida in a little bag tied about my neck, I would never catch a disease.

If I looked at the sun through a piece of smoked glass on Easter Sunday morning, I would see the sun shouting in praise of a Risen Lord.

If a man confessed anything on his deathbed, it was the truth; for no man could stare death in the face and lie.

If you spat on each grain of corn that was planted, the corn would grow tall and bear well.

If I spilt salt, I should toss a pinch over my left shoulder to ward off misfortune.

If I covered a mirror when a storm was raging, the lightning would not strike me.

If I stepped over a broom that was lying on the floor, I would have bad luck.

If I walked in my sleep, then God was trying to lead me somewhere to do a good deed for Him.

Anything seemed possible, likely, feasible, because I wanted everything to be possible . . . Because I had no power to make things happen outside of me in the objective world, I made things happen within. Because my environment was bare and bleak, I endowed it with unlimited potentialities, redeemed it for the sake of my own hungry and cloudy yearning.

A dread of white people now came to live permanently in

my feelings and imagination. As the war drew to a close, racial conflict flared over the entire South, and though I did not witness any of it, I could not have been more thoroughly affected by it if I had participated directly in every clash. The war itself had been unreal to me, but I had grown able to respond emotionally to every hint, whisper, word, inflection, news, gossip, and rumor regarding conflicts between the races. Nothing challenged the totality of my personality so much as this pressure of hate and threat that stemmed from the invisible whites. I would stand for hours on the doorsteps of neighbors' houses listening to their talk, learning how a white woman had slapped a black woman, how a white man had killed a black man. It filled me with awe, wonder, and fear, and I asked ceaseless questions.

One evening I heard a tale that rendered me sleepless for nights. It was of a Negro woman whose husband had been seized and killed by a mob. It was claimed that the woman vowed she would avenge her husband's death and she took a shotgun, wrapped it in a sheet, and went humbly to the whites, pleading that she be allowed to take her husband's body for burial. It seemed that she was granted permission to come to the side of her dead husband while the whites, silent and armed, looked on. The woman, so went the story, knelt and prayed, then proceeded to unwrap the sheet; and, before the white men realized what was happening, she had taken the gun from the sheet and had slain four of them, shooting at them from her knees.

I did not know if the story was factually true or not, but it was emotionally true because I had already grown to feel that there existed men against whom I was powerless, men who could violate my life at will. I resolved that I would emulate the black woman if I were ever faced with a white mob; I would conceal a weapon, pretend that I had been crushed by the wrong done to one of my loved ones; then, just when they thought I had accepted their cruelty as the law of my life, I would let go with my gun and kill as many of them as possible before they killed me. The story of the woman's deception gave form and meaning to confused defensive feelings that had long been sleeping in me.

My imaginings, of course, had no objective value whatever.

My spontaneous fantasies lived in my mind because I felt completely helpless in the face of this threat that might come upon me at any time, and because there did not exist to my knowledge any possible course of action which could have saved me if I had ever been confronted with a white mob. My fantasies were a moral bulwark that enabled me to feel I was keeping my emotional integrity whole, a support that enabled my personality to limp through days lived under the threat of violence.

These fantasies were no longer a reflection of my reaction to the white people, they were a part of my living, of my emotional life; they were a culture, a creed, a religion. The hostility of the whites had become so deeply implanted in my mind and feelings that it had lost direct connection with the daily environment in which I lived; and my reactions to this hostility fed upon itself, grew or diminished according to the news that reached me about the whites, according to what I aspired or hoped for. Tension would set in at the mere mention of whites and a vast complex of emotions, involving the whole of my personality, would be aroused. It was as though I was continuously reacting to the threat of some natural force whose hostile behavior could not be predicted. I had never in my life been abused by whites, but I had already become as conditioned to their existence as though I had been the victim of a thousand lynchings.

I lived in West Helena an undeterminedly long time before I returned to school and took up regular study. My mother luckily secured a job in a white doctor's office at the unheard-of wages of five dollars per week and at once she announced that her "sons were going to school again." I was happy. But I was still shy and half paralyzed when in the presence of a crowd, and my first day at the new school made me the laughingstock of the classroom. I was sent to the blackboard to write my name and address; I knew my name and address, knew how to write it, knew how to spell it; but standing at the blackboard with the eyes of the many girls and boys looking at my back made me freeze inside and I was unable to write a single letter.

"Write your name," the teacher called to me.

I lifted the white chalk to the blackboard and, as I was

about to write, my mind went blank, empty; I could not remember my name, not even the first letter. Somebody giggled and I stiffened.

"Just forget us and write your name and address," the teacher coaxed.

An impulse to write would flash through me, but my hand would refuse to move. The children began to twitter and I flushed hotly.

"Don't you know your name?" the teacher asked.

I looked at her and could not answer. The teacher rose and walked to my side, smiling at me to give me confidence. She placed her hand tenderly upon my shoulder.

"What's your name?" she asked.

"Richard," I whispered.

"Richard what?"

"Richard Wright."

"Spell it."

I spelled my name in a wild rush of letters, trying desperately to redeem my paralyzing shyness.

"Spell it slowly so I can hear it," she directed me.

I did.

"Now, can you write?"

"Yes, ma'am."

"Then write it."

Again I turned to the blackboard and lifted my hand to write, then I was blank and void within. I tried frantically to collect my senses, but I could remember nothing. A sense of the girls and boys behind me filled me to the exclusion of everything. I realized how utterly I was failing and I grew weak and leaned my hot forehead against the cold blackboard. The room burst into a loud and prolonged laugh and my muscles froze.

"You may go to your seat," the teacher said.

I sat and cursed myself. Why did I always appear so dumb when I was called upon to perform something in a crowd? I knew how to write as well as any pupil in the classroom, and no doubt I could read better than any of them, and I could talk fluently and expressively when I was sure of myself. Then why did strange faces make me freeze? I sat with my ears and neck burning, hearing the pupils whisper about me, hating myself, hating them; I sat still as stone and a storm of emotion surged through me.

While sitting in class one day I was startled to hear whistles blowing and bells ringing. Soon the bedlam was deafening. The teacher lost control of her class and the girls and boys ran to the windows. The teacher left the room and when she returned she announced:

"Everybody, pack your things and go home!"

"Why?"

"What's happened?"

"The war is over," the teacher said.

I followed the rest of the children into the streets and saw that white and black people were laughing and singing and shouting. I felt afraid as I pushed through crowds of white people, but my fright left when I entered my neighborhood and saw smiling black faces. I wandered among them, trying to realize what war was, what it meant, and I could not. I noticed that many girls and boys were pointing at something in the sky; I looked up too and saw what seemed to be a tiny bird wheeling and sailing.

"Look!"

"A plane!"

I had never seen a plane.

"It's a bird," I said.

The crowd laughed.

"That's a plane, boy," a man said.

"It's a bird," I said. "I see it."

A man lifted me upon his shoulder.

"Boy, remember this," he said. "You're seeing man fly."

I still did not believe it. It still looked like a bird to me. That night at home my mother convinced me that men could fly.

Christmas came and I had but one orange. I was hurt and would not go out to play with the neighborhood children who were blowing horns and shooting firecrackers. I nursed my orange all of Christmas Day; at night, just before going to bed, I ate it, first taking a bite out of the top and sucking the juice from it as I squeezed it; finally I tore the peeling into bits and munched them slowly.

Chapter III

H AVING GROWN taller and older, I now associated with
older boys and I had to pay for my admittance into
their company by subscribing to certain racial sentiments. The
touchstone of fraternity was my feeling toward white people,
how much hostility I held toward them, what degrees of
value and honor I assigned to race. None of this was premed-
itated, but sprang spontaneously out of the talk of black boys
who met at the crossroads.

It was degrading to play with girls and in our talk we rele-
gated them to a remote island of life. We had somehow
caught the spirit of the role of our sex and we flocked together for common moral schooling. We spoke boastfully in
bass voices; we used the word "nigger" to prove the tough
fiber of our feelings; we spouted excessive profanity as a sign
of our coming manhood; we pretended callousness toward
the injunctions of our parents; and we strove to convince one
another that our decisions stemmed from ourselves and ourselves alone. Yet we frantically concealed how dependent we
were upon one another.

Of an afternoon when school had let out I would saunter
down the street, idly kicking an empty tin can, or knocking a
stick against the palings of a wooden fence, or whistling, until
I would stumble upon one or more of the gang loitering at a
corner, standing in a field, or sitting upon the steps of somebody's house.

"Hey." Timidly.

"You eat yet?" Uneasily trying to make conversation.

"Yeah, man. I done really fed my face." Casually.

"I had cabbage and potatoes." Confidently.

"I had buttermilk and black-eyed peas." Meekly informational.

"Hell, I ain't gonna stand near you, nigger!" Pronouncement.

"How come?" Feigned innocence.

" 'Cause you gonna smell up this air in a minute!" A
shouted accusation.

Laughter runs through the crowd.

"Nigger, your mind's in a ditch." Amusingly moralistic.

"Ditch, nothing! Nigger, you going to break wind any minute now!" Triumphant pronouncement creating suspense.

"Yeah, when them black-eyed peas tell that buttermilk to move over, that buttermilk ain't gonna wanna move and there's gonna be war in your guts and your stomach's gonna swell up and bust!" Climax.

The crowd laughs loud and long.

"Man, them white folks oughta catch you and send you to the zoo and keep you for the next war!" Throwing the subject into a wider field.

"Then when that fighting starts, they oughta feed you on buttermilk and black-eyed peas and let you break wind!" The subject is accepted and extended.

"You'd win the war with a new kind of poison gas!" A shouted climax.

There is high laughter that simmers down slowly.

"Maybe poison gas is something good to have." The subject of white folks is associationally swept into the orbit of talk.

"Yeah, if they hava race riot round here, I'm gonna kill all the white folks with my poison." Bitter pride.

Gleeful laughter. Then silence, each waiting for the other to contribute something.

"Them white folks sure scared of us, though." Sober statement of an old problem.

"Yeah, they send you to war, make you lick them Germans, teach you how to fight and when you come back they scared of you, want to kill you." Half boastful and half complaining.

"My mama says that old white woman where she works talked 'bout slapping her and Ma said: 'Miz Green, if you slaps me, I'll kill you and go to hell and pay for it!' " Extension, development, sacrificial boasting.

"Hell, I woulda just killed her if she hada said that to me." An angry grunt of supreme racial assertion.

Silence.

"Man, them white folks sure is mean." Complaining.

"That's how come so many colored folks leaving the South." Informational.

"And, man, they sure hate for you to leave." Pride of personal and racial worth implied.

"Yeah. They wanna keep you here and work you to death."

"The first white sonofabitch that bothers me is gonna get a hole knocked in his head!" Naïve rebellion.

"That ain't gonna do you no good. Hell, they'll catch you." Rejection of naïve rebellion.

"Ha-ha-ha . . . Yeah, goddammit, they really catch you, now." Appreciation of the thoroughness of white militancy.

"Yeah, white folks set on their white asses day and night, but leta nigger do something, and they get every bloodhound that was ever born and put 'em on his trail." Bitter pride in realizing what it costs to defeat them.

"Man, you reckon these white folks is ever gonna change?" Timid, questioning hope.

"Hell, no! They just born that way." Rejecting hope for fear that it could never come true.

"Shucks, man. I'm going north when I get grown." Rebelling against futile hope and embracing flight.

"A colored man's all right up north." Justifying flight.

"They say a white man hit a colored man up north and that colored man hit that white man, knocked him cold, and nobody did a damn thing!" Urgent wish to believe in flight.

"Man for man up there." Begging to believe in justice.

Silence.

"Listen, you reckon them buildings up north is as tall as they say they is?" Leaping by association to something concrete and trying to make belief real.

"They say they gotta building in New York forty stories high!" A thing too incredible for belief.

"Man, I'd be scareda them buildings!" Ready to abandon the now suppressed idea of flight.

"You know, they say that them buildings sway and rock in the wind." Stating a miracle.

"Naw, nigger!" Utter astonishment and rejection.

"Yeah, they say they do." Insisting upon the miracle.

"You reckon that could be?" Questioning hope.

"Hell, naw! If a building swayed and rocked in the wind, hell, it'd fall! Any fool knows that! Don't let people maka fool outta you, telling you them things!" Moving body agitatedly, stomping feet impatiently, and scurrying back to safe reality.

Silence. Somebody would pick up a stone and toss it across a field.

"Man, what makes white folks so mean?" Returning to grapple with the old problem.

"Whenever I see one I spit." Emotional rejection of whites.

"Man, ain't they ugly?" Increased emotional rejection.

"Man, you ever get right close to a white man, close enough to smell 'im?" Anticipation of statement.

"They say we stink. But my ma says white folks smell like dead folks." Wishing the enemy was dead.

"Niggers smell from sweat. But white folks smell *all* the time." The enemy is an animal to be killed on sight.

And the talk would weave, roll, surge, spurt, veer, swell, having no specific aim or direction, touching vast areas of life, expressing the tentative impulses of childhood. Money, God, race, sex, color, war, planes, machines, trains, swimming, boxing, anything . . . The culture of one black household was thus transmitted to another black household, and folk tradition was handed from group to group. Our attitudes were made, defined, set, or corrected; our ideas were discovered, discarded, enlarged, torn apart, and accepted. Night would fall. Bats would zip through the air. Crickets would cry from the grass. Frogs would croak. The stars would come out. Dew would dampen the earth. Yellow squares of light would glow in the distance as kerosene lamps were lit in our homes. Finally, from across the fields or down the road a long slow yell would come:

"Youuuuuuuu, Daaaaaaaavee!"

Easy laughter among the boys, but no reply.

"Calling the hogs."

"Go home, pig."

Laughter again. A boy would slowly detach himself from the gang.

"Youuuuuuuu, Daaaaaaaavee!"

He would not answer his mother's call, for that would have been a sign of dependence.

"I'll do you-all like the farmer did the potato," the boy would say.

"How's that?"

"Plant you now and dig you later!"

The boy would trot home slowly and there would be more easy laughter. More talk. One by one we would be called home to fetch water from the hydrant in the back yard, to go to the store and buy greens and meal for tomorrow, to split wood for kindling.

On Sundays, if our clothes were presentable, my mother would take me and my brother to Sunday school. We did not object, for church was not where we learned of God or His ways, but where we met our school friends and continued our long, rambling talks. Some of the Bible stories were interesting in themselves, but we always twisted them, secularized them to the level of our street life, rejecting all meanings that did not fit into our environment. And we did the same to the beautiful hymns. When the preacher intoned:

Amazing grace, how sweet it sounds

we would wink at one another and hum under our breath:

A bulldog ran my grandma down

We were now large enough for the white boys to fear us and both of us, the white boys and the black boys, began to play our traditional racial roles as though we had been born to them, as though it was in our blood, as though we were being guided by instinct. All the frightful descriptions we had heard about each other, all the violent expressions of hate and hostility that had seeped into us from our surroundings, came now to the surface to guide our actions. The roundhouse was the racial boundary of the neighborhood, and it had been tacitly agreed between the white boys and the black boys that the whites were to keep to the far side of the roundhouse and we blacks were to keep to our side. Whenever we caught a white boy on our side we stoned him; if we strayed to their side, they stoned us.

Our battles were real and bloody; we threw rocks, cinders, coal, sticks, pieces of iron, and broken bottles, and while we threw them we longed for even deadlier weapons. If we were hurt, we took it quietly; there was no crying or whimpering. If our wounds were not truly serious, we hid them from our parents. We did not want to be beaten for fighting. Once, in a battle with a gang of white boys, I was struck behind the ear with a piece of broken bottle; the cut was deep and bled profusely. I tried to stem the flow of blood by dabbing at the cut with a rag and when my mother came from work I was forced to tell her that I was hurt, for I needed medical attention. She rushed me to a doctor who stitched my scalp; but when she took me home she beat me, telling me that I must never fight white boys again, that I might be killed by them, that she had to work and had no time to worry about my fights. Her words did not sink in, for they conflicted with the code of the streets. I promised my mother that I would not fight, but I knew that if I kept my word I would lose my standing in the gang, and the gang's life was my life.

My mother became too ill to work and I began to do chores in the neighborhood. My first job was carrying lunches to the men who worked in the roundhouse, for which I received twenty-five cents a week. When the men did not finish their lunches, I would salvage what few crumbs remained. Later I obtained a job in a small café carting wood in my arms to keep the big stove going and taking trays of food to passengers when trains stopped for a half hour or so in a near-by station. I received a dollar a week for this work, but I was too young and too small to perform the duties; one morning while trying to take a heavily loaded tray up the steps of a train, I fell and dashed the tray of food to the ground.

Inability to pay rent forced us to move into a house perched atop high logs in a section of the town where flood waters came. My brother and I had great fun running up and down the tall, shaky steps.

Again paying rent became a problem and we moved nearer the center of town, where I found a job in a pressing shop, delivering clothes to hotels, sweeping floors, and listening to Negro men boast of their sex lives.

Yet again we moved, this time to the outskirts of town, near a wide stretch of railroad tracks to which, each morning before school, I would take a sack and gather coal to heat our frame house, dodging in and out between the huge, black, puffing engines.

My mother, her health failing rapidly, spoke constantly now of Granny's home, of how ardently she wanted to see us grow up before she died. Already there had crept into her speech a halting, lisping quality that, though I did not know it, was the shadow of her future. I was more conscious of my mother now than I had ever been and I was already able to feel what being completely without her would mean. A slowly rising dread stole into me and I would look at my mother for long moments, but when she would look at me I would look away. Then real fear came as her illness recurred at shorter intervals. Time stood still. My brother and I waited, hungry and afraid.

One morning a shouting voice awakened me.

"Richard! Richard!"

I rolled out of bed. My brother came running into the room.

"Richard, you better come and see Mama. She's very sick," he said.

I ran into my mother's room and saw her lying upon her bed, dressed, her eyes open, her mouth gaped. She was very still.

"Mama!" I called.

She did not answer or turn her head. I reached forward to shake her, but drew back, afraid that she was dead.

"Mama!" I called again, my mind unable to grasp that she could not answer.

Finally I went to her and shook her. She moved slightly and groaned. My brother and I called her repeatedly, but she did not speak. Was she dying? It seemed unthinkable. My brother and I looked at each other; we did not know what to do.

"We better get somebody," I said.

I ran into the hallway and called a neighbor. A tall, black woman bustled out of a door.

"Please, won't you come and see my mama? She won't talk. We can't wake her up. She's terribly sick," I told her.

She followed me into our flat.

"Mrs. Wright!" she called to my mother.

My mother lay still, unseeing, silent. The woman felt my mother's hands.

"She ain't dead," she said. "But she's sick, all right. I better get some more of the neighbors."

Five or six of the women came and my brother and I
waited in the hallway while they undressed my mother and
put her to bed. When we were allowed back in the room, a
woman said:

"Looks like a stroke to me."

"Just like paralysis," said another.

"And she's so young," someone else said.

My brother and I stood against a wall while the bustling
women worked frantically over my mother. A stroke? Paralysis? What were those things? Would she die? One of the
women asked me if there was any money in the house; I did
not know. They searched through the dresser and found a
dollar or two and sent for a doctor. The doctor arrived. Yes,
he told us, my mother had suffered a stroke of paralysis. She
was in a serious condition. She needed someone with her day
and night; she needed medicine. Where was her husband? I
told him the story and he shook his head.

"She'll need all the help that she can get," the doctor said.
"Her entire left side is paralyzed. She cannot talk and she will
have to be fed."

Later that day I rummaged through drawers and found
Granny's address; I wrote to her, pleading with her to come
and help us. The neighbors nursed my mother day and night,
fed us and washed our clothes. I went through the days with
a stunned consciousness, unable to believe what had happened. Suppose Granny did not come? I tried not to think of
it. She *had* to come. The utter loneliness was now terrifying. I
had been suddenly thrown emotionally upon my own. Within
an hour the half-friendly world that I had known had turned
cold and hostile. I was too frightened to weep. I was glad that
my mother was not dead, but there was the fact that she
would be sick for a long, long time, perhaps for the balance of
her life. I became morose. Though I was a child, I could no
longer feel as a child, could no longer react as a child. The
desire for play was gone and I brooded, wondering if Granny
would come and help us. I tried not to think of a tomorrow
that was neither real nor wanted, for all tomorrows held questions that I could not answer.

When the neighbors offered me food, I refused, already
ashamed that so often in my life I had to be fed by strangers.

And after I had been prevailed upon to eat I would eat as little as possible, feeling that some of the shame of charity would be taken away. It pained me to think that other children were wondering if I were hungry, and whenever they asked me if I wanted food, I would say no, even though I was starving. I was tense during the days I waited for Granny, and when she came I gave up, letting her handle things, answering questions automatically, obeying, knowing that somehow I had to face things alone. I withdrew into myself.

I wrote letters that Granny dictated to her eight children—there were nine of them, including my mother—in all parts of the country, asking for money with which "to take Ella and her two little children to our home." Money came and again there were days of packing household effects. My mother was taken to the train in an ambulance and put on board upon a stretcher. We rode to Jackson in silence and my mother was put abed upstairs. Aunt Maggie came from Detroit to help nurse and clean. The big house was quiet. We spoke in lowered voices. We walked with soft tread. The odor of medicine hung in the air. Doctors came and went. Night and day I could hear my mother groaning. We thought that she would die at any moment.

Aunt Cleo came from Chicago. Uncle Clark came from Greenwood, Mississippi. Uncle Edward came from Carters, Mississippi. Uncle Charles from Mobile, Alabama. Aunt Addie from a religious school in Huntsville, Alabama. Uncle Thomas from Hazelhurst, Mississippi. The house had an expectant air and I caught whispered talk of "what is to become of her children?" I felt dread, knowing that others—strangers even though they were relatives—were debating my destiny. I had never seen my mother's brothers and sisters before and their presence made live again in me my old shyness. One day Uncle Edward called me to him and he felt my skinny arms and legs.

"He needs more flesh on him," he commented impersonally, addressing himself to his brothers and sisters.

I was horribly embarrassed, feeling that my life had somehow been full of nameless wrong, an unatonable guilt.

"Food will make him pick up in weight," Granny said.

Out of the family conferences it was decided that my

brother and I would be separated, that it was too much of a
burden for any one aunt or uncle to assume the support of
both of us. Where was I to go? Who would take me? I became more anxious than ever. When an aunt or an uncle
would come into my presence, I could not look at them. I
was always reminding myself that I must not do anything that
would make any of them feel they would not want me in their
homes.

At night my sleep was filled with wild dreams. Sometimes
I would wake up screaming in terror. The grownups would
come running and I would stare at them, as though they
were figures out of my nightmare, then go back to sleep. One
night I found myself standing in the back yard. The moon
was shining bright as day. Silence surrounded me. Suddenly I
felt that someone was holding my hand. I looked and saw an
uncle. He was speaking to me in a low, gentle voice.

"What's the matter, son?"

I stared at him, trying to understand what he was saying. I
seemed to be wrapped in a kind of mist.

"Richard, what are you doing?"

I could not answer. It seemed that I could not wake up. He
shook me. I came to myself and stared about at the moon-
drenched yard.

"Where are we going?" I asked him.

"You were walking in your sleep," he said.

Granny gave me fuller meals and made me take naps in the
afternoon and gradually my sleepwalking passed. The uneasy
days and nights made me resolve to leave Granny's home as
soon as I was old enough to support myself. It was not that
they were unkind, but I knew that they did not have money
enough to feed me and my brother. I avoided going into my
mother's room now; merely to look at her was painful. She
had grown very thin; she was still speechless, staring, quiet as
stone.

One evening my brother and I were called into the front
room where a conference of aunts and uncles was being
held.

"Richard," said an uncle, "you know how sick your
mother is?"

"Yes, sir."

"Well, Granny's not strong enough to take care of you two boys," he continued.

"Yes, sir," I said, waiting for his decision.

"Well, Aunt Maggie's going to take your brother to Detroit and send him to school."

I waited. Who was going to take me? I had wanted to be with Aunt Maggie, but I did not dare contest the decision.

"Now, where would you like to go?" I was asked.

The question caught me by surprise; I had been waiting for a fiat, and now a choice lay before me. But I did not have the courage to presume that anyone wanted me.

"Anywhere," I said.

"Any of us are willing to take you," he said.

Quickly I calculated which of them lived nearest to Jackson. Uncle Clark lived in Greenwood, which was but a few miles distant.

"I'd like to live with Uncle Clark, since he's close to the home here," I said.

"Is that what you really want?"

"Yes, sir."

Uncle Clark came to me and placed his hand upon my head.

"All right. I'll take you back with me and send you to school. Tomorrow we'll go and buy clothes."

My tension eased somewhat, but stayed with me. My brother was happy. He was going north. I wanted to go, but I said nothing.

A train ride and I was in yet another little southern town. Home in Greenwood was a four-room bungalow, comprising half of a double house that sat on a quiet shady road. Aunt Jody, a medium-sized, neat, silent, mulatto girl, had a hot supper waiting on the table. She baffled me with her serious, reserved manner; she seemed to be acting in conformity with a code unknown to me, and I assumed that she regarded me as a "wrong one," a boy who for some reason did not have a home; I felt that in her mind she would push me to the outskirts of life and I was awkward and self-conscious in her presence. Both Uncle Clark and Aunt Jody talked to me as though I were a grownup and I wondered if I could do what was expected of me. I had always felt a certain warmth with my mother, even when we had lived in squalor; but I felt none here. Perhaps I was too apprehensive to feel any.

During supper it was decided that I was to be placed in school the next day. Uncle Clark and Aunt Jody both had jobs and I was told that at noon I would find lunch on the stove.

"Now, Richard, this is your new home," Uncle Clark said.

"Yes, sir."

"After school, bring in wood and coal for the fireplaces."

"Yes, sir."

"Split kindling and lay a fire in the kitchen stove."

"Yes, sir."

"Bring in a bucket of water from the yard so that Jody can cook in the mornings."

"Yes, sir."

"After your chores are done, you may spend the afternoon studying."

"Yes, sir."

I had never been assigned definite tasks before and I went to bed a little frightened. I lay sleepless, wondering if I should have come, feeling the dark night holding strange people, strange houses, strange streets. What would happen to me here? How would I get along? What kind of woman was Aunt Jody? How ought I act around her? Would Uncle Clark let me make friends with other boys? I awakened the next morning to see the sun shining into my room; I felt more at ease.

"Richard!" my uncle was calling me.

I washed, dressed, and went into the kitchen and sat wordlessly at the table.

"Good morning, Richard," Aunt Jody said.

"Oh, good morning," I mumbled, wishing that I had thought to say it first.

"Don't people say good morning where you come from?" she asked.

"Yes, ma'am."

"I thought they did," she said pointedly.

Aunt Jody and Uncle Clark began to question me about my life and I grew so self-conscious that my hunger left me. After breakfast, Uncle Clark took me to school, introduced me to the principal. The first half of the school day passed without

incident. I sat looking at the strange reading book, following
the lessons. The subjects seemed simple and I felt that I could
keep up. My anxiety was still in me; I was wondering how I
would get on with the boys. Each new school meant a new
area of life to be conquered. Were the boys tough? How hard
did they fight? I took it for granted that they fought.

At noon recess I went into the school grounds and a group
of boys sauntered up to me, looked at me from my head to
my feet, whispering among themselves. I leaned against a
wall, trying to conceal my uneasiness.

"Where you from?" a boy asked abruptly.

"Jackson," I answered.

"How come they make you people so ugly in Jackson?" he
demanded.

There was loud laughter.

"You're not any too good-looking yourself," I countered
instantly.

"Oh!"

"Aw!"

"You hear what he told 'im?"

"You think you're smart, don't you?" the boy asked, sneering.

"Listen, I ain't picking a fight," I said. "But if you want to
fight, I'll fight."

"Hunh, hard guy, ain't you?"

"As hard as you."

"Do you know who you can tell that to?" he asked me.

"And you know who you can tell it back to?" I asked.

"Are you talking about my mama?" he asked, edging forward.

"If you want it that way," I said.

This was my test. If I failed now, I would have failed at
school, for the first trial came not in books, but in how one's
fellows took one, what value they placed upon one's willing-
ness to fight.

"Take back what you said," the boy challenged me.

"Make me," I said.

The crowd howled, sensing a fight. The boy hesitated,
weighing his chances of beating me.

"You ain't gonna take what that new boy said, is you?"
someone taunted the boy.

The boy came close. I stood my ground. Our faces were four inches apart.

"You think I'm scared of you, don't you?" he asked.

"I told you what I think," I said.

Somebody, eager and afraid that we would not fight, pushed the boy and he bumped into me. I shoved him away violently.

"Don't push me!" the boy said.

"Then keep off me!" I said.

He was pushed again and I struck out with my right and caught him in the mouth. The crowd yelled, milled, surging so close that I could barely lift my arm to land a blow. When either of us tried to strike the other, we would be thrown off balance by the screaming boys. Every blow landed elicited shouts of delight. Knowing that if I did not win or make a good showing I would have to fight a new boy each day, I fought tigerishly, trying to leave a scar, seeking to draw blood as proof that I was not a coward, that I could take care of myself. The bell rang and the crowd pulled us apart. The fight seemed a draw.

"I ain't through with you!" the boy shouted.

"Go to hell!" I answered.

In the classroom the boys asked me questions about myself; I was someone worth knowing. When the bell rang for school to be dismissed, I was set to fight again; but the boy was not in sight.

On my way home I found a cheap ring in the streets and at once I knew what I was going to do with it. The ring had a red stone held by tiny prongs which I loosened, took the stone out, leaving the sharp tiny prongs jutting up. I slid the ring on to my finger and shadow boxed. Now, by God, let a goddamn bully come and I would show him how to fight; I would leave a crimson streak on his face with every blow.

But I never had to use the ring. After I had exhibited my new weapon at school, a description of it spread among the boys. I challenged my enemy to another fight, but he would not respond. Fighting was not now necessary. I had been accepted.

No sooner had I won my right to the school grounds than a new dread arose. One evening, before bedtime, I was sitting in the front room, reading, studying. Uncle Clark, who was a contracting carpenter, was at his drawing table, drafting models of houses. Aunt Jody was darning. Suddenly the doorbell rang and Aunt Jody admitted the next-door neighbor, the owner of the house in which we lived and its former occupant. His name was Burden; he was a tall, brown, stooped man and when I was introduced to him I rose and shook his hand.

"Well, son," Mr. Burden told me, "it's certainly a comfort to see another boy in this house."

"Is there another boy here?" I asked eagerly.

"My son was here," Mr. Burden said, shaking his head. "But he's gone now."

"How old is he?" I asked.

"He was about your age," Mr. Burden mumbled sadly.

"Where did he go?" I asked stupidly.

"He's dead," Mr. Burden said.

"Oh," I said.

I had not understood him. There was a long silence. Mr. Burden looked at me wistfully.

"Do you sleep in there?" he asked, pointing to my room.

"Yes, sir."

"That's where my boy slept," he said.

"In *there*?" I asked, just to make sure.

"Yes, right in there."

"On *that* bed?" I asked.

"Yes, that was his bed. When I heard that you were coming, I gave your uncle that bed for you," he explained.

I saw Uncle Clark shaking his head vigorously at Mr. Burden, but he was too late. At once my imagination began to weave ghosts. I did not actually believe in ghosts, but I had been taught that there was a God and I had given a kind of uneasy assent to His existence, and if there was a God, then surely there must be ghosts. In a moment I built up an intense loathing for sleeping in the room where the boy had died. Rationally I knew that the dead boy could not bother me, but he had become alive for me in a way that I could not dismiss. After Mr. Burden had gone, I went timidly to Uncle Clark.

"I'm scared to sleep in there," I told him.

"Why? Because a boy died in there?"

"Yes, sir."

"But, son, that's nothing to be afraid of."

"I know. But I am scared."

"We all must die someday. So why be afraid?"

I had no answer for that.

"When you die, do you want people to be afraid of *you*?"

I could not answer that either.

"This is nonsense," Uncle Clark went on.

"But I'm scared," I told him.

"You'll get over it."

"Can't I sleep somewhere else?"

"There's nowhere else for you to sleep."

"Can I sleep here on the sofa?" I asked.

"*May* I sleep here on the sofa?" Aunt Jody corrected me in a mocking tone.

"May I sleep here on the sofa?" I repeated after her.

"No," Aunt Jody said.

I groped into the dark room and fumbled for the bed; I had the illusion that if I touched it I would encounter the dead boy. I trembled. Finally I jumped roughly into the bed and jerked the covers over my face. I did not sleep that night and my eyes were red and puffy the next morning.

"Didn't you sleep well?" Uncle Clark asked me.

"I can't sleep in that room," I said.

"You slept in it before you heard of that boy who died in there, didn't you?" Aunt Jody asked me.

"Yes, ma'am."

"Then why can't you sleep in it now?"

"I'm just scared."

"You stop being a baby," she told me.

The next night was the same; fear kept me from sleeping. After Uncle Clark and Aunt Jody had gone to bed, I rose and crept into the front room and slept in a tight ball on the sofa, without any cover. I awakened the next morning to find Uncle Clark shaking me.

"Why are you doing this?" he asked.

"I'm scared to sleep in there," I said.

"You go back into that room and sleep tonight," he told me. "You've got to get over this thing."

I spent another sleepless, shivering night in the dead boy's room—it was not my room any longer—and I was so frightened that I sweated. Each creak of the house made my heart stand still. In school the next day I was dull. I came home and spent another long night of wakefulness and the following day I went to sleep in the classroom. When questioned by the teacher, I could give no answer. Unable to free myself from my terror, I began to long for home. A week of sleeplessness brought me near the edge of nervous collapse.

Sunday came and I refused to go to church and Uncle Clark and Aunt Jody were astonished. They did not understand that my refusal to go to church was my way of silently begging them to let me sleep somewhere else. They left me alone in the house and I spent the entire day sitting on the front steps; I did not have enough courage to go into the kitchen to eat. When I became thirsty, I went around the house and drank water from the hydrant in the back yard rather than venture into the house. Desperation made me raise the issue of the room again at bedtime.

"Please, let me sleep on the sofa in the front room," I pleaded.

"You've got to get out of that fear," my uncle said.

I made up my mind to ask to be sent home. I went to Uncle Clark, knowing that he had incurred expense in bringing me here, that he had thought he was helping me, that he had bought my clothes and books.

"Uncle Clark, send me back to Jackson," I said.

He was bent over a little table and he straightened and stared at me.

"You're not happy here?" he asked.

"No, sir," I answered truthfully, fearing that the ceiling would crash down upon my head.

"And you really want to go back?"

"Yes, sir."

"Things will not be as easy for you at home as here," he said. "There's not much money for food and things."

"I want to be where my mother is," I said, trying to strengthen my plea.

"It's really about the room?"

"Yes, sir."

"Well, we tried to make you happy here," my uncle said, sighing. "Maybe we didn't know how. But if you want to go back, then you may go."

"When?" I asked eagerly.

"As soon as school term has ended."

"But I want to go now!" I cried.

"But you'll break up your year's schooling," he said.

"I don't mind."

"You will, in the future. You've never had a single year of steady schooling," he said.

"I want to go home," I said.

"Have you felt this way a long time?" he asked.

"Yes, sir."

"I'll write Granny tonight," he said, his eyes lit with surprise.

Daily I asked him if he had heard from Granny only to learn that there had been no word. My sleeplessness made me feel that my days were a hot, wild dream and my studies suffered at school. I had been making high marks and now I made low ones and finally began to fail altogether. I was fretful, living from moment to moment.

One evening, in doing my chores, I took the water pail to the hydrant in the back yard to fill it. I was half asleep, tired, tense, all but swaying on my feet. I balanced the handle of the pail on the jutting tip of the metal faucet and waited for it to fill; the pail slipped and water drenched my pants and shoes and stockings.

"That goddamn lousy bastard sonofabitching bucket!" I spoke in a whisper of hate and despair.

"Richard!" Aunt Jody's amazed voice sounded in the darkness behind me.

I turned. Aunt Jody was standing on the back steps. She came into the yard.

"What did you say, boy?" she asked.

"Nothing," I mumbled, looking contritely at the ground.

"Repeat what you said!" she demanded.

I did not answer. I stooped and picked up the pail. She snatched it from me.

"What did you say?" she asked again.

I still kept my head down, vaguely wondering if she were

intimidating me or if she really wanted me to repeat my curses.

"I'm going to tell your uncle on you," she said at last.

I hated her then. I thought that hanging my head and looking mutely at the ground was a kind of confession and a petition for forgiveness, but she had not accepted it as such.

"I don't care," I said.

She gave me the pail, which I filled with water and carried to the house. She followed me.

"Richard, you are a very bad, bad boy," she said.

"I don't care," I repeated.

I avoided her and went to the front porch and sat. I had had no intention of letting her hear me curse, but since she had heard me and since there was no way to appease her, I decided to let things develop as they would. I would go home. But where was home? Yes, I would run away.

Uncle Clark came and called me into the front room.

"Jody says that you've been using bad language," he said.

"Yes, sir."

"You admit it?"

"Yes, sir."

"Why did you do it?"

"I don't know."

"I'm going to whip you. Pull off your shirt."

Wordlessly I bared my back and he lashed me with a strap. I gritted my teeth and did not cry.

"Are you going to use that language again?" he asked me.

"I want to go home," I said.

"Put on your shirt."

I obeyed.

"I want to go home," I said again.

"But this is your home."

"I want to go to Jackson."

"You have no home in Jackson."

"I want to go to my mother."

"All right," he relented. "I'll send you home Saturday." He looked at me with baffled eyes. "Tell me, where did you learn those words Jody heard you say?"

I looked at him and did not answer; there flashed through my mind a quick, running picture of all the squalid hovels in

which I had lived and it made me feel more than ever a
stranger as I stood before him. How could I have told him
that I had learned to curse before I had learned to read? How
could I have told him that I had been a drunkard at the age
of six?

When he took me to the train that Saturday morning, I
felt guilty and did not want to look at him. He gave me my
ticket and I climbed hastily aboard the train. I waved a stiff
good-bye to him through the window as the train pulled out.
When I could see his face no longer, I wilted, relaxing. Tears
blurred my vision. I leaned back and closed my eyes and slept
all the way.

I was glad to see my mother. She was much better, though
still abed. Another operation had been advised by the doctor
and there was hope for recovery. But I was anxious. Why
another operation? A victim myself of too many hopes that
had never led anywhere, I was for letting my mother remain
as she was. My feelings were governed by fear and I spoke to
no one about them. I had already begun to sense that my
feelings varied too far from those of the people around me for
me to blab about what I felt.

I did not re-enter school. Instead, I played alone in the
back yard, bouncing a rubber ball off the fence, drawing figures in the soft clay with an old knife, or reading what books
I found about the house. I ached to be of an age to take care
of myself.

Uncle Edward arrived from Carters to take my mother to
Clarksdale for the operation; at the last moment I insisted
upon being taken with them. I dressed hurriedly and we went
to the station. Throughout the journey I sat brooding, afraid
to look at my mother, wanting to return home and yet wanting to go on. We reached Clarksdale and hired a taxi to the
doctor's office. My mother was jolly, brave, smiling, but I
knew that she was as doubtful as I was. When we reached the
doctor's waiting room the conviction settled in me that my
mother would never be well again. Finally the doctor came
out in his white coat and shook hands with me, then took my
mother inside. Uncle Edward left to make arrangements for a

room and a nurse. I felt crushed. I waited. Hours later the doctor came to the door.

"How's my mother?"

"Fine!" he said.

"Will she be all right?"

"Everything'll clear up in a few days."

"Can I see her now?"

"No, not now."

Later Uncle Edward returned with an ambulance and two men who carried a stretcher. They entered the doctor's office and brought out my mother; she lay with closed eyes, her body swathed in white. I wanted to run to the stretcher and touch her, but I could not move.

"Why are they taking mama that way?" I asked Uncle Edward.

"There are no hospital facilities for colored, and this is the way we have to do it," he said.

I watched the men take the stretcher down the steps; then I stood on the sidewalk and watched them lift my mother into the ambulance and drive away. I knew that my mother had gone out of my life; I could feel it.

Uncle Edward and I stayed at a boardinghouse; each morning he went to the rooming house to inquire about my mother and each time he returned gloomy and silent. Finally he told me that he was taking my mother back home.

"What chance has mama, really?" I asked him.

"She's very sick," he said.

We left Clarksdale; my mother rode on a stretcher in the baggage car with Uncle Edward attending her. Back home, she lay for days, groaning, her eyes vacant. Doctors visited her and left without making any comment. Granny grew frantic. Uncle Edward, who had gone home, returned and still more doctors were called in. They told us that a blod clot had formed on my mother's brain and that another paralytic stroke had set in.

Once, in the night, my mother called me to her bed and told me that she could not endure the pain, that she wanted to die. I held her hand and begged her to be quiet. That night I ceased to react to my mother; my feelings were frozen. I merely waited upon her, knowing that she was suffering. She remained abed ten years, gradually growing better, but never completely recovering, relapsing periodically into her paralytic state. The family had stripped itself of money to fight my mother's illness and there was no more forthcoming. Her illness gradually became an accepted thing in the house, something that could not be stopped or helped.

My mother's suffering grew into a symbol in my mind, gathering to itself all the poverty, the ignorance, the helplessness; the painful, baffling, hunger-ridden days and hours; the restless moving, the futile seeking, the uncertainty, the fear, the dread; the meaningless pain and the endless suffering. Her life set the emotional tone of my life, colored the men and women I was to meet in the future, conditioned my relation to events that had not yet happened, determined my attitude to situations and circumstances I had yet to face. A somberness of spirit that I was never to lose settled over me during the slow years of my mother's unrelieved suffering, a somberness that was to make me stand apart and look upon excessive joy with suspicion, that was to make me self-conscious, that was to make me keep forever on the move, as though to escape a nameless fate seeking to overtake me.

At the age of twelve, before I had had one full year of formal schooling, I had a conception of life that no experience would ever erase, a predilection for what was real that no argument could ever gainsay, a sense of the world that was mine and mine alone, a notion as to what life meant that no education could ever alter, a conviction that the meaning of living came only when one was struggling to wring a meaning out of meaningless suffering.

At the age of twelve I had an attitude toward life that was to endure, that was to make me seek those areas of living that would keep it alive, that was to make me skeptical of everything while seeking everything, tolerant of all and yet critical. The spirit I had caught gave me insight into the sufferings of others, made me gravitate toward those whose feelings were like my own, made me sit for hours while others told me of their lives, made me strangely tender and cruel, violent and peaceful.

It made me want to drive coldly to the heart of every

question and lay it open to the core of suffering I knew I would find there. It made me love burrowing into psychology, into realistic and naturalistic fiction and art, into those whirlpools of politics that had the power to claim the whole of men's souls. It directed my loyalties to the side of men in rebellion; it made me love talk that sought answers to questions that could help nobody, that could only keep alive in me that enthralling sense of wonder and awe in the face of the drama of human feeling which is hidden by the external drama of life.

Chapter IV

GRANNY was an ardent member of the Seventh-Day Adventist Church and I was compelled to make a pretense of worshiping her God, which was her exaction for my keep. The elders of her church expounded a gospel clogged with images of vast lakes of eternal fire, of seas vanishing, of valleys of dry bones, of the sun burning to ashes, of the moon turning to blood, of stars falling to the earth, of a wooden staff being transformed into a serpent, of voices speaking out of clouds, of men walking upon water, of God riding whirlwinds, of water changing into wine, of the dead rising and living, of the blind seeing, of the lame walking; a salvation that teemed with fantastic beasts having multiple heads and horns and eyes and feet; sermons of statues possessing heads of gold, shoulders of silver, legs of brass, and feet of clay; a cosmic tale that began before time and ended with the clouds of the sky rolling away at the Second Coming of Christ; chronicles that concluded with the Armageddon; dramas thronged with all the billions of human beings who had ever lived or died as God judged the quick and the dead . . .

While listening to the vivid language of the sermons I was pulled toward emotional belief, but as soon as I went out of the church and saw the bright sunshine and felt the throbbing life of the people in the streets I knew that none of it was true and that nothing would happen.

Once again I knew hunger, biting hunger, hunger that made my body aimlessly restless, hunger that kept me on edge, that made my temper flare, hunger that made hate leap out of my heart like the dart of a serpent's tongue, hunger that created in me odd cravings. No food that I could dream of seemed half so utterly delicious as vanilla wafers. Every time I had a nickel I would run to the corner grocery store and buy a box of vanilla wafers and walk back home, slowly, so that I could eat them all up without having to share them with anyone. Then I would sit on the front steps and dream of eating another box; the craving would finally become so acute that I would force myself to be active in order to forget.

I learned a method of drinking water that made me feel full temporarily whether I had a desire for water or not; I would put my mouth under a faucet and turn the water on full force and let the stream cascade into my stomach until it was tight. Sometimes my stomach ached, but I felt full for a moment.

No pork or veal was ever eaten at Granny's, and rarely was there meat of any kind. We seldom ate fish and then only those that had scales and spines. Baking powder was never used; it was alleged to contain a chemical harmful to the body. For breakfast I ate mush and gravy made from flour and lard and for hours afterwards I would belch it up into my mouth. We were constantly taking bicarbonate of soda for indigestion. At four o'clock in the afternoon I ate a plate of greens cooked with lard. Sometimes on Sundays we bought a dime's worth of beef which usually turned out to be uneatable. Granny's favorite dish was a peanut roast which she made to resemble meat, but which tasted like something else.

My position in the household was a delicate one; I was a minor, an uninvited dependent, a blood relative who professed no salvation and whose soul stood in mortal peril. Granny intimated boldly, basing her logic on God's justice, that one sinful person in a household could bring down the wrath of God upon the entire establishment, damning both the innocent and the guilty, and on more than one occasion she interpreted my mother's long illness as the result of my faithlessness. I became skilled in ignoring these cosmic threats and developed a callousness toward all metaphysical preachments.

But Granny won an ally in her efforts to persuade me to confess her God; Aunt Addie, her youngest child, had just finished the Seventh-Day Adventist religious school in Huntsville, Alabama, and came home to argue that if the family was compassionate enough to feed me, then the least I could do in return was to follow its guidance. She proposed that, when the fall school term started, I should be enrolled in the religious school rather than a secular one. If I refused, I was placing myself not only in the position of a horrible infidel but of a hardhearted ingrate. I raised arguments and objections, but my mother sided with Granny and Aunt Addie and I had to accept.

The religious school opened and I put in a sullen attendance. Twenty pupils, ranging in age from five to nineteen
and in grades from primary to high school, were crowded
into one room. Aunt Addie was the only teacher and from the
first day an acute, bitter antagonism sprang up between us.
This was the first time she had ever taught school and she was
nervous, self-conscious because a blood relative of hers—a
relative who would not confess her faith and who was not a
member of her church—was in her classroom. She was determined that every student should know that I was a sinner of
whom she did not approve, and that I was not to be granted
consideration of any kind.

The pupils were a docile lot, lacking in that keen sense of
rivalry which made the boys and girls who went to public
school a crowd in which a boy was tested and weighed, in
which he caught a glimpse of what the world was. These boys
and girls were will-less, their speech flat, their gestures vague,
their personalities devoid of anger, hope, laughter, enthusiasm, passion, or despair. I was able to see them with an objectivity that was inconceivable to them. They were claimed
wholly by their environment and could imagine no other,
whereas I had come from another plane of living, from the
swinging doors of saloons, the railroad yard, the round-
houses, the street gangs, the river levees, an orphan home;
had shifted from town to town and home to home; had mingled with grownups more than perhaps was good for me. I
had to curb my habit of cursing, but not before I had shocked
more than half of them and had embarrassed Aunt Addie to
helplessness.

As the first week of school drew to a close, the conflict that
smoldered between Aunt Addie and me flared openly. One
afternoon she rose from her desk and walked down the aisle
and stopped beside me.

"You know better than that," she said, tapping a ruler
across my knuckles.

"Better than what?" I asked, amazed, nursing my hand.

"Just look at that floor," she said.

I looked and saw that there were many tiny bits of walnut
meat scattered about; some of them had been smeared into
grease spots on the clean, white pine boards. At once I knew

that the boy in front of me had been eating them; my walnuts were in my pocket, uncracked.

"I don't know anything about that," I said.

"You know better than to eat in the classroom," she said.

"I haven't been eating," I said.

"Don't lie! This is not only a school, but God's holy ground," she said with angry indignation.

"Aunt Addie, my walnuts are here in my pocket . . ."

"I'm Miss Wilson!" she shouted.

I stared at her, speechless, at last comprehending what was really bothering her. She had warned me to call her Miss Wilson in the classroom, and for the most part I had done so. She was afraid that if I called her Aunt Addie I would undermine the morale of the students. Each pupil knew that she was my aunt and many of them had known her longer than I had.

"I'm sorry," I said, and turned from her and opened a book.

"Richard, get up!"

I did not move. The room was tense. My fingers gripped the book and I knew that every pupil in the room was watching. I had not eaten the nuts; I was sorry that I had called her Aunt Addie; but I did not want to be singled out for gratuitous punishment. And, too, I was expecting the boy who sat in front of me to devise some lie to save me, since it was really he who was guilty.

"I asked you to get up!" she shouted.

I still sat, not taking my eyes off my book. Suddenly she caught me by the back of my collar and yanked me from the seat. I stumbled across the room.

"I spoke to you!" she shouted hysterically.

I straightened and looked at her; there was hate in my eyes.

"Don't you look at me that way, boy!"

"I didn't put those walnuts on the floor!"

"Then who did?"

My street gang code was making it hard for me. I had never informed upon a boy in the public school, and I was waiting for the boy in front of me to come to my aid, lying, making up excuses, anything. In the past I had taken punishment that was not mine to protect the solidarity of the gang, and I had seen other boys do the same. But the religious boy, God helping him, did not speak.

"I don't know who did it," I said finally.

"Go to the front of the room," Aunt Addie said.

I walked slowly to her desk, expecting to be lectured; but my heart quickened when I saw her go to the corner and select a long, green, limber switch and come toward me. I lost control of my temper.

"I haven't done anything!" I yelled.

She struck me and I dodged.

"Stand still, boy!" she blazed, her face livid with fury, her body trembling.

I stood still, feeling more defeated by the righteous boy behind me than by Aunt Addie.

"Hold out your hand!"

I held out my hand, vowing that never again would this happen to me, no matter what the price. She stung my palm until it was red, then lashed me across my bare legs until welts rose. I clamped my teeth to keep from uttering a single whimper. When she finished I continued to hold out my hand, indicating to her that her blows could never really reach me, my eyes fixed and unblinking upon her face.

"Put down your hand and go to your seat," she said.

I dropped my hand and turned on my heels, my palm and legs on fire, my body taut. I walked in a fog of anger toward my desk.

"And I'm not through with you!" she called after me.

She had said one word too much; before I knew it, I had whirled and was staring at her with an open mouth and blazing eyes.

"Through with me?" I repeated. "But what have I done to you?"

"Sit down and shut up!" Aunt Addie bellowed.

I sat. I was sure of one thing: I would not be beaten by her again. I had often been painfully beaten, but almost always I had felt that the beatings were somehow right and sensible, that I was in the wrong. Now, for the first time, I felt the equal of an adult; I knew that I had been beaten for a reason that was not right. I sensed some emotional problem in Aunt

Addie other than her concern about my eating in school. Did my presence make her feel so insecure that she felt she had to punish me in front of the pupils to impress them? All afternoon I brooded, wondering how I could quit the school.

The moment Aunt Addie came into the house—I reached home before she did—she called me into the kitchen. When I entered, I saw that she was holding another switch. My muscles tightened.

"You're not going to beat me again!" I told her.

"I'm going to teach you some manners!" she said.

I stood fighting, fighting as I had never fought in my life, fighting with myself. Perhaps my uneasy childhood, perhaps my shifting from town to town, perhaps the violence I had already seen and felt took hold of me, and I was trying to stifle the impulse to go to the drawer of the kitchen table and get a knife and defend myself. But this woman who stood before me was my aunt, my mother's sister, Granny's daughter; in her veins my own blood flowed; in many of her actions I could see some elusive part of my own self; and in her speech I could catch echoes of my own speech. I did not want to be violent with her, and yet I did not want to be beaten for a wrong I had not committed.

"You're just mad at me for something!" I said.

"Don't tell me I'm mad!"

"You're too mad to believe anything I say."

"Don't speak to me like that!"

"Then how can I talk to you? You beat me for throwing walnuts on the floor! But I didn't do it!"

"Then who did?"

Since I was alone now with her, and desperate, I cast my loyalties aside and told her the name of the guilty boy, feeling that he merited no consideration.

"Why didn't you tell me before?" she asked.

"I don't want to tell tales on other people."

"So you lied, hunh?"

I could not talk; I could not explain how much I valued my code of solidarity.

"Hold out your hand!"

"You're not going to beat me! I didn't do it!"

"I'm going to beat you for lying!"

"Don't, don't hit me! If you hit me I'll fight you!"

For a moment she hesitated, then she struck at me with the switch and I dodged and stumbled into a corner. She was upon me, lashing me across the face. I leaped, screaming, and ran past her and jerked open the kitchen drawer; it spilled to the floor with a thunderous sound. I grabbed up a knife and held it ready for her.

"Now, I told you to stop!" I screamed.

"You put down that knife!"

"Leave me alone or I'll cut you!"

She stood debating. Then she made up her mind and came at me. I lunged at her with the knife and she grasped my hand and tried to twist the knife loose. I threw my right leg about her legs and gave her a shove, tripping her; we crashed to the floor. She was stronger than I and I felt my strength ebbing; she was still fighting for my knife and I saw a look on her face that made me feel she was going to use it on me if she got possession of it. I bit her hand and we rolled, kicking, scratching, hitting, fighting as though we were strangers, deadly enemies, fighting for our lives.

"Leave me alone!" I screamed at the top of my voice.

"Give me that knife, you boy!"

"I'll kill you! I'll kill you if you don't leave me alone!"

Granny came running; she stood thunderstruck.

"Addie, what are you doing?"

"He's got a knife!" she gasped. "Make 'im put it down!"

"Richard, put down that knife!" Granny shouted.

My mother came limping to the door.

"Richard, stop it!" she shouted.

"I won't! I'm not going to let her beat me!"

"Addie, leave the boy alone," my mother said.

Aunt Addie rose slowly, her eyes on the knife, then she turned and walked out of the kitchen, kicking the door wide open before her as she went.

"Richard, give me that knife," my mother said.

"But, mama, she'll beat me, beat me for nothing," I said. "I'm not going to let her beat me; I don't care what happens!"

"Richard, you are bad, bad," Granny said, weeping.

I tried to explain what had happened, but neither of them would listen. Granny came toward me to take the knife, but I dodged her and ran into the back yard. I sat alone on the back steps, trembling, emotionally spent, crying to myself. Grandpa came down; Aunt Addie had told him what had happened.

"Gimme that knife, mister," he said.

"I've already put it back," I lied, hugging my arm to my side to conceal the knife.

"What's come over you?" he asked.

"I don't want her to beat me," I said.

"You're a child, a boy!" he thundered.

"But I don't want to be beaten!"

"What did you do?"

"Nothing."

"You can lie as fast as a dog can trot," Grandpa said. "And if it wasn't for my rheumatism, I'd take down your pants and tan your backside good and proper. The very idea of a little snot like you threatening somebody with a knife!"

"I'm not going to let her beat me," I said again.

"You're bad," he said. "You better watch your step, young man, or you'll end up on the gallows."

I had long ceased to fear Grandpa; he was a sick old man and he knew nothing of what was happening in the house. Now and then the womenfolk called on him to throw fear into someone, but I knew that he was feeble and was not frightened of him. Wrapped in the misty memories of his young manhood, he sat his days out in his room where his Civil War rifle stood loaded in a corner, where his blue uniform of the Union Army lay neatly folded.

Aunt Addie took her defeat hard, holding me in a cold and silent disdain. I was conscious that she had descended to my own emotional level in her effort to rule me, and my respect for her sank. Until she married, years later, we rarely spoke to each other, though we ate at the same table and slept under the same roof, though I was but a skinny, half-frightened boy and she was the secretary of the church and the church's day-school teacher. God blessed our home with the love that binds . . .

I continued at the church school, despite Aunt Addie's never calling upon me to recite or go to the blackboard. Consequently I stopped studying. I spent my time playing with the boys and found that the only games they knew were brutal ones. Baseball, marbles, boxing, running were tabooed recreations, the Devil's work; instead they played a wildcat game called popping-the-whip, a seemingly innocent diversion whose excitement came only in spurts, but spurts that could hurl one to the edge of death itself. Whenever we were discovered standing idle on the school grounds, Aunt Addie would suggest that we pop-the-whip. It would have been safer for our bodies and saner for our souls had she urged us to shoot craps.

One day at noon Aunt Addie ordered us to pop-the-whip. I had never played the game before and I fell in with good faith. We formed a long line, each boy taking hold of another boy's hand until we were stretched out like a long string of human beads. Although I did not know it, I was on the tip end of the human whip. The leading boy, the handle of the whip, started off at a trot, weaving to the left and to the right, increasing speed until the whip of flesh was curving at breakneck gallop. I clutched the hand of the boy next to me with all the strength I had, sensing that if I did not hold on I would be tossed off. The whip grew taut as human flesh and bone could bear and I felt that my arm was being torn from its socket. Suddenly my breath left me. I was swung in a small, sharp arc. The whip was now being popped and I could hold on no more; the momentum of the whip flung me off my feet into the air, like a bit of leather being flicked off a horsewhip, and I hurtled headlong through space and landed in a ditch. I rolled over, stunned, head bruised and bleeding. Aunt Addie was laughing, the first and only time I ever saw her laugh on God's holy ground.

In the home Granny maintained a hard religious regime. There were prayers at sunup and sundown, at the breakfast table and dinner table, followed by a Bible verse from each member of the family. And it was presumed that I prayed before I got into bed at night. I shirked as many of the weekday church services as possible, giving as my excuse that I had to study; of course, nobody believed me, but my lies were accepted because nobody wanted to risk a row. The daily prayers were a torment and my knees became sore from kneeling so long and often. Finally I devised a method of kneeling that was not really kneeling; I learned, through arduous repetition, how to balance myself on the toes of my shoes and rest my head against a wall in some convenient corner. Nobody, except God, was any the wiser, and I did not think that He cared.

Granny made it imperative, however, that I attend certain all-night ritualistic prayer meetings. She was the oldest member of her church and it would have been unseemly if the only grandchild in her home could not be brought to these important services; she felt that if I were completely remiss in religious conformity it would cast doubt upon the stanchness of her faith, her capacity to convince and persuade, or merely upon her ability to apply the rod to my backside.

Granny would prepare a lunch for the all-night praying session, and the three of us—Granny, Aunt Addie, and I—would be off, leaving my mother and Grandpa at home. During the passionate prayers and the chanted hymns I would sit squirming on a bench, longing to grow up so I could run away, listening indifferently to the theme of cosmic annihilation, loving the hymns for their sensual caress, but at last casting furtive glances at Granny and wondering when it would be safe for me to stretch out on the bench and go to sleep. At ten or eleven I would munch a sandwich and Granny would nod her permission for me to take a nap. I would awaken at intervals to hear snatches of hymns or prayers that would lull me to sleep again. Finally Granny would shake me and I would open my eyes and see the sun streaming through stained-glass windows.

Many of the religious symbols appealed to my sensibilities and I responded to the dramatic vision of life held by the church, feeling that to live day by day with death as one's sole thought was to be so compassionately sensitive toward all life as to view all men as slowly dying, and the trembling sense of fate that welled up, sweet and melancholy, from the hymns blended with the sense of fate that I had already caught from life. But full emotional and intellectual belief never came. Perhaps if I had caught my first sense of life from the church I would have been moved to complete acceptance, but the hymns and sermons of God came into my heart only long after my personality had been shaped and formed by uncharted conditions of life. I felt that I had in me a sense of living as deep as that which the church was trying to give me, and in the end I remained basically unaffected.

My body grew, even on mush and lard gravy, a miracle which the church certainly should have claimed credit for. I survived my twelfth year on a diet that would have stunted an average-sized dog, and my glands began to diffuse through my blood, like sap rising upward in trees in spring, those strange chemicals that made me look curiously at girls and women. The elder's wife sang in the choir and I fell in love with her as only a twelve-year-old can worship a distant and unattainable woman. During the services I would stare at her, wondering what it was like to be married to her, pondering over how passionate she was. I felt no qualms about my first lust for the flesh being born on holy ground; the contrast between budding carnal desires and the aching loneliness of the hymns never evoked any sense of guilt in me.

It was possible that the sweetly sonorous hymns stimulated me sexually, and it might have been that my fleshy fantasies, in turn, having as their foundation my already inflated sensibility, made me love the masochistic prayers. It was highly likely that the serpent of sin that nosed about the chambers of my heart was lashed to hunger by hymns as well as dreams, each reciprocally feeding the other. The church's spiritual life must have been polluted by my base yearnings, by the leaping hunger of my blood for the flesh, because I would gaze at the elder's wife for hours, attempting to draw her eyes to mine, trying to hypnotize her, seeking to communicate with her with my thoughts. If my desires had been converted into a concrete religious symbol, the symbol would have looked something like this: a black imp with two horns; a long, curving, forked tail; cloven hoofs, a scaly, naked body; wet, sticky fingers; moist, sensual lips; and lascivious eyes feasting upon the face of the elder's wife . . .

A religious revival was announced and Granny felt that it was her last chance to bring me to God before I entered the precincts of sin at the public school, for I had already given loud and final notice that I would no longer attend the church school. There was a discernible lessening in Aunt Addie's hostility; perhaps she had come to the conclusion that my lost soul was more valuable than petty pride. Even my mother's attitude was: "Richard, you ought to know God through *some* church."

The entire family became kind and forgiving, but I knew the motives that prompted their change and it drove me an even greater emotional distance from them. Some of my classmates—who had, on the advice of their parents, avoided me—now came to visit and I could tell in a split second that they had been instructed in what to say. One boy, who lived across the street, called on me one afternoon and his self-consciousness betrayed him; he spoke so naïvely and clumsily that I could see the bare bones of his holy plot and hear the creaking of the machinery of Granny's maneuvering.

"Richard, do you know we are all worried about you?" he asked.

"Worried about me? Who's worried about me?" I asked in feigned surprise.

"All of us," he said, his eyes avoiding mine.

"Why?" I asked.

"You're not saved," he said sadly.

"I'm all right," I said, laughing.

"Don't laugh, Richard. It's serious," he said.

"But I tell you that I'm all right."

"Say, Richard, I'd like to be a good friend of yours."

"I thought we were friends already," I said.

"I mean true brothers in Christ," he said.

"We know each other," I said in a soft voice tinged with irony.

"But not in Christ," he said.

"Friendship is friendship with me."

"But don't you want to save your soul?"

"I simply can't feel religion," I told him in lieu of telling him that I did not think I had the kind of soul he thought I had.

"Have you really tried to feel God?" he asked.

"No. But I know I can't feel anything like that."

"You simply can't let the question rest there, Richard."

"Why should I let it rest?"

"Don't mock God," he said.

"I'll never feel God, I tell you. It's no use."

"Would you let the fate of your soul hang upon pride and vanity?"

"I don't think I have any pride in matters like this."

"Richard, think of Christ's dying for you, shedding His blood, His precious blood on the cross."

"Other people have shed blood," I ventured.

"But it's not the same. You don't understand."

"I don't think I ever will."

"Oh, Richard, brother, you are lost in the darkness of the world. You must let the church help you."

"I tell you, I'm all right."

"Come into the house and let me pray for you."

"I don't want to hurt your feelings . . ."

"You can't. I'm talking for God."

"I don't want to hurt God's feelings either," I said, the words slipping irreverently from my lips before I was aware of their full meaning.

He was shocked. He wiped tears from his eyes. I was sorry.

"Don't say that. God may never forgive you," he whispered.

It would have been impossible for me to have told him how I felt about religion. I had not settled in my mind whether I believed in God or not; His existence or nonexistence never worried me. I reasoned that if there did exist an all-wise, all-powerful God who knew the beginning and the end, who meted out justice to all, who controlled the destiny of man, this God would surely know that I doubted His existence and He would laugh at my foolish denial of Him. And if there was no God at all, then why all the commotion? I could not imagine God pausing in His guidance of unimaginably vast worlds to bother with me.

Embedded in me was a notion of the suffering in life, but none of it seemed like the consequences of original sin to me; I simply could not feel weak and lost in a cosmic manner. Before I had been made to go to church, I had given God's existence a sort of tacit assent, but after having seen His creatures serve Him at first hand, I had had my doubts. My faith, such as it was, was welded to the common realities of life, anchored in the sensations of my body and in what my mind could grasp, and nothing could ever shake this faith, and surely not my fear of an invisible power.

"I'm not afraid of things like that," I told the boy.

"Aren't you afraid of God?" he asked.

"No. Why should I be? I've done nothing to Him."

"He's a jealous God," he warned me.

"I hope that He's a kind God," I told him.

"If *you* are kind to Him, He is a kind God," the boy said. "But God will not look at you if you don't look at Him."

During our talk I made a hypothetical statement that summed up my attitude toward God and the suffering in the world, a statement that stemmed from my knowledge of life as I had lived, seen, felt, and suffered it in terms of dread, fear, hunger, terror, and loneliness.

"If laying down my life could stop the suffering in the world, I'd do it. But I don't believe anything can stop it," I told him.

He heard me but he did not speak. I wanted to say more to him, but I knew that it would have been useless. Though older than I, he had neither known nor felt anything of life for himself; he had been carefully reared by his mother and father and he had always been told what to feel.

"Don't be angry," I told him.

Frightened and baffled, he left me. I felt sorry for him.

Immediately following the boy's visit, Granny began her phase of the campaign. The boy had no doubt conveyed to her my words of blasphemy, for she talked with me for hours, warning me that I would burn forever in the lake of fire. As the day of the revival grew near, the pressure upon me intensified. I would go into the dining room upon some petty errand and find Granny kneeling, her head resting on a chair, uttering my name in a tensely whispered prayer. God was suddenly everywhere in the home, even in Aunt Addie's scowling and brooding face. It began to weigh upon me. I longed for the time when I could leave. They begged me so continuously to come to God that it was impossible for me to ignore them without wounding them. Desperately I tried to think of some way to say no without making them hate me. I was determined to leave home before I would surrender.

Then I blundered and wounded Granny's soul. It was not

my intention to hurt or humiliate her; the irony of it was
that the plan I conceived had as its purpose the salving of
Granny's frustrated feelings toward me. Instead, it brought
her the greatest shame and humiliation of her entire religious
life.

One evening during a sermon I heard the elder—I took my
eyes off his wife long enough to listen, even though she slumbered in my senses all the while—describe how Jacob had
seen an angel. Immediately I felt that I had found a way to
tell Granny that I needed proof before I could believe, that I
could not commit myself to something I could not feel or see.
I would tell her that if I were to see an angel I would accept
that as infallible evidence that there was a God and would
serve Him unhesitatingly; she would surely understand an attitude of that sort. What gave me courage to voice this argument was the conviction that I would never see an angel; if I
had ever seen one, I had enough common sense to have gone
to a doctor at once. With my bright idea bubbling in my
mind, wishing to allay Granny's fears for my soul, wanting to
make her know that my heart was not all black and wrong,
that I was actually giving serious thought to her passionate
pleadings, I leaned to her and whispered:

"You see, granny, if I ever saw an angel like Jacob did, then
I'd believe."

Granny stiffened and stared at me in amazement; then a
glad smile lit up her old wrinkled white face and she nodded
and gently patted my hand. That ought to hold her for a
while, I thought. During the sermon Granny looked at me
several times and smiled. Yes, she knows now that I'm not
dismissing her pleas from my mind . . . Feeling that my plan
was working, I resumed my worship of the elder's wife with a
cleansed conscience, wondering what it would be like to kiss
her, longing to feel some of the sensuous emotions of which
my reading had made me conscious. The service ended and
Granny rushed to the front of the church and began talking
excitedly to the elder; I saw the elder looking at me in surprise. Oh, goddamn, she's telling him! I thought with anger.
But I had not guessed one-thousandth of it.

The elder hurried toward me. Automatically I rose. He extended his hand and I shook it.

"Your grandmother told me," he said in awed tones.

I was speechless with anger.

"I didn't want her to tell you that," I said.

"She says that you have seen an angel." The words literally poured out of his mouth.

I was so overwhelmed that I gritted my teeth. Finally I could speak and I grabbed his arm.

"No . . . N-nooo, sir! No, sir!" I stammered. "I didn't say that. She misunderstood me."

The last thing on earth I wanted was a mess like this. The elder blinked his eyes in bewilderment.

"What did you tell her?" he asked.

"I told her that if I ever saw an angel, then I would believe," I said, feeling foolish, ashamed, hating and pitying my believing granny. The elder's face became bleak and stricken. He was stunned with disappointment.

"You . . . you didn't see an angel?" he asked.

"No, *sir*!" I said emphatically, shaking my head vigorously so that there could be no possible further misunderstanding.

"I see," he breathed in a sigh.

His eyes looked longingly into a corner of the church.

"With God, you know, anything is possible," he hinted hopefully.

"But I didn't see *anything*," I said. "I'm sorry about this."

"If you pray, then God will come to you," he said.

The church grew suddenly hot. I wanted to bolt out of it and never see it again. But the elder took hold of my arm and would not let me move.

"Elder, this is all a mistake. I didn't want anything like this to happen," I said.

"Listen, I'm older than you are, Richard," he said. "I think that you have in your heart the gift of God." I must have looked dubious, for he said: "Really, I do."

"Elder, please don't say anything to anybody about this," I begged.

Again his face lit with vague hope.

"Perhaps you don't want to tell me because you are bashful?" he suggested. "Look, this is serious. If you saw an angel, then tell me."

I could not deny it verbally any more; I could only shake

my head at him. In the face of his hope, words seemed useless.

"Promise me you'll pray. If you pray, then God will answer," he said.

I turned my head away, ashamed for him, feeling that I had unwittingly committed an obscene act in rousing his hopes so wildly high, feeling sorry for his having such hopes. I wanted to get out of his presence. He finally let me go, whispering:

"I want to talk to you sometime."

The church members were staring at me. My fists doubled. Granny's wide and innocent smile was shining on me and I was filled with dismay. That she could make such a mistake meant that she lived in a daily atmosphere that urged her to expect something like this to happen. She had told the other members and everybody knew it, including the elder's wife! There they stood, the church members, with joyous astonishment written on their faces, whispering among themselves. Perhaps at that moment I could have mounted the pulpit and led them all; perhaps that was to be my greatest moment of triumph!

Granny rushed to me and hugged me violently, weeping tears of joy. Then I babbled, speaking with emotional reproof, censuring her for having misunderstood me; I must have spoken more loudly and harshly than was called for— the others had now gathered about me and Granny—for Granny drew away from me abruptly and went to a far corner of the church and stared at me with a cold, set face. I was crushed. I went to her and tried to tell her how it had happened.

"You shouldn't've spoken to me," she said in a breaking voice that revealed the depths of her disillusionment.

On our way home she would not utter a single word. I walked anxiously beside her, looking at her tired old white face, the wrinkles that lined her neck, the deep, waiting black eyes, and the frail body, and I knew more than she thought I knew about the meaning of religion, the hunger of the human heart for that which is not and can never be, the thirst of the human spirit to conquer and transcend the implacable limitations of human life.

Later, I convinced her that I had not wanted to hurt her

and she immediately seized upon my concern for her feelings as an opportunity to have one more try at bringing me to God. She wept and pleaded with me to pray, really to pray, to pray hard, to pray until tears came . . .

"Granny, don't make me promise," I begged.

"But you must, for the sake of your soul," she said.

I promised; after all, I felt that I owed her something for inadvertently making her ridiculous before the members of her church.

Daily I went into my room upstairs, locked the door, knelt, and tried to pray, but everything I could think of saying seemed silly. Once it all seemed so absurd that I laughed out loud while on my knees. It was no use. I could not pray. I could never pray. But I kept my failure a secret. I was convinced that if I ever succeeded in praying, my words would bound noiselessly against the ceiling and rain back down upon me like feathers.

My attempts at praying became a nuisance, spoiling my days; and I regretted the promise I had given Granny. But I stumbled on a way to pass the time in my room, a way that made the hours fly with the speed of the wind. I took the Bible, pencil, paper, and a rhyming dictionary and tried to write verses for hymns. I justified this by telling myself that, if I wrote a really good hymn, Granny might forgive me. But I failed even in that; the Holy Ghost was simply nowhere near me . . .

One day while killing my hour of prayer, I remembered a series of volumes of Indian history I had read the year before. Yes, I knew what I would do; I would write a story about the Indians . . . But what about them? Well, an Indian girl . . . I wrote of an Indian maiden, beautiful and reserved, who sat alone upon the bank of a still stream, surrounded by eternal twilight and ancient trees, waiting . . . The girl was keeping some vow which I could not describe and, not knowing how to develop the story, I resolved that the girl had to die. She rose slowly and walked toward the dark stream, her face stately and cold; she entered the water and walked on until the water reached her shoulders, her chin; then it covered her. Not a murmur or a gasp came from her, even in dying.

"And at last the darkness of the night descended and softly

kissed the surface of the watery grave and the only sound was
the lonely rustle of the ancient trees," I wrote as I penned the
final line.

I was excited; I read it over and saw that there was a yawning void in it. There was no plot, no action, nothing save
atmosphere and longing and death. But I had never in my life
done anything like it; I had made something, no matter how
bad it was; and it was mine . . . Now, to whom could I show
it? Not my relatives; they would think I had gone crazy. I
decided to read it to a young woman who lived next door. I
interrupted her as she was washing dishes and, swearing her
to secrecy, I read the composition aloud. When I finished she
smiled at me oddly, her eyes baffled and astonished.

"What's that for?" she asked.

"Nothing," I said.

"But why did you write it?"

"I just wanted to."

"Where did you get the idea?"

I wagged my head, pulled down the corners of my mouth,
stuffed my manuscript into my pocket and looked at her in a
cocky manner that said: Oh, it's nothing at all. I write stuff
like this all the time. It's easy, if you know how. But I merely
said in an humble, quiet voice:

"Oh, I don't know. I just thought it up."

"What're you going to do with it?"

"Nothing."

God only knows what she thought. My environment contained nothing more alien than writing or the desire to
express one's self in writing. But I never forgot the look of
astonishment and bewilderment on the young woman's face
when I had finished reading and glanced at her. Her inability
to grasp what I had done or was trying to do somehow
gratified me. Afterwards whenever I thought of her reaction I
smiled happily for some unaccountable reason.

Chapter V

N O LONGER set apart for being sinful, I felt that I could breathe again, live again, that I had been released from a prison. The cosmic images of dread were now gone and the external world became a reality, quivering daily before me. Instead of brooding and trying foolishly to pray, I could run and roam, mingle with boys and girls, feel at home with people, share a little of life in common with others, satisfy my hunger to be and live.

Granny and Aunt Addie changed toward me, giving me up for lost; they told me that they were dead to the world, and those of their blood who lived in that world were therefore dead to them. From urgent solicitude they dropped to coldness and hostility. Only my mother, who had in the meantime recovered somewhat, maintained her interest in me, urging me to study hard and make up for squandered time.

Freedom brought problems; I needed textbooks and had to wait for months to obtain them. Granny said that she would not buy worldly books for me. My clothes were a despair. So hostile did Granny and Aunt Addie become that they ordered me to wash and iron my own clothes. Eating was still skimpy, but I had now adjusted myself to the starch, lard, and greens diet. I went to school, feeling that my life depended not so much upon learning as upon getting into another world of people.

Until I entered Jim Hill public school, I had had but one year of unbroken study; with the exception of one year at the church school, each time I had begun a school term something happened to disrupt it. Already my personality was lopsided; my knowledge of feeling was far greater than my knowledge of fact. Though I was not aware of it, the next four years were to be the only opportunity for formal study in my life.

The first school day presented the usual problem and I was emotionally prepared to meet it. Upon what terms would I be allowed to remain upon the school grounds? With pencil and tablet, I walked nonchalantly into the schoolyard, wearing a cheap, brand-new straw hat. I mingled with the boys, hoping to pass unnoticed, but knowing that sooner or later I would be spotted for a newcomer. And trouble came quickly. A black boy bounded past me, thumping my straw hat to the ground, and yelling:

"Straw katy!"

I picked up my hat and another boy ran past, slapping my hat even harder.

"Straw katy!"

Again I picked up my hat and waited. The cry spread. Boys gathered around, pointing, chanting:

"Straw katy! Straw katy!"

I did not feel that I had been really challenged so far; no particular boy had stood his ground and taunted me. I was hoping that the teasing would cease, and tomorrow I would leave my straw hat at home. But the boy who had begun the game came close.

"Mama bought me a straw hat," he sneered.

"Watch what you're saying," I warned him.

"Oh, look! He talks!" the boy said.

The crowd howled with laughter, waiting, hoping.

"Where you from?" the boy asked me.

"None of your business," I said.

"Now, look, don't you go and get sassy, or I'll cut you down," he said.

"I'll say what I please," I said.

The boy picked up a tiny rock and put in on his shoulder and walked close again.

"Knock it off," he invited me.

I hesitated for a moment, then acted; I brushed the rock from his shoulder and ducked and grabbed him about the legs and dumped him to the ground. A volcano of screams erupted from the crowd. I jumped upon the fallen boy and started pounding him. Then I was jerked up. Another boy had begun to fight me. My straw hat had been crushed and forgotten.

"Don't you hit my brother!" the new boy yelled.

"Two fighting one ain't fair!" I yelled.

Both of them now closed in on me. A blow landed on the back of my head. I turned and saw a brick rolling away and I felt blood oozing down my back. I looked around and saw several brickbats scattered about. I scooped up a handful. The two boys backed away. I took aim as they circled me; I made a motion as if to throw and one of the boys turned and ran. I let go with the brick and caught him in the middle of his back. He screamed. I chased the other halfway around the schoolyard. The boys howled their delight; they crowded around me, telling me that I had fought with two bullies. Then suddenly the crowd quieted and parted. I saw a woman teacher bearing down upon me. I dabbed at the blood on my neck.

"Was it you who threw that brick?" she asked.

"Two boys were fighting me," I told her.

"Come," she said, taking my hand.

I entered school escorted by the teacher, under arrest. I was taken to a room and confronted with the two brothers.

"Are these the boys?" she asked.

"Both of 'em fought me," I said. "I had to fight back."

"He hit me first!" one brother yelled.

"You're lying!" I yelled back.

"Don't you use that language in here," the teacher said.

"But they're not telling the truth," I said. "I'm new here and they tore up my hat."

"He hit me first," the boy said again.

I reached around the teacher, who stood between us, and smacked the boy. He screamed and started at me. The teacher grabbed us.

"The very idea of you!" the teacher shouted at me. "You are trying to fight right in school! What's the matter with you?"

"He's not telling the truth," I maintained.

She ordered me to sit down; I did, but kept my eyes on the two brothers. The teacher dragged them out of the room and I sat until she returned.

"I'm in a good mind not to let you off this time," she said.

"It wasn't my fault," I said.

"I know. But you hit one of those boys right in here," she said.

"I'm sorry."

She asked me my name and sent me to a room. For a

reason I could not understand, I was assigned to the fifth grade. Would they detect that I did not belong there? I sat and waited. When I was asked my age I called it out and was accepted.

I studied night and day and within two weeks I was promoted to the sixth grade. Overjoyed, I ran home and babbled the news. The family had not thought it possible. How could a bad, bad boy do that? I told the family emphatically that I was going to study medicine, engage in research, make discoveries. Flushed with success, I had not given a second's thought to how I would pay my way through a medical school. But since I had leaped a grade in two weeks, anything seemed possible, simple, easy.

I was now with boys and girls who were studying, fighting, talking; it revitalized my being, whipped my senses to a high, keen pitch of receptivity. I knew that my life was revolving about a world that I had to encounter and fight when I grew up. Suddenly the future loomed tangibly for me, as tangible as a future can loom for a black boy in Mississippi.

Most of my schoolmates worked mornings, evenings, and Saturdays; they earned enough to buy their clothes and books, and they had money in their pockets at school. To see a boy go into a grocery store at noon recess and let his eyes roam over filled shelves and pick out what he wanted—even a dime's worth—was a hairbreadth short of a miracle to me. But when I broached the idea of my working to Granny, she would have none of it; she laid down the injunction that I could not work on Saturdays while I slept under her roof. I argued that Saturdays were the only days on which I could earn any worth-while sum, and Granny looked me straight in the eyes and quoted Scripture:

But the seventh day is the sabbath of the Lord thy God: in it thou shalt not do any work, thou, nor thy son, nor thy daughter, nor thy manservant, nor thy maidservant, nor thine ox, nor thine ass, nor any of thy cattle, nor thy stranger that is within thy gates; that thy manservant and thy maidservant may rest as well as thou . . .

And that was the final word. Though we lived just on the borders of actual starvation, I could not bribe Granny with a promise of half or two-thirds of my salary; her answer was no and never. Her refusal wrought me up to a high pitch of nervousness and I cursed myself for being made to live a different and crazy life. I told Granny that she was not responsible for my soul, and she replied that I was a minor, that my soul's fate rested in her hands, that I had no word to say in the matter.

To protect myself against pointed questions about my home and my life, to avoid being invited out when I knew that I could not accept, I was reserved with the boys and girls at school, seeking their company but never letting them guess how much I was being kept out of the world in which they lived, valuing their casual friendships but hiding it, acutely self-conscious but covering it with a quick smile and a ready phrase. Each day at noon I would follow the boys and girls into the corner store and stand against a wall and watch them buy sandwiches, and when they would ask me: "Why don't you eat a lunch?" I would answer with a shrug of my shoulders: "Aw, I'm not hungry at noon, ever." And I would swallow my saliva as I saw them split open loaves of bread and line them with juicy sardines. Again and again I vowed that someday I would end this hunger of mine, this apartness, this eternal difference; and I did not suspect that I would never get intimately into their lives, that I was doomed to live with them but not of them, that I had my own strange and separate road, a road which in later years would make them wonder how I had come to tread it.

I now saw a world leap to life before my eyes because I could explore it, and that meant not going home when school was out, but wandering, watching, asking, talking. Had I gone home to eat my plate of greens, Granny would not have allowed me out again, so the penalty I paid for roaming was to forfeit my food for twelve hours. I would eat mush at eight in the morning and greens at seven or later at night. To starve in order to learn about my environment was irrational, but so were my hungers. With my books slung over my shoulder, I would tramp with a gang into the woods, to rivers, to creeks, into the business district, to the doors of poolrooms, into the movies when we could slip in without paying, to neighborhood ball games, to brick kilns, to lumberyards, to cottonseed mills to watch men work. There were hours when hunger would make me weak, would make me sway while walking, would make my heart give a sudden wild spurt of beating that would shake my body and make me breathless; but the happiness of being free would lift me beyond hunger, would enable me to discipline the sensations of my body to the ex tent that I could temporarily forget.

In my class was a tall, black, rebellious boy who was bright in his studies and yet utterly fearless in his assertion of himself; he could break the morale of the class at any moment with his clowning and the teacher never found an adequate way of handling him. It was he who detected my plaguing hunger and suggested to me a way to earn some money.

"You can't sit in school all day and not eat," he said.

"What am I going to eat?" I asked.

"Why don't you do like me?"

"What do you do?"

"I sell papers."

"I tried to get a paper route, but they're all full," I said. "I'd like to sell papers because I could read them. I can't find things to read."

"You too?" he asked, laughing.

"What do you mean?" I asked.

"That's why I sell papers. I like to read 'em and that's the only way I can get hold of 'em," he explained.

"Do your parents object to your reading?" I asked.

"Yeah. My old man's a damn crackpot," he said.

"What papers are you selling?"

"It's a paper published in Chicago. It comes out each week and it has a magazine supplement," he informed me.

"What kind of a paper is it?"

"Well, I never read the newspaper. It isn't much. But, boy, the magazine supplement! What stories . . . I'm reading the serial of Zane Grey's *Riders of the Purple Sage*."

I stared at him in complete disbelief.

"*Riders of the Purple Sage!*" I exclaimed.

"Yes."

"Do you think I can sell those papers?"

"Sure. I make over fifty cents a week and have stuff to read," he explained.

I followed him home and he gave me a copy of the newspaper and the magazine supplement. The newspaper was thin, ill-edited, and designed to circulate among rural, white Protestant readers.

"Hurry up and start selling 'em," he urged me. "I'd like to talk to you about the stories."

I promised him that I would order a batch of them that night. I walked home through the deepening twilight, reading, lifting my eyes now and then from the print in order not to collide with strangers. I was absorbed in the tale of a renowned scientist who had rigged up a mystery room made of metal in the basement of his palatial home. Prompted by some obscure motive, he would lure his victims into this room and then throw an electric switch. Slowly, with heart-racking agony, the air would be sucked from the metal room and his victims would die, turning red, blue, then black. This was what I wanted, tales like this. I had not read enough to have developed any taste in reading. Anything that interested me satisfied me.

Now, at last, I could have my reading in the home, could have it there with the approval of Granny. She had already given me permission to sell papers. Oh, boy, how lucky it was for me that Granny could not read! She had always burned the books I had brought into the house, branding them as worldly; but she would have to tolerate these papers if she was to keep her promise to me. Aunt Addie's opinion did not count, and she never paid any attention to me anyway. In her eyes, I was dead. I told Granny that I planned to make some money by selling papers and she agreed, thinking that at last I was becoming a serious, right-thinking boy. That night I ordered the papers and waited anxiously.

The papers arrived and I scoured the Negro area, slowly building up a string of customers who bought the papers more because they knew me than from any desire to read. When I returned home at night, I would go to my room and lock the door and revel in outlandish exploits of outlandish men in faraway, outlandish cities. For the first time in my life I became aware of the life of the modern world, of vast cities, and I was claimed by it; I loved it. Though they were merely stories, I accepted them as true because I wanted to believe them, because I hungered for a different life, for

something new. The cheap pulp tales enlarged my knowledge of the world more than anything I had encountered so
far. To me, with my roundhouse, saloon-door, and river-levee
background, they were revolutionary, my gateway to the
world.

I was happy and would have continued to sell the newspaper and its magazine supplement indefinitely had it not
been for the racial pride of a friend of the family. He was a
tall, quiet, sober, soft-spoken black man, a carpenter by trade.
One evening I called at his home with the paper. He gave me
a dime, then looked at me oddly.

"You know, son," he said, "I sure like to see you make a
little money each week."

"Thank you, sir," I said.

"But tell me, who told you to sell these papers?" he asked.

"Nobody."

"Where do you get them from?"

"Chicago."

"Do you ever read 'em?"

"Sure. I read the stories in the magazine supplement," I
explained. "But I never read the newspaper."

He was silent a moment.

"Did a white man ask you to sell these papers?" he asked.

"No, sir," I answered, puzzled now. "Why do you ask?"

"Do your folks know you are selling these papers?"

"Yes, sir. But what's wrong?"

"How did you know where to write for these papers?" he
asked, ignoring my questions.

"A friend of mine sells them. He gave me the address."

"Is this friend of yours a white man?"

"No, sir. He's colored. But why are you asking me all
this?"

He did not answer. He was sitting on the steps of his front
porch. He rose slowly.

"Wait right here a minute, son," he said. "I want to show
you something."

Now what was wrong? The papers were all right; at least
they seemed so to me. I waited, annoyed, eager to be gone on
my rounds so that I could have time to get home and lie in
bed and read the next installment of a thrilling horror story

The man returned with a carefully folded copy of the newspaper. He handed it to me.

"Did you see this?" he asked, pointing to a lurid cartoon.

"No, sir," I said. "I don't read the newspaper; I only read the magazine."

"Well, just look at that. Take your time and tell me what you think," he said.

It was the previous week's issue and I looked at the picture of a huge black man with a greasy, sweaty face, thick lips, flat nose, golden teeth, sitting at a polished, wide-topped desk in a swivel chair. The man had on a pair of gleaming yellow shoes and his feet were propped upon the desk. His thick lips nursed a big, black cigar that held white ashes an inch long. In the man's red-dotted tie was a dazzling horseshoe stickpin, glaring conspicuously. The man wore red suspenders and his shirt was striped silk and there were huge diamond rings on his fat black fingers. A chain of gold girded his belly and from the fob of his watch a rabbit's foot dangled. On the floor at the side of the desk was a spittoon overflowing with mucus. Across the wall of the room in which the man sat was a bold sign, reading:

The White House

Under the sign was a portrait of Abraham Lincoln, the features distorted to make the face look like that of a gangster. My eyes went to the top of the cartoon and I read:

> The only dream of a nigger is to be president
> and to sleep with white women! Americans, do
> we want this in our fair land? Organize and save
> white womanhood!

I stared, trying to grasp the point of the picture and the captions, wondering why it all seemed so strange and yet familiar.

"Do you know what this means?" the man asked me.

"Gee, I don't know," I confessed.

"Did you ever hear of the Ku Klux Klan?" he asked me softly.

"Sure. Why?"

"Do you know what the Ku Kluxers do to colored people?"

"They kill us. They keep us from voting and getting good jobs," I said.

"Well, the paper you're selling preaches the Ku Klux Klan doctrines," he said.

"Oh, no!" I exclaimed.

"Son, you're holding it in your hands," he said.

"I read the magazine, but I never read the paper," I said vaguely, thoroughly rattled.

"Listen, son," he said. "Listen. You're a black boy and you're trying to make a few pennies. All right. I don't want to stop you from selling these papers, if you want to sell 'em. But I've read these papers now for two months and I know what they're trying to do. If you sell 'em, you're just helping white people to kill you."

"But these papers come from Chicago," I protested naïvely, feeling unsure of the entire world now, feeling that racial propaganda surely could not be published in Chicago, the city to which Negroes were fleeing by the thousands.

"I don't care where the paper comes from," he said. "Just you listen to this."

He read aloud a long article in which lynching was passionately advocated as a solution for the problem of the Negro. Even though I heard him reading it, I could not believe it.

"Let me see that," I said.

I took the paper from him and sat on the edge of the steps; in the paling light I turned the pages and read articles so brutally anti-Negro that goose pimples broke out over my skin.

"Do you like that?" he asked me.

"No, sir," I breathed.

"Do you see what you are doing?"

"I didn't know," I mumbled.

"Are you going to sell those papers now?"

"No, sir. Never again."

"They tell me that you are smart in school, and when I read those papers you were selling I didn't know what to make of it. Then I said to myself that that boy doesn't know what he's selling. Now, a lot of folks wanted to speak to you about these papers, but they were scared. They thought you were mixed up with some white Ku Kluxers and if they told you to stop you would put the Kluxers on 'em. But I said, shucks, that boy just don't know what he's doing."

I handed him his dime, but he would not take it.

"Keep the dime, son," he said. "But for God's sake, find something else to sell."

I did not try to sell any more of the papers that night; I walked home with them under my arm, feeling that some Negro would leap from a bush or fence and waylay me. How on earth could I have made so grave a mistake? The way I had erred was simple but utterly unbelievable. I had been so enthralled by reading the serial stories in the magazine supplement that I had not read a single issue of the newspaper. I decided to keep my misadventure secret, that I would tell no one that I had been unwittingly an agent for pro-Ku Klux Klan literature. I tossed the papers into a ditch and when I reached home I told Granny, in a quiet, offhand way, that the company did not want to send me any more papers because they already had too many agents in Jackson, a lie which I thought was an understatement of the actual truth. Granny did not care one way or the other, since I had been making so little money in selling them that I had not been able to help much with household expenses.

The father of the boy who had urged me to sell the papers also found out their propagandistic nature and forbade his son to sell them. But the boy and I never discussed the subject; we were too ashamed of ourselves. One day he asked me guardedly:

"Say, are you still selling those papers?"

"Oh, no. I don't have time," I said, my eyes avoiding his.

"I'm not either," he said, pulling down the corners of his mouth. "I'm too busy."

I burned at my studies. At the beginning of the school term I read my civics and English and geography volumes through and only referred to them when in class. I solved all my mathematical problems far in advance; then, during school hours, when I was not called on to recite, I read tattered, second-hand copies of *Flynn's Detective Weekly* or the *Argosy All-Story Magazine*, or dreamed, weaving fantasies about cities I had never seen and about people I had never met.

School ended. I could not get a job that would let me rest on Granny's holy Sabbath. The long hot idle summer days palled on me. I sat at home brooding, nursing bodily and spiritual hunger. In the afternoons, after the sun had spent its force, I played ball with the neighborhood boys. At night I sat on the front steps and stared blankly at the passing people, wagons, cars . . .

On one such lazy, hot summer night Granny, my mother, and Aunt Addie were sitting on the front porch, arguing some obscure point of religious doctrine. I sat huddled on the steps, my cheeks resting sullenly in my palms, half listening to what the grownups were saying and half lost in a daydream. Suddenly the dispute evoked an idea in me and, forgetting that I had no right to speak without permission, I piped up and had my say. I must have sounded reekingly blasphemous, for Granny said, "Shut up, you!" and leaned forward promptly to chastise me with one of her casual, back-handed slaps on my mouth. But I had by now become adept at dodging blows and I nimbly ducked my head. She missed me; the force of her blow was so strong that she fell down the steps, headlong, her aged body wedged in a narrow space between the fence and the bottom step. I leaped up. Aunt Addie and my mother screamed and rushed down the steps and tried to pull Granny's body out. But they could not move her. Grandpa was called and he had to tear the fence down to rescue Granny. She was barely conscious. They put her to bed and summoned a doctor.

I was frightened. I ran to my room and locked the door, fearing that Grandpa would rend me to pieces. Had I done right or had I done wrong? If I had held still and let Granny slap me, she would not have fallen. But was it not natural to dodge a blow? I waited, trembling. But no one came to my room. The house was quiet. Was Granny dead? Hours later I unlocked the door and crept downstairs. Well, I told myself, if Granny died, I would leave home. There was nothing else to do. Aunt Addie confronted me in the hallway with burning, black eyes.

"You see what you've done to Granny," she said.

"I didn't touch her," I said. I had wanted to ask how Granny was, but my fear made me forget that.

"You were trying to kill her," Aunt Addie said.

"I didn't touch Granny, and you know it!"

"You are evil. You bring nothing but trouble!"

"I was trying to dodge her. She was trying to hit me. I had done nothing wrong . . ."

Her lips moved silently as she sought to formulate words to place me in a position of guilt.

"Why do you butt in when grown people are talking?" she demanded, finding her weapon at last.

"I just wanted to talk," I mumbled sullenly. "I sit in this house for hours and I can't even talk."

"Hereafter, you keep your mouth shut until you're spoken to," she advised me.

"But Granny oughtn't always be hitting at me like that," I said as delicately as possible.

"Boy, don't you stand there and say what Granny *ought* to do," she blazed, finding her ground of accusation. "If you don't keep your mouth shut, then *I'll* hit you!" she continued.

"I'm only trying to explain why Granny fell," I said.

"Shut up, now! Or I'll wring your neck, you fool!"

"You're another fool!" I came back at her, angry now.

She trembled with fury.

"I'll fix you this night!" she said, rushing at me.

I dodged her and ran into the kitchen and grabbed the long bread knife. She followed me and I confronted her. I was so hysterical that I was crying.

"If you touch me, I'll cut you, so help me," I said in gasps. "I'm going to leave here as soon as I can work and make a living. But as long's I'm here, you better not touch me."

We stood looking into each other's eyes, our bodies trembling with hate.

"I'm going to get you for this," she vowed in a low, serious voice. "I'll get you when you haven't got a knife."

"I'll always keep a knife for you," I told her.

"You've got to sleep at night," she whimpered with rage. "I'll get you then."

"If you touch me when I'm sleeping, I'll kill you," I told her.

She walked out of the kitchen, kicking the door open before her as she went. Aunt Addie had a habit of kicking doors; she always paused before a partly opened door and kicked it open; if the door swung in, she flung it back with her foot; or, if the door was shut, she opened it with her hand for an inch or two, then opened it the rest of the way with her foot; she acted as though she wanted to get a glimpse into the room beyond before she entered it, perhaps to see if it contained anything dreadful or unholy.

For a month after that I took a kitchen knife to bed with me each night, hiding it under my pillow so that when Aunt Addie came I could protect myself. But she never came. Perhaps she prayed.

Granny was abed for six weeks; she had wrenched her back when her slap missed me.

There were more violent quarrels in our deeply religious home than in the home of a gangster, a burglar, or a prostitute, a fact which I used to hint gently to Granny and which did my cause no good. Granny bore the standard for God, but she was always fighting. The peace that passes understanding never dwelt with us. I, too, fought; but I fought because I felt I had to keep from being crushed, to fend off continuous attack. But Granny and Aunt Addie quarreled and fought not only with me, but with each other over minor points of religious doctrine, or over some imagined infraction of what they chose to call their moral code. Wherever I found religion in my life I found strife, the attempt of one individual or group to rule another in the name of God. The naked will to power seemed always to walk in the wake of a hymn.

As summer waned I obtained a strange job. Our next-door neighbor, a janitor, decided to change his profession and become an insurance agent. He was handicapped by illiteracy and he offered me the job of accompanying him on trips into the delta plantation area to write and figure for him, at wages of five dollars a week. I made several trips with Brother Mance, as he was called, to plantation shacks, sleeping on shuck mattresses, eating salt pork and black-eyed peas for breakfast, dinner, and supper; and drinking, for once, all the milk I wanted.

I had all but forgotten that I had been born on a plantation and I was astonished at the ignorance of the children I met. I had been pitying myself for not having books to read, and now I saw children who had never read a book. Their chronic shyness made me seem bold and city-wise; a black mother would try to lure her brood into the room to shake hands with me and they would linger at the jamb of the door, peering at me with one eye, giggling hysterically. At night, seated at a crude table, with a kerosene lamp spluttering at my elbow, I would fill out insurance applications, and a sharecropper family, fresh from laboring in the fields, would stand and gape. Brother Mance would pace the floor, extolling my abilities with pen and paper. Many of the naïve black families bought their insurance from us because they felt that they were connecting themselves with something that would make their children "write 'n speak lak dat pretty boy from Jackson."

The trips were hard. Riding trains, autos, or buggies, moving from morning till night, we went from shack to shack, plantation to plantation. Exhausted, I filled out applications. I saw a bare, bleak pool of black life and I hated it; the people were alike, their homes were alike, and their farms were alike. On Sundays Brother Mance would go to the nearest country church and give his sales talk, preaching it in the form of a sermon, clapping his hands as he did so, spitting on the floor to mark off his paragraphs, and stomping his feet in the spit to punctuate his sentences, all of which captivated the black sharecroppers. After the performance the walleyed yokels would flock to Brother Mance, and I would fill out applications until my fingers ached.

I returned home with a pocketful of money that melted into the bottomless hunger of the household. My mother was proud; even Aunt Addie's hostility melted temporarily. To Granny, I had accomplished a miracle and some of my sinful qualities evaporated, for she felt that success spelled the reward of righteousness and that failure was the wages of sin. But God called Brother Mance to heaven that winter and, since the insurance company would not accept a minor as an agent, my status reverted to a worldly one; the holy household was still burdened with a wayward boy to whom, in spite of all, sin somehow insisted upon clinging.

School opened and I began the seventh grade. My old hunger was still with me and I lived on what I did not eat. Perhaps the sunshine, the fresh air, and the pot liquor from greens kept me going. Of an evening I would sit in my room reading, and suddenly I would become aware of smelling meat frying in a neighbor's kitchen and would wonder what it was like to eat as much meat as one wanted. My mind would drift into a fantasy and I would imagine myself a son in a family that had meat on the table at each meal; then I would become disgusted with my futile daydreams and would rise and shut the window to bar the torturing scent of meat.

When I came downstairs one morning and went into the dining room for my bowl of mush and lard gravy I felt at once that something serious was happening in the family. Grandpa, as usual, was not at the table; he always had his meals in his room. Granny nodded me to my seat; I sat and bowed my head. From under my brows I saw my mother's tight face. Aunt Addie's eyes were closed, her forehead furrowed, her lips trembling. Granny buried her face in her hands. I wanted to ask what had happened, but I knew that I would not get an answer.

Granny prayed and invoked the blessings of God for each of us, asking Him to guide us if it was His will, and then she told God that "my poor old husband lies sick this beautiful morning" and asked God, if it was His will, to heal him. That was how I learned of Grandpa's final illness. On many occasions I learned of some event, a death, a birth, or an impending visit, some happening in the neighborhood, at her church, or at some relative's home, first through Granny's informative prayers at the breakfast or dinner table.

Grandpa was a tall, black, lean man with a long face, snow-white teeth, and a head of woolly white hair. In anger he bared his teeth—a habit, Granny said, that he had formed while fighting in the trenches of the Civil War—and hissed, while his fists would clench until the veins swelled. In his rare laughs he bared his teeth in the same way, only now his teeth did not flash long and his body was relaxed. He owned a sharp pocketknife—which I had been forbidden to touch—

and sat for long hours in the sun, whittling, whistling quietly, or maybe, if he was feeling well, humming some strange tune.

I had often tried to ask him about the Civil War, how he had fought, what he had felt, had he seen Lincoln, but he would never respond.

"You, git 'way from me, you young'un," was all that he would ever say.

From Granny I learned — over a course of years — that he had been wounded in the Civil War and had never received his disability pension, a fact which he hugged close to his heart with bitterness. I never heard him speak of white people; I think he hated them too much to talk of them. In the process of being discharged from the Union Army, he had gone to a white officer to seek help in filling out his papers. In filling out the papers, the white officer misspelled Grandpa's name, making him Richard Vinson instead of Richard Wilson. It was possible that Grandpa's southern accent and his illiteracy made him mispronounce his own name. It was rumored that the white officer had been a Swede and had had a poor knowledge of English. Another rumor had it that the white officer had been a Southerner and had deliberately falsified Grandpa's papers. Anyway, Grandpa did not discover that he had been discharged in the name of Richard Vinson until years later; and when he applied to the War Department for a pension, no trace could be found of his ever having served in the Union Army under the name of Richard Wilson.

I asked endless questions about Grandpa's pension, but information was always denied me on the grounds that I was too young to know what was involved. For decades a long correspondence took place between Grandpa and the War Department; in letter after letter Grandpa would recount events and conversations (always dictating these long accounts to others); he would name persons long dead, citing their ages and descriptions, reconstructing battles in which he had fought, naming towns, rivers, creeks, roads, cities, villages, citing the names and numbers of regiments and companies with which he had fought, giving the exact day and the exact hour of the day of certain occurrences, and send it all to the War Department in Washington.

I used to get the mail early in the morning and whenever there was a long, businesslike envelope in the stack, I would know that Grandpa had got an answer from the War Department and I would run upstairs with it. Grandpa would lift his head from the pillow, take the letter from me and open it himself. He would stare at the black print for a long time, then reluctantly, distrustfully hand the letter to me.

"Well?" he would say.

And I would read him the letter—reading slowly and pronouncing each word with extreme care—telling him that his claims for a pension had not been substantiated and that his application had been rejected. Grandpa would not blink an eye, then he would curse softly under his breath.

"It's them goddamn rebels," he would hiss.

As though doubting what I had read, he would dress up and take the letter to at least a dozen of his friends in the neighborhood and ask them to read it to him; finally he would know it from memory. At last he would put the letter away carefully and begin his brooding again, trying to recall out of his past some telling fact that might help him in getting his pension. Like "K" of Kafka's novel, *The Castle*, he tried desperately to persuade the authorities of his true identity right up to the day of his death, and failed.

Often, when there was no food in the house, I would dream of the Government's sending a letter that would read something like this:

Dear Sir:
    Your claim for a pension has been verified. The matter of your name has been satisfactorily cleared up. In accordance with official regulations, we are hereby instructing the Secretary of the Treasury to compile and compute and send to you, as soon as it is convenient, the total amount of all moneys past due, together with interest, for the past ____ years, the amount being $____.
    We regret profoundly that you have been so long delayed in this matter. You may be assured that your sacrifice has been a boon and a solace to your country.

But no letter like that ever came, and Grandpa was so sullen most of the time that I stopped dreaming of him and his hopes. Whenever he walked into my presence I became silent,

waiting for him to speak, wondering if he were going to up-
braid me for something. I would relax when he left. My will
to talk to him gradually died.

It was from Granny's conversations, year after year, that the
meager details of Grandpa's life came to me. When the Civil
War broke out, he ran off from his master and groped his way
through the Confederate lines to the North. He darkly boasted
of having killed "mo'n mah fair share of them damn rebels"
while en route to enlist in the Union Army. Militantly resentful
of slavery, he joined the Union Army to kill southern whites;
he waded in icy streams; slept in mud; suffered, fought . . .
Mustered out, he returned to the South and, during elections,
guarded ballot boxes with his army rifle so that Negroes
could vote. But when the Negro had been driven from political power, his spirit had been crushed. He was convinced
that the war had not really ended, that it would start again.

And now as we ate breakfast—we ate in silence; there
was never any talk at our table; Granny said that talking while
eating was sinful, that God might make the food choke you
—we thought of Grandpa's pension. During the days that followed letters were written, affidavits were drawn up and sworn
to, conferences were held, but nothing came of it all. (It was
my conviction, supported by no evidence save my own emotional fear of whites, that Grandpa had been cheated out of
his pension because of his opposition to white supremacy.)

I came in from school one afternoon and Aunt Addie met me
in the hallway. Her face was trembling and her eyes were red.

"Go upstairs and say good-bye to your grandpa," she said.

"What's happened?"

She did not answer. I ran upstairs and was met by Uncle
Clark, who had come from Greenwood. Granny caught my
hand.

"Come and say good-bye to your grandpa," she said.

She led me to Grandpa's room; he was lying fully dressed
upon the bed, looking as well as he ever looked. His eyes
were open, but he was so still that I did not know if he was
dead or alive.

"Papa, here's Richard," Granny whispered.

Grandpa looked at me, flashed his white teeth for a fraction
of a second.

"Good-bye, grandpa," I whispered.

"Good-bye, son," he spoke hoarsely. "Rejoice, for God has picked out my s-s-e . . . in-in h-heaven . . ."

His voice died. I had not understood what he had said and I wondered if I should ask him to repeat it. But Granny took my hand and led me from the room. The house was quiet; there was no crying. My mother sat silent in her rocking chair, staring out the window; now and then she would lower her face to her hands. Granny and Aunt Addie moved silently about the house. I sat mute, waiting for Grandpa to die. I was still puzzled about what he had tried to say to me; it seemed important that I should know his final words. I followed Granny into the kitchen.

"Granny, what did Grandpa say? I didn't quite hear him," I whispered.

She whirled and gave me one of her back-handed slaps across my mouth.

"Shut up! The angel of death's in the house!"

"I just wanted to know," I said, nursing my bruised lips.

She looked at me and relented.

"He said that God had picked out his seat in heaven," she said. "Now you know. So sit down and quit asking fool questions."

When I awakened the next morning my mother told me that Grandpa had "gone home."

"Get on your hat and coat," Granny said.

"What do you want me to do?" I asked.

"Quit asking questions and do what you are told," she said. I dressed for the outdoors.

"Go to Tom and tell him that Papa's gone home. Ask him to come here and take charge of things," Granny said.

Tom, her eldest son, had recently moved from Hazelhurst to Jackson and lived near the outskirts of town. Feeling that I was bearing an important message, I ran every inch of the two miles; I thought that news of a death should be told at once. I came in sight of my uncle's house with a heaving chest; I bounded up the steps and rapped on the door. My little cousin, Maggie, opened the door.

"Where's Uncle Tom?" I asked.

"He's sleeping," she said.

I ran into his room, went to his bed, and shook him.

"Uncle Tom, Granny says to come at once. Grandpa's dead," I panted.

He stared at me a long time.

"You certainly are a prize fool," he said quietly. "Don't you know that that's no way to tell a person that his father's dead?"

I stared at him, baffled, panting.

"I ran all the way out here," I gasped. "I'm out of breath. I'm sorry."

He rose slowly and began to dress, ignoring me; he did not utter a word for five minutes.

"What're you waiting for?" he asked me.

"Nothing," I said.

I walked home slowly, asking myself what on earth was the matter with me, why it was I never seemed to do things as people expected them to be done. Every word and gesture I made seemed to provoke hostility. I had never been able to talk to others, and I had to guess at their meanings and motives. I had not intentionally tried to shock Uncle Tom, and yet his anger at me seemed to outweigh his sorrow for his father. Finding no answer, I told myself that I was a fool to worry about it, that no matter what I did I would be wrong somehow as far as my family was concerned.

I was not allowed to go to Grandpa's funeral; I was ordered to stay home "and mind the house." I sat reading detective stories until the family returned from the graveyard. They told me nothing and I asked no questions. The routine of the house flowed on as usual; for me there was sleep, mush, greens, school, study, loneliness, yearning, and then sleep again.

My clothing became so shabby that I was ashamed to go to school. Many of the boys in my class were wearing their first long-pants suits. I grew so bitter that I decided to have it out with Granny; I would tell her that if she did not let me work on Saturdays I would leave home. But when I opened the subject, she would not listen. I followed her about the house, demanding the right to work on Saturday. Her answer was no and no and no.

"Then I'll quit school," I declared.

"Quit then. See how much I care," she said.

"I'll go away from here and you'll never hear from me!"

"No, you won't," she said tauntingly.

"How can I ever learn enough to get a job?" I asked her, switching my tactics. I showed her my ragged stockings, my patched pants. "Look, I won't go to school like this! I'm not asking you for money or to do anything. I only want to work!"

"I have nothing to do with whether you go to school or not," she said. "You left the church and you are on your own. You are with the world. You're dead to me, dead to Christ."

"That old church of yours is messing up my life," I said.

"Don't you say that in this house!"

"It's true and you know it!"

"God's punishing you," she said. "And you're too proud to ask Him for help."

"I'm going to get a job anyway."

"Then you can't live here," she said.

"Then I'll leave," I said, trembling violently.

"You won't leave," she repeated.

"You think I'm joking, don't you?" I asked, determined to make her know how I felt. "I'll leave this minute!"

I ran to my room, got a battered suitcase, and began packing my ragged clothes. I did not have a penny, but I was going to leave. She came to the door.

"You little fool! Put that suitcase down!"

"I'm going where I can work!"

She snatched the suitcase out of my hands; she was trembling.

"All right," she said. "If you want to go to hell, then go. But God'll know that it was not my fault. He'll forgive me, but He won't forgive you."

Weeping, she rushed from the door. Her humanity had triumphed over her fear. I emptied the suitcase, feeling spent. I hated these emotional outbursts, these tempests of passion, for they always left me tense and weak. Now I was truly dead to Granny and Aunt Addie, but my mother smiled when I told her that I had defied them. She rose and hobbled to me on her paralytic legs and kissed me.

Chapter VI

THE NEXT DAY at school I inquired among the students about jobs and was given the name of a white family who wanted a boy to do chores. That afternoon, as soon as school had let out, I went to the address. A tall, dour white woman talked to me. Yes, she needed a boy, an honest boy. Two dollars a week. Mornings, evenings, and all day Saturdays. Washing dishes. Chopping wood. Scrubbing floors. Cleaning the yard. I would get my breakfast and dinner. As I asked timid questions, my eyes darted about. What kind of food would I get? Was the place as shabby as the kitchen indicated?

"Do you want this job?" the woman asked.

"Yes, ma'am," I said, afraid to trust my own judgment.

"Now, boy, I want to ask you one question and I want you to tell me the truth," she said.

"Yes, ma'am," I said, all attention.

"Do you steal?" she asked me seriously.

I burst into a laugh, then checked myself.

"What's so damn funny about that?" she asked.

"Lady, if I was a thief, I'd never tell anybody."

"What do you mean?" she blazed with a red face.

I had made a mistake during my first five minutes in the white world. I hung my head.

"No, ma'am," I mumbled. "I don't steal."

She stared at me, trying to make up her mind.

"Now, look, we don't want a sassy nigger around here," she said.

"No, ma'am," I assured her. "I'm not sassy."

Promising to report the next morning at six o'clock, I walked home and pondered on what could possibly have been in the woman's mind to have made her ask me point-blank if I stole. Then I recalled hearing that white people looked upon Negroes as a variety of children, and it was only in the light of that that her question made any sense. If I had been planning to murder her, I certainly would not have told her and, rationally, she no doubt realized it. Yet habit had overcome her rationality and had made her ask me: "Boy, do you steal?" Only an idiot would have answered: "Yes, ma'am. I steal."

What would happen now that I would be among white people for hours at a stretch? Would they hit me? Curse me? If they did, I would leave at once. In all my wishing for a job I had not thought of how I would be treated, and now it loomed important, decisive, sweeping down beneath every other consideration. I would be polite, humble, saying yes sir and no sir, yes ma'am and no ma'am, but I would draw a line over which they must not step. Oh, maybe I'm just thinking up trouble, I told myself. They might like me . . .

The next morning I chopped wood for the cook stove, lugged in scuttles of coal for the grates, washed the front porch and swept the back porch, swept the kitchen, helped wait on the table, and washed the dishes. I was sweating. I swept the front walk and ran to the store to shop. When I returned the woman said:

"Your breakfast is in the kitchen."

"Thank you, ma'am."

I saw a plate of thick, black molasses and a hunk of white bread on the table. Would I get no more than this? They had had eggs, bacon, coffee . . . I picked up the bread and tried to break it; it was stale and hard. Well, I would drink the molasses. I lifted the plate and brought it to my lips and saw floating on the surface of the black liquid green and white bits of mold. Goddamn . . . I can't eat this, I told myself. The food was not even clean. The woman came into the kitchen as I was putting on my coat.

"You didn't eat," she said.

"No, ma'am," I said. "I'm not hungry."

"You'll eat at home?" she asked hopefully.

"Well, I just wasn't hungry this morning, ma'am," I lied.

"You don't like molasses and bread," she said dramatically.

"Oh, yes, ma'am, I do," I defended myself quickly, not wanting her to think that I dared criticize what she had given me.

"I don't know what's happening to you niggers nowadays," she sighed, wagging her head. She looked closely at the molasses. "It's a sin to throw out molasses like that. I'll put it up for you this evening."

"Yes, ma'am," I said heartily.

Neatly she covered the plate of molasses with another plate, then felt the bread and dumped it into the garbage. She turned to me, her face lit with an idea.

"What grade are you in school?"

"Seventh, ma'am."

"Then why are you going to school?" she asked in surprise.

"Well, I want to be a writer," I mumbled, unsure of myself; I had not planned to tell her that, but she had made me feel so utterly wrong and of no account that I needed to bolster myself.

"A what?" she demanded.

"A writer," I mumbled.

"For what?"

"To write stories," I mumbled defensively.

"You'll never be a writer," she said. "Who on earth put such ideas into your nigger head?"

"Nobody," I said.

"I didn't think anybody ever would," she declared indignantly.

As I walked around her house to the street, I knew that I would not go back. The woman had assaulted my ego; she had assumed that she knew my place in life, what I felt, what I ought to be, and I resented it with all my heart. Perhaps she was right; perhaps I would never be a writer; but I did not want her to say so.

Had I kept the job I would have learned quickly just how white people acted toward Negroes, but I was too naïve to think that there were many white people like that. I told myself that there were good white people, people with money and sensitive feelings. As a whole, I felt that they were bad, but I would be lucky enough to find the exceptions.

Fearing that my family might think I was finicky, I lied to them, telling them that the white woman had already hired a boy. At school I continued to ask about jobs and was directed to another address. As soon as school was out I made for the house. Yes, the woman said that she wanted a boy who could milk a cow, feed chickens, gather vegetables, help serve breakfast and dinner.

"But I can't milk a cow, ma'am," I said.

"Where are you from?" she asked incredulously.

"Here in Jackson," I said.

"You mean to stand there, nigger, and tell me that you live in Jackson and don't know how to milk a cow?" she demanded in surprise.

I said nothing, but I was quickly learning the reality—a Negro's reality—of the white world. One woman had assumed that I would tell her if I stole, and now this woman was amazed that I could not milk a cow, I, a nigger who dared live in Jackson . . . They were all turning out to be alike, differing only in detail. I faced a wall in the woman's mind, a wall that she did not know was there.

"I just never learned," I said finally.

"I'll show you how to milk," she said, as though glad to be charitable enough to repair a nigger's knowledge on that score. "It's easy."

The place was large; they had a cow, chickens, a garden, all of which spelled food and that decided me. I told her that I would take the job and I reported for work the next morning. My tasks were simple but many; I milked the cow under her supervision, gathered eggs, swept, and was through in time to serve breakfast. The dining-room table was set for five; there were eggs, bacon, toast, jam, butter, milk, apples . . . That seemed promising. The woman told me to bring the food in as they called for it, and I familiarized myself with the kitchen so that I could act quickly when called upon. Finally the woman came into the dining room followed by a pale young man who sat down and stared at the food.

"What the hell!" he snarled. "Every morning it's these damn eggs for breakfast."

"Listen, you sonofabitch," the woman said, sitting too, "you don't have to eat 'em."

"You might try serving some dirt," he said, and forked up the bacon.

I felt that I was dreaming. Were they like that all the time? If so, I would not stay here. A young girl came and flopped into her chair.

"That's right, you bitch," the young man said. "Knock the food right out of my goddamn mouth."

"You know what you can do," the girl said.

I stared at them so intently that I was not aware that the young man was watching me.

"Say, what in hell are you glaring at me for, you nigger bastard?" he demanded. "Get those goddamn biscuits off that stove and put 'em on the table."

"Yes, sir."

Two middle-aged men came in and sat down. I never learned who was in the family, who was related to whom, or if it was a family. They cursed each other in an amazingly offhand manner and nobody seemed to mind. As they hurled invectives, they barely looked at each other. I was tense each moment, trying to anticipate their wishes and avoid a curse, and I did not suspect that the tension I had begun to feel that morning would lift itself into the passion of my life. Perhaps I had waited too long to start working for white people; perhaps I should have begun earlier, when I was younger—as most of the other black boys had done—and perhaps by now the tension would have become an habitual condition, contained and controlled by reflex. But that was not to be my lot; I was always to be conscious of it, brood over it, carry it in my heart, live with it, sleep with it, fight with it.

The morning was physically tiring, but the nervous strain, the fear that my actions would call down upon my head a storm of curses, was even more damaging. When the time came for me to go to school, I was emotionally spent. But I clung to the job because I got enough to eat and no one watched me closely and measured out my food. I had rarely tasted eggs and I would put hunks of yellow butter into a hot skillet and hurriedly scramble three or four eggs at a time and gobble them down in huge mouthfuls so that the woman would not see me. And I would take tumblers of milk behind a convenient door and drain them in a swallow, as though they contained water.

Though the food I ate strengthened my body, I acquired another problem: I had fallen down in my studies at school. Had I been physically stronger, had not my new tensions sapped my already limited energy, I might have been able to work mornings and evenings and still carry my studies successfully. But in the middle of the day I would grow groggy; in the classroom I would feel that the teacher and the pupils

were receding from me and I would know that I was drifting
off to sleep. I would go to the water fountain in the corridor
and let cold water run over my wrists, chilling my blood,
hoping in that way to keep awake.

But the job had its boon. At the midday recess I would
crowd gladly into the corner store and eat sandwiches with
the boys, slamming down my own money on the counter for
what I wanted, swapping descriptions of the homes of white
folks in which we worked. I used to divert them with vivid
word pictures of the cursing family, their brooding silences,
their indifference toward one another. I told them of the food
I managed to eat when the woman's back was turned, and
they were filled with friendly envy.

The boys would now examine some new article of clothing
I had bought; none of us allowed a week to pass without
buying something new, paying fifty cents down and fifty cents
per week. We knew that we were being cheated, but we never
had enough cash to buy in any other way.

My mother began a rapid recovery. I was happy when she
expressed the hope that someday soon we might have a home
of our own. Though Granny was angry and disgusted, my
mother began to attend a Methodist church in the neighborhood, and I went to Sunday school, not because my mother
begged me to—which she did—but to meet and talk with
my classmates.

In the black Protestant church I entered a new world; prim,
brown, puritanical girls who taught in the public schools;
black college students who tried to conceal their plantation
origin; black boys and girls emerging self-consciously from
adolescence; wobbly-bosomed black and yellow church
matrons; black janitors and porters who sang proudly in
the choir; subdued redcaps and carpenters who served as
deacons; meek, blank-eyed black and yellow washerwomen
who shouted and moaned and danced when hymns were sung;
jovial, potbellied black bishops; skinny old maids who were
constantly giving rallies to raise money; snobbery, clannish-
ness, gossip, intrigue, petty class rivalry, and conspicuous dis-
plays of cheap clothing . . . I liked it and I did not like it; I
longed to be among them, yet when with them I looked at

them as if I were a million miles away. I had been kept out of their world too long ever to be able to become a real part of it.

Nevertheless, I was so starved for association with people that I allowed myself to be seduced by it all, and for a few months I lived the life of an optimist. A revival began at the church and my classmates at school urged me to attend. More because I liked them than from any interest in religion, I consented. As the services progressed night after night, my mother tried to persuade me to join, to save my soul at last, to become a member of a responsible community church. Despite the fact that I told them I could never feel any religion, the boys of my gang begged me to "come to God."

"You believe in God, don't you?" they asked.

I evaded the question.

"But this is a new day," they said, pulling down the corners of their lips. "We don't holler and moan in church no more. Come to church and be a member of the community."

"Oh, I don't know," I said.

"We don't want to push you," they said delicately, implying that if I wanted to associate with them I would have to join.

On the last night of the revival, the preacher asked all those who were members of the church to stand. A good majority of those present rose. Next the preacher called upon the Christians who were not members of any church to stand. More responded. There remained now but a few young men who, belonging to no church and professing no religion, were scattered sheepishly about the pews. Having thus isolated the sinners, the preacher told the deacons to prevail upon those who lived "in darkness to discuss the state of their souls with him." The deacons sped to their tasks and asked us to go into a room and talk with a man "chosen and anointed of God." They held our arms and smiled as they bent and talked to us. Surrounded by people I knew and liked, with my mother's eyes looking pleadingly into mine, it was hard to refuse. I followed the others into a room where the preacher stood; he smiled and shook our hands.

"Now, you young men," he began in a brisk, clipped tone, "I want all of you to know God. I'm not asking you to join the church, but it's my duty as a man of God to tell you that you are in danger. Your peril is great; you stand in the need of

prayer. Now, I'm going to ask each of you a personal favor. I want you to let the members of this church send up a prayer to God for you. Now, is there any soul here so cold, so hard, so lost, that he would say no to that? Can you refuse to let the good people of this community pray for you?"

He paused dramatically and no one answered. All the techniques of his appeal were familiar to me and I sat there feeling foolish, wanting to leap through the window and go home and forget about it. But I sat still, filled more with disgust than sin.

"Would any man in this room dare fling no into God's face?" the preacher asked.

There was silence.

"Now, I'm going to ask all of you to rise and go into the church and take a seat on the front bench," he said, edging on to more definite commitments. "Just stand up," he said, lifting his hands, palms up, as though he had the power to make us rise by magic. "That's it, young man," he encouraged the first boy who rose.

I followed them and we sat like wet ducks on a bench facing the congregation. Some part of me was cursing. A low, soft hymn began.

This may be the last time, I don't know . . .

They sang it, hummed it, crooned it, moaned it, implying in sweet, frightening tones that if we did not join the church then and there we might die in our sleep that very night and go straight to hell. The church members felt the challenge and the volume of song swelled. Could they sing so terrifyingly sweet as to make us join, burst into tears and drop to our knees? A few boys rose and gave their hands to the preacher. A few women shouted and danced with joy. Another hymn began.

It ain't my brother, but it's me, Oh, Lord,
Standing in the need of prayer . . .

During the singing the preacher tried yet another ruse; he intoned mournfully, letting his voice melt into the singing, yet casting his words above it:

"How many mothers of these young men are here tonight?"

Among others, my mother rose and stood proudly.

"Now, good sweet mothers, come right down in front here," said the preacher.

Hoping that this was the night of my long-deferred salvation, my mother came forward, limping, weeping, smiling. The mothers ringed their sons around, whispering, pleading.

"Now, you good sweet mothers, symbols of Mother Mary at the tomb, kneel and pray for your sons, your only sons," the preacher chanted.

The mothers knelt. My mother grabbed my hands and I felt hot tears scalding my fingers. I tried to stifle my disgust. We young men had been trapped by the community, the tribe in which we lived and of which we were a part. The tribe, for its own safety, was asking us to be at one with it. Our mothers were kneeling in public and praying for us to give the sign of allegiance. The hymn ended and the preacher launched into a highly emotional and symbolic sermon, recounting how our mothers had given birth to us, how they had nursed us from infancy, how they had tended us when we were sick, how they had seen us grow up, how they had watched over us, how they had always known what was best for us. He then called for yet another hymn, which was hummed. He chanted above it in a melancholy tone:

"Now, I'm asking the first mother who really loves her son to bring him to me for baptism!"

Goddamn, I thought. It had happened quicker than I had expected. My mother was looking steadily at me.

"Come, son, let your old mother take you to God," she begged. "I brought you into the world, now let me help to save you."

She caught my hand and I held back.

"I've been as good a mother as I could," she whispered through her tears.

"God is hearing every word," the preacher underscored her plea.

This business of saving souls had no ethics; every human relationship was shamelessly exploited. In essence, the tribe was asking us whether we shared its feelings; if we refused to join the church, it was equivalent to saying no, to placing ourselves in the position of moral monsters. One mother led her beaten and frightened son to the preacher amid shouts of amen and hallelujah.

"Don't you love your old crippled mother, Richard?" my mother asked. "Don't leave me standing here with my empty hands," she said, afraid that I would humiliate her in public.

It was no longer a question of my believing in God; it was no longer a matter of whether I would steal or lie or murder; it was a simple, urgent matter of public pride, a matter of how much I had in common with other people. If I refused, it meant that I did not love my mother, and no man in that tight little black community had ever been crazy enough to let himself be placed in such a position. My mother pulled my arm and I walked with her to the preacher and shook his hand, a gesture that made me a candidate for baptism. There were more songs and prayers; it lasted until well after midnight. I walked home limp as a rag; I had not felt anything except sullen anger and a crushing sense of shame. Yet I was somehow glad that I had got it over with; no barriers now stood between me and the community.

"Mama, I don't feel a thing," I told her truthfully.

"Don't you worry; you'll grow into feeling it," she assured me.

And when I confessed to the other boys that I felt nothing, they too admitted that they felt nothing.

"But the main thing is to be a member of the church," they said.

The Sunday of the baptism arrived. I dressed in my best and showed up sweating. The candidates were huddled together to listen to a sermon in which the road of salvation was mapped out from the cradle to the grave. We were then called to the front of the church and lined up. The preacher, draped in white robes, dipped a small branch of a tree in a huge bowl of water and hovered above the head of the first candidate.

"I baptize thee in the name of the Father, the Son, and the Holy Ghost," he pronounced sonorously as he shook the wet branch. Drops trickled down the boy's face.

From one boy to another he went, dipping the branch each time. Finally my turn came and I felt foolish, tense; I wanted to yell for him to stop; I wanted to tell him that all this was so much nonsense. But I said nothing. The dripping branch was shaken above my head and drops of water wet my face and scalp, some of it rolling down my neck and wetting my back, like insects crawling. I wanted to squirm, but I held still. Then it was over. I relaxed. The preacher was now shaking the branch over another boy's head. I sighed. I had been baptized.

Even after receiving the "right hand of fellowship," Sunday school bored me. The Bible stories seemed slow and meaningless when compared to the bloody thunder of pulp narrative. And I was not alone in feeling this; other boys went to sleep in Sunday school. Finally the boldest of us confessed that the entire thing was a fraud and we played hooky from church.

As summer neared, my mother suffered yet another stroke of paralysis and again I had to watch her suffer, listen to her groans, powerless to help. I used to lie awake nights and think back to the early days in Arkansas, tracing my mother's life, reliving events, wondering why she had apparently been singled out for so much suffering, meaningless suffering, and I would feel more awe than I had ever felt in church. My mind could find no answer and I would feel rebellious against all life. But I never felt humble.

Another change took place at home. We needed money badly and Granny and Aunt Addie decided that we could no longer share the entire house, and Uncle Tom and his family were invited to live upstairs at a nominal rental. The dining room and the living room were converted into bedrooms and for the first time we were squeezed for living space. We began to get on each other's nerves. Uncle Tom had taught school in country towns for thirty years and as soon as he was under the roof he proceeded to tell me what was wrong with my life. I ignored him and he resented it.

Rattling pots and pans in the kitchen would now awaken me in the mornings and I would know that Uncle Tom and his family were getting breakfast. One morning I was roused by my uncle's voice calling gently but persistently. I opened my eyes and saw the dim blob of his face peering from behind the jamb of the kitchen door.

"What time have you?" I thought he asked me, but I was not sure.

"Hunh?" I mumbled sleepily.

"What time have you got?" he repeated.

I lifted myself on my elbow and looked at my dollar watch, which lay on the chair at the bedside.

"Eighteen past five," I mumbled.

"Eighteen past five?" he asked.

"Yes, sir."

"Now, is that the right time?" he asked again.

I was tired, sleepy; I did not want to look at the watch again, but I was satisfied that, on the whole, I had given him the correct time.

"It's right," I said, snuggling back down into my pillow. "If it's a little slow or fast, it's not far wrong."

There was a short silence; I thought he had gone.

"What on earth do you mean, boy?" he asked in loud anger.

I sat up, blinking, staring into the shadows of the room, trying to see the expression on his face.

"What do I mean?" I asked, bewildered. "I mean what I said." Had I given him the wrong time? I looked again at my watch. "It's twenty past now."

"Why, you impudent black rascal!" he thundered.

I pushed back the covers of the bed, sensing trouble.

"What are you angry about?" I asked.

"I never heard a sassier black imp than you in all my life," he spluttered.

I swung my feet to the floor so that I could watch him.

"What are you talking about?" I asked. "You asked me the time and I told you."

" 'If it's a little fast or slow, it's not far wrong,' " he said, imitating me in an angry, sarcastic voice. "I've taught school for thirty years, and by God I've never had a boy say anything like that to me."

"But what's wrong with what I said?" I asked, amazed.

"Shut up!" he shouted. "Or I'll take my fist and ram it down your sassy throat! One more word out of you, and I'll get a limb and teach you a lesson."

"What's the matter with you, Uncle Tom?" I asked. "What's wrong with what I said?"

I could hear his breath whistling in his throat; I knew that he was furious.

"This day I'm going to give you the whipping some man ought to have given you long ago," he vowed.

I got to my feet and grabbed my clothes; the whole thing seemed unreal. I had been confronted so suddenly with struggle that I could not pull all the strings of the situation together at once. I did not feel that I had given him cause to say I was sassy. I had spoken to him just as I spoke to everybody. Others did not resent my words, so why should he? I heard him go out of the kitchen door and I knew that he had gone into the back yard. I pulled on my clothes and ran to the window; I saw him tearing a long, young, green switch from the elm tree. My body tightened. I was damned if he was going to beat me with it. Until a few days ago he had never lived near me, had never had any say in my rearing or lack of rearing. I was working, eating my meals out, buying my own clothes, giving what few pennies I could to Granny to help out in the house. And now a strange uncle who felt that I was impolite was going to teach me to act as I had seen the backward black boys act on the plantations, was going to teach me to grin, hang my head, and mumble apologetically when I was spoken to.

My senses reeled in protest. No, that could not be. He would not beat me. He was only bluffing. His anger would pass. He would think it over and realize that it was not worth all the bother. Dressed, I sat on the edge of the bed and waited. I heard his footsteps come onto the back porch. I felt weak all over. How long was this going to last? How long was I going to be beaten for trifles and less than trifles? I was already so conditioned toward my relatives that when I passed them I actually had a nervous tic in my muscles, and now I was going to be beaten by someone who did not like the tone of voice in which I spoke. I ran across the room and pulled out the dresser drawer and got my pack of razor blades; I opened it and took a thin blade of blue steel in each hand. I stood ready for him. The door opened. I was hoping desperately that this was not true, that this dream would end.

"Richard!" he called me in a cold, even tone.

"Yes, sir!" I answered, striving to keep my tension out of my voice.

"Come here."

I walked into the kitchen, my eyes upon him, my hands holding the razors behind my back.

"Now, Uncle Tom, what do you want with me?" I asked him.

"You need a lesson in how to live with people," he said.

"If I do need one, you're not going to give it to me," I said.

"You'll swallow those words before I'm through with you," he vowed.

"Now, listen, Uncle Tom," I said, "you're not going to whip me. You're a stranger to me. You don't support me. I don't live with you."

"You shut that foul mouth of yours and get into the back yard," he snapped.

He had not seen the razors in my hand. I ducked out the kitchen door and jumped lightly off the porch to the ground. He ran down the steps and advanced with the lifted switch.

"I've got a razor in each hand!" I warned in a low, charged voice. "If you touch me, I'll cut you! Maybe I'll get cut too, but I'll cut you, so help me God!"

He paused, staring at my lifted hands in the dawning light of morning. I held a sharp blue edge of steel tightly between thumb and forefinger of each fist.

"My God," he gasped.

"I didn't mean to hurt your feelings this morning," I told him. "You insist I did. Now, I'll be damned if I'm going to be beaten because of your hurt feelings."

"You're the worst criminal I ever saw," he exclaimed softly.

"If you want to fight, I'll fight. That's the way it'll be between us," I told him.

"You'll never amount to anything," he said, shaking his head and blinking his eyes in astonishment.

"I'm not worried about that," I said. "All I want you to do is keep away from me, now and always . . ."

"You'll end on the gallows," he predicted.

"If I do, you'll have nothing to do with it," I said.

He stared at me in silence; evidently he did not believe me, for he took a step forward to test me.

"Put those razors down," he commanded.

"I'll cut you! I'll cut you!" I said, hysteria leaping into my voice, my hands slicing out with points of steel as I backed away.

He stopped; he had never in his life faced a person more grimly determined. Now and then he blinked his eyes and shook his head.

"You fool!" he bellowed suddenly.

"I'll make you bloody if you hit me!" I warned him.

His chest heaved and his body seemed to droop.

"Somebody will yet break your spirit," he said.

"It won't be you!"

"You'll get yours someday!"

"You won't be the one to give it to me!"

"And you've just been baptized," he said heavily.

"The hell with that," I said.

We stood in the early morning light and a touch of sun broke on the horizon. Roosters were crowing. A bird chirped near-by somewhere. Perhaps the neighbors were listening. Finally Uncle Tom's face began to twitch. Tears rolled down his cheeks. His lips trembled.

"Boy, I'm sorry for you," he said at last.

"You'd better be sorry for yourself," I said.

"You think you're a man," he said, dropping his arm and letting the switch drag in the dust of the yard. His lips moved as he groped for words. "But you'll learn, and you'll learn the hard way. I wish I could be an example to you . . ."

I knew that I had conquered him, had rid myself of him mentally and emotionally; but I wanted to be sure.

"You are not an example to me; you could never be," I spat at him. "You're a *warning*. Your life isn't so hot that you can tell me what to do." He repaired chairs for a living now, since he had retired from teaching. "Do you think I want to grow up and weave the bottoms of chairs for people to sit in?"

He twitched violently, trying to control himself.

"You'll be sorry you said that," he mumbled.

He turned his tall, lean, bent body and walked slowly up the steps. I sat on the porch a long time, waiting for my emotions to ebb. Then I crept cautiously into the house, got my hat, coat, books, and went to work, went to face the whims of the white folks.

Chapter VII

SUMMER. Bright hot days. Hunger still a vital part of my consciousness. Passing relatives in the hallways of the crowded home and not speaking. Eating in silence at a table where prayers are said. My mother recovering slowly, but now definitely crippled for life. Will I be able to enter school in September? Loneliness. Reading. Job hunting. Vague hopes of going north. But what would become of my mother if I left her in this queer house? And how would I fare in a strange city? Doubt. Fear. My friends are buying long-pants suits that cost from seventeen to twenty dollars, a sum as huge to me as the Alps! This was my reality in 1924.

Word came that a near-by brickyard was hiring and I went to investigate. I was frail, not weighing a hundred pounds. At noon I sneaked into the yard and walked among the aisles of damp, clean-smelling clay and came to a barrow full of wet bricks just taken from the machine that shaped them. I caught hold of the handles of the barrow and was barely able to lift it; it weighed perhaps four times as much as I did. If I were only stronger and heavier!

Later I asked questions and found that the water boy was missing; I ran to the office and was hired. I walked in the hot sun lugging a big zinc pail from one laboring gang of black men to another for a dollar a day; a man would lift the tin dipper to his lips, take a swallow, rinse out his mouth, spit, and then drink in long, slow gulps as sweat dripped into the dipper. And off again I would go, chanting:

"Water!"

And somebody would yell:

"Here, boy!"

Deep into wet pits of clay, into sticky ditches, up slippery slopes I would struggle with the pail. I stuck it out, reeling at times from hunger, pausing to get my breath before clambering up a hill. At the end of the week the money sank into the endless expenses at home. Later I got a job in the yard that paid a dollar and a half a day, that of bat boy. I went between the walls of clay and picked up bricks that had cracked open;

when my barrow was full, I would wheel it out onto a wooden scaffold and dump it into a pond.

I had but one fear here: a dog. He was owned by the boss of the brickyard and he haunted the clay aisles, snapping, growling. The dog had been wounded many times, for the black workers were always hurling bricks at it. Whenever I saw the animal, I would take a brick from my load and toss it at him; he would slink away, only to appear again, showing his teeth. Several of the Negroes had been bitten and had been ill; the boss had been asked to leash the dog, but he had refused. One afternoon I was wheeling my barrow toward the pond when something sharp sank into my thigh. I whirled; the dog crouched a few feet away, snarling. I had been bitten. I drove the dog away and opened my trousers; teeth marks showed deep and red.

I did not mind the stinging hurt, but I was afraid of an infection. When I went to the office to report that the boss's dog had bitten me, I was met by a tall blonde white girl.

"What do you want?" she asked.

"I want to see the boss, ma'am."

"For what?"

"His dog bit me, ma'am, and I'm afraid I might get an infection."

"Where did he bite you?"

"On my leg," I lied, shying from telling her where the bite was.

"Let's see," she said.

"No, ma'am. Can't I see the boss?"

"He isn't here now," she said, and went back to her typing.

I returned to work, stopping occasionally to examine the teeth marks; they were swelling. Later in the afternoon a tall white man wearing a cool white suit, a Panama hat, and white shoes came toward me.

"Is this the nigger?" he asked a black boy as he pointed at me.

"Yes, sir," the black boy answered.

"Come here, nigger," he called me.

I went to him.

"They tell me my dog bit you," he said.

"Yes, sir."

I pulled down my trousers and he looked.

"Humnnn," he grunted, then laughed. "A dog bite can't hurt a nigger."

"It's swelling and it hurts," I said.

"If it bothers you, let me know," he said. "But I never saw a dog yet that could really hurt a nigger."

He turned and walked away and the black boys gathered to watch his tall form disappear down the aisles of wet bricks.

"Sonofabitch!"

"He'll get his someday!"

"Boy, their hearts are hard!"

"Lawd, a white man'll do anything!"

"Break up that prayer meeting!" the white straw boss yelled.

The wheelbarrows rolled again. A boy came close to me.

"You better see a doctor," he whispered.

"I ain't got no money," I said.

Two days passed and luckily the redness and swelling went away.

Summer wore on and the brickyard closed; again I was out of work. I heard that caddies were wanted and I tramped five miles to the golf links. I was hired by a florid-faced white man at the rate of fifty cents for nine holes. I did not know the game and I lost three balls in as many minutes; it seemed that my eyes could not trace the flight of the balls. The man dismissed me. I watched the other boys do their jobs and within half an hour I had another golf bag and was following a ball. I made a dollar. I returned home, disgusted, tired, hungry, hating the sight of a golf course.

School opened and, though I had not prepared myself, I enrolled. The school was far across town and the walking distance alone consumed my breakfast of mush and lard gravy. I attended classes without books for a month, then got a job working mornings and evenings for three dollars a week.

I grew silent and reserved as the nature of the world in which I lived became plain and undeniable; the bleakness of the future affected my will to study. Granny had already thrown out hints that it was time for me to be on my own. But what had I learned so far that would help me to make a living? Nothing. I could be a porter like my father before me, but what else? And the problem of living as a Negro was cold and hard. What was it that made the hate of whites for blacks so steady, seemingly so woven into the texture of things? What kind of life was possible under that hate? How had this hate come to be? Nothing about the problems of Negroes was ever taught in the classrooms at school; and whenever I would raise these questions with the boys, they would either remain silent or turn the subject into a joke. They were vocal about the petty individual wrongs they suffered, but they possessed no desire for a knowledge of the picture as a whole. Then why was I worried about it?

Was I really as bad as my uncles and aunts and Granny repeatedly said? Why was it considered wrong to ask questions? Was I right when I resisted punishment? It was inconceivable to me that one should surrender to what seemed wrong, and most of the people I had met seemed wrong. Ought one to surrender to authority even if one believed that that authority was wrong? If the answer was yes, then I knew that I would always be wrong, because I could never do it. Then how could one live in a world in which one's mind and perceptions meant nothing and authority and tradition meant everything? There were no answers.

The eighth grade days flowed in their hungry path and I grew more conscious of myself; I sat in classes, bored, wondering, dreaming. One long dry afternoon I took out my composition book and told myself that I would write a story; it was sheer idleness that led me to it. What would the story be about? It resolved itself into a plot about a villain who wanted a widow's home and I called it *The Voodoo of Hell's Half-Acre*. It was crudely atmospheric, emotional, intuitively psychological, and stemmed from pure feeling. I finished it in three days and then wondered what to do with it.

The local Negro newspaper! That's it . . . I sailed into the office and shoved my ragged composition book under the nose of the man who called himself the editor.

"What is that?" he asked.

"A story," I said.

"A news story?"

"No, fiction."

"All right. I'll read it," he said.

He pushed my composition book back on his desk and looked at me curiously, sucking at his pipe.

"But I want you to read it *now*," I said.

He blinked. I had no idea how newspapers were run. I thought that one took a story to an editor and he sat down then and there and read it and said yes or no.

"I'll read this and let you know about it tomorrow," he said.

I was disappointed; I had taken time to write it and he seemed distant and uninterested.

"Give me the story," I said, reaching for it.

He turned from me, took up the book and read ten pages or more.

"Won't you come in tomorrow?" he asked. "I'll have it finished then."

I honestly relented.

"All right," I said. "I'll stop in tomorrow."

I left with the conviction that he would not read it. Now, where else could I take it after he had turned it down? The next afternoon, en route to my job, I stepped into the newspaper office.

"Where's my story?" I asked.

"It's in galleys," he said.

"What's that?" I asked; I did not know what galleys were.

"It's set up in type," he said. "We're publishing it."

"How much money will I get?" I asked, excited.

"We can't pay for manuscript," he said.

"But you sell your papers for money," I said with logic.

"Yes, but we're young in business," he explained.

"But you're asking me to *give* you my story, but you don't *give* your papers away," I said.

He laughed.

"Look, you're just starting. This story will put your name before our readers. Now, that's something," he said.

"But if the story is good enough to sell to your readers, then you ought to give me some of the money you get from it," I insisted.

He laughed again and I sensed that I was amusing him.

"I'm going to offer you something more valuable than money," he said. "I'll give you a chance to learn to write."

I was pleased, but I still thought he was taking advantage of me.

"When will you publish my story?"

"I'm dividing it into three installments," he said. "The first installment appears this week. But the main thing is this: Will you get news for me on a space rate basis?"

"I work mornings and evenings for three dollars a week," I said.

"Oh," he said. "Then you better keep that. But what are you doing this summer?"

"Nothing."

"Then come to see me before you take another job," he said. "And write some more stories."

A few days later my classmates came to me with baffled eyes, holding copies of the *Southern Register* in their hands.

"Did you really write that story?" they asked me.

"Yes."

"Why?"

"Because I wanted to."

"Where did you get it from?"

"I made it up."

"You didn't. You copied it out of a book."

"If I had, no one would publish it."

"But what are they publishing it for?"

"So people can read it."

"Who told you to do that?"

"Nobody."

"Then why did you do it?"

"Because I wanted to," I said again.

They were convinced that I had not told them the truth. We had never had any instruction in literary matters at school; the literature of the nation or the Negro had never been mentioned. My schoolmates could not understand why anyone would want to write a story; and, above all, they could not understand why I had called it *The Voodoo of Hell's Half-Acre*. The mood out of which a story was written was the most alien thing conceivable to them. They looked at me with new eyes, and a distance, a suspiciousness came between us. If I had thought anything in writing the story, I had thought that perhaps it would make me more acceptable to

them, and now it was cutting me off from them more completely than ever.

At home the effects were no less disturbing. Granny came
into my room early one morning and sat on the edge of my
bed.

"Richard, what is this you're putting in the papers?" she
asked.

"A story," I said.

"About what?"

"It's just a story, granny."

"But they tell me it's been in three times."

"It's the same story. It's in three parts."

"But what is it about?" she insisted.

I hedged, fearful of getting into a religious argument.

"It's just a story I made up," I said.

"Then it's a lie," she said.

"Oh, Christ," I said.

"You must get out of this house if you take the name of the
Lord in vain," she said.

"Granny, please . . . I'm sorry," I pleaded. "But it's hard
to tell you about the story. You see, granny, everybody knows
that the story isn't true, but . . ."

"Then why write it?" she asked.

"Because people might want to read it."

"That's the Devil's work," she said and left.

My mother also was worried.

"Son, you ought to be more serious," she said. "You're
growing up now and you won't be able to get jobs if you let
people think that you're weak-minded. Suppose the superintendent of schools would ask you to teach here in Jackson,
and he found out that you had been writing stories?"

I could not answer her.

"I'll be all right, mama," I said.

Uncle Tom, though surprised, was highly critical and contemptuous. The story had no point, he said. And whoever
heard of a story by the title of *The Voodoo of Hell's Half-Acre*?
Aunt Addie said that it was a sin for anyone to use the word
"hell" and that what was wrong with me was that I had
nobody to guide me. She blamed the whole thing upon my
upbringing.

In the end I was so angry that I refused to talk about the story. From no quarter, with the exception of the Negro newspaper editor, had there come a single encouraging word. It was rumored that the principal wanted to know why I had used the word "hell." I felt that I had committed a crime. Had I been conscious of the full extent to which I was pushing against the current of my environment, I would have been frightened altogether out of my attempts at writing. But my reactions were limited to the attitude of the people about me, and I did not speculate or generalize.

I dreamed of going north and writing books, novels. The North symbolized to me all that I had not felt and seen; it had no relation whatever to what actually existed. Yet, by imagining a place where everything was possible, I kept hope alive in me. But where had I got this notion of doing something in the future, of going away from home and accomplishing something that would be recognized by others? I had, of course, read my Horatio Alger stories, my pulp stories, and I knew my Get-Rich-Quick Wallingford series from cover to cover, though I had sense enough not to hope to get rich; even to my naïve imagination that possibility was too remote. I knew that I lived in a country in which the aspirations of black people were limited, marked-off. Yet I felt that I had to go somewhere and do something to redeem my being alive.

I was building up in me a dream which the entire educational system of the South had been rigged to stifle. I was feeling the very thing that the state of Mississippi had spent millions of dollars to make sure that I would never feel; I was becoming aware of the thing that the Jim Crow laws had been drafted and passed to keep out of my consciousness; I was acting on impulses that southern senators in the nation's capital had striven to keep out of Negro life; I was beginning to dream the dreams that the state had said were wrong, that the schools had said were taboo.

Had I been articulate about my ultimate aspirations, no doubt someone would have told me what I was bargaining for; but nobody seemed to know, and least of all did I. My classmates felt that I was doing something that was vaguely wrong, but they did not know how to express it. As the outside world grew more meaningful, I became more concerned, tense; and my classmates and my teachers would say: "Why do you ask so many questions?" Or: "Keep quiet."

I was in my fifteenth year; in terms of schooling I was far behind the average youth of the nation, but I did not know that. In me was shaping a yearning for a kind of consciousness, a mode of being that the way of life about me had said could not be, must not be, and upon which the penalty of death had been placed. Somewhere in the dead of the southern night my life had switched onto the wrong track and, without my knowing it, the locomotive of my heart was rushing down a dangerously steep slope, heading for a collision, heedless of the warning red lights that blinked all about me, the sirens and the bells and the screams that filled the air.

Chapter VIII

SUMMER AGAIN. The old problem of hunting for a job. I told the woman for whom I was working, a Mrs. Bibbs, that I needed an all-day job that would pay me enough money to buy clothes and books for the next school term. She took the matter up with her husband, who was a foreman in a sawmill.

"So you want to work in the mill, hunh?" he asked.

"Yes, sir."

He came to me and put his hands under my arms and lifted me from the floor, as though I were a bundle of feathers.

"You're too light for our work," he said.

"But maybe I could do *something* there," I said.

"That's the problem," he said soberly. "The work's heavy and dangerous." He was silent and I knew that he considered the matter closed. That was the way things were between whites and blacks in the South; many of the most important things were never openly said; they were understated and left to seep through to one. I, in turn, said nothing; but I did not leave the room; my standing silent was a way of asking him to reconsider, telling him that I wanted ever so much to try for a job in his mill. "All right," he said finally. "Come to the mill in the morning. I'll see what I can do. But I don't think that you'll like it."

I was at the mill at dawn the next morning and saw men lifting huge logs with tackle blocks. There were scores of buzzing steel saws biting into green wood with loud whines.

"Watch out!" somebody yelled.

I looked around and saw a black man pointing above my head; I glanced up. A log was swinging toward me. I scrambled out of its path. The black man came to my side.

"What do you want here, boy?"

"Mr. Bibbs, the foreman, told me to look around. I'm looking for a job," I said.

The man gazed at me intently.

"I wouldn't try for this if I was you," he said. "If you know this game, all right. But this is dangerous stuff for a guy that's green." He held up his right hand from which three fingers were missing. "See?"

I nodded and left.

Empty days. Long days. Bright hot days. The sun heated the pavements until they felt like the top of an oven. I spent the mornings hunting for jobs and I read during the afternoons. One morning I was walking toward the center of town and passed the home of a classmate, Ned Greenley. He was sitting on his porch, looking glum.

"Hello, Ned. What's new?" I asked.

"You've heard, haven't you?" he asked.

"About what?"

"My brother, Bob?"

"No, what happened?"

Ned began to weep softly.

"They killed him," he managed to say.

"The white folks?" I asked in a whisper, guessing.

He sobbed his answer. Bob was dead; I had met him only a few times, but I felt that I had known him through his brother.

"What happened?"

"Th-they t-took him in a c-car . . . Out on a c-country road . . . Th-they shot h-him," Ned whimpered.

I had heard that Bob was working at one of the hotels in town.

"Why?"

"Th-they said he was fooling with a white prostitute there in the hotel," Ned said.

Inside of me my world crashed and my body felt heavy. I stood looking down the quiet, sun-filled street. Bob had been caught by the white death, the threat of which hung over every male black in the South. I had heard whispered tales of black boys having sex relations with white prostitutes in the hotels in town, but I had never paid any close attention to them; now those tales came home to me in the form of the death of a man I knew.

I did not search for a job that day; I returned home and sat on my porch too, and stared. What I had heard altered the look of the world, induced in me a temporary paralysis of will and impulse. The penalty of death awaited me if I made a false move and I wondered if it was worth-while to make any move at all. The things that influenced my conduct as a Negro did not have to happen to me directly; I needed but to hear of them to feel their full effects in the deepest layers of my consciousness. Indeed, the white brutality that I had not seen was a more effective control of my behavior than that which I knew. The actual experience would have let me see the realistic outlines of what was really happening, but as long as it remained something terrible and yet remote, something whose horror and blood might descend upon me at any moment, I was compelled to give my entire imagination over to it, an act which blocked the springs of thought and feeling in me, creating a sense of distance between me and the world in which I lived.

A few days later I sought out the editor of the local Negro newspaper and found that he could not hire me. I had doubts now about my being able to enter school that fall. The empty days of summer rolled on. Whenever I met my classmates they would tell me about the jobs they had found, how some of them had left town to work in summer resorts in the North. Why did they not tell me of these jobs? I demanded of them. They said that they simply had not thought of it, and as I heard the words fall from their lips my sense of isolation became doubly acute. But, after all, what would make them think of me in connection with jobs when for years I had encountered them only casually in the classroom? I had had no association with them; the religious home in which I lived, my mush-and-lard-gravy poverty had cut me off from the normal processes of the lives of black boys my own age.

One afternoon I made a discovery in the home that stunned me. I was talking to my cousin, Maggie, who was a few months younger than I, when Uncle Tom entered the room. He paused, stared at me with silent hostility, then called his daughter. I gave the matter no thought. A few moments later I rose from my chair, where I had been reading, and was on my way down the hall when I heard Uncle Tom scolding his daughter. I caught a few phrases:

"Do you want me to break your neck? Didn't I tell you to stay away from him? That boy's a dangerous fool, I tell you! Then why don't you keep away from him? And make the other children keep away from him! Ask me no questions, but do as I tell you! Keep away from him, or I'll skin you!"

And I could hear my cousin's whimpering replies. My throat grew tight with anger. I wanted to rush into the room and demand an explanation, but I held still. How long had this been going on? I thought back over the time since Uncle Tom and his family had moved into the house, and I was filled with dismay as I recalled that on scarcely any occasion had any of his children ever been alone with me. Be careful now, I told myself; don't see what isn't there . . . But no matter how carefully I weighed my memories, I could recall no innocent intimacy, no games, no playing, none of the association that usually exists between young people living in the same house. Then suddenly I was reliving that early morning when I had held Uncle Tom at bay with my razors. Though I must have seemed brutal and desperate to him, I had never thought of myself as being so, and now I was appalled at how I was regarded. It was a flash of insight which revealed to me the true nature of my relations with my family, an insight which altered the entire course of my life. I was now definitely decided upon leaving home. But I would remain until the ninth grade term had ended. There were many days when I spoke to no one in the home except my mother. My life was falling to pieces and I was acutely aware of it. I was poised for flight, but I was waiting for some event, some word, some act, some circumstance to furnish the impetus.

I returned to my job at Mrs. Bibbs's and bought my schoolbooks; my clothing remained little better than rags. Luckily the studies in the ninth—my last year at school—were light; and, during a part of the term the teacher turned over the class to my supervision, an honor that helped me emotionally and made me hope faintly. It was even hinted that, if I kept my grades high, it would be possible for me to teach in the city school system.

During that winter my brother came home from Chicago; I was glad to see him, though we were strangers. But it was not long before I felt that the affection shown him by the family was far greater than that which I had ever had from them. Slowly my brother grew openly critical of me, taking his cue from those about him, and it hurt. My loneliness became organic. I felt walled in and I grew irritable. I associated less and less with my classmates, for their talk was now full of the schools they planned to attend when the term was over. The cold days dragged mechanically: up early and to my job, splitting wood, carrying coal, sweeping floors, then off to school and boredom.

The school term ended. I was selected as valedictorian of my class and assigned to write a paper to be delivered at one of the public auditoriums. One morning the principal summoned me to his office.

"Well, Richard Wright, here's your speech," he said with smooth bluntness and shoved a stack of stapled sheets across his desk.

"What speech?" I asked as I picked up the papers.

"The speech you're to say the night of graduation," he said.

"But, professor, I've written my speech already," I said.

He laughed confidently, indulgently.

"Listen, boy, you're going to speak to both *white* and colored people that night. What can you alone think of saying to them? You have no experience . . ."

I burned.

"I know that I'm not educated, professor," I said. "But the people are coming to hear the students, and I won't make a speech that you've written."

He leaned back in his chair and looked at me in surprise.

"You know, we've never had a boy in this school like you before," he said. "You've had your way around here. Just how you managed to do it, I don't know. But, listen, take this speech and say it. I know what's best for you. You can't afford to just say *anything* before those white people that night." He paused and added meaningfully: "The superintendent of schools will be there; you're in a position to make a good impression on him. I've been a principal for more years than you are old, boy. I've seen many a boy and girl graduate from this school, and none of them was too proud to recite a speech I wrote for them."

I had to make up my mind quickly; I was faced with a

matter of principle. I wanted to graduate, but I did not want to make a public speech that was not my own.

"Professor, I'm going to say my own speech that night," I said.

He grew angry.

"You're just a young, hotheaded fool," he said. He toyed with a pencil and looked up at me. "Suppose you don't graduate?"

"But I passed my examinations," I said.

"Look, mister," he shot at me, "I'm the man who says who passes at this school."

I was so astonished that my body jerked. I had gone to this school for two years and I had never suspected what kind of man the principal was; it simply had never occurred to me to wonder about him.

"Then I don't graduate," I said flatly.

I turned to leave.

"Say, you. Come here," he called.

I turned and faced him; he was smiling at me in a remote, superior sort of way.

"You know, I'm glad I talked to you," he said. "I was seriously thinking of placing you in the school system, teaching. But, now, I don't think that you'll fit."

He was tempting me, baiting me; this was the technique that snared black young minds into supporting the southern way of life.

"Look, professor, I may never get a chance to go to school again," I said. "But I like to do things right."

"What do you mean?"

"I've no money. I'm going to work. Now, this ninth-grade diploma isn't going to help me much in life. I'm not bitter about it; it's not your fault. But I'm just not going to do things this way."

"Have you talked to anybody about this?" he asked me.

"No, why?"

"Are you sure?"

"This is the first I've heard of it, professor," I said, amazed again.

"You haven't talked to any white people about this?"

"No, sir!"

"I just wanted to know," he said.

My amazement increased; the man was afraid now for his job!

"Professor, you don't understand me." I smiled.

"You're just a young, hot fool," he said, confident again. "Wake up, boy. Learn the world you're living in. You're smart and I know what you're after. I've kept closer track of you than you think. I know your relatives. Now, if you play safe," he smiled and winked, "I'll help you to go to school, to college."

"I want to learn, professor," I told him. "But there are some things I don't want to know."

"Good-bye," he said.

I went home, hurt but determined. I had been talking to a "bought" man and he had tried to "buy" me. I felt that I had been dealing with something unclean. That night Griggs, a boy who had gone through many classes with me, came to the house.

"Look, Dick, you're throwing away your future here in Jackson," he said. "Go to the principal, talk to him, take his speech and say it. I'm saying the one he wrote. So why can't you? What the hell? What can you lose?"

"No," I said.

"Why?"

"I know only a hell of a little, but my speech is going to reflect that," I said.

"Then you're going to be blacklisted for teaching jobs," he said.

"Who the hell said I was going to teach?" I asked.

"God, but you've got a will," he said.

"It's not will. I just don't want to do things that way," I said.

He left. Two days later Uncle Tom came to me. I knew that the principal had called him in.

"I hear that the principal wants you to say a speech which you've rejected," he said.

"Yes, sir. That's right," I said.

"May I read the speech you've written?" he asked.

"Certainly," I said, giving him my manuscript.

"And may I see the one that the principal wrote?"

I gave him the principal's speech too. He went to his room and read them. I sat quiet, waiting. He returned.

"The principal's speech is the better speech," he said.

"I don't doubt it," I replied. "But why did they ask me to write a speech if I can't deliver it?"

"Would you let me work on your speech?" he asked.

"No, sir."

"Now, look, Richard, this is your future . . ."

"Uncle Tom, I don't care to discuss this with you," I said.

He stared at me, then left. The principal's speech was simpler and clearer than mine, but it did not say anything; mine was cloudy, but it said what I wanted to say. What could I do? I had half a mind not to show up at the graduation exercises. I was hating my environment more each day. As soon as school was over, I would get a job, save money, and leave.

Griggs, who had accepted a speech written by the principal, came to my house each day and we went off into the woods to practice orating; day in and day out we spoke to the trees, to the creeks, frightening the birds, making the cows in the pastures stare at us in fear. I memorized my speech so thoroughly that I could have recited it in my sleep.

The news of my clash with the principal had spread through the class and the students became openly critical of me.

"Richard, you're a fool. You're throwing away every chance you've got. If they had known the kind of fool boy you are, they would never have made you valedictorian," they said.

I gritted my teeth and kept my mouth shut, but my rage was mounting by the hour. My classmates, motivated by a desire to "save" me, pestered me until I all but reached the breaking point. In the end the principal had to caution them to let me alone, for fear I would throw up the sponge and walk out.

I had one more problem to settle before I could make my speech. I was the only boy in my class wearing short pants and I was grimly determined to leave school in long pants. Was I not going to work? Would I not be on my own? When my desire for long pants became known at home, yet another storm shook the house.

"You're trying to go too fast," my mother said.

"You're nothing but a child," Uncle Tom pronounced.

"He's beside himself," Granny said.

I served notice that I was making my own decisions from then on. I borrowed money from Mrs. Bibbs, my employer, made a down payment on a pearl-gray suit. If I could not pay for it, I would take the damn thing back after graduation.

On the night of graduation I was nervous and tense; I rose and faced the audience and my speech rolled out. When my voice stopped there was some applause. I did not care if they liked it or not; I was through. Immediately, even before I left the platform, I tried to shunt all memory of the event from me. A few of my classmates managed to shake my hand as I pushed toward the door, seeking the street. Somebody invited me to a party and I did not accept. I did not want to see any of them again. I walked home, saying to myself: The hell with it! With almost seventeen years of baffled living behind me, I faced the world in 1925.

Chapter IX

M Y LIFE now depended upon my finding work, and I was so anxious that I accepted the first offer, a job as a porter in a clothing store selling cheap goods to Negroes on credit. The shop was always crowded with black men and women pawing over cheap suits and dresses. And they paid whatever price the white man asked. The boss, his son, and the clerk treated the Negroes with open contempt, pushing, kicking, or slapping them. No matter how often I witnessed it, I could not get used to it. How can they accept it? I asked myself. I kept on edge, trying to stifle my feelings and never quite succeeding, a prey to guilt and fear because I felt that the boss suspected that I resented what I saw.

One morning, while I was polishing brass out front, the boss and his son drove up in their car. A frightened black woman sat between them. They got out and half dragged and half kicked the woman into the store. White people passed and looked on without expression. A white policeman watched from the corner, twirling his night stick; but he made no move. I watched out of the corner of my eyes, but I never slackened the strokes of my chamois upon the brass. After a moment or two I heard shrill screams coming from the rear room of the store; later the woman stumbled out, bleeding, crying, holding her stomach, her clothing torn. When she reached the sidewalk, the policeman met her, grabbed her, accused her of being drunk, called a patrol wagon and carted her away.

When I went to the rear of the store, the boss and his son were washing their hands at the sink. They looked at me and laughed uneasily. The floor was bloody, strewn with wisps of hair and clothing. My face must have reflected my shock, for the boss slapped me reassuringly on the back.

"Boy, that's what we do to niggers when they don't pay their bills," he said.

His son looked at me and grinned.

"Here, hava cigarette," he said.

Not knowing what to do, I took it. He lit his and held the

match for me. This was a gesture of kindness, indicating that, even if they had beaten the black woman, they would not beat me if I knew enough to keep my mouth shut.

"Yes, sir," I said.

After they had gone, I sat on the edge of a packing box and stared at the bloody floor until the cigarette went out.

The store owned a bicycle which I used in delivering purchases. One day, while returning from the suburbs, my bicycle tire was punctured. I walked along the hot, dusty road, sweating and leading the bicycle by the handle bars.

A car slowed at my side.

"What's the matter there, boy?" a white man called.

I told him that my bicycle was broken and that I was walking back to town.

"That's too bad," he said. "Hop on the running board."

He stopped the car. I clutched hard at my bicycle with one hand and clung to the side of the car with the other.

"All set?"

"Yes, sir."

The car started. It was full of young white men. They were drinking. I watched the flask pass from mouth to mouth.

"Wanna drink, boy?" one asked.

The memory of my six-year-old drinking came back and filled me with caution. But I laughed, the wind whipping my face.

"Oh, no!" I said.

The words were barely out of my mouth before I felt something hard and cold smash me between the eyes. It was an empty whisky bottle. I saw stars, and fell backwards from the speeding car into the dust of the road, my feet becoming entangled in the steel spokes of the bicycle. The car stopped and the white men piled out and stood over me.

"Nigger, ain't you learned no better sense'n that yet?" asked the man who hit me. "Ain't you learned to say *sir* to a white man yet?"

Dazed, I pulled to my feet. My elbows and legs were bleeding. Fists doubled, the white man advanced, kicking the bicycle out of the way.

"Aw, leave the bastard alone. He's got enough," said one.

They stood looking at me. I rubbed my shins, trying to

stop the flow of blood. No doubt they felt a sort of contemptuous pity, for one asked:

"You wanna ride to town now, nigger? You reckon you know enough to ride now?"

"I wanna walk," I said simply.

Maybe I sounded funny. They laughed.

"Well, walk, you black sonofabitch!"

Before they got back into their car, they comforted me with:

"Nigger, you sure ought to be glad it was us you talked to that way. You're a lucky bastard, 'cause if you'd said that to some other white man, you might've been a dead nigger now."

I was learning rapidly how to watch white people, to observe their every move, every fleeting expression, how to interpret what was said and what left unsaid.

Late one Saturday night I made some deliveries in a white neighborhood. I was pedaling my bicycle back to the store as fast as I could when a police car, swerving toward me, jammed me into the curbing.

"Get down, nigger, and put up your hands!" they ordered.

I did. They climbed out of the car, guns drawn, faces set, and advanced slowly.

"Keep still!" they ordered.

I reached my hands higher. They searched my pockets and packages. They seemed dissatisfied when they could find nothing incriminating. Finally, one of them said:

"Boy, tell your boss not to send you out in white neighborhoods at this time of night."

"Yes, sir," I said.

I rode off, feeling that they might shoot at me, feeling that the pavement might disappear. It was like living in a dream, the reality of which might change at any moment.

Each day in the store I watched the brutality with growing hate, yet trying to keep my feelings from registering in my face. When the boss looked at me I would avoid his eyes. Finally the boss's son cornered me one morning.

"Say, nigger, look here," he began.

"Yes, sir."

"What's on your mind?"

"Nothing, sir," I said, trying to look amazed, trying to fool him.

"Why don't you laugh and talk like the other niggers?" he asked.

"Well, sir, there's nothing much to say or smile about," I said, smiling.

His face was hard, baffled; I knew that I had not convinced him. He whirled from me and went to the front of the store; he came back a moment later, his face red. He tossed a few green bills at me.

"I don't like your looks, nigger. Now, get!" he snapped.

I picked up the money and did not count it. I grabbed my hat and left.

I held a series of petty jobs for short periods, quitting some to work elsewhere, being driven off others because of my attitude, my speech, the look in my eyes. I was no nearer than ever to my goal of saving enough money to leave. At times I doubted if I could ever do it.

One jobless morning I went to my old classmate, Griggs, who worked for a Capitol Street jeweler. He was washing the windows of the store when I came upon him.

"Do you know where I can find a job?" I asked.

He looked at me with scorn.

"Yes, I know where you can find a job," he said, laughing.

"Where?"

"But I wonder if you can hold it," he said.

"What do you mean?" I asked. "Where's the job?"

"Take your time," he said. "You know, Dick, I know you. You've been trying to hold a job all summer, and you can't. Why? Because you're impatient. That's your big fault."

I said nothing, because he was repeating what I had already heard him say. He lit a cigarette and blew out smoke leisurely.

"Well," I said, egging him on to speak.

"I wish to hell I could talk to you," he said.

"I think I know what you want to tell me," I said.

He clapped me on the shoulder; his face was full of fear, hate, concern for me.

"Do you want to get killed?" he asked me.

"Hell, no!"

"Then, for God's sake, learn how to live in the South!"

"What do you mean?" I demanded. "Let white people tell me that. Why should you?"

"See?" he said triumphantly, pointing his finger at me. "There it is, *now*! It's in your face. You won't let people tell you things. You rush too much. I'm trying to help you and you won't let me." He paused and looked about; the streets were filled with white people. He spoke to me in a low, full tone. "Dick, look, you're black, black, *black*, see? Can't you understand that?"

"Sure. I understand it," I said.

"You don't act a damn bit like it," he spat.

He then reeled off an account of my actions on every job I had held that summer.

"How did you know that?" I asked.

"White people make it their business to watch niggers," he explained. "And they pass the word around. Now, my boss is a Yankee and he tells me things. You're marked already."

Could I believe him? Was it true? How could I ever learn this strange world of white people?

"Then tell me how must I act?" I asked humbly. "I just want to make enough money to leave."

"Wait and I'll tell you," he said.

At that moment a woman and two men stepped from the jewelry store; I moved to one side to let them pass, my mind intent upon Griggs's words. Suddenly Griggs reached for my arm and jerked me violently, sending me stumbling three or four feet across the pavement. I whirled.

"What's the matter with you?" I asked.

Griggs glared at me, then laughed.

"I'm teaching you how to get out of white people's way," he said.

I looked at the people who had come out of the store; yes, they were *white*, but I had not noticed it.

"Do you see what I mean?" he asked. "White people want you out of their way." He pronounced the words slowly so that they would sink into my mind.

"I know what you mean," I breathed.

"Dick, I'm treating you like a brother," he said. "You act

around white people as if you didn't know that they were white. And they *see* it."

"Oh, Christ, I can't be a slave," I said hopelessly.

"But you've got to eat," he said.

"Yes, I got to eat."

"Then start acting like it," he hammered at me, pounding his fist in his palm. "When you're in front of white people, *think* before you act, *think* before you speak. Your way of doing things is all right among *our* people, but not for *white* people. They won't stand for it."

I stared bleakly into the morning sun. I was nearing my seventeenth birthday and I was wondering if I would ever be free of this plague. What Griggs was saying was true, but it was simply utterly impossible for me to calculate, to scheme, to act, to plot all the time. I would remember to dissemble for short periods, then I would forget and act straight and human again, not with the desire to harm anybody, but merely forgetting the artificial status of race and class. It was the same with whites as with blacks; it was my way with everybody. I sighed, looking at the glittering diamonds in the store window, the rings and the neat rows of golden watches.

"I guess you're right," I said at last. "I've got to watch myself, break myself . . ."

"No," he said quickly, feeling guilty now. Someone—a white man—went into the store and we paused in our talk. "You know, Dick, you may think I'm an Uncle Tom, but I'm not. I hate these white people, hate 'em with all my heart. But I can't show it; if I did, they'd kill me." He paused and looked around to see if there were any white people within hearing distance. "Once I heard an old drunk nigger say:

> *All these white folks dressed so fine*
> *Their ass-holes smell just like mine . . .*"

I laughed uneasily, looking at the white faces that passed me. But Griggs, when he laughed, covered his mouth with his hand and bent at the knees, a gesture which was unconsciously meant to conceal his excessive joy in the presence of whites.

"That's how I feel about 'em," he said proudly after he had finished his spasm of glee. He grew sober. "There's an optical company upstairs and the boss is a Yankee from Illinois. Now, he wants a boy to work all day in summer, mornings and evenings in winter. He wants to break a colored boy into the optical trade. You know algebra and you're just cut out for the work. I'll tell Mr. Crane about you and I'll get in touch with you."

"Do you suppose I could see him now?" I asked.

"For God's sake, take your *time!*" he thundered at me.

"Maybe that's what's wrong with Negroes," I said. "They take too much time."

I laughed, but he was disturbed. I thanked him and left. For a week I did not hear from him and I gave up hope. Then one afternoon Griggs came to my house.

"It looks like you've got a job," he said. "You're going to have a chance to learn a trade. But remember to keep your head. Remember you're black. You start tomorrow."

"What will I get?"

"Five dollars a week to start with; they'll raise you if they like you," he explained.

My hopes soared. Things were not quite so bad, after all. I would have a chance to learn a trade. And I need not give up school. I told him that I would take the job, that I would be humble.

"You'll be working for a Yankee and you ought to get along," he said.

The next morning I was outside the office of the optical company long before it opened. I was reminding myself that I must be polite, must think before I spoke, must think before I acted, must say "yes sir, no sir," that I must so conduct myself that white people would not think that I thought I was as good as they. Suddenly a white man came up to me.

"What do you want?" he asked me.

"I'm reporting for a job, sir," I said.

"O.K. Come on."

I followed him up a flight of steps and he unlocked the door of the office. I was a little tense, but the young white man's manner put me at ease and I sat and held my hat in my hand. A white girl came and began punching the typewriter. Soon another white man, thin and gray, entered and went into the rear room. Finally a tall, red-faced white man arrived, shot me a quick glance and sat at his desk. His brisk manner branded him a Yankee.

"You're the new boy, eh?"

"Yes, sir."

"Let me get my mail out of the way and I'll talk with you," he said pleasantly.

"Yes, sir."

I even pitched my voice to a low plane, trying to rob it of any suggestion or overtone of aggressiveness.

Half an hour later Mr. Crane called me to his desk and questioned me closely about my schooling, about how much mathematics I had had. He seemed pleased when I told him that I had had two years of algebra.

"How would you like to learn this trade?" he asked.

"I'd like it fine, sir. I'd like nothing better," I said.

He told me that he wanted to train a Negro boy in the optical trade; he wanted to help him, guide him. I tried to answer in a way that would let him know that I would try to be worthy of what he was doing. He took me to the stenographer and said:

"This is Richard. He's going to be with us."

He then led me into the rear room of the office, which turned out to be a tiny factory filled with many strange machines smeared with red dust.

"Reynolds," he said to a young white man, "this is Richard."

"What you saying there, boy!" Reynolds grinned and boomed at me.

Mr. Crane took me to the older man.

"Pease, this is Richard, who'll work with us."

Pease looked at me and nodded. Mr. Crane then held forth to the two white men about my duties; he told them to break me in gradually to the workings of the shop, to instruct me in the mechanics of grinding and polishing lenses. They nodded their assent.

"Now, boy, let's see how clean you can get this place," Mr. Crane said.

"Yes, sir."

I swept, mopped, dusted, and soon had the office and the shop clean. In the afternoons, when I had caught up with my work, I ran errands. In an idle moment I would stand and watch the two white men grinding lenses on the machines. They said nothing to me and I said nothing to them. The first day passed, the second, the third, a week passed and I received my five dollars. A month passed. But I was not learning anything and nobody had volunteered to help me. One afternoon I walked up to Reynolds and asked him to tell me about the work.

"What are you trying to do, get smart, nigger?" he asked me.

"No, sir," I said.

I was baffled. Perhaps he just did not want to help me. I went to Pease, reminding him that the boss had said that I was to be given a chance to learn the trade.

"Nigger, you think you're white, don't you?"

"No, sir."

"You're acting mighty like it," he said.

"I was only doing what the boss told me to do," I said.

Pease shook his fist in my face.

"This is a *white* man's work around here," he said.

From then on they changed toward me; they said good morning no more. When I was just a bit slow in performing some duty, I was called a lazy black sonofabitch. I kept silent, striving to offer no excuse for worsening of relations. But one day Reynolds called me to his machine.

"Richard, how long is your thing?" he asked me.

"What thing?" I asked.

"You know what I mean," he said. "The thing the bull uses on the cow."

I turned away from him; I had heard that whites regarded Negroes as animals in sex matters and his words made me angry.

"I heard that a nigger can stick his prick in the ground and spin around on it like a top," he said, chuckling. "I'd like to see you do that. I'd give you a dime, if you did it."

I ignored him. Mr. Pease was watching me closely; then I saw them exchange glances. My job was not leading to what Mr. Crane had said it would. I had been humble, and now I was reaping the wages of humility.

"Come here, boy," Pease said.

I walked to his bench.

"You didn't like what Reynolds just said, did you?" he asked.

"Oh, it's all right," I said smiling.

"You didn't like it. I could see it on your face," he said.

I stared at him and backed away.

"Did you ever get into any trouble?" he asked.

"No, sir."

"What would you do if you got into trouble?"

"I don't know, sir."

"Well, watch yourself and don't get into trouble," he warned.

I wanted to report these clashes to Mr. Crane, but the thought of what Pease or Reynolds would do to me if they learned that I had "snitched" stopped me. I worked through the days and tried to hide my resentment under a nervous, cryptic smile.

The climax came at noon one summer day. Pease called me to his workbench; to get to him I had to go between two narrow benches and stand with my back against a wall.

"Richard, I want to ask you something," Pease began pleasantly, not looking up from his work.

"Yes, sir."

Reynolds came over and stood blocking the narrow passage between the benches; he folded his arms and stared at me solemnly. I looked from one to the other, sensing trouble. Pease looked up and spoke slowly, so there would be no possibility of my not understanding.

"Richard, Reynolds here tells me that you called me Pease," he said.

I stiffened. A void opened up in me. I knew that this was the showdown.

He meant that I had failed to call him Mr. Pease. I looked at Reynolds; he was gripping a steel bar in his hand. I opened my mouth to speak, to protest, to assure Pease that I had never called him simply *Pease*, and that I had never had any intention of doing so, when Reynolds grabbed me by the collar, ramming my head against a wall.

"Now, be careful, nigger," snarled Reynolds, baring his teeth. "I heard you call 'im *Pease*. And if you say you didn't, you're calling me a liar, see?" He waved the steel bar threateningly.

If I had said: No, sir, Mr. Pease, I never called you *Pease*, I would by inference have been calling Reynolds a liar; and if I had said: Yes, sir, Mr. Pease, I called you *Pease*, I would have been pleading guilty to the worst insult that a Negro can offer to a southern white man. I stood trying to think of a neutral course that would resolve this quickly risen nightmare, but my tongue would not move.

"Richard, I asked you a question!" Pease said. Anger was creeping into his voice.

"I don't remember calling you *Pease*, Mr. Pease," I said cautiously. "And if I did, I sure didn't mean . . ."

"You black sonofabitch! You called me *Pease*, then!" he spat, rising and slapping me till I bent sideways over a bench.

Reynolds was up on top of me demanding:

"Didn't you call him *Pease*? If you say you didn't, I'll rip your gut string loose with this f—k—g bar, you black granny dodger! You can't call a white man a liar and get away with it!"

I wilted. I begged them not to hit me. I knew what they wanted. They wanted me to leave the job.

"I'll leave," I promised. "I'll leave right now!"

They gave me a minute to get out of the factory, and warned me not to show up again or tell the boss. Reynolds loosened his hand on my collar and I ducked out of the room. I did not see Mr. Crane or the stenographer in the office. Pease and Reynolds had so timed it that Mr. Crane and the stenographer would be out when they turned on the terror. I went to the street and waited for the boss to return. I saw Griggs wiping glass shelves in the jewelry store and I beckoned to him. He came out and I told him what had happened.

"Then what are you standing there like a fool for?" he demanded. "Won't you ever learn? Get home! They might come down!"

I walked down Capitol Street feeling that the sidewalk was unreal, that I was unreal, that the people were unreal, yet expecting somebody to demand to know what right I had to be on the streets. My wound went deep; I felt that I had been slapped out of the human race. When I reached home, I did not tell the family what had happened; I merely told them that I had quit, that I was not making enough money, that I was seeking another job.

That night Griggs came to my house; we went for a walk.

"You got a goddamn tough break," he said.

"Can you say it was my fault?" I asked.

He shook his head.

"Well, what about your goddamn philosophy of meekness?" I asked him bitterly.

"These things just happen," he said, shrugging.

"They owe me money," I said.

"That's what I came about," he said. "Mr. Crane wants you to come in at ten in the morning. Ten sharp, now, mind you, because he'll be there and those guys won't gang up on you again."

The next morning at ten I crept up the stairs and peered into the office of the optical shop to make sure that Mr. Crane was in. He was at his desk. Pease and Reynolds were at their machines in the rear.

"Come in, Richard," Mr. Crane said.

I pulled off my hat and walked into the office; I stood before him.

"Sit down," he said.

I sat. He stared at me and shook his head.

"Tell me, what happened?"

An impulse to speak rose in me and died with the realization that I was facing a wall that I would never breech. I tried to speak several times and could make no sounds. I grew tense and tears burnt my cheeks.

"Now, just keep control of yourself," Mr. Crane said.

I clenched my fists and managed to talk.

"I tried to do my best here," I said.

"I believe you," he said. "But I want to know what happened. Which one bothered you?"

"Both of 'em," I said.

Reynolds came running to the door and I rose. Mr. Crane jumped to his feet.

"Get back in there," he told Reynolds.

"That nigger's lying!" Reynolds said. "I'll kill 'im if he lies on me!"

"Get back in there or get out," Mr. Crane said.

Reynolds backed away, keeping his eyes on me.

"Go ahead," Mr. Crane said. "Tell me what happened."

Then again I could not speak. What could I accomplish by telling him? I was black; I lived in the South. I would never learn to operate those machines as long as those two white men in there stood by them. Anger and fear welled in me as I felt what I had missed; I leaned forward and clapped my hands to my face.

"No, no, now," Mr. Crane said. "Keep control of yourself. No matter what happens, keep control . . ."

"I know," I said in a voice not my own. "There's no use of my saying anything."

"Do you want to work here?" he asked me.

I looked at the white faces of Pease and Reynolds; I imagined their waylaying me, killing me. I was remembering what had happened to Ned's brother.

"No, sir," I breathed.

"Why?"

"I'm scared," I said. "They would kill me."

Mr. Crane turned and called Pease and Reynolds into the office.

"Now, tell me which one bothered you. Don't be afraid. Nobody's going to hurt you," Mr. Crane said.

I stared ahead of me and did not answer. He waved the men inside. The white stenographer looked at me with wide eyes and I felt drenched in shame, naked to my soul. The whole of my being felt violated, and I knew that my own fear had helped to violate it. I was breathing hard and struggling to master my feelings.

"Can I get my money, sir?" I asked at last.

"Just sit a minute and take hold of yourself," he said.

I waited and my roused senses grew slowly calm.

"I'm awfully sorry about this," he said.

"I had hoped for a lot from this job," I said. "I'd wanted to go to school, to college . . ."

"I know," he said. "But what are you going to do now?"

My eyes traveled over the office, but I was not seeing.

"I'm going away," I said.

"What do you mean?"

"I'm going to get out of the South," I breathed.

"Maybe that's best," he said. "I'm from Illinois. Even for me, it's hard here. I can do just so much."

He handed me my money, more than I had earned for the week. I thanked him and rose to leave. He rose. I went into the hallway and he followed me. He reached out his hand.

"It's tough for you down here," he said.

I barely touched his hand. I walked swiftly down the hall, fighting against crying again. I ran down the steps, then paused and looked back up. He was standing at the head of the stairs, shaking his head. I went into the sunshine and walked home like a blind man.

Chapter X

FOR WEEKS after that I could not believe in my feelings. My personality was numb, reduced to a lumpish, loose, dissolved state. I was a non-man, something that knew vaguely that it was human but felt that it was not. As time separated me from the experience, I could feel no hate for the men who had driven me from the job. They did not seem to be individual men, but part of a huge, implacable, elemental design toward which hate was futile. What I did feel was a longing to attack. But how? And because I knew of no way to grapple with this thing, I felt doubly cast out.

I went to bed tired and got up tired, though I was having no physical exercise. During the day I overreacted to each event, my banked emotions spilling around it. I refused to talk to anyone about my affairs, because I knew that I would only hear a justification of the ways of the white folks and I did not want to hear it. I lived carrying a huge wound, tender, festering, and I shrank when I came near anything that I thought would touch it.

But I had to work because I had to eat. My next job was that of a helper in a drugstore, and the night before I reported for work I fought with myself, telling myself that I had to master this thing, that my life depended upon it. Other black people worked, got along somehow, then I must, *must*, MUST get along until I could get my hands on enough money to leave. I would make myself fit in. Others had done it. I would do it. I had to do it.

I went to the job apprehensive, resolving to watch my every move. I swept the sidewalk, pausing when a white person was twenty feet away. I mopped the store, cautiously waiting for the white people to move out of my way in their own good time. I cleaned acres of glass shelving, changing my tempo now to work faster, holding every nuance of reality within the focus of my consciousness. Noon came and the store was crowded; people jammed to the counters for food. A white man behind the counter ran up to me and shouted:

"A jug of Coca-Cola, quick, boy!"

My body jerked taut and I stared at him. He stared at me.

"What's wrong with you?"

"Nothing," I said.

"Well, move! Don't stand there gaping!"

Even if I had tried, I could not have told him what was wrong. My sustained expectation of violence had exhausted me. My preoccupation with curbing my impulses, my speech, my movements, my manner, my expressions had increased my anxiety. I became forgetful, concentrating too much upon trivial tasks. The men began to yell at me and that made it worse. One day I dropped a jug of orange syrup in the middle of the floor. The boss was furious. He caught my arm and jerked me into the back of the drugstore. His face was livid. I expected him to hit me. I was braced to defend myself.

"I'm going to deduct that from your pay, you black bastard!" he yelled.

Words had come instead of blows and I relaxed.

"Yes, sir," I said placatingly. "It was my fault."

My tone whipped him to a frenzy.

"You goddamn right it was!" he yelled louder.

"I'm new at this," I mumbled, realizing that I had said the wrong thing, though I had been striving to say the right.

"We're only trying you out," he warned me.

"Yes, sir. I understand," I said.

He stared at me, speechless with rage. Why could I not learn to keep my mouth shut at the right time? I had said just one short sentence too many. My words were innocent enough, but they indicated, it seemed, a consciousness on my part that infuriated white people.

Saturday night came and the boss gave me my money and snapped: "Don't come back. You won't do."

I knew what was wrong with me, but I could not correct it. The words and actions of white people were baffling signs to me. I was living in a culture and not a civilization and I could learn how that culture worked only by living with it. Misreading the reactions of whites around me made me say and do the wrong things. In my dealing with whites I was conscious of the entirety of my relations with them, and they were con-

scious only of what was happening at a given moment. I had
to keep remembering what others took for granted; I had to
think out what others felt.

I had begun coping with the white world too late. I could
not make subservience an automatic part of my behavior. I
had to feel and think out each tiny item of racial experience in
the light of the whole race problem, and to each item I
brought the whole of my life. While standing before a white
man I had to figure out how to perform each act and how to
say each word. I could not help it. I could not grin. In the
past I had always said too much, now I found that it was
difficult to say anything at all. I could not react as the world
in which I lived expected me to; that world was too baffling,
too uncertain.

I was idle for weeks. The summer waned. Hope for school
was now definitely gone. Autumn came and many of the
boys who held jobs returned to school. Jobs were now
numerous. I heard that hallboys were needed at one of the
hotels, the hotel in which Ned's brother had lost his life.
Should I go there? Would I, too, make a fatal slip? But I had
to earn money. I applied and was accepted to mop long white
tiled hallways that stretched around the entire perimeter of
the office floors of the building. I reported each night at ten,
got a huge pail of water, a bushel of soap flakes and, with a
gang of moppers, I worked. All the boys were Negroes and I
was happy; at least I could talk, joke, laugh, sing, say what I
pleased.

I began to marvel at how smoothly the black boys acted
out the roles that the white race had mapped out for them.
Most of them were not conscious of living a special, separate,
stunted way of life. Yet I knew that in some period of their
growing up—a period that they had no doubt forgotten—
there had been developed in them a delicate, sensitive controlling mechanism that shut off their minds and emotions from
all that the white race had said was taboo. Although they
lived in an America where in theory there existed equality of
opportunity, they knew unerringly what to aspire to and what
not to aspire to. Had a black boy announced that he aspired
to be a writer, he would have been unhesitatingly called crazy
by his pals. Or had a black boy spoken of yearning to get a

seat on the New York Stock Exchange, his friends—in the boy's own interest—would have reported his odd ambition to the white boss.

There was a pale-yellow boy who had gonorrhea and was proud of it.

"Say," he asked me one night, "you ever have the clap?"

"God, no," I said. "Why do you ask?"

"I got it," he said matter-of-factly. "I thought you could tell me something to use."

"Haven't you been to a doctor?" I asked.

"Aw, hell. Them doctors ain't no good."

"Don't be foolish," I said.

"What's the matter with you?" he demanded of me. "You talk like you'd be 'shamed of the clap."

"I would," I said.

"Hell, you ain't a man 'less you done had it three times," he said.

"Don't brag about it," I said.

"'Tain't nothing worse'n a bad cold," he said.

But I noticed that when he urinated he would grab hold of a steam pipe, a doorjamb, or a window sill and strain with tear-filled eyes and a tortured face, as though he were attempting to lift the hotel up from its foundations. I laughed to cover my disgust.

When I was through mopping, I would watch the never-ending crap games that went on in the lockers, but I could never become interested enough to participate. Gambling had never appealed to me. I could not conceive of any game holding more risks than the life I was living. Curses and sex stories sounded round the clock and blue smoke choked the air. I would sit listening for hours, wondering how on earth they could laugh so freely, trying to grasp the miracle that gave their debased lives the semblance of a human existence.

Several Negro girls were employed as maids in the hotel, some of whom I knew. One night when I was about to go home I saw a girl who lived in my direction and I fell in beside her to walk part of the distance together. As we passed the white night watchman, he slapped her playfully on her buttocks. I turned around, amazed. The girl twisted out of his reach, tossed her head saucily, and went down the hallway. I had not moved from my tracks.

"Nigger, you look like you don't like what I did," he said.

I could not move or speak. My immobility must have seemed a challenge to him, for he pulled his gun.

"Don't you like it, nigger?"

"Yes, sir," I whispered with a dry throat.

"Well, talk like it, then, goddammit!"

"Oh, yes, sir!" I said with as much heartiness as I could muster.

I walked down the hall, knowing that the gun was pointed at me, but afraid to look back. When I was out of the door, my throat felt as though it were swelling and bursting with fire. The girl was waiting for me. I walked past her. She caught up with me.

"God, how could you let him do that?" I exploded.

"It don't matter. They do that all the time," she said.

"I wanted to do something," I said.

"You woulda been a fool if you had," she said.

"But how must you feel?"

"They never get any further with us than that, if we don't want 'em to," she said dryly.

"Yes, I would've been a fool," I said, but she did not catch the point.

I was afraid to go to work the following night. What would the watchman think? Would he decide to teach me a lesson? I walked slowly through the door, wondering if he would continue his threat. His eyes looked at and through me. Evidently he considered the matter closed, or else he had had so many experiences of that kind that he had already forgotten it.

Out of my salary I had begun to save a few dollars, for my determination to leave had not lessened. But I found the saving exasperatingly slow. I pondered continuously ways of making money, and the only ways that I could think of involved transgressions of the law. No, I must not do that, I told myself. To go to jail in the South would mean the end. And there was the possibility that if I were ever caught I would never reach jail.

This was the first time in my life that I had ever consciously entertained the idea of violating the laws of the land. I had felt that my intelligence and industry could cope with all situations, and, until that time, I had never stolen a penny from anyone. Even hunger had never driven me to appropriate what was not my own. The mere idea of stealing had been repugnant. I had not been honest from deliberate motives, but being dishonest had simply never occurred to me.

Yet, all about me, Negroes were stealing. More than once I had been called a "dumb nigger" by black boys who discovered that I had not availed myself of a chance to snatch some petty piece of white property that had been carelessly left within my reach.

"How in hell you gonna git ahead?" I had been asked when I had said that one ought not steal.

I knew that the boys in the hotel filched whatever they could. I knew that Griggs, my friend who worked in the Capitol Street jewelry store, was stealing regularly and successfully. I knew that a black neighbor of mine was stealing bags of grain from a wholesale house where he worked, though he was a stanch deacon in his church and prayed and sang on Sundays. I knew that the black girls who worked in white homes stole food daily to supplement their scanty wages. And I knew that the very nature of black and white relations bred this constant thievery.

No Negroes in my environment had ever thought of organizing, no matter in how orderly a fashion, and petitioning their white employers for higher wages. The very thought would have been terrifying to them, and they knew that the whites would have retaliated with swift brutality. So, pretending to conform to the laws of the whites, grinning, bowing, they let their fingers stick to what they could touch. And the whites seemed to like it.

But I, who stole nothing, who wanted to look them straight in the face, who wanted to talk and act like a man, inspired fear in them. The southern whites would rather have had Negroes who stole, work for them than Negroes who knew, however dimly, the worth of their own humanity. Hence, whites placed a premium upon black deceit; they encouraged irresponsibility; and their rewards were bestowed upon us blacks in the degree that we could make them feel safe and superior.

My objections to stealing were not moral. I did not approve of it because I knew that, in the long run, it was futile, that it was not an effective way to alter one's relationship to one's environment. Then, how could I change my relationship to my environment? Almost my entire salary went to feed the eternally hungry stomachs at home. If I saved a dollar a week, it would take me two years to amass a hundred dollars, the amount which for some reason I had decided was necessary to stake me in a strange city. And, God knows, anything could happen to me in two years . . .

I did not know when I would be thrown into a situation where I would say the wrong word to the wrong white man and find myself in trouble. And, above all, I wanted to avoid trouble, for I feared that if I clashed with whites I would lose control of my emotions and spill out words that would be my sentence of death. Time was not on my side and I had to make some move. Often, when perplexed, I longed to be like the smiling, lazy, forgetful black boys in the noisy hotel locker rooms, with no torrential conflicts to resolve. Many times I grew weary of the secret burden I carried and longed to cast it down, either in action or in resignation. But I was not made to be a resigned man and I had only a limited choice of actions, and I was afraid of all of them.

A new anxiety was created in me by my desire to leave quickly. I had now seen at close quarters the haughty white men who made the laws; I had seen how they acted, how they regarded black people, how they regarded me; and I no longer felt bound by the laws which white and black were supposed to obey in common. I was outside those laws; the white people had told me so. Now when I thought of ways to escape from my environment I no longer felt the inner restraint that would have made stealing impossible, and this new freedom made me lonely and afraid.

My feelings became divided; in spite of myself I would dream of a locked cupboard in a near-by neighbor's house where a gun was kept. If I stole it, how much would it bring? When the yearning to leave would become strong in me, I could not keep out of my mind the image of a storehouse at a near-by Negro college that held huge cans of preserved fruits. Yet fear kept me from making any move; the idea of stealing floated tentatively in me. My inability to adjust myself to the white world had already shattered a part of the structure of my personality and had broken down the inner barriers to crime; the only thing that now stood in the way was lack of immediate opportunity, a final push of circumstance. And that came.

I was promoted to bellboy, which meant a small increase in income. But I soon learned that the substantial money came from bootlegging liquor to the white prostitutes in the hotel. The other bellboys were taking these risks, and I fell in. I learned how to walk past a white policeman with contraband upon my hip, sauntering, whistling like a nigger ought to whistle when he is innocent. The extra dollars were coming in, but slowly. How, how, how could I get my hands on more money before I was caught and sent to jail for some trivial misdemeanor? If I were going to violate the law, then I ought to get something out of it. My larcenous aims were modest. A hundred dollars would give me, temporarily, more freedom of movement than I had ever known in my life. I watched and waited, living with the thought.

While waiting for my chance to grab and run, I grew used to seeing the white prostitutes naked upon their beds, sitting nude about their rooms, and I learned new modes of behavior, new rules in how to live the Jim Crow life. It was presumed that we black boys took their nakedness for granted, that it startled us no more than a blue vase or a red rug. Our presence awoke in them no sense of shame whatever, for we blacks were not considered human anyway. If they were alone, I would steal sidelong glances at them. But if they were receiving men, not a flicker of my eyelids would show.

A huge, snowy-skinned blonde took a room on my floor. One night she rang for service and I went to wait upon her. She was in bed with a thickset man; both were nude and uncovered. She said that she wanted some liquor, and slid out of bed and waddled across the floor to get her money from the dresser drawer. Without realizing it, I watched her.

"Nigger, what in hell are you looking at?" the white man asked, raising himself upon his elbows.

"Nothing, sir," I answered, looking suddenly miles deep into the blank wall of the room.

"Keep your eyes where they belong if you want to be healthy!"

"Yes, sir."

I would have continued at the hotel until I left had not a short-cut presented itself. One of the boys at the hotel whispered to me one night that the only local Negro movie house wanted a boy to take tickets at the door.

"You ain't never been in jail, is you?" he asked me.

"Not yet," I answered.

"Then you can get the job," he said. "I'd take it, but I done six months and they know me."

"What's the catch?"

"The girl who sells tickets is using a system," he explained. "If you get the job, you can make some good gravy."

If I stole, I would have a chance to head northward quickly; if I remained barely honest, piddling with pints of bootleg liquor, I merely prolonged my stay, increased my chances of being caught, exposed myself to the possibility of saying the wrong word or doing the wrong thing and paying a penalty that I dared not think of. The temptation to venture into crime was too strong, and I decided to work quickly, taking whatever was in sight, amass a wad of money, and flee. I knew that others had tried it before me and had failed, but I was hoping to be lucky.

My chances for getting the job were good; I had no past record of stealing or violating the laws. When I presented myself to the Jewish proprietor of the movie house I was immediately accepted. The next day I reported for duty and began taking tickets. The boss man warned me:

"Now, look, I'll be honest with you if you'll be honest with me. I don't know who's honest around this joint and who isn't. But if *you* are honest, then the rest are bound to be. All tickets will pass through your hands. There can be no stealing unless you steal."

I gave him a pledge of my honesty, feeling absolutely no qualms about what I intended to do. He was white, and I could never do to him what he and his kind had done to me. Therefore, I reasoned, stealing was not a violation of my ethics, but of his; I felt that things were rigged in his favor and any action I took to circumvent his scheme of life was justified. Yet I had not convinced myself.

During the first afternoon the Negro girl in the ticket office watched me closely and I knew that she was sizing me up, trying to determine when it would be safe to break me into her graft. I waited, leaving it to her to make the first move.

I was supposed to drop each ticket that I took from a customer into a metal receptacle. Occasionally the boss would go to the ticket window and look at the serial number on the roll of unsold tickets and then compare that number with the number on the last ticket I had dropped into the receptacle. The boss continued his watchfulness for a few days, then began to observe me from across the street; finally he absented himself for long intervals.

A tension as high as that I had known when the white men had driven me from the job at the optician's returned to live in me. But I had learned to master a great deal of tension now; I had developed, slowly and painfully, a capacity to contain it within myself without betraying it in any way. Had this not been true, the mere thought of stealing, the risks involved, the inner distress would have so upset me that I would have been in no state of mind to calculate coldly, would have made me so panicky that I would have been afraid to steal at all. But my inner resistance had been blasted. I felt that I had been emotionally cast out of the world, had been made to live outside the normal processes of life, had been conditioned in feeling *against* something daily, had become accustomed to living on the side of those who watched and waited.

While I was eating supper in a near-by café one night, a strange Negro man walked in and sat beside me.

"Hello, Richard," he said.

"Hello," I said. "I don't think I know you."

"But I know *you*," he said, smiling.

Was he one of the boss's spies?

"How do you know me?" I asked.

"I'm Tel's friend," he said, naming the girl who sold the tickets at the movie.

I looked at him searchingly. Was he telling me the truth? Or was he trying to trap me for the boss? I was already thinking and feeling like a criminal, distrusting everybody.

"We start tonight," he said.

"What?" I asked, still not admitting that I knew what he was talking about.

"Don't be scared. The boss trusts you. He's gone to see some friends. Somebody's watching him and if he starts back to the movie, they'll phone us," he said.

I could not eat my food. It lay cold upon the plate and sweat ran down from my armpits.

"It'll work this way," he explained in a low, smooth tone. "A guy'll come to you and ask for a match. You give him five tickets that you'll hold out of the box, see? We'll give you the signal when to start holding out. The guy'll give the tickets to Tel; she'll resell them all at once, when a crowd is buying at the rush hour. You get it?"

I did not answer. I knew that if I were caught I would go to the chain gang. But was not my life already a kind of chain gang? What, really, did I have to lose?

"Are you with us?" he asked.

I still did not answer. He rose and clapped me on the shoulder and left. I trembled as I went back to the theater. Anything might happen, but I was used to that. Had I not felt that same sensation when I lay on the ground and the white men towered over me, telling me that I was a lucky nigger? Had I not felt it when I walked home from the optical company that morning with my job gone? Had I not felt it when I walked down the hallway of the hotel with the night watchman pointing a gun at my back? Had I not felt it all a million times before? I took the tickets with sweaty fingers. I waited. I was gambling: freedom or the chain gang. There were times when I felt that I could not breathe. I looked up and down the street; the boss was not in sight. Was this a trap? If it were, I would disgrace my family. Would not all of them say that my attitude had been leading to this all along? Would they not rake up the past and find clues that had led to my fate?

The man I had met in the café came through the door and put a ticket in my hand.

"There's a crowd at the box office," he whispered. "Save ten, not five. Start with this one."

Well, here goes, I thought. He gave me the ticket and sat looking at the moving shadows upon the screen. I held on to the ticket and my body grew tense, hot as fire; but I was used to that too. Time crawled through the cells of my brain. My muscles ached. I discovered that crime means suffering. The crowd came in and gave me more tickets. I kept ten of them tucked into my moist palm. No sooner had the crowd thinned than a black boy with a cigarette jutting from his mouth came up to me.

"Gotta match?"

With a slow movement I gave him the tickets. He went out and I kept the door cracked and watched. He went to the ticket office and laid down a coin and I saw him slip the tickets to the girl. Yes, the boy was honest. The girl shot me a quick smile and I went back inside. A few moments later the same tickets were handed to me by other customers.

We worked it for a week and after the money was split four ways, I had fifty dollars. Freedom was almost within my grasp. Ought I risk any more? I dropped the hint to Tel's friend that maybe I would quit; it was a casual hint to test him out. He grew violently angry and I quickly consented to stay, fearing that someone might turn me in for revenge, or to get me out of the way so that another and more pliable boy could have my place. I was dealing with cagey people and I would be cagey.

I went through another week. Late one night I resolved to make that week the last. The gun in the neighbor's house came to my mind, and the cans of fruit preserves in the store-house of the college. If I stole them and sold them, I would have enough to tide me over in Memphis until I could get a job, work, save, and go north. I crept from bed and found the neighbor's house empty. I looked about; all was quiet. My heart beat so fast that it ached. I forced a window with a screwdriver and entered and took the gun; I slipped it in my shirt and returned home. When I took it out to look at it, it was wet with sweat. I pawned it under an assumed name.

The following night I rounded up two boys whom I knew to be ready for adventure. We broke into the college storehouse and lugged out cans of fruit preserves and sold them to restaurants.

Meanwhile I bought clothes, shoes, a cardboard suitcase, all of which I hid at home. Saturday night came and I sent word to the boss that I was sick. Uncle Tom was upstairs. Granny and Aunt Addie were at church. My brother was sleeping. My mother sat in her rocking chair, humming to herself. I packed my suitcase and went to her.

"Mama, I'm going away," I whispered.

"Oh, no," she protested.

"I've got to, mama. I can't live this way."

"You're not running away from something you've done?"

"I'll send for you, mama. I'll be all right."

"Take care of yourself. And send for me quickly. I'm not happy here," she said.

"I'm sorry for all these long years, mama. But I could not have helped it."

I kissed her and she cried.

"Be quiet, mama. I'm all right."

I went out the back way and walked a quarter of a mile to the railroad tracks. It began to rain as I tramped down the crossties toward town. I reached the station soaked to the skin. I bought my ticket, then went hurriedly to the corner of the block in which the movie house stood. Yes, the boss was there, taking the tickets himself. I returned to the station and waited for my train, my eyes watching the crowd.

An hour later I was sitting in a Jim Crow coach, speeding northward, making the first lap of my journey to a land where I could live with a little less fear. Slowly the burden I had carried for many months lifted somewhat. My cheeks itched and when I scratched them I found tears. In that moment I understood the pain that accompanied crime and I hoped that I would never have to feel it again. I never did feel it again, for I never stole again; and what kept me from it was the knowledge that, for me, crime carried its own punishment.

Well, it's my life, I told myself. I'll see now what I can make of it . . .

Chapter XI

I ARRIVED in Memphis on a cold November Sunday morning, in 1925, and lugged my suitcase down quiet, empty sidewalks through winter sunshine. I found Beale Street, the street that I had been told was filled with danger: pickpockets, prostitutes, cutthroats, and black confidence men. After walking several blocks, I saw a big frame house with a sign in the window: ROOMS. I slowed, wondering if it was a rooming house or a whorehouse. I had heard of the foolish blunders that small-town boys made when they went to big cities and I wanted to be very cautious. I walked past the house to the end of the block, then turned and walked slowly past it again. Well, whatever it was, I would stay in it for a day or two, until I found something I was certain of. I had nothing valuable in my suitcase. My money was strapped to my body; in order for anyone to get it, they would have to kill me.

I walked up the steps and was about to ring the bell when I saw a big mulatto woman staring at me through the window. Oh, hell, I thought. This *is* a whorehouse . . . I stopped. The woman smiled. I turned around and went back down the walk. As I neared the street, I looked back in time to see the woman's face leave the window. A moment later she appeared in the doorway.

"Come here, boy!" she called to me.

I hesitated. Goddamn, I've run into a whore right off . . .

"Come here, boy," she commanded loudly. "I'm not going to hurt you."

I turned and walked slowly toward her.

"Come inside," she said.

I stared at her a moment, then stepped into a warm hallway. The woman smiled, turned on a light, and looked at me from my head to my feet.

"How come you was walking past this house so many times?" she asked.

"I was looking for a room," I said.

"Didn't you see the sign?"

"Yes, ma'am."

"Then how come you didn't come in?"

"Well, I don't know. You see, I'm a stranger here . . ."

"Lord, and don't I know it!" She dropped heavily into a chair and went into a gale of laughter that made her big bosom shake as though it were going to fly off. "Anybody could tell that." She gasped, giggled, and grew quiet. She said: "I'm Mrs. Moss."

I told her my name.

"That's a real nice name," she said after a moment's serious thought.

I blinked. What the hell kind of place was this? And who was this woman? I stood with my suitcase in my hand, poised to leave.

"Boy, Lord, this ain't no whorehouse," she said at last. "Folks get the craziest notions about Beale Street. I own this place; this is my home. I'm a church member. I got a daughter seventeen years old, and, by God, I sure make her walk a straight chalk line. Sit down, son. You in safe hands here."

I laughed and sat.

"Where might you be from?" she asked.

"Jackson, Mississippi."

"You act mighty bright to be from there," she commented.

"There are bright people in Jackson," I said.

"If there is, I got yet to see some of 'em. Most of 'em can't talk. They just stand with their heads down, with one foot on top of the other and you have to guess at what they're trying to say."

I was at ease now. I liked her.

"My husband works in a bakery," she rattled on pleasantly, openly, as though she had known me for years. "We take in roomers to help out. We just simple people here. You can call this home, if you got a mind to. The rent's three dollars."

"That's a little high," I said.

"Then give me two dollars and a half till you get yourself a job," she said.

I accepted and she showed me my room. I set my suitcase down.

"You run off, didn't you?" she asked.

I jerked in surprise.

"How did you know?"

"Boy, your heart's like an open book," she said. "I know things. Lotta boys run off to Memphis from little towns. They think they gonna find it easy here, but they don't." She looked at me searchingly. "You drink?"

"Oh, no, ma'am."

"Didn't mean no harm, son," she said. "Just wanted to know. You can drink here, if you like. Just don't make a fool of yourself. You can bring your girl here too. Do anything you want, but be decent."

I sat on the edge of the bed and stared at her in amazement. It was on reputedly disreputable Beale Street in Memphis that I had met the warmest, friendliest person I had ever known, that I discovered that all human beings were not mean and driving, were not bigots like the members of my family.

"You can eat dinner with us when we come from church," she said.

"Thank you. I'd like to."

"Maybe you want to come to church with us?"

"Well . . ." I hedged.

"Naw, you're tired," she said, closing the door.

I lay on the bed and reveled in the delightful sensation of living out a long-sought dream. I had always flinched inwardly from the lonely terror that I had thought I would feel in a strange city, and now I had found a home with friendly people. I relaxed completely and dozed off to sleep, for I had not slept much for many nights. Later I came awake with a sudden start, remembering the fright and tension that had accompanied my foray into crime. Well, all that was gone now. I could start anew. I did not like to feel tension and fear. I wanted something else, to be human, to be caught up in something meaningful. But I must first get a job.

Late that afternoon Mrs. Moss called me for dinner and introduced me to her daughter, Bess, whom I liked at once. She was young, simple, sweet, and brown. Mrs. Moss apologized for her husband, who was still at work. Why was she treating me so kindly? It made me self-conscious. We were eating dessert when Bess spoke.

"Mama's done told me all about you," she said.

"I'm afraid that there isn't much to tell," I said.

"She said you was walking up and down in the street in front of the house, and didn't know whether to come in," Bess said, giggling. "What kind of place did you think this was?"

I hung my head and smiled. Mrs. Moss went into a storm of laughter and left the room.

"Mama says she said to herself soon's she saw you out there on that street with your suitcase, 'That boy's looking for a clean home to live in,'" Bess said. "Mama's good about knowing what folks feel."

"She seems to be," I said, helping Bess to wash the dishes.

"You can eat with us any time you like," Bess said.

"Thanks," I said. "But I couldn't do that."

"How come?" Bess asked. "We got a plenty."

"I know. But a man ought to pay his own way."

"Mama said you'd be like that," Bess said with satisfaction. Mrs. Moss returned to the kitchen.

"Bess's going to be married soon," she announced.

"Congratulations!" I said. "Who's the lucky man?"

"Oh, I ain't got nobody yet," Bess said.

I was puzzled. Mrs. Moss laughed and nudged me.

"I say gals oughta marry young," she said. "Now, if Bess found a nice young man like *you*, Richard . . ."

"Mama!" Bess wailed, hiding her face in the dishcloth.

"I mean it," Mrs. Moss said. "Richard's a heap better'n them old ignorant nigger boys you been running after at school."

I gaped at one and then the other. What was happening here? They barely knew me; I had been in the house but a few hours.

"The minute I laid eyes on that boy in the street this morning," Mrs. Moss said, "I said to myself, 'That's the kind of boy for Bess.'"

Bess came to me and leaned her head on my shoulder. I was stunned. How on earth could she act like this?

"Mama, don't," Bess pleaded teasingly.

"I mean it," Mrs. Moss said. "Richard, I'm worried about whose hands this house is going to fall into. I ain't too long for this old world."

"Bess'll find a boy who'll love her," I said uneasily.

"I ain't so sure," Mrs. Moss said, shaking her head.

"I'm going up front," Bess said, giggling, burying her face in her hands, and running out.

Mrs. Moss came close to me and spoke confidently.

"A gal's a funny thing," she said, laughing. "They has to be tamed. Just like wild animals."

"She's all right," I said, wiping the table, thinking furiously, not wanting to become involved too deeply with the family.

"You like Bess, Richard?" Mrs. Moss asked me suddenly.

I stared at her, doubting my ears.

"I've been in the house only a couple of hours," I said hesitantly. "She's a fine girl."

"Now. I mean do you *like* her? Could you *love* her?" she asked insistently.

I stared at Mrs. Moss, wondering if something was wrong with Bess. What kind of people were these?

"You people don't know me. I didn't exist for you five hours ago," I said seriously. Then I shot at her: "I could be a robber or a burglar for all you know."

"Son, I know you," she said emphatically.

Oh, Christ, I thought. I'll have to leave this place.

"You go on up front with Bess," Mrs. Moss said.

"Look, Mrs. Moss, I'm just a poor nobody," I said.

"You got something in you I like," she said. "Money ain't everything. You got a good Christian heart and everybody ain't got that."

I winced and turned my head away. Her naïve simplicity was overwhelming. I felt as though I had been accused of something.

"I worked twenty years and bought this house myself," she went on. "I'd be happy when I died if I thought Bess had a husband like you."

"Oh, mama!" Bess shrieked with protesting laughter from the front room.

I went into a warm, cozy front room and sat on the sofa. Bess was sitting on a little bench, looking out the window. How must I act toward this girl? I did not want to be drawn into something I did not want, and neither did I wish to wound anybody's feelings.

"Don't you wanna set here with me?" Bess said.

I rose and sat with her. Neither of us spoke for a long time.

"I'm the same age as you," Bess said. "I'm seventeen."

"Do you go to school?" I asked to make conversation.

"Yes," she said. "Wanna see my books?"

"I'd like to."

She rose and brought her schoolbooks to me. I saw that she was in the fifth grade.

"I ain't so good in school," she said, tossing her head. "But I don't care."

"Well, school's kind of important, you know," I said cautiously.

"Love is the important thing," she countered strongly.

I wondered if she were demented. The behavior of the mother and the daughter ran counter to all I had ever seen or known. Mrs. Moss came into the room.

"I think I'll go out and look for a job," I said, wanting to escape them.

"On a Sunday!" Mrs. Moss exclaimed. "Wait till in the morning."

"But I can learn the streets tonight anyway," I said.

"That's really a good thought," Mrs. Moss said after a moment's reflection. "You see, Bess? That boy thinks."

I felt awkward, embarrassed, called upon to say something.

"I'll be glad to help you with your lessons, Bess," I said.

"You think you can?" she asked, doubting.

"Well, I used to take charge of classes at school last year," I said.

"Now ain't that nice?" Mrs. Moss said in a honeyed tone.

I went to my room and lay on the bed and tried to fathom out the kind of home I had come to. That they were serious, I had no doubt. Would they be angry with me when they learned that my life was a million miles from theirs? How could I avoid that? Was it wise to remain here with a seventeen-year-old girl eager for marriage and a mother equally anxious to have her marry me? What on earth had they seen in me to have made them act toward me as they had? My clothes were not good. True, I had manners, manners that had been drilled into me at home, at school, manners that had been kicked into me on jobs; but anybody could have manners. I had learned to know these people better in five hours than I had learned to know my own family in five years.

Later, after I had grown to understand the peasant mentality of Bess and her mother, I learned the full degree to which my life at home had cut me off, not only from white people but from Negroes as well. To Bess and her mother, money was important, but they did not strive for it too hard. They had no tensions, unappeasable longings, no desire to do something to redeem themselves. The main value in their lives was simple, clean, good living and when they thought they had found those same qualities in one of their race, they instinctively embraced him, liked him, and asked no questions. But such simple unaffected trust flabbergasted me. It was impossible.

I walked down Beale Street and into the heart of Memphis. My body was thin, my overcoat shabby, and each gust of wind chilled my blood. On Main Street I saw a sign in a café window:

Dish Washer Wanted

I went in and spoke to the manager and was hired to come to work the following night. The salary was ten dollars for the first week and twelve thereafter.

"Don't hire anyone else," I told him. "I'll be here."

I would get two meals at the café. But how would I eat in the daytime? I went into a store and bought a can of pork and beans and a can opener. Well, that problem was solved. I would pay two dollars and a half a week for my room and I would save the balance for my trip to Chicago. All my thoughts and movements were dictated by distant hopes.

Mrs. Moss was astonished when I told her that I had a job.

"You see, Bess," she said. "That boy's got a job his first day here. That's get-up for you. He's going somewhere. He just don't sit and gab. He moves."

Bess smiled at me. It seemed that every move I made captivated her. Mrs. Moss went upstairs to bed. I was uneasy.

"Lemme rest your coat," Bess said.

She took my coat and felt the can in the pocket.

"What you got in there?" she asked.

"Oh, nothing," I mumbled, trying to take the coat from her.

She pulled out the beans and the can opener. Her eyes widened with pity.

"Richard, you hungry, ain't you?" she asked me.

"Naw," I mumbled.

"Then let's eat some chicken," she said.

"Oh, all right," I said.

Bess ran to the stairway.

"Mama!" she called.

"Don't disturb her," I said, knowing that she was going to tell Mrs. Moss about my wanting to eat out of a can and feeling my heart fill with shame. My muscles flexed to hit her.

Mrs. Moss came down in her house robe.

"Mama, look what Richard was gonna do," Bess said, showing the can. "He was gonna eat this in his room."

"Lord, boy," Mrs. Moss said. "You don't have to do that."

"I'm used to it," I said. "I've got to save money."

"I just won't let you eat out of a can in my house," she said. "You don't have to pay me to eat. Go in the kitchen and eat. That's all."

"But I wouldn't dirty your room with the can," I said.

"It ain't that, son," Mrs. Moss said. "Why do you want to eat out of a can when you can set at the table with us?"

"I don't want to be a burden to anybody," I said.

Mrs. Moss stared at me, then hung her head and cried. I was stunned. It was incredible that what I did or the way I lived could evoke tears from anyone. Then my shame made me angry.

"You just ain't never had no home life," she said. "I'm sorry for you."

I stiffened. I did not like that. She was reaching into my inner life, where it was sore, and I did not want anyone there.

"I'm all right," I mumbled.

Mrs. Moss shook her head and went upstairs. I sighed. I was afraid that the family was getting too good a hold on me. Bess and I ate chicken, but I did not have much appetite. Bess was looking at me with melting eyes. We went back to the front room.

"I wanna get married," she whispered to me.

"You have a lot of time yet for that," I said, tense and uneasy.

"I wanna get married now. I wanna love," she said.

I had never met anyone like her, so direct, so easy in the expression of her feelings.

"Do you know what this means?" she asked me as she rose and went to a table and picked up a comb and came and stood before me.

I stared at the comb, then at her.

"What're you talking about?" I asked.

She did not answer. She smiled, then came close to me and reached out with the comb and touched my head. I drew back.

"What're you doing?"

She laughed and drew the comb through my hair. I stared at her, completely baffled.

"But my hair doesn't need combing," I said.

"I know it," she said, still combing.

"But why are you doing this?"

"Because I want to."

"What does it mean?"

She laughed again. I tried to get up and she caught hold of my arm and held me in the chair.

"You have nice hair," she said.

"It's just common nigger hair," I said.

"It's nice hair," she repeated.

"But why are you combing my hair?" I asked again.

"You know," she said.

"I don't."

" 'Cause I like you," she purred.

"Is this your way of telling me that?"

"It's a custom," she said. "You just fooling me. You know that. Everybody knows that. When a girl likes a man, she combs his hair."

"You're young. Give yourself a chance," I said.

"Don't you like me?" she asked.

"I do," I said. "We're friends."

"But I want more'n a friend," she sighed.

Her simplicity frightened me. The girls I had known had been hard and calculating, those who had worked at the hotel and those whom I had met at school. We were silent for a while.

"Say, what's them books in your room?" she asked.

"Were you in my room?" I asked with soft pointedness.

"Sure," she said without batting an eye. "I looked through your suitcase."

What could I do with a girl like this? Was I dumb or was she dumb? I felt that it would be easy to have sex relations with her and I was tempted. But what would happen? Love simply did not come to me that quickly and easily. And she was talking of marriage. Could I ever talk to her about what I felt, hoped? Could she ever understand my life? What had I above sex to share with her, and what had she? But I knew that such questions did not bother her. I did not love her and did not want to marry her. The prize of the house did not tempt me. Yet I sat beside her, feeling the attraction of her body increasing and deepening for me. What if I made her pregnant? I was sure that the fear of becoming pregnant did not bother her. Perhaps she would have liked it. I had come from a home where feelings were never expressed, except in rage or religious dread, where each member of the household lived locked in his own dark world, and the light that shone out of this child's heart—for she was a child—blinded me.

She leaned over and kissed me. What the hell, I thought. Have it out with her, and if anything happens, leave . . . I kissed and petted her. She was warm, eager, childish, pliable. She threw her arms and legs about me and hugged me fiercely. I began to wonder how old she was.

"What would your mother say?" I asked in a whisper.

"She's sleeping."

"But what if she saw us?"

"I don't care."

She was crazy. Plainly she would have married me that instant, knowing no more about me than she did.

"Let's go to my room," I said.

"Naw. Mama wouldn't like that," she said.

She would let me do anything to her in her own front room, but she did not want me to do it to her in my room. It was crazy, utterly crazy.

"Mama's sleeping," she observed.

I began to suspect that she had had every boy in the block.

"You love me?" she asked in a whisper.

I stared at her, becoming more aware each minute of the terrible simplicity of her life. That was life for her, simple, direct. She just did not attach to words the same meanings I did. She caught my hands in a viselike grip. I looked at her and could not believe in her existence.

"I love you," she said.

"Don't say that," I said, then was sorry that I had said it.

"But I do love you," she said again.

Her voice had come so clearly that I could no longer doubt her. For Christ's sake, I said to myself. The girl was astoundingly simple, yet vital in a way that I had never known. What kind of life had I lived that made the reality of this girl so strange? I sat thinking of Aunt Addie, her stern face, her forbidding nature, her caution, her restraint, her keen struggle to be good and holy.

"I'd make a good wife," she said.

I disengaged my hand from hers. I looked at her and wanted either to laugh or to slap her. I was about to hurt her and I did not want to. I rose. Oh, hell . . . This girl's crazy . . . I heard her crying and I bent to her.

"Look," I whispered. "You don't know me. Let's get to know each other better."

Her eyes were beaten, baffled. Love was that simple to her; it could be turned on or off in a moment.

"You just think I'm nothing," she whimpered.

I reached out my hand to touch her, to speak to her, to try to tell her of my life, my feelings, my doubts; and she leaped to her feet.

"I hate you," she burst out in a passionate whisper and ran out of the room.

I lit a cigarette and sat for a long time. I had never dreamed that anyone would accept me so simply, so completely, without question or the least hint of personal aggrandizement. The truth was that I had—even though I had fought against it—grown to accept the value of myself that my old environment had created in me, and I had thought that no other kind of environment was possible. My life had changed too suddenly. Had I met Bess upon a Mississippi plantation, I would have expected her to act as she had. But in Memphis, on Beale Street, how could there be such hope, belief, faith in others? I wanted to go to Bess and talk to her, but I knew no words to say to her.

When I awakened the next morning and recalled Bess's naïve hopes, I was glad that I had the can of pork and beans. I did not want to face her across the breakfast table. I dressed to go out; then, with my coat and hat on, I sat on the edge of the bed and propped my feet on a chair. Taking puffs from a cigarette, I scooped the beans out of the can with my fingers and ate them. I slipped out of the house and went to the water front and sat on a knoll of earth in the cold wind and sun, looking at the boats on the Mississippi River. Tonight I would begin my new job. I knew how to save money, thanks to my long starvation in Mississippi. My heart was at peace. I was freer than I had ever been.

A black boy came up to me.

"Hy," he said.

"Hy," I said.

"What you doing these days?" he asked.

"Nothing. Waiting for night. I got a job in a café," I said.

"Shucks," he said. "I'm looking for a buddy." He was trying to act tough, but I thought that he was lonely. "I wanna hop a freight and go north."

"Why not hop one alone?" I asked.

He grinned nervously.

"Did you run off from home?" I asked.

"Yeah. Four years ago," he said.

"What have you been doing?"

"Nothing."

That should have warned me, but I was not yet wise in the ways of the world or the road.

We talked a while longer, then walked down a path toward the river's edge, skirting high weeds. The boy stopped suddenly and pointed.

"What's that?"

"Looks like a can of some sort," I said.

I saw a huge can partially screened by high weeds. We went

to it and found that it was full of something heavy. I pulled out the stopper and smelt it.

"This stuff is liquor," I said.

The boy smelt it and his eyes widened.

"Reckon we can sell it?" he asked.

"But whose is it?" I asked.

"Gee, I wish I could sell this stuff," he said.

"Maybe somebody's watching," I suggested.

We looked about, but no one was in sight.

"This belongs to a bootlegger," I said.

"Let's see if we can sell it," he said.

"I wouldn't take that can out of here," I said. "The cops might see us."

"I need money," the boy said. "This'll help me on the road."

We agreed to look for a white buyer. We went into the streets and looked over the white men who passed. Finally we spotted one sitting alone in his car. We went up to him.

"Mister," the boy said, "we found a big can of liquor over there in the weeds. You want to buy it?"

The man screwed up his eyes and studied us.

"Is it good liquor?" he asked.

"I don't know," I said. "Go and see it."

"You niggers ain't lying to me, are you?" he asked suspiciously.

"Come on. I'll show it to you," I said.

We led the white man to the liquor; he unstoppered it and smelt it, then tasted the wetness on the cork.

"Holy cats," he said. He looked at us. "Did you really find this here?"

"Oh, yes, sir," we said.

"If you two niggers are lying, I'll kill both of you," he breathed.

"We're telling the truth," I said.

The other boy stood awkwardly and looked on. I wondered why he did not say anything. Some vague thought was trying to worm its way into my dense, naïve, childlike mind. But it did not come clear and I brushed it away.

"You boys bring this can to my car," the white man said.

I was afraid. But the other boy was eager and willing. With

the white man encouraging us, we lugged the can to his car
and put it into the back upon the floor.

"Here," the white man said, extending a five-dollar bill to
the boy. The car drove off and I could see the white man
looking about anxiously, fearing a trap; or so it seemed to me.

"Gee, let's get this changed," the boy said.

"All right," I said. "We'll split it."

The boy pointed across the street.

"There's a store over there," he said. "I'll run over and get
change."

"O.K.," I said, angel-like.

I sat on a sloping embankment and waited. He ran off in
the direction of the store, but I was so confident that I did
not even watch him. I felt amused. I was going to get two
and one-half dollars for finding a cache of liquor. I was a
hijacker already. Last night a girl had thrown herself at me.
And all this had happened within forty-eight hours of my
leaving home. I wanted to laugh out loud. Things could happen to one when one was not at home. I looked up, waiting
for the boy to return. But I did not see him. He's sure taking
his time, I thought, pushing down other ideas that were trying to bubble into my mind. I waited longer, then rose and
went quickly to the store and peered through the window.
The boy was not inside. I went in and asked the proprietor if
a boy had been in.

"Yeah," he said. "A nigger boy came in here, looked
around, then went out of the back door. He went like a light.
Did he have something of yours?"

"Yes," I said.

"Well, you'll never see that nigger again," the man said.

I walked along the streets in the winter sun, thinking: Well,
that's good enough for you, you fool. You had no business
monkeying in that liquor business anyway. Then I stopped in
my tracks. *They had been together!* The white man and the
black boy had seen me loitering in the vicinity of their liquor
and had thought I was a hijacker; and they had used me in
disposing of their liquor.

Last night I had found a naïve girl. This morning I had
been a naïve boy.

Chapter XII

WHILE WANDERING aimlessly about the streets of Memphis, gaping at the tall buildings and the crowds, killing time, eating bags of popcorn, I was struck by an odd and sudden idea. If I had attempted to work for an optical company in Jackson and had failed, why should I not try to work for an optical company in Memphis? Memphis was not a small town like Jackson; it was urban and I felt that no one would hold the trivial trouble I had had in Jackson against me.

I looked for the address of a company in a directory and walked boldly into the building, rode up in the elevator with a fat, round, yellow Negro of about five feet in height. At the fifth floor I stepped into an office. A white man rose to meet me.

"Pull off your hat," he said.

"Oh, yes, sir," I said, jerking off my hat.

"What do you want?"

"I was wondering if you needed a boy," I said. "I worked for an optical company for a short while in Jackson."

"Why did you leave?" he asked.

"I had a little trouble there," I said honestly.

"Did you steal something?"

"No, sir," I said. "A white boy there didn't want me to learn the optical trade and ran me off the job."

"Come and sit down."

I sat and recounted the story from beginning to end.

"I'll write Mr. Crane," he said. "But you won't get a chance to learn the optical trade here. That's not our policy."

I told him that I understood and accepted his policy. I was hired at eight dollars per week and promised a raise of a dollar a week until my wages reached ten. Though this was less than I had been offered for the café job, I accepted it. I liked the open, honest way in which the man talked to me; and, too, the place seemed clean, brisk, businesslike.

I was assigned to run errands and wash eyeglasses after they had come from the rouge-smeared machines. Each evening I had to take sacks of packages to the post office for mailing. It was light work and I was fast on my feet. At noon I would forgo my lunch hour and run errands for the white men who were employed in the shop. I would buy their lunches, take their suits out to have them pressed, pay their light, telephone, and gas bills, and deliver notes for them to their stenographer girl friends in near-by office buildings. The first day I made a dollar and a half in tips. I deposited the money I had left from my trip and resolved to live off my tips.

I was now rapidly learning to contain the tension I felt in my relations with whites, and the people in Memphis had an air of relative urbanity that took some of the sharpness off the attitude of whites toward Negroes. There were about a dozen white men in the sixth-floor shop where I spent most of my time; they varied from Ku Klux Klanners to Jews, from theosophists to just plain poor whites. Although I could detect disdain and hatred in their attitudes, they never shouted at me or abused me. It was fairly easy to contemplate the race issue in the shop without reaching those heights of fear that devastated me. A measure of objectivity entered into my observations of white men and women. Either I could stand more mental strain than formerly or I had discovered deep within me ways of handling it.

When I returned to Mrs. Moss's that Monday night, she was surprised that I had changed my plans and had taken a new job. I showed her my bankbook and told her my plan for saving money and bringing my mother to Memphis. As I talked to her I tried to tell from her manner if Bess had said anything about what had happened between us, but Mrs. Moss was bland and motherly as always.

Bess avoided me, refusing to speak when we were alone together; but when her mother was present, she was polite. A few days later Mrs. Moss came to me with a baffled look in their eyes.

"What's happened between you and Bess?" she asked.

"Nothing," I lied, burning with shame.

"She don't seem to like you no more," she said. "I wanted you-all to kinda hit it off." She looked at me searchingly. "Don't you like her none?"

I could not answer or look at her; I wondered if she had told Bess to give herself to me.

"Well," she drawled, sighing, "I guess folks just have to love each other naturally. You can't make 'em." Tears rolled down her cheeks. "Bess'll find somebody."

I felt sick, filled with a consciousness of the woman's helplessness, of her naïve hope. Time and again she told me that Bess loved me, wanted me. She even suggested that I "try Bess and see if you like her. Ain't no harm in that." And her words evoked in me a pity for her that had no name.

Finally it became unbearable. One night I returned home from work and found Mrs. Moss sitting by the stove in the hall, nodding. She blinked her eyes and smiled.

"How're you, son?" she asked.

"Pretty good," I said.

"Ain't you and Bess got to be friends or something yet?"

"No, ma'am," I said softly.

"How come you don't like Bess?" she demanded.

"Oh, I don't know." I was becoming angry.

"It's 'cause she ain't so bright?"

"No, ma'am. Bess's bright," I lied.

"Then how come?"

I still could not tell her.

"You and Bess could have this house for your home," she went on. "You-all could bring up your children here."

"But people have to find their own way to each other," I said.

"Young folks ain't got no sense these days," she said at last. "If somebody had fixed things for me when I was a gal, I sure would've taken it."

"Mrs. Moss," I said, "I think I'd better move."

"Move then!" she exploded. "You ain't got no sense!"

I went to my room and began to pack. A knock came at the door. I opened it. Mrs. Moss stood in the doorway, weeping.

"Son, forgive me," she said. "I didn't mean it. I wouldn't hurt you for nothing. You just like a son to me."

"That's all right," I said. "But I'd better move."

"No!" she wailed. "Then you ain't forgive me! When a body asks forgiveness, they means it!"

I stared. Bess appeared in the doorway.

"Don't leave, Richard," she said.

"We won't bother you no more," Mrs. Moss said.

I wilted, baffled, sorry, ashamed. Mrs. Moss took Bess's hand and led her away.

I centered my attention now upon making enough money to send for my mother and brother. I saved each penny I came by, stinting myself on food, walking to work, eating out of paper bags, living on a pint of milk and two sweet rolls for breakfast, a hamburger and peanuts for lunch, and a can of beans which I would eat at night in my room. I was used to hunger and I did not need much food to keep me alive.

I now had more money than I had ever had before, and I began patronizing secondhand bookstores, buying magazines and books. In this way I became acquainted with periodicals like *Harper's Magazine*, the *Atlantic Monthly*, and the *American Mercury*. I would buy them for a few cents, read them, then resell them to the bookdealer.

Once Mrs. Moss questioned me about my reading.

"What you reading all them books for, boy?"

"I just like to."

"You studying for law?"

"No, ma'am."

"Well, I reckon you know what you doing," she said.

Though I did not have to report for work until nine o'clock each morning, I would arrive at eight and go into the lobby of the downstairs bank—where I knew the Negro porter—and read the early edition of the Memphis *Commercial Appeal*, thereby saving myself five cents each day, which I spent for lunch. After reading, I would watch the black porter perform his morning ritual: he would get a mop, bucket, soap flakes, water, then would pause dramatically, roll his eyes to the ceiling and sing out:

"Lawd, today! Ahm still working for white folks!"

And he would mop until he sweated. He hated his job and talked incessantly of leaving to work in the post office.

The most colorful of the Negro boys on the job was Shorty, the round, yellow, fat elevator operator. He had tiny, beady eyes that looked out between rolls of flesh with a hard but humorous stare. He had the complexion of a Chinese, a short forehead, and three chins. Psychologically he was the most amazing specimen of the southern Negro I had ever met. Hardheaded, sensible, a reader of magazines and books, he was proud of his race and indignant about its wrongs. But in the presence of whites he would play the role of a clown of the most debased and degraded type.

One day he needed twenty-five cents to buy his lunch.

"Just watch me get a quarter from the first white man I see," he told me as I stood in the elevator that morning.

A white man who worked in the building stepped into the elevator and waited to be lifted to his floor. Shorty sang in a low mumble, smiling, rolling his eyes, looking at the white man roguishly.

"I'm hungry, Mister White Man. I need a quarter for lunch."

The white man ignored him. Shorty, his hands on the controls of the elevator, sang again:

"I ain't gonna move this damned old elevator till I get a quarter, Mister White Man."

"The hell with you, Shorty," the white man said, ignoring him and chewing on his black cigar.

"I'm hungry, Mister White Man. I'm dying for a quarter," Shorty sang, drooling, drawling, humming his words.

"If you don't take me to my floor, you will die," the white man said, smiling a little for the first time.

"But this black sonofabitch sure needs a quarter," Shorty sang, grimacing, clowning, ignoring the white man's threat.

"Come on, you black bastard, I got to work," the white man said, intrigued by the element of sadism involved, enjoying it.

"It'll cost you twenty-five cents, Mister White Man; just a quarter, just two bits," Shorty moaned.

There was silence. Shorty threw the lever and the elevator went up and stopped about five feet shy of the floor upon which the white man worked.

"Can't go no more, Mister White Man, unless I get my quarter," he said in a tone that sounded like crying.

"What would you do for a quarter?" the white man asked, still gazing off.

"I'll do anything for a quarter," Shorty sang.

"What, for example?" the white man asked.

Shorty giggled, swung around, bent over, and poked out his broad, fleshy ass.

"You can kick me for a quarter," he sang, looking impishly at the white man out of the corners of his eyes.

The white man laughed softly, jingled some coins in his pocket, took out one and thumped it to the floor. Shortly stooped to pick it up and the white man bared his teeth and swung his foot into Shorty's rump with all the strength of his body. Shorty let out a howling laugh that echoed up and down the elevator shaft.

"Now, open this door, you goddamn black sonofabitch," the white man said, smiling with tight lips.

"Yeeeess, siiiiir," Shorty sang; but first he picked up the quarter and put it into his mouth. "This monkey's got the peanuts," he chortled.

He opened the door and the white man stepped out and looked back at Shorty as he went toward his office.

"You're all right, Shorty, you sonofabitch," he said.

"I know it!" Shorty screamed, then let his voice trail off in a gale of wild laughter.

I witnessed this scene or its variant at least a score of times and I felt no anger or hatred, only disgust and loathing. Once I asked him:

"How in God's name can you do that?"

"I needed a quarter and I got it," he said soberly, proudly.

"But a quarter can't pay you for what he did to you," I said.

"Listen, nigger," he said to me, "my ass is tough and quarters is scarce."

I never discussed the subject with him after that.

Other Negroes worked in the building: an old man whom we called Edison; his son, John; and a night janitor who answered to the name of Dave. At noon, when I was not running errands, I would join the rest of the Negroes in a little room at the front of the building overlooking the street. Here, in this underworld pocket of the building, we munched our lunches and discussed the ways of white folks toward Negroes. When two or more of us were talking, it was impossible for this subject not to come up. Each of us hated and feared the whites, yet had a white man put in a sudden appearance we would have assumed silent, obedient smiles.

To our minds the white folks formed a kind of superworld: what was said by them during working hours was rehashed and weighed here; how they looked; what they wore; what moods they were in; who had outdistanced whom in business; who was replacing whom on the job; who was getting fired and who was getting hired. But never once did we openly say that we occupied none but subordinate positions in the building. Our talk was restricted to the petty relations which formed the core of life for us.

But under all our talk floated a latent sense of violence; the whites had drawn a line over which we dared not step and we accepted that line because our bread was at stake. But within our boundaries we, too, drew a line that included our right to bread regardless of the indignities or degradations involved in getting it. If a white man had sought to keep us from obtaining a job, or enjoying the rights of citizenship, we would have bowed silently to his power. But if he had sought to deprive us of a dime, blood might have been spilt. Hence, our daily lives were so bound up with trivial objectives that to capitulate when challenged was tantamount to surrendering the right to life itself. Our anger was like the anger of children, passing quickly from one petty grievance to another, from the memory of one slight wrong to another.

"You know what the bastard Olin said to me this morning?" John would ask, biting into a juicy hamburger.

"What?" Shorty would ask.

"Well, I brought him his change from paying his gas bill and he said: 'Put it here in my pocket; my hands are dirty,'" John said. "Hunh . . . I just laid the money on the bench besides him. I ain't no personal slave to him and I'll be damned if I'll put his *own* money in his *own* pocket."

"Hell, you're right," Shorty would say.

"White folks just don't think," old man Edison would say.

"You sure got to watch 'em," Dave, the night janitor, would say. (He would have slept in the room on a cot after his night's cleaning; he would be ready now to keep a date with some girl friend.)

"Falk sent me to have his suit pressed," I would say. "He didn't give me a penny. Told me he would remember it on payday."

"Ain't that some nerve?" John would say.

"You can't eat his memories," Shorty would say.

"But you got to keep on doing them favors," old man Edison would say. "If you don't, they won't like you."

"I'm going north one of these days," Shorty would say.

We would all laugh, knowing that Shorty would never leave, that he depended too much upon the whites for the food he ate.

"What would you do up north?" I would ask Shorty.

"I'd pass for Chinese," Shorty would say.

And we would laugh again. The lunch hour would pass and we would go back to work, but there would be in our faces not one whit of the sentiment we had felt during the hour of discussion.

One day I went to the optical counter of a department store to deliver a pair of eyeglasses. The counter was empty of customers and a tall, florid-faced white man looked at me curiously. He was unmistakably a Yankee, for his physical build differed sharply from that of the lanky Southerner.

"Will you please sign for this, sir?" I asked, presenting the account book and the eyeglasses.

He picked up the book and the glasses, but his eyes were still upon me.

"Say, boy, I'm from the North," he said quietly.

I held very still. Was this a trap? He had mentioned a tabooed subject and I wanted to wait until I knew what he meant. Among the topics that southern white men did not like to discuss with Negroes were the following: American white women; the Ku Klux Klan; France, and how Negro soldiers fared while there; Frenchwomen; Jack Johnson; the entire northern part of the United States; the Civil War; Abraham Lincoln; U. S. Grant; General Sherman; Catholics; the Pope; Jews; the Republican party; slavery; social equality; Communism; Socialism; the 13th, 14th, and 15th Amendments to the Constitution; or any topic calling for positive knowledge or manly self-assertion on the part of the Negro. The most accepted topics were sex and religion. I did not look at the man or answer. With one sentence he had lifted out of the silent dark the race question and I stood on the edge of a precipice.

"Don't be afraid of me," he went on. "I just want to ask you one question."

"Yes, sir," I said in a waiting, neutral tone.

"Tell me, boy, are you hungry?" he asked seriously.

I stared at him. He had spoken one word that touched the very soul of me, but I could not talk to him, could not let him know that I was starving myself to save money to go north. I did not trust him. But my face did not change its expression.

"Oh, no, sir," I said, managing a smile.

I was hungry and he knew it; but he was a white man and I felt that if I told him I was hungry I would have been revealing something shameful.

"Boy, I can see hunger in your face and eyes," he said.

"I get enough to eat," I lied.

"Then why do you keep so thin?" he asked me.

"Well, I suppose I'm just that way, naturally," I lied.

"You're just scared, boy," he said.

"Oh, no, sir," I lied again.

I could not look at him. I wanted to leave the counter, yet he was a white man and I had learned not to walk abruptly away from a white man when he was talking to me. I stood, my eyes looking away. He ran his hand into his pocket and pulled out a dollar bill.

"Here, take this dollar and buy yourself some food," he said.

"No, sir," I said.

"Don't be a fool," he said. "You're ashamed to take it. God, boy, don't let a thing like that stop you from taking a dollar and eating."

The more he talked the more it became impossible for me to take the dollar. I wanted it, but I could not look at it. I wanted to speak, but I could not move my tongue. I wanted him to leave me alone. He frightened me.

"Say something," he said.

All about us in the store were piles of goods; white men and women went from counter to counter. It was summer and from a high ceiling was suspended a huge electric fan that whirred. I stood waiting for the white man to give me the signal that would let me go.

"I don't understand it," he said through his teeth. "How far did you go in school?"

"Through the ninth grade, but it was really the eighth," I told him. "You see, our studies in the ninth grade were more or less a review of what we had in the eighth grade."

Silence. He had not asked me for this long explanation, but I had spoken at length to fill up the yawning, shameful gap that loomed between us; I had spoken to try to drag the unreal nature of the conversation back to safe and sound southern ground. Of course, the conversation was real; it dealt with my welfare, but it had brought to the surface of day all the dark fears I had known all my life. The Yankee white man did not know how dangerous his words were.

(There are some elusive, profound, recondite things that men find hard to say to other men; but with the Negro it is the little things of life that become hard to say, for these tiny items shape his destiny. A man will seek to express his relation to the stars; but when a man's consciousness has been riveted upon obtaining a loaf of bread, that loaf of bread is as important as the stars.)

Another white man walked up to the counter and I sighed with relief.

"Do you want the dollar?" the man asked.

"No, sir," I whispered.

"All right," he said. "Just forget it."

He signed the account book and took the eyeglasses. I stuffed the book into my bag and turned from the counter and walked down the aisle, feeling a physical tingling along my spine, knowing that the white man knew I was really hungry. I avoided him after that. Whenever I saw him I felt in a queer way that he was my enemy, for he knew how I felt and the safety of my life in the South depended upon how well I concealed from all whites what I felt.

One summer morning I stood at a sink in the rear of the factory washing a pair of eyeglasses that had just come from the polishing machines whose throbbing shook the floor upon which I stood. At each machine a white man was bent forward, working intently. To my left sunshine poured through a window, lighting up the rouge smears and making the factory look garish, violent, dangerous. It was nearing noon and my mind was drifting toward my daily lunch of a hamburger and a bag of peanuts. It had been a routine day, a day more or less like the other days I had spent on the job as errand boy and washer of eyeglasses. I was at peace with the world, that is, at peace in the only way in which a black boy in the South can be at peace with a world of white men.

Perhaps it was the mere sameness of the day that soon made it different from the other days; maybe the white men who operated the machines felt bored with their dull, automatic tasks and hankered for some kind of excitement. Anyway, I presently heard footsteps behind me and turned my head. At my elbow stood a young white man, Mr. Olin, the immediate foreman under whom I worked. He was smiling and observing me as I cleaned emery dust from the eyeglasses.

"Boy, how's it going?" he asked.

"Oh, fine, sir!" I answered with false heartiness, falling quickly into that nigger-being-a-good-natured-boy-in-the-presence-of-a-white-man pattern, a pattern into which I could now slide easily; although I was wondering if he had any criticism to make of my work.

He continued to hover wordlessly at my side. What did he want? It was unusual for him to stand there and watch me; I wanted to look at him, but was afraid to.

"Say, Richard, do you believe that I'm your friend?" he asked me.

The question was so loaded with danger that I could not reply at once. I scarcely knew Mr. Olin. My relationship to him had been the typical relationship of Negroes to southern whites. He gave me orders and I said, "Yes, sir," and obeyed them. Now, without warning, he was asking me if I thought that he was my friend; and I knew that all southern white men fancied themselves as friends of niggers. While fishing for an answer that would say nothing, I smiled.

"I mean," he persisted, "do you think I'm your friend?"

"Well," I answered, skirting the vast racial chasm between us, "I hope you are."

"I am," he said emphatically.

I continued to work, wondering what motives were prompting him. Already apprehension was rising in me.

"I want to tell you something," he said.

"Yes, sir," I said.

"We don't want you to get hurt," he explained. "We like you round here. You act like a good boy."

"Yes, sir," I said. "What's wrong?"

"You don't deserve to get into trouble," he went on.

"Have I done something that somebody doesn't like?" I asked, my mind frantically sweeping over all my past actions, weighing them in the light of the way southern white men thought Negroes should act.

"Well, I don't know," he said and paused, letting his words sink meaningfully into my mind. He lit a cigarette. "Do you know Harrison?"

He was referring to a Negro boy of about my own age who worked across the street for a rival optical house. Harrison and I knew each other casually, but there had never been the slightest trouble between us.

"Yes, sir," I said. "I know him."

"Well, be careful," Mr. Olin said. "He's after you."

"After me? For what?"

"He's got a terrific grudge against you," the white man explained. "What have you done to him?"

The eyeglasses I was washing were forgotten. My eyes were upon Mr. Olin's face, trying to make out what he meant. Was this something serious? I did not trust the white man, and neither did I trust Harrison. Negroes who worked on jobs in the South were usually loyal to their white bosses; they felt that that was the best way to ensure their jobs. Had Harrison felt that I had in some way jeopardized his job? Who was my friend: the white man or the black boy?

"I haven't done anything to Harrison," I said.

"Well, you better watch that nigger Harrison," Mr. Olin said in a low, confidential tone. "A little while ago I went down to get a Coca-Cola and Harrison was waiting for you at the door of the building with a knife. He asked me when you were coming down. Said he was going to get you. Said you called him a dirty name. Now, we don't want any fighting or bloodshed on the job."

I still doubted the white man, yet thought that perhaps Harrison had really interpreted something I had said as an insult.

"I've got to see that boy and talk to him," I said, thinking out loud.

"No, you'd better not," Mr. Olin said. "You'd better let some of us white boys talk to him."

"But how did this start?" I asked, still doubting but half believing.

"He just told me that he was going to get even with you, going to cut you and teach you a lesson," he said. "But don't you worry. Let me handle this."

He patted my shoulder and went back to his machine. He was an important man in the factory and I had always respected his word. He had the authority to order me to do this or that. Now, why would he joke with me? White men did not often joke with Negroes, therefore what he had said was serious. I was upset. We black boys worked long hard hours for what few pennies we earned and we were edgy and tense. Perhaps that crazy Harrison was really after me. My appetite was gone. I had to settle this thing. A white man had walked into my delicately balanced world and had tipped it and I had to right it before I could feel safe. Yes, I would go directly to Harrison and ask what was the matter, what I had said that he resented. Harrison was black and so was I; I would ignore the warning of the white man and talk face to face with a boy of my own color.

At noon I went across the street and found Harrison sitting on a box in the basement. He was eating lunch and reading a pulp magazine. As I approached him, he ran his hand into his pocket and looked at me with cold, watchful eyes.

"Say, Harrison, what's this all about?" I asked, standing cautiously four feet from him.

He looked at me a long time and did not answer.

"I haven't done anything to you," I said.

"And I ain't got nothing against you," he mumbled, still watchful. "I don't bother nobody."

"But Mr. Olin said that you came over to the factory this morning, looking for me with a knife."

"Aw, naw," he said, more at ease now. "I ain't been in your factory all day." He had not looked at me as he spoke.

"Then what did Mr. Olin mean?" I asked. "I'm not angry with you."

"Shucks, I thought *you* was looking for me to cut me," Harrison explained. "Mr. Olin, he came over here this morning and said you was going to kill me with a knife the moment you saw me. He said you was mad at me because I had insulted you. But I ain't said nothing about you." He still had not looked at me. He rose.

"And I haven't said anything about you," I said.

Finally he looked at me and I felt better. We two black boys, each working for ten dollars a week, stood staring at each other, thinking, comparing the motives of the absent white man, each asking himself if he could believe the other.

"But why would Mr. Olin tell me things like that?" I asked.

Harrison dropped his head; he laid his sandwich aside.

"I . . . I . . ." he stammered and pulled from his pocket a long, gleaming knife; it was already open. "I was just waiting to see what you was gonna do to me . . ."

I leaned weakly against a wall, feeling sick, my eyes upon the sharp steel blade of the knife.

"You were going to cut me?" I asked.

"If you had cut me, I was gonna cut you first," he said. "I ain't taking no chances."

"Are you angry with me about something?" I asked.

"Man, I ain't mad at nobody," Harrison said uneasily.

I felt how close I had come to being slashed. Had I come suddenly upon Harrison, he would have thought I was trying to kill him and he would have stabbed me, perhaps killed me. And what did it matter if one nigger killed another?

"Look here," I said. "Don't believe what Mr. Olin says."

"I see now," Harrison said. "He's playing a dirty trick on us."

"He's trying to make us kill each other for nothing."

"How come he wanna do that?" Harrison asked.

I shook my head. Harrison sat, but still played with the open knife. I began to doubt. Was he really angry with me? Was he waiting until I turned my back to stab me? I was in torture.

"I suppose it's fun for white men to see niggers fight," I said, forcing a laugh.

"But you might've killed me," Harrison said.

"To white men we're like dogs or cocks," I said.

"I don't want to cut you," Harrison said.

"And I don't want to cut you," I said.

Standing well out of each other's reach, we discussed the problem and decided that we would keep silent about our conference. We would not let Mr. Olin know that we knew that he was egging us to fight. We agreed to ignore any further provocations. At one o'clock I went back to the factory. Mr. Olin was waiting for me, his manner grave, his face serious.

"Did you see that Harrison nigger?" he asked.

"No, sir," I lied.

"Well, he still has that knife for you," he said.

Hate tightened in me. But I kept a dead face.

"Did you buy a knife yet?" he asked me.

"No, sir," I answered.

"Do you want to use mine?" he asked. "You've got to protect yourself, you know."

"No, sir. I'm not afraid," I said.

"Nigger, you're a fool," he spluttered. "I thought you had some sense! Are you going to just let that nigger cut your heart out? His boss gave *him* a knife to use against *you*! Take this knife, nigger, and stop acting crazy!"

I was afraid to look at him; if I had looked at him I would have had to tell him to leave me alone, that I knew he was lying, that I knew he was no friend of mine, that I knew if anyone had thrust a knife through my heart he would simply have laughed. But I said nothing. He was the boss and he could fire me if he did not like me. He laid an open knife on the edge of his workbench, about a foot from my hand. I had a fleeting urge to pick it up and give it to him, point first into his chest. But I did nothing of the kind. I picked up the knife and put it into my pocket.

"Now, you're acting like a nigger with some sense," he said.

As I worked Mr. Olin watched me from his machine. Later when I passed him he called me.

"Now, look here, boy," he began. "We told that Harrison nigger to stay out of this building, and leave you alone, see?

But I can't protect you when you go home. If that nigger starts at you when you are on your way home, you stab him before he gets a chance to stab you, see?"

I avoided looking at him and remained silent.

"Suit yourself, nigger," Mr. Olin said. "But don't say I didn't warn you."

I had to make my round of errands to deliver eyeglasses and I stole a few minutes to run across the street to talk to Harrison. Harrison was sullen and bashful, wanting to trust me, but afraid. He told me that Mr. Olin had telephoned his boss and had told him to tell Harrison that I had planned to wait for him at the back entrance of the building at six o'clock and stab him. Harrison and I found it difficult to look at each other; we were upset and distrustful. We were not really angry at each other; we knew that the idea of murder had been planted in each of us by the white men who employed us. We told ourselves again and again that we did not agree with the white men; we urged ourselves to keep faith in each other. Yet there lingered deep down in each of us a suspicion that maybe one of us was trying to kill the other.

"I'm not angry with you, Harrison," I said.

"I don't wanna fight nobody," Harrison said bashfully, but he kept his hand in his pocket on his knife.

Each of us felt the same shame, felt how foolish and weak we were in the face of the domination of the whites.

"I wish they'd leave us alone," I said.

"Me too," Harrison said.

"There are a million black boys like us to run errands," I said. "They wouldn't care if we killed each other."

"I know it," Harrison said.

Was he acting? I could not believe in him. We were toying with the idea of death for no reason that stemmed from our own lives, but because the men who ruled us had thrust the idea into our minds. Each of us depended upon the whites for the bread we ate, and we actually trusted the whites more than we did each other. Yet there existed in us a longing to trust men of our own color. Again Harrison and I parted, vowing not to be influenced by what our white boss men said to us.

The game of egging Harrison and me to fight, to cut each

other, kept up for a week. We were afraid to tell the white men that we did not believe them, for that would have been tantamount to calling them liars or risking an argument that might have ended in violence being directed against us.

One morning a few days later Mr. Olin and a group of white men came to me and asked me if I was willing to settle my grudge with Harrison with gloves, according to boxing rules. I told them that, though I was not afraid of Harrison, I did not want to fight him and that I did not know how to box. I could feel now that they knew I no longer believed them.

When I left the factory that evening, Harrison yelled at me from down the block. I waited and he ran toward me. Did he want to cut me? I backed away as he approached. We smiled uneasily and sheepishly at each other. We spoke haltingly, weighing our words.

"Did they ask you to fight me with gloves?" Harrison asked.

"Yes," I told him. "But I didn't agree."

Harrison's face became eager.

"They want us to fight four rounds for five dollars apiece," he said. "Man, if I had five dollars, I could pay down on a suit. Five dollars is almost half a week's wages for me."

"I don't want to," I said.

"We won't hurt each other," he said.

"But why do a thing like that for white men?"

"To get that five dollars."

"I don't need five dollars that much."

"Aw, you're a fool," he said. Then he smiled quickly.

"Now, look here," I said. "Maybe you *are* angry with me . . ."

"Naw, I'm not." He shook his head vigorously.

"I don't want to fight for white men. I'm no dog or rooster."

I was watching Harrison closely and he was watching me closely. Did he really want to fight me for some reason of his own? Or was it the money? Harrison stared at me with puzzled eyes. He stepped toward me and I stepped away. He smiled nervously.

"I need that money," he said.

"Nothing doing," I said.

He walked off wordlessly, with an air of anger. Maybe he will stab me now, I thought. I got to watch that fool . . .

For another week the white men of both factories begged us to fight. They made up stories about what Harrison had said about me; and when they saw Harrison they lied to him in the same way. Harrison and I were wary of each other whenever we met. We smiled and kept out of arm's reach, ashamed of ourselves and of each other.

Again Harrison called to me one evening as I was on my way home.

"Come on and fight," he begged.

"I don't want to and quit asking me," I said in a voice louder and harder than I had intended.

Harrison looked at me and I watched him. Both of us still carried the knives that the white men had given us.

"I wanna make a payment on a suit of clothes with that five dollars," Harrison said.

"But those white men will be looking at us, laughing at us," I said.

"What the hell," Harrison said. "They look at you and laugh at you every day, nigger."

It was true. But I hated him for saying it. I ached to hit him in his mouth, to hurt him.

"What have we got to lose?" Harrison asked.

"I don't suppose we have anything to lose," I said.

"Sure," he said. "Let's get the money. We don't care."

"And now they know that we know what they tried to do to us," I said, hating myself for saying it. "And they hate us for it."

"Sure," Harrison said. "So let's get the money. You can use five dollars, can't you?"

"Yes."

"Then let's fight for 'em."

"I'd feel like a dog."

"To them, both of us are dogs," he said.

"Yes," I admitted. But again I wanted to hit him.

"Look, let's fool them white men," Harrison said. "We won't hurt each other. We'll just pretend, see? We'll show 'em we ain't dumb as they think, see?"

"I don't know."

"It's just exercise. Four rounds for five dollars. You scared?"

"No."

"Then come on and fight."

"All right," I said. "It's just exercise. I'll fight."

Harrison was happy. I felt that it was all very foolish. But what the hell. I would go through with it and that would be the end of it. But I still felt a vague anger that would not leave.

When the white men in the factory heard that we had agreed to fight, their excitement knew no bounds. They offered to teach me new punches. Each morning they would tell me in whispers that Harrison was eating raw onions for strength. And—from Harrison—I heard that they told him I was eating raw meat for strength. They offered to buy me my meals each day, but I refused. I grew ashamed of what I had agreed to do and wanted to back out of the fight, but I was afraid that they would be angry if I tried to. I felt that if white men tried to persuade two black boys to stab each other for no reason save their own pleasure, then it would not be difficult for them to aim a wanton blow at a black boy in a fit of anger, in a passing mood of frustration.

The fight took place one Saturday afternoon in the basement of a Main Street building. Each white man who attended the fight dropped his share of the pot into a hat that sat on the concrete floor. Only white men were allowed in the basement; no women or Negroes were admitted. Harrison and I were stripped to the waist. A bright electric bulb glowed above our heads. As the gloves were tied on my hands, I looked at Harrison and saw his eyes watching me. Would he keep his promise? Doubt made me nervous.

We squared off and at once I knew that I had not thought sufficiently about what I had bargained for. I could not pretend to fight. Neither Harrison nor I knew enough about boxing to deceive even a child for a moment. Now shame filled me. The white men were smoking and yelling obscenities at us.

"Crush that nigger's nuts, nigger!"

"Hit that nigger!"

"Aw, fight, you goddamn niggers!"

"Sock 'im in his f—k—g piece!"

"Make 'im bleed!"

I lashed out with a timid left. Harrison landed high on my head and, before I knew it, I had landed a hard right on Harrison's mouth and blood came. Harrison shot a blow to my nose. The fight was on, was on against our will. I felt trapped and ashamed. I lashed out even harder, and the harder I fought the harder Harrison fought. Our plans and promises now meant nothing. We fought four hard rounds, stabbing, slugging, grunting, spitting, cursing, crying, bleeding. The shame and anger we felt for having allowed ourselves to be duped crept into our blows and blood ran into our eyes, half blinding us. The hate we felt for the men whom we had tried to cheat went into the blows we threw at each other. The white men made the rounds last as long as five minutes and each of us was afraid to stop and ask for time for fear of receiving a blow that would knock us out. When we were on the point of collapsing from exhaustion, they pulled us apart.

I could not look at Harrison. I hated him and I hated myself. I clutched my five dollars in my fist and walked home. Harrison and I avoided each other after that and we rarely spoke. The white men attempted to arrange other fights for us, but we had sense enough to refuse. I heard of other fights being staged between other black boys, and each time I heard those plans falling from the lips of the white men in the factory I eased out of earshot. I felt that I had done something unclean, something for which I could never properly atone.

Chapter XIII

O NE MORNING I arrived early at work and went into the bank lobby where the Negro porter was mopping. I stood at a counter and picked up the Memphis *Commercial Appeal* and began my free reading of the press. I came finally to the editorial page and saw an article dealing with one H. L. Mencken. I knew by hearsay that he was the editor of the *American Mercury*, but aside from that I knew nothing about him. The article was a furious denunciation of Mencken, concluding with one, hot, short sentence: Mencken is a fool.

I wondered what on earth this Mencken had done to call down upon him the scorn of the South. The only people I had ever heard denounced in the South were Negroes, and this man was not a Negro. Then what ideas did Mencken hold that made a newspaper like the *Commercial Appeal* castigate him publicly? Undoubtedly he must be advocating ideas that the South did not like. Were there, then, people other than Negroes who criticized the South? I knew that during the Civil War the South had hated northern whites, but I had not encountered such hate during my life. Knowing no more of Mencken than I did at that moment, I felt a vague sympathy for him. Had not the South, which had assigned me the role of a non-man, cast at him its hardest words?

Now, how could I find out about this Mencken? There was a huge library near the riverfront, but I knew that Negroes were not allowed to patronize its shelves any more than they were the parks and playgrounds of the city. I had gone into the library several times to get books for the white men on the job. Which of them would now help me to get books? And how could I read them without causing concern to the white men with whom I worked? I had so far been successful in hiding my thoughts and feelings from them, but I knew that I would create hostility if I went about this business of reading in a clumsy way.

I weighed the personalities of the men on the job. There was Don, a Jew; but I distrusted him. His position was not much better than mine and I knew that he was uneasy and insecure; he had always treated me in an offhand, bantering way that barely concealed his contempt. I was afraid to ask him to help me to get books; his frantic desire to demonstrate a racial solidarity with the whites against Negroes might make him betray me.

Then how about the boss? No, he was a Baptist and I had the suspicion that he would not be quite able to comprehend why a black boy would want to read Mencken. There were other white men on the job whose attitudes showed clearly that they were Kluxers or sympathizers, and they were out of the question.

There remained only one man whose attitude did not fit into an anti-Negro category, for I had heard the white men refer to him as a "Pope lover." He was an Irish Catholic and was hated by the white Southerners. I knew that he read books, because I had got him volumes from the library several times. Since he, too, was an object of hatred, I felt that he might refuse me but would hardly betray me. I hesitated, weighing and balancing the imponderable realities.

One morning I paused before the Catholic fellow's desk.

"I want to ask you a favor," I whispered to him.

"What is it?"

"I want to read. I can't get books from the library. I wonder if you'd let me use your card?"

He looked at me suspiciously.

"My card is full most of the time," he said.

"I see," I said and waited, posing my question silently.

"You're not trying to get me into trouble, are you, boy?" he asked, staring at me.

"Oh, no, sir."

"What book do you want?"

"A book by H. L. Mencken."

"Which one?"

"I don't know. Has he written more than one?"

"He has written several."

"I didn't know that."

"What makes you want to read Mencken?"

"Oh, I just saw his name in the newspaper," I said.

"It's good of you to want to read," he said. "But you ought to read the right things."

I said nothing. Would he want to supervise my reading?

"Let me think," he said. "I'll figure out something."

I turned from him and he called me back. He stared at me quizzically.

"Richard, don't mention this to the other white men," he said.

"I understand," I said. "I won't say a word."

A few days later he called me to him.

"I've got a card in my wife's name," he said. "Here's mine."

"Thank you, sir."

"Do you think you can manage it?"

"I'll manage fine," I said.

"If they suspect you, you'll get in trouble," he said.

"I'll write the same kind of notes to the library that you wrote when you sent me for books," I told him. "I'll sign your name."

He laughed.

"Go ahead. Let me see what you get," he said.

That afternoon I addressed myself to forging a note. Now, what were the names of books written by H. L. Mencken? I did not know any of them. I finally wrote what I thought would be a foolproof note: *Dear Madam: Will you please let this nigger boy*—I used the word "nigger" to make the librarian feel that I could not possibly be the author of the note—*have some books by H. L. Mencken?* I forged the white man's name.

I entered the library as I had always done when on errands for whites, but I felt that I would somehow slip up and betray myself. I doffed my hat, stood a respectful distance from the desk, looked as unbookish as possible, and waited for the white patrons to be taken care of. When the desk was clear of people, I still waited. The white librarian looked at me.

"What do you want, boy?"

As though I did not possess the power of speech, I stepped forward and simply handed her the forged note, not parting my lips.

"What books by Mencken does he want?" she asked.

"I don't know, ma'am," I said, avoiding her eyes.

"Who gave you this card?"

"Mr. Falk," I said.

"Where is he?"

"He's at work, at the M—— Optical Company," I said. "I've been in here for him before."

"I remember," the woman said. "But he never wrote notes like this."

Oh, God, she's suspicious. Perhaps she would not let me have the books? If she had turned her back at that moment, I would have ducked out the door and never gone back. Then I thought of a bold idea.

"You can call him up, ma'am," I said, my heart pounding.

"You're not using these books, are you?" she asked pointedly.

"Oh, no, ma'am. I can't read."

"I don't know what he wants by Mencken," she said under her breath.

I knew now that I had won; she was thinking of other things and the race question had gone out of her mind. She went to the shelves. Once or twice she looked over her shoulder at me, as though she was still doubtful. Finally she came forward with two books in her hand.

"I'm sending him two books," she said. "But tell Mr. Falk to come in next time, or send me the names of the books he wants. I don't know what he wants to read."

I said nothing. She stamped the card and handed me the books. Not daring to glance at them, I went out of the library, fearing that the woman would call me back for further questioning. A block away from the library I opened one of the books and read a title: *A Book of Prefaces*. I was nearing my nineteenth birthday and I did not know how to pronounce the word "preface." I thumbed the pages and saw strange words and strange names. I shook my head, disappointed. I looked at the other book; it was called *Prejudices*. I knew what that word meant; I had heard it all my life. And right off I was on guard against Mencken's books. Why would a man want to call a book *Prejudices*? The word was so stained with all my memories of racial hate that I could not conceive of anybody using it for a title. Perhaps I had made a mistake about Mencken? A man who had prejudices must be wrong.

When I showed the books to Mr. Falk, he looked at me and frowned.

"That librarian might telephone you," I warned him

"That's all right," he said. "But when you're through reading those books, I want you to tell me what you get out of them."

That night in my rented room, while letting the hot water run over my can of pork and beans in the sink, I opened *A Book of Prefaces* and began to read. I was jarred and shocked by the style, the clear, clean, sweeping sentences. Why did he write like that? And how did one write like that? I pictured the man as a raging demon, slashing with his pen, consumed with hate, denouncing everything American, extolling everything European or German, laughing at the weaknesses of people, mocking God, authority. What was this? I stood up, trying to realize what reality lay behind the meaning of the words . . . Yes, this man was fighting, fighting with words. He was using words as a weapon, using them as one would use a club. Could words be weapons? Well, yes, for here they were. Then, maybe, perhaps, I could use them as a weapon? No. It frightened me. I read on and what amazed me was not what he said, but how on earth anybody had the courage to say it.

Occasionally I glanced up to reassure myself that I was alone in the room. Who were these men about whom Mencken was talking so passionately? Who was Anatole France? Joseph Conrad? Sinclair Lewis, Sherwood Anderson, Dostoevski, George Moore, Gustave Flaubert, Maupassant, Tolstoy, Frank Harris, Mark Twain, Thomas Hardy, Arnold Bennett, Stephen Crane, Zola, Norris, Gorky, Bergson, Ibsen, Balzac, Bernard Shaw, Dumas, Poe, Thomas Mann, O. Henry, Dreiser, H. G. Wells, Gogol, T. S. Eliot, Gide, Baudelaire, Edgar Lee Masters, Stendhal, Turgenev, Huneker, Nietzsche, and scores of others? Were these men real? Did they exist or had they existed? And how did one pronounce their names?

I ran across many words whose meanings I did not know, and I either looked them up in a dictionary or, before I had a chance to do that, encountered the word in a context that made its meaning clear. But what strange world was this? I concluded the book with the conviction that I had somehow overlooked something terribly important in life. I had once tried to write, had once reveled in feeling, had let my crude imagination roam, but the impulse to dream had been slowly beaten out of me by experience. Now it surged up again and I hungered for books, new ways of looking and seeing. It was not a matter of believing or disbelieving what I read, but of feeling something new, of being affected by something that made the look of the world different.

As dawn broke I ate my pork and beans, feeling dopey, sleepy. I went to work, but the mood of the book would not die; it lingered, coloring everything I saw, heard, did. I now felt that I knew what the white men were feeling. Merely because I had read a book that had spoken of how they lived and thought, I identified myself with that book. I felt vaguely guilty. Would I, filled with bookish notions, act in a manner that would make the whites dislike me?

I forged more notes and my trips to the library became frequent. Reading grew into a passion. My first serious novel was Sinclair Lewis's *Main Street*. It made me see my boss, Mr. Gerald, and identify him as an American type. I would smile when I saw him lugging his golf bags into the office. I had always felt a vast distance separating me from the boss, and now I felt closer to him, though still distant. I felt now that I knew him, that I could feel the very limits of his narrow life. And this had happened because I had read a novel about a mythical man called George F. Babbitt.

The plots and stories in the novels did not interest me so much as the point of view revealed. I gave myself over to each novel without reserve, without trying to criticize it; it was enough for me to see and feel something different. And for me, everything was something different. Reading was like a drug, a dope. The novels created moods in which I lived for days. But I could not conquer my sense of guilt, my feeling that the white men around me knew that I was changing, that I had begun to regard them differently.

Whenever I brought a book to the job, I wrapped it in newspaper—a habit that was to persist for years in other cities and under other circumstances. But some of the white men pried into my packages when I was absent and they questioned me.

"Boy, what are you reading those books for?"

"Oh, I don't know, sir."

"That's deep stuff you're reading, boy."

"I'm just killing time, sir."

"You'll addle your brains if you don't watch out."

I read Dreiser's *Jennie Gerhardt* and *Sister Carrie* and they revived in me a vivid sense of my mother's suffering; I was overwhelmed. I grew silent, wondering about the life around me. It would have been impossible for me to have told anyone what I derived from these novels, for it was nothing less than a sense of life itself. All my life had shaped me for the realism, the naturalism of the modern novel, and I could not read enough of them.

Steeped in new moods and ideas, I bought a ream of paper and tried to write; but nothing would come, or what did come was flat beyond telling. I discovered that more than desire and feeling were necessary to write and I dropped the idea. Yet I still wondered how it was possible to know people sufficiently to write about them? Could I ever learn about life and people? To me, with my vast ignorance, my Jim Crow station in life, it seemed a task impossible of achievement. I now knew what being a Negro meant. I could endure the hunger. I had learned to live with hate. But to feel that there were feelings denied me, that the very breath of life itself was beyond my reach, that more than anything else hurt, wounded me. I had a new hunger.

In buoying me up, reading also cast me down, made me see what was possible, what I had missed. My tension returned, new, terrible, bitter, surging, almost too great to be contained. I no longer *felt* that the world about me was hostile, killing; I *knew* it. A million times I asked myself what I could do to save myself, and there were no answers. I seemed forever condemned, ringed by walls.

I did not discuss my reading with Mr. Falk, who had lent me his library card; it would have meant talking about myself and that would have been too painful. I smiled each day, fighting desperately to maintain my old behavior, to keep my disposition seemingly sunny. But some of the white men discerned that I had begun to brood.

"Wake up there, boy!" Mr. Olin said one day.

"Sir!" I answered for the lack of a better word.

"You act like you've stolen something," he said.

I laughed in the way I knew he expected me to laugh, but I resolved to be more conscious of myself, to watch my every act, to guard and hide the new knowledge that was dawning within me.

If I went north, would it be possible for me to build a new life then? But how could a man build a life upon vague, unformed yearnings? I wanted to write and I did not even know the English language. I bought English grammars and found them dull. I felt that I was getting a better sense of the language from novels than from grammars. I read hard, discarding a writer as soon as I felt that I had grasped his point of view. At night the printed page stood before my eyes in sleep.

Mrs. Moss, my landlady, asked me one Sunday morning:

"Son, what is this you keep on reading?"

"Oh, nothing. Just novels."

"What you get out of 'em?"

"I'm just killing time," I said.

"I hope you know your own mind," she said in a tone which implied that she doubted if I had a mind.

I knew of no Negroes who read the books I liked and I wondered if any Negroes ever thought of them. I knew that there were Negro doctors, lawyers, newspapermen, but I never saw any of them. When I read a Negro newspaper I never caught the faintest echo of my preoccupation in its pages. I felt trapped and occasionally, for a few days, I would stop reading. But a vague hunger would come over me for books, books that opened up new avenues of feeling and seeing, and again I would forge another note to the white librarian. Again I would read and wonder as only the naïve and unlettered can read and wonder, feeling that I carried a secret, criminal burden about with me each day.

That winter my mother and brother came and we set up housekeeping, buying furniture on the installment plan, being cheated and yet knowing no way to avoid it. I began to eat warm food and to my surprise found that regular meals enabled me to read faster. I may have lived through many illnesses and survived them, never suspecting that I was ill. My brother obtained a job and we began to save toward the trip north, plotting our time, setting tentative dates for departure.

I told none of the white men on the job that I was planning to go north; I knew that the moment they felt I was thinking of the North they would change toward me. It would have made them feel that I did not like the life I was living, and because my life was completely conditioned by what they said or did, it would have been tantamount to challenging them.

I could calculate my chances for life in the South as a Negro fairly clearly now.

I could fight the southern whites by organizing with other Negroes, as my grandfather had done. But I knew that I could never win that way; there were many whites and there were but few blacks. They were strong and we were weak. Outright black rebellion could never win. If I fought openly I would die and I did not want to die. News of lynchings were frequent.

I could submit and live the life of a genial slave, but that was impossible. All of my life had shaped me to live by my own feelings and thoughts. I could make up to Bess and marry her and inherit the house. But that, too, would be the life of a slave; if I did that, I would crush to death something within me, and I would hate myself as much as I knew the whites already hated those who had submitted. Neither could I ever willingly present myself to be kicked, as Shorty had done. I would rather have died than do that.

I could drain off my restlessness by fighting with Shorty and Harrison. I had seen many Negroes solve the problem of being black by transferring their hatred of themselves to others with a black skin and fighting them. I would have to be cold to do that, and I was not cold and I could never be.

I could, of course, forget what I had read, thrust the whites out of my mind, forget them; and find release from anxiety and longing in sex and alcohol. But the memory of how my father had conducted himself made that course repugnant. If I did not want others to violate my life, how could I voluntarily violate it myself?

I had no hope whatever of being a professional man. Not only had I been so conditioned that I did not desire it, but the fulfillment of such an ambition was beyond my capabilities. Well-to-do Negroes lived in a world that was almost as alien to me as the world inhabited by whites.

What, then, was there? I held my life in my mind, in my consciousness each day, feeling at times that I would stumble and drop it, spill it forever. My reading had created a vast sense of distance between me and the world in which I lived and tried to make a living, and that sense of distance was increasing each day. My days and nights were one long, quiet, continuously contained dream of terror, tension, and anxiety. I wondered how long I could bear it.

Chapter XIV

THE ACCIDENTAL VISIT of Aunt Maggie to Memphis formed a practical basis for my planning to go north. Aunt Maggie's husband, the "uncle" who had fled from Arkansas in the dead of night, had deserted her; and now she was casting about for a living. My mother, Aunt Maggie, my brother, and I held long conferences, speculating on the prospects of jobs and the cost of apartments in Chicago. And every time we conferred, we defeated ourselves. It was impossible for all four of us to go at once; we did not have enough money.

Finally sheer wish and hope prevailed over common sense and facts. We discovered that if we waited until we were prepared to go, we would never leave, we would never amass enough money to see us through. We would have to gamble. We finally decided that Aunt Maggie and I would go first, even though it was winter, and prepare a place for my mother and brother. Why wait until next week or next month? If we were going, why not go at once?

Next loomed the problem of leaving my job cleanly, smoothly, without arguments or scenes. How could I present the fact of leaving to my boss? Yes, I would pose as an innocent boy; I would tell him that my aunt was taking me and my paralyzed mother to Chicago. That would create in his mind the impression that I was not asserting my will; it would block any expression of dislike on his part for my act. I knew that southern whites hated the idea of Negroes leaving to live in places where the racial atmosphere was different.

It worked as I had planned. When I broke the news of my leaving two days before I left—I was afraid to tell it sooner for fear that I would create hostility on the part of the whites with whom I worked—the boss leaned back in his swivel chair and gave me the longest and most considerate look he had ever given me.

"Chicago?" he repeated softly.

"Yes, sir."

"Boy, you won't like it up there," he said.

"Well, I have to go where my family is, sir," I said.

The other white office workers paused in their tasks and listened. I grew self-conscious, tense.

"It's cold up there," he said.

"Yes, sir. They say it is," I said, keeping my voice in a neutral tone.

He became conscious that I was watching him and he looked away, laughing uneasily to cover his concern and dislike.

"Now, boy," he said banteringly, "don't you go up there and fall into that lake."

"Oh, no, sir," I said, smiling as though there existed the possibility of my falling accidentally into Lake Michigan.

He was serious again, staring at me. I looked at the floor.

"You think you'll do any better up there?" he asked.

"I don't know, sir."

"You seem to've been getting along all right down here," he said.

"Oh, yes, sir. If it wasn't for my mother's going, I'd stay right here and work," I lied as earnestly as possible.

"Well, why not stay? You can send her money," he suggested.

He had trapped me. I knew that staying now would never do. I could not have controlled my relations with the whites if I had remained after having told them that I wanted to go north.

"Well, I want to be with my mother," I said.

"You want to be with your mother," he repeated idly. "Well, Richard, we enjoyed having you with us."

"And I enjoyed working here," I lied.

There was silence; I stood awkwardly, then moved to the door. There was still silence; white faces were looking strangely at me. I went upstairs, feeling like a criminal. The word soon spread through the factory and the white men looked at me with new eyes. They came to me.

"So you're going north, hunh?"

"Yes, sir. My family's taking me with 'em."

"The North's no good for your people, boy."

"I'll try to get along, sir."

"Don't believe all the stories you hear about the North."

"No, sir. I don't."

"You'll come back here where your friends are."

"Well, sir. I don't know."

"How're you going to act up there?"

"Just like I act down here, sir."

"Would you speak to a white girl up there?"

"Oh, no, sir. I'll act there just like I act here."

"Aw, no, you won't. You'll change. Niggers change when they go north."

I wanted to tell him that I was going north precisely to change, but I did not.

"I'll be the same," I said, trying to indicate that I had no imagination whatever.

As I talked I felt that I was acting out a dream. I did not want to lie, yet I had to lie to conceal what I felt. A white censor was standing over me and, like dreams forming a curtain for the safety of sleep, so did my lies form a screen of safety for my living moments.

"Boy, I bet you've been reading too many of them damn books."

"Oh, no, sir."

I made my last errand to the post office, put my bag away, washed my hands, and pulled on my cap. I shot a quick glance about the factory; most of the men were working late. One or two looked up. Mr. Falk, to whom I had returned my library card, gave me a quick, secret smile. I walked to the elevator and rode down with Shorty.

"You lucky bastard," he said bitterly.

"Why do you say that?"

"You saved your goddamn money and now you're gone."

"My problems are just starting," I said.

"You'll never have any problems as hard as the ones you had here," he said.

"I hope not," I said. "But life is tricky."

"Sometimes I get so goddamn mad I want to kill everybody," he spat in a rage.

"You can leave," I said.

"I'll never leave this goddamn South," he railed. "I'm always saying I am, but I won't . . . I'm lazy. I like to sleep too goddamn much. I'll die here. Or maybe they'll kill me."

I stepped from the elevator into the street, half expecting someone to call me back and tell me that it was all a dream, that I was not leaving.

This was the culture from which I sprang. This was the terror from which I fled.

Part Two:

THE HORROR AND THE GLORY

Sometimes I wonder, huh,
Wonder if other people wonder, huh,
Sometimes I wonder, huh,
Wonder if other people wonder, huh,
Just like I do, oh, my Lord, just like I do!
—NEGRO FOLK SONG

Chapter XV

My FIRST GLIMPSE of the flat black stretches of Chicago depressed and dismayed me, mocked all my fantasies. Chicago seemed an unreal city whose mythical houses were built of slabs of black coal wreathed in palls of gray smoke, houses whose foundations were sinking slowly into the dank prairie. Flashes of steam showed intermittently on the wide horizon, gleaming translucently in the winter sun. The din of the city entered my consciousness, entered to remain for years to come. The year was 1927.

What would happen to me here? Would I survive? My expectations were modest. I wanted only a job. Hunger had long been my daily companion. Diversion and recreation, with the exception of reading, were unknown. In all my life—though surrounded by many people—I had not had a single satisfying, sustained relationship with another human being and, not having had any, I did not miss it. I made no demands whatever upon others.

The train rolled into the depot. Aunt Maggie and I got off and walked slowly through the crowds into the station. I looked about to see if there were signs saying: For White— For Colored. I saw none. Black people and white people moved about, each seemingly intent upon his private mission. There was no racial fear. Indeed, each person acted as though no one existed but himself. It was strange to pause before a crowded newsstand and buy a newspaper without having to wait until a white man was served. And yet, because everything was so new, I began to grow tense again, although it was a different sort of tension than I had known before. I knew that this machine-city was governed by strange laws and I wondered if I would ever learn them.

As we waited for a streetcar to take us to Aunt Cleo's home for temporary lodging, I looked northward at towering buildings of steel and stone. There were no curves here, no trees; only angles, lines, squares, bricks and copper wires. Occasionally the ground beneath my feet shook from some faraway pounding and I felt that this world, despite its massiveness, was somehow dangerously fragile. Streetcars screeched past over steel tracks. Cars honked their horns. Clipped speech sounded about me. As I stood in the icy wind, I wanted to talk to Aunt Maggie, to ask her questions, but her tight face made me hold my tongue. I was learning already from the frantic light in her eyes the strain that the city imposed upon its people. I was seized by doubt. Should I have come here? But going back was impossible. I had fled a known terror, and perhaps I could cope with this unknown terror that lay ahead.

The streetcar came. Aunt Maggie motioned for me to get on and pushed me toward a seat in which a white man sat looking blankly out the window. I sat down beside the man and looked straight ahead of me. After a moment I stole a glance at the white man out of the corners of my eyes; he was still staring out the window, his mind fastened upon some inward thought. I did not exist for him; I was as far from his mind as the stone buildings that swept past in the street. It would have been illegal for me to sit beside him in the part of the South that I had come from.

The car swept past soot-blackened buildings, stopping at each block, jerking again into motion. The conductor called street names in a tone that I could not understand. People got on and off the car, but they never glanced at one another. Each person seemed to regard the other as a part of the city landscape. The white man who sat beside me rose and I turned my knees aside to let him pass, and another white man sat beside me and buried his face in a newspaper. How could that possibly be? Was he conscious of my blackness?

We went to Aunt Cleo's address and found that she was living in a rented room. I had imagined that she lived in an apartment and I was disappointed. I rented a room from Aunt Cleo's landlady and decided to keep it until I got a job. I was baffled. Everything seemed makeshift, temporary. I caught an abiding sense of insecurity in the personalities of the people around me. I found Aunt Cleo aged beyond her years. Her husband, a product of a southern plantation, had, like my father, gone off and left her. Why had he left? My aunt could not answer. She was beaten by the life of the city, just as my mother had been beaten. Wherever my eyes turned they saw stricken, frightened black faces trying vainly to cope with a civilization that they did not understand. I felt lonely. I had fled one insecurity and had embraced another.

When I rose the next morning the temperature had dropped below zero. The house was as cold to me as the southern streets had been in winter. I dressed, doubling my clothing. I ate in a restaurant, caught a streetcar and rode south, rode until I could see no more black faces on the sidewalks. I had now crossed the boundary line of the Black Belt and had entered that territory where jobs were perhaps to be had from white folks. I walked the streets and looked into shop windows until I saw a sign in a delicatessen: PORTER WANTED.

I went in and a stout white woman came to me.

"Vat do you vant?" she asked.

The voice jarred me. She's Jewish, I thought, remembering with shame the obscenities I used to shout at Jewish store-keepers in Arkansas.

"I thought maybe you needed a porter," I said.

"Meester 'Offman, he eesn't here yet," she said. "Vill you vait?"

"Yes, ma'am."

"Seet down."

"No, ma'am. I'll wait outside."

"But eet's cold out zhere," she said.

"That's all right," I said.

She shrugged. I went to the sidewalk. I waited for half an hour in the bitter cold, regretting that I had not remained in the warm store, but unable to go back inside. A bald, stoutish white man went into the store and pulled off his coat. Yes, he was the boss man . . . I went in.

"Zo you vant a job?" he asked.

"Yes, sir," I answered, guessing at the meaning of his words.

"Vhere you vork before?"

"In Memphis, Tennessee."

"My brudder-in-law vorked in Tennessee vonce," he said.

I was hired. The work was easy, but I found to my dismay that I could not understand a third of what was said to me. My slow southern ears were baffled by their clouded, thick accents. One morning Mrs. Hoffman asked me to go to a neighboring store—it was owned by a cousin of hers—and get a can of chicken à la king. I had never heard the phrase before and I asked her to repeat it.

"Don't you know nosing?" she demanded of me.

"If you would write it down for me, I'd know what to get," I ventured timidly.

"I can't vite!" she shouted in a sudden fury. "Vat kinda boy ees you?"

I memorized the separate sounds that she had uttered and went to the neighboring store.

"Mrs. Hoffman wants a can of Cheek Keeng Awr Lar Keeng," I said slowly, hoping that he would not think I was being offensive.

"All vight," he said, after staring at me a moment.

He put a can into a paper bag and gave it to me; outside in the street I opened the bag and read the label: Chicken à La King. I cursed, disgusted with myself. I knew those words. It had been her thick accent that had thrown me off. Yet I was not angry with her for speaking broken English; my English, too, was broken. But why could she not have taken more patience? Only one answer came to my mind. I was black and she did not care. Or so I thought . . . I was persisting in reading my present environment in the light of my old one. I reasoned thus: Though English was my native tongue and America my native land, she, an alien, could operate a store and earn a living in a neighborhood where I could not even live. I reasoned further that she was aware of this and was trying to protect her position against me.

(It was not until I had left the delicatessen job that I saw how grossly I had misread the motives and attitudes of Mr. Hoffman and his wife. I had not yet learned anything that would have helped me to thread my way through these perplexing racial relations. Accepting my environment at its face value, trapped by my own emotions, I kept asking myself what had black people done to bring this crazy world upon them?

(The fact of the separation of white and black was clear to me; it was its effect upon the personalities of people that stumped and dismayed me. I did not feel that I was a dyou a to anybody; yet, as soon as I had grown old enough to think I had learned that my entire personality, my aspirations had long ago been discounted; that, in a measure, the very meaning of the words I spoke could not be fully understood.

(And when I contemplated the area of No Man's Land into which the Negro mind in America had been shunted I wondered if there had ever existed in all human history a more corroding and devastating attack upon the personalities of men than the idea of racial discrimination. In order to escape the racial attack that went to the roots of my life, I would have gladly accepted any way of life but the one in which I found myself. I would have agreed to live under a system of feudal oppression, not because I preferred feudalism but because I felt that feudalism made use of a limited part of a man, defined him, his rank, his function in society. I would have consented to live under the most rigid type of dictatorship, for I felt that dictatorships, too, defined the use of men, however degrading that use might be.

(While working in Memphis I had stood aghast as Shorty had offered himself to be kicked by the white men; but now, while working in Chicago, I was learning that perhaps even a kick was better than uncertainty . . . I had elected, in my fevered search for honorable adjustment to the American scene, not to submit and in doing so I had embraced the daily horror of anxiety, of tension, of eternal disquiet. I could now sympathize with—though I could never bring myself to approve—those tortured blacks who had given up and had gone to their white tormentors and had said: "Kick me, if that's all there is for me; kick me and let me feel at home, let me have peace!"

(Color hate defined the place of black life as below that of white life; and the black man, responding to the same dreams as the white man, strove to bury within his heart his awareness of this difference because it made him lonely and afraid. Hated by whites and being an organic part of the culture that hated him, the black man grew in turn to hate in himself that which others hated in him. But pride would make him hide his self-hate, for he would not want whites to know that he was so thoroughly conquered by them that his total life was conditioned by their attitude; but in the act of hiding his self-hate, he could not help but hate those who evoked his self-hate in him. So each part of his day would be consumed in a war with himself, a good part of his energy would be spent in keeping control of his unruly emotions, emotions which he had not wished to have, but could not help having. Held at bay by the hate of others, preoccupied with his own feelings, he was continuously at war with reality. He became inefficient, less able to see and judge the objective world. And when he reached that state, the white people looked at him and laughed and said:

("Look, didn't I tell you niggers were that way?"

(To solve this tangle of balked emotion, I loaded the empty part of the ship of my personality with fantasies of ambition to keep it from toppling over into the sea of senselessness. Like any other American, I dreamed of going into business and making money; I dreamed of working for a firm that would allow me to advance until I reached an important position; I even dreamed of organizing secret groups of blacks to fight all whites . . . And if the blacks would not agree to organize, then they would have to be fought. I would end up again with self-hate, but it was now a self-hate that was projected outward upon other blacks. Yet I knew—with that part of my mind that the whites had given me—that none of my dreams was possible. Then I would hate myself for allowing my mind to dwell upon the unattainable. Thus the circle would complete itself.

(Slowly I began to forge in the depths of my mind a mechanism that repressed all the dreams and desires that the Chicago streets, the newspapers, the movies were evoking in me. I was going through a second childhood; a new sense of the limit of the possible was being born in me. What could I dream of that had the barest possibility of coming true? I could think of nothing. And, slowly, it was upon exactly that nothingness that my mind began to dwell, that constant sense of wanting without having, of being hated without reason. A dim notion of what life meant to a Negro in America was coming to consciousness in me, not in terms of external events, lynchings, Jim Crowism, and the endless brutalities, but in terms of crossed-up feeling, of psyche pain. I sensed that Negro life was a sprawling land of unconscious suffering, and there were but few Negroes who knew the meaning of their lives, who could tell their story.)

Word reached me that an examination for postal clerk was impending and at once I filed an application and waited. As the date for the examination drew near, I was faced with another problem. How could I get a free day without losing my job? In the South it would have been an unwise policy for a Negro to have gone to his white boss and asked for time to take an examination for another job. It would have implied that the Negro did not like to work for the white boss, that he felt he was not receiving just consideration and, inasmuch as most jobs that Negroes held in the South involved a personal, paternalistic relationship, he would have been risking an argument that might have led to violence.

I now began to speculate about what kind of man Mr. Hoffman was, and I found that I did not know him; that is, I did not know his basic attitude toward Negroes. If I asked him, would he be sympathetic enough to allow me time off with pay? I needed the money. Perhaps he would say: "Go home and stay home if you don't like this job"? I was not sure of him. I decided, therefore, that I had better not risk it. I would forfeit the money and stay away without telling him.

The examination was scheduled to take place on a Monday; I had been working steadily and I would be too tired to do my best if I took the examination without the benefit of rest. I decided to stay away from the shop Saturday, Sunday, and Monday. But what could I tell Mr. Hoffman? Yes, I would tell him that I had been ill. No, that was too thin. I would tell him that my mother had died in Memphis and that I had gone down to bury her. That lie might work.

I took the examination and when I came to the store on Tuesday, Mr. Hoffman was astonished, of course.

"I didn't sink you vould ever come back," he said.

"I'm awfully sorry, Mr. Hoffman."

"Vat happened?"

"My mother died in Memphis and I had to go down and bury her," I lied.

He looked at me, then shook his head.

"Rich, you lie," he said.

"I'm not lying," I lied stoutly.

"You vanted to do somesink, zo you zayed ervay," he said, shrugging.

"No, sir. I'm telling you the truth," I piled another lie upon the first one.

"No. You lie. You disappoint me," he said.

"Well, all I can do is tell you the truth," I lied indignantly.

"Vy didn't you use the phone?"

"I didn't think of it," I told a fresh lie.

"Rich, if your mudder die, you vould tell me," he said.

"I didn't have time. Had to catch the train," I lied yet again.

"Vhere did you get the money?"

"My aunt gave it to me," I said, disgusted that I had to lie and lie again.

"I don't vant a boy vat tells lies," he said.

"I don't lie," I lied passionately to protect my lies.

Mrs. Hoffman joined in and both of them hammered at me.

"Ve know. You come from ze Zouth. You feel you can't tell us ze truth. But ve don't bother you. Ve don't feel like people in ze Zouth. Ve treat you nice, don't ve?" they asked.

"Yes, ma'am," I mumbled.

"Zen vy lie?"

"I'm not lying," I lied with all my strength.

I became angry because I knew that they knew that I was lying. I had lied to protect myself, and then I had to lie to protect my lie. I had met so many white faces that would have violently disapproved of my taking the examination that I could not have risked telling Mr. Hoffman the truth. But how could I now tell him that I had lied because I was so unsure of myself? Lying was bad, but revealing my own sense of insecurity would have been worse. It would have been shameful and I did not like to feel ashamed.

Their attitudes had proved utterly amazing. They were taking time out from their duties in the store to talk to me, and I had never encountered anything like that from whites before. A southern white man would have said: "Get to hell out of here!" or "All right, nigger. Get to work." But no white people had ever stood their ground and probed at me, questioned me at such length. It dawned upon me that they were trying to treat me as an equal, which made it even more impossible for me ever to tell them that I had lied, why I had lied. I felt that if I confessed I would give them a moral advantage over me that would be unbearable.

"All vight, zday and vork," Mr. Hoffman said. "I know you're lying, but I don't care, Rich."

I wanted to quit. He had insulted me. But I liked him in spite of myself. Yes, I had done wrong, but how on earth could I have known the kind of people I was working for? Perhaps Mr. Hoffman would have gladly consented for me to take the examination, but my hopes had been far weaker than my powerful fears.

Working with them from day to day and knowing that they knew I had lied from fear crushed me. I knew that they pitied me and pitied the fear in me. I resolved to quit and risk hunger rather than stay with them. I left the job that following Saturday, not telling them that I would not be back, not possessing the heart to say good-bye. I just wanted to go quickly and have them forget that I had ever worked for them.

After an idle week, I got a job as a dishwasher in a North Side café that had just opened. My boss, a white woman, directed me in unpacking barrels of dishes, setting up new tables, painting, and so on. I had charge of serving breakfast; in the late afternoons I carted trays of food to patrons in the hotel who did not want to come down to eat. My wages were fifteen dollars a week; the hours were long, but I ate my meals on the job.

The cook was an elderly Finnish woman with a sharp, bony face. There were several white waitresses. I was the only Negro in the café. The waitresses were a hard, brisk lot and I was keenly aware of how their attitudes contrasted with those of southern white girls. They had not been taught to keep a gulf between me and themselves; they were relatively free of the heritage of racial hate.

One morning as I was making coffee, Cora came forward with a tray loaded with food and squeezed against me to draw a cup of coffee.

"Pardon me, Richard," she said.

"Oh, that's all right," I said in an even tone.

But I was aware that she was a white girl and that her body was pressed closely against mine, an incident that had never happened to me before in my life, an incident charged with the memory of dread. But she was not conscious of my blackness or of what her actions would have meant in the South. And had I not been born in the South, her trivial act would have been as unnoticed by me as it was by her. As she stood close to me, I could not help thinking that if a southern white girl had wanted to draw a cup of coffee, she would have commanded me to step aside so that she might not come in contact with me. The work of the hot and busy kitchen would have had to cease for the moment so that I could have taken my tainted body far enough away to allow the southern white girl a chance to get a cup of coffee. There lay a deep, emotional safety in knowing that the white girl who was now leaning carelessly against me was not thinking of me, had no deep, vague, irrational fright that made her feel that I was a creature to be avoided at all costs.

One summer morning a white girl came late to work and rushed into the pantry where I was busy. She went into the women's room and changed her clothes; I heard the door open and a second later I was surprised to hear her voice:

"Richard, quick! Tie my apron!"

She was standing with her back to me and the strings of her apron dangled loose. There was a moment of indecision on my part, then I took the two loose strings and carried them around her body and brought them again to her back and tied them in a clumsy knot.

"Thanks a million," she said grasping my hand for a split second, and was gone.

I continued my work, filled with all the possible meanings that that tiny, simple, human event could have meant to any Negro in the South where I had spent most of my hungry days.

I did not feel any admiration for the girls, nor any hate. My attitude was one of abiding and friendly wonder. For the most part I was silent with them, though I knew that I had a firmer grasp of life than most of them. As I worked I listened to their talk and perceived its puzzled, wandering, superficial fumbling with the problems and facts of life. There were many things they wondered about that I could have explained to them, but I never dared.

During my lunch hour, which I spent on a bench in a near-by park, the waitresses would come and sit beside me, talking at random, laughing, joking, smoking cigarettes. I learned about their tawdry dreams, their simple hopes, their home lives, their fear of feeling anything deeply, their sex problems, their husbands. They were an eager, restless, talkative, ignorant bunch, but casually kind and impersonal for all that. They knew nothing of hate and fear, and strove instinctively to avoid all passion.

I often wondered what they were trying to get out of life, but I never stumbled upon a clue, and I doubt if they themselves had any notion. They lived on the surface of their days; their smiles were surface smiles, and their tears were surface tears. Negroes lived a truer and deeper life than they, but I wished that Negroes, too, could live as thoughtlessly, serenely as they. The girls never talked of their feelings; none of them possessed the insight or the emotional equipment to understand themselves or others. How far apart in culture we stood! All my life I had done nothing but feel and cultivate my feelings; all their lives they had done nothing but strive for petty goals, the trivial material prizes of American life. We shared a common tongue, but my language was a different language from theirs.

It was in the psychological distance that separated the races that the deepest meaning of the problem of the Negro lay for me. For these poor, ignorant white girls to have understood my life would have meant nothing short of a vast revolution in theirs. And I was convinced that what they needed to make them complete and grown-up in their living was the inclusion in their personalities of a knowledge of lives such as I lived and suffered containedly.

(As I, in memory, think back now upon those girls and their lives I feel that for white America to understand the significance of the problem of the Negro will take a bigger and tougher America than any we have yet known. I feel that America's past is too shallow, her national character too superficially optimistic, her very morality too suffused with color hate for her to accomplish so vast and complex a task. Culturally the Negro represents a paradox: Though he is an organic part of the nation, he is excluded by the entire tide and direction of American culture. Frankly, it is felt to be right to exclude him, and it is felt to be wrong to admit him freely. Therefore if, within the confines of its present culture, the nation ever seeks to purge itself of its color hate, it will find itself at war with itself, convulsed by a spasm of emotional and moral confusion. If the nation ever finds itself examining its real relation to the Negro, it will find itself doing infinitely more than that; for the anti-Negro attitude of whites represents but a tiny part—though a symbolically significant one—of the moral attitude of the nation. Our too-young and too-new America, lusty because it is lonely, aggressive because it is afraid, insists upon seeing the world in terms of good and bad, the holy and the evil, the high and the low, the white and the black; our America is frightened of fact, of history, of processes, of necessity. It hugs the easy way of damning those whom it cannot understand, of excluding those who look different, and it salves its conscience with a self-draped cloak of righteousness. Am I damning my native land? No; for I, too, share these faults of character! And I really do not think that America, adolescent and cocksure, a stranger to suffering and travail, an enemy of passion and sacrifice, is ready to probe into its most fundamental beliefs.

(I know that not race alone, not color alone, but the daily values that give meaning to life stood between me and those white girls with whom I worked. Their constant outward-looking, their mania for radios, cars, and a thousand other trinkets made them dream and fix their eyes upon the trash of life, made it impossible for them to learn a language which could have taught them to speak of what was in their or others' hearts. The words of their souls were the syllables of popular songs.

(The essence of the irony of the plight of the Negro in America, to me, is that he is doomed to live in isolation while those who condemn him seek the basest goals of any people on the face of the earth. Perhaps it would be possible for the Negro to become reconciled to his plight if he could be made to believe that his sufferings were for some remote, high, sacrificial end; but sharing the culture that condemns him, and seeing that a lust for trash is what blinds the nation to his claims, is what sets storms to rolling in his soul.)

Though I had fled the pressure of the South, my outward conduct had not changed. I had been schooled to present an unalteringly smiling face and I continued to do so despite the fact that my environment allowed more open expression. I hid my feelings and avoided all relationships with whites that might cause me to reveal them.

One afternoon the boss lady entered the kitchen and found me sitting on a box reading a copy of the *American Mercury*.

"What on earth are you reading?" she demanded.

I was at once on guard, though I knew I did not have to be.

"Oh, just a magazine," I said.

"Where did you get it?" she asked.

"Oh, I just found it," I lied; I had bought it.

"Do you understand it?" she asked.

"Yes, ma'am."

"Well," she exclaimed, "the colored dishwasher reads the *American Mercury*!"

She walked away, shaking her head. My feelings were mixed. I was glad that she had learned that I was not completely dumb, yet I felt a little angry because she seemed to think it odd for dishwashers to read magazines. Thereafter I kept my books and magazines wrapped in newspaper so that no one would see them, reading them at home and on the streetcar to and from work.

Tillie, the Finnish cook, was a tall, ageless, red-faced, raw-boned woman with long, snow-white hair which she balled in a knot at the nape of her neck. She cooked expertly and was superbly efficient. One morning as I passed the sizzling stove I thought I heard Tillie cough and spit. I paused and looked carefully to see where her spittle had gone, but I saw nothing; her face, obscured by steam, was bent over a big pot. My senses told me that Tillie had coughed and spat into that pot, but my heart told me that no human being could possibly be so filthy. I decided to watch her. An hour or so later I heard Tillie clear her throat with a grunt, saw her cough, and spit into the boiling soup. I held my breath; I did not want to believe what I had seen.

Should I tell the boss lady? Would she believe me? I watched Tillie for another day to make sure that she was spitting into the food. She was; there was no doubt of it. But who would believe me if I told them what was happening? I was the only black person in the café. Perhaps they would think that I hated the cook? I stopped eating my meals there and bided my time.

The business of the café was growing rapidly and a Negro girl was hired to make salads. I went to her at once.

"Look, can I trust you?" I asked.

"What are you talking about?" she asked.

"I want you to say nothing, but watch that cook."

"For what?"

"Now, don't get scared. Just watch the cook."

She looked at me as though she thought I was crazy; and, frankly, I felt that perhaps I ought not to say anything to anybody.

"What do you mean?" she demanded.

"All right," I said. "I'll tell you. That cook spits in the food."

"What are you saying?" she asked aloud.

"Keep quiet," I said.

"Spitting?" she asked me in a whisper. "Why would she do that?"

"I don't know. But watch her."

She walked away from me with a funny look in her eyes. But half an hour later she came rushing to me, looking ill, sinking into a chair.

"Oh, God, I feel awful!"

"Did you see it?"

"She *is* spitting in the food!"

"What ought we do?" I asked.

"Tell the lady," she said.

"She wouldn't believe me," I said.

She widened her eyes as she understood. We were black and the cook was white.

"But I can't work here if she's going to do that," she said.

"Then you tell her," I said.

"She wouldn't believe me either," she said.

She rose and ran to the women's room. When she returned she stared at me. We were two Negroes and we were silently asking ourselves if the white boss lady would believe us if we told her that her expert white cook was spitting in the food all day long as it cooked upon the stove.

"I don't know," she wailed in a whisper and walked away.

I thought of telling the waitresses about the cook, but I could not get up enough nerve. Many of the girls were friendly with Tillie. Yet I could not let the cook spit in the food all day. That was wrong by any human standard of conduct. I washed dishes, thinking, wondering; I served breakfast, thinking, wondering; I served meals in the apartments of patrons upstairs, thinking, wondering. Each time I picked up a tray of food I felt like retching. Finally the Negro salad girl came to me and handed me her purse and hat.

"I'm going to tell her and quit, goddamn," she said.

"I'll quit too, if she doesn't fire her," I said.

"Oh, she won't believe me," she wailed in agony.

"You tell her. You're a woman. She might believe you."

Her eyes welled with tears and she sat for a long time; then she rose and went abruptly into the dining room. I went to the door and peered. Yes, she was at the desk, talking to the boss lady. She returned to the kitchen and went into the pantry; I followed her.

"Did you tell her?" I asked.

"Yes."

"What did she say?"

"She said I was crazy."

"Oh, God!" I said.

"She just looked at me with those gray eyes of hers," the girl said. "Why would Tillie do that?"

"I don't know," I said.

The boss lady came to the door and called the girl; both of them went into the dining room. Tillie came over to me; a hard, cold look was in her eyes.

"What's happening here?" she asked.

"I don't know," I said, wanting to slap her across the mouth.

She muttered something and went back to the stove,

coughed, spat into a bubbling pot. I left the kitchen and went into the back areaway to breathe. The boss lady came out.

"Richard," she said.

Her face was pale. I was smoking a cigarette and I did not look at her.

"Is this true?"

"Yes, ma'am."

"It couldn't be. Do you know what you're saying?"

"Just watch her," I said.

"I don't know," she moaned.

She looked crushed. She went back into the dining room, but I saw her watching the cook through the doors. I watched both of them, the boss lady and the cook, praying that the cook would spit again. She did. The boss lady came into the kitchen and stared at Tillie, but she did not utter a word. She burst into tears and ran back into the dining room.

"What's happening here?" Tillie demanded.

No one answered. The boss lady came out and tossed Tillie her hat, coat, and money.

"Now, get out of here, you dirty dog!" she said.

Tillie stared, then slowly picked up her hat, coat, and the money; she stood a moment, wiped sweat from her forehead with her hand, then spat, this time on the floor. She left.

Nobody was ever able to fathom why Tillie liked to spit into the food.

Brooding over Tillie, I recalled the time when the boss man in Mississippi had come to me and had tossed my wages to me and said:

"Get out, nigger! I don't like your looks."

And I wondered if a Negro who did not smile and grin was as morally loathsome to whites as a cook who spat into the food . . .

I worked at the café all spring and in June I was called for temporary duty in the post office. My confidence soared; if I obtained an appointment as a regular clerk, I could spend at least five hours a day writing.

I reported at the post office and was sworn in as a temporary clerk. I earned seventy cents an hour and I went to bed each night now with a full stomach for the first time in my life. When I worked nights, I wrote during the day; when I worked days, I wrote during the night.

But the happiness of having a job did not keep another worry from rising to plague me. Before I could receive a permanent appointment I would have to take a physical examination and the weight requirement was one hundred and twenty-five pounds and I—with my long years of semistarvation—barely tipped the scales at a hundred and ten. Frantically I turned all of my spare money into food and ate. But my skin and flesh would not respond to the food. Perhaps I was not eating the right diet? Perhaps my chronic anxiety kept my weight down. I drank milk, ate steak, but it did not give me an extra ounce of flesh. I visited a doctor who told me that there was nothing wrong with me except malnutrition, that I must eat and sleep long hours. I did and my weight remained the same. I knew now that my job was temporary and that when the time came for my appointment I would have to resume my job hunting again.

While I crammed my stomach I read Stein's *Three Lives*, Crane's *The Red Badge of Courage*, and Dostoevski's *The Possessed*, all of which revealed new realms of feeling. But the most important discoveries came when I veered from fiction proper into the field of psychology and sociology. I ran through volumes that bore upon the causes of my conduct and the conduct of my family. I studied tables of figures relating population density to insanity, relating housing to disease, relating school and recreational opportunities to crime, relating various forms of neurotic behavior to environment, relating racial insecurities to the conflicts between whites and blacks . . .

I still had no friends, casual or intimate, and felt the need for none. I had developed a self-sufficiency that kept me distant from others, emotionally and psychologically. Occasionally I went to house-rent parties, parties given by working-class families to raise money to pay the landlord, the admission to which was a quarter or a half dollar. At these affairs I drank home-brewed beer, ate spaghetti and chitterlings, laughed and talked with black, southern-born girls who worked as domestic servants in white middle-class homes. But with none of them did my relations rest upon my deepest feelings. I discussed what I read with no one, and to none did I confide. Emotionally, I was withdrawn from the objective world; my desires floated loosely within the walls of my consciousness, contained and controlled.

As a protective mechanism, I developed a terse, cynical mode of speech that rebuffed those who sought to get too close to me. Conversation was my way of avoiding expression; my words were reserved for those times when I sat down alone to write. My face was always a deadpan or a mask of general friendliness; no word or event could jar me into a gesture of enthusiasm or despair. A slowly, hesitantly spoken "Yeah" was my general verbal reaction to almost everything I heard. "That's pretty good," said with a slow nod of the head, was my approval. "Aw, naw," muttered with a cold smile, was my rejection. Even though I reacted deeply, my true feelings raced along underground, hidden.

I did not act in this fashion deliberately; I did not prefer this kind of relationship with people. I wanted a life in which there was a constant oneness of feeling with others, in which the basic emotions of life were shared, in which common memory formed a common past, in which collective hope reflected a national future. But I knew that no such thing was possible in my environment. The only ways in which I felt that my feelings could go outward without fear of rude rebuff or searing reprisal was in writing or reading, and to me they were ways of living.

Aunt Maggie had now rented an apartment in which I shared a rear room. My mother and brother came and all three of us slept in that one room; there was no window, just four walls and a door. My excessive reading puzzled Aunt Maggie; she sensed my fiercely indrawn nature and she did not like it. Being of an open, talkative disposition, she declared that I was going about the business of living wrongly, that reading books would not help me at all. But nothing she said had any effect. I had long ago hardened myself to criticism.

"Boy, are you reading for law?" my aunt would demand.

"No."

"Then why are you reading all the time?"

"I like to."

"But what do you get out of it?"

"I get a great deal out of it."

And I knew that my words sounded wild and foolish in my environment, where reading was almost unknown, where the highest item of value was a dime or a dollar, an apartment or a job; where, if one aspired at all, it was to be a doctor or a lawyer, a shopkeeper or a politician. The most valued pleasure of the people I knew was a car, the most cherished experience a bottle of whisky, the most sought-after prize somebody else's wife. I had no sense of being inferior or superior to the people about me; I merely felt that they had had no chance to learn to live differently. I never criticized them or praised them, yet they felt in my neutrality a deeper rejection of them than if I had cursed them.

Repeatedly I took stabs at writing, but the results were so poor that I would tear up the sheets. I was striving for a level of expression that matched those of the novels I read. But I always somehow failed to get onto the page what I thought and felt. Failing at sustained narrative, I compromised by playing with single sentences and phrases. Under the influence of Stein's *Three Lives*, I spent hours and days pounding out disconnected sentences for the sheer love of words.

I would write:

"The soft melting hunk of butter trickled in gold down the stringy grooves of the split yam."

Or:

"The child's clumsy fingers fumbled in sleep, feeling vainly for the wish of its dream."

"The old man huddled in the dark doorway, his bony face lit by the burning yellow in the windows of distant skyscrapers."

My purpose was to capture a physical state or movement that carried a strong subjective impression, an accomplishment which seemed supremely worth struggling for. If I could fasten the mind of the reader upon words so firmly that he would forget words and be conscious only of his response, I felt that I would be in sight of knowing how to write narrative. I strove to master words, to make them disappear, to make them important by making them new, to make them melt into a rising spiral of emotional stimuli, each greater than the other, each feeding and reinforcing the other, and all ending in an emotional climax that would drench the reader with a sense of a new world. That was the single aim of my living.

Autumn came and I was called for my physical examination for the position of regular postal clerk. I had not told my mother or brother or aunt that I knew I would fail. On the morning of the examination I drank two quarts of buttermilk, ate six bananas, but it did not hoist the red arrow of the government scales to the required mark of one hundred and twenty-five pounds. I went home and sat disconsolately in my back room, hating myself, wondering where I could find another job. I had almost got my hands upon a decent job and had lost it, had let it slip through my fingers. Waves of self-doubt rose to haunt me. Was I always to hang on the fringes of life? What I wanted was truly modest, and yet my past, my diet, my hunger, had snatched it from before my eyes. But these self-doubts did not last long; I dulled the sense of loss through reading, reading, writing and more writing.

The loss of my job did not evoke in me any hostility toward the system of rules that had barred my first grasp at the material foundations of American life. I felt that it was unfair that my lack of a few pounds of flesh should deprive me of a chance at a good job, but I had long ago emotionally rejected the world in which I lived and my reaction was: Well, this is the system by which people want the world to run whether it helps them or not. To me, my losing was only another manifestation of that queer, material way of American living that computed everything in terms of the concrete: weight, color, race, fur coats, radios, electric refrigerators, cars, money . . . It seemed that I simply could not fit into a materialistic life.

The living arrangement of my mother, brother, and Aunt Maggie—now that I had no promise of being a postal clerk—quickly deteriorated. In Aunt Maggie's eyes I was a plainly marked failure and she feared that perhaps she would have to feed me. The emotional atmosphere in the cramped quarters became tense, ugly, petty, bickering. Fault was found with my reading and writing; it was claimed that I was swelling the electric bill. Though I had saved almost no money, I decided to rent an apartment. Aunt Cleo was living in a rented room and I invited her to share the apartment with me, my mother, and brother, and she consented. We moved into a tiny, dingy two-room den in whose kitchen a wall bed fitted snugly into a corner near the stove. The place was alive with vermin and the smell of cooking hung in the air day and night.

I asked for my job back at the café and the boss lady allowed me to return; again I served breakfast, washed dishes, carted trays of food up into the apartments. Another postal examination was scheduled for spring and to that end I made eating an obsession. I ate when I did not want to eat, drank milk when it sickened me. Slowly my starved body responded to food and overcame the lean years of Mississippi, Arkansas, and Tennessee, counteracting the flesh-sapping anxiety of fear-filled days.

I spent my nights reading Proust's *A Remembrance of Things Past*, admiring the lucid, subtle but strong prose, stupefied by its dazzling magic, awed by the vast, delicate, intricate, and psychological structure of the Frenchman's epic of death and decadence. But it crushed me with hopelessness, for I wanted to write of the people in my environment with an equal thoroughness, and the burning example before my eyes made me feel that I never could.

My ability to endure tension had now grown amazingly. From the accidental pain of southern years, from anxiety that I had sought to avoid, from fear that had been too painful to bear, I had learned to like my unintermittent burden of feeling, had become habituated to acting with all of my being, had learned to seek those areas of life, those situations, where I knew that events would complement my own inner mood. I was conscious of what was happening to me; I knew that my attitude of watchful wonder had usurped all other feelings, had become the meaning of my life, an integral part of my personality; that I was striving to live and measure all things by it. Having no claims upon others, I bent the way the wind blew, rendering unto my environment that which was my environment's, and rendering unto myself that which I felt was mine.

It was a dangerous way to live, far more dangerous than violating laws or ethical codes of conduct; but the danger was for me and me alone. Had I not been conscious of what I was doing, I could have easily lost my way in the fogbound regions of compelling fantasy. Even so, I floundered, staggered; but somehow I always groped my way back to that path where I felt a tinge of warmth from an unseen light.

Hungry for insight into my own life and the lives about me, knowing my fiercely indrawn nature, I sought to fulfill more than my share of all obligations and responsibilities, as though offering libations of forgiveness to my environment. Indeed, the more my emotions claimed my attention, the sharper—as though in ultimate self-defense—became my desire to measure accurately the reality of the objective world so that I might more than meet its demands. At twenty years of age the mold of my life was set, was hardening into a pattern, a pattern that was neither good nor evil, neither right nor wrong.

Chapter XVI

IN THE SPRING I took the postal examination again. Time had somewhat repaired the ravages of hunger and I was able to meet the required physical weight. We moved to a larger apartment. My increased pay made better food possible. I was happy in my own way.

Working nights, I spent my days in experimental writing, filling endless pages with stream-of-consciousness Negro dialect, trying to depict the dwellers of the Black Belt as I felt and saw them. My reading in sociology had enabled me to discern many strange types of Negro characters, to identify many modes of Negro behavior; and what moved me above all was the frequency of mental illness, that tragic toll that the urban environment exacted of the black peasant. Perhaps my writing was more an attempt at understanding than self-expression. A need that I did not comprehend made me use words to create religious types, criminal types, the warped, the lost, the baffled; my pages were full of tension, frantic poverty, and death.

But something was missing in my imaginative efforts; my flights of imagination were too subjective, too lacking in reference to social action. I hungered for a grasp of the framework of contemporary living, for a knowledge of the forms of life about me, for eyes to see the bony structures of personality, for theories to light up the shadows of conduct.

While sorting mail in the post office, I met a young Irish chap whose sensibilities amazed me. We would take a batch of mail in our fingers and, while talking in low monotones out of the sides of our mouths, toss them correctly into their designated holes and suddenly our hands would be empty and we would have no memory of having worked. Most of the clerks could work in this automatic manner. The Irish chap and I had read a lot in common and we laughed at the same sacred things. He was as cynical as I was regarding uplift and hope, and we were proud of having escaped what we called the "childhood disease of metaphysical fear." I was introduced to the Irish chap's friends and we formed a "gang" of Irish,

Jewish, and Negro wits who poked fun at government, the masses, statesmen, and political parties. We assumed that all people were good to the degree to which they amused us, or to the extent to which we could make them objects of laughter. We ridiculed all ideas of protest, of organized rebellion or revolution. We felt that all businessmen were thoroughly stupid and that no other group was capable of rising to challenge them. We sneered at voting, for we felt that the choice between one political crook and another was too small for serious thought. We believed that man should live by hard facts alone, and we had so long ago put God out of our minds that we did not even discuss Him.

During this cynical period I met a Negro literary group on Chicago's South Side; it was composed of a dozen or more boys and girls, all of whom possessed academic learning, economic freedom, and vague ambitions to write. I found them more formal in manner than their white counterparts; they wore stylish clothes and were finicky about their personal appearance. I had naïvely supposed that I would have much in common with them, but I found them preoccupied with twisted sex problems. Coming from a station in life which they no doubt would have branded "lower class," I could not understand why they were so all-absorbed with sexual passion. I was encountering for the first time the full-fledged Negro Puritan invert—the emotionally sick—and I discovered that their ideas were but excuses for sex, leads to sex, hints at sex, substitutes for sex. In speech and action they strove to act as un-Negro as possible, denying the racial and material foundations of their lives, accepting their class and racial status in ways so oblique that one had the impression that no difficulties existed for them. Though I had never had any assignments from a college professor, I had made much harder and more prolonged attempts at self-expression than any of them. Swearing love for art, they hovered on the edge of Bohemian life. Always friendly, they could never be anybody's friend; always reading, they could really never learn; always boasting of their passions, they could never really feel and were afraid to live.

The one group I met during those exploring days whose lives enthralled me was the Garveyites, an organization of

black men and women who were forlornly seeking to return
to Africa. Theirs was a passionate rejection of America, for
they sensed with that directness of which only the simple are
capable that they had no chance to live a full human life in
America. Their lives were not cluttered with ideas in which
they could only half believe; they could not create illusions
which made them think they were living when they were not;
their daily lives were too nakedly harsh to permit of camouflage. I understood their emotions, for I partly shared them.

The Garveyites had embraced a totally racialistic outlook
which endowed them with a dignity that I had never seen
before in Negroes. On the walls of their dingy flats were maps
of Africa and India and Japan, pictures of Japanese generals
and admirals, portraits of Marcus Garvey in gaudy regalia, the
faces of colored men and women from all parts of the world. I
gave no credence to the ideology of Garveyism; it was, rather,
the emotional dynamics of its adherents that evoked my admiration. Those Garveyites I knew could never understand why
I liked them but would never follow them, and I pitied them
too much to tell them that they could never achieve their
goal, that Africa was owned by the imperial powers of Europe, that their lives were alien to the mores of the natives of
Africa, that they were people of the West and would forever
be so until they either merged with the West or perished. It
was when the Garveyites spoke fervently of building their
own country, of someday living within the boundaries of a
culture of their own making, that I sensed the passionate
hunger of their lives, that I caught a glimpse of the potential
strength of the American Negro.

Rumors of unemployment came, but I did not listen to
them. I heard of the organizational efforts of the Communist
party among the Negroes of the South Side, but Communist
activities were too remote to strike my mind with any degree
of vividness. Whenever I met a person whom I suspected of
being a Communist, I talked to him affably but from an emotional distance. I sensed that something terrible was beginning to happen in the world, but I tried to shut it out of my
mind by reading and writing.

When the time came for my appointment as a regular clerk,
I was told that no appointments would be made for the time

being. The volume of mail dropped. My hours of work dwindled. My paychecks grew small. Food became scarce at home. The hunger I thought I had left behind returned. One winter afternoon, in 1929, en route to work from the library, I passed a newsstand on which papers blazed:

Stocks Crash—Billions Fade

Most of what I had seen in newspapers had never concerned me, so why should this? Newspapers reported the doings in a life I did not share. But the volume of mail fell so low that I worked but one or two nights a week. In the post-office canteen the boys stood about and talked.

"The cops beat up some demonstrators today."

"The Reds had a picket line around the City Hall."

"Wall Street's cracking down on the country."

"Surplus production's throwing millions out of work."

"There're more than two million unemployed."

"They don't count. They're always out of work."

"Read Karl Marx and get the answer, boys."

"There'll be a revolution if this keeps up."

"Hell, naw. Americans are too dumb to make a revolution."

The post-office job ended and again I was out of work. I could no longer think that the tides of economics were not my concern. But how could I have had any possible say in how the world had been run? I had grown up in complete ignorance of what created jobs. Having been thrust out of the world because of my race, I had accepted my destiny by not being curious about what shaped it.

The following summer I was again called for temporary duty in the post office, and the work lasted into the winter. Aunt Cleo succumbed to a severe cardiac condition and, hard on the heels of her illness, my brother developed stomach ulcers. To rush my worries to a climax, my mother also became ill. I felt that I was maintaining a private hospital. Finally the post-office work ceased altogether and I haunted the city for jobs. But when I went into the streets in the morning I saw sights that killed my hope for the rest of the day. Unemployed men loitered in doorways with blank looks in their eyes, sat dejectedly on front steps in shabby clothing, congregated in sullen groups on street corners, and filled all the empty benches in the parks of Chicago's South Side.

Luck of a sort came when a distant cousin of mine, who was a superintendent in a Negro burial society, offered me a position on his staff as an agent. The thought of selling insurance policies to ignorant Negroes disgusted me.

"Well, if you don't sell them, somebody else will," my cousin told me. "You've got to eat, haven't you?"

During that year I worked for several burial and insurance societies that operated among Negroes, and I received a new kind of education. I found that the burial societies, with some exceptions, were mostly "rackets." Some of them conducted their businesses legitimately, but there were many that exploited the ignorance of their black customers.

I was paid under a system that netted me fifteen dollars for every dollar's worth of new premiums that I placed upon the company's books, and for every dollar's worth of old premiums that lapsed I was penalized fifteen dollars. In addition, I was paid a commission of ten per cent on total premiums collected, but during the depression it was extremely difficult to persuade a black family to buy a policy carrying even a dime premium. I considered myself lucky if, after subtracting lapses from new business, there remained fifteen dollars that I could call my own.

This "gambling" method of remuneration was practiced by some of the burial companies because of the tremendous "turnover" in policyholders, and the companies had to have a constant stream of new business to keep afloat. Whenever a black family moved or suffered a slight reverse in fortune, it usually let its policy lapse and later bought another policy from some other company.

Each day now I saw how the Negro in Chicago lived, for I visited hundreds of dingy flats filled with rickety furniture and ill-clad children. Most of the policyholders were illiterate and did not know that their policies carried clauses severely restricting their benefit payments, and, as an insurance agent, it was not my duty to tell them.

After tramping the streets and pounding on doors to collect premiums, I was dry, strained, too tired to read or write. I hungered for relief and, as a salesman of insurance to many young black girls, I found it. There were many comely black housewives who, trying desperately to keep up their insurance payments, were willing to make bargains to escape paying a ten-cent premium. I had a long, tortured affair with one girl by paying her ten-cent premium each week. She was an illiterate black child with a baby whose father she did not know. During the entire period of my relationship with her, she had but one demand to make of me: She wanted me to take her to a circus. Just what significance circuses had for her, I was never able to learn.

After I had been with her one morning—in exchange for the dime premium—I sat on the sofa in the front room and began to read a book I had with me. She came over shyly.

"Lemme see that," she said.

"What?" I asked.

"That book," she said.

I gave her the book; she looked at it intently. I saw that she was holding it upside down.

"What's in here you keep reading?" she asked.

"Can't you really read?" I asked.

"Naw," she giggled. "You know I can't read."

"You can read *some*," I said.

"Naw," she said.

I stared at her and wondered just what a life like hers meant in the scheme of things, and I came to the conclusion that it meant absolutely nothing. And neither did my life mean anything.

"How come you looking at me that way for?" she asked.

"Nothing."

"You don't talk much."

"There isn't much to say."

"I wished Jim was here," she sighed.

"Who's Jim?" I asked, jealous. I knew that she had other men, but I resented her mentioning them in my presence.

"Just a friend," she said.

I hated her then, then hated myself for coming to her.

"Do you like Jim better than you like me?" I asked.

"Naw. Jim just likes to talk."

"Then why do you be with me, if you like Jim better?" I

asked, trying to make an issue and feeling a wave of disgust because I wanted to.

"You all right," she said, giggling. "I like you."

"I could kill you," I said.

"What?" she exclaimed.

"Nothing," I said, ashamed.

"Kill me, you said? You crazy, man," she said.

"Maybe I am," I muttered, angry that I was sitting beside a human being to whom I could not talk, angry with myself for coming to her, hating my wild and restless loneliness.

"You oughta go home and sleep," she said. "You tired."

"What do you ever think about?" I demanded harshly.

"Lotta things."

"What, for example?"

"You," she said, smiling.

"You know I mean just one dime to you each week," I said.

"Naw, I thinka lotta you."

"Then what do you think?"

" 'Bout how you talk when you talk. I wished I could talk like you," she said seriously.

"Why?" I taunted her.

"When you gonna take me to a circus?" she demanded suddenly.

"You ought to be in a circus," I said.

"I'd like it," she said, her eyes shining.

I wanted to laugh, but her words sounded so sincere that I could not laugh.

"There's no circus in town," I said.

"I bet there is and you won't tell me 'cause you don't wanna take me," she said, pouting.

"But there's no circus in town, I tell you!"

"When will one come?"

"I don't know."

"Can't you read it in the papers?" she asked.

"There's nothing in the papers about a circus."

"There is," she said. "If I could read, I'd find it."

I laughed and she was hurt.

"There *is* a circus in town," she said stoutly.

"There's no circus in town," I said. "But if you want to learn to read, then I'll teach you."

She nestled at my side, giggling.

"See that word?" I said, pointing.

"Yeah."

"That's an 'and,' " I said.

She doubled, giggling.

"What's the matter?" I asked.

She rolled on the floor, giggling.

"What's so funny?" I demanded.

"You," she giggled. "You so funny."

I rose.

"The hell with you," I said.

"Don't you go and cuss me now," she said. "I don't cuss you."

"I'm sorry," I said.

I got my hat and went to the door.

"I'll see you next week?" she asked.

"Maybe," I said.

When I was on the sidewalk, she called to me from a window.

"You promised to take me to a circus, remember?"

"Yes." I walked close to the window. "What is it you like about a circus?"

"The animals," she said simply.

I felt that there was a hidden meaning, perhaps, in what she had said; but I could not find it. She laughed and slammed the window shut.

Each time I left her I resolved not to visit her again. I could not talk to her; I merely listened to her passionate desire to see a circus. She was not calculating; if she liked a man, she just liked him. Sex relations were the only relations she had ever had; no others were possible with her, so limited was her intelligence.

Most of the other agents also had their bought girls and they were extremely anxious to keep other agents from tampering with them. One day a new section of the South Side was given to me as a part of my collection area and the agent from whom the territory had been taken suddenly became very friendly with me.

"Say, Wright," he asked, "did you collect from Ewing at —— Champlain Avenue yet?"

"Yes," I answered, after consulting my book.

"How did you like her?" he asked, staring at me.

"She's a good-looking number," I said.

"You had anything to do with her yet?" he asked.

"No, but I'd like to," I said, laughing.

"Look," he said. "I'm a friend of yours."

"Since when?" I countered.

"No, I'm really a friend," he said.

"What's on your mind?"

"Listen, that gal's sick," he said seriously.

"What do you mean?"

"She's got the clap," he said. "Keep away from her. She'll lay with anybody."

"Gee, I'm glad you told me," I said.

"You had your eye on her, didn't you?" he asked.

"Yes, I did," I said.

"Leave her alone," he said. "She'll get you down."

That night I told my cousin what the agent had said about Miss Ewing. My cousin laughed.

"That gal's all right," he said. "That agent's been fooling around with her. He told you she had a disease so that you'd be scared to bother her. He was protecting her from you."

That was the way the black women were regarded by the black agents. Some of the agents were vicious; if they had claims to pay to a sick black woman and if the woman was able to have sex relations with them, they would insist upon it, using the claim money as a bribe. If the woman refused, they would report to the office that the woman was a malingerer. The average black woman would submit because she needed the money badly.

As an insurance agent, it was necessary for me to take part in one swindle. It appears that the burial society had originally issued a policy that was—from their point of view—too liberal in its provisions, and the officials decided to exchange the policies then in the hands of their clients for other policies carrying stricter clauses; of course, this had to be done in a manner that would not allow the policyholder to know that his policy was being switched, that he was being swindled. I did not like it, but there was only one thing I could do to keep from being a party to it: I could quit and starve. But I did not feel that being honest was worth the price of starvation.

The swindle worked in this way. In my visits to the homes of policyholders to collect premiums, I was accompanied by the superintendent who claimed to the policyholder that he was making a routine inspection. The policyholder, usually an illiterate black woman, would dig up her policy from the bottom of a trunk or a chest and hand it to the superintendent. Meanwhile I would be marking the woman's premium book, an act which would distract her from what the superintendent was doing. The superintendent would exchange the old policy for a new one which was identical in color, serial number, and beneficiary, but which carried much smaller payments. It was dirty work and I wondered how I could stop it. And when I could think of no safe way I would curse myself and the victims and forget about it. (The black owners of the burial societies were leaders in the Negro communities and were respected by whites.)

As I went from house to house collecting money, I saw black men mounted upon soapboxes at street corners, bellowing about bread, rights, and revolution. I liked their courage, but I doubted their wisdom. The speakers claimed that Negroes were angry, that they were about to rise and join their white fellow workers to make a revolution. I was in and out of many Negro homes each day and I knew that the Negroes were lost, ignorant, sick in mind and body. I saw that a vast distance separated the agitators from the masses, a distance so vast that the agitators did not know how to appeal to the people they sought to lead.

Some mornings I found leaflets on my steps telling of China, Russia, and Germany; on some days I witnessed as many as five thousand jobless Negroes, led by Communists, surging through the streets. I would watch them with an aching heart, firmly convinced that they were being duped; but if I had been asked to give them another solution for their problems, I would not have known how.

It became a habit of mine to visit Washington Park of an afternoon after collecting a part of my premiums, and I would wander through crowds of unemployed Negroes, pausing here and there to sample the dialectic or indignation of

Communist speakers. What I heard and saw baffled and angered me. The Negro Communists were deliberately careless in their personal appearance, wearing their shirt collars turned in to make V's at their throats, wearing their caps—they wore caps because Lenin had worn caps—with the visors turned backward, tilted upward at the nape of their necks. Many of their mannerisms, pronunciations, and turns of speech had been consciously copied from white Communists whom they had recently met. While engaged in conversation, they stuck their thumbs in their suspenders or put their left hands into their shirt bosoms or hooked their thumbs into their back pockets as they had seen Lenin or Stalin do in photographs. Though they did not know it, they were naïvely practicing magic; they thought that if they acted like the men who had overthrown the czar, then surely they ought to be able to win their freedom in America.

In speaking they rolled their "r's" in Continental style, pronouncing "party" as "parrrtee," stressing the last syllable, having picked up the habit from white Communists. "Comrades" became "cumrrrades," and "distribute," which they had known how to pronounce all their lives, was twisted into "distrrribuuute," with the accent on the last instead of the second syllable, a mannerism which they copied from Polish Communist immigrants who did not know how to pronounce the word. Many sensitive Negroes agreed with the Communist program but refused to join their ranks because of the shabby quality of those Negroes whom the Communists had already admitted to membership.

When speaking from the platform, the Negro Communists, eschewing the traditional gestures of the Negro preacher—as though they did not possess the strength to develop their own style of Communist preaching—stood straight, threw back their heads, brought the edge of the right palm down hammerlike into the outstretched left palm in a series of jerky motions to pound their points home, a mannerism that characterized Lenin's method of speaking. When they walked, their stride quickened; all the peasant hesitancy of their speech vanished as their voices became clipped, terse. In debate they interrupted their opponents in a tone of voice that was an octave higher, and if their opponents raised their voices to be heard, the Communists raised theirs still higher until shouts rang out over the park. Hence, the only truth that prevailed was that which could be shouted and quickly understood.

Their emotional certainty seemed buttressed by access to a fund of knowledge denied to ordinary men, but a day's observation of their activities was sufficient to reveal all their thought processes. An hour's listening disclosed the fanatical intolerance of minds sealed against new ideas, new facts, new feelings, new attitudes, new hints at ways to live. They denounced books they had never read, people they had never known, ideas they could never understand, and doctrines whose names they could not pronounce. Communism, instead of making them leap forward with fire in their hearts to become masters of ideas and life, had frozen them at an even lower level of ignorance than had been theirs before they met Communism.

When Hoover threatened to drive the bonus marchers from Washington, one Negro Communist speaker said:

"If he drives the bonus marchers out of Washington, the people will rise up and make a revolution!"

I went to him, determined to get at what he really meant.

"You know that even if the United States Army actually kills the bonus marchers, there'll be no revolution," I said.

"You don't know the indignation of the masses!" he exploded.

"But you don't seem to know what it takes to make a revolution," I explained. "Revolutions are rare occurrences."

"You underestimate the masses," he told me.

"No, I know the masses of Negroes very well," I said. "But I don't believe that a revolution is pending. Revolutions come through concrete historical processes . . ."

"You're an intellectual," he said, smiling disdainfully.

A few days later, after Hoover had had the bonus marchers driven from Washington at the point of bayonets, I accosted him:

"What about that revolution you predicted if the bonus marchers were driven out?" I asked.

"The prerequisite conditions did not exist," he shrugged and muttered.

I left him, wondering why he felt it necessary to make so many ridiculous overstatements. I could not refute the general Communist analysis of the world; the only drawback was that their world was just too simple for belief. I liked their readiness to act, but they seemed lost in folly, wandering in a fantasy. For them there was no yesterday or tomorrow, only the living moment of today; their only task was to annihilate the enemy that confronted them in any manner possible.

At times their speeches, glowing with rebellion, were downright offensive to lowly, hungry Negroes. Once a Negro Communist speaker, inveighing against religion, said:

"There ain't no goddamn God! If there is, I hereby challenge Him to strike me dead!"

He paused dramatically before his vast black audience for God to act, but God declined. He then pulled out his watch.

"Maybe God didn't hear me!" he yelled. "I'll give Him two more minutes!" Then, with sarcasm: "Mister God, kill me!"

He waited, looking mockingly at his watch. The audience laughed uneasily.

"I'll tell you where to find God," the speaker went on in a hard, ranting voice. "When it rains at midnight, take your hat, turn it upside down on a floor in a dark room, and you'll have God!"

I had to admit that I had never heard atheism of so militant a nature; but the Communist speaker seemed to be amusing and frightening the people more than he was convincing them.

"If there is a God up there in that empty sky," the speaker roared on, "I'll reach up there and grab Him by His beard and jerk Him down here on this hungry earth and cut His throat!" He wagged his head. "Now, let God dare me!"

The audience was shocked into silence for a moment, then it yelled with delight. I shook my head and walked away. That was not the way to destroy people's outworn beliefs . . . They were acting like irresponsible children . . .

I was now convinced that they did not know the complex nature of Negro life, did not know how great was the task to which they had set themselves. They had rejected the state of things as they were, and that seemed to me to be the first step toward embracing a creative attitude toward life. I felt that it was not until one wanted the world to be different that one could look at the world with will and emotion. But these men had rejected what was before their eyes without quite knowing what they had rejected and why.

I felt that the Negro could not live a full, human life under the conditions imposed upon him by America; and I felt, too, that America, for different reasons, could not live a full, human life. It seemed to me, then, that if the Negro solved his problem, he would be solving infinitely more than his problem alone. I felt certain that the Negro could never solve his problem until the deeper problem of American civilization had been faced and solved. And because the Negro was the most cast-out of all the outcast people in America, I felt that no other group in America could tackle this problem of what our American lives meant so well as the Negro could.

But, as I listened to the Communist Negro speakers, I wondered if the Negro, blasted by three hundred years of oppression, could possibly cast off his fear and corruption and rise to the task. Could the Negro ever possess himself, learn to know what had happened to him in relation to the aspirations of Western society? It seemed to me that for the Negro to try to save himself he would have to forget himself and try to save a confused, materialistic nation from its own drift toward self-destruction. Could the Negro accomplish this miracle? Could he take up his bed and walk?

Election time was nearing and a Negro Republican precinct captain asked me to help him round up votes. I had no interest in the candidates, but I needed the money. I went from door to door with the precinct captain and discovered that the whole business was one long process of bribery, that people voted for three dollars, for the right to continue their illicit trade in sex or alcohol. On election day I went into the polling booth and drew the curtain behind me and unfolded my ballots. As I stood there the sordid implications of politics flashed through my mind. "Big Bill" Thompson headed the local Republican machine and I knew that he was using the Negro vote to control the city hall; in turn, he was engaged in vast political deals of which the Negro voters, political innocents, had no notion. With my pencil I wrote in a determined scrawl across the face of the ballots:

I Protest This Fraud

I knew that my gesture was futile. But I wanted somebody to know that out of that vast sea of ignorance in the Black Belt there was at least one person who knew the game for what it was. I collected my ten dollars and went home.

The depression deepened and I could not sell insurance to hungry Negroes. I sold my watch and scouted for cheaper rooms; I found a rotting building and rented an apartment in it. The place was dismal; plaster was falling from the walls; the wooden stairs sagged. When my mother saw it, she wept. I felt bleak. I had not done what I had come to the city to do.

One morning I rose and my mother told me that there was no food for breakfast. I knew that the city had opened relief stations, but each time I thought of going into one of them I burned with shame. I sat for hours, fighting hunger, avoiding my mother's eyes. Then I rose, put on my hat and coat, and went out. As I walked toward the Cook County Bureau of Public Welfare to plead for bread, I knew that I had come to the end of something.

Chapter XVII

WHEN I REACHED the relief station, I felt that I was making a public confession of my hunger. I sat waiting for hours, resentful of the mass of hungry people about me. My turn finally came and I was questioned by a middle-class Negro woman who asked me for a short history of my life. As I waited again I became aware of something happening in the room. The black men and women were mumbling quietly among themselves; they had not known one another before they had come here, but now their timidity and shame were wearing off and they were exchanging experiences. Before this they had lived as individuals, each somewhat afraid of the other, each seeking his own pleasure, each stanch in that degree of Americanism that had been allowed him. But now life had tossed them together, and they were learning to know the sentiments of their neighbors for the first time; their talking was enabling them to sense the collectivity of their lives, and some of their fear was passing.

Did the relief officials realize what was happening? No. If they had, they would have stopped it. But they saw their "clients" through the eyes of their profession, saw only what their "science" allowed them to see. As I listened to the talk I could see black minds shedding many illusions. These people now knew that the past had betrayed them, had cast them out; but they did not know what the future would be like, did not know what they wanted. Yes, some of the things that the Communists said were true; they maintained that there came times in history when a ruling class could no longer rule, and I sat looking at the beginnings of anarchy. To permit the birth of this new consciousness in these people was proof that those who ruled did not quite know what they were doing, assuming that they were trying to save themselves and their class. Had they understood what was happening, they would never have allowed millions of perplexed and defeated people to sit together for long hours and talk, for out of their talk was rising a new realization of life. And once this new conception of themselves had formed, no power on earth could alter it.

I left the relief station with the promise that food would be sent to me, but I also left with a knowledge that the relief officials had not wanted to give to me. I had felt the possibility of creating a new understanding of life in the minds of people rejected by the society in which they lived, people to whom the Chicago *Daily Tribune* referred contemptuously as the "idle" ones, as though these people had deliberately sought their present state of helplessness.

Who would give these people a meaningful way of life? Communist theory defined these people as the molders of the future of mankind, but the Communist speeches I had heard in the park had mocked that definition. These people, of course, were not ready for a revolution; they had not abandoned their past lives by choice, but because they simply could not live the old way any longer. Now, what new faith would they embrace? The day I begged bread from the city officials was the day that showed me I was not alone in my loneliness, society had cast millions of others with me. But how could I be with them? How many understood what was happening? My mind swam with questions that I could not answer.

I was slowly beginning to comprehend the meaning of my environment; a sense of direction was beginning to emerge from the conditions of my life. I began to feel something more powerful than I could express. My speech and manner changed. My cynicism slid from me. I grew open and questioning. I wanted to know.

(If I were a member of the class that rules, I would post men in all the neighborhoods of the nation, not to spy upon or club rebellious workers, not to break strikes or disrupt unions; but to ferret out those who no longer respond to the system in which they live. I would make it known that the real danger does not stem from those who seek to grab their share of wealth through force, or from those who try to defend their property through violence, for both of these groups, by their affirmative acts, support the values of the system in which they live. The millions that I would fear are those who do not dream of the prizes that the nation holds forth, for it is in them, though they may not know it, that a revolution has taken place and is biding its time to translate itself into a new and strange way of life.

(I feel that the Negroes' relation to America is symbolically peculiar, and from the Negroes' ultimate reactions to their trapped state a lesson can be learned about America's future. Negroes are told in a language they cannot possibly misunderstand that their native land is not their own; and when they, acting upon impulses which they share with whites, try to assert a claim to their birthright, whites retaliate with terror, never pausing to consider the consequences should the Negroes give up completely. They never dream that they would face a situation far more terrifying if they were confronted by Negroes who made no claims at all than by those who are buoyed by social aggressiveness. My knowledge of how Negroes react to their plight makes me declare that no man can possibly be individually guilty of treason, that an insurgent act is but a man's desperate answer to those who twist his environment so that he cannot fully share the spirit of his native land. Treason is a crime of the state.)

Christmas came and I was once more called to the post office for temporary work. Again I met the Irish chap and we discussed world happenings, the vast armies of unemployed, the rising tide of radical action. I now detected a change in the attitudes of the whites I met; their privations were making them regard Negroes with new eyes, and for the first time I was invited to their homes.

When the work in the post office ended, I was assigned by the relief system as an orderly to a medical research institute in one of the largest and wealthiest hospitals in Chicago. I cleaned operating rooms, dog, rat, mice, cat, and rabbit pens, and fed guinea pigs. Four of us Negroes worked there and we occupied an underworld position, remembering that we must restrict ourselves—when not engaged upon some task—to the basement corridors so that we would not mingle with white nurses, doctors, or visitors.

The sharp line of racial division drawn by the hospital authorities came to me the first morning when I walked along an underground corridor and saw two long lines of women coming toward me. A line of white girls marched past, clad in starched uniforms that gleamed white; their faces were alert, their steps quick, their bodies lean and shapely, their shoulders erect, their faces lit with the light of purpose. And after them came a line of black girls, old, fat, dressed in ragged gingham, walking loosely, carrying tin cans of soap powder, rags, mops, brooms . . . I wondered what law of the universe kept them from being mixed? The sun would not have stopped shining had there been a few black girls in the first line, and the earth would not have stopped whirling on its axis had there been a few white girls in the second line. But the two lines I saw graded status in purely racial terms.

Of the three Negroes who worked with me, one was a boy of about my own age, Bill, who was either sleepy or drunk most of the time. Bill straightened his hair and I suspected that he kept a bottle hidden somewhere in the piles of hay which we fed to the guinea pigs. He did not like me and I did not like him, though I tried harder than he to conceal my dislike. We had nothing in common except that we were both black and lost. While I contained my frustration, he drank to drown his. Often I tried to talk to him, tried in simple words to convey to him some of my ideas, and he would listen in sullen silence. Then one day he came to me with an angry look on his face.

"I got it," he said.

"You've got what?" I asked.

"This old race problem you keep talking about," he said.

"What about it?"

"Well, it's this way," he explained seriously. "Let the government give every man a gun and five bullets, then let us all start over again. Make it just like it was in the beginning. The ones who come out on top, white or black, let them rule."

His simplicity terrified me. I had never met a Negro who was so irredeemably brutalized. I stopped pumping my ideas into Bill's brain for fear that the fumes of alcohol might send him reeling toward some fantastic fate.

The two other Negroes were elderly and had been employed in the institute for fifteen years or more. One was Brand, a short, black, morose bachelor; the other was Cooke, a tall, yellow, spectacled fellow who spent his spare time keeping track of world events through the Chicago *Daily Tribune*. Brand and Cooke hated each other for a reason that I was

never able to determine, and they spent a good part of each
day quarreling.

When I began working at the institute, I recalled my adolescent dream of wanting to be a medical research worker.
Daily I saw young Jewish boys and girls receiving instruction
in chemistry and medicine that the average black boy or girl
could never receive. When I was alone, I wandered and poked
my fingers into strange chemicals, watched intricate machines
trace red and black lines upon ruled paper. At times I paused
and stared at the walls of the rooms, at the floors, at the wide
desks at which the white doctors sat; and I realized—with a
feeling that I could never quite get used to—that I was looking at the world of another race.

My interest in what was happening in the institute amused
the three other Negroes with whom I worked. They had no
curiosity about "white folks' things," while I wanted to know
if the dogs being treated for diabetes were getting well; if
the rats and mice in whom cancer had been induced showed
any signs of responding to treatment. I wanted to know the
principle that lay behind the Aschheim-Zondek tests that
were made with rabbits, the Wassermann tests that were made
with guinea pigs. But when I asked a timid question I found
that even Jewish doctors had learned to imitate the sadistic
method of humbling a Negro that the native-born whites
had cultivated.

"If you know too much, boy, your brains might explode," a
doctor said one day.

Each Saturday morning I assisted a young Jewish doctor in
slitting the vocal cords of a fresh batch of dogs from the
city pound. The object was to devocalize the dogs so that
their howls would not disturb the patients in the other parts
of the hospital. I held each dog as the doctor injected nembutal into its veins to make it unconscious; then I held the
dog's jaws open as the doctor inserted the scalpel and severed
the vocal cords. Later, when the dogs came to, they would lift
their heads to the ceiling and gape in a soundless wail. The
sight became lodged in my imagination as a symbol of silent
suffering.

To me nembutal was a powerful and mysterious liquid
but when I asked questions about its properties I could not

obtain a single intelligent answer. The young Jewish doctor simply ignored me with:

"Come on. Bring the next dog. I haven't got all day."

One Saturday morning, after I had held the dogs for their vocal cords to be slit, the doctor left the nembutal on a bench. I picked it up, uncorked it, and smelt it. It was odorless. Suddenly Brand ran to me with a stricken face.

"What're you doing?" he asked.

"I was smelling this stuff to see if it had any odor," I said.

"Did you really smell it?" he asked me.

"Yes."

"Oh, God!" he exclaimed.

"What's the matter?" I asked.

"You shouldn't've done that!" he shouted.

"Why?"

He grabbed my arm and jerked me across the room.

"Come on!" he yelled, snatching open the door.

"What's the matter?" I asked.

"I gotta get you to a doctor 'fore it's too late," he gasped.

Had my foolish curiosity made me inhale something dangerous?

"But . . . Is it poisonous?"

"Run, boy!" he said, pulling me. "You'll fall dead."

Filled with fear, with Brand pulling my arm, I rushed out of the room, raced across a rear areaway, into another room, then down a long corridor. I wanted to ask Brand what symptoms I must expect, but we were running too fast. Brand finally stopped, gasping for breath. My heart beat wildly and my blood pounded in my head. Brand then dropped to the concrete floor, stretched out on his back and yelled with laughter, shaking all over. He beat his fists against the concrete; he moaned, giggled.

I tried to master my outrage, wondering if some of the white doctors had told him to play the joke. He rose and wiped tears from his eyes, still laughing. I walked away from him. He knew that I was angry and he followed me.

"Don't get mad," he gasped through his laughter.

"Go to hell," I said.

"I couldn't help it," he giggled. "You looked at me like you'd believe anything I said. Man, you was scared . . ."

He leaned against the wall, laughing again, stomping his feet. I was angry, for I felt that he would spread the story. I knew that Bill and Cooke never ventured beyond the safe bounds of Negro living, and they would never blunder into anything like this. And if they heard about this, they would laugh for months.

"Brand, if you mention this, I'll kill you," I swore.

"You ain't mad?" he asked, laughing, staring at me through tears.

Sniffing, Brand walked ahead of me. I followed him back into the room that housed the dogs. All day, while at some task, he would pause and giggle, then smother it with his hand, looking at me out of the corner of his eyes, shaking his head. He laughed at me for a week. I kept my temper and let him amuse himself. I finally found out the properties of nembutal by consulting medical books, but I never told Brand.

One summer morning, just as I began work, a young Jewish boy came to me with a stop watch in his hand.

"Dr. —— wants me to time you when you clean a room," he said. "We're trying to make the institute more efficient."

"I'm doing my work and getting through on time," I said.

"This is the boss's order," he said.

"Why don't you work for a change?" I blurted, angry.

"Now, look," he said. "*This* is my work. Now *you* work."

I got mop and pail, sprayed a room with disinfectant, and scrubbed at coagulated blood and hardened dog, rat, and rabbit feces. The normal temperature of a room was ninety, but as the sun beat down upon the skylights, the temperature rose above a hundred. Stripped to my waist, I slung the mop, moving steadily like a machine, hearing the Jewish boy press the button on the stop watch as I finished cleaning a room. I worked from seven in the morning until noon, and I was limp, washed-out.

"Well, how is it?" I asked.

"It took you seventeen minutes to clean that last room," he said. "That ought to be the time for each room."

"That room was not very dirty," I said.

"You have seventeen rooms to clean," he went on as though I had not spoken. "Seventeen times seventeen make four hours and forty-nine minutes." He wrote upon a little pad. "After lunch, clean the five flights of stone stairs. I timed a boy who scrubbed one step and multiplied that time by the number of steps. You ought to be through at six."

"Suppose I want relief?" I asked.

"You'll manage," he said and left.

Never had I felt so much the slave as when I scoured those stone steps each afternoon. Working against time, I would wet five steps, sprinkle soap powder, then a white doctor or a nurse would come and, instead of avoiding the soppy steps, walk on them and track the dirty water onto the steps that I had already cleaned. To obviate this, I cleaned but two steps at a time, a distance over which a ten-year-old child could step. But it did no good. The white people still plopped their feet down into the dirty water and muddied the other clean steps. If I ever really hotly hated unthinking whites, it was then. Not once during my entire stay at the institute did a single white person show enough courtesy to avoid a wet step. I would be on my knees, scrubbing, sweating, pouring out what limited energy my body could wring from my meager diet, and I would hear feet approaching. I would pause and curse with tense lips:

"These sonofabitches are going to dirty these steps again, goddamn their souls to hell!"

Sometimes a sadistically observant white man would notice that he had tracked dirty water up the steps, and he would look back down at me and smile and say:

"Boy, we sure keep you busy, don't we?"

And I would not be able to answer.

The feud that went on between Brand and Cooke continued. Although they were working daily in a building where scientific history was being made, the light of curiosity was never in their eyes. They were conditioned to their racial "place," had learned to see only a part of the whites and the white world; and the whites, too, had learned to see only a part of the lives of the blacks and their world.

Perhaps Brand and Cooke, lacking interests that could absorb them, fuming like children over trifles, simply invented their hate of each other in order to have something to feel deeply about. Or perhaps there was in them a vague psyche pain stemming from their chronically frustrating way of life, a pain whose cause they did not know; and, like those de-vocalized dogs, they would whirl and snap at the air when their old pain struck them. Anyway, they argued about the weather, sports, sex, war, race, politics, and religion; neither of them knew the subjects they debated, but it seemed that the less they knew the better they could argue.

The tug of war between the two elderly men reached a cli-max one winter day at noon. It was incredibly cold and an icy gale swept up and down the Chicago streets with blizzard force. The door of the animal-filled room was locked, for we always insisted that we be allowed one hour in which to eat and rest. Bill and I were sitting on wooden boxes, eating our lunches out of paper bags. Brand was washing his hands at the sink. Cooke was sitting on a rickety stool, munching an apple and reading the Chicago *Daily Tribune*.

Now and then a devocalized dog lifted his nose to the ceil-ing and howled soundlessly. The room was filled with many rows of high steel tiers. Perched upon each of these tiers were layers of steel cages containing the dogs, rats, mice, rabbits, and guinea pigs. Each cage was labeled in some indecipher-able scientific jargon. Along the walls of the room were long charts with zigzagging red and black lines that traced the success or failure of some experiment. The lonely piping of guinea pigs floated unheeded about us. Hay rustled as a rab-bit leaped restlessly about in its pen. A rat scampered around in its steel prison. Cooke tapped the newspaper for attention.

"It says here," Cooke mumbled through a mouthful of apple, "that this is the coldest day since 1888."

Bill and I sat unconcerned. Brand chuckled softly.

"What in hell you laughing about?" Cooke demanded of Brand.

"You can't believe what that damn *Tribune* says," Brand said.

"How come I can't?" Cooke demanded. "It's the world's greatest newspaper."

Brand did not reply; he shook his head pityingly and chuckled again.

"Stop that damn laughing at me!" Cooke said angrily.

"I laugh as much as I wanna," Brand said. "You don't know

what you talking about. The *Herald-Examiner* says it's the coldest day since 1873."

"But the *Trib* oughta know," Cooke countered. "It's older'n that *Examiner*."

"That damn *Trib* don't know nothing!" Brand drowned out Cooke's voice.

"How in hell you know?" Cooke asked with rising anger.

The argument waxed until Cooke shouted that if Brand did not shut up he was going to "cut his black throat."

Brand whirled from the sink, his hands dripping soapy water, his eyes blazing.

"Take that back," Brand said.

"I take nothing back! What you wanna do about it?" Cooke taunted.

The two elderly Negroes glared at each other. I wondered if the quarrel was really serious, or if it would turn out harmlessly as so many others had done.

Suddenly Cooke dropped the Chicago *Daily Tribune* and pulled a long knife from his pocket; his thumb pressed a button and a gleaming steel blade leaped out. Brand stepped back quickly and seized an ice pick that was stuck in a wooden board above the sink.

"Put that knife down," Brand said.

"Stay 'way from me, or I'll cut your throat," Cooke warned.

Brand lunged with the ice pick. Cooke dodged out of range. They circled each other like fighters in a prize ring. The cancerous and tubercular rats and mice leaped about their cages. The guinea pigs whistled in fright. The diabetic dogs bared their teeth and barked soundlessly in our direction. The Aschheim-Zondek rabbits flopped their ears and tried to hide in the corners of their pens. Cooke now crouched and sprang forward with the knife. Bill and I jumped to our feet, speechless with surprise. Brand retreated. The eyes of both men were hard and unblinking; they were breathing deeply.

"Say, cut it out!" I called in alarm.

"Them damn fools is really fighting," Bill said in amazement.

Slashing at each other, Brand and Cooke surged up and down the aisles of steel tiers. Suddenly Brand uttered a bellow and charged into Cooke and swept him violently backward.

Cooke grasped Brand's hand to keep the ice pick from sinking into his chest. Brand broke free and charged Cooke again, sweeping him into an animal-filled steel tier. The tier balanced itself on its edge for an indecisive moment, then toppled.

Like kingpins, one steel tier lammed into another, then they all crashed to the floor with a sound as of the roof falling. The whole aspect of the room altered quicker than the eye could follow. Brand and Cooke stood stock-still, their eyes fastened upon each other, their pointed weapons raised; but they were dimly aware of the havoc that churned about them.

The steel tiers lay jumbled; the doors of the cages swung open. Rats and mice and dogs and rabbits moved over the floor in wild panic. The Wassermann guinea pigs were squealing as though judgment day had come. Here and there an animal had been crushed beneath a cage.

All four of us looked at one another. We knew what this meant. We might lose our jobs. We were already regarded as black dunces, and if the doctors saw this mess they would take it as final proof. Bill rushed to the door to make sure that it was locked. I glanced at the clock and saw that it was 12:30. We had one half hour of grace.

"Come on," Bill said uneasily. "We got to get this place cleaned."

Brand and Cooke stared at each other, both doubting.

"Give me your knife, Cooke," I said.

"Naw! Take Brand's ice pick *first*," Cooke said.

"The hell you say!" Brand said. "Take his knife *first!*"

A knock sounded at the door.

"Sssshh," Bill said.

We waited. We heard footsteps going away. We'll all lose our jobs, I thought.

Persuading the fighters to surrender their weapons was a difficult task, but at last it was done and we could begin to right things. Slowly Brand stooped and tugged at one end of a steel tier. Cooke stooped to help him. Both men seemed to be acting in a dream. Soon, however, all four of us were working frantically, watching the clock.

As we labored we conspired to keep the fight a secret: we agreed to tell the doctors—if any should ask—that we had not been in the room during our lunch hour; we felt that that lie would explain why no one had unlocked the door when the knock had come.

We righted the tiers and replaced the cages; then we were faced with the impossible task of sorting the cancerous rats and mice, the diabetic dogs, the Aschheim-Zondek rabbits, and the Wassermann guinea pigs. Whether we kept our jobs or not depended upon how shrewdly we could cover up all evidence of the fight. It was pure guesswork, but we had to try to put the animals back into the correct cages. We knew that certain rats or mice went into certain cages, but we did not know *what* rat or mouse went into *what* cage. We did not know a tubercular mouse from a cancerous mouse; the white doctors had made sure that we would not know. They had never taken time to answer a single question; though we worked in the institute, we were as remote from the meaning of the experiments as if we lived in the moon. The doctors had laughed at what they felt was our childlike interest in the fate of the animals.

First we sorted the dogs; that was fairly easy, for we could remember the size and color of most of them. But the rats and mice and guinea pigs baffled us completely.

We put our heads together and pondered, down in the underworld of the great scientific institute. It was a strange scientific conference; the fate of the entire medical research institute rested in our ignorant, black hands.

We remembered the number of rats, mice, or guinea pigs—we had to handle them several times each day—that went into a given cage, and we supplied the number helter-skelter from those animals that we could catch running loose on the floor. We discovered that many rats, mice, and guinea pigs were missing; they had been killed in the scuffle. We solved that problem by taking healthy stock from other cages and putting them into cages with sick animals. We repeated this process until we were certain that, numerically at least, all the animals with which the doctors were experimenting were accounted for.

The rabbits came last. We broke the rabbits down into two general groups: those that had fur on their bellies and those that did not. We knew that all those rabbits that had shaven bellies—our scientific knowledge adequately covered this point because it was our job to shave the rabbits—were undergoing Aschheim-Zondek tests. But in what pen did a given rabbit belong? We did not know. I solved the problem very simply. I counted the shaven rabbits; they numbered seventeen. I counted the pens labeled "Aschheim-Zondek," then proceeded to drop a shaven rabbit into each pen at random. And again we were numerically successful. At least white America had taught us how to count . . .

Lastly we carefully wrapped all the dead animals in newspapers and hid their bodies in a garbage can.

At a few minutes to one the room was in order; that is, the kind of order that we four Negroes could figure out. I unlocked the door and we sat waiting, whispering, vowing secrecy, wondering what the reaction of the doctors would be.

Finally a doctor came, gray-haired, white-coated, spectacled, efficient, serious, taciturn, bearing a tray upon which sat a bottle of mysterious fluid and a hypodermic needle.

"My rats, please."

Cooke shuffled forward to serve him. We held our breath. Cooke got the cage which he knew the doctor always called for at that hour and brought it forward. One by one, Cooke took out the rats and held them as the doctor solemnly injected the mysterious fluid under their skins.

"Thank you, Cooke," the doctor murmured.

"Not at all, sir," Cooke mumbled with a suppressed gasp.

When the doctor had gone we looked at one another, hardly daring to believe that our secret would be kept. We were so anxious that we did not know whether to curse or laugh. Another doctor came.

"Give me A-Z rabbit number 14."

"Yes, sir," I said.

I brought him the rabbit and he took it upstairs to the operating room. We waited for repercussions. None came.

All that afternoon the doctors came and went. I would run into the room—stealing a few seconds from my step scrubbing—and ask what progress was being made and would learn that the doctors had detected nothing. At quitting time we felt triumphant.

"They won't never know," Cooke boasted in a whisper.

I saw Brand stiffen. I knew that he was aching to dispute Cooke's optimism, but the memory of the fight he had just had was so fresh in his mind that he could not speak.

Another day went by and nothing happened. Then another day. The doctors examined the animals and wrote in their little black books, in their big black books, and continued to trace red and black lines upon the charts.

A week passed and we felt out of danger. Not one question had been asked.

· Of course, we four black men were much too modest to make our contribution known, but we often wondered what went on in the laboratories after that secret disaster. Was some scientific hypothesis, well on its way to validation and ultimate public use, discarded because of unexpected findings on that cold winter day? Was some tested principle given a new and strange refinement because of fresh, remarkable evidence? Did some brooding research worker—those who held stop watches and slopped their feet carelessly in the water of the steps I tried so hard to keep clean—get a wild, if brief, glimpse of a new scientific truth? Well, we never heard . . .

I brooded, of course, upon whether I should have gone to the director's office and told him what had happened, but each time I thought of it I remembered that the director had been the man who had ordered the boy to stand over me while I was working and time my movements with a stop watch. He did not regard me as a human being. I did not share his world. I earned thirteen dollars a week and I had to support four people with it, and should I risk that thirteen dollars by acting idealistically? Brand and Cooke would have hated me and would have eventually driven me from the job had I "told" on them. The hospital kept us four Negroes, as though we were close kin to the animals we tended, huddled together down in the underworld corridors of the hospital, separated by a vast psychological distance from the significant processes of the rest of the hospital—just as America had kept us locked in the dark underworld of American life for three hundred years—and we had made our own code of ethics, values, loyalty.

Chapter XVIII

O NE THURSDAY NIGHT I received an invitation from a group of white boys I had known in the post office to meet in a South Side hotel and argue the state of the world. About ten of us gathered and ate salami sandwiches, drank beer, and talked. I was amazed to discover that many of them had joined the Communist party. I challenged them by reciting the antics of the Negro Communists I had seen in the parks, and I was told that those antics were "tactics" and were all right. I was dubious.

Then one Thursday night Sol, a Jewish chap, startled us by announcing that he had had a short story accepted by a little magazine called the *Anvil*, edited by Jack Conroy, and that he had joined a revolutionary artists' organization, the John Reed Club. Sol repeatedly begged me to attend the meetings of the club, but I always found an easy excuse for refusing.

"You'd like them," Sol said.

"I don't want to be organized," I said.

"They can help you to write," he said.

"Nobody can tell me how or what to write," I said.

"Come and see," he urged. "What have you to lose?"

I felt that Communists could not possibly have a sincere interest in Negroes. I was cynical and I would rather have heard a white man say that he hated Negroes, which I could have readily believed, than to have heard him say that he respected Negroes, which would have made me doubt him. I did not think that there existed many whites who, through intellectual effort, could lift themselves out of the traditions of their times and see the Negro objectively.

One Saturday night, sitting home idle, not caring to visit the girls I had met on my former insurance route, bored with reading, I decided to appear at the John Reed Club in the capacity of an amused spectator. I rode to the Loop and found the number. A dark stairway led upwards; it did not look welcoming. What on earth of importance could transpire in so dingy a place? Through the windows above me I saw

vague murals along the walls. I mounted the stairs to a door
that was lettered:

The Chicago John Reed Club

I opened it and stepped into the strangest room I had ever
seen. Paper and cigarette butts lay on the floor. A few benches
ran along the walls, above which were vivid colors depicting
colossal figures of workers carrying streaming banners. The
mouths of the workers gaped in wild cries; their legs were
sprawled over cities.

"Hello."

I turned and saw a white man smiling at me.

"A friend of mine, who's a member of this club, asked me
to visit here. His name is Sol ——," I told him.

"You're welcome here," the white man said. "We're not
having an affair tonight. We're holding an editorial meeting.
Do you paint?" He was slightly gray and he had a mustache.

"No," I said. "I try to write."

"Then sit in on the editorial meeting of our magazine, *Left
Front*," he suggested.

"I know nothing of editing," I said.

"You can learn," he said.

I stared at him, doubting.

"I don't want to be in the way here," I said.

"My name's Grimm," he said.

I told him my name and we shook hands. He went to a
closet and returned with an armful of magazines.

"Here are some back issues of the *Masses*," he said. "Have
you ever read it?"

"No," I said.

"Some of the best writers in America publish in it," he explained. He also gave me copies of a magazine called *International Literature*. "There's stuff here from Gide, Gorky . . ."

I assured him that I would read them. He took me to an
office and introduced me to a Jewish boy who was to become
one of the nation's leading painters, to a chap who was to
become one of the eminent composers of his day, to a writer
who was to create some of the best novels of his generation,
to a young Jewish boy who was destined to film the Nazi
invasion of Czechoslovakia. I was meeting men and women

whom I would know for decades to come, who were to form the first sustained relationships in my life.

I sat in a corner and listened while they discussed their magazine, *Left Front*. Were they treating me courteously because I was a Negro? I must let cold reason guide me with these people, I told myself. I was asked to contribute something to the magazine, and I said vaguely that I would consider it. After the meeting I met an Irish girl who worked for an advertising agency, a girl who did social work, a schoolteacher, and the wife of a prominent university professor. I had once worked as a servant for people like these and I was skeptical. I tried to fathom their motives, but I could detect no condescension in them.

I went home full of reflection, probing the sincerity of the strange white people I had met, wondering how they *really* regarded Negroes. I lay on my bed and read the magazines and was amazed to find that there did exist in this world an organized search for the truth of the lives of the oppressed and the isolated. When I had begged bread from the officials, I had wondered dimly if the outcasts could become united in action, thought, and feeling. Now I knew. It was being done in one-sixth of the earth already. The revolutionary words leaped from the printed page and struck me with tremendous force.

It was not the economics of Communism, nor the great power of trade unions, nor the excitement of underground politics that claimed me; my attention was caught by the similarity of the experiences of workers in other lands, by the possibility of uniting scattered but kindred peoples into a whole. My cynicism—which had been my protection against an America that had cast me out—slid from me and, timidly, I began to wonder if a solution of unity was possible. My life as a Negro in America had led me to feel—though my helplessness had made me try to hide it from myself—that the problem of human unity was more important than bread, more important than physical living itself; for I felt that without a common bond uniting men, without a continuous current of shared thought and feeling circulating through the social system, like blood coursing through the body, there could be no living worthy of being called human.

I hungered to share the dominant assumptions of my time and act upon them. I did not want to feel, like an animal in a jungle, that the whole world was alien and hostile. I did not want to make individual war or individual peace. So far I had managed to keep humanly alive through transfusions from books. In my concrete relations with others I had encountered nothing to encourage me to believe in my feelings. It had been by denying what I saw with my eyes, disputing what I felt with my body, that I had managed to keep my identity intact. But it seemed to me that here at last in the realm of revolutionary expression was where Negro experience could find a home, a functioning value and role. Out of the magazines I read came a passionate call for the experiences of the disinherited, and there were none of the lame lispings of the missionary in it. It did not say: "Be like us and we will like you, maybe." It said: "If you possess enough courage to speak out what you are, you will find that you are not alone." It urged life to believe in life.

I read on into the night; then, toward dawn, I swung from bed and inserted paper into the typewriter. Feeling for the first time that I could speak to listening ears, I wrote a wild, crude poem in free verse, coining images of black hands playing, working, holding bayonets, stiffening finally in death . . . I read it and felt that in a clumsy way it linked white life with black, merged two streams of common experience.

I heard someone poking about the kitchen.

"Richard, are you ill?" my mother called.

"No. I'm reading."

My mother opened the door and stared curiously at the pile of magazines that lay upon my pillow.

"You're not throwing away money buying those magazines, are you?" she asked.

"No. They were given to me."

She hobbled to the bed on her crippled legs and picked up a copy of the *Masses* that carried a lurid May Day cartoon. She adjusted her glasses and peered at it for a long time.

"My God in heaven," she breathed in horror.

"What's the matter, mama?"

"What is this?" she asked, extending the magazine to me, pointing to the cover. "What's wrong with that man?"

With my mother standing at my side, lending me her eyes, I stared at a cartoon drawn by a Communist artist; it was the figure of a worker clad in ragged overalls and holding aloft a red banner. The man's eyes bulged; his mouth gaped as wide as his face; his teeth showed; the muscles of his neck were like ropes. Following the man was a horde of nondescript men, women, and children, waving clubs, stones, and pitchforks.

"What are those people going to do?" my mother asked.

"I don't know," I hedged.

"Are these Communist magazines?"

"Yes."

"And do they want people to act like this?"

"Well . . ." I hesitated.

My mother's face showed disgust and moral loathing. She was a gentle woman. Her ideal was Christ upon the Cross. How could I tell her that the Communist party wanted her to march in the streets, chanting, singing?

"What do Communists think people are?" she asked.

"They don't quite mean what you see there," I said, fumbling with my words.

"Then what do they mean?"

"This is symbolic," I said.

"Then why don't they speak out what they mean?"

"Maybe they don't know how."

"Then why do they print this stuff?"

"They don't quite know how to appeal to people yet," I admitted, wondering whom I could convince of this if I could not convince my mother.

"That picture's enough to drive a body crazy," she said, dropping the magazine, turning to leave, then pausing at the door. "You're not getting mixed up with those people?"

"I'm just reading, mama," I dodged.

My mother left and I brooded upon the fact that I had not been able to meet her simple challenge. I looked again at the cover of the *Masses* and I knew that the wild cartoon did not reflect the passions of the common people. I reread the magazine and was convinced that much of the expression embodied what the artists thought would appeal to others, what they thought would gain recruits. They had a program, an ideal, but they had not yet found a language.

Here, then, was something that I could do, reveal, say. The Communists, I felt, had oversimplified the experience of those whom they sought to lead. In their efforts to recruit masses, they had missed the meaning of the lives of the masses, had conceived of people in too abstract a manner. I would make voyages, discoveries, explorations with words and try to put some of that meaning back. I would address my words to two groups: I would tell Communists how common people felt, and I would tell common people of the self-sacrifice of Communists who strove for unity among them.

That following Thursday night, when I joined my friends at the hotel for beer, I pulled out my crude verses and laid them on the table. Sol read them.

"This can be published," he said.

"That's not the point," I said. "What do they mean to you?"

"This is the vision of the disinherited," he said.

"If you're going to publish these to recruit me into the party, then nothing doing," I said.

"They'll be published whether you join or not," he said.

I told the group of my mother's reaction to the *Masses* cartoon.

"She'll have to learn the symbolism of the revolution," somebody said.

"But why can't Communism speak a language she understands?" I asked.

There was a lot of argument that went nowhere.

Still suspicious, my eyes watching for the slightest anti-Negro gesture, I attended the next meeting of the club. In the end I had to admit that they were glad to have me with them. But I still doubted their motives. Were they trying to get my head bashed in a picket line so that they could capitalize on the publicity? Or did the discipline of the club demand that they be friendly with me? If that was true, then those who did not want a Negro in the club could resign. But no one made a move to resign. How had these people, denying profit and home and God, made that hurdle that even the churches of America had not been able to make?

The editor of *Left Front* accepted two of my crude poems for publication, sent two of them to Jack Conroy's *Anvil*, and

sent another to the *New Masses*, the successor of the *Masses*.
Doubts still lingered in my mind.

"Don't send them if you think they're aren't good
enough," I said.

"They're good enough," he said.

"Are you doing this to get me to join up?" I asked.

"No," he said. "Your poems are crude, but good for us.
You see, we're all new in this. We write articles about Negroes, but we never see any Negroes. We need your stuff."

I sat through several meetings of the club and was impressed by the scope and seriousness of its activities. The club
was demanding that the government create jobs for unemployed artists; it planned and organized art exhibits; it raised
funds for the publication of *Left Front*; and it sent scores of
speakers to trade-union meetings. The members were fervent,
democratic, restless, eager, self-sacrificing. I was convinced,
and my response was to set myself the task of making Negroes know what Communists were. While mopping the operating rooms of the medical research institute, I got the
notion of writing a series of biographical sketches of Negro
Communists. I told no one of my intentions, and I did not
know how fantastically naïve my ambition was.

I had attended but a few meetings before I realized that a
bitter factional fight was in progress between two groups of
members of the club. But when I tried to learn the nature of
the fight, no one would tell me anything. Sharp arguments
rose at every meeting. I noticed that a small group of painters
actually led the club and dominated its policies. The group of
writers that centered about *Left Front* resented the leadership
of the painters. Being primarily interested in *Left Front*, I
sided in simple loyalty with the writers. Then came a strange
development. The *Left Front* group declared that the incum-
bent leadership did not reflect the wishes of the club. A special meeting was called and a motion was made to reelect an
executive secretary. When nominations were made for the
office, my name was included. I declined the nomination, telling the members that I was too ignorant of their aims to be
seriously considered. The debate lasted all night. A vote was
taken in the early hours of morning by a show of hands, and I

was elected. I had been a member of the club for less than two months and did not fully understand the purposes of the organization.

Later I learned what had happened: the writers of the club had decided to "use" me to oust the painters, who were party members, from the leadership of the club. Without my knowledge and consent, they confronted the members of the party with a Negro, knowing that it would be difficult for Communists to refuse to vote for a man representing the largest single racial minority in the nation, inasmuch as Negro equality was one of the main tenets of Communism.

Though I was not a Communist, cynical rivalry had put me in charge of one of the party's leading cultural organizations. At once I offered my resignation, but the members would not hear of it. I could not determine if they were acting sincerely. I was afraid that the defeated secretary, being white, would resent losing to a Negro, but his conduct showed nothing but friendliness.

As the club's leader, I soon learned the nature of the fight. The Communists had secretly organized a "fraction" in the club; that is, a small portion of the club's members were secret members of the Communist party. They would meet outside of the club, decide what policies the club should follow; and when they put forth their proposals in open meetings, the sheer strength of their arguments usually persuaded nonparty members to vote with them. The crux of the fight was that the nonparty members resented the excessive demands made upon the club by the local party authorities through the fraction. For example, the fraction demanded that the *Daily Worker* and the *New Masses*, official periodicals of the Communist party, be put on sale at all meetings. The nonparty group declared that this would limit the club's membership to those who already believed in Communism.

The demands of the local party authorities for money, speakers, and poster painters were so great that the publication of *Left Front* was in danger. Many young writers had joined the club because of their hope of publishing in *Left Front*, and when the Communist party sent word through the fraction that the magazine should be dissolved, the writers rejected the decision, an act which was interpreted as hostility toward party authority.

I pleaded with the party members for a more liberal program for the club. Feelings waxed violent and bitter. Then the showdown came. I was informed that if I wanted to continue as secretary of the club I would have to join the Communist party. I stated that I favored a policy that allowed for the development of writers and artists. My policy was accepted. I signed the membership card.

As the club's leader, I strove to keep the quarrels within limits by striking a series of compromises: for example, the sale of the *Daily Worker* was withdrawn, but the sale of the *New Masses* was continued. My position was in the "middle"; the fraction urged me to collect money from the members for the Communist party, and the members urged me to fight for the continuance of *Left Front*, which had been branded as "useless" by the Communist party. Trying to please everybody, I pleased nobody. The club's energies were sapped by internal strife. Bills piled up. Rent fell past due. I wanted the club to continue at all hazards; my feelings were intensely personal. The club was my first contact with the modern world. I had lived so utterly isolated a life that the club filled for me a need that could not be imagined by the white members who were becoming disgusted with it, whose normal living had given them what I was so desperately trying to get.

One night a Jewish chap appeared at one of our meetings and introduced himself as Comrade Young of Detroit. He told us that he was a member of the Communist party, a member of the Detroit John Reed Club, that he planned to make his home in Chicago. He was a short, friendly, black-haired, well-read fellow with hanging lips and bulging eyes. Shy of forces to execute the demands of the Communist party, we welcomed him. But I could not make out Young's personality; whenever I asked him a simple question, he looked off and stammered a confused answer. I decided to send his references to the Communist party for checking and forthwith named him for membership in the club. He's okay, I thought. Just a queer artist . . .

After the meeting Comrade Young confronted me with a problem. He had no money, he said, and asked if he could sleep temporarily on the club's premises. Believing him loyal, I gave him permission. Straightway Young became one of the most ardent members of our organization, admired by all. His paintings—which I did not understand—impressed our best artists. No report about Young had come from the Communist party, but since Young seemed a conscientious worker, I did not think the omission serious in any case.

At a meeting one night Young asked that his name be placed upon the agenda; when his time came to speak, he rose and launched into one of the most violent and bitter political attacks upon Swann, one of our best young artists, in the club's history. We were aghast. Young accused Swann of being a traitor to the workers, an opportunist, a collaborator with the police, and an adherent of Trotsky. Naturally most of the club's members assumed that Young, a member of the party, was voicing the ideas of the party. Surprised and baffled, I moved that Young's statement be referred to the executive committee for decision. Swann rightfully protested; he declared that he had been attacked in public and would answer in public.

It was voted that Swann should have the floor. He refuted Young's wild charges, but the majority of the club's members were bewildered, did not know whether to believe him or not. We all liked Swann, did not believe him guilty of any misconduct; but we did not want to offend the party. A verbal battle ensued. Finally the members who had been silent in deference to the party rose and demanded of me that the foolish charges against Swann be withdrawn. Again I moved that the matter be referred to the executive committee, and again my proposal was voted down. The membership had now begun to distrust the party's motives. They were afraid to let an executive committee, the majority of whom were party members, pass upon the charges made by party member Young.

Three meetings were consumed in bitter debate. Between meetings we urged Young to tell us who had given him the authority to castigate Swann, and Young hinted darkly that he was acting under the orders of either the Central Committee of the Communist party or the Communist International. And we were naturally impressed. Who were we to question the decisions of political bodies so highly placed? I sympathized with Swann, but was afraid to say a word in his behalf for fear that I, too, would be charged.

A delegation of members asked me if I had anything to do with Young's charges. I was so hurt and humiliated that I disavowed all relations with Young. Determined to end the farce, I cornered Young and demanded to know who had given him authority.

"I've been asked to rid the club of traitors," he said.

"But Swann isn't a traitor," I said.

"We must have a purge," he said, his eyes bulging, his face quivering with passion.

I admitted his great revolutionary fervor, but I felt that his zeal was a trifle excessive. The situation became worse. A delegation of members informed me that if the charges against Swann were not withdrawn, they would resign in a body. I was frantic. I wrote to the Communist party to ask why orders had been issued to punish Swann, and a reply came back that no such orders had been issued. Then what was Young up to? Who was prompting him? I finally begged the club to let me place the matter before the leaders of the Communist party for decision. After a violent debate, my proposal was accepted.

One night ten of us met in an office of a leader of the party to hear Young restate his charges against Swann. The party leader, aloof and amused, gave Young the signal to begin. Young unrolled a sheaf of papers and declaimed a list of political charges that excelled in viciousness his previous charges. An instinct warned me that something was wrong, but I could not make out what it was. I stared at Young, feeling that he was making a dreadful mistake, but fearing him because he had, by his own account, the sanction of high political authority. When Young had finished, the party leader asked:

"Will you allow me to read these charges?"

"Of course," said Young, surrendering a copy of his indictment. "You may keep that copy. I have ten carbons."

"Why did you make so many carbons?" the leader asked.

"I didn't want anyone to steal them," Young said.

"If this man's charges against me are taken seriously," Swann said, "I'll resign and publicly denounce the club."

"You see!" Young yelled. "He's with the police!"

I was sick. The meeting ended with a promise from the party leader to read the charges carefully and render a verdict as to whether Swann should be placed on trial or not. I was convinced that something was wrong, but I could not figure it out. One afternoon I went to the club to have a long talk with Young; but when I arrived, he was not there. Nor was he there the next day. For a week I sought Young in vain. What had become of the man? I asked about him far and wide, but could get no word. Meanwhile the club's members asked his whereabouts and they would not believe me when I told them that I did not know. Was he ill? Had he been picked up by the police?

Somebody suggested that we search Young's luggage which was still in the club's back room. One afternoon Comrade Grimm and I sneaked into the club's headquarters and opened Young's luggage. What we saw amazed and puzzled us. First of all, there was a scroll of paper twenty yards long— one page pasted to another—which had drawings depicting the history of the human race from a Marxist point of view. The first page was titled:

A Pictorial Record of Man's Economic Progress

"This is terribly ambitious," I said.

"He's very studious," Grimm said.

There were long dissertations written in long hand; some were political and others dealt with the history of art. Finally we found a letter with a Detroit return address and I promptly wrote asking news of our esteemed member. A few days later a letter came which said in part:

Dear Sir:

In reply to your letter of the ——, we beg to inform you that Mr. Young, who was a patient in our institution and who escaped from our custody a few months ago, has been apprehended and returned to this institution for mental treatment.

I was thunderstruck. Was this true? Undoubtedly it was. Then what kind of club did we run that a lunatic could step into it and help run it? Were we all so mad that we could not detect a madman when we saw one? I called a meeting of a few of the most trusted members of the club and laid the matter before them. They were dumfounded. We swore ourselves to secrecy and decided to suppress the matter. We agreed that we had made a terrible mistake.

But, of course, we had no power to restrain the other members from asking questions. Swann hammered at us from meeting to meeting.

"Where is Comrade Young? Is he sick? Is he dead? Is he in jail? Did the Communist party order him to stay away from the club?"

And to these questions I could but lie:

"I've had no word from Comrade Young. As soon as any is received, I'll inform the club."

Meanwhile I made a motion that all charges against Swann be dropped, which was done. I offered Swann an apology but, as the leader of the Chicago John Reed Club, I was a completely sober and chastened Communist.

Chapter XIX

I HAD READ widely in revolutionary literature, had observed many Communists, white and black, and had learned to know the daily hazards they faced and the sacrifices they made. I now wanted to give time to writing the book of biographical sketches I had planned. I did not know Negro Communists as well as I wanted to, and when, on many occasions, I had sought to question them about their feelings, their work, and their actions, they had been reticent. My zeal made me forget these rebuffs, for I was sure that an atmosphere of trust would be created as soon as I had explained my project to them.

The Communist party fraction in the John Reed Club instructed me to ask my party cell—or "unit," as it was called—to assign me to full duty in the work of the club. I was instructed to give my unit a report of my activities, writing, organizing, speaking. I agreed to do this and wrote a report.

A unit, membership in which is obligatory for all Communists, is the party's basic form of organization. Unit meetings are held on certain nights which are kept secret for fear of police raids. Nothing treasonable transpires at these meetings; but, once one is a Communist, one does not have to be guilty of wrongdoing to attract the attention of the police. At these meetings members pay their dues, are given party tasks, are instructed in the party's interpretation of world events.

I went to my first unit meeting—which was held in the Black Belt of the South Side—and introduced myself to the Negro organizer.

"Welcome, comrade," he said, grinning. "We're glad to have a writer with us."

"I'm not much of a writer," I said.

The meeting started. About twenty Negroes were gathered. The time came for me to make my report and I took out my notes and told them how I had come to join the party, what few stray items I had published, what my duties were in the John Reed Club. I finished and waited for comment. There was silence. I looked about. Most of the comrades sat with bowed heads. Then I was surprised to catch a twitching smile on the lips of a Negro woman. Minutes passed. The Negro woman lifted her head and looked at the organizer. The organizer smothered a smile. Then the woman broke into unrestrained laughter, bending forward and burying her face in her hands. I stared. Had I said something funny?

"What's the matter?" I asked.

The giggling became general. The unit organizer, who had been dallying with his pencil, looked up.

"It's all right, comrade," he said. "We're glad to have a writer in the party."

There was more smothered laughter. Some of the more intelligent ones were striving to keep deadpan faces. What kind of people were these? I had made a serious report and now I heard giggles.

"I did the best I could," I said uneasily. "I realize that writing is not basic or important. But, given time, I think I can make a contribution."

"We know you can, comrade," the black organizer said.

His tone was more patronizing than that of a southern white man. I grew angry. I thought I knew these people, but evidently I did not. I wanted to take issue with their attitude, but caution urged me to talk it over with others first. I left the meeting baffled.

During the following days I learned through discreet questioning that I had seemed a fantastic element to the black Communists. I was shocked to hear that I, who had been only to grammar school, had been classified as an *intellectual*. What was an intellectual? I had never heard the word used in the sense in which it was applied to me. I had thought that they might refuse me on the grounds that I was not politically advanced; I had thought they might place me on probation; I had thought they might say I would have to be investigated. But they had simply laughed. And I began to realize why so few sensitive Negroes had had the gall to come as close to them as I had.

I learned, to my dismay, that the black Communists in my unit had commented upon my shined shoes, my clean shirt, and the tie I had worn. Above all, my manner of speech had seemed an alien thing to them.

"He talks like a book," one of the Negro comrades had said. And that was enough to condemn me forever as bourgeois.

The more I learned of the Negro Communists the more I found that they were not vicious, that they had no intention to hurt. They just did not know anything and did not want to learn anything. They felt that all questions had been answered, and anyone who asked new ones or tried to answer old ones was dangerous. The word "writer" was enough to make a black Chicago Communist feel that the man to whom the word applied had gone wrong.

I discovered that it was not wise to be seen reading books that were not endorsed by the Communist party. On one occasion I was asked to show a book that I carried under my arm. The comrade looked at it and shook his head.

"What're you reading this for?" he asked.

"It's interesting," I said.

"Reading bourgeois books can only confuse you, comrade," he said, returning the book.

"You seem convinced that I'm easily confused," I said.

"You know," he said, his voice dropping to a low, confidential tone, "many comrades go wrong by reading the books of the bourgeoisie. The party in the Soviet Union had trouble with people like that."

"Didn't Lenin read bourgeois books?" I asked.

"But you're not Lenin," he shot at me.

"Are there some books reserved for some people to read, while others cannot read them?" I asked.

"Comrade, you do not understand," he said.

An invisible wall was building slowly between me and the people with whom I had cast my lot. Well, I would show them that all men who wrote books were not their enemies. I would communicate the meaning of their lives to people whom they could not reach; then, surely, my intentions would merit their confidence. I dismissed the warning about the Soviet Union's trouble with intellectuals. I felt that it simply did not apply to me. The problem I faced seemed a much simpler one. I had to win the confidence of people who had been misled so often that they were afraid of anybody who differed from themselves. Yet deep down I feared their militant ignorance.

*   *   *

In my party work I met a Negro Communist, Ross, who was under indictment for "inciting to riot." I decided to use him in my series of biographical sketches. His trial was pending and he was organizing support in his behalf. Ross was typical of the effective, street agitator. Southern-born, he had migrated north and his life reflected the crude hopes and frustrations of the peasant in the city. Distrustful but aggressive, he was a bundle of the weaknesses and virtues of a man struggling blindly between two societies, of a man living on the margin of a culture. I felt that if I could get his story I would make known some of the difficulties inherent in the adjustment of a folk people to an urban environment; I would make his life more intelligible to others than it was to himself. I would reclaim his disordered days and cast them into a form that people could grasp, see, understand, and accept.

I approached Ross and explained my plan. He was agreeable. He invited me to his home, introduced me to his Jewish wife, his young son, his friends. I talked to Ross for hours, explaining what I was about, cautioning him not to relate anything that he did not want to divulge.

"I'm after the things that made you a Communist," I said.

It was arranged that I was to visit Ross each morning and take notes for two hours. At last, I thought, I would reveal dramas of hope, fear, love, and hate that existed in these humble people. I would make these lives merge with the lives of the mass of mankind. I knew I could. My life had prepared me for this.

Word spread in the Communist party that I was taking notes on the life of Ross and strange things began to happen. A quiet black Communist came to my home one night and called me out to the street to speak to me in private. He made a prediction about my future that frightened me.

"Intellectuals don't fit well into the party, Wright," he said solemnly.

"But I'm not an intellectual," I protested. "I sweep the streets for a living." I had just been assigned by the relief system to sweep the streets for thirteen dollars a week.

"That doesn't make any difference," he said. "We've kept records of the trouble we've had with intellectuals in the past. It's estimated that only 13 per cent of them remain in the party."

"Why do they leave, since you insist upon calling me an intellectual?" I asked.

"Most of them drop out of their own accord," he said.

"Well, I'm not dropping out," I said.

"Some are expelled," he hinted gravely.

"For what?"

"General opposition to the party's policies," he said.

"But I'm not opposing anything in the party."

"But you have to prove yourself."

"What do you mean?"

"You'll have to prove your revolutionary loyalty."

"That's what I'm trying to do through writing."

"That's not the way to do it," he said. "You must act."

"How?"

"The party has a way of testing people."

"Well, talk. What is this?"

"How do you react to police?"

"I don't react to them," I said. "I've never been bothered by them."

"Do you know Evans?" he asked, referring to a local, militant Negro Communist.

"Yes. I've seen him; I've met him."

"Did you notice that he was injured?"

"Yes. His head was bandaged."

"He got that wound from the police in a demonstration," he explained. "That's proof of revolutionary loyalty."

"Do you mean that I must get whacked over the head by cops to prove that I'm sincere?" I asked.

"I'm not suggesting anything," he said. "I'm explaining."

"That's a primitive way to measure sincerity," I gasped.

"It's a practical way," he said.

"Look, suppose a cop whacks me over the head and I suffer a brain concussion. Suppose I'm nuts after that? Can I write then? What will I have proven?"

He did not answer. He shook his head.

"The Soviet Union has had to shoot a lot of intellectuals," he said.

"Good God!" I exclaimed. "Do you know what you're

saying? You're not in Russia. You're standing on a sidewalk in Chicago. You talk like a man lost in a fantasy."

He said nothing. I did not know that the notes I was taking of Ross's life were being discussed by the local Communist leaders, that my motives were already being questioned; and no doubt my rash words did not help any.

"You've heard of Trotsky, haven't you?" he asked.

"Yes."

"Do you know what happened to him?"

"He was banished from the Soviet Union," I said.

"Do you know why?"

"Well," I stammered, trying not to reveal my ignorance of politics, for I had not followed the details of Trotsky's fight against the Communist party of the Soviet Union, "it seems that after a decision had been made, he broke that decision by organizing against the party."

"It was for counterrevolutionary activity," he snapped impatiently; I learned afterwards that my answer had not been satisfactory, had not been couched in the acceptable phrases of bitter, anti-Trotsky denunciation.

"I understand," I said. "But I've never read Trotsky. What's his stand on minorities?"

"Why ask me?" he asked. "I don't read Trotsky."

"Look," I asked, "if you found me reading Trotsky, what would that mean to you?"

"You have no need to read Trotsky," he said.

"Don't you think I can read Trotsky and not be influenced to follow him?" I asked.

"Comrade, you don't understand," he said in an annoyed tone.

That ended the conversation. But that was not the last time I was to hear the phrase: "Comrade, you don't understand." I had not been aware of holding wrong ideas. I had not read any of Trotsky's works; indeed, the very opposite had been true. It had been Stalin's *The National and Colonial Question* that had captured my interest.

Stalin's book showed how diverse minorities could be welded into unity, and I regarded it as a most politically sensitive volume that revealed a new way of looking upon lost and beaten peoples. Of all the developments in the Soviet

Union, the method by which scores of backward peoples had been led to unity on a national scale was what had enthralled me. I had read with awe how the Communists had sent phonetic experts into the vast regions of Russia to listen to the stammering dialects of peoples oppressed for centuries by the czars. I had made the first total emotional commitment of my life when I read how the phonetic experts had given these tongueless people a language, newspapers, institutions. I had read how these forgotten folk had been encouraged to keep their old cultures, to see in their ancient customs meanings and satisfactions as deep as those contained in supposedly superior ways of living. And I had exclaimed to myself how different this was from the way in which Negroes were sneered at in America.

Then what was the meaning of the warning I had received from the black Communist? Why was it that I was a suspected man because I wanted to reveal the vast physical and spiritual ravages of Negro life, the profundity latent in these rejected people, the dramas as old as man and the sun and the mountains and the seas that were transpiring in the poverty of black America? What was the danger in showing the kinship between the sufferings of the Negro and the sufferings of other people?

I sat one morning in Ross's home with his wife and child. I was scribbling furiously upon my yellow sheets of paper. The doorbell rang and Ross's wife admitted a black Communist, one Ed Green. He was tall, taciturn, soldierly, square-shouldered. I was introduced to him and he nodded stiffly.

"What's happening here?" he asked bluntly.

Ross explained my project to him, and as Ross talked I could see Ed Green's face darken. He had not sat down and when Ross's wife offered him a chair, he did not hear her.

"What're you going to do with these notes?" he asked me.

"I hope to weave them into stories," I said.

"What're you asking the party members?"

"About their lives in general."

"Who suggested this to you?" he asked.

"Nobody. I thought of it myself."

"Were you ever a member of any other political group?"

"I worked with the Republicans once," I said.

"I mean, revolutionary organizations?" he asked.

"No. Why do you ask?"

"What kind of work do you do?"

"I sweep the streets for a living."

"How far did you go in school?"

"Through the grammar grades."

"You talk like a man who went further than that," he said.

"Why would I lie to you about my education?" I asked.

"I don't know," he said, looking directly at me.

"I've read books. I taught myself."

"You know about Ross's indictment?" he asked.

"Yes."

"I don't know," he said, looking off.

"What do you mean?" I asked. "What's wrong?"

"To whom have you shown this material?"

"I've shown it to no one yet."

What was the meaning of his questions? Naïvely I thought that he himself would make a good model for a biographical sketch.

"I'd like to interview you next," I said.

"I'm not interested," he snapped.

His manner was so rough that I did not urge him. He called Ross into a rear room. I sat feeling that I was guilty of something. In a few minutes Ed Green returned, stared at me wordlessly, then marched out.

"Who does he think he is?" I asked Ross.

"He's a member of the Central Committee," Ross said.

"But why does he act like that?"

"Oh, he's always like that," Ross said uneasily.

There was a long silence.

"He's wondering what you're doing with this material," Ross said finally.

I looked at him. He, too, had been captured by suspicion. He was trying to hide the fear in his face.

"You don't have to tell me anything you don't want to," I said.

That seemed to enable him for a moment. But the seed of doubt had already been planted. I felt dizzy. Was I mad? Or were these people mad?

"You see, Dick," Ross's wife said, "Ross's under an indictment. Ed Green is the representative of the International Labor Defense for the South Side. It's his duty to keep track of the people he's trying to defend. He wanted to know if Ross has given you anything that could be used against him in court."

I was speechless.

"What does he think I am?" I demanded.

There was no answer.

"You lost people!" I cried and banged my fist on the table.

Ross was shaken and ashamed.

"Aw, Ed Green's just supercautious," he mumbled.

"Ross," I asked, "do you trust me?"

"Oh, yes," he said uneasily.

We two black men sat in the same room looking at each other in fear. Both of us were hungry. Both of us depended upon public charity to eat and for a place to sleep. Yet we had more doubt in our hearts of each other than of the men who had cast the mold of our lives.

Self-consciously we went on with the work, but something was gone out of it. Did they think I was gathering material for the police? How could I make them understand what I was trying to do? I found that when I talked to them in abstract terms, my ideas were not understood. The irony of it was that I, who had all but to steal books to read, had been branded as an intellectual by the one group that claimed it was dedicated to educating the oppressed and informing them with a vision of life. I was doubted by those who shared more of my life than any others could possibly share of it.

I could not doubt the sincerity of Ed Green. His was a long and militant record in the Communist party. Then why was he suspicious of me? And, if he doubted me, whom could he ever trust? If I was an intellectual, then what was a Negro doctor, lawyer, teacher? The thing just did not make sense. Yet there it was . . .

Ed Green was afterwards killed in action while fighting for the Spanish Loyalists. He knew how to die better than he knew how to live. He was organically capable of only the most elementary reactions. His fear-haunted life made him suspicious of everything that did not look as he looked, that did not act as he acted, that did not talk as he talked, that did not feel as he felt. His existence both gladdened and frightened me. I was glad that he was militant, but I was frightened when I pondered upon what he could do with his militancy. The only people he could move to believe in him were those who shared his own world of fear, and all the world that lay beyond his terribly restricted vision was enemy ground.

I wanted to make the lives of these men known through the images already accepted as the common coin of communication. I wanted to make them know that they had allies, that more people than they knew, and in ways they did not understand, were their friends, and that I was their friend. I wanted to voice the words in them that they could not say, to be a witness for their living. And they were wondering if I were in league with the police!

I had embraced their aims with the freest impulse I had ever known. I, the chary cynic, the man who had felt that no idea on earth was worthy of self-sacrifice, had publicly identified myself with them, and now their suspicion of me hit me with a terrific impact, froze me within. I groped in the noon sun. What was I after? they wanted to know. And when I tried to explain, I always, it seemed, said the wrong things. There were no concrete charges that they could bring against me. They were simply afraid of that which was not familiar. They were more fearful of my ideas than they would have been had I held a gun on them; they could have taken the gun away from me and shot me with it, but they did not know what to do with ideas.

I talked with white Communists about my experiences with black Communists, and I could not make them understand what I was talking about. White Communists had idealized all Negroes to the extent that they did not see the same Negroes I saw. And the more I tried to explain my ideas the more they, too, began to suspect that I was somehow dreadfully wrong. Words lost their usual meanings. Simple motives took on sinister colors. Attitudes underwent quick and startling transformations. Ideas turned into their opposites while you were talking to a person you thought you knew. I began to feel an emotional isolation that I had not known in the depths of the hate-ridden South.

*   *   *

I continued to take notes on Ross's life, but each succes-
sive morning found him more reticent. I pitied him and did
not argue with him, for I knew that persuasion would not
nullify his fears. Instead I sat and listened to him and his
friends tell tales of southern Negro experience, noting them
down in my mind, not daring to ask questions for fear they
would become alarmed. In spite of their fears, I became quite
drenched in the details of their lives. I gave up the idea of the
biographical sketches and settled finally upon writing a series
of short stories, using the material I had got from Ross and
his friends, building upon it, inventing. I wove a tale of a
group of black boys trespassing upon the property of a
white man and the lynching that followed. The story was
published in an anthology under the title of *Big Boy Leaves
Home*, but its appearance came too late to influence the
Communists who were questioning the use to which I was
putting their lives.

My fitful work assignments from the relief officials ceased
and I looked for work that did not exist. I borrowed money
to ride to and fro on the club's business. I found a cramped
attic for my mother and aunt and brother behind some railroad tracks. At last the relief authorities placed me in the
South Side Boys' Club and my wages were just enough to
provide a deficient diet.

Then political problems rose to plague me. Ross, whose life
I had tried to write, was charged by the Communist party
with "antileadership tendencies," "class collaborationist attitudes," and "ideological factionalism," phrases so fanciful that
I gaped when I heard them. And it was rumored that I, too,
would face similar charges. It was known that I had visited
Ross, had taken notes on his life, and it was believed that I
had been politically influenced by him, though in what way
was not stated. As before, the more I tried to explain the
guiltier I seemed in the eyes of my comrades. I had taken part
in the formation of none of the policies of the Communist
party, had expressed no opinion regarding its leadership or
work. But the rumors of my disaffection persisted.

One night a group of black comrades came to my house
and warned me against believing in Ross's ideas. When I as-

sured them that I did not share Ross's views, they ordered me
to stay away from him.

"But why?" I demanded.

"He's an unhealthy element," they said. "Can't you accept a
decision?"

"Is this a decision of the Communist party?"

"Yes," they said.

"If I were guilty of something, I'd feel bound to keep your
decision," I said. "But I've done nothing."

"Comrade, you don't understand," they said. "Members of
the party do not violate the party's decisions."

"But your decision does not apply to me," I said. "I'll be
damned if I'll act as if it does."

"Your attitude does not merit our trust," they said.

I was angry.

"Look," I exploded, rising and sweeping my arms at the
bleak attic in which I lived, "what is it here that frightens
you? You know where I work! You know what I earn! You
know my friends! Now, what in God's name is wrong?"

They left with mirthless smiles which implied that I would
soon know what was wrong.

But there was relief from these shadowy political bouts.
I found my work in the South Side Boys' Club deeply engrossing. Each day black boys between the ages of eight and
twenty-five came to swim, draw, and read. They were a wild
and homeless lot, culturally lost, spiritually disinherited,
candidates for the clinics, morgues, prisons, reformatories,
and the electric chair of the state's death house. For hours I
listened to their talk of planes, women, guns, politics, and
crime. Their figures of speech were as forceful and colorful as
any ever used by English-speaking people. I kept pencil and
paper in my pocket to jot down their word-rhythms and reactions. These boys did not fear people to the extent that every
man looked like a spy. The Communists who doubted my
motives did not know these boys, their twisted dreams, their
all-too-clear destinies; and I doubted if I would ever be able
to convey to them the tragedy I saw here.

Wrestling with words gave me my moments of deepest
meaning. The short story, *Big Boy Leaves Home*, had posed a
question: What quality of will must a Negro possess to live

and die with dignity in a country that denied his humanity? There took shape in my mind—as though an answer was trying to grope its way out of the depths of me—the tale of a flood, *Down by the Riverside*. I waded into it, feeling my way, trying to find the answer to my question. But it dissatisfied me when I had finished it; so, casting it aside, I tried to say the same thing in yet another way in *Long Black Song*. But that did not catch the quality of the experience I was looking for.

Party duties broke into my efforts at expression. The club decided upon a conference of all the left-wing writers in the Middle West. I supported the idea and argued that the conference should deal with craft problems. My arguments were rejected. The conference, the club decided, would deal with political questions. I asked for a definition of what was expected from the writers, books or political activity. Both, was the answer. Write a few hours a day and march on the picket line the other hours. I pointed out that the main concern of a revolutionary artist was to produce revolutionary art, and that the future of the club was in doubt if a clear policy could not be found.

The conference convened with a leading Communist attending as adviser. The question debated was: What did the Communist party expect from the club? The answer of the Communist leader ran from organizing to writing novels. I argued that either a man organized or he wrote novels. The party leader said that both must be done. The attitude of the party leader prevailed and *Left Front*, for which I had worked so long, was voted out of existence.

The party leader demanded that writers be assigned the task of producing pamphlets for the use of trade unions. I contended that it would be a mistake for the Communist party to persuade writers to abandon imaginative work to write pamphlets. I explained the advantages that could be derived from the long-term artistic products of the club's writers, and pointed out that these more durable products would outweigh all the pamphleteering. This, too, was rejected by vote. I then appealed for an organizational structure that would include provisions for artistic work of all types, hoping in this way to eliminate constant quarrels over tactics and strategy. But all my proposals were voted down.

I knew now that the club was nearing its end, and I rose and stated my gloomy conclusions, recommending that the club dissolve. My "defeatism," as it was called, brought upon my head the sharpest disapproval of the party leader. The conference ended with the passing of a multitude of resolutions dealing with China, India, Germany, Japan, and conditions afflicting various parts of the earth. But not one idea regarding writing had emerged.

The ideas I had expounded at the conference were linked with the suspicions I had roused among the Negro Communists on the South Side, and the Communist party was now certain that it had a dangerous enemy in its midst. It was whispered that I was trying to lead a secret group in opposition to the party. I had learned that denial of accusations was useless. It was now painful to meet a Communist, for I did not know what his attitude would be.

Following the conference, a national John Reed Club congress was called. It convened in the summer of 1934 with left-wing writers attending from all states. But, as the sessions got under way, there was a sense of looseness, bewilderment, and dissatisfaction among the writers, most of whom were young, eager, and on the verge of doing their best work. No one knew what was expected of him, and out of the congress came no unifying idea. Through conversations I learned that the members of the New York John Reed Club were in despair at the way in which the congress was drifting, but they took care to conceal their disapproval. This puzzled me, for I felt that the problem should be brought into the open for discussion. But I was glad to hear the New York Communists express horror at the brutal way in which the Chicago Communists made demands upon the Chicago John Reed Club membership. One astonished New York comrade declared:

"A Chicago Communist is a walking terror!"

As the congress drew to a close, I attended a caucus to plan the future of the clubs. Ten of us met in a Loop hotel room and, to my amazement, the leaders of the club's national board confirmed my criticisms of the manner in which the clubs had been conducted. I was excited. Now, I thought, the clubs will be given a new lease on life. Writers would now be free to make their political contributions in the form of their creative work.

Then I was stunned when I heard a nationally known Communist announce a decision to dissolve the clubs. Why? I asked. Because the clubs do not serve the new People's Front policy, I was told. That can be remedied; the clubs can be made healthy and broad, I said. No; a bigger and better organization must be launched, one in which the leading writers of the nation could be included, they said. I was informed that the People's Front policy was now the correct vision of life and that the clubs could no longer exist. I asked what was to become of the young writers whom the Communist party had implored to join the clubs and who were ineligible for the new group, and there was no answer. This thing is cold! I exclaimed to myself. To effect a swift change in policy, the Communist party was dumping one organization, scattering its members, then organizing a new scheme with entirely new people!

I had sacrificed energy to recruit writers who subscribed to a revolutionary point of view, and now my feelings fought against the waste and meaninglessness to which my efforts were being reduced. This was the first time I had sat with a Communist policy-making body; I had had the illusion that each man would have his say and, out of the facts presented, a decision would be made. I was naïve. I had merely been called in to give my approval to a decision previously made. It angered me.

I found myself arguing alone against the majority opinion and then I made still another amazing discovery. I saw that even those who agreed with me would not support me. At that meeting I learned that when a man was informed of the wish of the party he submitted, even though he knew with all the strength of his brain that the wish was not a wise one, was one that would ultimately harm the party's interests. I had heard Communists discuss discipline in the abstract, but when I saw it in its concrete form it tore my feelings.

It was not courage that made me oppose the party. I simply did not know any better. It was inconceivable to me, though bred in the lap of southern hate, that a man could not have his say. I had spent a third of my life traveling from the place of my birth to the North just to talk freely, to escape the pressure of fear. And now I was facing fear again, though I had no notion that I was slowly adding fagots to a flame that would soon blaze over my head with all the violence of the assault I had sustained when I had naïvely thought I could learn the optical trade in Mississippi.

(The artist and the politician stand at opposite poles. The artist enhances life by his prolonged concentration upon it, while the politician emphasizes the impersonal aspect of life by his attempts to fit men into groups. The artist's enhancement of life may emphasize, at certain times, those aspects that a politician can use. But the politician, at other times, eager to do good for man, may sneer at the artist because the art product cannot be used by him. Hence, the two groups of men, driving in the same direction, committed to the same vision, often find themselves locked in a struggle more desperate than either of them wanted, while their mutual enemies gape at the spectacle in amazement.

(Why did not we writers leave the realm of politics and organize ourselves? We simply did not know how. We were hostile toward our environment and we did not know how other American writers had met such problems. Totally at odds with our culture, we wanted nothing less than to make anew; and, for our examples, we looked toward Russia, Germany, and France. Out of step with our times, it was but natural for us to respond to the Communist party, which said: "Your rebellion is right. Come with us and we will support your vision with militant action."

(Indeed, we felt that we were lucky. Why cower in towers of ivory and squeeze out private words when we had only to speak and millions listened? Our writing was translated into French, German, Russian, Chinese, Spanish, Japanese . . . Who had ever, in all human history, offered to young writers an audience so vast? True, our royalties were small or less than small, but that did not matter.

(We wrote what we felt. Confronted with a picture of a revolutionary and changing world, there spilled out of our hearts our reaction to that world, our hope, our anger at oppression, our dreams of a new life; it spilled without coercion, without the pleading of anyone.)

Before the congress adjourned, it was decided that another congress of American writers would be called in New York the following summer, 1935. I was lukewarm to the proposal and tried to make up my mind to stand alone, write alone. I was already afraid that the stories I had written would not fit into the new, official mood. Must I discard my plot-ideas and seek new ones? No. I could not. My writing was my way of seeing, my way of living, my way of feeling; and who could change his sight, his notion of direction, his senses?

My relationship with Communists reached a static phase. I shunned them and they shunned me. Buddy Nealson, a member of the Communist International, had arrived in Chicago to assume charge of Negro work. This man, it was rumored, was the party's theoretician on the Negro Question, and word reached me that he had launched a campaign to rid the Communist party of all its "Negro Trotskyite elements." Of all the Negro Communists I knew, I tried to determine who could be called a Trotskyite, and I could think of none. None of the black Communists I knew possessed the intellectual capacity to formulate a Trotskyite position in politics. Most of them were illiterate migrants from southern plantations and they had never been vitally interested in politics until they had entered the Communist party. Nevertheless, the drive against Negro Trotskyism went on, though I was too remote from it to know what was happening.

The spring of 1935 came and the plans for the writers' congress went on apace. For some obscure reason—it might have been to "save" me—I was urged by the local Communists to attend and I was named as a delegate. I got time off from my job at the South Side Boys' Club and, along with several other delegates, hitchhiked to New York.

Long used to the flat western prairie, I was startled by my first view of New York. We came in along the Hudson River and I stared at the sweep of clean-kept homes and grounds. But where was the smoke pall? The soot? Grain elevators? Factories? Stack-pipes? The flashes of steam on the horizon? The people on the sidewalks seemed better dressed than the people of Chicago. Their eyes were bold and impersonal.

They walked with a quicker stride and seemed intent upon reaching some destination in a great hurry.

We arrived in the early evening and registered for the congress sessions. The opening mass meeting was being held at Carnegie Hall. I asked about housing accommodations and the New York John Reed Club members, all white members of the Communist party, looked embarrassed. I waited while one white Communist called another white Communist to one side and discussed what could be done to get me, a black Chicago Communist, housed. During the trip I had not thought of myself as a Negro; I had been mulling over the problems of the young left-wing writers I knew. Now, as I stood watching one white comrade talk frantically to another about the color of my skin, I felt disgusted. The white comrade returned.

"Just a moment, comrade," he said to me. "I'll get a place for you."

"But haven't you places already?" I asked. "Matters of this sort are ironed out in advance."

"Yes," he admitted in an intimate tone. "We have some addresses here, but we don't know the people. You understand?"

"Yes, I understand," I said, gritting my teeth.

"But just wait a second," he said, touching my arm to reassure me. "I'll find something."

"Listen, don't bother," I said, trying to keep anger out of my voice.

"Oh, no," he said, shaking his head determinedly. "This is a problem and I'll solve it."

"It oughtn't to be a problem," I could not help saying.

"Oh, I didn't mean that," he caught himself quickly.

Goddamn, I cursed under my breath. Several people standing near-by observed the white Communist trying to find a black Communist a place to sleep. I burned with shame. A few minutes later the white Communist returned, frantic-eyed, sweating.

"Did you find anything?" I asked.

"No, not yet," he said, panting. "Just a moment. I'm going to call somebody I know. Jay, give me a nickel for the phone."

"Forget it," I said. My legs felt like water. "I'll find a place."

But I'd like to put my suitcase somewhere until after the meeting tonight."

"Do you really think you can find a place?" he asked, trying to keep a note of desperate hope out of his voice.

"Of course, I can," I said.

He was still uncertain. He wanted to help me, but he did not know how. He locked my bag in a closet and I stepped to the sidewalk wondering where Harlem was, wondering where I would sleep that night. Before I had left Chicago I had thought of a thousand arguments to present for the retention of the John Reed Clubs, but now the retention of those clubs did not seem important. I stood on the sidewalks of New York with a black skin, practically no money, and I was not absorbed with the burning questions of the left-wing literary movement in the United States, but with the problem of how to get a bath. I presented my credentials at Carnegie Hall. The building was jammed with people. As I listened to the militant speeches, I found myself wondering why in hell I had come.

I went to the sidewalk and stood studying the faces of the people. The white Communist, who had been scouting for a room in which I could sleep, ran up to me.

"Did you find a place yet?"

"No," I answered.

"Well, here's a name and address," he said proudly. "Go there and they'll put you up for tonight."

"Thanks," I said, glad to have a place to flop.

When the meeting ended, I retrieved my bag from the club and found the address in a dark alley of Greenwich Village. I knocked at the door. A white man opened it, took one quick look at my face, then pushed the door almost shut again, as though in desperate defense of himself and his home.

"What do you want?" the words spilled out of him.

I asked for the name of the person written on the slip of paper I had.

"They aren't here," he said.

"When will they return?" I asked.

"I don't know," he spluttered, inching the door to.

I walked away. How could I sleep in a home where the sight of my face struck fear into people? I returned to the club and saw a few of the white comrades standing about the side-walk. I crossed to the opposite side of the street to avoid them. I approached a newsstand merchant. It was nearing three o'clock.

"Where is Harlem?" I asked.

He stared at me. I lost my temper.

"For God's sake!" I exploded. "I'm a stranger here. I'm asking you where Harlem is!"

He blinked and pointed vaguely.

"That way," he said.

His directions did not help me. I walked on. I met a Chicago club member.

"Didn't you find a place yet?" he asked.

"No," I said. "I'd like to try one of the hotels, but, God, I'm in no mood to argue with a hotel clerk about my color."

"Oh, goddamn, wait a minute," he said.

I waited as he scooted off. He returned in a few moments with a big heavy white woman. He introduced us.

"You can sleep in my place, tonight," she said.

I walked with her to her apartment and she introduced me to her husband. I thanked them for their hospitality and went to sleep on a cot in the kitchen. I got up at six, dressed, tapped on their door and bade them good-bye. I went to the sidewalk, sat on a bench, took out pencil and paper and tried to jot down notes for the argument I wanted to make in defense of the John Reed Clubs. But again the problem of the clubs did not seem important. What did seem important was: Could a Negro ever live halfway like a human being in this goddamn country?

That day I sat through the congress sessions, but what I heard did not touch me. That night I found my way to Harlem and walked pavements filled with black life. I was amazed, when I asked passers-by, to learn that there were practically no hotels for Negroes in Harlem. I kept walking. Finally I saw a tall, clean hotel; black people were passing the doors and no white people were in sight. Confidently I entered and was surprised to see a white clerk behind the desk. I hesitated.

"I'd like a room," I said.

"Not here," he said.

"But isn't this Harlem?" I asked.

"Yes, but this hotel is for white only," he said.

"Where is a hotel for colored?"

"You might try the Y," he said.

"In what direction is it?"

"Keep walking that way," he said, pointing.

Half an hour later I found the Negro Young Men's Christian Association, that bulwark of Jim Crowism for young black men, got a room, took a bath, and slept for twelve hours. When I awakened, I did not want to go to the congress. I lay in bed thinking: I've got to go it alone . . . I've got to learn how again . . .

I dressed and attended the meeting that was to make the final decision to dissolve the clubs. It started briskly. A New York Communist writer summed up the history of the clubs and made a motion for their dissolution. Debate started and I rose and explained what the clubs had meant to young writers and begged for their continuance. I sat down amid silence. Debate was closed. The vote was called. The room filled with uplifted hands to dissolve. Then there came a call for those who disagreed and my hand went up alone. I knew that my stand would be interpreted as one of opposition to the Communist party, but I thought: The hell with it . . .

New York held no further interest and the next morning I left for home.

With the clubs now dissolved, I was free of all party relations. I avoided unit meetings for fear of being subjected to discipline. Occasionally a Negro Communist—defying the code that enjoined him to shun suspect elements—came to my home and informed me of the current charges that Communists were bringing against one another. To my astonishment I heard that Buddy Nealson had branded me a "smuggler of reaction."

"Why does he call me that?" I asked.

"He says that you are a petty bourgeois degenerate," I was told.

"What does that mean?"

"He says that you are corrupting the party with your ideas," I was told.

"How?"

There was no answer. I decided that my relationship with the party was about over; I would have to leave it. The attacks were growing worse, and my refusal to react incited Nealson into coining more absurd phrases. I was termed a "bastard intellectual," an "incipient Trotskyite"; it was claimed that I possessed an "antileadership attitude" and that I was manifesting "seraphim tendencies," the latter phrase meaning that one has withdrawn from the struggle of life and considers oneself an infallible angel.

I could not dismiss these charges lightly, for a frantic, hysterical hunt was going on then in the ranks of the party for Trotskyites. In the Soviet Union men were being shot for Trotskyism. I used to lie awake nights wondering what would happen to me if I lived in the Soviet Union.

Working all day and writing half the night brought me down with a severe chest ailment. I was in constant pain, scarcely able to breathe. I lay reviewing the life I had lived in the party and I found it distasteful. I realized that I had not been objective in my quixotic fight to save the clubs. I had been fighting as much for myself as for them. But was that wrong? Again I resolved to leave the party, for the emotional cost of membership was too high.

While I was ill, a knock came at my door one morning. My mother admitted Ed Green, the man who had demanded to know what use I planned to make of the material I was collecting from the comrades. I stared at him as I lay abed and I knew that he considered me a clever and sworn enemy of the party. Bitterness welled up in me.

"What do you want?" I asked bluntly. "You see I'm ill."

"I have a message from the party for you," he said.

I had not said good day, and he had not offered to say it. He had not smiled, and neither had I. He looked curiously at my bleak room.

"This is the home of a bastard intellectual," I cut at him.

He stared without blinking. I could not endure his standing there so stone-like. Common decency made me say:

"Sit down."

His shoulders stiffened.

"I'm in a hurry." He spoke like an army officer.

"What do you want to tell me?"

"Do you know Buddy Nealson?" he asked.

"No," I said. "But I've heard of him."

I was suspicious. Was this a political trap? They had hurled baseless accusations at me and I felt that there could be no ground of trust between us. Was he trying to discover if I knew someone whom, politically, I should not know? But, after all, Buddy Nealson was a member of the Communist International. But what if Buddy Nealson had suddenly been accused of something and Ed Green was here trying to find out if I knew him?

"What about Buddy Nealson?" I asked, committing myself to nothing until I knew the kind of reality I was grappling with.

"He wants to see you," Ed Green said.

I breathed easier. I could not meet Communists now without feeling a degree of fear.

"What about?" I asked, still suspicious.

"He wants to talk with you about your party work," he said.

"I'm ill and can't see him until I'm well," I said.

Ed Green stood for a fraction of a second, then turned on his heel and marched out of the room.

Ought I see Buddy Nealson? He was the man who had formulated the Communist position for the American Negro; he had made speeches in the Kremlin; he had spoken before Stalin himself. Then perhaps he could explain many of the aspects of Communism that had baffled me. Anyway, I resolved to confront him and ask him some direct, simple questions and hear what he had to say.

When my chest healed, I sought an appointment with Buddy Nealson. He was a short, black man with an ever-ready smile, thick lips, a furtive manner, and a greasy, sweaty look. His bearing was nervous, self-conscious; he seemed always to be hiding some deep irritation. He spoke in short, jerky sentences, hopping nimbly from thought to thought, as though his mind worked in a free, associational manner. He suffered from asthma and would snort at unexpected intervals. Now and then he would punctuate his flow of words by taking a nip from a bottle of whisky. He had traveled half around the world and his talk was pitted with vague allusions to European citics. I met him in his apartment, listened to him intently, observed him minutely, for I knew that I was facing one of the leaders of World Communism.

"Hello, Wright," he snorted. "I've heard about you."

As we shook hands he burst into a loud, seemingly cause-less laugh; and as he guffawed I could not tell whether his mirth was directed at me or was meant to hide his uneasiness.

"I hope what you've heard about me is good," I parried.

"Sit down," he laughed again, waving me to a chair. "Yes, they tell me you write . . ."

"I try to," I said.

"You can write," he snorted. "I read that article you wrote for the *New Masses* about Joe Louis. Good stuff . . . First political treatment of sports we've yet had. Ha-ha . . ."

"I'm trying to reveal the meaning of Negro experience," I said.

"We need a man like you," he said flatteringly.

I waited. I had thought that I would encounter a man of ideas, but he was not that. Then perhaps he was a man of action? But that was not indicated either. As we talked, I tried to grasp the frame of reference of his words, so that I would know how to talk to him.

"They tell me that you are a friend of Ross's," he shot at me.

I paused before answering. He had not asked me directly, but had hinted in a neutral, teasing way. Mentally I prodded myself into remembering that I was speaking to a member of the Communist International. Ross, I had been told, was slated for expulsion on the grounds that he was "antileader-ship"; and if a member of the Communist International was asking me if I were a friend of a man about to be expelled, he was indirectly asking me if I were loyal or not.

"Ross is not particularly a friend of mine," I said frankly. "But I know him well; in fact, quite well."

"If he isn't your friend, how do you happen to know him so well?" he asked, laughing to soften the hard threat of his question.

"I was writing an account of his life and I know him as well, perhaps, as anybody," I told him.

"I heard about that," he said. "Wright . . . Ha-ha . . . Say, let me call you Dick, hunh?"

"Go ahead," I said.

"Dick," he said, "Ross is a nationalist." He paused to let the weight of his accusation sink in. He meant that Ross's militancy was extreme. "We Communists don't dramatize Negro nationalism," he said in a voice that laughed, accused, and drawled.

"What do you mean?" I asked.

"We're not advertising Ross," he spoke directly now.

"We're talking about two different things," I said. "You seem worried about my making Ross popular because he is your political opponent. But I'm not concerned about Ross's politics at all. The man struck me as one who typified certain traits of the Negro migrant. I've already sold a story based upon an incident in his life."

Nealson became excited.

"What was the incident?" he asked.

"Some trouble he got into when he was thirteen years old," I said.

His face looked blank for a second, then he laughed.

"Oh, I thought it was political," he said, shrugging.

"But I'm telling you that you are wrong about that," I explained. "I'm not trying to fight you with my writing. I've no political ambitions. I'm not trying to hurt or help any particular comrade. You must believe that. I'm trying to depict Negro life."

"Have you finished writing about Ross?" he asked.

"No," I said. "I dropped the idea. Our party members were suspicious of me and were afraid to talk."

He laughed.

"You've got to know us better, Dick," he grinned. "I hold a high position in the party. I'll straighten out this misunderstanding."

"I'm not looking for a patron," I said.

"I don't mean that," he said, grinning, snorting. "Here, Dick, hava drink."

"No, thank you."

"Don't you drink?"

"Sometimes."

There are men with whom one can drink and there are men with whom one cannot drink. Nealson was one of the men with whom I could not drink. He drank and put the bottle back; he shot me a quick, self-conscious glance. I was tense, but rigidly controlled.

"Dick," he began, "we're short of forces. We're facing a grave crisis."

"The party's always facing a crisis," I said.

His smile left and he stared at me.

"You're not cynical, are you, Dick?" he asked.

"No," I said. "But it's the truth. Each week, each month there's a crisis."

"You're a funny guy," he said, laughing, snorting again. "But we've got a job to do. We're altering our work. Fascism's the danger, the danger now to all people."

"I understand," I said.

"You were in New York not long ago," he said unexpectedly.

"Yes."

"Did you talk with any of the party leaders?"

"No."

"You said nothing to anyone about your work here?"

I stared at him. Was he trying to find out whether I had taken up any of his accusations with the national leadership of the party? Was he trying to determine whether I had influential enough political connections to make trouble for him?

"I told you that I have no political ambitions," I said.

"Yes," he said. "They say that you didn't want the clubs dissolved."

"No, I didn't," I said truthfully. "I felt that the ground was being cut from under the feet of the party's best writers."

"We've got to defeat the Fascists," he said, snorting from asthma, switching his line of thought. "We've discussed you and know your abilities. We want you to work with us. We've got to crash out of our narrow way of working and get our message to the church people, students, club people, professionals, middle class . . ."

"I've been called names," I said softly. "Is that crashing out of the narrow way?"

"Forget that," he said, laughing.

He had not denied the name-calling. That meant that, if I did not obey him, the name-calling would begin again.

"I don't know if I fit into things," I said openly.

"We want to trust you with an important assignment," he said.

"What do you want me to do?"

"We want you to organize a committee against the high cost of living . . ."

"The high cost of living?" I exclaimed. "What do I know about such things?"

"It's easy. You can learn," he said.

I was in the midst of writing a novel and he was calling me from it to tabulate the price of groceries. He doesn't think much of what I'm trying to do, I thought.

"Comrade Nealson," I said, "a writer who hasn't written anything worth-while is a most doubtful person. Now, I'm in that category. Yet I think I can write. I don't want to ask for special favors, but I'm in the midst of a book which I hope to complete in six months or so. Let me convince myself that I'm wrong about my hankering to write and then I'll be with you all the way."

"The party can't wait," he said. "You'll find time to write."

"I work every day for a living," I said, remembering that he was being paid by the party to talk to me.

"Look, we want to make you a mass leader," he said.

"But suppose I'm not that kind of material?"

He laughed. Not one word that I had said had been seriously considered by him. Our talk was a game; he was trying to outwit me. The feelings of others meant nothing to him.

"Dick," he said, turning in his chair and waving his hand as though to brush away an insect that was annoying him, "you've got to get to the masses of people . . ."

"You've seen some of my work," I said. "Isn't it just barely good enough to warrant my being given a chance?"

"The party can't deal with your feelings," he said.

"Maybe I don't belong in the party," I stated it in full.

"Oh, no! Don't say that," he said, snorting. He looked at me. "You're blunt."

"I put things the way I feel them," I said. "I want to start in right with you. I've had too damn much crazy trouble in the party."

He laughed and lit a cigarette.

"Dick," he said, shaking his head, "the trouble with you is that you've been around with those white artists on the North Side too much . . . You even talk like 'em. You've got to know your own people . . ."

"I think I know them," I said, realizing that I could never really talk with him. "I've been inside of three-fourths of the Negroes' homes on the South Side . . ."

"But you've got to work with 'em," he said.

"I was working with Ross until I was suspected of being a spy," I said.

There was silence. The doorbell rang and he admitted his wife, a dark, attractive, European white woman who carried a book under her arm. She came forward with a wide smile. Nealson introduced us.

"What are you reading?" I asked.

"A Dracula mystery story," she said, eagerly exhibiting her book. "You know, Dick, you and I ought to build Negro culture on the South Side."

"I'm asking Nealson for that chance right now," I said, wondering what connection there could be between a Dracula mystery and Negro culture.

"I want him to organize against high prices," Nealson told his wife. "But he's writing a book . . ."

"That oughtn't interfere with his book," she said, sliding easily into a verbal solution of my problem.

"I work in the day," I said.

"Oh, you'll find time," she said lightly.

She left the room and there was silence. The next word was due to come from the member of the Communist International.

"Dick," he spoke seriously now, "the party has decided that you are to accept this task."

I was silent. I knew the meaning of what he had said. A decision was the highest injunction that a Communist could receive from his party, and to break a decision was to break the effectiveness of the party's ability to act. In principle I heartily agreed with this, for I knew that it was impossible for working people to forge instruments of political power until they had achieved unity of action. Oppressed for centuries, divided, hopeless, corrupted, misled, they were cynical—as I had once been—and the Communist method of unity had been found historically to be the only means of achieving discipline. In short, Nealson had asked me directly if I were a Communist or not. I wanted to be a Communist, but my kind of Communist. I wanted to shape people's feelings, awaken their hearts. But I could not tell Nealson that; he would only have snorted.

"I'll organize the committee and turn it over to someone else," I suggested.

"You don't want to do this, do you?" he asked.

"No," I said firmly.

"You worked willingly enough to organize white writers," he cut at me.

"I was organizing people I understood," I said.

"What would you like to do on the South Side, then?"

"I'd like to organize Negro artists," I said.

"But the party doesn't need that now," he said.

I rose, knowing that he had no intention of letting me go after I had organized the committee. I wanted to tell him that I was through, but I was not ready to bring matters to a head. I went out, angry with myself, angry with him, angry with the party. Well, I had not broken the decision, but neither had I accepted it wholly. I had dodged, trying to save time for writing, time to think.

Again I urged myself to quit, but I could not do it. I knew that Nealson was not a leader. His mind was too rigid, too limited. I had not discerned in him any understanding of life or politics. His approach had been to offer me a drink, and when that had failed he had threatened; he had tried flattery, and when that had failed he had hinted at expulsion. If I had been wrong, he certainly had not convinced me. In the end I resolved to work a month, then confront him with my original compromise.

My task consisted in attending meetings until the late hours of the night, taking part in discussions, or lending myself generally along with other Communists in leading the people of the South Side. We debated the housing situation, the best means of forcing the city to authorize open hearings on conditions among Negroes. I gritted my teeth as the daily value of pork chops was tabulated, longing to be at home with my writing. I felt that pork chops were a fundamental item in life, but I preferred that someone else chart their rise and fall in price.

Nealson was cleverer than I and he confronted me before I had a chance to confront him. I was summoned one night to meet Nealson and a "friend." When I arrived at a South Side hotel I was introduced to a short, yellow man who carried himself like Napoleon. He wore glasses, kept his full lips pursed as though he were engaged in perpetual thought. He swaggered when he walked. He spoke slowly, precisely, trying to charge each of his words with more meaning than the words were able to carry. He talked of trivial things in lofty tones. He said that his name was Smith, that he was from Washington, that he planned to launch a national organization among Negroes to federalize all existing Negro institutions so as to achieve a broad unity of action. The three of us sat at a table, facing one another. There were no smiles now. I knew that another and last offer was about to be made to me, and if I did not accept it, there would be open warfare.

"Wright, how would you like to go to Switzerland?" Smith asked with dramatic suddenness.

"I'd like it," I said. "But I'm tied up with work now."

"You can drop that," Nealson said. "This is important."

"What would I do in Switzerland?" I asked.

"You'll go as a youth delegate," Smith said. "From there you can go to the Soviet Union."

"Much as I'd like to, I'm afraid I can't make it," I said honestly. "I simply cannot drop the writing I'm doing now."

We sat looking at one another, smoking silently.

"Has Nealson told you how I feel?" I asked Smith.

Smith did not answer. He stared at me a long time, then spat:

"Wright, you're a fool!"

I rose. Smith turned away from me. A breath more of anger and I would have driven my fist into his face. Nealson laughed sheepishly, snorting.

"Was that necessary?" I asked, trembling.

I stood recalling how, in my boyhood, I would have fought until blood ran had anyone said anything like that to me. But I was a man now and master of my rage, able to control the surging emotions. I put on my hat and walked to the door. Keep cool, I said to myself. Don't let this get out of hand . . .

"This is good-bye," I said.

I walked home. My mind was made up. I would attend the next unit meeting and announce my withdrawal, telling the comrades that I still adhered to the ideological program of the party, but that I did not want to be bound any longer by the party's decisions.

I attended the next unit meeting and asked for a place on the agenda, which was readily granted. Nealson was there. Evans was there. Ed Green was there. When my time came to speak, I rose and said:

"Comrades, for the past two years I've worked daily with most of you. Despite this, I have for some time found myself in a difficult position in the party. What has caused this difficulty is a long story which I do not care to recite now; it would serve no purpose. But I tell you honestly that I think I've found a solution of my difficulty. I am proposing here tonight that my membership be dropped from the party rolls. No ideological differences impel me to say this. I simply do not wish to be bound any longer by the party's decisions. I would like to retain my membership in those organizations in which the party has influence, and I shall comply with the party's program in those organizations. I hope that my words will be accepted in the spirit in which they are said. Perhaps sometime in the future I would like to meet and talk with the leaders of the party as to what tasks I can best perform."

I sat down amid a profound silence. The Negro secretary of the meeting looked frightened, glancing at Nealson, Evans, and Ed Green.

"Is there any discussion on Comrade Wright's statement?" the secretary asked finally.

"I move that discussion on Wright's statement be deferred," Nealson said.

A quick vote confirmed Nealson's motion. I looked about the silent room, then reached for my hat and rose.

"I would like to go now," I said.

No one said anything. I walked to the door and out into the night and a heavy burden seemed to lift from my shoulders. I was free. And I had done it in a decent and forthright manner. I had not been bitter. I had not raked up a single recrimination. I had attacked no one. I had disavowed nothing. I remembered, as I walked the night streets, how I had stolen money from the movie house in Jackson, Mississippi; how I had forced the window and had stolen the gun; how I had broken into the college storehouse and had stolen cans of fruit preserves; I remembered how I had lied to my boss man in Memphis when I had wanted to leave my job and come to Chicago; how I had lied to Mr. Hoffman; how I had forged notes to the library in Memphis when I had wanted books to read . . . But I had changed; I had none of that fear, none of those wild impulses now. I had merely confronted my comrades, stated what I felt, and had let it go at that.

The Communist party could not say that I was an enemy, that I had attacked them. A Trotskyite or a man bent upon wrecking or disrupting the work of the Communist party would have remained within the organization so as better to quarrel, obstruct. But I had only asked to be free, had accused no one, and had denounced nothing. Perhaps, I told myself, when the Communist party has grown up, when it can work without tactics of terror, threat, invective, intimidation, suspicion, I would go back . . .

Aw, God . . . How naïve I was! I was young and brimming with confidence. I felt that my strength was unlimited. I had neatly solved a problem that had been worrying me for a long time, and now I thought that I could turn my energies to writing and justify myself. I did not know that night how little I understood the political party to which I had belonged. But I soon learned, learned how simple were my motives, how trusting was my attitude, how wide and innocent were my eyes, as round and open and dew-wet as morning-glories . . .

The next night two Negro Communists called at my home. They pretended to be ignorant of what had happened at the unit meeting. Patiently I explained what had occurred.

"Your story does not agree with what Nealson says," they said, revealing the motive of their visit.

"And what does Nealson say?" I asked.

"He says that you are in league with a Trotskyite group, and that you made an appeal for other party members to follow you in leaving the party . . ."

"What?" I gasped. "That's not true. I asked that my membership be dropped. I raised no political issues." What did this mean? I sat pondering. "Look, maybe I ought to make my break with the party clean. If Nealson's going to act this way, I'll resign . . ."

"You can't resign," they told me.

"What do you mean?" I demanded.

"No one can resign from the Communist party," they said.

I looked at them and laughed.

"You're talking crazy," I said.

"Nealson would expel you publicly, cut the ground from under your feet if you resigned," they said. "People would think that something was wrong if someone like you quit here on the South Side."

I was angry. Was the party so weak and uncertain of itself that it could not accept what I had said at the unit meeting? Who thought up such tactics? Then, suddenly, I understood. These were the secret, underground tactics of the political movement of the Communists under the czars of Old Russia! The Communist party felt that it had to assassinate me morally merely because I did not want to be bound by its decisions. I saw now that my comrades were acting out a fantasy that had no relation whatever to the reality of their environment.

"Tell Nealson that if he fights me, then, by God, I'll fight him," I said. "If he leaves this damn thing where it is, then all right. If he thinks I won't fight him publicly, he's crazy!"

I was not able to know if my statement reached Nealson, but there was no public outcry against me. But in the ranks of the party itself a storm broke loose and I was branded a traitor, an unstable personality, and one whose faith had failed.

What a weird experience I had had! At no time had I felt at home in the Communist party. I had always felt that the possibility was there, but always I was not quite sure of the

motives of the people with whom I worked and they never
seemed quite sure of mine. My comrades had known me, my
family, my friends; they, God knows, had known my aching
poverty. But they had never been able to conquer their fear of
the individual way in which I acted and lived, an individuality
which life had seared into my blood and bones.

I now avoided the comrades as much as possible, and, as I
was losing touch with the party, many other young Negroes
of the South Side were entering it for the first time. The ex-
pansion of the party's activity under the People's Front policy
offered many opportunities to young Negroes who, because
of race and status, had led cramped lives. The invitation to go
to Switzerland as a youth delegate, which I had refused, was
accepted by a young Negro who had fought the Communist
party and all its ideas until he had seen a chance to take a trip
to Europe.

I was transferred by the relief authorities from the South
Side Boys' Club to the Federal Negro Theater to work as a
publicity agent. There were days when I was acutely hungry
for the incessant analyses that went on among the comrades,
but whenever I heard news of the party's inner life, it was of
charges and countercharges, reprisals and counterreprisals. I
was glad to be out of it. All its energies, it seemed, were absorbed in factional fights, hair-splitting political definitions.

The Federal Negro Theater, for which I was doing publicity, had run a series of ordinary plays, all of which had been
revamped to "Negro style," with jungle scenes, spirituals, and
all. For example, the skinny white woman who directed it, an
elderly missionary type, would take a play whose characters
were white, whose theme dealt with the Middle Ages, and
recast it in terms of southern Negro life with overtones of
African backgrounds. Contemporary plays dealing realistically
with Negro life were spurned as being controversial. There
were about forty Negro actors and actresses in the theater,
lolling about, yearning, disgruntled, not knowing what to do
with themselves.

What a waste of talent, I thought. Here was an opportunity
for the production of a worth-while Negro drama and no one
was aware of it. I studied the situation, then laid the matter

before white friends of mine who held influential positions in the Works Progress Administration. I asked them to replace the white woman—including her quaint aesthetic notions— with someone who knew the Negro and the theater. They promised me that they would act.

Within a month the white woman director had been transferred. We moved from the South Side to the Loop and were housed in a first-rate theater. I successfully recommended Charles DeSheim, a talented Jew, as director. DeSheim and I held long talks during which I outlined what I thought could be accomplished. I urged that our first offering should be a bill of three one-act plays, including Paul Green's *Hymn to the Rising Sun*, a grim, poetical, powerful one-acter dealing with chain gang conditions in the South.

I was happy. At last I was in a position to make suggestions and have them acted upon. I was convinced that we had a rare chance to build a genuine Negro theater. I convoked a meeting and introduced DeSheim to the Negro company, telling them that he was a man who knew the theater, who would lead them toward serious dramatics. DeSheim made a speech wherein he said that he was not at the theater to direct it, but to help the Negroes to direct it. He spoke so simply and eloquently that they rose and applauded him.

I then proudly passed out copies of Paul Green's *Hymn to the Rising Sun* to all members of the company. DeSheim assigned reading parts. I sat down to enjoy adult Negro dramatics. But something went wrong. The Negroes stammered and faltered in their lines. Finally they stopped reading altogether. DeSheim looked frightened. One of the Negro actors rose.

"Mr. DeSheim," he began, "we think this play is indecent. We don't want to act in a play like this before the American public. I don't think any such conditions exist in the South. I lived in the South and I never saw any chain gangs. Mr. DeSheim, we want a play that will make the public love us."

I could not believe my ears. I had assumed that the heart of the Negro actor was pining for adult expression in the American theater, that he was ashamed of the stereotypes of clowns, mammies, razors, dice, watermelon, and cotton fields . . . Now they were protesting against dramatic realism! I tried to defend the play and I was heckled down.

"What kind of play do you want?" DeSheim asked them.

They did not know. I went to the office and looked up their records and found that most of them had spent their lives playing cheap vaudeville. I had thought that they played vaudeville because the legitimate theater was barred to them, and now it turned out that they wanted none of the legitimate theater, that they were scared spitless at the prospects of appearing in a play that the public might not like, even though they did not understand that public and had no way of determining its likes or dislikes.

I felt—but only temporarily—that perhaps the whites were right, that Negroes were children and would never grow up. DeSheim informed the company that he would produce any play they liked, and they sat like frightened mice, possessing no words to make known their vague desires.

When I arrived at the theater a few mornings later, I was horrified to find that the company had drawn up a petition demanding the ousting of DeSheim. I was asked to sign the petition and I refused.

"Don't you know your friends?" I asked them.

They glared at me. I called DeSheim to the theater and we went into a frantic conference.

"What must I do?" he asked.

"Take them into your confidence," I said. "Let them know that it is their right to petition for a redress of their grievances."

DeSheim thought my advice sound and, accordingly, he assembled the company and told them that they had a right to petition against him if they wanted to, but that he thought any misunderstandings that existed could be settled smoothly.

"Who told you that we were getting up a petition?" a black man demanded.

DeSheim looked at me and stammered wordlessly.

"There's an Uncle Tom in the theater!" a black girl yelled.

After the meeting a delegation of Negro men came to my office and took out their pocketknives and flashed them in my face.

"You get the hell off this job before we cut your belly button out!" they said.

I tried to talk to them, but could not. That day a huge, fat, black woman, a blues singer, found an excuse to pass me as often as possible and she hissed under her breath in a menacing singsong:

"Lawd, Ah sho hates a white man's nigger."

I telephoned my white friends in the Works Progress Administration:

"Transfer me at once to another job, or I'll be murdered."

Within twenty-four hours DeSheim and I were given our papers. We shook hands and went our separate ways.

I was transferred to a white experimental theatrical company as a publicity agent and I resolved to keep my ideas to myself, or, better, to write them down and not attempt to translate them into reality. I dodged the Negro theatrical world and kept rigorously clear of all members of the Communist party. Whenever I met any of my erstwhile comrades, they refused to acknowledge my existence in accordance with a party principle that made it imperative that all "traitors be isolated from the working class."

One evening a group of Negro Communists called at my home and asked to speak to me in strict secrecy. I took them into my room and locked the door.

"Dick," they began abruptly, "the party wants you to attend a meeting Sunday."

"Why?" I asked. "I'm no longer a member."

"That's all right. They want you to be present," they said.

"Communists don't speak to me on the street," I said. "Now, why do you want me at a meeting?"

They hedged. They did not want to tell me.

"If you can't tell me, then I can't come," I said.

They whispered among themselves and finally decided to take me into their confidence.

"Dick, Ross is going to be tried," they said.

"For what?"

They recited a long list of political offenses of which they alleged that he was guilty.

"But what has this got to do with me?"

"If you come, you'll find out," they said.

"I'm not that naïve," I said, smiling. I was suspicious now.

Were they trying to lure me to a trial and expel me? "This trial might turn out to be mine . . ."

They swore that they had no intention of placing me on trial, that the party merely wanted me to observe Ross's trial so that I might learn what happened to "enemies of the working class."

"But I'm not your enemy," I said.

"We want to save you," they said.

"Save me from what?" I asked. "I'm not lost."

"We have your welfare at heart," they said.

"Then why did you-all lie and call me a Trotskyite?"

"Nealson lost his head," they said. "When you left the party, he had to hit at you some way."

"Why do you spend your time in these crazy witch hunts?" I asked them. "You claim to be fighting oppression, but you spend more of your time fighting each other than in fighting your avowed enemies." As I spoke to them I recalled the time when my mother had slapped me when I had asked her—in the far-off days of Arkansas—why my "uncle" had run away from the white people, why he had not fought back; my mother had given me a ringing slap—fear had made her do it. And I felt that it was the fear of their enemies that made Communists—unconsciously compensating for their fear— fight one another so doggedly and persistently. But I did not tell them that; they would not have understood. "Look, Ross is a minor street agitator. Forget him. And in two weeks he'd be no issue at all."

"We're going to make an example out of Ross," they told me. "His trial will be an education for the working class, and for you, too, if you'll come."

As they talked, my old love of witnessing something new came over me. I wanted to see this trial, but I did not want to risk being placed on trial myself.

"Listen," I told them. "I'm not guilty of Nealson's charges. If I showed up at this trial, it would seem that I am."

"No, it won't. Please come."

"All right. But, listen . . . If I'm tricked, I'll fight. You hear! I don't trust Nealson. I'm not a politician and I cannot anticipate all the funny moves of a man who spends his waking hours plotting."

Ross's trial took place that following Sunday afternoon. Comrades stood inconspicuously on guard about the meeting hall, at the doors, down the street, and along the hallways. When I appeared, I was ushered in quickly. I was tense. It was a rule that once you had entered a meeting of this kind you could not leave until the meeting was over; it was feared that you might go to the police and denounce them all.

Acting upon the loftiest of impulses, filled with love for those who suffer, urged toward fellowship with the rebellious, committed to sacrifice, why was it that there existed among Communists so much hate, suspicion, bitterness, and internecine strife? I stood in the midst of people I loved and I was afraid of them. I felt profoundly that they were traveling in the right direction, yet if their having power to rule had depended merely upon my lifting my right hand, I would have been afraid to do so. My heart throbbed and I whispered to myself: God, I love these people, but I'm glad that they're not in power, or they'd shoot me!

No one spoke to me. Some of the party leaders shot me hostile glances and looked away. Why had I been called in to witness this trial? I sat with jumpy nerves, impatient for the trial to get under way. Despite my fear, I was keenly curious. But I was determined not to participate in any way, for that would have surely, by implication, incriminated me in a network of guilt which I did not share.

Ross, the accused, sat alone at a table in the front of the hall, his face distraught. I felt sorry for him, yet I could not escape feeling that he enjoyed this. For him, this was perhaps the highlight of an otherwise bleak existence.

I was for these people. Being a Negro, I could not help it. They did not hate Negroes. They had no racial prejudices. Many of the white men in the hall were married to Negro women, and many of the Negro men were married to white women. Jews, Germans, Russians, Spaniards, all races and nationalities were represented without any distinctions whatever.

Racial hate had been the bane of my life, and here before my eyes was concrete proof that it could be abolished. Yet a new hate had come to take the place of the rankling racial hate. It was irrational that Communists should hate what they called "intellectuals," or anybody who tried to think for himself. I had fled men who did not like the color of my skin, and now I was among men who did not like the tone of my thoughts.

In trying to grasp why Communists hated intellectuals, my mind was led back again to the accounts I had read of the Russian Revolution. There had existed in Old Russia millions of poor, ignorant people who were exploited by a few, educated, arrogant noblemen, and it became natural for the Russian Communists to associate betrayal with intellectualism. But there existed in the Western world an element that baffled and frightened the Communist party: the prevalence of self-achieved literacy. Even a Negro, entrapped by ignorance and exploitation—as I had been—could, if he had the will and the love for it, learn to read and understand the world in which he lived. And it was these people that the Communists could not understand. The American Communists, enjoying legality, were using the methods forged by the underground Russian Bolshevik fire, and therefore had to have their followers willing to accept all explanations of reality, even when the actual situation did not call for it.

The heritage of free thought,—which no man could escape if he read at all,—the spirit of the Protestant ethic which one suckled, figuratively, with one's mother's milk, that self-generating energy that made a man feel, whether he realized it or not, that he had to work and redeem himself through his own acts, all this was forbidden, taboo. And yet this was the essence of that cultural heritage which the Communist party had sworn to carry forward, whole and intact, into the future. But the Communist party did not recognize the values that it had sworn to save when it saw them; the slightest sign of any independence of thought or feeling, even if it aided the party in its work, was enough to make one suspect, to brand one as a dangerous traitor.

The trial began in a quiet, informal manner. The comrades acted like a group of neighbors sitting in judgment upon one of their kind who had stolen a chicken. Anybody could ask and get the floor. There was absolute freedom of speech. Yet the meeting had an amazingly formal structure of its own, a structure that went as deep as the desire of men to live together.

A member of the Central Committee of the Communist party rose and gave a description of the world situation. He spoke without emotion and piled up hard facts. He painted a horrible but masterful picture of Fascism's aggression in Germany, Italy, and Japan.

I accepted the reason why the trial began in this manner. It was imperative that there be postulated against what or whom Ross's crimes had been committed. Therefore there had to be established in the minds of all present a vivid picture of mankind under oppression. And it was a true picture. Perhaps no organization on earth, save the Communist party, possessed so detailed a knowledge of how workers lived, for its sources of information stemmed directly from the workers themselves.

The next speaker discussed the role of the Soviet Union as the world's lone workers' state, how the Soviet Union was hemmed in by enemies, how the Soviet Union was trying to industrialize itself, what sacrifices she was making to help the workers of the world to steer a path toward peace through the idea of collective security.

The facts presented so far were as true as any facts could be in this uncertain world. Yet not one word had been said of the accused, who sat listening like any other member. The time had not yet come to include him and his crimes in this picture of global struggle. An absolute had first to be established in the minds of the comrades so that they could measure the success or failure of their deeds by it. There was no mysticism, no invoking of God, merely a passionate identification of all present with a will to right wrongs. It was a simple, elemental morality. Communism had found a moral code that could control the conduct of men, yet it was a code that stemmed from practical living, and not from the injunctions of the supernatural.

Still another speaker rose and described the domestic situation in the United States and linked it with the world scene. This was done in a leisurely, painstaking manner; yet the people in the hall were charged with passion; a sense of human destiny lived; an atmosphere of human frailty was present.

Finally a speaker came forward and spoke of Chicago's South Side, its Negro population, their sufferings, and handicaps, linking all that, also, to the world struggle. Then still another speaker followed and described the tasks of the Communist party of the South Side. At last, the world, the national, and the local pictures had been fused into one overwhelming drama of moral struggle in which everybody in the hall was participating. This presentation had lasted for more than three hours, but it had enthroned a new sense of reality in the hearts of those present, a sense of man on earth. With the exception of the church and its myths and legends, there was no agency in the world so capable of making men feel the earth and the people upon it as the Communist party.

I knew, as I watched, that I was looking at the future of mankind, that this way of living would finally win out. I knew that in no other way could the emotional capacities, the passional nature of men be so deeply tapped. In no other system yet devised could man so clearly reveal his destiny on earth, a destiny to rise and grapple with the world in which he lives, to wring from it the satisfactions he feels he must have. I knew, as I watched and listened, that but few people understood the essence of Communism, its passional dynamics; but a few knew that Communism was more important than any of its individual parties, than the sum of all its tactics, strategies, theories, mistakes, and tragedies. I knew that once this system became entrenched on earth, for good or bad, it could not fail, that all Europe and her armies could not destroy the Soviet Union, that the spirit of self-sacrifice that Communism engendered in men would astound the world.

And these people had asked me to come and listen to another man being tried so that I might know what was in store for me if I went wrong. I was with them. Could I not rise up and tell them? But, even as I thought of it, I knew they would not be able to know when I was telling the truth. My kind of helping was something frightening to them. If I talked, I would only incriminate myself further.

I had wanted to tell others what these men felt. I understood their impulses, the long years' privation and hurt out of which they had come to Communism. I knew that I did not know as much politics as Buddy Nealson, as the members of the Central Committee, or the members of the Communist

International. Politics was not my game; the human heart was my game, but it was only in the realm of politics that I could see the depths of the human heart. I had wanted to make others see what was in the Communist heart, what the Communists were after; but I was on trial by proxy, condemned by them.

Toward evening the direct charges against Ross were made, not by the leaders of the party but by Ross's friends, those who knew him best! It was crushing. Ross wilted. His emotions could not withstand the weight of the moral pressure. No one was terrorized into giving information against him. They gave it willingly, citing dates, conversations, scenes. The black mass of Ross's wrongdoing emerged slowly and irrefutably. He could not deny it. No one could.

They did not place me on trial because they did not know how to give names to what they feared in me. I had not fought them as Ross had; I had not challenged a single policy of theirs. It was my way of thinking and feeling that they feared. The conditions under which I had to work were what baffled them. Writing had to be done in loneliness and Communism had declared war upon human loneliness. Alone, they said, a man was weak; united with others, he was strong. Therefore, they habitually feared a man who stood alone. Communism spelt the unity of human life, and when a Communist, newly risen from his oppressed isolation and feeling strange and lonely because of it, saw another man seeking seclusion, he became afraid of him. The Communism I looked upon was impatient of extended processes, of results that could not be obtained overnight, of an act that could not be performed within a day. This was how America had embraced Communism; this was America's first green fruit of materialistic rebellion.

The moment came for Ross to defend himself. I had been told that he had arranged for friends of his to testify in his behalf, but he called upon no one. He stood, trembling; he tried to talk and his words would not come. The hall was as still as death. Guilt was written in every pore of his black skin. His hands shook. He held onto the edge of the table to keep on his feet. His personality, his sense of himself, had been obliterated. Yet he could not have been so humbled unless he had shared and accepted the vision that had crushed him, the common vision that bound us all together.

"Comrades," he said in a low, charged voice, "I'm guilty of all the charges, all of them . . ."

His voice broke in a sob. No one prodded him. No one tortured him. No one threatened him. He was free to go out of the hall and never see another Communist. But he did not want to. He could not. The vision of a communal world had sunk down into his soul and it would never leave him until life left him. He talked on, outlining how he had erred, how he would reform.

I knew, as I sat there, that there were many people who thought they knew life who had been skeptical of the Moscow trials. But they could not have been skeptical had they witnessed this astonishing trial. Ross had not been doped; he had been awakened. It was not a fear of the Communist party that had made him confess, but a fear of the punishment that he would exact of himself that made him tell of his wrongdoings. The Communists had talked to him until they had given him new eyes with which to see his own crime. And then they sat back and listened to him tell how he had erred. He was one with all the members there, regardless of race or color; his heart was theirs and their hearts were his; and when a man reaches that state of kinship with others, that degree of oneness, or when a trial has made him kin after he has been sundered from them by wrongdoing, then he must rise and say, out of a sense of the deepest morality in the world:

"I'm guilty. Forgive me."

This, to me, was a spectacle of glory; and yet, because it had condemned me, because it was blind and ignorant, I felt that it was a spectacle of horror. The blindness of their limited lives—lives truncated and impoverished by the oppression they had suffered long before they had ever heard of Communism—made them think that I was with their enemies. American life had so corrupted their consciousness that they were unable to recognize their friends when they saw them. I knew that if they had held state power I would have been declared guilty of treason and my execution would have followed. And I knew that they felt, with all the strength of their black blindness, that they were right.

I could not stay until the end. I was anxious to get out of the hall and into the streets and shake free from the gigantic tension that had hold of me. I rose and went to the door; a comrade shook his head, warning me that I could not leave until the trial had ended.

"You can't leave now," he said.

"I'm going out of here," I said, my anger making my voice sound louder than I intended.

We glared at each other. Another comrade came running up. I stepped forward. The comrade who had rushed up gave the signal for me to be allowed to leave. They did not want violence, and neither did I. They stepped aside.

I went into the dark Chicago streets and walked home through the cold, filled with a sense of sadness. Once again I told myself that I must learn to stand alone. I did not feel so wounded by their rejection of me that I wanted to spend my days bleating about what they had done. Perhaps what I had already learned to feel in my childhood saved me from that futile path. I lay in bed that night and said to myself: I'll be for them, even though they are not for me.

The next morning a Negro Communist came to my house before I was out of bed. He sat and would not look at me.

"What do you want, Harold?" I asked.

"I don't know how to say what I want to say," he said.

"Say it anyhow. I can stand anything now."

"Gee, I'm sorrier than I've ever been in all my life," he cried. "I didn't know what they were going to do . . ."

"Do you mean that?" I asked.

"God, yes!"

"Thanks. I'm no enemy of the party."

"It was horrible," he said.

"There was a glimpse of glory in it, too," I said.

"What?"

"Nothing," I said.

He left. He was the only Communist who had enough courage to speak to me.

Chapter XX

From the Federal Experimental Theater I was transferred to the Federal Writers' Project, and I tried to earn my bread by writing guidebooks. Many of the writers on the project were members of the Communist party and they kept their revolutionary vows that restrained them from speaking to "traitors of the working class." I sat beside them in the office, ate next to them in restaurants, and rode up and down in the elevators with them, but they always looked straight ahead, wordlessly.

After working on the project for a few months, I was made acting supervisor of essays and straightway I ran into political difficulties. One morning the administrator of the project called me into his office.

"Wright, who are your friends on this project?" he asked.

"I don't know," I said. "Why?"

"Well, you ought to find out soon," he said.

"What do you mean?"

"Some people are asking for your removal on the grounds that you are incompetent," he said.

"Who are they?"

He named several of my erstwhile comrades. Yes, it had come to that. They were trying to take the bread out of my mouth, and I agreed with them too much to want to fight back.

"What do you propose to do about their complaints?" I asked.

"Nothing," he said, laughing. "I think I understand what's happening here. I'm not going to let them drive you off this job."

I thanked him and rose to go to the door. Something in his words had not sounded right. I turned and faced him.

"*This* job?" I repeated. "What do you mean?"

"You mean to say that you don't know?" he asked.

"Know what? What are you talking about?"

"Why did you leave the Federal Negro Theater?"

"I had trouble there. They drove me off the job, the Negroes did."

358

"And you don't think that they had any encouragement?" he asked me ironically.

I sat again. This was deadly. I gaped at him.

"You needn't fear here," he said. "You work, write . . ."

"It's hard to believe that," I murmured.

"Forget it," he said.

I returned to my desk and stared at the Communists who sat near me. I was not angry. I was sorry. How far can they go acting like this? I wondered. I knew that if they had succeeded in getting me fired they would have considered it a triumph of proletarian tactics. Why could they not forget me? I was opposing no policy of theirs. I was not speaking or writing against them. But the worst was yet to come.

One day at noon I closed my desk and went down in the elevator. When I reached the first floor of the building, I saw a picket line moving to and fro in the streets. Many of the men and women carrying placards were old friends of mine, and they were chanting for higher wages for Works Progress Administration artists and writers. It was not the kind of picket line that one was not supposed to cross, and as I started away from the door I heard my name shouted:

"There's Wright, that goddamn Trotskyite!"

"That sonofabitch Wright is with 'em, too!"

"We know you, you bastard!"

"Wright's a traitor, too!"

For a moment it seemed that I ceased to live. I had now reached that point where I was cursed aloud in the busy streets of America's second largest city. It shook me as nothing else had.

I decided upon a bold, open, and friendly move. I had to put a stop to this hounding of me. I would go directly to the head of the local Communist party and have it out with him, talk to him, explain things. I implored a friend of mine to use what influence he had to obtain an appointment for me with the secretary of the party.

Weeks passed and finally word came that I had an appointment, not with the secretary, but with the secretary's secretary, a girl, Alma Zetkin. I sighed and accepted it.

When I walked into the headquarters of the Communist party, I was ushered into Alma Zetkin's presence. She was plump, blonde, blue-eyed, with big braids of hair circling her head. She was shuffling a pile of papers in her hand. She did not look up.

"I've an appointment to see you," I said. "But I'd like to see Bernard, the party secretary."

"What do you want with him?" she asked, not lifting her head, her eyes glued to the papers in her hand.

"I want to discuss my party affiliation with him," I said.

"He cannot see you about such matters," she said.

"With whom can I talk?"

"I can listen to what you have to say," she said.

She was cold, distant; I knew that she had already made up her mind, that a decision had already been made about me.

"There're a lot of misunderstandings that I'd like to clear up," I said, forcing the words out of me, for I knew now that my errand was futile.

"What are they?" she asked, still not looking at me.

Quietly I outlined the story, sticking to bare facts, feeling that I was talking to a stone wall. When I had finished, she said:

"We can't help you with that problem."

"What do you mean?"

"If you can't get along with your comrades on the South Side, what do you expect us to do about it?" she snapped, her eyes flashing blue and cold and hard.

"They're not people with whom one can talk," I said. "I'm called a Trotskyite. WHY?"

"Are you a Trotskyite?" she asked, looking at me full now.

"No, and why would you think I was one?" I asked.

She laughed silently and turned to her papers again.

"Well, what have you to say?" I asked.

"There's nothing we can do for you here," she said.

I stood silent for a moment. I had had my answer. Yet the answer did not seem sensible, intelligible. I had not solved anything. I looked at her; she was still intent upon the papers.

"Good-bye," I said, turning and walking toward the door.

She did not answer. I paused at the door and stared at her again; she was still gazing at the papers. I went out.

That night I tossed sleepless, trying to imagine what had been in Alma Zetkin's mind, what she had been told, what were her motives. And my mind could find nothing but improbable answers. Had she been warned that I must under no circumstances be given encouragement? If so, why? Even Ross, who had actively fought the party within the ranks of the party, was still a member in good standing. But I, whom they had officially accused of nothing, was an open enemy in their eyes.

Nothing that I could think of could explain the reality I saw. My mind was like an ulcer whenever it touched upon what had happened to my relations with the party. I asked myself why a million times, and there were no answers.

Days passed. I continued on my job, where I functioned as the shop chairman of the union which I had helped to organize, though my election as shop chairman had been bitterly opposed by the party. In their efforts to nullify my influence in the union, my old comrades were willing to kill the union itself.

As May Day of 1936 approached, it was voted by the union membership that we should march in the public procession. On the morning of May Day I received printed instructions as to the time and place where our union contingent would assemble to join the parade. At noon I hurried to the spot and found that the parade was already in progress. In vain I searched for the banners of my union local. Where were they? I went up and down the streets, asking for the location of my local.

"Oh, that local's gone fifteen minutes ago," a Negro told me. "If you're going to march, you'd better fall in somewhere."

I thanked him and walked through the milling crowds. Suddenly I heard my name called. I turned. To my left was the Communist party's South Side section, lined up and ready to march.

"Come here!" an old party friend called me.

I walked over to him.

"Aren't you marching today?" he asked me.

"I missed my union local," I told him.

"What the hell," he said. "March with us."

"I don't know," I said, remembering my last visit to the headquarters of the party, and my status as an "enemy."

"This is May Day," he said. "Get into the ranks."

"You know the trouble I've had," I said.

"That's nothing," he said. "Everybody's marching today."

"I don't think I'd better," I said, shaking my head.

"Goddamn, are you scared?" he asked. "This is *May Day*."

He caught my right arm and pulled me into line beside him. I stood talking to him, asking him about his work, about common friends.

"Get out of our ranks!" a voice barked in my ears.

I turned. A white Communist, a leader of the district of the Communist party, Cy Perry, a slender, close-cropped fellow, stood glaring at me.

"I . . . It's May Day and I want to march," I said.

"Get out!" he shouted.

"I was invited here," I said.

I turned to the Negro Communist who had invited me into the ranks. I did not want public violence. I looked at my friend. He turned his eyes away. He was afraid. I did not know what to do.

"You asked me to march here," I said to him.

He did not answer.

"Tell him that you did invite me," I said, pulling his sleeve.

"I'm asking you for the last time to get out of our ranks!" Cy Perry shouted.

I did not move. I had intended to, but I was beset by so many impulses that I could not act. Another white Communist came to assist Perry. Perry caught hold of my collar and pulled at me. I resisted. They held me fast. I struggled to free myself.

"Turn me loose!" I said.

Hands lifted me bodily from the sidewalk; I felt myself being pitched headlong through the air. I saved myself from landing on my head by clutching a curbstone with my hands. Slowly I rose and stood. Perry and his assistant were glaring at me. The rows of white and black Communists were look-ing at me with cold eyes of nonrecognition. I could not quite believe what had happened, even though my hands were smarting and bleeding. I had suffered a public physical assault by two white Communists with black Communists looking on. I could not move from the spot. I was empty of any idea about what to do. But I did not feel belligerent. I had outgrown my childhood. I did not know how much time elapsed as I stood there, numb, astonished; but, suddenly, the vast ranks of the Communist party began to move. Scarlet banners with the hammer and sickle emblem of world revolution were lifted, and they fluttered in the May breeze. Drums beat. Voices were chanting. The tramp of many feet shook the earth. A long line of set-faced men and women, white and black, flowed past me.

I followed the procession to the Loop and went into Grant Park Plaza and sat upon a bench. I was not thinking; I could not think. But an objectivity of vision was being born within me. A surging sweep of many odds and ends came together and formed an attitude, a perspective. They're blind, I said to myself. Their enemies have blinded them with too much oppression. I lit a cigarette and I heard a song floating out over the sunlit air.

Arise, you pris'ners of starvation!

I remembered the stories I had written, the stories in which I had assigned a role of honor and glory to the Communist party and I was glad that they were down in black and white, were finished. For I knew in my heart that I would never be able to write that way again, would never be able to feel with that simple sharpness about life, would never again express such passionate hope, would never again make so total a commitment of faith.

Arise, you wretched of the earth . . .

The days of my past, of my youth, were receding from me like a rolling tide, leaving me alone upon high, dry ground, leaving me with a quieter and deeper consciousness.

For justice thunders condemnation . . .

My thoughts seemed to be coming from somewhere within me, as by a power of their own: It's going to take a long and bloody time, a lot of stumbling and a lot of falling, before they find the right road.

They will have to grope about blindly in the sunshine, butting their heads against every mistake, bruising their bodies against every illusion, making a million futile errors and suffering for them, bleeding for them, until they learn how to live, I thought.

Somehow man had been sundered from man and, in his search for a new unity, for a new wholeness, for oneness again, he would have to blunder into a million walls to find merely that he could not go in certain directions. No one could tell him. He would have to learn by marching down history's bloody road. He would have to purchase his wisdom of life with sacred death. He would have to pay dearly to learn just a little.

But perhaps that is the way it has always been with man . . .

A better world's in birth . . .

The procession still passed. Banners still floated. Voices of hope still chanted.

I headed toward home alone, really alone now, telling myself that in all the sprawling immensity of our mighty continent the least-known factor of living was the human heart, the least-sought goal of being was a way to live a human life. Perhaps, I thought, out of my tortured feelings I could fling a spark into this darkness. I would try, not because I wanted to but because I felt that I had to if I were to live at all.

I sat alone in my narrow room, watching the sun sink slowly in the chilly May sky. I was restless. I rose to get my hat; I wanted to visit some friends and tell them what I felt, to talk. Then I sat down. Why do that? My problem was here, here with me, here in this room, and I would solve it here alone or not at all. Yet, I did not want to face it; it frightened me. I rose again and went out into the streets. Halfway down the block I stopped, undecided. Go back . . . I returned to my room and sat again, determined to look squarely at my life.

Well, what had I got out of living in the city? What had I got out of living in the South? What had I got out of living in America? I paced the floor, knowing that all I possessed were words and a dim knowledge that my country had shown me no examples of how to live a human life. All my life I had been full of a hunger for a new way to live . . .

I heard a trolley lumbering past over steel tracks in the early dusk and I knew that underpaid, bewildered black men and women were returning to their homes from serving their white masters. In the front room of my apartment our radio was playing, pouring a white man's voice into my home, a voice that hinted of a coming war that would consume millions of lives.

Yes, the whites were as miserable as their black victims, I thought. If this country can't find its way to a human path, if it can't inform conduct with a deep sense of life, then all of us, black as well as white, are going down the same drain . . .

I picked up a pencil and held it over a sheet of white paper, but my feelings stood in the way of my words. Well, I would wait, day and night, until I knew what to say. Humbly now, with no vaulting dream of achieving a vast unity, I wanted to try to build a bridge of words between me and that world outside, that world which was so distant and elusive that it seemed unreal.

I would hurl words into this darkness and wait for an echo, and if an echo sounded, no matter how faintly, I would send other words to tell, to march, to fight, to create a sense of the hunger for life that gnaws in us all, to keep alive in our hearts a sense of the inexpressibly human.

THE OUTSIDER

Cruelty has a Human Heart,
And Jealousy a Human Face;
Terror the Human Form Divine,
And Secrecy the Human Dress.
—WILLIAM BLAKE

Mark me, and be astonished,
And lay your hand upon your mouth.
—JOB

For Rachel
my daughter who was born on alien soil

BOOK ONE

DREAD

Dread is an alien power which lays hold of an individual, and yet one cannot tear oneself away, nor has a will to do so; for one fears what one desires.

— KIERKEGAARD

FROM AN INVISIBLE February sky a shimmering curtain of snowflakes fluttered down upon Chicago. It was five o'clock in the morning and still dark. On a South Side street four masculine figures moved slowly forward shoulder to shoulder and the sound of their feet tramping and sloshing in the melting snow echoed loudly. The men were warmly dressed and wore mufflers about their throats. The brims of their hats, encrusted with snow, were pulled down at rakish tilts over their eyes. Behind turned-up overcoat collars their gruff voices exploded in jokes, laughter, and shouts. They jostled one another with rude affection and their hot breaths projected gusts of vapor on to the chilled morning air. One of the men threw out an arm and grabbed a companion about the neck and crooned:

"Booker, let me rest this tired old body on you, hunh?"

"Hell, naw! Stand on your own two big flat feet, Cross!" Booker, a short, black man protested with a laugh.

The man called Cross turned and flung his arm about the shoulders of a big, fat, black man and said, "Then how about you, Joe?"

"Look, Crossy, I'm tired too," Joe defended himself, shying off. "Why pick on me?"

" 'Cause you're soft as a mattress and can stand it," Cross explained.

"If you're cold, it's your own damn hard luck," Joe said. "You don't take care of yourself. Me, I ain't never cold. I know how come you're always so cold, Cross. You drink too much. Don't eat enough. Don't sleep. But, *me* . . . Ha-ha! I eat and sleep as much as I can. And my good old fat helps to keep me warm. Ain't that right, Pink?"

The man called Pink did not reply at once; he was reddish in color and older than the other three.

"Cross," Pink said seriously, "you ought to take some vitamins or something. Man, you *couldn't* be cold now. Hell, we just left that steamy Post Office *twenty* minutes ago."

Cross swiftly pulled the glove off his right hand and, grabbing Pink's shoulder, rammed his bare fingers down the collar of Pink's neck.

"How do they feel, Pink?" Cross demanded.

"Jeeesus! Your fingers're cold as *snakes!*" Pink gasped, his eyes lit with concern. "They ought to call you *Mr. Death!*"

"I just need some alcohol," Cross confessed grimly. "My old engine won't run without it."

"You better quit that bottle, Cross," Joe, the big, fat, black man warned. "When you start *living* on alcohol, you're traveling a road that ain't got no turning. You been hitting that bottle heavy for a month now. Better let up, boy."

"Man, whiskey ain't never hurt nobody," Pink said; he broke into song:

> *If the ocean was whiskey*
> *And I was a duck*
> *I'd dive right in*
> *And never come up*

A rich, rolling laughter erupted and died away over the snow-blanketed sidewalks.

"Crossy, how come you're drinking so much these days?" Booker asked in a tone free of moral objections.

"My soul needs it," Cross mumbled.

"Makes you feel better, hunh?" Booker asked.

"No. Makes me feel *less*," Cross corrected him.

"But how about your liver?" Joe demanded.

"My liver's in the death house," Cross admitted.

"Say, Pinkie, remember when Crossy used to be the life of the gang!" Joe asked. "Now he just swills and every word he says is a gripe."

"We all have blue days," Pink said.

"*Pink* has *blue* days," Cross's tongue played softly with the words.

They tossed wild laughter amidst the milling flakes of snow. All of them laughed except Cross whose lips shaped themselves into an ambiguous smile whose meaning might have been a jeering at or a participation in the merriment. He was tall but slightly built with a smooth, brown and yellow skin, and his body moved as though it had more nervous energy than it could contain.

"Aw, leave Cross alone," Pink said.

"Thanks, pal," Cross muttered.

Joe suddenly paused amid the flakes of dancing snow, laughing hysterically, slapping his thighs, sending blasts of steam on to the frigid air. The sheen of a street lamp sharply etched his ebony face.

"What's the matter, Joe?" Booker asked.

"Oh, God," Joe gasped, his fat cheeks trembling and tears gleaming at the corners of his eyes.

"All right; share the damn joke," Pink said.

The three men confronted Joe and waited for his mirth to subside.

"Today I heard somebody say the damndest thing about Cross—" Joe went off into another spasm of mirth, bending over, coughing, spluttering, sending tiny flecks of spittle into the run-away snowflakes. Joe finally straightened and placed a brotherly hand upon Cross's shoulder. "Now, listen, if I tell what I heard, you won't be mad, will you?"

"I don't give a damn what you heard," Cross muttered.

Tiny crystals trembled whitely between their dark faces. The shoulders of their overcoats were laced with icy filigrees; dapples of moisture glowed diamondlike on their eyebrows where the heat of their blood was melting the snow.

"Well, spill it, man," Pink urged impatiently.

Joe sobered only to give way to so much laughter that Pink and Booker joined in and laughed so infectiously that even Cross surrendered to the contagion and chuckled.

"Somebody said," Joe began, "that Cross was trying to imitate the United States' Government. They said the trouble with Cross was his four A's. *Alcohol. Abortions. Automobiles.* And *alimony*." Joe laughed so violently that his eyes were buried in fat and the pearly gleam of his white teeth vied with the translucence of the snow. Jerking out his words, he continued: "They called C-cross the Q-q-quadruple-A Program! Said that the best thing for Cross w-was to plow h-himself under . . ."

Cross stood aloof as the others bent double with their giggles. Cross did not resent what had been said; it was as though they were laughing at the foibles of an absent man who was well-known to him. He smiled, admitting to himself that the analogy was not badly put, that it fitted the snarled facts of his life pretty aptly, and that he could not have summed up his situation any better himself. The more Pink, Joe, and Booker guffawed, the longer Cross retained his nervous, ambiguous smile. Finally the laughter died and Joe, putting his arm about Cross's shoulder, promised consolingly: "Goddammit, Crossy, I'm gonna buy you a drink. Hell, I'm gonna buy you *two* damn drinks. You need 'em."

Still chuckling, they trudged on through the snow to a corner tavern whose neon sign dimly identified it as: THE SALTY DOG. They pushed through the door and went in. Cross followed solemnly, his hands dug into his overcoat pockets, a cigarette stub glowing in his lips. He sat with the others in a booth and looked at them with quiet eyes and an enigmatic smile. A short, fat, brown proprietor with a bald head and a grey goatee called to them from behind the bar: "Same old thing, boys?"

"Same old thing, Doc," Joe and Pink chorused.

"Crossy, what's the trouble?" Booker asked softly.

"You *know* what's wrong with 'im," Joe insisted. "His Quadruple-A Program's got 'im down."

They laughed again. Doc sat four whiskies before them and, at the sight of the little glasses of pale brown fluid, they grew sober, almost dignified; each took up his glass daintily and threw back his head and tossed the liquor down his throat.

"One of these days, Doc," Cross said, sighing and smacking his lips, "we're going to fool you. We're going to swallow the glasses too."

"Atta boy!" Joe approved.

"The spirit moved 'im at last," Booker commented.

"Crossy," Joe said, "you're losing your touch. Remember the time you used to pull them crazy stunts?" Joe turned to the others for confirmation. "When Cross first came to work in the Post Office, he was a nonstop riot, a real killer-diller. Early in the evening, when the rush hour was on, he used to—we were working on the 11th floor then—lift up the window, run his hand in his pocket and toss out every cent of silver he had. Just throw it all out of the window to the street. And then he'd lean out and watch the commotion of all them little antlike folks down there going wild, scrambling and scratching and clawing after them few pieces of money and then, when the money was all gone, they'd stand looking up to the window of the 11th floor with their mouths hanging open like fishes out of water. And Cross'd be laughing to beat all hell. And Cross'd say that them folks was praying when their faces were turned up like that, waiting for more money to fall. Ha-ha!

"Remember when two men jumped at the same time for the same quarter that Cross had tossed out? They dived toward each other and they butted head on and knocked each other out, cold? They just lay there, like a truck had hit 'em, and all the other folks crowded round, looking and wondering what had happened. They had to send the riot cars full of cops to break up the mob and take the two dopes who had been diving for the quarter to jail. Ha-ha! Honest to God, I thought I'd die laughing. Cross said that that was the only time he ever felt like God. Ha-ha!"

They laughed musingly, their eyes resting on Cross's face which carried a detached smile.

"Remember that wild gag he pulled at Christmas time in 19—?" Joe frowned thoughtfully and the others waited. "When the hell was that now? Oh, yes! It was in 1945. I'll never forget it. Cross bought a batch of magazines, *Harper's*, *Atlantic Monthly*, *Collier's*, *Ladies' Home Journal*, and clipped out those ads that say you can send your friends a year's subscription as a Christmas gift. Well, Cross signed 'em and sent 'em to his friends. But he didn't sign 'em with *his* name, see? He signed 'em with the names of friends of people he was sending the subscriptions to. He sent me one and it was signed by my wife. Ha-ha! Was she mad? But in the end, she really paid for it. Crossy sent one to James Harden and signed it with my name. Ha-ha! Christmas morning Harden calls me up and starts thanking me for the gift-subscription I'd sent 'im to *Harper's*. I didn't know what the hell Harden was talking about, and I was so 'shamed I sat right down and sent *Harper's* a check! Man, the whole South Side was in a dither that Christmas morning. Folks was thanking other folks for presents the others didn't know nothing about. And Crossy was listening and watching and saying nothing. Lord, it was a mess! Cross, how in God's name did you dream up such stuff? Any man who can do things like that is a man standing *outside* of the world! Know what I mean? Like somebody outside of your window was looking into your house and poking out his tongue at you." Joe went into a gale of laughter; then he pointed to Cross's smiling face. "Look at 'im, will you? He sits there, smiling, not saying a word, not letting on he used to pull stunts like that."

They laughed, looking at Cross with tenderness in their eyes.

"Say, remember all them big, deep books he used to read and tell us about?" Joe asked looking from Cross to the others. "He used to use so many big words I thought he'd choke! Every time I saw 'im, he had a batch of books under his arm."

"But what I couldn't understand," Pink recalled, "was why Cross wouldn't believe anything in the books he read. One time he was all hepped-up over one writer and the next time he was through with 'im and was gone on to another."

"And the books in Cross's room!" Booker exclaimed. "I went to see 'im one day when he was sick, and I could hardly get into the door! Big books, little books, books piled everywhere! He even had books in bed with 'im."

Their heads tilted back with laughter; Cross smiled without rancor.

"I told 'im," Booker continued, " 'Crossy, you better find a gal to sleep with you, 'cause them books can't keep you warm!' Man, in the clothes closet: books. In the bathroom: books. Under the bed: books. I said, 'Crossy, you ain't got no 'oo gains, you got bookworms!' "

They clapped their hands with laughter; Cross smiled and looked off.

"Cross, you ain't never said how come you was reading all them books," Joe pointed out.

"I was looking for something," Cross said quietly.

"What?" Pink asked.

"I don't know," Cross confessed gloomily.

"Did you find it?" Joe asked.

"No."

Joe, Pink, and Booker howled with delight.

"In those days Cross's mind was like a little mouse, running every which way— Say, Cross, how many books you got in your room?"

"I don't know," Cross mumbled.

"I wished I had a dollar for every book you got," Joe sighed. "Now, honest, Crossy, how come you don't read no more?"

"I've put away childish things," Cross said.

"Aw, be yourself, man," Booker said.

"I am what I am," Cross said. "I'm sparing you guys a lot. I'm not going to bother you with my troubles."

"Can't we help you any, Cross?" Joe asked seriously.

"Lay off, guys," Cross said, frowning for the first time. "I'm all right." He turned and beckoned to Doc. "Bring me a bottle, Doc!"

"Don't drink any more, Cross," Pink begged.

"Ain't you gonna eat some breakfast?" Booker asked.

"Whiskey ain't no good on an empty stomach," Joe reminded him.

"It's my stomach," Cross said.

"Aw, leave 'im alone," Booker said.

"But a man who drinks ought to eat," Joe insisted.

"Eating's all you think about, Joe," Cross growled.

"Hell, you got to eat to live!" Joe shouted with authoritative rudeness. "And you better stop drinking and eat and sleep some." Joe suddenly laughed and began a game of make-believe, imitating a baby's crying: "Awwwww—Awwww—Awwww—!" He altered his tone. "Now, what the little baby wants?" He bawled out the answer: "The bottle, the bottle, the *whiskey* bottle, Mama!"

Laughter seethed and Cross joined in to show his appreciation.

"Leave 'im alone," Booker said. "He knows his own mind."

"If he keeps up that drinking, he won't have no mind left," Joe said emphatically. "And it'll kill 'im."

"All right," Cross said darkly. "Do I want to live forever?"

"You're nuts," Joe said.

"It pleases me," Cross said without anger.

"Okay," Joe said.

"Sure; it's okay," Cross said, opening the bottle and taking a long swig.

"Wheeew," Joe whistled. "You can't *drink* like that, boy!"

"I *am*," Cross said calmly.

"You gonna finish that bottle today?" Booker asked softly.

"Maybe. How do I know?"

"Ain't you gonna sleep?"

"If I can."

"'If I can'," jeered Joe. "Stop drinking and you *can* sleep."

"I wouldn't sleep at all then," Cross said.

"What's *eating* you, Cross?" Pink implored softly. "We've been your friends for six years. Spill it. We'll help you—"

"Skip it," Cross said. "Am I complaining? You signed for my last loan and that took care of my Quadruple-A debts. That's enough."

They laughed at how Cross could laugh at himself.

"There're some things a man must do alone," Cross added.

The three men looked silently at Cross. He knew that they liked him, but he felt that they were outside of his life, that there was nothing that they could do that would make any difference. Now more than ever he knew that he was alone and that his problem was one of a relationship of himself to himself.

"We ain't your mama and your papa," Joe sighed, forcing a sad smile. "We can't hold your hand, Big Boy. And you're a big boy, you know."

"Yes, I'm a big boy," Cross smiled bitterly.

"It's between you and Your Maker, your problem," Joe said.

"Lucky Joe," Cross murmured in a tone of envy.

"What do you mean?" Joe asked.

Cross rose, smiled widely for the first time, pointed his

finger into Joe's fat, black, round face, and intoned: " 'And God made man in His own image . . .' "

Pink and Booker yelled with laughter. Joe passed his hand caressingly and self-consciously over his black face and looked puzzled. Cross demanded in a mockingly serious voice: "Did God really make *that* face? Is He guilty of *that*? If He did, then He was walking in His sleep!" Cross shook with laughter. "To blame God for making Joe is to degrade the very concept of God!"

Pink and Booker leaped to their feet and grabbed Joe about the waist.

"Did God really make you, Joe?" Pink demanded.

"Was God absent-minded when He cooked you up, Joe?" Booker asked.

Joe forced a smile, but underneath he was a little disturbed. Then he protested: "God made me, all right. He made my soul and He made my *body* too."

"But why did He make your body so *fat*, Joe?" Cross asked.

"I just ate too much and got fat," Joe replied sheepishly.

"But *God* gave you your appetite," Pink told him.

"And the body reflects the soul," Cross clenched it.

"Wow!" Pink screamed, covering his mouth with his hand. "I'm going home 'fore I laugh myself to death!"

They all rose except Cross; he still sat and smiled up at Joe.

"Go home and get some shut-eye, Cross," Joe advised him.

"God won't let me sleep," Cross said.

"God ain't got *nothing* to do with it!" Joe pronounced.

"Then who keeps me awake all day long?" Cross wanted to know.

"You, yourself," Joe said.

"Maybe you're right," Cross conceded.

"So long," Pink said.

"See you, Crossy," Joe said.

" 'Bye, now," Booker said.

"So long," Cross mumbled, not looking at them as they filed out.

"Some guys," Doc said from behind the bar.

"Yeah; *some* guys," Cross repeated, staring at the floor.

Yeah; it was time to sleep. He felt dead. How long could he last like this? His eyes suddenly clouded with displeasure. He had promised to see Dot this morning, but he didn't want to talk to her, much less see her . . . That was all he needed: seeing Dot and having one of those long, hysterical, weeping arguments. He knew what Dot wanted to ask and the answer was no and it would always be no! Oh, *damn* that Dot! But if he didn't call her, she'd soon be coming to his room and they'd argue all day long. And that was the last thing he wanted. Yes; he'd better call her; he'd tell her he was sick, feeling too bad to see her. He rose, jammed the whiskey bottle into his overcoat pocket, went into the telephone booth, dropped a coin into the slot and dialed. Almost at once Dot's voice sang over the wire: "How are you, darling?"

She was waiting in the hallway by the phone, he thought.

"I feel like hell," he growled.

"Have you eaten breakfast?"

"Naw; I just left the Post Office—"

"But honey, you got off from work at *four* o'clock and now it's nearly *six*. You've had plenty of time to eat."

"I was in a bar," he told her.

"Oh, God, Cross! You must stop *drinking*!"

"Do you think I can with what I've got on my mind?"

"Come over right *now*, hunh? I'll cook your breakfast—"

"Naw."

"Why?"

"I don't want to."

"You're mean! And you promised you'd see me this morning—"

"But I don't feel like it. I'm exhausted."

"You mean you're too *drunk*!" she said savagely.

"So?"

"Oh, God, Cross! Why did I ever get mixed up with you?"

"I've told you how to get *unmixed* with me, haven't I?"

"Don't you say that to me again!"

"I *am* saying it!"

"Listen, come here now! I want to talk to you!"

"I'm tired, I tell you!"

"I don't care! You come over *now!*"

"You're crazy, Dot! Do you think you can make people do things they don't want to do?" he asked her earnestly.

He heard her suck in her breath and when her voice came over the wire again it was so shrill that he had to hold the receiver away from his ear.

"If you *don't* see me this morning, you'll be *sorry!* You hear? Whatever happens'll be *your* fault! You can't treat me this way! I won't *let* you! You hear? I said I won't *let* you! You made me a promise and I want you to keep it! Now, come over here. I've got something to tell you—"

"Dot—"

"No; no; let me talk—"

"Listen, Dot—"

"I said let *me* talk!"

"Oh, Goddammit, Dot!"

"Don't cuss me! Oh, God, don't cuss me when I'm like this! Can't you understand? Have a little pity—" Her voice caught in her throat. "I'll *kill* myself—"

"Dot— Don't go on like that—"

"You don't think I'll kill myself, but I will—"

"You're crazy!"

"I'll get you for that!" she shouted. "I *will!*"

"If you keep shouting at me, I'll hang up!"

"I *will* shout at you!"

He hesitated, then slammed the receiver on to the hook. Damn her! He was trembling. He'd not wanted to call her because he'd known that it'd go like this and he'd be un-nerved for the rest of the day. He fumbled for the bottle and took a deep swallow. Yes; he had to get some sleep or go mad. He went out of the telephone booth and waved good-bye to Doc and kept on out of the door and walked along the snow-piled sidewalks. He caught a trolley and rode standing on the platform, swaying as much from the rocking of the car as from the influence of alcohol. He alighted in front of his apartment building, groped for his key, and let himself in. Fifteen minutes later he was undressed and in bed. He was so tired that he could scarcely feel the sensations of his body and he could not relax. He stared wakefully in the semi-darkness and wondered what he could do about Dot . . .

What a messy life he was living! It was crazy; it was killing
him; it was senseless; and he was a fool to go on living it.
What a stinking botch he'd made out of everything he had
touched! Why? He didn't know. *I could be teaching school,*
he told himself. He'd dropped out of the university right after
he'd married Gladys and after that nothing had gone right.

He lay still, his bloodshot eyes staring blankly before him,
and drifted into dreams of his problems, compulsively living
out dialogues, summing up emotional scenes with his mother,
reliving the reactions of his wife, Dot, and his friends. Repeatedly he chided himself to go to sleep, but it did no good,
for he was hungry for these waking visions that depicted his
dilemmas, yet he knew that such brooding did not help; in
fact, he was wasting his waning strength, for into these unreal
dramas he was putting the whole of his ardent being. The
long hours of the day dragged on.

He twisted on his crumpled bed, reshaped his lumpy pillow
until his head nestled into it exactly right; and, for the hun-
dredth time, he closed his eyes and lay still, trying to purge
his mind of anxiety, beseeching sleep. He felt his numbed
limbs slowly shedding tension and for a moment he floated
toward a world of dreams, seesawing softly between sleeping
and waking. Then, convulsively, his entire body jerked rigidly
to stem a fearful feeling of falling through space. His rebellious nerves twanged with a terror that his mind sought desperately to deny. He shook his head, his body seething with
hate against himself and the world.

He checked his watch: two o'clock. A grey day showed
through the curtained window and from the snowy street
rose the din of traffic. Today was like yesterday and he knew
that tomorrow would be the same. And it had been like this
now for many months. Each morning he'd come from work
and crawl wearily into bed and toss for hours, yearning for
the mercy of a sleep that was not his and at last he realized
that his search for surcease was hopeless. He sighed, stood,
crossed to the dresser and took another pull from the bottle.
At six o'clock he'd report to work and for eight long hours
he'd sway upon his feet, drugged with fatigue, straining
against collapse, sorting mail like a sleepwalker. He moist-

ened his lips with his tongue. He had not eaten all day and, as the alcohol deadened the raw nerves of his twitching stomach, he thought: I'll do it now; I'll end this farce . . . He hunched determinedly forward and his crinkled pyjamas bagged about his gaunt body and the muscles of his neck bulged. He'd not crawl like a coward through stupid days; to act quickly was the simplest way of jumping through a jungle of problems that plagued him from within and from without. A momentary dizziness swamped him; his throat tightened; his vision blurred; his chest heaved and he was defenseless against despair. He sprang to the dresser and yanked open a drawer and pulled forth his gun. Trembling, feeling the cold blue steel touching his sweaty palm, he lifted the glinting barrel to his right temple, then paused. His feelings were like tumbling dice . . . He wilted, cursed, his breath expiring through parted lips. Choked with self-hate, he flung himself on the bed and buried his face in his hands.

Broken thus in will, he relaxed for the first time in weeks; he could rest only when he was too drained of energy to fret further. At length he lifted his head and the fingers of his right hand pressed nervously against his lower lip, then tapped his knee as though to still the writhing of his spirit. He was despairingly aware of his body as an alien and despised object over which he had no power, a burden that was always cheating him of the fruits of his thought, mocking him with its stubborn and supine solidity.

Claimed at last by the needs of the hour, he proceeded to bathe and dress. Again he drank from the bottle and was grateful for the sense of depression caused by the alcohol which made him feel less of pleasure, pain, anxiety, and hope. Could he get through the night without collapsing? Suddenly he was filled with an idea: *He would take the gun with him!* And if the pressure from within or without became too great he would use it; his gun would be his final protection against the world as well as against himself . . . And if he was ever so unlucky as to be found sprawled from nervous collapse upon some frozen sidewalk or upon the floor of the Post Office, it would be manfully better to let others see a bloody hole gaping in his temple than to present to the eyes of strangers a mass of black flesh stricken by stupor. His decision renewed his courage; if he had not thought of the gun, he doubted if he could have gone to work.

He pulled on his overcoat and stood hesitantly by the door; he knew now that even the gun sagging in his pocket did not convince him that he was fit to work. During the past month he had been absent so often on excuses of illness that he did not dare telephone and report himself on the sick list. He would master his tricky sensations; he would force himself to carry on till he dropped. He usually found that he did not really collapse even when he had the consciousness of being about to pitch forward on his face . . .

He yearned to talk to someone; he felt his mere telling his story would have helped. But to whom could he talk? To his mother? No; she would only assure him that he was reaping the wages of sin and his sense of dread would deepen. Could he talk to his wife with whom he was not living? God, no! She'd laugh bitterly and say, "I told you so!" There was Dot, his sweetheart, but she was not capable of understanding anything. Moreover, she was partly the cause of his present state. And there was not a single man to whom he cared to confess the nightmare that was his life. He had sharp need of a confidant, and yet he knew that if he had had an ideal confidant before whom he could lay his whole story, he would have instantly regretted it, would have murdered his confidant the moment after he had confided to him his shame. How could he have gone on living knowing that someone else knew how things were with him? Cross was proud.

His hand touched the doorknob and the telephone shrilled. Now, who in hell could that be? Was it Dot? Or Gladys? He turned the doorknob and the telephone rang again. Hell! Anger flashed through him at some vague someone who was trying to snatch him from his futile wrestling with his problem, trying to pry him loose from the only thing that made his life possess meaning even though it made him suffer. Impatiently he picked up the receiver.

"Cross? Is that you?" It was his mother's quavering, high-pitched voice singing uncertainly over the wire.

"How are you, Ma?"

"Fine, Cross, I reckon," she said querulously, like those

who are over sixty and who feel uncommonly well but are too superstitious to admit it. "Can I see you, Cross? Sometime today . . . ?"

He bridled, trying to slap away the clutch of his mother's wrinkled hand as it reached invisibly for him.

"Anything wrong, Ma?"

"I want to see you," she said, evading his question.

His teeth clamped; he did not want to see her, certainly not now with this mood of bleak dread in him.

"Ma, I'm trying to sleep," he lied, speaking reprovingly.

Silence. He felt he had hurt her and he grew angry. He waited for her to speak further, but only the metallic hum of the line came to his ear.

"Ma," he called softly. "You're still there?"

"Yes, Cross." A note of firm patience in her voice frightened him.

"What is it, Ma? I work nights and I've got to get some rest."

Again silence.

"Is it about money?" he asked, trying to hasten it.

Another silence; then his mother's voice came clearly: "Cross, that Dot girl was just by here to see me . . ."

Her tone, charged and precise, was filled with a multitude of accusations that evoked a vast, hot void in him. His mother was still talking, but he did not hear her. His eyes darted like those of a bayed animal. Oh, God! *Why had Dot done that?* He had not kept his promise to see her this morning and she had gotten into a panic; that was it. But she had sworn to consult him before acting on her own, and now . . . His life was a delicate bridge spanning a gaping chasm and hostile hands were heaping heavy loads upon that bridge and it was about to crack and crash downward.

"What did you say, Ma?" He pretended that he had not heard.

How much did she know? Perhaps everything! That crazy Dot! He could wring her neck for this! She had no right to tell tales to his mother! Women had no sense of . . .

"You *know* what I'm talking about, boy," his mother scolded him sternly. "That girl's in trouble—"

"*Who* are you talking about, Ma?" He still stalled for time.

"Stop acting foolish, Cross! That girl's blaming *you*—"

"Blaming me for what?" he asked. He knew that he was acting silly, but he could not easily change his attitude now.

"She's in a family way, Cross," his mother spoke boldly, a woman lodging woman's ancient complaint against man. "And she says it's *you*! She's worried sick. She had to talk to somebody, so she came to me. Son, what have you done?" There came the sound of a sob being choked back. "You're married. You've three children. What're you going to do?"

"Just a sec. Somebody's at the door," he lied for respite.

Like always, he had doubled his burdens; he heard his mother's tirades and at the same time he pretended that he was not reacting to them, and this dual set of responses made him frantic. That harebrained Dot! Trying to save herself and ruining me, the only one who can save her . . . Dot's panic had made her deal him a dirty blow. He brought the receiver to his mouth.

"Is she still there, Ma?" His tone of voice confessed that he now knew what it was all about.

"Hunh? No; she's gone," his mother said. "She's gone to see Gladys . . . Cross, that girl's young, a child. She can get you into serious trouble . . ."

Dot was talking to his wife! This was the end! The void in him grew hotter. A widening circle of people were becoming acquainted with his difficulties. He knew that Gladys would do her damndest now; she would be merciless. Her knowing about Dot would redouble her hate for him. She would bare the details of his private blunderings before the domestic courts . . . He had to try to stop her. But could he? Maybe it was already too late?

"I'll be right over," he said, hanging up abruptly.

He took another drink and went out of the door. As he descended the stairs, his mother's scolding intensified his mood of self-loathing, a mood that had been his longer than he could recall, a mood that had been growing deeper with the increasing complexity of the events of his life. He knew himself too well not to realize the meaning of what he was feeling; yet his self-knowledge, born of a habit of incessant reflection, did not enable him to escape the morass in which his feelings were bogged. His insight merely augmented his emotional conflicts. He was aware, intimately and bitterly, that his dread had been his mother's first fateful gift to him. He had been born of her not only physically but emotionally too. The only psychological difference between them was that he was aware of having received this dark gift from her at a time when he was too young to reject it, and she had given it to him in a period of her life when her intense grief over the death of her husband had rendered her incapable of realizing the full import of what she had been doing. And he could never speak to her about this difference in emotional similarity; he could only pretend that it did not exist, for not only did his deep love of her forbid it, but he did not possess enough emotional detachment from her for that to happen. As her son, he was much too far from her and at the same time much too close, much too warm toward her and much too cold. To keep her life from crushing his own, he had slain the sense of her in his heart and at the same time had clung frantically to his memory of that sense. His feelings for her were widely distant: flight and embrace . . .

From the vestibule he stepped into a frozen world lit by a lemon-colored sun whose glare sparkled on mounds of ice. The snow had stopped and the sky stretched pale and blue; the air was dry and bitter cold. The sun disclosed in sharp detail the red brick buildings, glinted on the slow moving trolleys, and cast into the windowpanes liquid reflections that stung his eyes. His shoulders hunched forward and he shivered and clenched his teeth to keep them from chattering, his breath steaming against the freezing air.

He was conscious of himself as a frail object which had to protect itself against a pending threat of annihilation. This frigid world was suggestively like the one which his mother, without her having known it, had created for him to live in when he had been a child. Though she had loved him, she had tainted his budding feelings with a fierce devotion born of her fear of a life that had baffled and wounded her. His first coherent memories had condensed themselves into an image of a young woman whose hysterically loving presence had made his imagination conscious of an invisible God—Whose secret grace granted him life—hovering oppressively in space above him. His adolescent fantasies had symbolically telescoped this God into an awful face shaped in the form of a huge and crushing NO, a terrifying face which had, for a reason he could never learn, created him, had given him a part of Himself, and yet had threateningly demanded that he vigilantly deny another part of himself which He too had paradoxically given him. This God's NO-FACE had evoked in his pliable boy's body an aching sense of pleasure by admonishing him to shun pleasure as the tempting doorway opening blackly on to hell; had too early awakened in him a sharp sense of sex by thunderingly denouncing sex as the sin leading to eternal damnation; had posited in him an unbridled hunger for the sensual by branding all sensuality as the monstrous death from which there was no resurrection; had made him instinctively choose to love himself over and against all others because he felt himself menaced by a mysterious God Whose love seemed somehow like hate. Mother love had cleaved him in twain: a wayward sensibility that distrusted itself, a consciousness that was conscious of itself. Despite this, his sensibilities had not been repressed by God's fearful negations as represented by his mother; indeed, his sense of life had been so heightened that desire boiled in him to a degree that made him afraid. Afraid of what? Nothing exactly, precisely . . . And this constituted his sense of dread.

As he neared his mother's rooming house, he could already feel the form of her indictment, could divine the morally charged words she would hurl at him. And he knew that his reaction would be one of sullen and guilty anger. Why, then, was he going to see her? Because he really wanted her to rail at him, denounce him, and he would suffer, feel his hurt again, and, in doing so, would know intuitively that somewhere in the depths of his raw wound lay the blood of his salvation or the pus of his disaster. This obscure knowledge had stayed his finger on the trigger of the gun whose barrel had touched his temple this morning . . .

He entered a dilapidated building, went down a dark hallway and tapped upon a door. Sounds of muffled movement came to him; the door opened and framed his mother's solemnly lined face, the white hair pulled severely back from a wide forehead, a gnarled right hand holding a woolen shawl about stooped shoulders. Her mouth was a tight, flat slit and her eyes peered through cloudy spectacles.

"Hi, Ma."

Without answering, she widened the door and he walked past her into a tiny, shabby room that smelt of a sweetish odor of decaying flesh that seemed to cling to the aged who are slowly dying while still living.

He noticed, as he did each time he visited her, that she appeared to have shrunken a bit more; and he knew that it was her chronic fretting, her always tearing at her emotions that was whitening the hairs of her head, deepening the lines in her face, and accentuating the stoop of her back. His mother could no more relax than he could. Like me, she's using up herself too fast, and she's just a little over sixty . . . If she cared for herself more, judged life less severely, time would deal easier with her . . . Why were some people fated, like Job, to live a never-ending debate between themselves and their sense of what they believed life should be? Why did some hearts feel insulted at being alive, humiliated at the terms of existence? It was as though one felt that one had been promised something and when that promise had not been kept, one felt a sense of loss that made life intolerable; it was as though one was angry, but did not know toward what or whom the anger should be directed; it was as though one felt betrayed, but could never determine the manner of the betrayal. And this was what was making his mother old before her time . . .

He smoked, looked about vacantly, avoiding her accusing eyes, and was already fighting down a feeling of defensive guilt. She turned and began rummaging aimlessly in a dresser drawer and he knew that she was deliberately making him wait before she spoke, attempting to reduce him again to the status of a fearfully impressionable child. Before pronouncing her condemnations, she would make him feel that she was weighing him in the scales of her drastic judgment and was finding, to her horror, that he was a self-centered libertine ruthlessly ridden by this lust for pleasure, an irresponsible wastrel thoughtlessly squandering his life's substance. And afterwards he would listen with a face masked in indifference and he would know that she was right; but he would also know that there was nothing that neither he nor she could do about it, that there was no cure for his malady, and, above all, that this dilemma was the meaning of his life.

Long ago, in his fourteenth year, while standing waiting for her preachments, he had demanded to know why she always pinioned him in solitude before handing down her moral laws, and she had replied that it was to make him develop the habit of reflecting deeply, that he knew as well as she when he had done wrong and she wanted to teach him to be his own judge. Anger now rose in him and he sought for some way to make her feel it. He grew suddenly resentful of the rickety furniture of the room. It's her own damn fault if she lives like this . . . She could be living comfortably with Gladys . . .

Yet, even as he thought it, he knew that he was wrong. Gladys and his mother hated each other; once, when they had lived together during the early days of his marriage, Gladys and his mother had vied for female dominance in the home and it had ended with his mother's packing and leaving, declaring that she preferred to live alone rather than with a wilful daughter-in-law who did not respect her.

"Why do you insist on living like this?" he broke the ice.

"We're not going to talk about how *I'm* living," she countered.

"No matter. But why do you live like this?" he asked again.

"And why do you live as *you're* living?" she demanded bitterly turning to him. "You're drinking again. I can *smell* it."

"Not much," he said; his voice was clipped but controlled.

Her right hand dabbed clumsily at a tear on her wrinkled cheek. She slid into a chair and cried, her withered lips twisting, her false teeth wobbling loosely in shrunken gums.

"You've started spoiling little girls, taking advantage of children . . . Son, can't you *control* yourself? Where's all this leading you? Why in God's name do you lie to a little girl like Dot and seduce her?"

"I didn't lie—"

"You *did!*" she blazed. "You let her hope for what you couldn't do, and that's lying. I'm no fool! If you didn't lie to her, that's worse. Then she's just a little whore. And if she's a whore, why did you take up with her? Cross, it's easy to fool a young girl. If you're proud of this cheap trick, you've fallen lower than I thought you had."

She had done it; she had evoked in him that shameful mood of guilt born of desire and fear of desire. He knew that she was not lamenting for him alone, but for her own betrayed maidenhood, for how she had once been so treacherously beguiled into trusting surrender; she was blaming him somehow for its having gone wrong, confusedly seeking his masculine sympathy for her sexually blighted life! Goddamn her! Hadn't she no sense of shame? He imagined himself rising and with a single sweep of his palm slapping her to the floor. And in the same instant a poignant pity for her seized him. Poor, lost, lonely woman clinging for salvation to a son who she knew was as lost as she was. He was too close to her and too far from her; much too warm toward her and much too cold. If only he understood her less! But he was cut off from that; he was anchored in a knowledge that offended him. And this image of his mother's incestuously-tinged longings would linger with him for days and he could curse her for it, and finally he would curse himself for living in a crazy world that he could not set right.

"Promising a child and knowing you don't mean it," she sobbed in despair. "How can men *do* that?"

He knew that now she was reliving her own experience, grieving over the thwarted hopes that had driven her into the arms of religion for the sake of her sanity. And he? Where could he be driven? Nowhere. His mother was lucky; she had a refuge, even if that refuge was only an illusion. But he could only get out of this world or stay in it and bear it. His anger waxed as he saw that she had a balm, however delusory, and he had none. And yet *she* was complaining to *him*! If she knew what he lived each day, she would be horrified. But his mother was convinced that he was hardhearted, that he was withholding his help out of selfish malice. An ironic smile stole across his lips.

"You can laugh!" she stormed at him. "But God'll punish you! He *will*! You'll see before you die! You'll weep! God is a just God! And He's a hard and jealous God! If you mock Him, He'll show you His Power!"

He shuddered and again projected his pity out upon her, then his pity recoiled back upon himself, for he knew that she would never understand him. A second later he pushed even this self-pity from him, realizing that it too was useless, would only depress him.

"I'm sorry, Ma," he sighed.

"Sorry for what?" she railed. "You can't undo what you've done. You've sinned, Cross, and it's to God you must confess with a contrite heart. Even if that girl gets rid of her child, she'll be forever hurt. She'll remember what you promised—"

"But I didn't *promise* her anything," he protested.

"Oh, stop lying," she said. "You *did*! You promised by the way you *acted* . . ."

A hopeless silence rose between them. Through the years his mother had related to him how, when she had been a country school teacher in a tiny southern community, she had met his father during the early days of the First World War. A Negro regiment had been camped nearby and excitement was everywhere. Her heart was ready and full of love. They first met at a church dance and he had straightaway declared his love. In her romantic eyes he was a huge boy going away to die on some distant battlefield and her heart had gone impulsively out to him, and finally her body also.

They married a month after they met and his regiment moved northward. She followed, feeling glad that she was giving him her life. But she soon learned that there were other girls foolish enough to look at him through romantic eyes and give him their hearts and bodies too. She finally upbraided him and he was cynical and defiant; then, more to avoid her than from motives of patriotism, he had, after returning from France, joined the army as a regular soldier. She trailed him dismally from army camp to army camp, begging for an understanding. Instead, the gap grew wider. Even before her son was born in 1924, she knew that she was only in his way, a worrisome wife. It was then that she took her sorrow and her infant son to God in copious tears. A year later she learned that somewhere in the reaches of Harlem, in a dirty, vacant lot at midnight, the police had found him lying wounded. He had been in a drunken street brawl, had lain unconscious in sub-zero weather, and had died a day later in an army hospital . . .

With Cross in her arms, she had returned South and resumed her teaching, but her real profession was a constant rehearsal in her memory of her tiny but pathetic drama, a continuous clutching of it to her heart in the form of a blend of complaint and accusation.

Cross looked at her; tears were still streaming on her cheeks.

"Son, can't you deny yourself sometimes and not hurt others?" she begged of him humbly; she was again, in the evening of her life, supplicating the fateful world of man. "You're destroying yourself. I know you believe only in your own pleasure, but must you hurt other people? If you feel you can't master yourself, then take your problem to God. He'll teach you how to live with others before it's too late. Life is a promise, son; God promised it to us and we must promise it to others. Without that promise, life's nothing . . . Oh, God, to think that at twenty-six you're lost . . . What're you going to do, Cross?"

He stood and gazed solemnly down at her.

"I don't know, Ma."

"Is it really over between you and Gladys?"

"Yeah. There's nothing there."

"Why?"

"I don't know. We can't make it."

"But your children? They *need* you . . . Cross, you can lose your job. Gladys can ruin you, and so can that girl. A wronged woman is a hard woman, Cross."

On wobbly legs he waited for her to grow quiet; he was frantic to see Gladys.

"To think I named you Cross after the Cross of Jesus," she sighed.

"I got to go," he said brusquely. The longer he stayed the more she would bewail the past and grate her heart as well as his nerves. "You need anything, Ma?"

"I need to know that you've found God, Cross," she whispered. "For months now everything I've heard about you is bad."

"I'll—" He felt the need to be kind. "See you tomorrow, hunh?"

"And pray, son."

He went out of the door quickly to escape this fountain of emotion that made him feel guilty. He had to see Gladys and attempt to arrange a roughshod compromise to curb any rashness she might be contemplating as a result of Dot's crazy visit. But the thought of Gladys made him quail; he knew that she would grasp eagerly upon his predicament and turn it against him, would try to use it to hold him at her mercy. Goddammit, if necessary, he would threaten to throw up his job . . . That ought to make her think a little. After all, the only thing Gladys really wanted was money.

Of all the mad things on earth, the maddest was Dot's talking to Gladys. Damn . . . He paused in the snow and stared. He ought to see Dot *first* and learn what had happened between her and Gladys. And he would give Dot the dressing down of her life! Didn't she know that Gladys was her enemy, that she would never befriend her, would do all in her power to humiliate her? Yes; instinct should have warned Dot not to reveal her plight to the wife of the man she claimed to love. He stopped at a street corner and looked at his watch. He had three hours before reporting to work; he had to hurry.

The sun had waned and already a touch of darkness was in the sky. It was growing rapidly colder and an icy wind swept through the streets. Hunger and emotional tension had drained him; he had to eat to stave off that incessant grinding in his stomach. He saw a dingy lunchstand with a sweaty plate glass window. He'd grab a bite to eat . . . He turned, crossed the ice-packed pavement, pushed through a narrow doorway and saw a crowd of working class Negroes and heard babbling voices. He perched himself atop a high stool and propped his elbows upon a greasy counter.

"A hamburger and a cup of coffee," he told the girl who came toward him.

"Right," she sang out.

The girl turned to prepare his order and his eyes, trained by habit, followed the jellylike sway of her sloping hips. At once his imagination began a reconstruction of the contours of her body, using the clues of her plump arms, her protruding breasts, the gently curving shape of her legs, and the width of her buttocks. Through the bluish haze of tobacco smoke and amidst the hub of laughter coming from the rear of the cafe, his senses dreamily seized upon woman as body of woman, not the girl standing by the steam table, but just woman as an image of a body and he drifted toward a state of desire, his consciousness stirring vaguely with desire for desire. His feelings, set off by the sight of the girl, now turned inward, then they projected themselves outwardly again, not so much upon the girl but in a seeking for a girl, to an image that fetched him toward something to embrace as desirable: woman as body of woman . . . The girl came toward him now and he looked fully at her; she slid the plate with the hamburger to him and he saw her face: hard, with small reddish eyes; a full, coarsely formed mouth; huge cheek bones that slanted to a stubborn chin; sullen lips . . . An intractable bitch, he thought. He sighed as the girl's too-solid reality eroded his deepening mood of desire for the desirable: woman as body of woman . . .

He munched his hamburger and fell into a melancholy brooding upon the mysterious movements of his consciousness. What was this thing of desire that haunted him? It seems that I just desire desire, he told himself. And there's no apparent end or meaning to it . . . And then there came to his mind the memory of the many sultry, smoky nights when he had been drunk with his friends in cheap dives and had seen girls like this. And, on those times, like today, a drive toward desire had risen imperiously in him and he had been just drunk enough for this desire for desire to hold fast to itself in spite of the girl's blatant ugliness and he had sordidly bargained with her and had had her; and, like now, in the end, he had recoiled from her in self-disgust while lying beside her in bed just as he had recoiled a moment ago from this one without ever having gone to bed with her. On those drunken occasions he had gone back alone to his empty room to reflect moodily upon the obscurity of what he had been seeking when he had wanted the girl. Surely it had not been *that* girl he had so ardently wanted. No. But, yes, it had been the girl and it had *not* been the girl; he saw clearly that he had wanted the girl because his desire-impulse had pointed to her; but

after having had her, desire was still not satisfied, still sought
to encompass something within desire and hold it steady, to
possess it, to become one with it. And that's impossible, he
told himself. One's crazy to try to do it . . . Yet, he did try,
and his trying seemed to be the essence of living. And marriage, could he build a marriage upon desire? Should one give
pledges, make promises, swear vows the sacredness of which
depended upon such running sands of feelings as desires . . . ?

And what about his desire for Dot? Although she was carrying his child, his desire for her had already gone . . . God
in Heaven! What could he do? When he had been a child he
had thought that life was a solidly organized affair, but when
he had grown up he had found that it had the disorganized
character of a nightmare. What crazy fool had thought up
these forms of human relations? Or had men and women just
drifted blindly through the centuries into such emotional arrangements? He was convinced that an idiot could have conceived of better ways of establishing emotional alliances, and
men must have felt uneasy about it too, for they had sought
to make desire and passion stable by subjecting them to legal
contracts! If human emotions fail to remain constant, then
draft laws stipulating that that which will not remain constant
must remain constant . . . As he brooded over the problem of
desire a quiet sense of awe drenched him. Moods like these
were the nearest he ever came to religious feelings.

He jerked to attention as a wave of guffaws rose from the
crowd of Negroes in the rear of the cafe. Most of them were
young and they were bent double with mirth. A tall Negro
lifted his voice with loud authority over the rolling laughter.

"Where there's lots of rumors, there's bound to be some
truth in 'em," he pronounced.

"You mean to tell me you believe Flying Saucers are *real*?"
a short, brown boy demanded with indignation. "You got
better sense than *that*!"

Cross had heard a hundred such arguments in bars and
cafes and he was primed to relax and listen to yet another one,
to see to what heights of fantasy it would soar.

"I say these white folks is hiding something," the tall Negro
maintained, "and what they're hiding *scares* 'em!"

"And what're they hiding?" the waitress asked.

"Things they don't want *you* to know," the tall Negro said cryptically.

Teasing laughter full of suspense went from man to man. Cross could feel that they wanted to believe this high mystery, but they needed more fantastic facts before their beliefs could jell. Their attitude was one of laughing scepticism underscored with seriousness.

"Know what they found in one of them Flying Saucers?" the tall man demanded. "One of 'em was full of little men, about two feet high, with skin like peach fuzz—"

A waterfall of laughter showered in the cafe. Men rose and stomped their feet, tossed back their heads, and bellowed.

"But what the white folks so scared about?" someone asked. "Little men can't hurt nobody."

Silence. All eyes were turned expectantly to the face of the tall man.

"THEM LITTLE MEN THE WHITE FOLKS FOUND IN THEM SAUCERS WAS COLORED MEN AND THEY WAS FROM MARS!" the tall man spoke in deep solemn tones. "That's why they hushed up the story. They didn't want the world to know that the rest of the universe is colored! Most of the folks on this earth is colored, and if the white folks knew that the other worlds was full of colored folks who wanted to come down here, what the hell chance would the white folks have?"

Screams of approval, leaping from chairs, and clapping of hands.

"You ought to be shot to think of a thing like that!"

"It fits in with the way white folks act!"

Laughter died slowly. The men wiped their mouths with the backs of their hands, gazing at one another with sly joy.

"But it *could* be true," a man said soberly. "White folks in America, France, England, and Italy are the scaredest folks that ever lived on this earth. They're scareda Reds, Chinese, Indians, Africans, *everybody*."

"But how come you reckon they so scared?" an elderly man asked.

" 'Cause they're guilty," the tall man explained. "And guilty folks are *scared* folks! For four hundred years these white folks done made everybody on earth feel like they ain't human, like they're outsiders. They done kicked 'em around and called 'em names . . . What's a Chinese to a white man? Chink-Chink Chinaman with pigtails down his back and he ain't fit for nothing but to cook and wash clothes. What's a Hindoo to a white man? A nigger who's in love with ghosts, who kisses cows and makes pets of vipers. What's a black man to a white man? An ape made by God to cut wood and draw water, and with an inborn yen to rape white girls. A Mexican? A greasy, stinking rascal who ought to be worked to death and then shot. A Jew? A Christ-killer, a cheat, a rat. A Japanese? A monkey with a yellow skin . . . Now our colored brothers are visiting us from Mars and Jupiter and the white folks is sweating in a panic—"

Negroes rolled in laughter, feeling that the powerful white world had been lowered to their own humble plane by the magic of comic words. One black boy danced ecstatically, then, holding his hands over his mouth as though he felt it unseemly to vent his savage mirth indoors, ran out of the cafe, leaving the door open. Upon the snowy sidewalk he screamed and howled and flapped his arms in the icy wind. For a moment he paused, then ran back to the door and, gasping for breath, said:

"Man, that's sure cool!" He lifted his eyes to the grey sky. "You colored brothers on Mars, come on down here and help us!"

Cross found himself joining in the laughter. His heart went out to these rejected men whose rebel laughter banished self-murder from his thoughts. If only he could lose himself in that kind of living! Were there not somewhere in this world rebels with whom he could feel at home, men who were outsiders not because they had been born black and poor, but because they had thought their way through the many veils of illusion? But where were they? How could one find them?

It was time to go. Amidst a tidal wave of laughter he paid his check and went out, passing the black boy on the sidewalk and looking back several times to see other Negroes leave the cafe to join the black boy laughing in the white snow. Their peals reached his ears for half a block.

Yes, he had to see Dot. The thought made tension rise in him and he went into a bar and had a double whiskey. When

he came out a bluish mist hung in the air and the sun was a
faint red ball. The outlines of the buildings were beginning to
blur. A freezing wind stung his face. He found a taxi and
climbed in.

"5743 Indiana," he told the driver.

Underneath all he had felt that day, Dot had rested as a
kind of uneasy undertow, a slow black tide that would not be
gainsaid. And, now that he was going to have it out with her,
he flinched with fear at the hurt she would sustain. It had
been six months ago that she had first floated into his mind as
just another image of desire, woman as body of woman; but,
for reasons which he had not foreseen, she had clung to him
and he had clung to her and slowly she had come to mean
more to him than just a woman's body. Now that the moment of what she so melodramatically liked to refer to as the
"payoff" was at hand, he did not like it. What bothered him
most was that he knew that he had to betray her, and this
betrayal was not springing from any innate perversity in him,
but from the very complexity of his relations with Gladys.
There was no way out but to hurt her, and he was convinced
that she knew it. He had helped her with money, advice, sharing with her his life; but it seemed that these gifts enraged
her. She had said that they were not enough and he knew
that, as a woman, she was right. Dot was so close to what she
wanted in life, that is, to marry him, that its impossibility
drove her almost out of her mind.

In her struggle for legal possession of him, Cross knew that
she was in the end counting heavily upon his weakness to
carry her through. Yes, he was weak, but he knew that he was
weak, and that made a difference. He also knew more about
the turnings and twistings of her mind than she knew he
knew, and this knowledge gave him an ironic insight into her
that he did not relish. How could he ever make her know
that, though he gave forth the appearance of weakness, that
this weakness was really a kind of strength of not wanting to
hurt others. His own experience had shown him that he was
cold-bloodedly brutal when trapped in situations involving
his self-respect. All his life he had been plagued by being
caught in relations where others had tried to take advantage
of him because they had thought him supine and gullible; and

when he had finally confronted them with the fact that he knew that they were playing him, they had hated him with a redoubled fury for his having deceived them! And he dreaded that happening with Dot.

He had never tried to conceal from Dot his situation; he had been transparently honest with her from the beginning; he had told her everything and if she had any illusions, they were of her own making. And what saddened him to inward tears was that he suspected that Dot had allowed herself to become impregnated in order to test the strength of their attachment, hoping that he would be so moved and harassed by her passionate appeals that he would find some way of breaking legally with Gladys and marrying her. And he knew that freedom was the last thing on earth that Gladys would ever grant him. Dot's just young and romantic enough to try such a fool thing, he thought bitterly.

He had met her, of all the places in a teeming city, in the liquor section of the South Center Department Store one Saturday morning last spring. There had been a widely advertised sale of Jamaica rum and long lines of people had queued up to buy at the unheard of rate of two bottles of rum for three dollars. The store had been jammed with milling crowds. He had taken his place at the end of a long queue and a moment later he had been aware that a young, willowy slip of a tall yellow girl had fallen in directly behind him. It was warm; he was without a coat and his shirt sleeves were rolled up past his elbows. He sniffed the perfume she wore, then gave her a quick survey; she was uncommonly pretty and was wearing a sheer pink print dress that showed the shape of her body with disturbing distinctness. She looks sweet, he thought. He glanced at her, trying to catch her eye; but the jostling crowd so distracted him that he forgot her until a few minutes later, when, all at once, he felt his naked elbow touching something yieldingly soft behind him. He looked around and she smiled shyly; a soft lump rose in his throat. Good God, what a gal! And so *young* . . . Did she know that his elbow was touching her left breast? If she did, she gave no outward sign; she still had that vague, sweet smile that could mean anything: coyness or just simple self-consciousness. Why, she's just a child, he thought with a twinge of shame.

He looked at her again, feeling his elbow still touching her breast; she smiled and looked off, yet she did not try to move away. She knows . . . But really, would a young girl with a face so sensitive and finely chiselled allow him to do that to her in public? Was she alone or was that man behind her her husband? The image of woman as body of woman filled him and his head felt pleasantly giddy. He was determined to know if she knew that his bare elbow was tantalizingly touching the tip of her breast. Perhaps she's so excited about the rum that she does not feel it . . . But his knowledge of the erotic made him feel that that was impossible. He sensed in her a quality of quiet waiting and it made him feel that she *did* know and did not mind, was even welcoming it. The line inched forward. The metallic ringing of cash registers sang out over the crowd. Traffic clanged through the streets outside. And all around was bubbling a cacophony of voices. He was now so near the counter that he could see the towering rows of bottles of dark yellow rum. Slowly, so slowly that no one could notice anything, he moved his bare elbow to and fro across the tip of her breast, realizing with sensual astonishment: She's not wearing a brassiere! Desire surged softly through him. Out of the corner of his eye he could see that she had not moved; she was staring steadily ahead, holding her purse primly in front of her. He tried it again; she did not move or seem aware that she was being touched at all; her face was sweet, composed, solemn, angel-like in its purity and remoteness from erotic passion. Was she aware or was she not? He had to know; it obsessed him. She could, of course, abruptly leave the line to indicate her disgust; or she could, if she were the hysterical breed, yell out that he was molesting her. But he did not believe that she would . . . Was she playing the same game that he was playing? And who was she? Again he moved his naked elbow across her left breast, caressing it, gently indenting the soft, surrendering flesh under the sheer cloth of her dress as much as he dared, and, this time, he knew that she knew, for he felt the tip of her loose breast gradually hardening, growing delicately into a pointed, taut nipple. He gazed at her directly now, but still she did not look at him; and her face was as passive and serene as a summer landscape. The line shortened and he fondled her breast with his elbow and she made no move to withdraw her body; instead, as the line snaked forward, she managed to keep her breast where his elbow could touch it. He was now certain that the man behind her was not her husband, did not know her. Finally he turned to her and smiled, still touching her breast, and said:

"It's a long time, hunh, to wait for two bottles of rum?"

"It's awful," she said, and they both laughed.

"You like rum?" he asked.

"Now, what do you think?" she countered teasingly.

"What do you make with it? Cuba Libres or Rum Punches?"

"Both," she said.

"You live around here?"

"Naw. Up near 37th Street."

He looked at her openly now, as a man looks at a woman he likes and wants.

"You *couldn't* be over sixteen," he ventured.

"You're wrong. I'm seventeen," she corrected him.

They had spoken in low tones, as though both were conspiring to keep secret the erotic link that was springing up between them. He noticed that she was trembling slightly and he knew that she was being claimed by a state he knew well: dread. This was perhaps the first time she had ever let herself be caressed in this manner and he must not frighten her. He cast about for something to say to let her know that, though he was after her, he was also a gentleman and that she need not be afraid of him, that she could rely on him for discreetness and good sense. It was then that he saw a Wendell Phillips High School pin on the collar of her dress.

"When did you get your sheepskin?" he asked her.

"Last June," she answered readily.

"Phillips was my school, too," he told her.

"Really?" she asked. She smiled broadly, relaxing completely for the first time.

They were at the counter now and he paid for his rum and stood aside, waiting for her. When she left the counter, he said:

"Here. Let me help you carry that."

"Thank you," she said with a charming degree of hesitation; then she allowed him to take her bottles.

They walked out of the store together, making small talk. She told him that she lived with her mother and a younger brother; but her mother was a terror, depriving her of all freedom. She said that she was thinking seriously of leaving home and living with Myrtle, a girl friend . . . During the first five minutes he had let her know that he was not free, that he worked in the Post Office, that he was married but not living with his wife. They passed a movie house and he asked her if she liked movies and she said yes. He invited her to see a show with him that afternoon and she demurred modestly. She doesn't want to seem too *forward*, he thought; and he laughed out loud about it when he was alone in his room.

"But you can call me sometimes, if you want to," she said, and she gave him her telephone number.

That was how it had begun. She had known from the beginning that he was not free and she had told him that it did not really matter for the time being. In their relationship he had found her a passionate child achingly hungry for emotional experience. Of an afternoon she would come to his room with the most disconcerting directness he had ever known in a woman. He would try to talk to her and as he talked he could tell that she was not listening; she was pulling off her dress, stripping down her nylon stockings, stepping out of her nylon slip and panties . . . And afterwards he would stare at her unbelievingly as she would stomp her foot and tell him with a childlike seriousness that was all the more serious because it was so childlike: "I never want to make love with anybody but you."

"You'll live and learn," he had told her, yawning.

"Don't *say* that," she had protested with sudden fury, and he realized with a sense of dismay that what had taken place was to her sacred.

But that did not prevent some nuance of perversity in him from trying to make her admit that she had been conscious of his elbow caressing her breast that warm, spring Saturday morning in the liquor store, but she would never confess it, would exhibit feelings of shame and indignation whenever he mentioned it; but beneath her ardent denials was a furtive sense of erotic pleasure. He was amused by the manner in which she balanced her moral notions with her emotional hungers. Under his questioning she would pause in her dressing and stare at him with wide, hurt eyes and exclaim:

"How can you *say* that? You sure have a *filthy* imagination!"

"But, Dot, dammit, you *knew*! I *swear* you did—"

"Do you think I'd let anybody do *that* to me in public?" she asked, her voice ringing with genuine incredulity.

"But you *did*, Dot!"

"I *didn't*!"

Tears would roll down her cheeks and he would take her in his arms and soothe her; but she never got angry about it. And until the end she would never concede that that morning was the first time that she had ever felt so keen a sensual pleasure. But Cross was certain of it and it made him marvel that she could deny it with such passionate consistency.

His bond with her grew deeper with the passing days, for it was with her that, for the first time in his life, he found himself talking freely, emptying out of his soul the dammed up waters of reflection and brooding thought. He told her of his morbidly tangled yet profound relation with his mother; he told her how, when he had been twenty-one years of age, he had naïvely been sucked into a stupid marriage with Gladys; and he confessed to her his incurable melancholy stemming from his mulling over his emotions. He never quite knew how much of what he told her she understood, but she always listened patiently, now and then timidly venturing a detached question or two, but never commending or blaming. He came at last to believe that she accepted the kind of talk in which he indulged as a mysterious part of a man's equipment, along with his sexual organs. But the mere fact that she listened to his analytical tirades had been a boon to him beyond his deepest hopes.

And now he had to hurt her. And what would she do? Once he had toyed with trying to find possible friends of his with whom she could fall in love; he had once even spoken to her in glowing terms of a man who worked with him on the job. And he had been amazed when she had turned to look at him and demanded:

"Are you trying to pawn me off on somebody?"

To hear her speak like that had so shamed him that he had never tried it again. Then, one Sunday evening over dinner in a crowded restaurant, she told him that she was carrying his child. His stupefication had been such that the food stuck in his throat. Later, in his room, she had wildly resisted his suggestion that she abort the child and it had maddened him. The scenes of emotional conflict that took place the following month had frayed him almost to madness.

He had just left one woman, his mother, who, in an outpouring, had hurled at him her life draped in the dark hues of complaint and accusation, had tried futilely to rouse compassion in him by dramatizing the forlorn nature of her abandoned plight; now he was on his way to struggle with yet another woman. And after Dot there loomed the formidable figure of his wife.

"Okay, Buddy; here you are," the taxi driver told him as the cab swerved to a curb hidden by snowflakes.

He paid, ran up the steps, pushed the bell of Dot's apartment three times, the signal they agreed upon when he was calling to see her. The buzzer was so long in answering that he thought that surely she was not in. Where could she be? He rang again and was about to leave when the buzzer suddenly responded in a long blast of sound that would not stop. He opened the vestibule door, feeling that something was wrong. He heard the buzzer still emitting its tinny throb long after he had passed the second floor. She must be upset or something . . . When he reached the door of Dot's apartment, he saw Myrtle, Dot's girl friend, looking at him with a face as devoid of expression as she could make it. Myrtle was a tall, dark girl with a handsome face and sardonic eyes. Cross slowed his movements, sensing knowledge of a crisis behind Myrtle's reserved manner.

"Hi," he greeted her.

Without answering, she caught hold of his arm and drew him forcibly into the hallway of the apartment.

"Where's Dot?" he asked, trying to keep his voice calm.

"In bed," she said flatly.

"What's happened?"

"*You* ought to be asking . . . All hell's broke loose, that's all."

"What do you mean? I want to see Dot."

"You can't now," she said with an air of petty satisfaction.

He started for Dot's bedroom and Myrtle held him back.

"The *doctor's* in there," she whispered fiercely.

"The doctor? Why? Tell me what's happening!"

"You *men!*" She curled her lips in scorn. "How much do you think a poor girl can stand?"

"Okay. You can can that," he told her roughly, unable to suppress hot resentment. "Dot can talk to me like that, but *you* can't!"

He had never liked her and she did not like him and the way she was now acting was something he had known she would do if she ever had gotten the chance; now she had it and was doing it. One instinct told him to ignore her, but she had cut too deeply into his bleeding feelings for him to leave off. He stood glaring at her, his fingers trembling.

"Look, I'm Dot's best friend, see?" she shot at him. "I'm taking care of her, trying to repair the damage you've done. I can say what I damn well like . . ."

"Not to *me*," Cross said.

"And why not?" she flipped at him.

"Because I don't sleep with you," he told her brutally, looking her straight in the eyes.

An anger so intense burned in Myrtle's face that her large eyes shrank in size.

"You dirty sonofabitch," she said in an even, low tone.

"Thanks," he said.

He opened the door of Dot's room and peered in.

"Who is it?" a loud masculine voice called out to him as he stood uncertainly.

It was the doctor who had yelled; Cross could see his back bent over Dot's bed. Dot was lying with her face to the wall.

"It's me, honey. Cross."

"Please, please, don't come in now, Cross."

"Will you be kind enough to wait outside until I'm through here?" the doctor asked brusquely. "What happens after I'm gone is your business."

Cross shut the door and turned to see the smirk on Myrtle's face.

"What happened?"

"I ought to spit right in your face for what you said to me," she said forming her lips as though about to spew something through them. "What she ever saw in your sullen heart, God only knows!"

"I'm sorry," he relented to get information. "But why don't you tell me what's happened?"

"Yeah, *sorry* . . . Men are always *sorry*," she derided him openly, keeping her voice low and charging it with hate.

"For Christ's sake!" he exploded. "Now's no time to carry on like that! Tell me what happened."

"Wait and she'll tell you," Myrtle said and went into the kitchen, closing the door behind her.

Cross sat and fumed. How crazy women could be sometimes . . . What did she think she was gaining by throwing dramatic fits? He looked up as she came briskly out of the kitchen, opened the door of the hall closet, took out her coat and put it on. She paused, not looking directly at him. The muscles of Cross's body tightened; he could have kicked her right through the brick wall into the snowdrifts piled outside.

"I've got to go down to the drugstore and get a prescription filled," she said matter-of-factly. "I'm leaving a hypodermic needle and a syringe boiling in a pan on the gas stove. Turn out the fire under it in two or three minutes, will you?" She shot him a sidelong glance. "You ought to be able to do *that* now."

"You can go to hell," he growled at her.

"I'd gladly go, if only I could take you along with me," she snapped at him and pulled the door shut behind her so violently that it sounded like a rifle shot.

His nerves twitched in protest, then he was conscious that the droning murmur of the doctor's voice in the bedroom had ceased and he heard Dot's distressed voice ringing out:

"Oh, Cross! What was that?"

Before he could reply the doctor had opened the door and was glaring at him.

"The girl slammed the door," Cross told the doctor sheepishly.

"This child's a nervous wreck," the doctor said, throwing up his hands in despair. "She's got to be kept quiet."

Cross huddled forward in his chair. The doctor went back into Dot's room, drawing the door shut.

Once more the masculine murmur of the doctor's voice resumed. What was he saying to her? And what had she told him? He was convinced that he was under discussion and it made him feel deprived of his humanity, converted into a condemned object, exposed to the baleful gaze of a million eyes. He crept softly to the door, cocked his head and listened, but he could not distinguish any words. Now and then he could hear Dot's silvery voice rising in a melody of complaint, of protest. Goddamn . . . Why had she called in that doctor without telling him? If she'd only trust me . . . But he knew that her trusting him would not get her what she wanted; he was in no position to marry her. All right; suppose Dot was in trouble? Did that justify her subjecting him to shame? The South Side was a small community and if Dot had revealed their relations to this doctor, their predicament would be on the lips of a thousand gossiping men and women in a day's time . . .

He had a hot impulse to rise and flee the apartment and disappear forever . . . What had he to lose by throwing up this fool's game? His job? It was not worth a damn, so mortgaged was he with debt. He really had nothing to lose. What a stupid situation for an intelligent man to find himself in! What greater shame was there for a man than to walk the streets cringing with fear of grasping women whose destructive strokes were draped in the guise of whimpers and accusations? Somehow he would shake loose from this and never in all his life let himself be caught again . . .

He was already supporting Dot, but she could, if she wanted to be brutal about it, compel him, at the behest of a court of law, to support the child after it was born. He knew that she would do such only if she were certain that he would never marry her. Had Gladys told her that a divorce was impossible? More than likely she had.

He ought to leave *now* . . . But he sat, hating himself. He yearned to roll himself into a tight little black ball and fling himself away as far as his strength would allow. But, no; there were his small sons, Cross, Junior, Peter, and Robert, whom he loved and did not want to leave. He would regain his influence over Dot; all was not lost. Dot had gone berserk because he had broken his promise to see her this morning and now he would have to be with her constantly to bring her around. Above all, he had to persuade her to abort the child for her sake, his sake . . .

A gurgle of water sounded in the kitchen. That pot that Myrtle had told him to look after! He ran and turned out the gas just in time, for there were but a few bubbles left in the pan.

The telephone rang. He entered the hallway and stood uncertainly.

"Shall I answer it, Dot?" he called through the door.

"Yes, please," Dot answered weakly.

He picked up the receiver.

"Dot? Is that you?" It was the voice of a woman speaking with breathless eagerness.

"No, this is not she," he said.

"Who's speaking?" the voice was cautious now, but still urgent.

"Just a friend," Cross said, disguising his tone. He was always afraid of Gladys' trapping him in Dot's apartment.

"Is this Mr. Damon?"

"No," he lied, hoping that his voice would not carry to Dot's room. "I'm a friend of Myrtle."

"Won't you please call Dot to the phone?"

"I'm afraid she can't come. She's in bed. The doctor's with her. Who's this?"

"Mary, a friend of Dot. Listen, tell Dot I've found her a lawyer. He's a whizz. She's to call me as soon as possible."

"I see." His eyes widened.

"Tell her that she'll have to act fast to tie up Damon—"

"I'll tell her." He struggled to keep his voice normal.

There was a hesitating silence.

"*Who's* this speaking?" Fear was in the voice.

"Brown's the name," he lied.

"Oh . . . For a moment I had the feeling you were Dot's friend, that Damon man," the voice sighed with relief.

"Oh, no. I wouldn't want to be in his shoes—"

"Nothing's seriously wrong with Dot, I hope?"

"No. She just needs some rest."

"Tell Dot that she's got to hang on to her birth certificate; it's her quickest way of proving that she's under sixteen. My lawyer says that as long as she's not sixteen, Damon's guilty of rape. Now, Dot's birthday comes in June, and that gives her four months of grace."

Cross felt a red horizon of danger closing in about him.

"What did you say?"

"Explain this to Dot," the voice spoke distinctly. "Wait a minute."

He held his breath as a faint rustle of paper came over the wire.

"I got it," the voice was edged with satisfaction. "I copied it down as my lawyer read it to me this morning. Here it is: '. . . Every male person of the age of seventeen years and upwards who shall have carnal knowledge of any female person under the age of sixteen years and not his wife, either with or without her consent shall be adjudged guilty of the crime of rape . . .' You know what *carnal* means, don't you?"

"Yes," Cross breathed; he felt wrapped in a nightmare.

" '. . . Every person convicted of the crime of rape shall be imprisoned in a penitentiary for a term of not less than one year and may extend to life . . .' You got that?"

"Yes."

"Now, this Damon's married, so he *can't* marry Dot and wriggle out that way," the voice went on in a tone of hard triumph. "So if Dot doesn't get mushy, she's got Damon where she wants him."

"I see," Cross said. "But are you sure Dot's *under* sixteen?"

"I've seen her birth certificate," the voice assured him.

"I'll tell her," Cross promised heavily.

" Goodby."

" 'Bye."

He hung up, swayed a bit, then sat. Dot was a minor!

How was that possible? He was certain that she had told him that she was seventeen. Jesus . . . Could this be true? He had been honest with her and she had tricked him! Yet, in casting back his mind, he remembered that he had often felt that she was younger than she had claimed. How in God's name had he stumbled into a situation of such deadly seriousness? He sat hunched over in the chair, too stunned to move. If ever, now was the time to act upon the impulse of flight. He had about fifty dollars in his pocket. He ought to buy a railroad ticket for as long a journey as the money would cover, and vanish. There was no doubt now but that Dot had made up her mind, and from now on he had to regard her as his enemy. Longing for a drink, he rummaged in the kitchen and found an inch of gin in a bottle and drained it.

The hall door lock clicked and Myrtle entered without glancing at him. Yes; she was in on this too. Her knowledge of his being a potential convict was what had made her so bold in sassing him. He glared at her as she pulled off her coat and went into the kitchen and returned with a tray; she went into Dot's room, closing the door behind her. That bitch . . . His talk with Dot would be decisive; either she called off the lawyer or he would drop her and let her do her worst. He had a last weapon, his gun, and it would change things and leave her dismayed . . .

At last the doctor emerged, leaving Dot's door open this time. Moving methodically, the doctor placed his black bag on a chair and proceeded to get into his overcoat. He pulled on his hat and looked at Cross with cold eyes. Abruptly he grabbed his bag and went unaided out of the door. Yes; Dot had identified him to the doctor. Cross felt sick and cheap.

On his tongue was a storm of reproaches he wanted to hurl at Dot, but he checked himself. To lose his temper would be playing into her hands, giving her an opportunity to wallow in an emotional scene. He walked slowly into the room and saw Dot lying with her face to the wall. Myrtle sat huddled on a side of the bed with her head bent forward, her body shaking; she was weeping. The hypodermic needle and the syringe lay on the tray at the foot of the bed. A medicinal odor hung in the air.

"Myrtle, what the hell's eating you?" he demanded.

As he had expected, they had been waiting for this signal; both women started to berate him at once. It was Dot's voice that won out.

"Please, Cross, in the name of God," Dot begged, without turning to look at him. "Be gentle with Myrtle. She's been waiting on me night and day. She's all I got. Don't insult her."

"I'm not insulting anybody—"

Myrtle jerked upright, her limbs trembling and her face wet with tears.

"You did! And what have I ever done to you?"

"You started slashing at me the moment I got into this apartment," he charged her.

"But can't you see what's happening?" Myrtle blazed at him. "This poor child's half out of her mind . . . Try to be *human!*"

"That's the trouble," he almost hissed. "I'm simply too *damned* human."

"If I was Dot, I wouldn't take this off you for a single minute," Myrtle burst out in a torrent of rage. "Oh, boy, I'd have you in a way that you'd never forget!"

"Do you think I don't know that?"

"I'd get your money, your job, and throw you smack into jail!"

"Oh, Myrtle, no . . ." Dot protested.

Yes, Myrtle was going further than Dot wanted. Cross looked at the two of them. When he spoke he was not smiling, but there was a note of hard irony in his voice that was worse than laughter.

"Yeah, I know. I'm just a big, bad, black brute. Pushing little girls around. Taking advantage of the helpless. Spoiling innocent children. I've no feelings. I'm just having a damn grand time and making others suffer." He summed up their case for them and then sat on the edge of the bed beside Myrtle.

"You're a man and you can't dodge your responsibilities," Myrtle told him wailingly.

"I'm not responsible to *you* for anything," Cross told her. "And I don't like your meddling. Now get the hell out of here and let me talk to Dot."

"You are a *real* bastard," Myrtle said. "You ought to marry Dot, but I pity her spending a lifetime with you."

"Don't worry," he taunted her. "I'm not going to spend a lifetime with *you*."

"Cross, for God's sake," Dot whimpered. "Don't be that way."

"That's the only way he can be," Myrtle said.

"Get out of here, Myrtle," Cross told her again.

There was silence. He stood his ground. He was determined to wreck their rehearsed appeal to him. He felt that instinct was guiding them, prompting their attitudes and the strategy of their attacks. Both of them were weeping now and he made no move. He would let their tears flow futilely for awhile; they would see that he was not to be easily overcome.

"You're lucky that it's Dot you're dealing with instead of me," Myrtle said. Weeping, she stood and walked from the room.

Cross heard the door close behind his back. He could almost see the little wheels turning in the brains of both girls as they planned their next move. Men had to consult together for concerted action; women simply gravitated together spontaneously, motivated by their situation in life as women. They knew without prior consultation the most effective assaults. Cross was conscious of their consciousness. He knew them as women better than they knew him as man.

"Dot, I want to talk to you," he began. "Are you up to it, or should I come back in the morning?"

Dot lay without moving. He knew that she was debating. Finally she slowly turned over and faced him, the mass of her tumbling brown tresses framing an oval of face delicate and demure. God, but she's really beautiful . . . Her deep brown eyes were haunted, empty. She lifted her head an inch from the damp pillow and then let it fall again, as though she was too weak to bear the strain of holding it erect. She managed a wan smile. What an actress! How do they learn it? Is it instinct?

"I'm sorry, Cross," she whispered.

And he was truly sorry too. He wanted in that instant to take her in his arms and comfort her, but he knew that she would at once take advantage of it, would exploit it, would try to wring out of a simple act of compassion a promise of marriage. Goddamn! He reined in his feelings. She was gazing toward the window and the thought shot through his mind: She's about to switch her tactics . . . His eyes traveled along the slight outlines of her body stretching under the blanket; she was so tiny and yet somehow so strong, this girl. Woman as body of woman was not in his consciousness now, but there was rolling teasingly through his memory a memory of it. He did not really want to hurt her, but what was he to do? How could he avoid it?

"Dot, let's start from the beginning," he commenced. "Are you going to do what I suggested?"

"What do you mean, Cross?" she hedged, sparring for time, her eyes swimming helplessly at him.

"About the child," he told her. "I've got it all arranged."

She leapt to a sitting position. Her body rocked to and fro; she clenched her fists and shook them at him, her mouth gaping in protest.

"No, no, no!" she pealed hysterically. "Don't ask me *that* again! Please, Cross, if you do—"

"I *am* asking you," he said. "There's nothing else I can do."

She sprang from the bed in her nylon gown and screamed, then ran on bare, scampering feet across the room to the window. He walked toward her, calmly. The door burst open and Myrtle stood staring at them with parted lips and tense eyes.

"If you ask me that again, I'll jump out of the window! I swear I will! I swear, I swear . . ." Dot sobbed, clawing blindly at the window latch.

"Oh, God!" Myrtle exclaimed, grabbing Dot with both arms. "Darling, don't! You don't know what you are doing!" She looked beseechingly at Cross who stood near Dot. Cross had not budged; he regarded Dot coldly. "Please, Cross, help me to get her back to bed . . ."

"Get back in bed, Dot," Cross said in a detached voice; he still did not touch her.

Dot sobbed brokenly, clinging convulsively to Myrtle. Then she slid heavily to the wooden floor, resting on her bare knees. The nylon gown was pulled taut across the curves of her firm, yellow thighs and through the sheer white translucence of the tissue he could see the dark smudge of her pubic hair. She beat her knees frantically with her fists, violently shaking her head, tears oozing from her eyes, her body rocking back and forth. She keened: "No, no! I'll *never* kill my child! I'll die first! You can't make me *murder* . . . ! It's my child and I'll keep it and love it like I love my own life . . . ! Oh, God, don't let this happen to me!" She gulped for breath and fell prone to the floor, her body jerking with nervous spasms.

"Help me, Cross," Myrtle begged, struggling with Dot.

He did not move; he stood looking silently at both of them. Myrtle stood over Dot, looking from him to Dot. Yes, she's trying to weigh how much influence this is having on me, he thought. A woman's business is emotion and her trade is carried on in cash of tears . . . He would help to keep Dot from leaping out of the window, but that was all he was prepared to do at the moment. And, besides, he was not convinced that she would leap.

"Come, darling," Myrtle coaxed, lifting Dot.

Dot allowed herself finally to be led back to the bed. Myrtle eased her upon it and Dot sat and sobbed with tears streaming through the fingers of her hands which covered her face.

"I won't kill my child," Dot took up the refrain. "I *won't* . . ."

"Darling, get in bed," Myrtle cooed. "The doctor said you had to be careful. You're not well, you know."

Cross knew that these words were aimed at him. When Dot was once more in bed, Myrtle turned to him.

"Why do you treat her like that?" she demanded. "The doctor said—"

"Leave me alone!" he shouted; he did not relent; he could not.

"I never dreamed anyone like you existed," Myrtle said.

"You know better now," he said tersely.

Myrtle ran from the room. Cross sat on the edge of the bed and tenderly touched Dot's shaking shoulder.

"Dot," he began, "try to listen calmly. This may be the last time I can talk to you like this—"

"Don't say that, Cross. You're going to leave me?" she asked.

"I don't know what I'm going to do," he said.

Dot lay very still. Cross heard an "L" train thundering past outside. Night was falling and a dark blue sheen of sky stood at the windowpane.

"You promised not to tell anybody about this without first telling me," he began.

"Oh, Cross, I *had* to tell the doctor," she said in a rush of words. "I was so nervous and he kept asking me what was the matter—"

"I'm not talking about *that*!"

Dot's eyes showed helpless bewilderment. He knew that her pretended naïveté was particularly dangerous, for in it was a pathetic appeal for love that his heart yearned to answer. He knew that her deception stemmed from her craving for security and that she was expecting him, if he ever caught her in it, to forgive her.

"Don't you know that if you destroy me, you're hurting yourself?" he asked her. "This calling in a lawyer—"

"Oh, Cross!" she wailed. "I didn't! You don't *understand*!"

"I understand more than you think," he told her.

She flung herself into his arms and clutched him frantically. All grief and despair vanished from her face as quickly as a summer rain, and he could not help but marvel at the weapons of a woman when she fought. Her volatile emotions altered with dialectical suddenness, changing into their opposites, disappearing, hiding under new guises.

"Mary phoned and told me to tell you that she had a lawyer for you," he told her.

"That was Mary on the phone a while back?" she asked with wide eyes.

"Yes."

Dot sighed with such relief that Cross wondered if she had other plots cooking . . .

"Oh, Mary . . . She's crazy," Dot explained it away in a childlike voice. "I don't have to obey her, Cross. The lawyer was her idea."

He would now try to see what was really on her mind.

"Dot, how old are you?" he asked her softly.

She did not look at him; her eyes were steadily before her and yet he knew that she knew that he was staring at her and waiting for an answer.

"Did you hear what I asked you, Dot?" he demanded.

She still did not answer or look at him. Well, he would wait her out. He had been intimately tender with this girl and now he had caught her acting most cruelly against him. What excuse would she give? Then he guessed her strategy; she would give none. She would just be a helpless, hard-put-upon, suffering woman playing her oldest and strongest role.

"Dot, I'm talking to you," he said. "How old are you?"

The knowledge of the criminal threat she held over him stood between them like an invisible wall. She still could not turn to look at him; then she bent suddenly forward, covered her face with her hands and sobbed.

"I don't know what to do," she gulped.

She had failed to answer; instead, she had let him see the emotional dilemma in which she was caught, let him glimpse the terrible weapon she held in her hand, let him surmise how reluctantly she would use it, but use it she would.

"Look, Dot, you can haul me before a court and get me convicted, but I swear to you that I'll find some way out, you hear?" he warned her. "You lied to me. You told me you were seventeen. You led me to this crime, if you call it a crime. Now, how old are you?"

"I'll be sixteen in June," she breathed, not looking at him.

Cross sighed. "Why did you lie to me?"

"I wanted you," she whispered, her eyelashes nestling against her cheeks.

"And now you want me put into jail for ten, maybe twenty years?"

Myrtle entered and lifted the tray from the bed.

"Darling, I'll never do that to you," Dot said sweetly, too sweetly.

"If you do, you'll never win," he warned her solemnly.

"Maybe Superman'll kill himself and escape everybody?" Myrtle gave forth a brittle laugh. "You *could* run off to South America, too."

She went briskly through the door and Cross balled his fingers in fury. He turned again to Dot.

"Look, start with Ma. Why did you go to her?"

Again Dot became too weak to talk; through tears she groped blindly for Cross's hand and gripped it.

"I was wild— Even my mother won't speak to me," she whimpered.

"Your mother? Does *she* know?" he demanded, amazed.

She gave him a look that begged forgiveness. She had not kept her word. He would never be dumb enough to trust anybody again. Dot's face suddenly brightened with joy.

"Your mother's wonderful," she sang.

Goddammit! Wouldn't Dot ever learn that these assumed poses would never work.

"I understand now why you love her so," Dot floated on warmly. "She has such a *noble* face . . . And she's *for* us, Crossy. She hates Gladys; she didn't tell me so, but I can feel it. She says your children are beautiful! Oh, Crossy, I'd love to take care of them. I *would*!"

She's out of her mind . . . Did she think that she could take away another woman's children? Were there no limits to her vanity? Dot turned and looked yearningly at him.

"The children, yours and mine, could all be together—"

"Did Gladys tell you that?" he asked with soft irony.

Dot's eyes narrowed as she conjured up the image of Gladys. "She hates me; she hates you— God, she's *awful*!"

"Look, Dot, I'm going to tell you the lay of the land, then you must let your common sense guide you. Gladys will not let me go; her keeping me is her revenge on me for leaving her. Let's live together and ride this out. Or, get rid of the child—"

Dot sat up and looked at him; she had changed.

"Cross, you *got* to get a divorce," she pronounced.

"*Somebody* has to give way in this," he insisted.

"I won't kill the child," she said simply.

She was telling him that she would not let go of the hold she had upon him, no matter what. He stood up.

"I don't give a damn," he muttered. "I couldn't care less—"

"Then, why do you blame me for getting a lawyer?" she demanded.

"I'm not talking to you. I'm talking to myself, about my-self," he said.

His eyes were hot and vacant. He was in a rage.

"You're threatening me with jail to make me get a divorce my wife won't give," the words growled out of him.

"Pull off your coat, honey," she seemed to relent.

"Naw; I got to go," he said. "I've got to see Gladys and try to undo some of the harm you've done."

"Aren't you going to tell me *something*?" she begged.

"*You* tell me what to tell you!" he shouted.

Myrtle came in and stood by the bed, and asked, "What did you decide about Dot, Cross?"

"Nothing," he told her bluntly.

"Wouldn't your wife take some money?"

"Sure; if I had it."

"Can't you borrow some?"

"I'm already up to my neck in debt."

"Give her monthly payments—"

"And what'll be left for Dot, then? I'm paying for the car—"

"Sell it," Myrtle suggested.

"I haven't got the car to sell. Gladys has it and she's hanging on to it and I've got to keep up the payments," he explained.

"Well, it's your funeral," Myrtle said. "You can't expect Dot to sit here and not defend herself; can you?"

"All right; put me in jail, if you want to," he spoke through tight lips.

He turned abruptly and walked out. He was so spent that he felt that he was floating down the steps. Through the night's mist the street lamps gleamed dully. He tramped over snow-carpeted sidewalks without knowing it. He had to see Gladys, but he did not know what he would say to her. He paused and rubbed his hand over his eyes. If those who were pressing him knew how little he felt himself as a real being, they would recoil in horror; he felt unreal, scarcely alive. How long could he go on like this? Shame flooded him as he recalled his attempt with the gun. He could not even do *that* . . .

He stopped at a street corner and waited for a southbound trolley. The snow enforced a hush over the city, muffling the sounds of traffic and the footsteps of passersby. Above him an invisible plane droned through the night sky. Icy wind flapped his overcoat and he turned his back to it to escape its knifelike pain on his face. His eyes caught a scrap of paper whirling uncertainly on currents of wind; he watched it rise, veer, hover, then vanish aimlessly around a corner. A clanging trolley heaved into view and he approached the tracks and sprang upon the trolley when it slowed to a stop. He paid and sat in the rear of the car and closed his eyes and leaned his head against a sweaty windowpane.

Dread was deep in him now; he had to tackle Gladys and he did not know how. The tussle between them had been so long and bitter that there was not much room left for jockeying. Over the years they had hurled at each other every curse word they knew and he felt that his present visit would be by far the most exacting. He had not seen her for more than three months; he made his payments to her by sending a check through the mails every two weeks. His not seeing her had made him forego his joy in seeing his sons and he missed them acutely, but Gladys had so adroitly managed their parting that she had extorted his not seeing the children as part of the price he had to pay for his being rid of her. After the terrible scene the last time he had seen her, he had told her that he did not intend to come again, and, in his black mood, he had given her the right to tell the children any damn thing she chose. And Gladys had seized literally upon his words and had written a special delivery letter to his mother informing her that he had disowned his children, branding him an unnatural monster. His mother had summoned him, had upbraided him, wept and prayed.

His head lolled as the trolley jolted through the snowy night streets and his mind drifted back to the time he had been attending day classes at the University of Chicago, majoring in philosophy and working the nightshift in the Post Office. In those days he had not had much time for fun and had been constantly hankering for relaxation. His mother had been in the South, living in the house that she had bought through her lifelong and morbid frugality, and he had been a lonely young man hankering after pleasures in a big city. A stream of her pious letters had urged him to marry, but he had ignored her naïve moralizing and had remained single.

Ideas had been his only sustained passion, but he knew that his love of them had that same sensual basis that drew him achingly to the sight of a girl's body swinging in a tight skirt along a sunny street.

He had been more than ready for Gladys when she had first risen on his horizon. He had congratulated himself on having tumbled upon a naïve girl who was gratefully receiving his amorous attentions, and it was not until long afterwards that he had discovered that she had waited patiently while he had gropingly strayed into her domain, and then she had quietly closed the trap door over him. If some ironic enemy had been intending to tangle him in an ill-suited marriage, his self-enforced abstinence could not have better prepared him for her. She had been living in his South Side rooming house and he had spoken to her only casually. A registered nurse, quiet, perhaps more than a little repressed and with maybe a tendency toward the hysterical, she was soft-spoken, brown-skinned, and well-made. Sometimes he had seen her in her handsome nurse's uniform and he had admitted that she looked distinctively attractive in it.

Early one rainy autumn afternoon five years ago he had gone down into the vestibule to go out to drive his Ford to work and had found her standing there, sheltering herself against the roaring downpour. He could see the edges of her white uniform showing around the hem of her coat. Surmising that she was trying to get to work, he had offered her a lift. Enroute he engaged her in a bantering conversation which had ended with her accepting an invitation to have a drink with him at the GOLDEN KEY the next afternoon.

That was how it began. The next afternoon—the rain was still falling—he sat waiting for her in a rear booth of the tavern, hunched over an unfinished drink. She presented herself a half hour late all done up in a smart, dark blue suit with a white silk blouse. A red silk scarf was tied over her head and flouncing over her whole body was a transparent, plastic raincoat. He helped her out of her coat and noticed that tiny drops of rain gleamed on her wide forehead and her pert nose. From her there drifted to him the odor of lilacs and autumn leaves . . .

As they drank they talked about themselves, their families,

racial problems. He found that she had no settled tastes or convictions, and he was not a little flattered to discover that she was curious about his notions and had the good sense to defer to him when he told her something of importance. Years later Cross realized that she had had enough sagacity to clear ample psychological ground about her so that he could move in at ease and without knowing that she was luring him. Her feminine instinct placed him at once in the role of a strong and reliable man and encouraged him to play it; he found himself liking to talk to her.

He had already made up his mind to invite her to dinner when she suddenly lifted her left wrist and looked at her watch, wailing:

"Oh, God! It's almost six. I've got to go."

"I thought you were going to be free," he said disappointedly.

"You didn't ask me to be," she said quickly. "I've got to go to a cocktail party. You know, the white and colored nurses' associations are merged and if a colored member doesn't show up when she's invited, they might get the notion that we don't want to belong." She frowned and stared off. "Really, I feel out of place in a roomful of whites. I'm afraid I'll be the only spook there."

"Guess I'll catch up on my sleep," he yawned.

"If that's all you've got to do, come with me to the party. Then I'll have dinner with you. And I'd feel better if you were with me."

They hustled out of the bar and drove to the Loop. The party was paralyzingly dull, with Cross and Gladys standing huddled together at one end of a huge, buzzing roomful of people, holding their drinks self-consciously, watching the others. He was amazed at how uneasy Gladys was in the presence of whites. She's too conscious of her color, he thought.

"Look, buck up," he sought to put some backbone in her. "Don't let the mere existence of these people intimidate you."

"They think they're *something* and we're *nothing*," she snapped.

"It's up to us to make ourselves something," he argued. "A man creates himself . . ."

"You are a *man*," she said simply.

He understood now; it was the helplessness of dependence that made her fret so. Men made themselves and women were made only through men.

They had been there only half an hour when Gladys whispered to him: "Let's get to goddamn hell out of here. They make me sick!"

"Okay," he assented. "But whites don't scare me."

They went straight to a bar on the South Side where Gladys sulked bitterly. He studied her, wondering what memories lay under her mood. Through gentle questioning he stumbled upon it; she had attended a racially mixed school in her adolescence and the snubs and ostracism had branded her with a deep sense of not belonging and a yearning to have her status as an outsider cleared of shame. Her consciousness of being an outcast moved him toward her, enabled him to drape about her a net of tender compassion. Underneath sex and common interests flowed a profounder tide of identity.

After dinner they began to drink in earnest, then they danced in a far South Side night club and it was while holding her in his arms on the dance floor that desire for her leaped in him and it carried an extra urge to bind her to him and make her feel her humanity; he hungered for her as an image of woman as body of woman, but also as a woman of his own color who was longing to conquer the shame imposed upon her by her native land because of her social and racial origin. Gladys finally said that she wanted some fresh air and they went to a little bar on 47th Street where they drank some more. They got quite drunk.

"I ought to be getting in," Gladys said. "It's late."

"Okay. I'll put the car up and we'll walk home; is that all right?"

"Anything you do is all right," she said, her head lolling and her eyes a little glazed.

He took her arm and guided her wandering steps to the car; he kissed her when they were inside and she went limp. But when he attempted to caress her further, she resisted. He put the car in the garage, then walked beside her, his arm about her waist.

"I'm drunk, really drunk," she said as though talking to herself.

"I am too," he confessed, chuckling.

It was raining and she began to stumble. Giggling, they supported each other. It was after three o'clock in the morning and they were fairly floating. The rain began to fall in broad, steady sheets and Cross, who wore no hat, let his coat flop open.

"Honey, you're getting wet," she said.

"I don't feel it," he said.

"But you'll catch cold!"

"Naw!"

He suggested another drink when they were near the rooming house and she agreed. They had three each. In the vestibule of their building, he kissed her; then, on the landing leading to their rooms, he kissed her again in the stillness and darkness.

Nestling close to him, she mumbled as out of a dream: "I hate white people."

"Why?"

"They're mean."

"Did white people ever bother you?"

"Hell, naw! I wouldn't let 'em," she said belligerently.

"Then why do you hate 'em?"

" 'Cause they're *different* from me. I don't like 'em even to look at me. They make me self-conscious, that's why. Ain't that enough?"

"If you say so, baby. But, listen, *I'm* not white."

"That's what's so nice about it," she said drunkenly.

He led her to his room and when he switched on the light she had a fleeting moment of soberness and shook her head, taking an aimless step backward. He tried to kiss her again and she twisted out of reach.

He switched off the light and kissed her and she melted, letting her lips cling fully to his; he carried her to the bed and they slept together in their damp clothes, being too drunk to undress. It was the beginning of the unleashing of a mutual, silent, and intense passion. During the following week, Cross had her in his bed, on the floor, standing up, in the bathroom . . . She made no demands, imposed no conditions, set no limits; she simply clung to him and when she spoke at all on general topics it was about how good it was to have someone to be with when the whole world was white and she was colored; he could say nothing to her about her color consciousness because he did not know how to handle it. In time he grew to accept it along with her womanness.

Cross's drunken carousal in the rain gave him pneumonia and Gladys stayed home from her job to nurse him. Quietly and all the time avoiding discussing it, she took total charge of him, created a situation that spelled unconditional surrender. She straightened out his disordered room, sent his piles of soiled linen to the laundry, gave him his penicillin injections, cooked and brought up his food. He accepted it all meekly, gazing up at her in humble gratitude when his fever was over one hundred and four. He had never been so comfortably looked after in all his life.

The climax of their relationship came unexpectedly when the fat, black, religious landlady told Cross that, now that he was well, she could no longer permit Miss Dennis "actually living in your room like that. You know it ain't decent. I want folks to respect my home".

He told Gladys and she wept; he held her in his arms till she quieted.

"What must people think of me?" she moaned.

"To hell with that landlady," Cross said.

"You think the others in the house feel the same way?"

"God, I don't know."

"I hope it doesn't get to my job . . ."

His head reeled. He had not thought of that.

"I don't want to leave you," she told him.

"So; it's settled."

"But what are we going to do?" her voice echoed with ringing meanings.

It was the first time he had thought of marriage and it frightened him. But could he abandon her like that? He felt that if he had said that he was through with her, she would have accepted it, humbly. And it made him feel guilty. Well, would he ever find anyone better than she? He studied her face for a moment, then said impulsively to her: "Let's get married."

She had wept again. They rented an apartment and were furnishing it when they were married. Gladys had definite

ideas about the home and Cross, having none, deferred to
her. She argued gently that the thing to do was to buy a
house and they did, arranging for the payments to fall due
monthly.

The advent of the birth of their first child, a son, Cross,
Junior, marked the commencement of protracted trouble.
After safely transporting Gladys, who was in violent labor,
to the hospital, Cross went out with a picked group of his
Post Office cronies—Pink, Joe, and Booker—to stage a cele-
bration which ended for his cronies after seven guzzling
hours, but which, for Cross, extended itself for two whole
days and nights during which he managed to pick up—he
never knew exactly where or how—a brown-skinned girl who
encouraged him to continue his "bat" as long as he had
money to spend.

As strenuously as he could try, he could never recall quite
clearly as to how he had come to bring the girl home with
him and he never saw her after that to inquire. He suspected
that he had drunkenly decided to do it after his money
had run out; he had confused recollections of being ejected
from bars for nonpayment of drinks. Before his nonstop
carousal, Gladys had tried to reach him by telephoning from
the hospital, and worried, she had come home with the
baby and a nurse to find Cross unshaven, bleary-eyed and
in bed with what Gladys chose to call his "whore". Gladys'
reaction had been so savage and intense that she had wept for
days, refused food, sat in deep moods of depression. Finally
she demanded of Cross despairingly: "Aren't you happy with
me?"

"Sure," he had said lightly, not wanting to think about it.

"Where did you meet the girl?"

"In a bar, I think . . ." he said vaguely.

"How in God's name can you pick up a girl in a bar?"

In a nervous rage he had demanded: "Do *you* want to
go? Or do you want *me* to go? I told you I was *drunk*,
didn't I?"

Gladys resisted an explanation that enthroned the demonical as a motive for his actions; she sensed the presence of
irrational forces that could trample her and her home.

Despite this they remained together, but the naturalness

and trust that had characterized their earlier relationship were gone. Cross hoped that Gladys had written off that shameful episode as an unrepeatable aberration which she would forget. But whenever he drank she would fling it at him and, in the end, a slow, mounting resentment rose in him toward her. More and more she sulked and, as he suffered her nagging, he felt increasingly walled off from her; but the more he felt it the more he sought to hide it, and finally there crept into his dealings with her a weird quality of irony. It first manifested itself in an innocent question: How could he help Gladys? And the moment he asked himself that question he knew that he did not love her and perhaps had never loved her . . . She had become for him an object of compassion. He was now haunted by the idea of finding some way to make her hate him. Her hatred would be a way of squaring their relationship, of curing her of her love for him, of setting her free as well as himself.

One winter when Cross was ill, Gladys nursed him and tried to reestablish over him her old emotional authority. It resulted in another pregnancy from which there issued two more sons, twins this time, Peter and Robert. Gladys had been hopeful, but not for long. Expenses increased and Cross's salary was squeezed. Gladys now had her hands full while Cross worked extra hours to pull in more money. The house was bedlam, filled with shouting, tumbling children. Cross found it all but impossible to sleep during the day and he became so nervous that Gladys would flare at him: "What are you trying to do? Drive us all out so that you can fill the house with your whores?"

Dating from this period, a wave of self-loathing began to engulf Cross. Each time he realized how much he had lost control of his life, his self-hatred swelled threateningly. He knew himself too well to blame Gladys and he was scrupulous enough to let her know it, which baffled and tortured her all the more. She longed for some simple definition of their troubles that she could grasp. She thought that she was losing her physical appeal for him and she went, without telling him— and submitted to an extraordinarily expensive operation to have her breasts lifted! That more than anything else had depressed Cross, filled him with a compassion mingled with disgust. He had been so stunned by it that he could never discuss it with her.

One afternoon in a bar, dawdling over a drink, he recalled how stunned Gladys had been when she had come home from the hospital with Junior and had found him in bed with the girl. That fantastic happening had now become accepted as an "accident". Well, why could not another "accident" happen? One so fatal and unique that it would make her re-member the last one as a guide by which to interpret it! He was far from planning anything overtly criminal; it was a complicated psychological attack whose consequences would clarify Gladys' feelings about him. But what on earth could that "accident" be? It would have to be so decisive that she would tell him to go and never come back. He would support her and the children, of course. He sipped his drink idly, turning his wish carefully over in his mind. His self-hate, his aversion for Gladys, his perpetual toying with his own feel-ings had resulted in there flashing into his mind a confound-ingly luminous image. He had it! By God, this was it! It could flow from him as naturally as it could be embraced by her, and it was simple. Though the seed of the idea came from the time when he had brought the girl home, it had only psychological affinities with it. Could he carry it out? It would take cool nerve, insight, timing, and ruthless execu-tion. What decided him was a cynical question: "If I fail, I'll be no worse off than I am now, will I?"

He finished his nightshift in the Post Office at four o'clock in the morning; then, with his cronies, he went to the SALTY DOG, a bar around the corner from his house, for what they jokingly called a "daycap", since they slept during the day. At five o'clock he went home for breakfast which Gladys was preparing in the kitchen in her kimono. After-wards he went directly to bed. But on *that* morning, he would not stop for his "daycap"; he would go back for his drink *after* he had done it. Such timing would make his ac-tions seem more *normal*. Furthermore, his going back to have a drink with the boys would give him an alibi, in case he needed one. Above all, the children should be sound asleep when he did it; he did not want to disturb them in any way.

He decided upon a Friday morning to carry his plan into action. After he left work he detached himself unobtrusively from his friends and went directly home, arriving shortly after four o'clock. Gladys had just gone into the kitchen and was putting a pot of coffee on the gas stove. He walked in and advanced wordlessly upon her, his eyes fastened on her face.

"Oh, good morning, Cross," she said, glancing at the electric clock on the wall. "You're early, aren't you?"

He stood directly in front of her, his eyes unblinking and his face a blank mask.

"What's the matter?" she asked, backing away a step.

He reached forward and gave her a slap with his open palm, not hard, but stinging and with enough force to send her stumbling backwards into a corner.

"Cross!" her voice was not loud, but charged with shock.

Then for a moment she was still as stone, staring at him, her lips parted, her hands lifted to shield her face. She lay against the wall, her kimono open and showing her full breasts. The sound that came from her now seemed to coincide with her recognition of danger.

"No, no, no . . ." she spoke in low, clipped words, the inflection of her voice rising.

As he advanced toward her again, her mouth opened slowly and her chest heaved as she sucked in her breath to scream. He roughly seized both of her hands in his left hand and slapped her once more, then stood leering down at her with a twisted face.

"Oh, God!" she screamed. "Don't kill me, Cross!"

As if pulled by cables of steel, he whirled and walked from the kitchen and out of the front door, hearing Gladys sobbing. He had not uttered a single syllable and the whole assault had taken no more than a minute. When he reached the door of the bar, he stood a moment to collect himself. He saw his pals sitting in the rear; he eased himself toward them and sat down.

"Where did you go, Crossy?" big, fat Joe asked carelessly.

"I was making a phone call," he said, lighting a cigarette and controlling his hand to keep it from trembling.

They began arguing politics. He spoke with composure, glancing now and then at the clock on the wall, wondering what was happening at home. He was pleased that the children had not heard him. Would she call the police? He doubted it; she would wait and talk to him first. Would she tell the children? He did not think so. Would she go to see his mother? Maybe. Her mind must be in a turmoil . . . At five-thirty, he said casually: "Well, guys, I've got to cut out and get some shut-eye."

He rose and waved good-bye. Now was the test. If his abrupt, physical attack upon Gladys provoked an immediate storm of reaction, then it would go badly for him; but if she was frantically trying to find some explanation for it, then all might go well. The main strategy was not to let her settle upon any one reason for it, to keep her judgment torturingly uncertain. Everything depended upon how much pretended incredulity he could demonstrate, how much simulated surprise he could convincingly sustain. As he turned into the walk leading to the house, he had a bad moment; a surging impulse made him want to turn about and dodge it all. He shook it off, went to the front door, entered the hallway and went into the bathroom. That had always been his routine and he adhered to it now. As he washed he whistled a tune, not steadily, but in snatches, not like a man intentionally trying to create an impression of carefreeness, but like a man with nothing serious on his mind. There was not a sound of movement in the house. Where was Gladys? Had she funked and fled? No; she would not leave the children . . . He emerged from the bathroom and went into the kitchen; he knew that she was not there, but he had to act as though he expected to find her frying his bacon and eggs. On the gas stove a blue flame glowed under the coffee pot and the scent of burning metal assailed his nostrils. He went to the stove and saw that the coffee had evaporated from the pot and that the metal around the bottom gleamed red hot. He shut off the gas and looked over his shoulder. That meant that Gladys had quit the kitchen the moment he had left the house. That's *normal* . . .

"Gladys!" he called out quietly, questioningly.

There was no answer. He made for the bedroom, calling again: "Gladys!"

Silence. He opened the bedroom door and asked into the semi-gloom: "Gladys, aren't you up yet?"

Silence. He hesitated a second, then switched on the wall light. Gladys was huddled on the bed, her eyes black with fear. She was so immobile that at first he thought that maybe she was dead, had died of shock. But, no; he could see her chest slowly rising and falling.

"What's the matter?" he asked softly.

She did not answer. Tears rolled down her cheeks and her fingers writhed.

"Didn't you know you left the coffee pot on the fire? All the water boiled out and it was red hot . . ."

She did not move.

"What's the matter? Are you ill?" he asked.

He walked toward her and she lunged violently backwards, falling from the bed to the floor, leaving one of her bedroom slippers on the quilt. He stopped, blinked his eyes in simulated bewilderment. He advanced upon her again and Gladys shook her head wildly.

"No, no, no . . . Don't hit me, Cross! *Don't* . . . !" she whimpered convulsively, barricading her face and head with her elbows.

He stared at her, his mouth drooping open in mock amazement. "What's the matter with you?"

"Cross," she sobbed. "I never thought you'd *hit* me."

He stepped away from her imperceptibly, as though stunned. "*Hit* you? What in the world are you talking about?"

He went to her and she shrank, burrowing herself against the wall. He caught hold of her shoulder and she lifted her eyes and stared at him and he returned her stare with make-believe astonishment until her eyes fell.

"What's the *matter*, Gladys! You're *shaking*! Here, let me put you to bed. I'll call a doctor . . ."

He was still holding onto her shoulder and felt a slight lessening of tension in her muscles. Trembling, she allowed him to lead her to the bed and push her gently upon it. She looked at him with eyes filled with shock.

"Lie down and keep still," he said hurriedly, feigning deep

anxiety. "I'll have the doctor here in a minute. If you felt like that, why didn't you phone me at the Post Office?"

Delicately he pulled the cover over her, went to the telephone at the bedside, picked it up, dialed the first letter and then glanced at her.

"No, no, no . . . No, Cross," she begged; her eyes were pools of bewilderment. She breathed uncertainly. Her gaze fell and her fingers fluttered.

"Now, listen, you'd better have the doctor take a look at you," he said, play-acting and pitching his voice to a tone of half-command and half-entreaty.

She began to sob again, burying her face in the pillow. He sat on the edge of the bed and patted her shoulder.

"Take it easy. Have you any pains? What's happened? Where are the children?"

She stared at him again, unable to believe the evidence of her senses. Her head rocked on its neck. Her mouth trembled and she had to move her lips several times before she could speak.

"Why did you do it?" she whimpered. Then she spoke fully, almost rising to a point of objectivity. "Do you hate me that much?"

"Do *what*?" he asked, replacing the receiver upon the hook of the transmitter. "*Hate* you? What *are* you talking about?"

"Oh, God!" she croaked. "You *know* what you did?"

Fear filled him for a second. She was in her crisis now; would she veer against him or would she still float in indecision?

"You're dreaming!" he shot at her. "Do you know what you are saying?"

"You hit me . . . You beat me . . . What *for*?" she asked insistently.

"*Beat* you?" he echoed, as though he had to repeat the word to believe in its reality. His face was the living personification of stupefied surprise. "You are out of your mind. Now, look here, be calm. Tell me what happened."

Her chest heaved, emptying her lungs, then she looked distractedly about the room like a rat searching for a hole. She was a tiny child hearing a grownup tell a tale that it did not believe, but it dared not challenge that tale because it had no way of successfully disputing it, feeling that its reasoning was not acceptable.

"Cross, you came into the kitchen and knocked me down," she explained in a low voice.

"You are crazy!" He stood and pretended to look suspiciously about the room. "*Who's* been here?"

"You!"

"Good Lord, you're wild!" He shook his head. "I *just* left the bar; I went there directly from work and had a drink, like always . . . Look, get hold of yourself." He wagged his head, aping bewilderment. "Have you been *drinking?*"

"Oh, Cross!"

"Listen, if you don't stop I'll call the doctor. You've got the children to look after," he copied tones of responsibility.

She stared at him, dumbfounded. Slowly, she shook her head. *Yes!* The idea was working in her mind. It was coming off much easier than he had thought. But he had to be firm and not retreat from his position.

"When do you think I hit you, Gladys?" he mimicked the compassion of one resolved to be lenient.

"I *didn't* imagine it," she whimpered.

It was working; she was beginning to wonder if what had happened had not been wiped from his memory. Silence followed. The restoration of normality must depend upon *his* initiative; what had so mysteriously occurred must seem to have been swallowed up in his mind as though it had never transpired; he must not in any way grant it one whit of objective reality.

"Look, kid," he began kindly, "I know we are not the loving couple one reads about in books. But you mustn't let our troubles break you down. There's no sense in brooding 'til you start imagining things. You need a rest . . ."

She clutched his arm. "Cross, don't you *remember* what you did?"

"Darling, really, I hate to say it, but you're *off!*"

"I'm sane, Cross," she said, unable to restrain her tears.

She collected her senses; she was no longer physically afraid; she was fearful of something more menacingly dark than a slap.

"I don't know what's happened to you," he played his role.

"Cross, you *remember* you hit me," she moaned.

"I *didn't*!" His face pretended to grow hard. "You're mixed up . . . Tell me, *who's* been here?"

"Nobody," she breathed.

"Who *else* saw me come in here?"

"Nobody," she whispered, her eyes widening with understanding.

"Look, Junior's coming," he spoke in a low, rapid voice. "Brace up . . . You'll upset 'im."

"Is it possible?" she asked herself in a despairing whisper.

She pulled herself unsteadily from the bed to the dresser and began arranging her hair with palsied hands. He could see her watching his reflection in the mirror; he had to be careful. She had forgotten her bedroom slipper on the quilt; he got it and held it out to her.

"Here; you better put it on," he said in a neutral voice.

"Oh," she said in confusion.

She obeyed him with movements charged with suppressed fear. But when he looked at her she glanced quickly away.

Junior, four years of age, came running in in his pyjamas. "I'm hungry," he sang, lifting an earnest, brown face to his father.

Cross swept the boy up in his arms and fondled him. Watching Cross out of the corners of her eyes, Gladys went hesitantly from the room to prepare breakfast. Cross burrowed his head playfully into Junior's stomach and the boy giggled. He was now certain that he could handle it. This was the beginning, the setup; next time would be the pay-off.

During the following week, under the cover of anxious solicitude, Cross craftily urged Gladys to see a doctor and she politely refused. A few days later she timidly begged *him* to see a doctor, telling him that she was *certain* that what had happened was a recurrence of what he had done with the girl. In a tone of play-acting shock, looking her levelly in the eyes, he scoffed at her interpretation and assured her that he was absolutely sane. He now made it a rigorous rule never to refer to the "accident"; all mention of it had to come from her.

And, as time went on, she found it more and more difficult to bring it up; but he knew that the thought of it was continuously hovering in the background of her mind.

One day, puckering up her lips and touching his cheek gently as she spoke — hoping by such a gesture to negate any hint that she thought him insane — she expressed concern that he might harm the children "while in one of your spells". He patted her shoulder and said soothingly: "Don't worry, darling. Everything's all right." She beseeched him to reduce his drinking, his smoking, to sleep more. She strove to keep more order in the house, chiding the children lovingly not to "make noise and get on poor papa's nerves".

He chose Easter Sunday morning for his next attack. He knew that nothing would be further from Gladys' mind then, for her attention would be involved in buying Easter egg coloring and arranging new clothes for the children's Easter outing. He worked the night of Easter Eve and went straight home and found Gladys alone in the kitchen; she whirled with fear as he came in, for she knew that he was as early as on that other fateful morning. Again he walked slowly toward her, wordlessly, his facial expression simulating dementia.

"No, no, no . . . !"

He slapped her resoundingly and she went down like a log.

"Junior!" she yelled. "Somebody help me!"

He stooped and slapped her once more, his face contorted in an imitation of rage; then he turned and rushed out, hurried to the bar and joined Joe, Pink and Booker who had not missed him this time. He sat coolly talking and drinking with them, but his mind was trying to picture what was happening at home. At a little past five he went back, let himself in with his key, and headed as usual to the bathroom to wash up. He lathered his hands and whistled softly. Suddenly he was still, hearing muffled footsteps moving haltingly along the hallway. What's she doing . . . ? Then all was quiet. He dried his face and hands and when he emerged he did not have to look for Gladys, for there she was at the door, confronting him with his gun, pointing it straight at his heart.

"Cross," she said heavily, struggling to manage her breathing, "I can't bear with you another minute. Pack your things and get out, *now*! You're crazy, a danger to yourself and others!"

He saw such craven fear in her face that he was afraid that she would lose control of herself and pull the trigger, causing him to die messily in a trap of his own devising.

"My God," his voice rang with sincerity. "Take it *easy* . . ."

His nervousness made Gladys step quickly away from him and wave the gun threateningly.

"If you come near me, I'll shoot!" she cried. "And I'll go free, for you're crazy!"

Her arm trembled and she reached toward him, the gun barrel coming within inches of his right temple.

"Gladys," he breathed, leaning weakly against a wall. "I can't get my clothes unless you let me pass."

"You're sick, Cross," she pronounced in neutral, distant tones.

Realizing that she was blocking his path, she stepped cautiously to one side. He went into the bedroom and began to pack. She waited in the doorway, still nervously clutching the gun.

"Gladys," he ventured to protest.

"Get out!" she ordered in a frenzy.

He packed a suitcase and stood looking at her out of the corners of his eyes. "I'll come back for the rest of my stuff later—"

"You let me know and I'll *send* you your things," she said. "Don't *ever* set foot in this house without *first* telling me, you hear! If you do, it'll be dangerous for you."

"I'll phone you," he mumbled.

She held open the front door, still brandishing the gun loosely in her shaking hand. He saw her legs wobbling; he walked over the threshold, sweating, fearing that he would stumble.

"See a doctor, Cross," she said, slamming the door.

On the sidewalk he paused and saw her peering at him from behind one of the lace window curtains in the living room, still grasping the gun. He walked on and filled his lungs with crisp morning air. It had worked without a hitch.

*   *   *

Cross roused himself on the jolting trolley, wiped a clear spot on the sweaty windowpane and saw that he had ridden past Gladys' place. Good God . . . He rushed to the front of the car and when it slowed he swung off. As he neared the house his steps faltered. He was doubtful if Gladys would help him, but his predicament was so knotty that he had to try, whatever the outcome. He mounted the steps and paused; his instincts warned him away from this Gladys whom he had made hate him too well. But he had to see her. He pushed the button of the doorbell and almost in the moment of his pushing it, the door flung open and Gladys stood before him, grim, erect. Out of a tightly organized face two deep-set eyes regarded him with composed hate.

"Hello, Gladys," he mumbled.

"I've been waiting for you," she said with placid irony. "I watched you creep up the walk like a doomed man. Are you scared of your home now?"

"I want to talk to you about something important," he told her.

A twisted smile played on Gladys' rouged lips. "I suppose it's about Miss Dorothy Powers, hunh?"

Anger flashed through him. No; he had to be calm.

"That's it, Gladys," he admitted, forcing a smile.

She stepped to one side and he moved gingerly into the hallway, feeling for the first time intimidated by Gladys. He glanced about apprehensively, his body screaming for a drink to brace him for this ordeal.

"Where're the kids?" he asked to fill the gaping silence.

"I knew you were coming," she announced, "so I sent them for the afternoon to the house of a friend of mine." Her voice was a midnight bell tolling tidings of bad news to come.

He walked into the living room and sat. Gladys followed and stood at the other end of the room and regarded him with hostile eyes. He could feel that she was clamoring for an emotional scene. Well, he would refuse her any such satisfaction. He would be polite, bantering, if possible.

"A young lady visited you this morning, I think," he said, trying to rid his voice of anxiety.

"You mean that bitch you sent—!" The hot lava of hate leaped out.

"Gladys, I didn't send anybody here," he cut in quickly.

"Cross, for God's sake, why do you insist on being such a crawling coward? You *sent* her here—"

"I didn't, I tell you!"

"You're lying!"

"Gladys, I know how you feel about me—"

"You ought to," she spat at him. "Do you think you can walk over me? Well, you won't, ever! You sent that little whore here to beg me . . ."

He tried to stop listening. It was going worse than he thought. Well, if she wanted to blast Dot, let her. The main thing was the question of divorce.

"There is one thing, by God," she roared, "that you are going to do! You are going to *respect* me. You can't send a filthy, stinking little tart like that to talk to me. You can be sure I gave your bitch a hot welcome, and she won't forget it, not soon!" Gladys groped for words, her mouth open. "And while I'm on it, let me settle one more question. You'll *not* get a divorce. For a rotten slut like her, *never*! That's the way I feel and I'm not ashamed of it! If you can be dirty, then so can I! Keep on living with her, but if she asks you to make her respectable, tell her you can't! Take your Dorothy and fuck her and let her give you a litter of bastards. That's all she's fit for, and you, too, it seems! Is that clear?"

Her hysterical tirade made him ashamed for her. The satisfaction she was deriving from it was obscene.

"Look, I'm not going to argue with your feelings," he clutched at words to stem the tide, striving to be judicious, balanced. "Let's arrange something. I'm supporting you and the children—"

"And by the living hell, you'll keep *on*!"

"Okay. I agree. But your welfare depends on my job—"

He jerked as she burst into a gale of cynical laughter. "So, you've been to the Post Office?" she asked. "They put the fear of God into you, hunh? That's why you came crawling to me . . ."

Cross froze. Had she already told the postal officials about the possibility of his being convicted of rape? He had come to bargain with her, but if she had already talked, the game was all but lost.

"What are you talking about?" he asked quietly.

"Cross, are you stupid?" There was a mocking pity in her tone. "I must protect myself . . . That little whore of yours had not been gone from here an hour before my lawyer and I had gone to the Post Office—"

"Why?"

He knew why she had gone, but he wanted to know how far she had gone. Maybe his job was already lost!

Gladys spoke quietly, as though she were a school teacher explaining a complicated problem to a dullard. She came to within a few feet of Cross and sat.

"Cross, you really cannot expect me to think of you and your troubles," she said. "You're intelligent and you know what you're doing. I had to act in my own defense. I went straight to the Postmaster and told him that your Miss Powers was about to charge you with rape—"

"Did she tell you that?" Cross asked, feeling that his chair was whirling him round.

"Of course she did," Gladys informed him with a smile. "Do you think she's informing you of her moves against you? The Postmaster knows, of course, that you cannot marry the girl . . . And if you are convicted, you're ruined. Now, the Postal Inspector has your case, see?"

Cross had no will to gainsay her; he knew that she was summing up his situation accurately.

"Cross, you must not be naïve," she continued. "There's nothing that Miss Powers can do but charge you, unless she's willing to live with you and bear your child . . . And I doubt if she loves you that much." She paused, lit a cigarette, eyeing Cross the while. "Now, there are some rather disagreeable things I must say to you." She lifted her left hand and with her right hand she pulled down the little finger of her left hand and said: "Number One: You're signing this house over to me at once. Number Two: You're signing over the car to me. Number Three: You're going to the Post Office tonight and borrow eight hundred dollars from the Postal Union on your salary. I've already made the arrangements with the Postal Inspector. He's okayed it. I want that money to clear the titles of both the house and the car." She stood, lifted her hand to bar his words. "I know you want to say no," she said. "But you can't. Cross, understand this: so far as I'm concerned, you're *through*! I'm squeezing you like a lemon. If you *don't* do what I'm asking, in the morning I shall keep an appointment with Miss Powers. She, *I*, and her lawyer will go to the 49th Street Police Station and I will help her bring charges against you. I'm not justifying my actions. I'm not apologizing, see? I'm just telling you. That's how things stand between us, Cross."

He was willing to sign over everything, but he did not want to borrow the money; it would mean indebtedness for him for two years to come. And he could use that money to try to bribe Dot . . .

"They may not let me have the money," he said.

"Mr. Dumb," she said scornfully, "if the Postal Union thought you were going to be indicted for rape, they'd not let you have the money, for you'd have no job. I led them to believe that the girl would abort the child, that you'd pay her off . . . I made sure with the Postmaster that your job was safe, and the Postal Union has been told that it's all right . . ."

"But the girl can *still* charge me," Cross protested without strength. "What game's this you're playing?"

"*My* game," Gladys said.

"The eight hundred dollars," he was pleading now, "could keep the girl and I could make payments to you—"

"I don't give a damn about that girl," she snapped. "What happens between you and her is your business!"

Gladys was using Dot to drag money from him and at the same time betraying Dot! Cross wanted to close his eyes and sleep this nightmare away.

"If you get eight hundred dollars, you'll not help the girl?"

"Hell, no! Why should I? Let that bitch rot!"

He was properly trapped. There was nothing more to say. This was a cold and vindictive Gladys created by him. He rose and moved toward the door.

"What's your answer?" she asked.

"Okay. I'll get the money. I'll phone you tonight."

"Oh, there's one other thing," she said, opening the door for him. "Is your life insurance paid up?"

"Hunh?" His voice sounded far away. "Yes; yes . . ."

"Have you changed the beneficiary?" she asked.

"No; why should I?"

"I just wanted to know," she said.

He felt as though he were already dead and was listening to her speak about him. He went out and did not glance back. He was so depressed that he was not aware of trampling through the deep snow. About him were sounds that had no meaning. When he came fully to himself, his feet were like two icy stumps. I must have fever . . . He paused and stared around him. He was tired. Oh, God, I got to get that money for Gladys . . . He looked about for a taxi. Oh, there's the "L" . . . He ran for the entrance, stumbled up the steps of the "L", fished a dime from his pocket, paid, and rushed to the platform just as a Loopbound train slid to a stop. He found a seat, fell into it, and sat hunched over, brooding.

His seeing Gladys had compounded his problems. If he obeyed her, he was lost; and if he did not obey her, he was lost. Yet, because he could not make up his mind to ditch it all, he had to follow her demands.

Before reaching Roosevelt Road the "L" dipped underground. Cross rose, swaying with the speed of the train, and traversed each coach until he came to the first car whose front window looked out upon a dim stretch of tunnel. He leaned his forehead against the glass and stared at the rushing ribbons of steel rails whose glinting surfaces vanished beneath his feet.

When his station arrived, he got off and went toward the Post Office, a mass of steel and stone with yellow windows glowing, a mass that rose sheerly toward an invisible sky. The night air was still; it had begun to grow a little warmer. It's going to snow again, he thought idly. Yes, he'd see about the loan right now, but he'd not work tonight. He hungered for sleep. He flashed his badge to the guard at the door and went inside. Where's that Postal Union office? Yes; there on the right . . . He pushed open the door and saw Finch, the union secretary, sitting quietly, his hat on, chewing an unlighted cigar and holding a deck of soiled playing cards in his hands. Cross approached Finch's desk and for a moment they stared at each other. He suddenly hated Finch's whiteness, not racially, but just because he was white and safe and calm and he was not.

"Damon, hunh?"

"Yes."

"I was waiting for you," Finch said. "Sit down."

Cross obeyed. He did not want to look at Finch; he knew that the man knew his troubles and it made him ashamed; instead, he stared stupidly at the pudgy, soft fingers as they shuffled the cards.

"You look like an accident going somewhere to happen," Finch commented.

"I'm under the weather," Cross confessed. "I want to renew that eight-hundred-dollar loan I had last year—"

"Oh, yes." Finch looked up. "Your wife's been in."

White fingers took the cigar from thin lips and a brown stream of tobacco juice spewed into a spittoon. Finch replaced the cigar, chewed it, and settled it carefully again in his jaw.

"You colored boys get into a lot of trouble on the South Side," Finch gave a superior smile. "You must have a hot time out there every day, hunh?"

Cross stiffened. His accepting Finch's sneering at his racial behavior was a kind of compound interest he had to pay on his loan.

"Is the loan possible?" Cross asked.

"The Postmaster said it's all right," Finch said, finally stacking the cards and flinging them to one side, as though ridding himself of something unpleasant. "Half of my time's spent taking care of you colored boys . . . What goes on on the South Side?"

Cross cleared his throat to control himself. "I don't know," he mumbled. "I'm offering my house as security—"

"I'm ahead of you, Damon," Finch said. "On the strength of your wife's plea, I've had the papers all drawn up. Boy, you've got a good wife. You ought to take care of her—"

"I do," Cross mumbled.

"If you did, you wouldn't be in this mess," Finch said. He pushed the contract toward Cross. "Here, sign . . ."

Cross signed clumsily, his nervousness letting a blob of ink smear blackly across the page. He fumbled with a blotter to soak it up.

"Let me do that," Finch said, taking the blotter from Cross. "Looks like a chicken with dirty feet ran over this contract." He handed Cross a carbon copy of the contract, then opened a drawer and pulled forth a sheaf of vouchers. "How do you want this? A check or cash?"

"Cash. I'd like the money tonight."

"Why not? It's your money."

Finch initialed a voucher for cash and flipped it at Cross.

"Okay. Get going," Finch said, yanking his thumb toward the door.

Cross stood and wanted to spit at the man. He edged forward and opened the door.

"Shut the door when you go out," Finch called, picking up his deck of cards and beginning to shuffle them again.

"Yes; of course," Cross said.

He pulled the door softly shut and sighed. Well, that was done. Then he stiffened. One of the Assistant Postmasters was bearing down upon him, his grey eyes intent on Cross's face.

"Damon, just a moment!"

"Yes, sir," Cross answered, waiting.

The Assistant Postmaster pointed a forefinger at Cross. "Damon, don't ever again come to this Post Office on an errand like this. If it hadn't been for your wife, I wouldn't touch this stink with a ten-foot pole. Look, you had one loan and paid it. Do the same with this. We're here to handle the mails, not emotional dramas. Now, this eight hundred ought to settle your little business, hunh?"

"Yes, sir," he lied; it would only settle the claim of Gladys, but it would not help him with Dot. "Let me explain, sir . . ."

"Don't tell me about it. I don't want to know."

"I'd like the night off, sir," Cross said. "I'll take it out of my vacation days."

"And what other service can I render you?" the Assistant Postmaster asked with mockery.

"I'm ill," Cross said peevishly.

"You look it," the Assistant Postmaster said. "Okay. Take it. But I know a guy called Damon who's going to find the Post Office a hard line to walk from this out."

Cross bit his lip, turned away and descended the stairs to the cashier's office of the Postal Union and presented his voucher.

"Cash, eh?" the teller asked, smiling. "What're you going to do with all that money? Buy the Tribune Tower?"

Cross pretended that he had not heard. He pushed the pile of fifty-dollar bills into his wallet, sought a telephone booth and dialed Gladys.

"I got the money," he told her.

"I want it first thing in the morning," she said flatly.

"I'll bring it by at noon."

"All right."

He made for the exit, showed his badge to the guard and stepped into the street. It was snowing again; fat, white flakes drifted lazily down from a night sky. An "L" train rattled past overhead. He sighed, feeling relieved. He had to be careful and not let a pickpocket rob him of the money. He put his badge, the duplicate copy of the loan contract into the pocket of his overcoat and stuffed his wallet into his shirt, next to his skin. His job now was to head off Dot.

Diving into a subway, he paid his fare and, two minutes later, when a train roared up, walked into the first coach and sank into a seat, closing his eyes. The train pulled into motion; he opened his eyes and noticed that another Negro, shabbily dressed, of about his own color and build, was sitting across the aisle from him. The movement of the coach rocked some of the tension out of him, but not enough to let him relax. Restlessness made him rise and go to the front window and stand looking at the twin ribbons of steel rails sliding under the train. A moment later, when the train was streaking through the underground, darkness suddenly gripped his eyes and a clap of thunder smote his ears. He was spinning through space, his body smashing against steel, then he was aware of being lifted and brutally catapulted through black space and, while he was tossed, screams of men and women rent the black air.

Afterwards Cross remembered that when the lights had gone out he had involuntarily blinked his eyes, instinctively feeling that the cause of sudden darkness was some fault of the functioning of his pupils. About him were sounds of ripping metals and then something thumped against his head, sending him to sleep. How long he was unconscious, he did not know. When he was aware of himself again he realized that his body was in a vaguely upright position, but jammed between what seemed like two walls of steel. The right side of his skull was gripped by pain and something wet and warm trickled down a side of his face. His left leg was being wrenched and his right leg was pinioned, crushed to numbness between what seemed like two vices. He groaned. The words: *It's a subway wreck!* shaped themselves in his consciousness.

Abruptly the thunder ceased and the only sounds he heard were screams. In the blackness that walled itself before his eyes, Cross was afraid to move. *How badly am I hurt? Is it over?* He became aware that he was holding his head tucked down to dodge another attack of annihilation. Lifting his eyes he saw far ahead of him a jutting spray of blue electric sparks showering down from somewhere. He had to get out of this, now, NOW . . . Gingerly, he groped with his fingers and what he touched made him project in terms of images what his fingers felt and he screamed. He imagined he saw the profile of a human face drenched in blood. He snatched his hand away and wiped it dry upon his coat.

He breathed softly, listening: a viscous liquid was slowly falling drop by drop somewhere near him: the whimper of a woman seemed to be issuing from a half-conscious body: a quiet coughing seemed to be trying to dislodge something thick and wet from a sticky throat: an incessant grunt grew fainter and fainter until it was heard no more . . .

He was calm now, thinking. His lighter must be in his left pants' pocket. Twisting, he reached for it, felt it with the ends of his fingers. Yes! Purpose gripped him and, squeezing the tips of his fingers together, he caught hold of the lighter and slowly pulled it out. He pushed the lever and a bluish flame

shed feeble light amid a welter of topsy-turvy forms. Lines
zigzagged and solids floated in shadows, vanishing into meaninglessness; images dissolved into other images and his mind
was full of a sense of shifting significances.

He saw that the seats of the train were above his head; the
coach had reversed itself, twisted within the tube of the underground and he was standing on the shattered lights of the
ceiling. Seats had ripped from the floor and had fallen to the
ceiling where he stood.

Cross shut his eyes and bit his lips, his ears assailed by
screams. He had to get out of here! He bent lower and
looked; a white face with unblinking eyes was wedged at the
level of his knees and beneath that face he could make out a
dark pool of fluid that reflected the flickering flame of his
lighter. He moved the flame over shards of glinting glass and
saw again that window and the shower of blue electric sparks
still sprinkling down . . . Yes; he had to get to that window
. . . But his legs . . . He had to get them free . . . He bent
and looked closer; his right leg was gripped between the steel
wall of the coach and a seat that had tumbled from the floor
to the ceiling. He pushed at the seat and it would not budge.
Again he shoved his weight mightily at the seat. Why didn't it
move? He stooped lower with the light and saw that the seat
that jammed his leg to the wall was anchored in place by the
man's head, which, in turn, was rammed by another seat. The
man's face was fronting Cross.

Cross lifted the pressure of his finger from the lever and the
flame went out. He thought: That man's head is keeping this
seat from moving . . . Could he get that head out of his way?
He pressed the lever again and looked. He could just reach
the man's head with his right hand. Yes; he had to shove it
out of the way. He held the lighter in his left hand, shut his
eyes, and felt the palm of his right hand touching the yielding
flesh of the man's face, expecting to hear a protest . . . He
opened his eyes; no breath seemed to be coming from the
nostrils or mouth. Cross shuddered. If the man was dead,
then any action he took to free himself was right . . . He held
his fingers to the man's parted lips and could feel no stir of
air. For a few seconds he watched the man's chest and could
detect no movement. The man's dead . . . But how could he

get that head out of his way . . . ? Again he pushed his right hand with all of his strength against the face and it budged only a fraction of an inch. Goddamn . . . He panted with despair, regarding the man's head as an obstacle; it was no longer flesh and blood, but a rock, a chuck of wood to be whacked at until it was gone . . .

He searched vainly in the moving shadows for something to hold in his hand, hearing still the sounds of screams. He felt in his overcoat pocket; the gun was there. Yes . . . He pulled it out. Could he beat down that foolishly staring face belonging to that head pushing against the seat wedging his leg to the wall? He shut his eyes and lifted the gun by the barrel and brought down the butt, and, even though his eyes were closed, he could see the gun butt crashing into the defenseless face . . . Sweat broke out on his face and rivulets of water oozed from his armpits.

He opened his eyes; the bloody face had sunk only a few inches; the nostrils, teeth, chin and eyes were pulped and blackened. Cross sucked in his breath; a few more blows would dislodge it. He shut his eyes and hammered again and suddenly he heard a splashing thud and he knew that the head had given way, for his blows were now falling on air . . . He looked; the mangled face was on the floor; most of the flesh had been ripped away and it already appeared skeletonlike. He had done it; he could move his leg.

Now, he had to free his other leg. Peering with the lighter, he saw that his left leg was hooked under a fallen seat. With his right leg free, he hoisted himself up and saw that he would get loose if he could use his left leg as a ramrod to shove at the seat. Pricked by splinters of glass, he hauled himself upward and perched himself on the back of an overturned seat and, with his left foot, he gave a wild kick against the seat and it did not move. Bracing himself, he settled his heel against the back of the seat, eased his overcoat— which was hindering his movements—down a little from his shoulders, and shut his eyes and pushed against the seat. It fell away. Both of his legs were free. An awful stench filled his nostrils.

He looked toward the gutted window; the blue electric sparks were still falling. From somewhere came a banging of

metal against metal, like an urgent warning. That window
was the way out. He crept forward over the ceiling of the
overturned coach, past twisted and bloody forms, crunching
shattered electric bulbs under his feet, feeling his shoes slop-
ping through sticky liquid. He moved on tiptoe, as though
afraid of waking the sleeping dead. He reached the window
and saw that a young woman's body had been crushed almost
flat just beneath it. The girl was dead, but, if he was to get
through that window, he had either the choice of standing
upon her crushed body or remaining where he was. He
stepped upon the body, feeling his shoes sinking into the lifeless flesh and seeing blood bubbling from the woman's mouth
as his weight bore down on her bosom. He reached for the
window, avoiding the jagged edges of glass. Outside the blue
electric sparks rained down, emitting a ghostly light. He did
not need his lighter now. He crawled through and lowered
his feet to the ground. He had to be careful and not step
upon any live wires or the third rail . . . His feet sought for
gravel.

He stood for a moment, collecting himself. His head
throbbed. When he moved his right leg it pained him. His
body was clammy and was trembling. For a moment he felt as
though he would lose consciousness, but he remained on his
feet. Screams, more distant now, came to his ears. He moved
forward in the bluish gloom. Yes, ahead of him were amber
lights! He pushed on and could hear distant voices and they
were not the voices of the wounded. He had been lucky. I'd
better let a doctor look at me . . . He now realized how fantastically fortunate he had been; had he remained in his seat,
he would have been crushed to death . . .

He picked his way catlike over wooden trestles and then
stopped. His overcoat . . . ? Oh, God, he had left it somewhere back in that death-filled darkness, but he could not
recall how it had gotten away from him. The gun was still
in his pants' pocket. With stiff and sweaty fingers he lit a
cigarette and walked on. From above ground he caught the
faint wail of sirens and ahead of him he saw dim traces
of light in the circular tunnel. Later he made out blurred,
white uniforms and he knew that they were doctors and
nurses.

He trudged past overturned coaches whose windows were gutted of glass. He could see doctors and nurses quite clearly now. He heard someone yell: "Here comes another one! He seems all right!"

They had seen him and were running to meet him. A doctor and a nurse caught hold of his arms.

"Are you all right?" the doctor asked.

"I guess so," he answered out of a daze.

"You are lucky," the nurse said.

"Get 'im to an ambulance," the doctor told the nurse. "I want to take a look back here."

The doctor hurried off into the tunnel of darkness, spotting his way with a flashlight.

"Can you walk all right?" the nurse asked him.

"Yeah."

"Does anything hurt you?"

"My leg, my right leg . . ."

"Come along, if you can manage," she said. "They'll see about it . . . What happened?"

"I don't know."

She led him toward a group of doctors and nurses who were congregated upon a subway station platform. He saw policemen pouring upon the underground tracks and heard someone shout: "Tell 'em the current's cut off!"

Cross felt hands lifting him on to the platform, and now another nurse had hold of his arm. About him was a babble of voices. He began to revive, feeling a little more like himself.

"I'm all right now," he told the nurse.

"But you must go to the hospital and be examined," the nurse told him. "Come. The ambulance is waiting."

She led him through a throng of policemen to the sidewalk where masses of excited people clogged the streets. The nurse tried to guide him through the crowd but they were brought to a standstill. A policeman saw them and attempted to help by clearing a path before them.

"That's one of 'em," Cross heard someone say. "But he doesn't seem hurt."

Cross could see the ambulances now; there were internes with stretchers rushing toward the subway station.

"You can get through now," the policeman said.

"Look," Cross told the nurse. "I'll go and get into an ambulance. I'm all right. Go back and help the others."

"Are you sure you're all right?" the nurse asked.

"Absolutely," Cross assured her.

She let go of him and he was alone. He felt fine. He started in the direction of the ambulances. The crowd ignored him. He looked down at his clothes; save for dried blood on his shoes, he was all right. His overcoat had protected him somewhat. He paused. Why in hell should he go to a hospital? He was not wounded, only bruised. What he wanted more than medicine was a good, stiff drink of whiskey. Were the doctors and nurses watching him? He looked around; they were not . . . And the policeman had disappeared. The hell with it . . . He crossed the street and peered at his dim reflection in the plate glass window of a clothing store. His eyes were muddy and his face was caked with dirt and dried blood. He mopped at his cheek with his coat sleeve, rubbing it clean. Otherwise, he looked quite normal. Some whiskey would fix me up, he told himself and went in search of a drink.

A fine snow was falling, hanging in the air like a delicate veil. He limped toward Roosevelt Road and found a second-rate bar that had sawdust on the floor and an odor of stale bread and beer. He was glad of the warmth that caressed his face; he had been too preoccupied to notice that he was half-frozen. But what happened to his overcoat? He ordered a double whiskey and thought back over the underground accident. Then he remembered that he must have lost his overcoat when he had climbed atop that overturned seat to free his leg. That was it; he had had to pull his arms out of the coat and had been in such a frenzy that he had forgotten to put it on again. Well, he would buy another one. An overcoat was indeed a small loss in such a holocaust. He fingered the lump at the right side of his head; it was sore, but not serious. A man sure needs luck, he told himself.

The bar was filled with foreign-born working men who did not find his disheveled clothing outlandish. Over his head a loud speaker blared. He was leaning on his elbow when he heard the radio commentator announce:

Ladies and Gentlemen, we interrupt this program to bring you a special news bulletin. One half hour ago, a Southbound subway train crashed headlong into another Southbound train that had come to a standstill about six hundred yards from the Roosevelt Road Subway Station. The cause of the accident is being investigated. Access to the wrecked trains is difficult because debris has blocked the underground tubes and rescuers are having to cut their way through thick steel beams with acetylene torches. Although it is too early to give any details, it is feared that the loss of life has been heavy. In the immediate area all subway traffic has been suspended. Doctors and nurses have been rushed to the scene of the disaster. Keep tuned to this station for further details.

Cross smiled. How quick they were! Then suddenly he started so violently that the white man drinking next to him drew back in astonishment. *That money!* He shoved his hand into his shirt . . . *It was there!* Thank God . . . He leaned weakly against the bar. If he had lost the eight hundred dollars, the only thing left for him would have been to jump into the Chicago River.

He paid his bill and hobbled back into the street where snow was still sifting down. Tomorrow at noon he had to see Gladys. And he'd go home now and wash up and then see Dot . . . He was hungry; yes, he'd first go to a South Side restaurant and have a decent meal. But he would not take a subway. Hell, no . . . He'd treat himself to something better this time. At a corner he limped into a taxi and called out: "47th and South Park."

He leaned back and wondered why his life had been spared. Or had it been? To say that he had been "spared" implied that some God was watching over him, and he did not believe that. It was simply the way the dice had rolled. He stretched out his right leg, testing it; the flesh was still sore to the touch, but he could keep on his feet. Funny, that morning he had been ready to blow his brains out, but when his body had been tossed about in that darkness, he had wanted to live.

His postal badge! The loan papers! They too were in the pocket of his overcoat. He'd have to report their being lost the first thing in the morning to the postal officials . . . The taxi swerved to a curb at 47th and South Park. He paid the driver, limped out, walked through tumbling snowflakes and entered Dug's, a small restaurant that served the kind of food he liked. He went into the men's room, washed himself and then examined his face in the mirror. Not bad . . . He looked as though he had been on a two-day drunk, that was all. He grinned, reentered the restaurant which was almost empty and ordered a steak, fried potatoes, coffee, and ice cream. He took a sip of water, listening to the radio that was going near the front window.

. . . This is John Harlan speaking. I'm broadcasting from the scene of the subway wreck at Roosevelt Road. It is snowing here and the visibility is rather bad. I have my microphone with me upon the "L" platform and I'm able to see directly down to the subway entrance where doctors, nurses, attendants, and policemen are working frantically to bring the wounded from the underground. The scene is being illuminated by huge spotlights attached to telephone poles. Beyond the subway entrance, stretching far into the street and blocking the traffic, is a crowd of more than five thousand people standing silently in the falling snow. They have been here for almost an hour waiting for news of friends or relatives believed to have been passengers on the ill-fated subway trains that collided with a heavy loss of life more than an hour ago . . .

I see the internes bringing out another victim. A body is on the stretcher. It is the body of a woman, it seems; yes, I can see her long brown hair . . . Wait a minute. I'll see if I can get the police to identify her for us.

So engrossed was Cross in listening that he did not see the waitress when she placed his food before him. They're acting like it's a baseball game, he thought with astonishment. He was glad now that he had walked so unceremoniously away from the accident. He surely would not have wanted anybody to blare out his name over the airways as a victim. He shrugged his shoulders. They'll give us a commercial soon, he thought. The radio commentator resumed:

The name of the last accident victim is: Mrs. Maybelle Broadman of 68 Green Street, Ravenswood Park. She is being taken directly to the Michael Reese Hospital . . .

Ladies and gentlemen, I see the internes coming out with another stretcher. I can't tell yet if the victim is a man or a woman, for the stretcher is completely covered. It's a man . . . I can tell by the blood-stained overcoat which is draped over the foot of the stretcher . . . That is the forty-fourth victim taken so far from the wreckage of underground trains. Just a minute; I'll try to get the identity of the last victim who was brought out . . .

In spite of himself, his interest was captured by the description of the happenings at the scene of the accident. As he waited for more news, he chewed and swallowed a mouthful of steak and lifted his cup of coffee to his lips.

Ladies and gentlemen, while we are endeavoring to establish the identity of the last man taken from the scene of the subway accident at Roosevelt Road, I'm going to ask one of the eyewitnesses, who was a passenger on the subway train, to say a few words about what he saw and felt when the disaster occurred. I have here at my side Mr. Glenn Williams, a salesman of 136 Rush Street, who escaped with but a few minor bruises. Mr. Williams, could you tell us what happened? Where were you on the train . . . ?

WELL, I WAS IN A COACH TOWARD THE MIDDLE OF THE TRAIN. EVERYTHING SEEMED TO BE GOING ALL RIGHT. I WAS READING THE EVENING PAPER. THE TRAIN WAS FULL. I WAS SEATED. I GUESS WE WERE ABOUT A MINUTE FROM THE ROOSEVELT ROAD STATION, WHERE I WAS TO GET OFF, WHEN A GREAT CRASH CAME AND ALL THE LIGHTS WENT OFF. I FELT MYSELF BEING KNOCKED OFF MY SEAT . . .

I must interrupt you, Mr. Williams. I'm sorry. Ladies and gentlemen, the police have just informed me of the identity of the last victim taken from the subway crash at Roosevelt Road. His name is Cross Damon, a 26-year-old postal clerk who lived at 244 East 57th Street on the South Side. Mr. Damon's body was crushed and mangled beyond recognition or hope of direct identification. His identity has been established, however, by his overcoat, private papers, and his post office badge . . . His body is being taken directly to the Cook County Morgue. Relatives must address all inquiries there . . .

Now, Mr. Williams, will you kindly . . . ?

Cross was still holding the cup of coffee in his right hand, his fingers tense upon the handle. He stared, stupefied. *What?* He half stood, then sat down again. Good God! He . . . *dead?* He had a wild impulse to laugh. The damn fools! They were really crazy! Well, it was his overcoat that had led them wrong . . . Yes, that was it. He ought to phone them right now! He looked around the restaurant; except for himself, the place was now empty of customers. That tall, black girl who had been eating in the corner had gone . . . Dug, the proprietor who knew him, was not there. The waitress was a new one and he did not know her and she did not know him. He saw her watching him curiously. She must think I'm loony, he thought.

"Is there anything wrong, sir?"

He did not answer. This was rich! *He was dead!* He had to tell this to the gang at THE SALTY DOG, right now! Old Doc Huggins would die laughing . . .

"Is the food all right, sir?"

"Hunh? Oh, yes. Look, what do I owe you?"

"Aren't you going to eat?"

"No. I've forgotten something. I got to go at once . . ."

"Well, sir. It's one seventy-five. You see, even if you don't eat, they had to prepare it. We can't serve that food to any-body else, sir, you know. So you'll have to pay . . ."

"That's all right. Here," he said, tossing her two one-dollar bills.

He hurried out into the spinning snow and headed for THE SALTY DOG. This was the damndest thing! It was even more freakish than his having escaped alive from the subway accident itself. When he reached the corner, some force jerked his body to an abrupt halt amidst the jumping snow. He was stunned and shaken by the power of an idea that took his breath away and left him standing open-mouthed like an idiot amid the crazy flakes.

He was dead . . . All right . . . Okay . . . Why the hell *not*? Why should he refute it? Why should he deny it? He, of all the people on earth, had a million reasons for being dead and staying dead! An intuitive sense of freedom flashed through his mind. Was there a slight chance here of his being able to start all over again? To live a new life? It would solve every problem he had if the world and all the people who knew him could think of him as dead . . . He felt dizzy as he tried to encompass the totality of the idea that had come so suddenly and unsought into his mind, for its implications rumbled in so many directions that he could not grasp them all at once. Was it possible that he could somehow make this false account of his death become real? Could he pull off a thing like that? What did one do in a case like this? These questions made him feel that the world about him held countless dangers; he suddenly felt like a criminal, and he was grateful for the nervous flakes of snow which screened his face from the eyes of passersby. Oh, God . . . He had to sit down somewhere alone and think this thing out; it was too new, too odd, too complicated. How could he let them go on believing that he was dead? But suppose later they found out that the body that they had dragged from the wreckage was not his? What then? Well, could he not hide away for a few days until they had made up their minds? If they buried that body as the body of Cross Damon, then he was dead, really, legally, morally dead. Had any of his friends seen him since he had come up out of the subway? No, not one. And no one had known him at the subway station. No doubt that doctor and those nurses had already, in their excitement, forgotten that they had ever seen him. He was certain that no one he knew had seen him in that dingy bar on Roosevelt Road. And if he was really serious about this, then he ought not go into THE SALTY DOG. What wild luck! And Dug had not been in! And that waitress was new and could not have known him from Adam . . . !

Then, if he was to do this thing, no one who knew him must see him now . . . From this moment on he had to vanish . . . Hide . . . Now! And his mother must not see him . . . And Dot must not see him . . . Gladys must be led to believe that he was dead . . . His sons . . . ? Good God . . . Doing this meant leaving them forever! Did he want to do that? He had to make up his mind . . . Well, they were not close to him as it was; so leaving them was merely making final and formal what had already happened. And how was Gladys to live? Ah, she'd get his insurance money, ten thousand dollars! His cheeks felt hot. Gladys would be taken care of. And no doubt his old mother would now swallow her pride and go and live with Gladys. And the stern logic of Dot's position would force her to have the child aborted . . . He trembled, looking about him in the snow-scattered street, his eyes smouldering with excitement. A keen sensation of vitality invaded every cell of his body and a slow, strange smile stole across his lips. It was as though he was living out a daring dream. If, after hiding away for a few days, they discovered that that body was not his, why, he could always come forth and say that the accident had wounded him in such a way that he had temporarily lost his memory! That would be his alibi . . . And were not such claims being made every day? He had often read of cases of amnesia . . . It might work. Why not? It was surely worth trying. What had he to lose? His job. It was already compromised by Dot's possible accusations against him. And only tonight he had signed an obligation to pay a debt that would take him two years to discharge . . . And if he were dead, all of that would be at an end!

All right; what next? He could not plot or plan this by talking it over with anybody. He would have to sit down alone and figure this thing out carefully. And he had to keep shy of those sections of the city where he might meet people who knew him. Where could he go? Yes, down around 22nd Street, the area of the bums and whores and sporting houses . . . And he had eight hundred dollars in cash in his shirt next to his skin! Holy Moses! It all made *sense*! This eight hundred dollars would be his stake until he could launch himself anew somewhere else . . . It all fitted . . . He would be a damn fool if he did not try it. All of his life he had been hankering after his personal freedom, and now freedom was knocking at his door, begging him to come out. He shivered in the cold. Yes, he had to go to his room and get his clothes . . . But, no . . . Someone would surely see him. He could not take that chance. Funny, it was hard to think straight about this. He had to break right now the chains of habit that bound him to the present. And that was not easy. Each act of his consciousness sought to drag him back to what he wanted to flee.

He had to act, NOW! Each second he stood here like this made it more dangerous for him to do what he wanted. Yet he remained standing as though some power over which he had no control held him rooted. His judgment told him to move on, and yet he stood. Already he felt like the hunted. Waves of realization rolled through him: he had to break with everything he had ever known and create a new life. Could he do it? If he could conceive of it, he should be able to do it.

This thing suited his personality, his leanings. Yes, take a taxi to 22nd Street . . . No, the driver might remember him; the South Side was a small place. The subway . . . ? No, he might meet another postal clerk. He would walk over to State Street and take a trolley northward to 22nd Street. He was not likely to meet anybody in that direction.

At last he moved through the shaking flakes of snow. If it did not work, he could explain it all away. But, by God, it *had* to work. It was up to him to *make* it work. He was walking fast, caught up in a sense of drama, trying to work out a new destiny.

He recalled now the other Negro passenger on the train who had sat across the aisle opposite him; the man had been about his own general build, size, and color. What had happened was simple; they had mistaken that man's body for his own! The body had been so disfigured that direct identification had been impossible, and, when they had found his overcoat with his postal badge and the contract papers in the pocket, they had leaped to the conclusion that it was the body of Cross Damon. Would anyone demand that that body be subjected to further examination to determine if it was really his? The insurance company? But why would they do that unless somebody put the idea in their heads? Would Gladys? Hell, no . . . She would be content to get the ten thousand dollars of insurance money and probably some more money from the subway company. Dot? She would not know what to do. His mother? Poor Mama . . . She'll just think that God has finally paid me off, he mused.

He seethed with impatience; he was both scared and glad, yearning to find shelter before meeting anyone he knew. Anxiety now drove a sharp sense of distance between him and his environment. Already the world around him seemed to be withdrawing, and he could feel in his heart a certain pathos about it. There was no racial tone to his reactions; he was just a man, *any* man who had had an opportunity to flee and had seized upon it. He was afraid of his surroundings and he knew that his surroundings did not know that he was afraid. In a way, he was a criminal, not so much because of what he was doing, but because of what he was feeling. It was for much more than merely criminal reasons that he was fleeing to escape his identity, his old hateful consciousness. There was a kind of innocence that made him want to shape for himself the kind of life he felt he wanted, but he knew that that innocence was deeply forbidden. In a debate with himself that went on without words, he asked himself if one had the right to such an attitude? Well, he would see . . .

He took a northbound trolley on State Street and pushed his way apprehensively into the packed crowd and stood swaying. Was there anything in his manner that would attract attention? Could others tell that he was nervous, trying to hide a secret? How could one act normally when one was *trying* to act normally? He caught hold of a strap and, his shoulders jostling others, rocked with the motion of the trolley.

He began to see that this project of deception he had taken upon himself back there in the winging snow of the street was much bigger than he had realized. It was a supreme challenge that went straight to the very heart of life. What was he to do with himself? For years he had been longing for his own way to live and act, and now that it was almost his, all he could feel was an uncomfortable sense of looseness. What puzzled him most was that he could not think of concrete things to do. He was going to a cheap hotel in order to hide for a few days, but beyond that he had no ideas, no plans. He would have to imagine this thing out, dream it out, invent it, like a writer constructing a tale, he told himself grimly as he watched the blurred street lamps flash past the trolley's frosted window.

As he neared 22nd Street he edged forward through the crowd, keeping his head down to conceal his face. He swung off and shivered from the penetrating dampness that bit into his bones. He was still limping, thinking: I got to find a hotel now . . . But . . . Who was he? His name? Age? Occupation? He slowed his feet. It was not easy to break with one's life. It was not difficult to see that one was always much, much more than what one thought one was. His past? What was his past if he wanted to become another person? His past had come to him without his asking and almost without his knowing; at some moment in the welter of his spent days he had just simply awakened to the fact that he had a past, and that was all. Now, his past would have to be a deliberately constructed thing. And how did one go about that? If he went into a hotel they would ask him his name and he would not be able to say that he was Cross Damon, postal clerk . . . He stood still in the flood of falling snow. Question upon question bombarded him. Could he imagine a past that would fit in with his present personality? Was there more than one way in which one could account for one's self? His mind came to a standstill. If he could not figure out anything about the past, then maybe it was the future that must determine what and who he was to be . . . The whole hastily conceived project all but crumpled. Maybe this dream of a new life was too mad? But I ought to be able to do this, he told himself. He liked the nature of this dare; there was in it something that appealed to him deeply. Others took their lives for granted; he, he would have to mold his with a conscious aim. Why not? Was he not free to do so? That all men were free was the fondest and deepest conviction of his life. And his acting upon this wild plan would be but an expression of his perfect freedom. He would do with himself what he would, what he liked.

He did not have to decide every detail tonight; just enough had to be fabricated in order to get a hotel room without rousing too much suspicion. Later, he would go into it more thoroughly, casting about for who he was or what he wanted to be.

He went into an ill-lighted tavern that reeked of disinfectant and sat in a rear booth and listened to the radio pour forth a demonical jazz music that linked itself with his sense of homelessness. The strains of blue and sensual notes were akin to him not only by virtue of their having been created by black men, but because they had come out of the hearts of men who had been rejected and yet who still lived and shared the lives of their rejectors. Those notes possessed the frightened ecstasy of the unrepentant and sent his feelings tumbling and coagulating in a mood of joyful abandonment. The tavern was filled with a mixture of white and black sporting people and no one turned to look at him. He ordered a beer and sat hunched over it, wondering who he would be for the next four or five days until he left for, say, New York. To begin his new life he would relive something he knew well, something that would not tax too greatly his inventive powers. He would be a Negro who had just come up fresh from the Deep South looking for work. His name? Well . . . Charles . . . Charles what? Webb . . . Yes, that was good enough for the time being. Charles Webb . . . Yes, he had just got in from Memphis; he had had a hard time with whites down there and he was damn glad of being in the North. What had he done in Memphis? He had been a porter in a drugstore . . . He repressed a smile. *He loved this!*

When he went out he bought a stack of newspapers to keep track of developments in the subway accident. He searched for a hotel, the cheaper and more disreputable the better. If there was the slightest doubt about his being dead, he would come forth with a story to square it all; but if all sailed smoothly, he was free.

He came finally to an eight-story hotel with tattered window shades and bare light bulbs burning in the lobby. The hotels in this district were so questionable that they rarely drew a color line. Next door was a liquor store in which he bought a bottle of whiskey. He entered the hotel and a short, fat white woman studied him appraisingly from behind a counter.

"I'm looking for a room," he said. "A single."

"For how long?"

"Maybe a week."

"You got any luggage?"

"No'm. Not with me."

"Then you have to pay in advance, you know."

"Oh, yes'm. I can do that. How much is it?"

"One-fifty a night. I'll put you on the top floor. But no noise in the room, see?"

"I don't make any noise," he told her.

"They all say that," she commented, sliding him a sheet of paper. "Here; fill that out."

He answered the questions, identifying himself as Charles Webb from Memphis. When he returned the form to her, she pointed to the bottle he had under his arm.

"Look," she said. "I don't care what you do in your room,

but I don't want any trouble, see? Some people get drunk and hurt others."

"Lady, I never really hurt anybody in my life but myself," he told her before he realized what he was saying.

The woman looked at him sharply; she opened her mouth to reply, but thought better of it. He knew that that had been a foolish thing to say; it was completely out of character. He had to be careful.

"Come on," the woman said, leading him down a narrow hallway to a skinny Negro with a small, black face who stood in a tiny elevator and eyed Cross sullenly.

"Take this man up to room 89, Buck. Here's the key," the woman ordered.

"Yes'm," Buck sang.

He rode up with Buck who weighed him with his eyes. Cross knew that a bundle of newspapers and a bottle of whiskey were not the normal accoutrements of a Negro migrant from Memphis. He would have to do better than this. Five minutes later he was settled in his garishly papered room which had the white lip of a stained sink jutting out. The floor was bare and dirty. He lay across the lumpy bed and sighed. His limbs ached from fatigue. The hard light of the bare electric bulb swinging from the smoky ceiling stung his eyes; he doubled a piece of newspaper and tied it about the bulb to reduce the glare. He opened the bottle and took a deep swig.

Undoubtedly Gladys had now heard about his being dead. How was she taking it? He was perversely curious to know if she was sorry. And, Good God, his poor old mother! She had always predicted that he would end up badly, but he had presented her with a morally clean way of dying, a way that would induce even in his enemies a feeling of forgiving compassion. And Dot . . . ? She would find out through the newspapers or over the radio. He could almost hear Myrtle telling Dot that she had the worst luck of any girl in the whole round world . . . He was foolishly toying with the idea of trying to disguise his voice and calling Dot on the telephone when he fell asleep . . .

Late the next morning, Cross awakened with a pale winter sun falling full into his eyes. He lay without moving, staring dully. Was this his room? Around him was a low murmur of voices and the subdued music of radios coming from other rooms. His body felt weak and he could not quickly orientate himself. He swung his feet to the floor, kicking over the whiskey bottle. For a moment he watched the bubbling liquid flow; then he righted the bottle, corked it, and the action helped to bring back in his mind the events of last night. He had quit, run off; *he was dead.*

He yearned for just one more glimpse of his mother, his three sons; he hungered for just one last embrace with Dot . . . But this was crazy. Either he went through with this thing or he did not; it was all or nothing. He was being brought gradually to a comprehension of the force of habit in his and others' lives. He had to break with others and, in breaking with them, he would break with himself. He must sever all ties of memory and sentimentality, blot out, above all, the insidious tug of longing. Only the future must loom before him so magnetically that it could condition his present and give him those hours and days out of which he could build a new past. Yes, it would help him greatly if he went to New York; other faces and circumstances would be a better setting out of which to forge himself anew. But first he had to make sure that he was dead . . .

He washed himself and mulled over his situation. When a man had been born and bred with other men, had shared and participated in their traditions, he was not required of himself to conceive the total meaning or direction of his life; broad, basic definitions of his existence were already contained implicitly in the general scope of other men's hopes and fears; and, by living and acting with them—a living and acting he will have commenced long before he could have been able to give his real consent—, he will have assumed the responsibility for promises and pledges made for him and in his name by others. Now, depending only upon his lonely will, he saw that to map out his life entirely upon his own assumptions was a task that terrified him just to think of it, for he knew that he first had to know what he thought life was, had to know autonomously all the multitude of assumptions which other men took for granted, and he did not know them and he knew that he did not know them. The question summed itself up: What's a man? He had unknowingly set himself a project of no less magnitude than contained in that awful question.

He looked through the newspapers, finding only more extended accounts of what he had heard last night on the radio. For the latest news he would have to buy today's papers. Yes; and the Negro weekly papers would be upon the newsstands in the Black Belt neighborhoods tonight or in the morning. They would tell the tale; they would carry detailed stories of all Negroes who had been involved in the accident.

He spent the morning shopping for an overcoat and other necessities in a poor West Side working class district where he was certain that he would not encounter any of his acquaintances. He prodded himself to be frugal, for he did not know what the coming days would bring. How would he spend his time? Yes; he would lay in a pile of good books . . . No. What the hell was he thinking of? Books? What he had before him was of far more interest than any book he would ever buy; it was out of realities such as this that books were made. He was full of excitement as he realized that eventually he would not only have to think and feel this out, but he would have to act and live it out.

The relationship of his consciousness to the world had become subtly altered in a way that nagged him uneasily because he could not define it. His break with the routine of his days had disturbed the tone and pitch of reality. His repudiation of his ties was as though his feelings had been water and those watery feelings had been projected by his desires out upon the surface of the world, like water upon pavements and roofs after a spring rain; and his loyalty to that world, like the sun, had brightened that world and made it glitter with meaning; and now, since last night, since he had broken all of the promises and pledges he had ever made, the water of meaning had begun to drain off the world, had begun to dry up and leave the look of things changed; and now he was seeing an alien and unjustifiable world completely different from him. It was no longer *his* world; it was just *a* world . . .

He bought a tiny radio and went back to his hotel room. He was so spent from yesterday's exertions that he slept again. In the late afternoon there was a soft tapping upon his door and he awakened in terror. Who was it? Had somebody tracked him down? Ought he answer? He tiptoed to the door in his stockinged feet and stooped and peered through the keyhole. It was a woman; he could see the falling folds of a polka dot dress. The landlady? The knock came again and he saw a tiny patch of white skin as the woman's hand fell to her side. She was white . . .

He made sure that his gun was handy, then scampered back to bed and called out sleepily: "Who is it?"

"May I speak to you a moment?"

It was a woman's voice. He hesitated, opened the door, and saw a young white girl of about eighteen standing before him.

"Gotta match?" she asked, lifting a cigarette to her mouth and keeping her eyes boldly on his face.

He caught on; she was selling herself. But was she safe? Was she stooling for the police?

"Sure," he said, taking out his lighter and holding the flame for her.

"You're new here," she said.

"Yeah," he said. "I got in last night."

"So I heard," she smiled.

"Seems like news travels pretty fast around here."

"Pretty fast for those who wanna find out things," she said.

She had black, curly hair, bluish-grey-green deep-set eyes, was about five feet two in height and seemed to weigh around a hundred and five or six pounds. Her breasts were ample, her legs large but shapely; her lips were full but over-rouged and she reeked of too much cheap perfume.

"Having fun in the city, Big Boy?" She arched her eyebrows as she spoke, then looked past him into the interior of his room.

Ought he bother with her? He wanted to, but his situation was too delicate for him to get mixed up with this fetching little tart. Yet he was suddenly hungry for her; she was woman as body of woman . . .

"I don't know anybody around here yet," he said.

"Are you stingy with that fire water?" she asked, nodding toward his whiskey bottle sitting on the night table.

"Naw," he laughed, making up his mind.

She entered slowly, glancing at him out of the corner of her eyes as she went past; he followed the movements of her body as she walked to the center of the room and sat, crossing her legs and tossing back her hair and letting her breasts take a more prominent place on her body. He closed the door and placed the bottle between them.

"What do they call you?" he asked, pouring her a drink.

"Jenny," she said. "You?"

"Charlie, just Good-Time Charlie," he said, laughing.

He saw her looking appraisingly about the room. "Traveling light, hunh?"

"Just passing through," he said. "Heading west."

She sipped her drink, then rose and turned on his radio; dance music came and she stood moving rhythmically. He rose and made dance movements with her, holding her close to him, seeing in his mind the sloping curves of her body.

"Want to spend the afternoon with me?" he asked.

"Why not?"

"Look, baby, seeing this is not the Gold Coast, what do you want?"

"I got to pay my rent," she said flatly.

"The hell with that," he told her. "How much do you want? That's all I asked you."

"I want five," she said at last.

"I'll give you three," he countered.

"I said five, you piker—"

"I said three, and you can take it or leave it; I don't want to argue with you."

"Okay," she said, shrugging.

"Let's drink some more."

"Suits me."

When the dance music stopped she turned off the radio, pulled down the window shade, and rolled back the covers of the bed. Wordlessly, she began to undress and he wondered what she was thinking of. Clad in nylon panties, she came to him and held out her hand. Her breasts were firm and the nipples were pink.

"I'll take it now, baby," she said.

"But why *now*?" he demanded.

"Listen, I'm selling; you're buying. Pay now or nothing

doing," she said. "I know how men feel when they get through."

Cross laughed; he liked her brassy manner. Nobody taught her that; sense of that order was derived only through experience. He handed her three one-dollar bills which she put into the pocket of her dress, looking at him solemnly as she did so. She pulled off her panties and climbed into bed and lay staring vacantly.

"They could paint this damn place," she said matter-of-factly.

"What?" he asked, surprised, looking vaguely around the room.

"They could paint that ceiling sometime," she repeated.

Cross studied her, then laughed. "Yes; I guess they could," he admitted.

"You're not from Memphis," she said suddenly.

He whirled and glared at her, a sense of hot danger leaping into his throat. Did she know something or was she merely guessing? Was he that bad an actor? If he had thought that she was spying on him, he would have grabbed the whiskey bottle and whacked her across the head with it and knocked her cold and run . . . Naw, she's just fishing, he told himself. But I got to be careful . . . So shaken were his feelings by sudden dread that he did not want to get into bed with her.

"How do you know?" he asked.

"You don't talk like it," she said, puffing at her cigarette.

He relaxed. It was true that his accent was not completely of the Deep South. He drew upon the bottle to stifle his anxiety and when he took her in his arms he did not recall the fear that had scalded him. She responded so mechanically and wearily that only sheer physical hunger kept him with her. The edge gone from his desire, he lay looking at her and wondering how a woman so young could have achieved so ravaged a sense of life. His loneliness was rekindled and he lit a cigarette and grumbled: "You could have at least tried a little."

"You're not from Memphis," she said with finality.

"You're dodging the point," he reminded her with anger in his voice. "I said that you could at least pretend when you're in bed."

"You think it's important?" She looked cynically at him. "What do you want for three dollars?"

"You agreed to the price," he said brusquely.

"Hell, that's nothing," she said casually, squinting her eyes against the smoke of her cigarette. "I might've done it for nothing. Why didn't you ask me?"

She was fishing around to know him and he did not want it. He washed and dressed while she still lolled in the nude on his bed, her eyes thoughtful. He should not act now with these girls as he used to; things were changed with him and he had to change too. And she was taking her own goddamn time about leaving. Resentment rose in him as he realized that he had made less impression on her physical feelings than if he had spat into the roaring waters of Niagara Falls . . .

"Haven't you got something to do?" he asked her.

"I can take a hint," she said pleasantly, rolling off the bed and getting into her panties.

"Be seeing you," she said after she had dressed.

"Not if I see you first."

"You'll be glad to see me if you're in a certain mood," she said; she touched him under the chin with her finger and left.

He lay on the bed, feeling spiteful toward even the scent of her perfume that lingered on in the room. He rose, opened the window wide, let in a blast of freezing air, and peered over the edge of the sill, his sight plunging downward eight floors to the street where tiny men and women moved like little black beetles in the white snow. I wouldn't like to fall down there, he thought aimlessly and turned back into the room, closing the window.

He went down for lunch and got the afternoon newspapers. The final list of the dead was over one hundred, making the accident the worst in Chicago's history. The mayor had appointed a committee to launch an investigation, for the cause of the tragedy was still obscure. The *Herald-Examiner* carried two full pages of photographs of some of the dead and Cross was pricked by a sense of the bizarre when he saw his own face staring back at him. He knew at once that Gladys had given that photograph to the newspapers, for she alone possessed the batch of old snaps from which it had been taken. By God, she really believes it, he thought with wry glee.

Then anxiousness seized him. If Jenny saw that photograph, would she not recognize him? He studied the photograph again; it showed him wearing football togs, sporting a mustache, and his face was much thinner and younger . . . No; Jenny wouldn't recognize him from that . . .

Early that evening the snow stopped falling and Chicago lay white and silent under huge drifts that made the streets almost impassable. Cross was glad, for it kept down the number of pedestrians and lessened his chances of being seen by anyone he knew. Near midnight he went to 35th Street and bought a batch of Negro weeklies and rushed back to his room, not daring to open them on the street or in the trolley. There, on the front pages, were big photographs of himself. His funeral had been set for Monday afternoon at 3 P.M. at the Church of the Good Shepherd. He laughed out loud. It was working like a charm! He wondered vaguely, while downing a drink, just how badly mangled his body was supposed to have been. Then he saw the answer; an odd item in the *Chicago Defender* reported:

> Subway officials stated that the body of Cross Damon had been so completely mangled that his remains had to be scooped up and wrapped in heavy cellophane before they could be placed in a coffin.

He giggled so long that tears came into his eyes.

A little after two o'clock that morning, when the snow-drenched streets were almost empty, he took a trolley to the neighborhood of his wife. He was afraid to loiter, for he was well-known in this area. From a distance of half a block he observed his home: lights were blazing in every window. She's got a plenty to do these days, he said to himself, repressing a desire to howl with laughter. But as the faces of his three sons rose before him, he sobered. He was never to see them again, except like this, from a distance. His eyes misted. They were his future self, and he had given up that future for a restricted but more intense future . . .

He went next to 37th and Indiana Avenue and crept into a snow-choked alleyway back of Dot's apartment building and figured out where her window would be. Yes, it was there, on the third floor . . . A light burned behind the shade. Was Dot really sorry? Had she wept over him? Or had her weeping been over her own state of unexpected abandonment? The light in her window went out suddenly and he wondered if she was going to bed. He hurried around to the street, watching like a cat for passersby, and secreted himself in a dark doorway opposite the entrance of the building in which she lived. Half an hour later he saw Dot and Myrtle come out, moving slowly through the snow and darkness with their heads and shoulders bent as under a weight of bewildered sorrow. He noticed that Myrtle was carrying a suitcase. Yes, Dot was no doubt on her way to see a doctor about the abortion. Only that could account for their having a suitcase with them. He could not have arranged things so neatly if he had really tried dying for real!

The next morning was Sunday and it was clear and cold, with a sharp, freezing wind sweeping in over the city from Lake Michigan. He felt driven to haunt the neighborhood of his mother. How was she taking his death? Her lonely plight saddened him more than anything else. She lived in an area that did not know him and he waited in a bar near a window to get a glimpse of her as she left for church. His overcoat was turned up about his chin and his hat was pulled low over his eyes. He smoked, toyed with a glass of beer, keeping his eyes hard upon the entrance of her house. True enough, at a quarter to eleven she came out, dressed in black, her face hidden by a veil, and picked her way gingerly over the deep snow toward her church some two blocks away. Cross felt hot tears stinging his cheeks for the first time since his childhood. He longed to run to her, fall on his knees in the snow and clasp her to him, begging forgiveness. His poor, sad, baffled old Mama . . . But if he went to her, she would collapse in the snow and might well die of the shock.

His worry that something might go wrong with his burial was what kept Cross awake the whole of the Sunday night before his funeral. Had there been no inquiries about the Negro's body that they had mistaken for his own? Who had that man been? Would his family come forward at the last moment and ask questions? Maybe his wife would claim the body? In fact, anybody's raising a question would endanger his whole plan. But perhaps no one had known that the Negro had been on the train. As he recalled now the man had seemed rather shabbily dressed. Perhaps the man's wife, if he had had a wife, thought that he had run off. Cross chided himself for worrying. In the minds of whites, what's one Negro more or less? If the rites went off without someone's raising a question, then he would consider the whole thing settled.

Monday morning was bright and cold; the temperature dipped to ten below zero. Gusts of wind swept in from Lake Michigan, setting up swirling eddies of powdered snow in the quiet streets. Cross stood moodily at his window and stared out at the frozen world, occupied with the question of how he was to spy on his burial. The *Chicago World* had reported that his body had been laid out at the Jefferson Resting Home and that "his postal colleagues and a host of friends" had sent numerous floral wreaths; his death had been referred to as a "great loss to the South Side community". He felt that if he could get a sneaking glimpse of Gladys and the funeral procession, he would feel certain in judging how soundly his death had been accepted. Spying upon the church was easy; he had, late one night, rented a top floor room in the building opposite the church, identifying himself to the old black landlady as John Clark, a student visiting Chicago as a tourist for a week. He had already made two visits to the room, bowing respectfully to the landlady, and had observed the church at leisure.

A little after ten that morning, just after he had returned from breakfast, Jenny came to see him and her manner was so friendly that one would have thought that she had known him for years. Cross was decidedly in no mood for her company, fearing that she might ask him where he was going when he was ready to leave to spy on his last rites.

"I got the blues today," he growled at her.

"Maybe I can cheer you up," she chirped, seating herself even though he had not asked her to. There was something in her manner that warned him to be on guard. She had a mouthful of chewing gum.

"Nothing to drink this morning?" she asked.

"Empty pocket, empty bottle," he lied.

"What kind of work did you do in Memphis?" she asked.

"Why in hell do you want to know that?" he demanded.

"Just curious, that's all," she answered innocently, chewing vigorously. "Something tells me you got some money."

"Yeah; I opened the safe with a bar of soap and got a million bucks," he joshed her. "Now tell me, are you working for the police?"

She paled. Her jaws stopped moving. Then she said: "Well, I never . . . !"

"Then why in hell do you keep on questioning me?"

"You *are* scared of something!" she exclaimed.

She had trapped him so neatly that he wanted to slap her. Yet he knew that it was he who had betrayed his fear and made her suspicious of him. He decided that she was honest; but honest or not, he could not use her. Her present attitude might be buttressed by good faith, but she was tough and if she found out that he had something to conceal, might she not blackmail him?

"Look— Why don't you tell Jenny about your troubles? Maybe we can team up together," she said seriously.

"Forget it, Jenny. You'll save yourself time."

"You're in no mood for talking today," she said, rising. "See you when you're feeling better."

She let herself out of the room and he sat brooding. Maybe he ought to play safe and move? Was Jenny stooling for the police? But he had no criminal record and even if the police should question him, there was nothing they could pin on him. He had only a day to wait; he would remain where he was. Later, after the descent of the catastrophe, he wondered why he had not acted upon his sense of foreboding and moved . . .

It was nearing two o'clock when Cross, filled with trepidation, took a trolley to the South Side. He found himself being irresistibly drawn to Gladys' home and, rashly, he boarded an "L" that passed in sight of the house and rode back and forth, snatching a quick glimpse of the front door each time the train sped past. He would ride a station past the house in one direction, get off, traverse the footbridge, and ride past the house again in the other direction to the station beyond it, get off again and return. It was not until nearly two-thirty

that he saw any signs of life; the front door opened and
Gladys and his mother—both dressed in deep black—came
out upon the sidewalk and stood in the snow. Junior, Peter,
and Robert followed, being led by a distant cousin of Gladys.
Excited, Cross got off the train, concealed himself behind a
billboard on the "L" platform, and saw a man garbed formally
in black go up to Gladys, his mother, and the children, and
tip his hat to them. No doubt the undertaker, Cross thought.
His eyes lingered on his mother and his sons and, as they left,
a light seemed to go out of the winter sky. He would never
see them again . . .

His heart bubbled with hot panic when a voice sounded in
his ear: "Do you know 'em?"

He spun and looked into the face of a young Negro dressed
in the uniform of the "L" company. He had never seen the
man before.

"No," he answered, relaxing.

"That's the family of a guy who was killed in the subway
accident last week," the man spoke in a detached voice. "I
reckon they must be going to the funeral."

"Oh," Cross said, keeping his face averted. "I read about
that."

"Man, that guy wasn't nothing but meatballs and spaghetti
when the subway got through with 'im," the man went on.

"What do you mean?" Cross asked.

"Brother, your blood is the tomato sauce. Your white guts
is the spaghetti. And your flesh is the meat, see? You'd be
surprised how like a plate of meatballs and spaghetti you look
when you get minced up in one of those subway wrecks. Ha-
ha-ha," the man laughed cynically.

An "L" train rolled to a stop and Cross hurried into it; he
had seen and heard enough. He rushed to his rented room
and sat at a window overlooking the church entrance. Fifteen
minutes later the hearse arrived. There's Tom . . . ! Tom was
his old friend from the Post Office and he was one of the
pallbearers. And there was Frank . . . And Pinkie . . . And
Booker . . . And Joe Thomas . . . He could not make out
the others, but their faces were turned. He watched them lift
the black coffin and march slowly into the church. The undertaker's assistants followed, carrying many wreaths of flowers

inside. He saw the undertaker lead Gladys, his mother, and his three sons into the church. He opened the window a crack and caught an echo of a melancholy hymn . . . The service was so long that he wondered what the preacher could have found to say about him. He was certain, however, of one thing: whatever was being said had no relationship at all to him, his life, or the feelings he was supposed to have had.

An hour later the church doors opened and the crowd began to file out, first Gladys, then his mother; finally his three sons came, led by the preacher and the undertaker. Again he saw them sliding the black coffin into the hearse. Soon a long procession of black cars pulled off through the snow. It was over. He had witnessed a scene about which he could never in his life talk with anybody. And he *did* hanker to talk about it. When men shared normal experiences, they could talk about them without fear, but he had to hug this black secret to his heart.

The procession had gone and the church doors had shut. He had to go back to his hotel and prepare to catch a train for New York. But he did not move. He was empty, face to face with a sense of dread more intense than anything he had ever felt before. He was alone. He was not only without friends, their hopes, their fears, and loves, to buoy him up, but he was a man tossed back upon himself when that self meant only a hope of hope. The church across the street was still there, but somehow it had changed into a strange pile of white, lonely stone, as bleak and denuded of meaning as he was. And the snowy street, like the church, assumed a dumb, lifeless aspect. He lit a cigarette and sat on the edge of the bed and stared about the room. His movements were mechanical. The dingy walls seemed to loom over against him, asking wordlessly questions that he could not answer. Nothing made meaning; his life seemed to have turned into a static dream whose frozen images would remain unchanged throughout eternity.

He told himself that he was brooding too much; he had to get out of this room. On the snow-cushioned sidewalk, his legs led him to a taxi, but when he reached his hotel, he did not want to go in. Instead he ambled into a nearby bar, THE CAT'S PAW, and ordered a whiskey. He drank eleven shots before he could feel the influence of the alcohol. He ordered his twelfth and the bartender told him: "If I were you, I'd get some air."

"I can pay you," Cross told him.

"That ain't the point," the bartender said. "Get rid of what you've got, then I'll sell you some more." The bartender studied him. "Worried about something, eh?"

He paid and went out. He was not drunk; there was simply no purpose in him. When he finally entered the hotel, he met Jenny in the corridor near the door of his room. Because she had no meaning, she meant everything to him now.

"Speak of the devil," she greeted him, smiling.

"Hi," he breathed.

"Look, I got a bottle," she said, showing it to him. "How about it?"

"I don't mind."

He needed a drink. He felt her take hold of his hand and squeeze it.

"You're freezing," she said.

"Yeah."

He unlocked the door and let her go in; he followed, pulled off his coat and flopped on the bed.

"You're all in," she commented sympathetically.

"Tired," he said and closed his eyes.

"You must relax," she said.

He was silently grateful when he felt her cool, soft hand moving slowly across his hot forehead. Her hand left him; he heard her pouring whiskey, felt the glass as she took his fingers and gently forced them about it. He pulled up and drank. She sat next to him on the bed, cradling her glass in her palms.

"Don't you want to know anything about me?" she asked him.

"Jenny, you don't understand," he said kindly.

"I'm a little better than you think I am," she said; she bent forward and fingered his ear.

"Maybe."

"You *would* do a lot more than me, and maybe you *could* do a lot better. But whatever it is, it's not for keeps," she told him.

"What are you trying to say?"

"Take me with you," she said. "When you're tired of me, then dump me. I don't care. I want to get out of Chicago."

"I can't."

"Why?"

Her soft arm went around his neck and his nostrils were full of the scent of her hair; he drained his glass and a moment later he heard her ask: "What's the matter? If you talk about it, it'll be easier."

She searched for his mouth and kissed him. His world was a blur. He needed what she was trying to give him but he was afraid.

"Why do you bother about me?" he asked.

"'Cause I like you. Ain't that enough?"

"Guess so," he mumbled. He was alone, empty. "Give me another drink."

She poured the glasses full. He drank again, stood, swayed, tugged at his tie.

"What're you doing?"

"Going to bed . . ."

"Wait, I'll help you undress," she said. "You're three sheets to the wind."

His limbs were like rubber. She aided him in pulling off his clothes, rolled back the blanket and pushed him into bed. His eyes closed; he heard her moving about, pulling down the shade, locking the door. Then he felt the sensual smoothness of her skin as she slid into bed beside him. She blended her body with his and he could feel the tender spread of her fingers on his back. His senses were dreaming. He looked at her and she was not a dangerous girl; those deep, tranquil, bluish-grey-green eyes were dark and helpful now and the heat of her body was filling him with thankfulness.

"Can't you talk to me?" she asked him.

"You wouldn't understand."

"I would. Just *try*."

He laughed, took her face between his palms and stared at her, feeling foolishly proud of the irony of his life.

"I'm dead," he said.

Her lips parted in bewilderment and she pushed his hands

roughly from her face. She looked off a second and then back to him.

"You're nuts," she said.

He wanted to tell her. He knew now that she was not working for the police, but for herself. She needed a man and had fastened her hope on him. If she had been well-known to him, he would never have had the impulse to tell her. But a strange girl was different and he would be leaving soon. Dammit, he had to tell somebody just to make sure that his situation was not a fantasy of his own mind. He was too much alone and it was insupportable.

"I'm in a funny fix," he began. "You remember that subway accident last week? Well, I was in it."

"You were hurt in it? Is that what's making you act so funny?"

"I wasn't really hurt," he continued, knowing that he ought not talk, but hearing the words spilling out in spite of himself. "Listen, they found a body down there all mangled and they think it's mine . . ."

"Are you *sure* you weren't hurt?" Her eyes were round with concern.

"No. I wasn't hurt," he went on, nettled that she was not believing him. "Today, just two hours ago, they buried that body thinking that it was mine . . ."

She pulled abruptly away from him, rose, walked across the room and got her cigarettes. She lit one and sat near him.

"Are you trying to shit me? Now, come on; tell me what you've done."

Cross buried his face in the pillow to stifle his laughter. She did not believe him. He knew that his story was wild, but he had not counted upon so much outright disbelief.

"This is funny," he chuckled.

"What's so goddamn funny?" she snapped at him.

"You asked me to tell you, now you don't believe me."

"If you had done something like that, you wouldn't tell me," she said.

"Why not?"

"Because the insurance companies would want to know about it," she explained. "And you're smarter than that."

He grew sober. Her intelligence was frightening.

"All right," he said, relieved. "I'm lying." He stood and got his bathrobe and struggled into it. *"I'm not dead, then."*

"Where're you going?" she asked.

"Down the hall to see a man about a coffin," he said.

He lumbered into the corridor, feeling swamped by confusion. This damn girl was making him lose control of the project he had planned. I'm really crazy to talk to her, he reproached himself. He resolved that upon his return from the bathroom he was going to get dressed and get the hell out of the city as fast as a train could carry him. And from now on he would keep firm hold on himself. He turned a bend in the corridor, his head lowered in reflection; he drew in his breath sharply as he felt his body colliding with that of another man. Before his senses could register what was happening, he heard a familiar voice bursting in his ears and saw an old, familiar smile of incredulous astonishment spreading over a fat, black face.

"As I live and breathe! You're either Cross or his twin!"

Cross stared at the face and had the stupid desire to shake his head and make it vanish. He was looking into the eyes of a man he had known for six years! Like he, the man wore a bathrobe and had evidently just come from the bathroom. He was done for; there was no way out of this except . . . *He had to decide what to do quickly!* Tension made him hot as fire; he had to check a crazy impulse to wave his arm and try to sweep this man from sight and keep his freedom. It was big, fat, black Joe Thomas who stood in front of him, the same man he had seen acting as a pallbearer around his coffin earlier that afternoon!

"Speak, man! They say you're dead, but you ain't no ghost and I damn well *know* it! We just put your coffin in the ground, man! What the *hell* is this?" Joe's eyes were dancing in his fat, black face; he threw out his hands, hesitated, then clapped both of them on Cross's shoulders. "I got to *touch* you to believe it!" Joe's face was a mixture of fear and gladness. "They *all* think you're dead, and *here* you are in a cat house with the chippies! Good God Almighty! I feel weak . . ." Joe blinked, his lips hanging open. "I just came in here to knock off a piece of tail 'fore going to work— Hell, the whole town's talking 'bout how you died—" Joe rocked

back on his heels and burst into a gale of hysterical laughter. "This is a new way to cover up cunt hunting! Oh, Jesus, this is hot!" Joe sobered for a moment; he was struggling with himself to adjust his mind to what his eyes saw. "But, *say* something! You *are* Cross, ain't you?"

"Yes," Cross heard himself speaking. "I'm Cross."

"Well, don't be ashamed of letting me catch you in a whorehouse, man," Joe said, blinking and trying to understand the strange expression that shrouded Cross's face. "Come on *in* here and let me *talk* to you." Joe grabbed Cross's hand and dragged him forward. He unlocked a door and pulled Cross inside a room. Cross's eyes darted about. The bed was unmade, the shades drawn, and a dim light glowed on the ceiling. Joe's clothing was flung pell-mell over the back of a chair. Cross's fingers ached to blot out this black man who grinned with bewilderment.

"Sit down, man," Joe spluttered. "Tell me what this *is* . . ."

Joe shut the door and Cross heard the click of the lock; that meant that no one could come in without warning; he was alone with Joe . . . Joe flopped on the bed, his eyes full on Cross, waiting for an explanation. Cross moved on cat's feet to the center of the room, noticing the window which had the exact position of the window in his room, that window through which he had peered only a few hours ago and looked at the distant, snow-drenched streets far below . . . He then stared at the almost empty whiskey bottle on the night table. Tension was so tight in him that he felt his skull would burst. Joe saw him gazing at the bottle.

"You want a drink, hunh? I scared you, didn't I?" Joe took the bottle and drained the whiskey into a glass. "This bottle's dead. But we've got another one on the way." He sat the bottle on the floor and handed the tumbler to Cross. "I reckon I'm about the last man on earth you ever expected to see, hunh?"

Cross emptied the glass with one swallow, and smiling tightly, said: "That's right, Joe."

"You *are* Cross!" Joe shouted and slapped his thighs. "For a minute, I thought maybe I was making a fool out of myself. God, I'm sweating—! Cross, you're the goddamndest man God ever made . . ."

Cross reached for the neck of the empty whiskey bottle and lifted it.

"Ain't no more whiskey in that bottle, man," Joe said. "I just sent Ruth down for another fifth. She'll be back in a minute. Sit down, man! Don't be scared . . . Lord, I can't get over this!"

"When's this Ruth coming back?" Cross asked quietly.

"In a minute," Joe said, a shadow of disquiet flickering over his face. He brightened quickly. "Say, who you're shacking up with in here? Bertha, Mamie, Della, or . . ."

"Jenny," Cross said.

"She's great!" Joe approved. "Boy, she can go when she feels like it. She's got some build . . ."

Joe went on talking and Cross stared at him. He had to do something. But what? This clown was tearing down his dream, smashing all he had so laboriously built up. And there he sat: fat, black, half-laughing and half-scared, with beads of sweat popping on his forehead, his black chest showing and his bare legs sprawled out from the bed, his blue silk bathrobe flowing around him . . .

"God, but you're sly, Cross," Joe went on. "Ain't you gonna tell me what happened? I didn't know you knew about this place. But there ain't no better place to get over the blues, is it? Kind of crummy here, but the gals are nice. Hell, man, if you ain't gonna say nothing, I'll tell 'em. They made a mistake in that damned church today. I'm gonna call up Pink. He'll die laughing . . ." Joe rose from the bed.

Cross grasped the neck of the bottle firmly; his arm trembled; his fingers gripped the bottle so hard that he thought the glass would crush in his palm. He lifted the bottle high in the air. Joe's lips moved soundlessly, his eyes black pools of mute protest. Joe was frozen, waiting, his lips open and about to utter a question and then Cross brought down the bottle with a crashing blow on Joe's head. Just before the blow landed Cross heard Joe utter in tones of deep amazement: "Say?" The bottle caught Joe on the temple, bursting from the force of the blow and Joe fell slowly backwards without having lifted a finger; he lay still, his thick lips hanging grotesquely open. Cross moved now with the speed of a panther. He let up the shade and a tide of greyish light swept into the

room; he opened the window and a blast of freezing air
turned his breath to steam. He turned and faced the inert
form sprawled on the bed in its bathrobe. He grabbed Joe's
right arm and slid his left arm under Joe's legs and lifted him
as one would a sick child. He stood a moment, looking at
Joe's black, quiet face, and then he looked at the open window. He struggled to the window with the body, hoisted it
up and for a moment the body was poised in space. He
pushed it through and shut the window at once, all in one
swift, merciless movement. He turned back to the room,
picked up the glass shards of whiskey bottle and opened the
door. The corridor was empty. He went out and hurried to
the bathroom and secreted the shards atop a tall, wooden cabinet. He examined himself minutely in the full mirror and saw
no telltale signs except sweat on his face. He mopped his
brow with the bottom of his bathrobe, then stood still, listening intently. He heard faint voices and the muffled music of
radios. Time seemed to be flowing on normally. Through the
window of the bathroom he could see that night was falling
upon the frozen city. He headed for his room, feeling un-
steady in his legs. He hesitated before going in, trying to
control himself. Again he mopped sweat from his face, then
opened the door of his room. Jenny still lay on the bed.

"I thought maybe you had flushed down the drain, you
took so long," she said.

He sank into a chair, fighting down a wild, foolish impulse
to tell her what he had done. She rose, smiling, and went to
him; he pushed her violently away.

"What's the matter with you? You're trembling and wring-
ing wet . . ." She paused and narrowed her eyes. "Say, are
you on the needle or something . . . ?"

"Leave me alone," he muttered.

"I wonder what you're up to," she said, turning away uneasily.

A knock came at the door. Cross stiffened and felt he could
not breathe. He would not have been too surprised if the
door had opened and Joe had walked into the room. But he
had tossed Joe out of that window; or had he? He struggled
to sort reality from fantasy. The knock came again, louder this
time.

"Aren't you going to answer it?" Jenny asked him.

"You answer it," Cross said.

"Jenny!" a woman's voice called through the door.

"Yeah?" Jenny answered, going to the door and opening it.

A tall, fleshy blonde woman stood in the doorway with a bottle of whiskey under her arm.

"Hello, Ruth," Jenny said. "What's the matter?"

"Sorry. Didn't mean to disturb you," the woman called Ruth said. Her eyes looked about the room, resting at last on Cross. "But Joe isn't here, is he?"

"No, honey," Jenny said, shrugging. "I haven't seen him."

Ruth's lips curled in scorn. "That black bastard's run out on me," she hissed. "If he's dumped me without paying, I'll kill him the next time I see him, so help me God! But I don't understand . . . All his clothes are still there."

"Oh, he'll come back," Jenny smiled. "He always does."

"He tried a new trick," Ruth blazed. "He sent me down for a bottle of liquor and took a powder." Ruth forced a smile for Cross. "I'm sorry to bother you with my troubles. But, you know, the fool left his clothes behind . . . You reckon he could be two-timing me? Maybe he's in some other room . . . ?"

"*Might* be," Jenny said, laughing at the possibility.

"I'll leave you now," Ruth said, her eyes baffled.

Jenny closed the door and turned to Cross, chuckling: "Ruth and her Joe. I do believe she's in love with him, but he doesn't give a damn about her."

"Who's Joe?" Cross asked listlessly.

"A colored postal clerk who comes here all the time," she told him as she sat on the bed again, her hands folded modestly over her pubic hair. "He's Ruth's star client; he even keeps his bathrobe and slippers in her room. God, he's a scream. Jet black, fat . . . A regular clown . . . Spends his money like water . . . Listen to this: He once told me . . ."

Cross was not listening though his eyes were on her face. He was wondering how Joe's body had fallen and where . . . Had it landed on the street? He wanted to open the window and look out, but he knew that would have aroused questions in Jenny's mind. He had done a horrible thing; he had killed so swiftly and brutally that he hardly recognized what he had done as he recalled it to his mind. It was he who had made that assault on Joe in that room; yes, he had done that to save himself. He heard Jenny laughing.

". . . don't you think so?" she was asking.

"I don't know," he mumbled.

"Hell, you're not even *listening*!" she said angrily. "At least Joe's a good sport!"

"Well, go to him," Cross told her, relishing his irony.

If Joe's body had landed on the street in the snow, then it would soon be seen by someone and there would be an out-cry. But maybe it had dropped into a deep drift? He was excited by such a prospect. If that had happened, no one would see it for awhile . . . He blinked when Jenny rose from the bed and came to him; she caught his hand and pulled him to his feet. Gently, she forced him to the bed, climbed in with him and drew the covers over them.

"Charlie, what's the matter?" she asked in a whisper. "Talk to me . . ."

Maybe at any moment now a knock would come at the door and it would be about Joe. He heard footsteps pass in the corridor outside and wondered if it was Ruth still hunting for her Joe . . . He had had no choice; it had been either he or Joe. He had known it the moment he had looked into that fat, black, laughing face.

"Your body is trembling," Jenny whispered. "I wish I could *help* you!"

She was getting on his nerves. Why didn't she leave . . . ?

"You're always watching me, questioning me," he complained in a distant voice.

"You're too goddamn fucking suspicious!" she cursed him, curling her lips back over her teeth.

He looked at her; there was an animal-like quality in her that made him like her, and that quality showed most clearly when she was angry.

"Okay, baby, spill your story," he consented. "You've been wanting to talk to me. Now, I'm listening . . ."

He lifted himself on an elbow, his eyes on her face, but he was really seeking over the snowdrifts outside, looking for Joe's body.

"You sure are a great help," she complained, her anger vanishing. "I'll try— Look, Charlie, you're black and I'm white— That's what this goddamn country says, but it's the bunk, and you know it and I know it. They say it to keep us apart, don't they?"

He nodded, not quite understanding what she had said. Maybe he had made a mistake in killing Joe like that . . . ? God, he had planned to be free, and now he had killed . . .

". . . I'd bet a million dollars that I've lived a much harder life than you have. I grew up in the slums of a small rotten town in the middle of Kansas. My father was a drunkard and a socialist of a sort . . ."

He was conscious that the more she talked the better she talked. The gal's got some sense . . . But wouldn't they raid the hotel when they found Joe's body . . . ?

". . . he was always yelling about the rights of Negroes and fighting for the underdog. My mother was the janitor in the town school. If it hadn't been for her, I wouldn't 've even learned to read and write. My mother really supported us, brought us up and nursed father when he had the D.T.'s. She was the only decent person I've ever known in my life . . . Surprised to hear *me* say things like that, hunh?"

He was looking at her, but was wondering what the police would say about finding Joe's body clad only in a bathrobe . . .

". . . and I spotted you as an educated guy after you'd said only two words. I respect education . . . It's too late for me to get one now, I reckon. But I want one; really, I do."

He nodded his head as she spoke, telling her that he was following her, but he was only reacting to the general sense of her words.

". . . everybody in our little town looked down on us. Me, my brothers and sisters, we were the drunkard's children, the scum of the earth. Then I got in trouble with a boy, got knocked up, and had to have an abortion. You wouldn't think it, Charlie, but 'til two years ago I didn't know where babies came from. Honest to Pete! I thought they came out of women's bowels . . . Isn't that crazy? But I know *now*. And how! But let me get back to the story. You're listening, aren't you? You're not bored?"

"Oh, no; go ahead," he said; he might be lost already. It was good that he had his gun; if the police found out about him, well, he would blow his brains out . . .

". . . and when I got knocked up, the whole town knew it. My father drove me out of the house. I lived in a dump for awhile, then got rid of the child. It was hell; I was sick with a fever of one hundred and four for three days. I thought I was a dead duck. Mama finally made father let me come back home. But just to walk down the street to the store to buy a loaf of bread was hell . . . When I passed people, they'd stop talking and just stare at me . . . I ran off and came to Chicago. The first week I worked in a Greek restaurant; like a dope, I went out with the Greek. He raped me . . ."

He wondered why she felt so deep a sense of inferiority; he was black, but he had never felt that humble in the face of life. And Joe? Maybe the sirens would start howling soon . . . ?

". . . sounds crazy, hunh? But I'm not asking for sympathy. The hell with it. I'm young. I'll fight, work. Now, why am I telling you all this? You said you were going west, didn't you? I want to go to California—"

"Movies?" he asked.

"Hell, no. I'm not pretty," she said.

Cross studied her face; she was much prettier than she thought.

"Then why California?"

"I just like the sunshine and want to be as far from Kansas and my family as I can get," she said. "Take me with you, won't you? I could be of some use, couldn't I? I don't care if you're colored. The hell with that crap—"

"Jenny," he began. "It won't work—"

"Why not? You can trust me."

"But my life— No. It won't work at all."

"I don't give a good goddamn *what* you've done," she said.

Cross smiled ruefully. She doesn't know what she's saying . . . "Look, baby, I like you. I believe you. But forget it, hunny. It's too complicated to explain."

She stood and her face grew red and her eyes blazed with anger. Would he have to do something to keep her quiet?

Was she going to threaten him and make him take her with him?

"Why am I so different?" she demanded. "Do you loathe me? What's wrong with me . . . ?" Tears welled in her eyes. "Only last week Pearl Bland got a ride to New York with a guy with dough," she said bitterly. "Me? I can't even get a *Negro* to trust me!" She bent to him and asked: "*Why?* Tell me why . . ."

"Come here, Jenny," he said.

He folded her in his arms. Good God, this child was bitter! In despair she began kissing him with passion, still weeping. He relaxed. Why not let her make him forget? He could not control the flow of events now anyway; he was probably already lost . . . Any minute the cops would be knocking on the door. What did he have to lose? He pressed his lips to Jenny's and this time he knew that she was allowing herself to be more of a woman because she wanted his trust. When the spasm was over he lay with his hand gently touching her face, mutely thanking her for the benediction that she had shed upon his distraught senses.

"Darling, what's your real name?" she asked him quietly.

The respite was over; he felt danger again. He had to shake this girl off him quickly. But, what about Joe? He had pushed Joe out of that window and time had flowed on as though nothing had happened. No one here knew his name or that he had known Joe. So, when they found Joe's body, there would be no thought of him in connection with his death. They might even think that Ruth had done it. He lay still, plotting. He would not hurt Jenny; killing her would be a sure way of putting the police on his trail. He would fool her and ditch her. She thought that he was heading west. All right; agree to take her, dump her at the last moment, and strike out for New York alone. Cunning was better than violence; he must not allow himself to be confronted again with the unexpected, as he had been with Joe . . .

"You really want to come with me?"

Her arms tightened about his neck in gratitude.

"Where're we going?" she asked.

"We'll take a bus to Denver, then later we'll go to the Far West," he said.

"But we have to have dough. How much have you got?"

"Leave that to me," he argued. "I'll get you to the West Coast, if you want to go."

"When do we leave?"

"Tonight." He rolled swiftly from the bed and began washing up. "I'll go down for the tickets now."

"I'll believe it when I see those tickets," she said, rising and commencing to dress also.

"You better start packing," he told her. "How much luggage have you got?"

"Just a suitcase." She studied him, then rubbed her fingers together. "I need some nylons and things . . ."

He gave her ten dollars.

"Aw, come on," she exploded. "Be a sport."

"I'll give you more tomorrow," he said. "Now, go." He pushed her out of the door, looked both ways in the corridor, then shut the door and locked it. He hurried to the window and opened it. A clear night sky sent a sheen over the snow-covered world. He stared down, searching for Joe's body. Ah . . . There it was, on that roof! He could see it lying straight out, a black mark on the white snow. The soft snow had no doubt cushioned its fall and the impact of the body on the roof had not been heard. He had time to get away before anyone discovered it. He closed the window and stood in the center of the room. Why had that damn fool come upon him at that time? But he could not think of Joe now; he had to plan how to ditch Jenny . . .

He rode down in the elevator with Buck who was grumbling: "Jesus! Why can't that bitch leave me alone?" He spoke to no one in particular. "She keeps yapping at me about Joe, Joe . . . What the hell do I care about Joe? It ain't my job to keep track of her damn men! These whores make me sick. Let a bobby pin get lost, and they come running to me."

"Don't let 'em break you down," Cross told him.

"You damn right I won't," Buck seethed with anger. "I don't do my day's work at night, like they do, flat on their backs. Man, a woman'd make a man jump out of a window; she would—"

Cross walked from the lobby on legs he did not feel. He knew that Buck knew nothing about how Joe had died, but his talking of jumping from a window had almost paralyzed him. His body was seized with ague and he felt so weak that he went into an alleyway and sank down upon an empty wooden soda water case under the spreading glare of a street lamp. He started when a door opened and an aproned man came out with a garbage can and dumped its contents near him; the man glanced curiously at Cross, then went back inside, slamming the door and bolting it securely. Cross rested his wrists on his knees and his eyes traveled without purpose over the steaming pile of refuse, the top of which was crowned with a mound of wet, black coffee grounds that gleamed in the light of the street lamp; some of the grounds spilled over a bloodstained Kotex which still retained the curving shape of having fitted tightly and recently against the lips of some vagina; there was a flattened grapefruit hull whose inner pulpy fibres held a gob of viscous phlegm; there was the part of a fried sausage with grease congealed white in the porous grains of meat; there was the crumpled cellophane wrapping from a pack of cigarettes glittering with tiny beads of moisture; there was a brass electric socket still holding its delicate filigreed web of wires even though its glass globe had been shattered; there was a bone from a piece of roast beef still holding traces of red and grey meat; there was a lemon rind molded to a light green color; there was a clump of cigarette butts whose ends were blackened and whose tips were stained red from the rouge of a woman's lips; there was a limp wad of lettuce whose leaves glistened with a fine film of oil; there was a clean piece of wood jutting out with a shining nail bent at the end of it; there were several egg shells showing bits of yellow yolk; there was the stump of a cigar bearing the marks of a man's teeth; and there was a clump of fluffy dust freshly gathered from some floor . . .

His blood felt chilled. He had to shake off this dead weight and move on. He pulled to his feet and took a cab to La Salle Street Railroad Station and went directly to the reservation window.

"Have you any sleeping accommodations for New York?"

"For tonight?" the clerk asked.

"For the earliest possible train," Cross said.

"Just a minute," the clerk said.

Cross waited nervously while the clerk telephoned.

"We have one, a lower 13," the clerk informed him.

"Okay. Fix it up. When does the train leave?"

"At six on track eight, sir."

He paid, received the tickets, then rushed by cab to the Greyhound Bus Terminal and bought two tickets to Denver. Back in the hotel, he settled his bill in full and rode up in the elevator to the eighth floor. Jenny was waiting for him at the door of his room with her suitcase. She smiled warmly, but there was nervousness in her manner. When they were inside, he handed her her ticket for the bus.

"Where's your ticket?" she asked suspiciously.

"Here," he said, showing it to her. He had thought that she would ask that; it was why he had bought two tickets. The extra money he had paid for his ticket was his insurance that she would believe in him long enough for him to take the six o'clock train to New York. When Joe's body was discovered or when any word was ever raised about the identification of that body found in the subway wreck, nothing of him must come into the mind of Jenny.

"You know where the Greyhound Bus Terminal is?" he asked.

"Sure."

"The bus leaves at eight. I've got to see some people; I'll be gone about an hour." He looked at his watch. "It's five now. I'll be back at six. We'll eat and then we're off. Now, give me your suitcase and I'll check it at the Bus Terminal."

With his suitcase and hers, he got into a cab, checked her suitcase at the Bus Terminal and then rode over to the La Salle Street Railroad Station. A porter guided him to his coach. He showed his reservation and ticket to the conductor, got on, and, when he was in his compartment, he locked the door.

He cursed softly: That damn fool Joe . . . ! And Jenny did not know how lucky she was. From now on he had to cope with this impulse of his to confide. If circumstances had been just a little different, he would have had to kill Jenny too, or give up the game. He had thought he was free. But was he? He was free from everything but himself. Loneliness had driven him to confess to Jenny, and fear could have made him kill her as he had killed Joe. He kept his fists tightly clenched as he waited impatiently for the train to pull out. At last he heard the distant calling:

"Alll aboooooard . . . !"

He stood at the window as the train began to move. A light snow was raining softly down upon the world. Two hours from now Jenny would be searching frantically for him at the bus station. And she would never know that he had done her the greatest favor of her life.

But what was he to do with this conflict of his? This urge to confide and the fear of the danger of confiding? The outside world had fallen away from him now and he was alone at the center of the world of the laws of his own feelings. And what was this world he was?

The dreary stretches of Chicago passed before his window; it was a dim, dead, dumb, sleeping city wrapped in a dream, a dream born of his frozen impulses. Could he awaken this world from its sleep? He recalled that pile of steaming garbage, the refuse the world had rejected; and he had rejected himself and was bowed, like that heap of garbage, under the weight of endurance and time.

As the train wheels clicked through the winter night, he knew where his sense of dread came from; it was from within himself, within the vast and mysterious world that was his and his alone, and yet not really known to him, a world that was his own and yet unknown. And it was into this strange but familiar world that he was now plunging . . .

BOOK TWO

DREAM

As silent as a mirror is believed
Realities plunge in silence by . . .
—HART CRANE

C ROSS'S WORLD was now sunk in sleep and, in his compulsiveness to rouse it from its slumber, the moments of his life became a dream of anxiety. He had lied, killed, and fled to get shunt of his old hated consciousness and now he was dismayed to find it redoubled in its density and still with him. He had merely shifted his cares from without to within him, from that which he could deny to that which he could not. Imprisoned he was in a state of consciousness that was so infatuated by its own condition that it could not dominate itself; so swamped was he by himself with himself that he could not break forth from behind the bars of that self to claim himself.

During the nightmarish weeks that followed his heightened sensibilities became responsive beyond his control. His turbulent mind developed a million mental eyes that ceaselessly hunted down non-existent dangers; and his tense emotions started in terror at the most casual phrases falling from the lips of strangers.

He found that he had been deprived of the will to make decisions, that he had, by his flight, abandoned himself to be tossed and buffeted by the tyranny of daily minutia. Thrust thus back upon himself, his actions were snared in a web of self-love that made the images of his mind assume a hypnotic sway over his body that was more decisive than the food he ate to sustain himself.

The train had been plunging through the wintry night for some hours before his memory of the happenings of the last days in Chicago had dimmed in his consciousness enough for him to feel somewhat relaxed. Whenever he recalled the past there returned to him not only the mere constellations of events through which he had lived, but also a psychological grasp of the role that his desires, hates, hopes, or loves had played in them. What helped him most was that he possessed the lucky capacity of reducing and referring his memories to an intense and personal basis, and could, therefore, once he was emotionally free of the concrete context from which they had sprung, live with them without a too-crushing sense of guilt.

His memory of his relationship with Dot was not only a recollection of a man's sensual affair with a pretty girl whom he had forsaken in the trouble he had brought upon her; but, above all, Dot had been to him an alluring representation of a personal hunger which he had projected out of his heart upon her and, the two of them—Dot and what she subjectively meant to him—had been something he had not been able to cope with with satisfaction to himself and honor to her. There had been no element of sadism in his love for Dot, and he would have gladly, if such had been possible, taken upon himself in a spirit of atonement the hurt she had sustained. But who can reverse time? What was done was done and the only part of the past that he could alter was that portion lingering on in his melancholy heart. The mirage of desire that he had sought so pathetically was still his to mull over in regretful recollection.

In breaking his life in two he had left his baffled mother to fend for herself as best she could, but that baleful gift of the sense of dread which she had, out of her life's hysteria, conferred upon him in his childhood, was still his beyond his right to surrender. More definitely than ever her fateful gift was shaping and toning his hours even now on this fleeing train, was subtly sculpturing the contours of his destiny, staining all the future that he was to embrace even to that lonely grave which he would some day have to fill alone.

His being quit of Gladys was infinitely more than his shedding a vindictive wife; it was his inheritance to the full of an insight into those quicksands of appalling loneliness that had sucked him into her waiting arms in the first place. He did not remember her in a way that made him yearn to return to

her; his memory assumed the form of an intense appropriation of that intimate part of himself which had seduced him
into embracing her, and toward that part of his being he had
now a change of heart of not wanting ever again to seek fulfillment of desire in that direction.

He was, however, far from being resigned; an urge to
launch again into life was still strong in him. His sorrow for
Dot, his mother, and Gladys originated in his knowing that
they had hoped for something from him which he did not
possess; his pity for them was his knowledge of himself, a
regret for his ever having allowed them to build their dreams
upon the mercurial instabilities of his emotions.

His memory of the death of Joe was of greater simplicity.
His killing of Joe had been dictated by his fear of exposure,
and he knew that what had happened with Joe could happen
again under conditions whose advent he could not gainsay or
choose. Given a situation of danger and the dreaded tension
that went with it, his impulse to save himself would sweep
him toward what horizons? He knew that his being able to
reflect coolly upon this did not mean that he was free of it,
that to see was not to control, that self-understanding was far
short of self-mastery. He was afraid of himself.

Had they discovered Joe's body yet? Or would that snowdrift on the roof hide it for a few days longer? He would
keep track by reading the Chicago newspapers . . . But he
had no real fear of his ever being accused of killing Joe,
for his relation to Joe had been twice removed and no
apparent motive for his having killed him could be easily
deduced. For days the Chicago police would no doubt sniff
about aimlessly in the hotel corridors, accusing first this
whore and that, and, in the end, they would probably mark it
down either as suicide or death at the hands of parties unknown . . . Or maybe they'd conclude that his death had
been accidental . . . ?

The next morning, as the train neared New York, he made
his way apprehensively into the dining car for breakfast. He
was afraid that his preoccupation with his burden of nonidentity and his fear of sudden surprise would distract him to
the point of robbing reality of its naturalness and innocence.

The serried white faces floating above the tables about him were signs whose meanings he had to decipher in terms of wondering if they suspected him. Or could he find with them some basis of relationship to still the howling loneliness of his heart?

Seating himself circumspectly at a vacant table, he looked about for the waiter. Coming from the front of the dining car, grinning broadly, holding aloft in his right palm a tray of steaming food, was a short, nervous, brown-skinned man who winked smilingly at Cross and kept on looking at him as he passed. The waiter had given him an innocent, racially fraternal greeting common among Negroes and Cross knew that most whites never dreamed that their behavior towards Negroes had bred in them, especially when Negroes were in the presence of whites, a situationally defensive solidarity that possessed no validity save that occasioned by the latent pressure of white hostility. He idly observed the waiter's movements as the brown hand deftly placed succulent dishes under the impassive faces of whites. Having emptied his tray, the waiter turned, paused at Cross's table, dusted his napkin at imaginary bread crumbs on the white table cloth, and whispered: "How you, guy?"

"Fine," Cross answered. "And you?"

"Just dragging my black ass, serving these white sonsof-bitches," the waiter said in a sniggling whisper. "Be with you in a sec. I'm the only waiter in this car. My pal took sick and got off in Cleveland. So I got my hands full of white shit." The waiter clapped his hands over his mouth and widened his eyes at Cross in a sign-language laugh.

"Take your time," Cross told him. "I'm in no hurry."

"Wish these white monkeys felt like you do," the waiter whispered in appreciation. He handed Cross a folded news-paper. "Want the paper?"

"Thanks," Cross mumbled.

He gave Cross another wink and moved swiftly on between the crowded tables. Cross opened the paper and glanced at the headlines. Was there any news of Joe? It was not until he had reached the bottom of page four that he saw a small caption:

POSTAL CLERK'S BODY FOUND

He lowered the paper quickly, reading:

> The almost nude body of a Negro postal clerk, Joe Thomas, 39, of 3433 St. Lawrence Avenue, was found dead early this morning on the near South Side by an emergency line repairman. The body was lying clad only in a bathrobe in a deep snowdrift atop the roof of a four-story dwelling.
>
> The victim had apparently been drunk and it has not been determined if Thomas leaped, was pushed, or died from exposure.

That was all. Could they trace Joe's death to him? But how could they discover that he, Cross Damon, had been in the hotel? He felt safe. He looked through the moisture-streaked window at the sunny fields of snow glittering and turning slowly outside. The train rumbled on clicking wheels of steel. Ice-encrusted telegraph wires shot past, rising and dipping like strings plucked by invisible fingers. It was a normal world whose events flowed intelligibly and each object had a sharp, precise meaning. He looked in the direction of the waiter and was surprised to see the waiter looking at him, winking, smiling . . .

Out of a void, anxiety rose and captured his senses; he could feel the reality of the dining car falling away as alien powers claimed his consciousness, projecting menacing meanings upon the look of the world. He fought against it feebly, but in the end he succumbed, trembling and embracing what he dreaded. Was he being followed on this train? Was not that waiter being especially friendly to allay any fears he might have that he was being watched? Had not that waiter cursed the white folks with the idea of inducing in him a false notion of security? His grasp of reality became confounded . . .

He had no objective evidence that anything extraordinary was happening in the dining car, but this rational perception did not down his fear. His mood sought restlessly for proof to feed his beast of terror. Why was that tall white man staring at him? And why had he looked off when his eyes met his? In vain his mind protested this mood of delusive reference that was stealing his sanity away . . .

Passing to get another tray of food, the waiter again paused at Cross's table, grinning, whispering: "These white bastards think they're smart, hunh? But one of these days we'll show 'em, won't we, boy?"

The waiter knew and was teasing him! He had spotted him for the police and was so sure of himself that he could joke about it! Cross blinked and fought to control the sensations of his body; he had the illusion of something crawling over the surface of his skin. When the waiter finally came to take his order, he was so confused that he kept his eyes on the menu and mumbled what he wanted to eat. He was conscious of the irrational nature of what was transpiring, but he could not master it. His sensibilities clamored to believe in this delusion; his emotions needed the certainty of this transparent fantasy; yet, in the end, his mind was tough enough to cling to its anchorage in the hard ambiguities of normal reality. When his bacon and eggs came, he had no desire to eat. But would not that make him conspicuous? He picked up his knife and fork and forced himself, praying for this spell to pass.

He was loading his fork with a bit of bacon and a part of egg yolk when a stretch of black cloth appeared before him. He lifted his eyes and saw a Catholic priest: tall, heavy, florid of face, and with a white, turned-about collar.

"Good morning," the priest said, smiling.

"Good morning," Cross answered.

The priest sat down, then nodded toward the white landscape. "We've had a lot of snow."

"Yes."

"Did you sleep well?" the priest asked.

"Yes," Cross lied.

"I didn't," the priest said. "I can never sleep on trains. By the way, do you live in Harlem?"

"Yes."

Why was he being so closely questioned? The priest stared thoughtfully out of the window and Cross wondered what he was thinking . . . He gripped his knife and fork hard. Goddamn . . . He had to keep his head above this dangerous water and not go under. As the waiter passed, the priest caught hold of his arm and asked: "May I keep this seat for my friend? He'll be here in a moment."

"Certainly, sir," the waiter said and, when he was out of the range of the vision of the priest, he made a grimace with his lips to Cross.

Cross's anxieties now condensed themselves into an attitude of sullenness toward the priest. He disliked most strongly all men of religion because he felt that they could take for granted an interpretation of the world that his sense of life made impossible. The priest was secure and walked the earth with a divine mandate, while Cross's mere breathing was an act of audacity, a confounding wonder at the daily mystery of himself. He felt that the attitude of the priest was predicated upon a scheme of good and evil ordained by a God whom he was constrained out of love and fear to obey; and Cross therefore regarded him as a kind of dressed-up savage intimidated by totems and taboos that differed in kind but not in degree from those of the most primitive of peoples. Cross had to discover what was good or evil through his own actions which were more exacting than the edicts of any God because it was he alone who had to bear the brunt of their consequences with a sense of absoluteness made intolerable by knowing that this life of his was all he had and would ever have. For him there was no grace or mercy if he failed.

The waiter paused with a loaded tray at his table and said: "I'll be serving your coffee, next."

"Good," Cross mumbled.

He saw the waiter bend with a dead-pan face to serve a white woman who sat across the aisle from him.

"I'm sorry I had to make you wait, Ma'm," the waiter mumbled.

Cross watched the waiter place a tumbler of orange juice before the woman, then a platter of ham and poached eggs. The waiter was about to lift a silver pot of steaming coffee to fill her cup when the woman turned abruptly with her whole body, opening her mouth to speak. Cross saw the woman's plump, naked elbow describe a tiny, swift arc and collide with the coffee pot as it left the tray. There was a ringing clatter of metal and a brown spout of boiling coffee, emitting a cloud of vapor, splashed over the woman's bare arm and on to her bosom. The waiter's movements froze and the woman leaped to her feet and screamed, her face distorted with fury and pain.

"Nigger, you're burning me!" she yelled.

The waiter stood paralyzed, his mouth open. The woman's frantic eyes swept the dining car, then rested upon the table. In one flowing movement, she seized the handle of a silver water pitcher and raised it above her head, her eyes bulging and her darkly rouged lips curled in pain.

Cross was on his feet before he knew it and had traversed the aisle and was standing between the woman and the waiter, fronting the woman, blocking her action with his up-lifted right hand which still clutched his napkin. The woman sighed and lowered her hand.

"You're not hitting me, nigger," the woman said quietly.

"You're not hitting anybody either," Cross said.

The priest rushed to the side of the woman, put his arm about her, then looked from Cross to the waiter. The dining car was full of the rumble of the train speeding over steel rails. In the middle of the car a tall, hard-faced man stood up and glared.

"What's the matter down there?" the man called.

"I'm sorry, lady," the waiter crooned in humility.

The woman pawed at her arm which gleamed a brick red where the coffee had scalded it. Steam still rose from her dress. She began to weep.

"I got something for that burn, Ma'm," the waiter found his tongue and ran toward the rear of the car. The tall, hard-faced man rushed to the side of the priest and now two men were holding the woman and looking at Cross. Cross's hand fell to his side. He was surprised to find that he was smiling; he had acted before he had known it. Another white woman came forward and took hold of the injured woman.

"Darling, I've got something in my purse for burns," the woman said and led her from sight, toward the women's lavatory. The waiter came running with a tube of salve and stood staring helplessly at the backs of the two retreating women.

"It wasn't my fault," he said, looking at the silent, thoughtful faces in the car. "She turned round—like this." He imitated the woman's movement. "And she knocked the pot out of my hand."

The train whistled a long, mournful blast and Cross could feel the centrifugal pull of its speed as it struck a stretch of curving track. He went to his seat and sat before his half-empty plate and stared out of the window. Low voices were murmuring in the car.

"It's a shame— Was she burnt badly?"

"But I *saw* her; she knocked the pot out of his hand . . ."

"What happened? Did somebody hit the woman?"

"Oh, no; it was an accident. It wasn't the waiter's fault."

Cross became aware that the priest had also sat and was staring at him; when their eyes met, the priest looked off toward the snow-filled fields. Cross realized that he had sprung without thinking to his feet to block the woman's tossing the pitcher into the waiter's face and he knew that the priest had leapt up to defend the woman. Both of them had acted before they had been fully conscious of what they had wanted to do. And now shame made them avoid each other's eyes.

"It's a strange world, isn't it?" Cross asked the priest softly.

The priest ruefully smiled his answer and nibbled thoughtfully at a slice of buttered toast.

The injured woman came briskly down the aisle with lips pursed and eyes glazed. The other woman followed.

"I'm going to report you," she told the waiter.

The waiter paused, stared, his lips hanging open in dismay. He shook his head and when he spoke his voice was so high-pitched that it was ludicrous.

"It wasn't my fault, Ma'm." It was a plea issuing from a soul that hated its shame and humility.

"You were careless and I'm going to sue," the woman said.

She tossed her blonde hair and flounced out of the car and another silence reigned. The waiter's face was a mask of distress and Cross chided himself upon ever having thought that he could have been spying on him.

"Oh, there you are!" a sonorous voice came from a hunched-back man who slid into the seat beside the priest.

"What kept you?" the priest asked.

"I went in the wrong direction looking for the diner," the man said, laughing and letting his eyes settle upon Cross's face.

Suddenly the priest beamed at Cross and spoke: "By the way, I'm Father Seldon and my friend here is District Attorney Ely Houston of New York City."

"How do you do?" Cross asked, full of fear, nodding to the hunchback. A District Attorney? *The* Ely Houston of whom he had heard? The celebrated crime-buster . . . ? At once his tensions began to deform the look of the world. Though the two white faces regarded him with friendliness, he projected out upon them an air of the sinister. Maybe the Chicago police had wired ahead and Houston had gotten on the train to apprehend him? How had they come to seat themselves *exactly* at his table? And he recalled that the priest had *expressly* asked the waiter to save the chair next to him for Houston . . . Was Houston armed? He imagined he could see a slight bulge under the man's right armpit and he mentally pictured a gun nestling there . . .

"You live in New York?" Houston asked.

"Yes."

Could this be a trap? He did not volunteer to tell his name and they did not ask him to do so. Would they think it odd that he had not identified himself?

"Mr. Houston and I are very much interested in your people," the priest said to Cross.

Cross knew exactly what the priest meant, but he allowed his eyebrows to lift in surprise. He did not want to be drawn into any discussion with them, yet he did not want to make them feel that he was afraid.

"*My* people? What do you mean?"

Father Seldon chewed industriously upon his mouthful of bacon and eggs and kept his eyes on his plate, answering: "I mean the colored people—"

"Oh," Cross said, giving a play-acting laugh. "But they were born that color. Nobody *colored* them."

Houston and the priest were startled for a moment, then

both of them laughed. Houston continued to examine Cross in a friendly manner; finally he nodded his head affirmatively.

"That's good. I must remember it," Houston said.

"Well, Ely," Father Seldon said, turning and smiling at Houston, "if you should ever run for the Senate, you'd know how not to make a mistake before an audience in Harlem."

"I sure would," Houston admitted.

Cross was through eating and he wanted to go back to his compartment. But he must not act too fast and arouse unnecessary suspicions. He lingered on, studying Houston closely. The man had a huge head of remarkably black, unruly hair; a long, strong, too-white face; clear, wide-apart brown eyes; and a well-shaped mouth that held always a hint of a smile at its corners. His shoulders were Herculean with long arms that terminated in huge hands with delicately strong fingers. The hump on the back was prominent but not in any way as noticeable as Cross would have thought it would be, so naturally did it blend in with the man's general build. Cross had not particularly noticed this deformity when Houston had first sat down, but now he remembered that Houston had moved forward to the table with a motion that slightly resembled that of a creeping animal, holding his body still as he walked. He reminded Cross of a giant, patiently waiting white spider whose temper was never ruffled but whose mental processes ground both fast and exceedingly fine. He had the impression of a man possessing stealthy reserves of physical and emotional strength, and he felt intuitively that this was exactly the kind of man whom he had to fear not only because he was a defender of the law, but because Houston had an ability to delve into life. He was afraid of this man and yet his fear made him want to know him.

"Where's your parish, Father?" Cross asked.

"In Harlem," Father Seldon said, obviously glad to speak of it. "We also operate a school for delinquent boys in Upstate New York. Maybe you've heard of it? The Sanctuary, it's called. We have about sixty Negro boys up there now."

"I see," Cross said.

Houston, whose deformity always made him seem hunched forward, now leaned even more over the table, dawdling his fork in his plate and speaking in a tone that made Cross know that he was expressing thoughts of deep interest to himself, thoughts touched and lighted by passion, almost.

"I'm profoundly interested in the psychological condition of the Negro in this country," Houston said. "Only a few people see and understand the complexity of this problem. And don't think that my interest is solely political. It's not; it was there long before I ever thought of entering politics." He smiled cryptically and let his eyes wander over the icy landscape flowing past the train's window. "My personal situation in life has given me a vantage point from which I've gained some insight into the problems of other excluded people."

Cross's impulses were at war. Was Houston raising the question of the Negro to mislead him before he was told that he was under arrest? Why did he not come right out with what he wanted? He had a foolish desire to reach forward and grab Houston's shoulder and say to him: All right; I know you're after me . . . Let's get it over with . . . His stomach muscles tightened as he checked himself. He knew that Houston, in identifying himself with Negroes, had been referring to his deformity. Houston was declaring himself to be an outsider like Cross and Cross was interested, but he kept his face passive to conceal it.

"The way Negroes were transported to this country and sold into slavery, then stripped of their tribal culture and held in bondage; and then allowed, so teasingly and over so long a period of time, to be sucked into our way of life is something which resembles the rise of all men from whatever it was we all came from," Houston said, the smile on his lips playful and knowing.

"I follow you," Cross said.

"Yes; I see you do," Houston smiled with satisfaction. "We are not now keeping the Negro on such a short chain and they are slowly entering into our culture. But that is not the end of this problem. It is the beginning . . ."

"What do you mean, Ely?" Father Seldon asked.

"I mean this," Houston hastened to explain. "Negroes, as they enter our culture, are going to inherit the problems we have, but with a difference. They are outsiders and they are going to *know* that they have these problems. They are going to be self-conscious; they are going to be gifted with a double vision, for, being Negroes, they are going to be both *inside* and *outside* of our culture at the same time. Every emotional and cultural convulsion that ever shook the heart and soul of Western man will shake them. Negroes will develop unique and specially defined psychological types. They will become psychological men, like the Jews . . . They will not only be Americans or Negroes; they will be centers of *knowing*, so to speak . . . The political, social, and psychological consequences of this will be enormous . . ."

"You are much too complicated, Ely," Father Seldon said. "The problem's bad enough without trying to make it into *everything*. All the colored people need is the right to jobs and living space."

"True," Houston said. "But their getting those elementary things is so long and drawn out that they must, while they wait, adjust themselves to living in a kind of No-Man's Land . . . Now, imagine a man inclined to think, to probe, to ask questions. Why, he'd be in a wonderful position to do so, would he not, if he were black and lived in America? A dreadful objectivity would be forced upon him."

"Oh, Ely, you're always climbing some rocky, goat track of speculation," Father Seldon protested. "Take the simple facts of life just as they are found—"

"That's what I'm doing," Houston said. "And when you look at them closely, those simple facts turn out to be not so simple."

"I think Mr. Houston's close to the truth," Cross said, pretending a smile, relishing an irony that came from his referring both to his own feelings that maybe Houston was trying to track him down and to the aptness of the man's remarks. "After many of the restraints have been lifted from the Negro's movements, and after certain psychological inhibitions have been overcome on his part, then the problem of the Negro in America really starts, not only for whites who will have to become acquainted with Negroes, but mainly for Negroes themselves. Perhaps not many Negroes, even, are aware of this today. But time will make them increasingly conscious of it. Once the Negro has won his so-called rights, he is going to be confronted with a truly knotty problem . . ."

Will he be able to settle down and live the normal, vulgar, day-to-day life of the average white American? Or will he still cling to his sense of outsidedness? For those who can see, this will be a wonderfully strange drama . . ."

"Right," Houston agreed by stabbing the air with his fork. "You're on the beam. Say, where did you go to school? Not that you learn things like that in school . . ."

"Fisk," Cross lied. He rose; this was getting too close. He had to go and hug his black secret. "I'm sorry, gentlemen," Cross smiled at them. "But I must leave. It's wonderful to talk like this."

"Well, sit down and talk," Houston said.

"No; really, I must go. I've a lot to do," Cross lied vaguely. "Good morning." He made his way nervously out of the dining car. Goddamn . . . He was frightened of that hunchback, that outsider who understood *too* much. Houston was a man crammed with guilty knowledge. What weird luck to encounter a kindred type to whom he wanted to talk and who wanted to talk to him. And this would be his life until he found himself an identity behind which he could hide.

The Pullman porter had made up his bed and he was alone; he sat and stared moodily out of the window. He who had a secret to hide loved talking! When one tried to conceal one's self, did not one make one's self conspicuous? And that seductive fear that always surged up in him, how was he to handle it? And why did he always yearn to embrace those delusive fantasies? What unearthly greed made him want to feed upon what he knew to be unreal? He could run away from Dot, Gladys, his mother, but he could not run away from this; it was he and he was it. A tapping came at the door and he rose in dread, his lips parting. Was it Houston? The tapping sounded again and he opened the door.

"Hey, guy," it was the waiter, holding a scared smile on his lips.

"Hello," Cross said, relieved.

"Can I speak to you a minute?"

"Sure; come on in."

The waiter came hesitantly into the compartment.

"Man, that bitch is raising hell," the waiter began. "She's gonna sue the company for damages, and she's saying it's all my fault. If she wins, it's my job." The waiter's eyes danced in his head.

"What're you going to do?" Cross asked.

"I got to get some witnesses," the waiter said. "You know, that priest won't witness for me. Can you feature that? Man, what can we do with these white folks?" He spoke in a low, nervous tone of voice charged with bitterness. "I'm gonna take it up with the union; they'll fight for me. But I got to have evidence, see?"

"Sure," Cross said.

"My name's Bob Hunter," the waiter said.

Cross knew that Hunter was waiting for him to give his name.

"Mine's Addison Jordan," Cross said, feeling that he was speaking out of a dream.

"Would you be a witness if that bitch makes trouble?"

"Sure," Cross said, beginning to hate the man.

"Give me your address and the union'll get in touch with you," Hunter said, taking a frayed address book from his pocket.

"It's 128 West 137th Street," Cross lied, never again wanting to look into Hunter's eyes. He could not explain his unavailability to this man, yet it was wrong to allow him to think that he had his help.

"Thanks," Hunter said, jotting down the address. "You don't live so far from me. Here; take my address. 142 West 144th. If you're ever up there, drop in and we can kill a bottle, hunh?"

"Sure," Cross agreed.

Hunter made him feel his impotence so keenly that he wanted to spit in his face. Hunter's manner of pronouncing certain words bothered Cross and Cross asked him: "Where were you born, Hunter?"

"Texas, man," Hunter said, eyeing Cross closely. "Why?"

"I don't know. Just curious, that's all."

"Say, you need any help with your bags?" Hunter asked.

"Oh, no," Cross said through clenched teeth. "I've only one suitcase."

"Just want to help you, man," Hunter smiled. "We colored folks got to stick together, don't we?"

"Oh, yes," Cross agreed with pretended heartiness.

"Good-bye, now," Hunter said, leaving and closing the door.

Christ Almighty! Hunter was believing that he had his help, that he would be a friend. He had made Hunter a promise that he could not keep, just as he had made his mother, his sons, Dot, Gladys, and Jenny promises that he could not keep . . . His nonidentity was making Hunter believe in the unreal. Cross sighed. He had to break out of this dream, or he would surely go mad. He had to be born again, come anew into the world. To live amidst others without an identity was intolerable. In a strict sense he was not really in the world; he was haunting it for his place, pleading for entrance into life . . . He sat and rested his head in his hands. He must eventually find Bob Hunter and try to square this deception. But why did he care about Bob Hunter? No; it was not Hunter himself that bothered him; it was Hunter's delusive belief in him that he found offensive. He started as another knock came. Hunter again? If so, he'd explain to the man that he could not help him. He rose and opened the door.

"I'm not disturbing you, am I?" Houston asked him, smiling.

"Oh, no," Cross lied. His body seemed suddenly made of soft, melting wax. "Come in."

"Are you sure? I just wanted to talk a little," Houston said.

Houston's manner seemed sincere. Maybe he was wrong? As he talked to Houston, he would be waiting for the trap to be sprung. Houston sat and held out his pack of cigarettes. Cross took one and Houston held his lighter. Cross strove for nonchalance, meeting Houston's gaze with a smile. Houston studied Cross for some minutes. Why in hell doesn't he speak . . . ?

"It's not often that one meets someone who can grasp ideas," Houston began. "If I'm bothering you now, it's a little of your own fault; you ought not to have agreed with me in the dining car." Houston laughed. "You know, to get to the point, I've never had a chance to talk to Negroes like I'd like to. There's something about the Negro in America that almost hypnotizes me, really . . . By the way, quite frankly, talking about this problem does not bother you, does it?"

"Not at all," Cross said, grinding his teeth in anxiety.

"People are so tender-skinned these days," Houston went on. "Everybody's trying to be other than what they really are: something official, approved of, safe—"

"They are afraid," Cross said, suppressing his own fear.

"You strike me as being a man of pretty cool judgment and having some insight into life," Houston said.

Cross wanted to laugh out loud. If the man only knew how lost and guilty and scared he was! How wrapped in anxiety . . . !

"I don't know," Cross said.

"Whenever I've tried to talk to most educated Negroes, I've felt a barrier," Houston continued. "I can understand why they feel constrained. They feel that I'm enjoying their humiliation. And many whites do enjoy talking to Negroes about this problem; it makes them feel superior and secure."

"That's all too true," Cross agreed.

"But this hump on my back ought to give me some licence," Houston argued. "I know what it means to be an object outside of the normal lives of men. I know how it feels to be stared at, to have some silly woman want to touch your hump for luck . . . When I was a child, I hated myself, cursed my ill-fortune; but now I'd not want to give up what my peculiar situation has taught me about life. This damned hump has given me more psychological knowledge than all the books I read at the university.

"My deformity made me free; it put me outside and made me feel as an outsider. It wasn't pleasant; hell, no. At first I felt inferior. But now I have to struggle with myself to keep from feeling superior to the people I meet . . . Do you understand what I mean?"

"I do," Cross said quietly.

"Some men are so placed in life by accident of race or birth or chance that what they see is terrifying," Houston said, carried away by his theme. "Life converts the lives of such men into something almost dreamlike. And I've often wondered why I could not detect this feeling of the outsider in the

Negroes I've met. In America the Negro is outside. Our laws and practices see to it that he stays outside . . . Or, am I mistaken in looking for this in Negroes, Mr.—?"

"Addison Jordan's the name," Cross lied, murmuring softly. Was Houston spying on him? If he acted afraid, Houston would wonder why. The best policy would be to talk frankly, and when he spoke he was talking of himself, a self pushed away from him and described in abstract terms. "Yes, Mr. Houston, the Negro feels exactly what you are asking about. But he hides it. The American Negro, because of his social and economic situation, is a congenital coward. He's scared to reveal what he feels. He fears reprisals from his white neighbors." Cross was feeling how much he was hiding from Houston.

"But they ought to be able to talk to *me* without fear," Houston said with a note of pleading in his voice. "After all, in a psychological sense, I'm a brother to them."

"They're even afraid of you," Cross said, smiling, wondering if Houston too was being ironical.

Cross could feel that Houston sensed the quality of the demonical in him, and he could feel the same in Houston. But this man, of all men, must not get too close to him. He represented the law and the law condemned what he was and what he had done. Cross felt the hot breath of danger as Houston continued.

"My position's difficult," he said. "I feel outside of the lives of men. Yet my job demands that I enforce the law against the outsider who breaks that law."

"How do you manage it?" Cross asked with a constricted throat.

Houston laughed and did not answer.

"Do you have sympathy for those who break the laws of civilization?" Cross felt compelled to ask.

"In a way, yes," Houston confessed. "But it all depends upon *how* the laws are broken. My greatest sympathy is for those who feel that they have a *right* to break the law. But do you know that there are not many criminals who feel that? Most of them almost beg you to punish them. They would be lost without the law. The law's vengeance is what gives meaning to their lives." Houston paused and stared at the floor. "You asked something about civilization . . . Ha-ha-ha! Civilization," Houston repeated the word, letting it roll slowly on his tongue. He looked at Cross, smiled, then asked teasingly: "You call this *civilization*? I don't. This is a jungle. We pretend that we have law and order. But we don't, really. We have imposed a visible order, but hidden under that veneer of order the jungle still seethes."

"But why do you call it a jungle?" Cross asked. "Isn't it normal life and we've tried to hide it with order because it is too terrible, maybe?"

"Maybe," Houston admitted.

"Is not life exactly what it ought to be, in a certain sense? Isn't it only the naïve who find all of this baffling? If you've a notion of what man's heart is, wouldn't you say that maybe the whole effort of man on earth to build a civilization is simply man's frantic and frightened attempt to hide himself from himself? That there is a part of man that man wants to reject? That man wants to keep from knowing what he is? That he wants to protect himself from seeing that he is something awful? And that this 'awful' part of himself might not be as awful as he thinks, but he finds it too strange and he does not know what to do with it? We talk about what to do with the atom bomb . . . But man's heart, his spirit is the deadliest thing in creation. Are not all cultures and civilizations just screens which men have used to divide themselves, to put between that part of themselves which they are afraid of and that part of themselves which they wish, in their deep timidity, to try to preserve? Are not all of man's efforts at order an attempt to still man's fear of himself?"

"And what is man that he has to hide from himself?" Houston asked, smiling; there was a look of frightened delight in his eyes.

Involuntarily Cross drew in his breath and looked past Houston to the bleak landscape of snow sweeping past the train's window. The conversation was making him feel a sense of intense isolation, and, even though Houston was there in the compartment with him, for a moment he was unaware of it. He was man who had killed and fled, man who had broken all of his ties and was free . . .

"Maybe man is nothing in particular," Cross said gropingly. "Maybe that's the terror of it. Man may be just anything at all. And maybe man deep down suspects this, really knows this, kind of dreams that it is true; but at the same time he does not want really to know it? May not human life on this earth be a kind of frozen fear of man at what he could possibly be? And every move he makes, might not these moves be just to *hide* this awful fact? To twist it into something which he feels would make him rest and breathe a little easier? What man is is perhaps too much to be borne by man . . ."

Houston rose quickly; there was intense excitement in his face and Cross grew afraid. Maybe he had talked too much?

"Maybe my theory is too wild," Cross said with hasty self-deprecation.

"No," Houston pulled down the corners of his mouth. "I've had the same notion and I can't get rid of it." Houston looked directly at Cross and smiled. "I *knew* that this existed! By God, I knew that someday I'd hear this from your side of the fence. The Negro *has* to know this. How could he escape knowing it . . . ? He looks right at it every day of his life, every hour . . ." Houston paused, smiled cynically. "All my life I've been haunted by the notion that this life we live is a pretense, and all the more deadly because it is a pretense. And woe to the man who tries to reveal that pretense. *He* is the *criminal* . . ." He pulled deeply at his cigarette and laughed softly. " 'Man's nothing in particular'," he repeated Cross's words. "I think you're pretty close to something there, guy. It's not often that one meets somebody with whom one can talk, somebody who sees that deeply into things . . . Say, we seem to be getting into the city . . . Look, here's my card. Call me up sometimes and we can chat a little, eh? I'd love it."

"Sure," Cross said, rising and taking the card. "I'd be glad to."

Houston left, smiling, seemingly satisfied. Alone, Cross sat again and stared unseeingly at the dreary apartment-building landscape of the Bronx as it heaved into view. Of one thing he was certain: he could never see Houston again. It was Houston's job to bring him to justice. The man's mind seemed to find its recreation by delving directly into problems of consciousness like those that were possessing him. He felt like a bird veering and fluttering toward the wide, unblinking eyes of the crouching cat . . . He had to master himself; he had to steer clear of being always drawn toward that which he dreaded. And, intuitively, he knew that Houston was caught in the same psychological trap. That was why Houston was a District Attorney sworn to uphold a system of law in which he did not really believe. Houston was an impulsive criminal who protected himself against himself by hunting down other criminals! How cleverly the man had worked out his life, had balanced his emotional drives! He could experience vicariously all destructive furies of the murderer, the thief, the sadist, without being held to accountability!

The train slowed and was passing 125th Street and Cross looked down at the wintry drabness of Harlem, at its rows of towering tenements, at black men and women huddled in overcoats, trudging through snowy streets. Well, here I am . . . I've made no promises . . . I'm nobody . . . I'm responsible for nothing . . . He sighed as the train slid into the underground, making for Grand Central Station.

Half an hour later, Cross, lugging his heavy suitcase, followed the crowd down the ramp toward the waiting rooms. As he edged forward, his anxieties began to mount. Care seemed to bring him these compulsive moods which, when they first made their presence felt, when they first declared their emotional authority, were nothing definite. They simply rose seemingly out of nowhere and in defiance of his rational capacity and began seeking their own object; failing to find it, they created it out of what was at hand, anything . . . Cross knew that this was himself acting, and that self was alien to him.

He passed the train's huge, sighing, black engine and longed to become as uncaring and passively brutish as that monster of steel and steam that lived on coal. But, no, his was to feel all of these anxieties in his shivering flesh. Goddamn! To swap the burden of this sorry consciousness for something else! To be a God who could master feeling! If not that, then a towering rock that could feel nothing at all! His life was becoming a tense prayer interspersed with curses. He wondered if the priest felt life as keenly as he did. Or had not the priest become a priest precisely in order *not* to feel it?

Through the bars of the gate he saw crowds milling in the station; porters rushed to and fro; hand-trucks piled with luggage rolled toward the exits; he heard shouts of friends greeting friends. If his apprehensions were true, if Houston were playing a game, he could expect the police to accost him. When he was out of the gate, he saw Houston and Father Seldon smiling and waving at him and he smiled and waved back. He was still safe.

Twice before he had been in New York with Gladys on summer vacations and he knew his way about. He headed for the Grand Central subway station and took the shuttle to Times Square where he changed for a Harlem train and stood at the front window of the first coach with his back to the other passengers, his emotions reading a secret language in the red and amber and green lights that swept past in the noisy night of the underground. At 110th Street he began to wonder where he would get off. Such were now the tiny decisions that clogged his consciousness. He was *too* free! For no reason at all he rode past 110th Street and at 125th Street he decided to get off simply because it was one of the best known thoroughfares in Harlem. Standing uncertainly on the platform, he debated: Maybe 125th Street is *too* crowded; it's just possible I might meet somebody I know . . . He waited for a local and rode to 135th Street and got off and climbed the stairs to the upper world.

Loitering, holding his suitcase, his cheeks stinging from the icy wind, he pondered what direction to take to find a room. When he finally ambled forward, he avoided looking into the faces of the passersby, feeling instinctively that he did not have the right to do so. He was without a name, a past, a future; no promises or pledges bound him to those about him. He had to become human before he could mingle again with people. Yet he needed those people and could become human only with them. Dimly he realized that his dilemma, though personal, bore the mark of the general. The lives of children, too, were subjected to this same necessity; they, too, could become human only by growing up with human beings . . .

He came to Seventh Avenue and walked up to 136th Street, turned left, looking for FOR RENT signs. At last he saw a brick house set well back from the sidewalk with shutters closed and it appealed to him. It was as though his doubt about his right to exist blended with the closed shutters and the distance the house was from the street. He mounted stone steps and rang the bell; the opening door disclosed a woman with a brown face,—a burning cigarette slanting across her chin made her seem sluttish at first—wearing a dark blue dressing gown. He saw the tip of a soiled brassiere struggling to keep her bulging breasts to the dimensions of modesty. She was about twenty-eight or thirty, had hard surfacy eyes that might have indicated that she was limited in her thinking. Woman as body of woman shot through his senses, but he pushed the impulse from him; he was in too much danger now to play around . . .

"What can I do for you?" she asked bluntly.

"You have a room for rent, I think," Cross said, a little taken aback by her abrupt manner. Yet he liked her. She was the kind of woman who would most likely take him for granted and not pry into his past; her attitude seemed to place her in the sane, ordinary events of Harlem life.

"Come on in if you want to see it," she said.

He stepped inside, sat his suitcase in a corner, and followed her down a hallway and up a flight of steps to a second floor. She trailed an odor of tobacco smoke. She opened the door of a large room and threw him a defiant glance.

"There it is," she spoke flatly.

He sized her up as a naïve woman who had created about herself a hard-boiledness of manner to protect a too-believing nature that had been tramped on and abused by sundry men. In appearance, she was intensely feminine, seemingly ready to surrender in a yearning for a happiness which she was certain that she would be cheated out of in the end.

"How much is the rent?" he asked her.

"Ten dollars a week," she said.

"I'll take it."

"You don't have to decide right now," she told him; she seemed to be uncertain of herself.

"I want a room and here is one: large, airy, clean. I'll take it," he smiled at her, took out his wallet and gave her a ten-dollar bill.

"When do you want to move in?" she asked.

"I'm here," he said. "My bag's downstairs. It's simple."

Having identified himself as Addison Jordan, Cross, half an hour later, was lying on his bed, trying to plot out his life.

The weather continued bitterly cold. An icy wind swooped from a bleak sky, ripped against windowpanes, and clawed at passersby in the streets. Cross, overcome by a listlessness which he could not shake off, spent his days either lounging in his room or in the consoling shadows of movie houses. He was Mrs. Hattie Turner's only paying guest and he heard rather than saw her, slightly in her cups at times, stumbling around downstairs in her dining room or kitchen. He learned from a gossipy drugstore clerk that she was a widow who owned her own home, that she drank a little too much, and that she had recently begun to receive the attentions of two men. Most of the time he could hear her playing blues or jazz records whose wild rhythms wailed up to him through the thin flooring. His morbid mood was susceptible to the lonely melodies and, as he tapped his feet to the beat of the tunes, his sense of estrangement became accentuated and he felt more inclined than ever to avoid contact with reality.

The raucous blue-jazz welling up from downstairs was his only emotional home now and he listened with an appreciation he had never had before. He came to feel that this music was the rhythmic flauntings of guilty feelings, the syncopated outpourings of frightened joy existing in guises forbidden and despised by others. He sensed how Negroes had been made to live in but not of the land of their birth, how the injunctions of an alien Christianity and the strictures of white laws had evoked in them the very longings and desires that that religion and law had been designed to stifle. He realized that this blue-jazz was a rebel art blooming seditiously under the condemnations of a Protestant ethic just like his own consciousness had sprung conditioned to defiance from his relationship to his mother who had shrilly evoked in him exactly what she had so desperately tried to smother, had posited in him that which she loathed above all in the world by bringing it too insistently to his attention. Blue-jazz was the scornful gesture of men turned ecstatic in their state of rejection; it was the musical language of the satisfiedly amoral, the boastings of the contentedly lawless, the recreations of the innocently criminal . . . Cross smiled with depressed joy as he paced about his room, his ears full of the woeful happiness of the blues and the orgiastic culpability of jazz.

He had enough money to keep him for awhile, but his pile of dollars was dwindling fast. Each night he vowed that on the following morning he would do something practical about his problem of identity, but the morning found him ready with excuses for inaction. He avoided trying to justify his fear of activity, but in his heart he knew that to exert himself was to invite down upon him those spells of dread; so he remained inert, hoping that by blending his bleak mood with the empty hours he would elude his compulsions.

Of a morning or of an evening he would encounter Mrs. Turner in the downstairs hallway and they would exchange greetings. Whenever she asked him if he were comfortable, he would tell her that everything was all right in a tone of voice that sought to hold her off from him, for he sensed slumbering in her strained manner a nervousness whose content he did not want to know. Now and then he noticed two well-dressed Negroes coming to visit her, but they roused neither his interest nor jealousy.

When she did finally break in on his jealous solitude, it was with a naïve brusqueness that swept him before it and he was again acting with swift heartlessness to save himself. His anxiety rose when he noticed her staring at him. Inflamed, his dread sucked all innocent events into its greedy maw. Was she not suspicious about his background? Why did those two men come to see her? Why were they always *together*? Did not policemen act that way? Why was not Mrs. Turner more relaxed with him of late? He even wondered if she searched his suitcase when he was out . . .

On the morning of the day of the eruption, the coming storm was presaged by the brittle manner of Mrs. Turner who failed to return his greeting in the hallway. At noon she knocked on his door. He made sure that his gun was handy, then rose and opened the door. She stared at him blankly, embarrassed.

"God, I'm rattled today," she complained. "I came up here to say something, and now, for the life of me, I can't remember what it was." She tapped the knuckles of her hand against her forehead. "It'll come back to me in a minute. If it doesn't, then it couldn't've been so *very* important, could it? I'm silly." She forced a smile and left.

Cross was frantic. Had she come up to make sure that he was in his room? He ached to grab her and shake the truth out of her. He was certain that she had not forgotten the object of her errand; a mere failure of nerve had swamped her before she could speak. Quickly he packed his suitcase. Maybe she was trying to tempt him . . . ? Or maybe the cops were waiting downstairs? He sat on the side of the bed and sweated.

What stalled his fleeing was his recollection of past times when he had misread events under the hot promptings of anxiety. Was he wrong now? But too many unanswered questions stood between him and Mrs. Turner's nervousness. He fretted, listening for sounds in the house. No blue-jazz came up now, yet he knew that she was downstairs, alone. If the police cornered him in this room, what could he do? He looked out of the window upon a backyard whose deep snow gleamed bluish in the night. He could jump for it . . . He was suddenly alert, hearing slow footsteps on the upper stairs. Finally the sound of her heels tapped hesitantly along the hallway, then stopped at his door and all was quiet. He ran to the window, hoisted it, shivering in a stream of freezing air. He would never unlock that door until he was satisfied that she was alone. If the police were with her, they would have to bash in the door; meanwhile, he would leap out of the window . . . His suitcase? Hell, he'd just leave it . . .

She was standing quietly at his door. But why? He fingered his gun and waited. At last there came the sound of a congested throat being cleared, then a light sigh. He stiffened as he heard Mrs. Turner's voice:

"Have you gone to bed yet?"

Why hadn't she knocked? And why hadn't she called him by his name? Perhaps she wasn't speaking to him? He decided not to answer. Then a timid rap came at his door.

"Are you sleeping?" she called loudly this time.

"Just a second," he said. He closed the window, adjusted his gun, turned the key, and opened the door cautiously, keeping his weight back of it to slam it shut. She was standing quietly with her back to him. He had opened the door so noiselessly that she was unaware that he was looking at her.

"Yes?"

She whirled, drawing in her breath, looking at him in blank fright.

"You scared me," she sighed, her hands flutteringly protecting her breasts. Then she laughed nervously. "I'm so jittery. I hate like hell to bother you."

A mute begging swam in her dark eyes and his dread vanished.

"What's the matter?" he asked.

"You've *got* to help me," she spoke as though she had debated for days on how to talk to him. "I need your advice about something terribly important."

"Come in," he said.

The dark blue dressing gown made her seem somehow naked, gave her an abandoned air that clothed her body in an appeal of sex. Cross fought shy of it. She moved to the center of the room, not looking at him. He left his door ajar as protection against any unexpected entry. Luckily, his packed suitcase was under the bed, out of sight. She seemed afraid of him; why? Was it the severe reserve that he had imposed upon himself that made her hesitate? He was poised, his feelings mobilized to react violently and suddenly in any direction.

"Mr.—" she looked helpfully at him. "*What's* your name? I must be going out of my mind." She sat and closed her eyes in confusion.

He smouldered. He knew it; she was fishing for information. Did she think that he was so naïve that he would inadvertently blurt out that he was Cross Damon? Yet, he was dubious; his mind behaved.

"Jordan's the name," he flung it at her and waited for her to challenge it.

"Oh, yes. Mr. *Jordan*, I've something to ask you—"

"What is it?"

"I'm in trouble and worried sick . . ."

Cross relaxed a bit. This silly woman . . . Suppose she had *his* trouble? She'd jump out of a window, he thought.

"Okay, Mrs. Turner. What's bothering you?"

"I'm not trying to be fresh— But if you call me Mrs. Turner again, I'll *scream!*" she protested in a sob of complaint.

"All right, Hattie," he relented. "I'll help you if I can."

His words produced a convulsion in her and she clapped her hands to her face and wept. He wanted to console her, but he was afraid of his gesture committing him to more than he knew. She wiped her eyes on the sleeve of her dressing gown and looked off.

"What do you want to tell me?" he asked her gently.

"Maybe I've waited too late to talk," she stammered. "And I don't know what to do . . ." A tremor went through her. "I'm scared I'm being cheated. Oh, why was I such a fool to believe them?" Her face darkened. "If they cheat me, I'll *kill* them!" A crazy light lit her eyes.

"Who are you talking about?" Cross asked.

"They *call* themselves my friends." She was composed now and talked more coherently. "I'm a widow. My husband died six months ago. He left me this house. It's all I got . . . He was a good provider and took care of me. Now, I'm alone, and it's hell when you're a woman and all alone. I'm hounded by men running to me but for one reason: to steal this house. Every time I get to know a man, he's up to some lousy trick . . . I didn't know people were so *bad*." She wagged her head and swallowed, overcome with self-pity. "About a month ago I met two men. One's a real estate broker, Mr. White. The other's a plain-clothes detective, Mr. Mills . . ."

A wave of voluptuous dread engulfed him. He stood, flexed for action. She was pulling a crude confidence trick by pretending to be in trouble and winning his sympathy and trapping him for the police! She noticed his agitation.

"What's the matter? Oh, you'll like Mr. Mills—"

"He's on the police force?" he asked.

"Yes."

"Where's he now?"

"At home, I guess," she answered vaguely.

If she was really trying to deceive him, would she talk about a detective like that?

"How did you meet these men?"

She hung her head bashfully.

"Come on; tell me. How did you meet 'em?" he demanded.

"In a bar," she answered coyly; it had been modesty that had made her hesitate. "Well, they told me how to make some quick money—"

"You mean you're building a printing plant here?" he asked her; she was beginning to amuse him now.

"Oh, no! *That* would be wrong!" she protested, her eyes widening with shock. "They know an old, blind, sick man who wants to sell a $100,000 apartment building. Now, I can get an $8,000 mortgage on my house and they can persuade this old, sick man to sell me his building for $8,000— It's a beauty; I've seen it." Her eyes shone with hope.

"But why's he selling a $100,000 building for $8,000?" Cross asked, trying to make sense out of the picture.

"That's the point," she explained eagerly. "You see, they're friends of the old man. He's about to die; he's blind and'll sign what they ask. I'll get the $8,000 and they'll draw up the papers and the old man'll sign 'em. He'll be dead in a month and can't make trouble, see? Now, that's an attractive proposition to me." She added in a tone of regret: "Of course, I'm giving fifty percent to Mr. White and Mr. Mills."

"Hattie, you're joking," Cross accused her.

"But it's true," she swore. "Ask Mr. White or Mr. Mills if you don't believe me."

"I doubt if they'll talk to me," he said.

"That may be," she admitted. "They're *very* high class men."

Every time he thought that he was going mad, he met somebody else who had already gone mad, but in a nice, sweet sort of way.

"Don't touch a deal like that," he advised her.

"Why not? I'm alone and I need security—"

"But you've got your home—"

"But I want to *do* something! I don't read and I'm tired of listening to jazz all day." She brought her life's problem to him.

"Hattie," he spoke in a stilted manner to force the absurdity of her story upon her, "who's this sick, blind fool who signs strange papers, who's giving you a $100,000 apartment building for $8,000, and who's dying in a month so you'll have things clear?"

"You don't understand," she chided him gently; she was debating if Cross was intelligent enough to grasp the subtlety of her project. "It's not quite fair for the old man," she conceded. "But it's legal. Mr. White says so."

For days he had crept about the house with loaded gun, shaking in fear—all because of a woman with fantasies like these!

"How old are you, Hattie?"

"What's that got to do with it?" she asked indignantly.

Cross knew the game: the sick, blind man, together with White and Mills, had chosen Hattie who didn't like reading and who was tired of jazz as their sucker. Cross studied her full breasts, her plump thighs, her smooth arms . . . Her husband had protected her, but no one else ever would. Men would either want her money or her body, and no doubt they would take both.

"Do any of your friends know White or Mills?"

"No. They don't associate with people like me, Mr. Jordan."

"Hattie, you ever see Mills in the company of his fellow officers?"

"No," she answered readily. "He works alone on very important cases." What Cross was driving at finally hit her and she demanded: "Say, you act like Mr. Mills isn't a real person, like I'm making this up—"

"Oh, Mr. Mills is real, all right. Too real. Hattie, have you a lawyer?"

"No," she laughed gaily. "Mr. White calls 'em *liars*!"

"Hattie, these men are trying to cheat you," Cross told her.

Her eyes widened and she covered her mouth with her hand to smother words she wanted to speak but did not want to hear.

"You *think* so?"

"They're *crooks*!"

"Oh, Mr. Jordan, how *could* they be?"

He ought to leave right now and find another room. Was it his business if this woman wanted to lose her money? If he saved her now, she'd not rest until she had found others to deceive her. Hers was the kind of personality that bred the desire to cheat, and he was certain that, despite her tears of protest, she loved her role. Then why should he hinder her? If Hattie's life was what living was without the screen of civilization, why did he not leave her with it? But it was not for Hattie that he was worrying. What was happening to her made a mockery of his conception of life, offended him and he wanted to stop it.

"Don't see these men anymore," he told her. "And don't give them one damn red cent of your money, see?"

Hattie's mouth gaped open; she stood abruptly, looked wildly about her, then flopped weakly on the bed, shaking with sobs.

"I don't know," she wailed.

"Now, don't cry," he told her. "Everything's all right."

"Men are so *awful*," she lamented.

"They tried to take you," he told her. "Now, you're wise. Break with 'em."

She turned on the bed and looked at him with stricken eyes and he wondered if she had already given them her money. Then suddenly he knew; she had given them her money and did not want to tell him, hoping that before she did, he would tell her something that would redeem the horror and undo her actions!

"What have I done?" she begged him meekly.

"You *didn't* give them your money?"

Her weeping took on a quality of laughter, high-pitched and painful. Cross wanted to kick her. How could anyone be so avariciously dumb? And could he help her now?

"You gave them the money? A check?"

"No," she gasped in reply. "Cash."

"But why cash? We could stop the payment of a check."

"They said deals went quicker with cash. They wanted to close the deal before the old man died . . ."

Had she a right to be alive? Was anybody bound to respect a creature like this?

"How old are you, Hattie?"

"You asked me before," she complained. "Why do you want to know? I'm twenty-nine."

She began talking in a whimper, reliving the events of the morning. "We took a taxi to Mr. White's office and signed the mortgage, then we went to my bank and got a certified check and I cashed it. We stopped and had a drink—"

"Who paid for the taxi?"

"Me. Why?"

"And the drinks?"

"Me. They said I was making the biggest profit. That's the way men do it. I want to be business-like and I did what they said." She dabbed softly at her eyes. "What can I *do* now?"

"Hattie, I want to ask you something and you must answer truthfully. I want you to understand what you've done, see?" he argued gently.

"Yes," she answered, looking at him with dark, placid eyes.

"You were trying to steal a building, weren't you?"

"But it was *legal!*" she defended herself.

"You're lying!" he shouted at her. "I asked you to tell the truth!"

She did not answer; it was odd how respectable she really was. The crime did not offend her; but the idea of it did.

"You don't have to talk to me," he said, rising. "I've been thinking of moving—"

She whirled and clutched him with both of her hands.

"Don't leave me! I need you, God knows— Don't be mad at me. I'll do anything you *say!*" She collapsed on the bed again.

"Hattie, you turned thief and while you were trying to steal from the blind man, they stole your $8,000. It's an old trick," he explained.

"I'll lose my *house*," she wailed. "What must I *do?*"

"Tell the police at once—"

"And I'll get my money back?"

"I doubt it. They're not so foolish to keep that money. That so-called blind man's got it. Mills and White are watching you to see if you get wise. When arc you seeing Mills and White?"

"They're coming tonight."

"I'll talk to them," he said.

She rested quietly against him on the bed and he could feel the heavy, slow beat of her heart. He would try to scare those crooks into giving her her money back, and then he would move at once. He feared getting involved; it was possible that something would go wrong and he would be questioned by the police and his identity would come out. And under no conceivable conditions could he allow his fingerprints to be taken; if that happened, he was lost, for his prints were on file in the Post Office in Chicago and in Washington.

The doorbell rang and Hattie locked her arms about his neck.

"That's them now," she whispered.

"Let's go down," he said.

She rose and went to the mirror and began rearranging her hair, tucking stray curls into their accustomed niches. She turned to him and asked coyly:

"Do I look all right?"

"You're wonderful," he assured her.

"You're so kind to me," she said with eyes round with gratitude. "Come on."

He followed her down the stairs and was standing behind her when she opened the door.

"Good evening, my lady," a tall black man called.

"How are you, Mrs. Turner?" a short brown man boomed.

"Come in," Hattie said. When the men were in the hallway, Hattie gestured toward the tall black man and said:

"Mr. Jordan, this is Mr. White."

"How are you?" Cross asked.

"Fine," White said, eyeing Cross intently. "You're a friend of Mrs. Turner?"

"Sort of," Cross said, turning to the brown man. "And you're Mr. Mills, I take it?"

"That's right," Mills came out with a hearty voice; but his eyes were cold and watchful.

"Come into the living room and sit down, won't you?" Hattie asked them.

"We'd like to speak to you alone, if it's all right, Mrs. Turner," White said, smiling at Hattie.

"But Mr. Jordan wants to ask you some questions about my business," Hattie told them.

"I'm looking after her, gentlemen," Cross said.

There was a split-second silence. The eyes of White and Mills were directly on the face of Cross.

"Sure, sure," White said suddenly, entering the living room.

"Why not?" Mills said, following White in.

Cross knew that he had two tough men on his hands and he had no stomach for the job. White and Mills sat, their overcoats still on, their hats on their knees, their eyes never straying from Cross's face. Hattie stood in the doorway, demure and anxious. Cross lingered in the center of the room, cleared his throat and waded in.

"Let's get to the point," he began. "I'm wise to the game. You want to cough up her money and call it quits?"

"Who in hell are you?" White shot at him.

"Does it matter?" Cross countered.

"Are you interested in real estate?" Mills asked him.

Cross knew that Mills was asking if he would be *their* partner in cheating Hattie.

"No deals," Cross said. "Can we settle this between ourselves?" He found himself referring obliquely to the police long before he had wanted to. "Where's the money you took from her?"

White turned to Hattie and asked:

"Mrs. Turner, are you letting *him* horn in on this? He's after money, that's all! Is this the man who walked in one morning with a suitcase? Haven't we been fair with you? Are you out of your senses?"

Hattie blinked and Cross knew that she was already influenced by White's words.

"I don't want her money," Cross said. "I advised her to get a lawyer. Then she can make any deal she likes. Where's her money?"

"In a bank," Mills said flatly and laughed. "You think I carry money like that around on me at night?"

"When can you give her her money?" Cross demanded.

"If she wants to drop the deal," Mills said, "she can. She can have her money in four days—"

"She wants it now," Cross said. "Look, you were going to tell her that the blind man ran off with her money, or some such tale. And you're here tonight to see how she's feeling. Four days from now, you'll be in California . . ."

Mills rose and stood before him, his eyes hard and his lips flexed with anger. Cross grasped the gun in his pocket.

"Don't accuse me of being a thief," Mills warned. "I know a thing or two. I've got police connections here in Harlem—"

"You're no cop," Cross shot at him.

"No cop, hunh? Listen, I can have you put on ice 'til this deal is cleaned up! Now, get *wise!*"

Cross's ardor suddenly waned. Mills was no policeman, but he could slip a ten-dollar bill to a cop and he could be picked up and put in the Tombs for investigation. The police could always say that he resembled somebody they were looking for. His fingerprints would be taken . . . He looked at Hattie who was waiting for him to save her and he cursed himself. He would stall for time, coach Hattie to talk to the police, and then vanish. He plotted his next move, hating himself. He had to make Hattie think that he was not backing down and, at the same time, he had to appear to compromise with White and Mills.

"You can get her money in four days?" he asked, feeling that self-loathing would choke him.

White looked at Mills; they were uncertain.

"Sure," Mills said, trying to hide his surprise.

"Will you give her that in writing?" Cross asked.

"Sure; why not?" White agreed, but he was baffled. He took out his fountain pen and a sheet of paper and began writing.

"Oh, I'm so glad," Hattie sighed.

Cross dared not look at her. Mills backed off into a corner and stared appraisingly at Cross. Cross knew that the man was trying to figure him out.

"Why don't you come in on this deal with us?" Mills asked again.

"I'd feel safe then," Hattie said.

"No," Cross growled. He longed to be as far from this dopey Hattie and these wily crooks as space could take him.

"Are you on the level?" Mills asked.

"Are *you?*" Cross countered cynically.

Hattie suspected nothing. Of what use was pity? Did not

pity only choke up your life and make it into something which others ought to pity? White handed him a slip of paper which he did not bother to read, for he knew that it was worthless; he handed the paper to Hattie and watched her eyes devour it.

"Thank you," she breathed.

"Is everything all right?" Mills asked.

"Of course," Hattie said, smiling sweetly.

"Well, I suppose we'll be getting on," White said.

"Yes," Mills said. "We're late now."

"I'll see you Thursday?" Hattie asked.

"Of course; good night," White said.

The door closed and Cross watched them rush down the steps to the sidewalk. They paused, looked back, all round them, then hailed a taxi and climbed in; the taxi, no doubt at their bidding, shot off wildly down the snow-covered street.

"They seemed to be in a hurry," Hattie sighed.

He saw her eyes grow thoughtful and he wondered what processes of ratiocination were transpiring in her brain.

"You think maybe they were honest after all?" she asked.

If one good smack on her chin could have awakened her to the truth, he would have given it. Instead he pushed her violently from him.

"Get away from me," he growled.

She backed off, trembling. "What's the matter? I don't understand you," she gasped. "You helped me, then you turn wild!"

He saw her bleak face and relented. What good was there in punishing this irresponsible creature?

"I'm sorry," he breathed.

She waited to see if danger had gone out of him, then she circled his waist with her plump arm and led him toward the stairs.

"Are you angry with me?"

"No."

"I could go for you," she crooned, regaining confidence and hugging him tightly. "You saved me. Say, how about a drink?"

"God, yes; I need one," he said.

"Go to your room. I'll bring up a bottle."

He was lying on his bed when she came with a bottle and two glasses. He had a big swig and felt the whiskey numbing his stomach; he felt better. He saw her moist, round, giving eyes.

"Why are you so blue?" she asked.

"I'm thinking," he said.

"About me?"

"How could anybody be with you and not think about you?"

She bent forward and kissed him. He smelt the odor of her hair and wondered what could one do with a woman like this but love her even when one did not love her? She was woman as body of woman for him now and he wanted her. He laid her on the bed and she struggled up.

"Wait," she murmured. "I'll be back in a minute."

She kissed him and went quickly out of the room. A moment later he heard water running in the bathroom. He leaped from the bed, grabbed his suitcase and softly groped his way out, tiptoeing. In the hallway he heard the sound of water still coming from the bathroom and he could see a light shining from beneath the sill. He crept down the stairs to the front door and paused; he opened it and saw a bluish haze hanging in the dim streets. It was late, far past midnight; the world was wrapped in silence. He scampered over the snow to the sidewalk with Hattie hovering as a poignant image in his mind. He reached Seventh Avenue, walked to Lexington and ducked into a subway, relieved that he was free, free to wrestle again with the tyranny of himself. The fear induced in him by the cheap threat of White and Mills drove home to him the unreal nature of his life; he was defenseless. He had to break out of this dream. Hattie was already the melancholy memory of a woman he had tried to help and failed. He felt that his fleeing was best for her, not the best that could be for her, but *his* best.

Cross's opportunistic rejection of his former life had been spurred by his shame at what a paltry man he had made of himself. What little external pressure had compelled him to this stance was also a part of that self which he had rejected, for he alone had been responsible for what he had done to

Gladys and Dot. His consciousness of the color of his skin had played no role in it. Militating against racial consciousness in him were the general circumstances of his upbringing which had somewhat shielded him from the more barbaric forms of white racism; also the insistent claims of his own inner life had made him too concerned with himself to cast his lot wholeheartedly with Negroes in terms of racial struggle. Practically he was with them, but emotionally he was not of them. He felt keenly their sufferings and would have battled desperately for any Negro trapped in a racial conflict, but his character had been so shaped that his decisive life struggle was a personal fight for the realization of himself.

What really obsessed him was his nonidentity which negated his ability to relate himself to others. He realized that what was happening to him now had been buried implicitly all along in his past life, had slumbered there in the form of a habit of acute reflection, in the guise of a propensity toward a certain coldness in judging even those closest to him, in a manner of forgetting too quickly what had been a long time in or with him, all because none of it really interested him.

He had long yearned to be free of all responsibilities of a certain sort, but that did not imply that he had no capacity for responsibility in general. What irked him about his past responsibilities had been their dullness, their tenuity, their tendency simply to bore him. What he needed, demanded, was the hardest, the most awful responsibility, something that would test him and make him feel his worth. And his South Side Chicago environment had held forth no hope of his ever being able to find any such responsibility in it.

Where could he find such experiences, such spheres of existence? In the main he accepted the kind of world that the Bible claimed existed; but, for the sufferings, terrors, accidental births, and meaningless deaths of that world, he rejected the Biblical prescriptions of repentance, prayer, faith, and grace. He was persuaded that what started on this earth had to be rounded off and somehow finished here.

He had reckoned that his getting rid of the claims of others would have automatically opened up to him what he wanted, but it had merely launched him to live in the empty possibility of action whose spell, by purging reality of its aliveness, had bound him more securely in foolish drifting that he had experienced in all the past. The world became distant, opaque; he was not related to it and could find no way of becoming so.

It was this static dreamworld that had elicited from him those acts of compulsion, those futile attempts to coerce reality to his emotional demands. There was in him a need for a stabilization of his surroundings. The world of most men is given to them by their culture, and, in choosing to make his own world, Cross had chosen to do that which was more daringly dangerous than he had thought.

One walks along a street and strays unknowingly from one's path; one then looks up suddenly for those familiar landmarks of orientation, and, seeing none, one feels lost. Panic drapes the look of the world in strangeness, and the more one stares blankly at that world, the stranger it looks, the more hideously frightening it seems. There is then born in one a wild, hot wish to project out upon that alien world the world that one is seeking. This wish is a hunger for power, to be in command of one's self. Because Cross had lied, killed, and fled, it was to a sense of guilt that his heart leaped when he looked about him and felt his lostness . . .

Toward the ideology of Communism his attitude was ambivalent; he found as much in it to hate as to admire. He knew the imperialistic wars of the Western World far too well to be snared into believing that Stalin was the historic essence of the Satanic; even if Stalin had personally eaten fifteen million human beings, it did not cancel the destructions of entire civilizations and the barbarous slaughter of countless millions by the arms of the Western World during the past four hundred years. Further, he was constrained by logic to accept Marxism as an intellectual instrument whose absence from the human mind would reduce the picture of the processes of modern industrial society to a meaningless ant heap. He was also compelled by facts to accept the Communist notion that one form of social consciousness, designated as bourgeois, had been outlived, but he emphatically spurned the slavish class consciousness with which the Communists sought to replace it. Above all he loathed the Communist attempt to destroy human subjectivity; for him, his subjectivity was the essence of his life, and for him to deny it was as impossible as it would have been for him to deny himself the right to live.

In his weighing of ideas, Fascism possessed the same vitally negative merit of Communism in sensing the imminent end of a system of economic domination in the Western World, but what revulsed him in the fascist doctrine was its boast that it needed no ideological justification for its desire to rule. Life was denuded of all meaning when a Hitler could kill millions of men by an efficiently scientific method of mass industrial extermination simply because he did not like the color of their skins or the shape of their nostrils.

All of these rejections, plus that of himself and his past, were behind the man Cross as he walked up the exit of the stairway of the 116th Street subway station the night he had fled from Hattie and started looking again for a room in which to hide and try to think out his future. When he reached the sidewalk the weather had turned to sleet and it was bitter cold. Lugging his suitcase through the slush underfoot, he leaned against the stinging wind and squinted his eyes, seeking a FOR RENT sign. He was tired; it was after two o'clock in the morning. Now and then he felt the pavement beneath his feet trembling from the rush of underground trains. Ahead he saw faint blobs of traffic lights wink from red to green and back again. Here and there a few neon signs glowed, half lost in murkiness. He went into a little bar that was almost empty and ordered a whiskey.

As he sipped his drink, his eyes fell upon a series of crude signs on the dingy walls. He smiled as he read: IF YOU SPIT ON THE FLOOR AT HOME, YOU MAY DO SO HERE. Under the wording was a drawing of a coarse-faced man in a nicely furnished room reclining in an easy chair; his legs were stretched out and his feet rested upon a sofa. He was expectorating upon the floor, much to the horror of his long-suffering wife who was on her hands and knees with a scrub rag trying to keep the floor clean.

Another sign read: NO PROFANITY IN HERE, PLEASE. IF YOU DON'T BELIEVE IN GOD, THEN WHY DO YOU CURSE HIM ALL THE TIME? Cross gave a silent laugh and studied the drawing illustrating the philosophical profundity of that question. There was a drunkard at a bar with a half-filled bottle before him and he was represented as giving forth a string of vile oaths whose meaning was conveyed by exclamation points, question marks, and asterisks.

There was still another sign which read: DO NOT ASK FOR MR. CREDIT. HE DIED A LONG TIME AGO AND WE BURIED HIM. Under this drawing was the picture of a neglected grave in a hideously dilapidated cemetery. Engraved on the headstone was: MR. BROKE, BORN APRIL 1, 1949—DIED APRIL 2, 1949.

Cross wondered who thought up such legends. Oh, yes . . . That image of the grave! That reminded him that *he* was supposed to be dead! How fantastic it seemed! How did his grave look? And where was it? He did not even know the name of the cemetery . . . He sighed and closed his eyes. Wonder what did Gladys engrave on my tombstone . . . ? He visualized big words hewn into marble:

CROSS DAMON

1924——1950

In Loving Memory

Would Gladys say more than that? Hell, would she even say *that* much . . . ? Perhaps she might; people had a way of forgiving you when you were dead. And why not? You could not hurt them then and maybe their forgiving you was an expression of their joy at your being dead . . . ?

He downed his last drop of whiskey, then held his breath, caught in the grip of a paralyzing idea. Good God! Why in the name of all that was reasonable had he not thought of it before? It was *too* easy, that's why. He had often read about such things in newspapers; it had been reliably reported that underground Communists had established new identities by such methods. Why not? It more than answered his problem. Sure; all he had to do was to go to a cemetery and find the name of a man born on his birthday or any birthday that would make his present age and appearance seem normal! Why, if he were clever about it, he could even have a birth certificate! He had been pounding his brain for days for a new identity, and all he had to do was go to a graveyard and copy down a name. And there might be a hell of a wide choice; he could even afford to be critical about whose name he took. First thing in the morning he would go. He was excited.

"Hey, another whiskey here," he called to the bartender. When he was being served, he asked: "Say, you know where a guy can find a room for rent in this neighborhood?"

The bartender pursed his lips, put down the whiskey bottle and stood thoughtfully.

"I know a Mrs. Crawford who lives up the street," the bartender told him. "She's been asking me to send her somebody. She's kind of old, but she's got a nice place. I lived there once myself, 'fore I got married."

Cross took down the number; he gulped his drink, thanked the bartender and was about to go when the door flew open and two Negro policemen entered. Dread froze him to his stool. One cop sat to one side of him and the other went to the end of the room and looked about the bar carefully, his eyes at last resting upon Cross's face. Cross scarcely breathed. Was this *it*? He kept his head down, hiding his features. Goddamn, why did he always have to have that suitcase with him? He looked up and saw one of the cops coldly examining the reflection of his face in the mirror opposite him. Yes, they were looking him over; there was no doubt about it. He slipped his hand slowly into his overcoat pocket and grasped the gun. Then he started violently.

"It's okay, Jerry. Set it up in the back," one of the cops boomed out.

"Right," the bartender said.

Both cops disappeared wordlessly into the rear and Cross felt his hot muscles relaxing. The bartender took a bottle of whiskey back to the cops. When he returned, Cross said in a whisper: "I thought they were raiding the joint."

"*Them?* Hell, naw. They want a drink. They're on duty this time of night and they're just making sure no spotters are about, that's all. Say, you gonna take that room?"

"Yeah, sure," Cross said. "Thanks a million."

Ten minutes later he was climbing dirty, smelly stairs to the door of Mrs. Crawford. He rang the bell, waited, then he heard an old woman's voice ask: "Who is it?"

Cross told her that Jerry, the bartender, had sent him for a room. She opened the door and peered at him. She was about sixty years old and had on a dressing gown. She'll be safe, Cross thought.

"Oh, you want a room? Kind of late, you know . . . Well, come in."

"I just got into the city," Cross lied.

"I see," she said, trudging slowly down the darkened hallway.

Mrs. Crawford was a brown-skinned, talkative, motherly, and slightly crippled old woman who was rather nervous at his sudden appearance.

"When did Jerry tell you 'bout this room?"

"A few minutes ago, Mrs. Crawford. I just left the bar," Cross assured her.

He accepted the room, paid his rent and an hour later he was in a warm bed and feeling more hopeful than he had felt in a long time. Soon he would have an identity. But what kind of man would he pretend to be? What kind of beliefs would he pretend to have? Would he pretend studiousness or gaiety? He would choose the kind of disposition that would make people like him and accept him. Was not that the way life was lived in this world? Didn't people select deliberately the types of personality that would get them the kind of attention that they thought would help them? He laughed silently on his bed, enjoying the insight into life that his outlandish position was giving him. He felt that at last he was beginning to grapple with his problem, was getting near its meaning.

The next morning near ten o'clock Cross was roused from sleep by the solicitously soft voice of Mrs. Crawford calling to him through the partly opened door.

"Good morning. Wouldn't you like a hot cup of coffee?" she asked, smiling shyly.

"I'd love some, Mrs. Crawford. Would you mind if I came out in my bathrobe?" he asked her.

"Come right along. Make yourself at home here, son," she said. "I've no dining room; you'll have to take it in the kitchen."

"That's all right with me," he told her.

He liked her and felt secure; she was homey. Unlike Hattie, her concerns were simple. He slipped into his bathrobe and lumbered into a spotlessly tiny kitchen.

"Hope I didn't wake you up too early," Mrs. Crawford mumbled.

"Not at all. I should have been up hours ago," Cross said, sipping black coffee and wondering about how to find a graveyard.

"That weather outdoors beats everything!" Mrs. Crawford exclaimed.

Through the fogged windowpane Cross could see a world of churning bits of snow and could hear the wind whimpering like a thing in agony as it tore past the corner of the building.

"Looks like we're in for it," Cross commented.

"A body needs something hot in the stomach first thing in the morning, especially on days like this," Mrs. Crawford proceeded to give her views on life.

She was skinny, brittle, fragile in her bone structure; her eyes were sunken, cloudy, weak.

"There's nothing better than a good cup of hot coffee," he agreed, feeling that this woman was lucky to have such elementary preoccupations.

"Planning to stay in Harlem long?"

"I don't know yet," he answered honestly.

"Where're you from, if you don't mind my asking?"

"Not at all; I'm from Maine," he lied, naming the first state that popped into his mind.

"Maine? Well, what do you know about that! Are many colored people up there?"

"Plenty," he continued lying, beginning to relish it.

"I didn't know that," Mrs. Crawford sighed over a world much too big and complex for her. "Well, you're young and you keep on the go," she philosophized. "Me, I'm old and I'm not too long for this life. I just pray and keep my house straight and wait for the Good Lord to call me home." Her voice was charged with courageous resignation.

"Oh, no! You'll be around for a long time yet," Cross spoke with make-believe sincerity. She looked as if she would die in two weeks. Malnutrition, maybe, he said to himself.

"The only thing I worry about is keeping up my insurance payments," the old woman went on, as though talking to herself. "I'll have just enough money to lay me away decently. I don't want a pack of strangers toting this old body of mine off to some Potter's Field. If I thought something like that would happen to me, why, I wouldn't be able to sleep at night. Before my poor husband died he bought us a little plot out in the Woodvale Cemetery. That's where my blessed husband's sleeping now. I'll be joining him soon, please God."

Cross's interest heightened. Woodvale Cemetery? And he was *looking* for a cemetery!

"Is Woodvale a nice cemetery?" he asked casually.

"It's simply *beautiful*," the old woman cried enthusiastically. "I'm so happy I'll be sleeping there till God calls me to rise from the dead." She paused and looked quizzically at Cross. "But son, you're young. How come you interested in cemeteries?"

"I was thinking about taking out some insurance," Cross explained. "I'm alone too and I've got to look out for myself. I may as well buy a plot somewhere . . ."

"You're wise," Mrs. Crawford approved. "Ain't too many young folks these days serious enough to worry about important things like that . . ." Her dim eyes shone. "Just a minute—I want to show you something." She rose and hobbled hurriedly out of the kitchen.

Poor woman, Cross thought. Mrs. Crawford returned with a huge bundle wrapped in thick brown paper. She placed it upon the kitchen floor and commenced to unwrap it. Cross saw a pile of filmy summer clothing, each piece of which was delicately folded in white tissue paper.

"This is what I'm going to wear," Mrs. Crawford said, looking at him appealingly. "Don't you think it's nice?"

"Yes; it's nice," Cross said, puzzled. "But where're you going to wear it?"

"When I pass to the other shore to meet Jesus, this is what they're going to dress me in," Mrs. Crawford told him sweetly.

Cross felt that he had blundered; he quickly bent forward and fingered the aged material. There was a pearl handled fan made of large, colored feathers; there was a faded silk, cream-colored parasol; there was a long, tea-colored ruffled voile dress which had huge pleats and a décolleté neck-line; and there was a pair of fragile, high-heeled slippers. Cross noticed that she had even included a pair of nicely starched drawers and a pair of nylon stockings from which the price tags had not been removed. Christ Almighty! The woman was acting as though she was preparing to go to a cocktail party. He opened his mouth to tell her that her burial wardrobe was for summer and not this raging blizzard that held forth outdoors, but thought better of it. Yes, each time he thought that he was mad, he met someone else with a head full of sane, socially acceptable madness.

"Where is Woodvale?" he asked gently, sighing.

"Out near White Plains—"

"Is it a colored cemetery?" he asked.

"*Strictly* colored," Mrs. Crawford assured him. "And only the best colored folks are buried there. You'd be surprised at how well they keep those graves. Why, in the summertime, it's like a garden. I was lucky to get my plot when I did, for the prices have gone up something awful."

"You're right," Cross said, thinking that he would go out to White Plains at once. "Thanks for the coffee, Mrs. Crawford."

"'Twasn't nothing, young man," she told him.

Half an hour later Cross was hurrying toward the subway through the raging blizzard. He was grateful for the lack of visibility, for that would obscure him when he was pillaging the tombstones of the graveyard for names and dates. He asked himself musingly if anything could be wrong with his taking the name of a dead man for his own? Did not parents every day bestow the names of the dead upon their children? Well, instead of letting someone give him the name of a dead man, he would take one.

Arriving at White Plains, he inquired his way to the Woodvale Cemetery, which he had to reach by a long bus ride and then tramp almost a mile through deep snowdrifts. At last the cemetery came into view, veiled by demonic snowflakes dancing crazily in the winter wind. Myriads of white marble crosses and tombstones stretched away in a white, shaking shroud. The huge, iron gate was locked; no one was about.

He climbed over the fence and stood in the white silence with a feeling of unreality filling him. He went to the nearest grave and peered at the inscription on the headstone: MARY HAWKINS. The hell with her . . . He searched farther and read: MAYBELLE SMITH. Shucks . . . Even people with the name of Smith have to die . . . He looked at yet another which said: BESSIE ROUNDTREE. Hell, were only women buried here? He walked a good way into the cemetery, looking over his shoulder to make certain that he was not being observed. He approached another batch of graves, bent and wiped snowflakes from a slab of marble with his hand and read: JAMES HOLIDAY—1934–1948. Hunh . . . Cross was thoughtful. Only fourteen years old, just a kid . . . He looked farther, reading: NEIL BROWN—1870–1950. That old bugger had a long span, he commented. But he's not for me . . .

It was proving harder to find a good birth date and a name than he thought. Snow was heaping up on the crown of his hat and his feet ached with cold. He stood, breathing gusts of vapor into the snowflakes that flitted about his face and clogged his eyelids at times. Dammit, he couldn't give up now. But an hour later he had not found what he wanted; he had seen graves containing young girls, old men, babies, middle-aged women, the twin graves of husband and wife, of brother and sister, all kinds of graves, white and eternally silent in the shuddering snow. But all these dead seemed to have died either too early or too late for him to use their abandoned names . . . Hell, there *must* be some young men here my age, he told himself bitterly, his teeth chattering, his body shivering in an icy gale. Finally, when he discovered that he was examining the same graves twice, he found that he had somehow overlooked a plain, obscure grave whose cheap, wooden board at the head of the mound read: LIONEL LANE—1924, June 29th–1950, March 3rd . . . Ah, this was something like it. The guy had been buried only two days ago . . . He scraped the clinging snowflakes from the headboard and read the rest of the inscription:

Sleeping secure in the Faith of the Second Coming of Our Lord and Savior, Jesus Christ, Amen . . .

Awkwardly, Cross took out his pen and ripped off a bit of paper from his notebook and copied down the name and the date; he hesitated at the expression of sentiment regarding Jesus' second coming; but, what the hell, take it all down; it couldn't do any harm. Had this guy been widely known? Would it be wise for him to go to the Bureau of Vital Statistics and ask for a birth certificate in the name of Lionel Lane? What proofs of identity would the clerks ask of him? He would have to invent a good pretext . . . Well, he would try it. What had he to lose? After all, the identity he was seeking did not have to be foolproof; he wanted a mask of normality just airtight enough to enable him to start living again without too much fear. He would create his own past if he could find a respite of but a few weeks.

But if he wanted to assume Lionel Lane's name, should he not try to learn something about him? Where he had worked? How he had lived? Did he have a family? His ardor ebbed somewhat when he realized that he had not the remotest idea of how to find out about the man. Oh, there must be a caretaker somewhere around this cemetery who could tell him if Lane had belonged to a church, or the name of the funeral home from which he had been buried . . . He looked about in the sea of frightened snowflakes, full again of that old sense of dread and criminality. But there's nothing to be scared of . . . Find the caretaker and tell him that Lionel Lane had been an old pal of his, that he had just come from the army and had learned that poor Lionel was dead, and that he was searching for Lionel's folks . . .

Cross struggled through the snowdrifts back to the huge, iron gate and peered about for signs of life, a house . . . Nothing but silence and flurrying flakes of white. He was about to leave when he noticed on the gate a square, wooden plaque whose face was obscured by a thick layer of snow crystals. He cleaned the flakes away with his coat sleeve and read: Address all inquiries to Mr. Sloane, 6 Pine Road, White Plains . . .

More frozen than alive, he dragged himself out of the cemetery and tramped back to the street. When the bus rolled silently toward him out of the scudding swirls of whiteness and stopped, he stumbled on board and had difficulty getting his money out of his pocket, so frozen were his fingers.

"Looks like you came out of a deep-freeze," the bus driver said.

"You can say that again," Cross mumbled.

At the office of the Woodvale Cemetery in White Plains, Cross found a colored girl of about eighteen years chewing gum behind a typewriter. In reply to his plea to find the relatives of his "long lost pal", Lionel Lane, the girl said:

"You'd better come back this afternoon at four when Mr. Sloane's in, because I'm not allowed to give out information like that to anybody—"

"What harm could that do?" Cross asked. "My friend's dead now. Come on, have a heart." Cross aped the sentiment of nostalgic distress. "I want to see his mother—"

"Why don't you try his pastor at his church?" the girl suggested.

"I don't know his church or his pastor—"

"And you say you were an old, dear friend of his, hunh?" the girl asked him in a light, taunting voice.

"But I never asked him about his religion—"

"He lived in Harlem," the girl said. "But that's all I can tell you. I'm sorry, but you'll have to see Mr. Sloane . . ." The girl resumed masticating her gum and turned back to her typewriter.

Though disappointed, he decided not to press her any further; he thanked her and left. If untoward events developed in the future, he did not want that girl to recall that a young man had been demanding details about Lionel Lane . . . Dammit, he had failed in his first essay. But perhaps he could phone the office later in the afternoon and pretend that he was . . . Whom could he pretend to be? He stood musing in the street amid the circling columns of snow, then he looked again at the scrap of paper upon which he had written the data he had taken from the wooden headboard of Lionel Lane's grave, rereading the words: Sleeping in the Faith of the Second Coming of our Lord and Savior, Jesus Christ, Amen . . . Where and when had he heard words like those before? They reminded him of something. Yes! Of course!

That inscription expressed the cardinal article of faith of the

Seventh Day Adventist Church! He had, in his childhood in the Deep South, met and known adherents of that denomination. True, it was a guess, but not at all a bad one. His task, now, was to find the Seventh Day Adventist Church from which Lane had been buried. The girl had said that Lane had lived in Harlem, and it would be safe to assume that the church was there . . .

During the subway ride to Harlem, he pondered over the difficulties involved in his quest. As the excitement wore off he realized that he was attempting a long shot gamble. For instance, he did not know if Lionel Lane had been born in the State of New York or not. Suppose it turned out that Lionel Lane had been born in, say, Ohio? What could he do then?

At 110th Street he got out of the subway, went into a drugstore and consulted a telephone directory. Ah . . . Here were three addresses of Seventh Day Adventist organizations in Harlem. One was on West 135th Street and another was on West 123rd Street; and there was still another organization called the Seventh Day Adventist Conference on West 150th Street . . . Yes, he'd call the Conference. He dialed and heard a suave, masculine voice answering:

"Hello."

"This is the Eastern Insurance Company," Cross lied smoothly. "I wonder if you'd be kind enough to give us some information, please?"

"Yes. What is it?"

"We are searching for the address of a man's family; the man, we believe, was buried from one of your Harlem churches about two or three days ago. The name is Lane, Lionel Lane. Could you tell us where his parents are living? Or do you know the last address of the deceased?"

"Just a moment, please."

Cross waited, looking uneasily over his shoulder at people shopping at the counter of the drugstore.

"We have no direct information here, sir. But I understand that there was a funeral three days ago at our Ephesus Church at 101 West 123rd Street. Why don't you get in touch with Elder Wiggins there?"

"Thank you," Cross said.

He dialed Elder Wiggins and, still impersonating an insurance official, asked for the whereabouts of the Lane family.

"Oh, yes," the gentle, tired voice of a man came over the wire. "We held services for the Departed at our church last Thursday. But I cannot help you very much, sir. My secretary's not here for the moment. But I know that the Lane family lives in Newark, New Jersey. The Departed lived here in Harlem, I'm fairly certain. You see, the Departed was not himself a member of our church. His mother, Mrs. Mary Lane, is one of our oldest members and, though she lives in Newark, she wanted her son buried from our church. If you'd care to phone later today . . ."

"It won't be necessary," Cross said. "Our Newark office will be able to locate the family. I thank you very much."

So Lionel Lane had parents in New Jersey. Well, he'd go there right now. Twenty minutes later Cross was in the Pennsylvania Station, hunched over a Newark telephone directory, feverishly thumbing the thin, crisp leaves, searching under L's. Good Lord, here was a long list of names of Lanes: there was an Albert Lane, a Bernard Lane, a Daniel Lane, a Harry Lane . . . and then there came Mary Lane . . . This undoubtedly was Lionel Lane's mother. He jotted down the address and an hour later he was in Newark, inquiring for the street on which the Lanes lived. He was so excited that he had to calm himself when he learned that the street was located in the heart of the local Black Belt: 17 Broome Street in the Hill District. *This* was it!

When he reached the bleak neighborhood, he slowed and mapped out his plan of attack. Presuming that he was on the track of the right family, to go to the Lane house directly and ask questions carried a risk. If, when carrying the name of Lionel Lane, something happened to him and caused that name to get into the newspapers, someone might recall that a stranger had been around asking vague questions. It would be better if he posed as a social worker or a salesman of some sort and in that way pick up bits of information from neighbors or shopkeepers. What kind of a family were the Lanes? Working class or professional? If they turned out to be a family of prominent citizens, then it would be almost impossible to go to the Bureau of Vital Statistics in a city like this and

impersonate Lionel Lane and demand a birth certificate without getting into serious trouble. He first had to get hold of
some basic facts.

The Lane house proved to be a ramshackle, wooden affair,
sitting unpainted on a run-down dirty, treeless street in a
bleak slum area. If Lionel Lane came out of this hellhole, then
not many people of any consequence could have known him.
But was this the house of the family of Lanes whose son was
buried in Woodvale?

At that moment he saw an elderly Negro postman bent
under the weight of a mailbag coming toward him over the
snowy street.

"Say," Cross stopped him, "have you got a minute? Maybe
you can help me?"

The postman paused, spat a stream of tobacco juice into a
snowdrift, eyed Cross cynically and mumbled: "That depends
on what kind of help you want. I'm on my rounds. But I'll
spare you a minute."

"I'm from the Central Credit Bureau of New York City,"
Cross lied fluently. "I'm trying to track down a young chap
by the name of Lionel Lane."

"Lionel Lane?" the postman echoed, smiling ironically. "He
owed money somewhere?"

"Confidentially, yes."

"Well, the people who let him have money didn't have
good sense," the postman observed, spitting another spout of
tobacco juice. "And you got a fat chance of collecting, 'cause
that baby's where you can't get at 'im. He's six feet deep
with snow in his face. He kicked off three days ago. Had
consumption—"

"Did he live with his family?"

"When he didn't have any dough, he did; and that was
almost all the time. He holed up somewhere in Harlem, I'm
told, with a dame. Didn't want his family to know where he
was when he was with that dame. Had to forward all his mail
there . . ."

"Can you give me his address in Harlem?"

"Sure; 145 West 147th Street, it was."

"What kind of a family has he got? Do you know 'em?"

"Ain't but one person in that outfit that you could call

human, and that's the mother . . . She's solid, religious. But
the rest of 'em—I've seen 'em, but I don't know 'em and
don't want to know 'em," the postman sought to disabuse
Cross of any illusions. "Boy, if you're thinking of giving the
Lanes any more credit, then just don't."

"What kind of work did Lionel Lane do?"

"Work?" the postman mocked Cross, chuckling. "He used
to work in a laundry, but for the past two years he used all his
energy pulling at the neck of a bottle—"

"Thanks, Buddy," Cross said.

He felt he had a chance. He went into a bar, THE FAT
MAN, and schemed out his next move over a whiskey.
How soon was a death reported to the clerks in the Bureau
of Vital Statistics? Lionel Lane had died in Harlem and it
was safe to assume that the Newark officials did not yet know
that he was dead . . . When he approached the clerks about
a birth certificate, there must not be in their minds any
doubt whatsoever that he was Lionel Lane. One blunder and
the whole structure he was so carefully building would tum-
ble. How was he to handle it? He reflected intensely, calling
upon his knowledge of white and black race relations to stand
him in good stead. If ever he could act convincingly the role
of a subservient Negro, this was the time. He would have to
present to the officials an appearance of a Negro so scared and
ignorant that any white American acting out the normal
content of his racial consciousness would never dream that
he was up to anything deceptive. But why would any black
wastrel be wanting a birth certificate? Cross was well aware
that the American authorities were chronically watchful these
days about handing out birth certificates, for spies were using
such documents to establish their claim to having been born
in the United States. In the end Cross decided that a simple,
an almost silly reason was the best reason that an ignorant
Negro could have in demanding a birth certificate; it would
have to be a reason that whites, long schooled in dealing
with Negroes as frightened inferiors, would accept without
question.

He went to the City Hall and presented himself at the window marked: DUPLICATE BIRTH CERTIFICATES. Looking apprehensively about, he took his place in line. When his turn

came to face the young white clerk, he said in a plaintive, querulous tone:

"He told me to come up here and get the paper."

The clerk blinked and looked annoyed. "*What?*" the clerk demanded.

"The paper, Mister. My boss told me to come and get it."

"What kind of paper are you talking about, boy?"

"The one that say I was born," Cross told him as though he, in his ignorance, had to teach this white man what to do.

The clerk smiled, then laughed: "Maybe you weren't born, boy. Are you *sure* you were?"

Cross batted his eyes stupidly. He saw that he was making this poorly paid clerk happy; his pretense of dumbness made the clerk feel superior, white.

"Well, they *say* I was born. If I wasn't born, I can't keep my job. That's why my boss told me to come here and get the paper." Cross let a tiny edge of indignation creep into his voice.

The clerk regarded him with benevolent amusement and turned and yelled behind him: "Say, Jack! Come here and get a load of this, will you?"

Another clerk, somewhat older, came forward and asked: "What's up?"

"This coon clown says he was born somewhere," the young clerk said.

"I *don't* believe it," the older clerk said.

"Oh, yes, sir. I *was* born," Cross said, his lips hanging open, his eyes wide with desperation.

"Can you prove it?" the first clerk said.

"Now, look here, Mister. I ain't done nothing to nobody, 'specially to no white folks," Cross wailed in deep distress, pleading innocent to a charge not even mentioned.

"The worst thing you did was to be born," the older clerk said.

"But I ain't done nothing wrong, Mister," Cross protested.

"You are always wrong," the young clerk said. "Say, Jack, what in hell do we do with 'im?"

The older clerk pulled down his mouth and muttered: "Hell, go ahead and give 'im a certificate if he was born around here. These clowns don't mean any harm."

"If I can't say I was born, I'll lose my job," Cross complained.

"Where do you work?" the young clerk asked.

"Machine Tools Company, in Brooklyn."

"What's the address?"

"I don't know the number, not exactly, Mister. But you take the Fulton Street bus and ride—"

"Can that," the old clerk said. "You were born in Newark, you are sure of that?"

"Yes, sir."

"Wait, Jack. He ought to know something about his job," the young clerk said. "Say, boy, what's your boss's name?"

Cross stared in blank amazement, then he shook his head as though trying to avoid the worst trap of a black man's life.

"Mister, I don't ask white folks their personal business," he told them.

The clerks shouted their laughter.

"Where were you born in Newark?" the young clerk asked.

Cross blinked again, then looked up brightly, as though his memory had returned, and said: "In the Third Ward." He pointed elaborately in the direction.

"Whereabouts in the Third Ward?"

"Over the hill— Why, Mister, everybody knows where that is."

The two clerks howled with laughter. The young clerk asked: "What street were you born on 'over the hill', as you call it? And on what date were you born? And what's your name? You got a name, I suppose?"

"Yes, sir. They gave me a name," he said, falling silent.

"Well, what in hell is it?"

"But you know," Cross said, amazement showing on his face. "They say you got all the names here."

The two clerks bent double with mirth. And as he stood there masterfully manipulating their responses, Cross knew exactly what kind of man he would pretend to be in order to allay suspicion if he ever got into trouble. In his role of an ignorant, frightened Negro, each white man—except those few who were free from the race bias of their group—he would encounter would leap to supply him with a background and an identity; each white man would project out upon him his own conception of the Negro and he could safely hide behind it.

"All right, boy," the young clerk agreed. "We'll give you your certificate if we can find your record. But we've got to have your name and the year of your birth. We're pretty smart here, I admit. But we're not so smart that we can guess your name."

"They call me Lionel," Cross admitted at last.

"Lionel what?"

"What Lionel what?" Cross asked stupidly.

"What kind of work do you do at Machine Tools?"

"I load up trucks."

"Do you carry anything upstairs in your head?"

"In my head?" Cross repeated. "I ain't got nothing in my head. What you mean?"

Laughter spilled out of the clerks.

"Boy, if your brains were baggage, you could ship them by air freight for nothing," the older clerk said.

"I ain't got nothing to ship nowhere," Cross defended himself.

"Now, look, everybody's got a first name and a last name, see? Now, for God's sake, tell us your *last* name—"

"Lane," Cross responded promptly.

"Why didn't you say that in the first place?"

"'Cause you didn't ask me."

The clerks threw up their hands in mock despair. People in the line behind Cross, all of whom were white, had begun to join in the merriment. Cross wondered who was laughing at whom.

"In what year were you born?"

"My mama told me it was in 1924; the 29th of June."

"Give us a dollar and we'll mail you a duplicate certificate," the young clerk said.

"But my boss told me to bring it in the morning, or I ain't got no job," Cross complained, whining a bit.

"Okay. Sit down over there on that bench. We'll see what we can do. We'll look it up," the older clerk said resignedly.

Two hours later Cross had the duplicate birth certificate of

Lionel Lane and had left in the minds of the clerks a picture of a Negro whom the nation loved and of whom the clerks would speak in the future with contemptuous affection. Maybe some day I could rule this nation with means like this, Cross mused as he rode back to New York. All you have to do is give the people what they want . . . He knew that deep in their hearts those two white clerks knew that no human being on earth was as dense as he had made himself out to be, but they wanted, needed to believe such of Negroes and it helped them to feel racially superior. They were pretending, just as he had been pretending. But maybe men sometimes pretended for much bigger and graver stakes?

Cross was now as solidly identified as he felt he could be for the time being, and the first desire that sprang into his mind was to try to redress, to some extent, the unintentional wrong he had done to that waiter, Bob Hunter, whom he had met in the dining car more than two weeks ago. He fished in his pocket for the address, made his way to Harlem, and found the grim tenement where Hunter lived. Climbing six flights of rickety stairs, he squinted in shadows from doorway to doorway until he came to a white card whose printed legend read:

MR. & MRS. ROBERT HUNTER

He pushed the bell and a moment later he was staring into Bob Hunter's brown and nervous face. The man was in his shirt sleeves and held a pamphlet with a yellow and red back in his left hand.

"Remember me?" Cross asked.

"Man, where in hell have you been?" Bob exclaimed, his face breaking in a broad grin. "I've been looking for you everywhere! Come in."

Cross walked into a large, clean, rather bare apartment and Bob led him into the living room.

"You *are* Mr. Jordan, ain't you?" Bob asked to make sure.

"How are you, Bob?" Cross asked, ignoring the question.

"Sit down, man," Bob said. "I ain't complaining, though I got a lot I could complain about." Bob's eyes were fixed intently upon Cross's face and the lips held a nervous smile.

Cross felt that he could not deceive the man any longer.

"Bob, I suppose you wondered about me, hunh?" Cross asked.

"Well, I sure needed you, man . . . I went to that address you gave me, but it was a funeral parlor and nobody knew you there. Is your name really Jordan?" Bob asked in an appealing yet venturesome tone of voice.

Cross placed his right hand reassuringly upon Bob's shoulder. "Take it easy, Bob. I'll explain everything. Say, how did you make out in that little trouble you had on the train?"

"Hunh? What trouble?" Bob asked.

Cross knew that Bob was pretending that he had not understood. *He's trying to save face . . .*

"Did that woman on the train make any trouble for you?" Cross asked.

Bob shrugged his shoulders and laughed, but there was no mirth in his voice. "*Trouble?* Hell, man, I got *fired*! I lost my goddamn job, that's all." Bob's eyes were evasive but he could not hide that he felt that Cross had betrayed him unpardonably. "I ain't blaming you none, man. After all, you did jump up and stop that bitch from hitting me with that water pitcher, didn't you? And if you gave me a bum steer 'bout your name and address— Well, you know your own business."

"But didn't the union help you?" Cross asked.

"Man, I'm too goddamn militant for my union," Bob explained. "I had a hell of a fight with 'em. My union's got a left wing, and I'm with the left. When the company brought me up on charges, the rightists piled in on me, and I was out. Man, only *you*, an eyewitness, could have saved me. How come you fooled me like that? You could've said you didn't want to help me— Maybe I could've found some other witnesses. But I didn't look for any 'til it was too late. I was counting on you . . ."

Bob related how the white woman had sued the company, how the company had charged him with carelessness, how the leftists in the union had tried to defend him, and how, in the end, because he could not get a single witness to establish independent corroboration of his version of the accident, he had lost.

"But what about that priest?" Cross asked.

"I went to see 'im," Bob said. "Told me he didn't want to get mixed up in it. Said his job was saving souls and stuff like that. Then he went off to Rome to see the Pope—"

"I'm sorry, Bob."

"Hell, man, it's nothing," Bob said defiantly. "Me and Sarah's making out."

"Are you working now? I can let you have a loan—"

"Man," Bob's face spread in a wide, glad grin, "I'm working for the biggest outfit in the world!"

"What's that?"

"The Party, man."

"What party?"

"Hell, man! There ain't but *one* Party and that's the Communist Party," Bob explained proudly.

"What are you doing for them?"

"Organizing! What the hell do you think?"

"Do you like it?"

"I'm just crazy 'bout it," Bob confessed with a smile. "I'm going to be a professional revolutionary, working twenty-four hours a day beating these rich white bastards. It makes me feel *good*!"

Bob went into the kitchen and brought out two bottles of cold beer and, opening them, sat them on the table.

"Listen, Bob," Cross began, "I don't trust many people in this world—"

"I know *that*!" Bob agreed. "You lied to me on that train so smooth that I would have died trusting your word. Man, you can *lie*!" Bob's howl of laughter was so infectious that Cross was forced to join in.

"Bob, I'm going to trust you as far as I *dare*—"

"Man, I'm black like you and you can trust me till death. Race means a lot to me. I love and trust my own," Bob swore his fidelity.

"Bob, my name's not Addison Jordan," Cross said.

"Hell, I found *that* out," Bob said, exploding with laughter. "But what is it? You don't have to tell me 'less you want to."

"Lionel Lane," Cross lied.

Bob looked at Cross with skeptical eyes and grinned, a light of admiration showing in his face. "You telling the truth now?"

"Well," Cross hedged, feeling that it was impossible to really fool Bob now. "I'm Lionel Lane for the moment." Cross could not help laughing at himself. "But it's the name I'm giving to everybody from now on."

"You did something to the white folks and they're looking for you, hunh?"

Cross looked away, chagrined. His life had become a vast system of pretense; one act of bad faith necessitated another, and in order to prove the sincerity of a new lie he had to fall back upon lying still further. Bob was asking him if he had committed some act of racial heroism against whites, and the only people he had wronged thus far had been black.

"Something like that, Bob," Cross lied vaguely with an embarrassed mumble.

"Brother!" Bob exclaimed seizing hold of Cross's hand and pumping it vigorously in fraternal friendship. "I'm with you till the curtain comes down."

Cross's teeth felt on edge, but he managed to say: "I feel I made you lose your job. Bob, I want to help you—"

"Just be my friend, man; that's all the help I want," Bob's voice rang with hope, his words pouring out in a gush of forgiving generosity. "Now, *I'll* tell you something, see? I ain't no American, I'm British, see? But I'm black, like you . . . I came to this goddamn country from Trinidad ten years ago . . . Had to run off; was an organizer and they were after me . . . So I got to be careful too."

"Your secret's safe with me, Bob," Cross told him; he now understood why Bob's accent had seemed strange to him on the train.

"Now, tell me what you did," Bob asked.

"Bob, you'll just have to trust me. I can't tell you . . ."

"You ain't no *spy*?"

"If I was, do you think I'd tell you?"

They laughed. Bob was overcome with wonder. Cross's secret loomed in his mind more important and intriguing than any concrete crime.

"You were Mr. Jordan on the train, and now you're Mr.

Lane," Bob mused, laughing. "That's all right with me." His eyes narrowed and he stared silently for a moment in deep thought. "Man, the Party could *use* you—"

"Really? Why do you say that?"

"You can be so *many* things at once—"

"Maybe I'm *too* many things," Cross said quickly.

"Lionel," Bob said, his mind working fast, "I'm sorry my wife, Sarah, ain't here to meet you. You'll like her, man. She's down to earth and takes nothing off nobody; she's militant . . . Say, we're having some folks over to dinner tonight. Why don't you come over 'bout nine-thirty and eat with us?"

Cross knew that Bob was trying to recruit him. He had no desire whatsoever to join the Communist Party, but he knew that he would feel somewhat at home with Communists, for they, like he, were outsiders. Would not Communism be the best temporary camouflage behind which he could hide from the law? Would not his secret past make Communists think that he was anxious for their help? To be with them was not at all a bad way of ending his isolation and loneliness . . .

"Who's going to be there?"

Bob's face beamed with a look akin to worship.

"Man, you talk just *like* the Party folks! I *declare* you do!" Bob laughed uproariously, delighted and amused.

"Why do you say that?"

"You're so *suspicious*— You don't want to take a step without knowing *where* you're going . . ." Bob sobered. "They're Party folks who's coming."

"Who are they?"

Bob shook his head with an air of deep approval. "Man, you're sure careful," Bob commended him. "There's gonna be Gil and Eva Blount, friends of mine. Gil's a member of the Central Committee of the Communist Party. A damn nice guy. Man, he's sharp, cold as ice. You'll like him; he's a lot like you— And there's gonna be my goddamn organizer, Jack Hilton. Then there's me and Sarah, that's all. And you, if you'll come."

"It's a deal," Cross said, his eyes deep and thoughtful

Cross said good-bye, descended into the streets, entered a bar and sat brooding over Bob's believing mind. He found himself amused and a little intrigued at the prospects of meeting some Communists tonight. In all of his cudgeling of his brain to find some disguise for his outlaw existence, he had never seriously considered Communism. But why not? Did not the Communists, like he, have a secret to hide? And what was the Communist secret? Cross felt that at the heart of all political movements the concept of the basic inequality of man was enthroned and practiced, and the skill of politicians consisted in how cleverly they hid this elementary truth and gained votes by pretending the contrary . . . If, by pretending, he could find a hiding place, why, he would pretend that he believed in the Communist pretensions . . . Why not? They are deceivers and so am I . . . That ought to be fair enough, he thought as he took a long gulp of beer.

But the Communists were shrewd; they'd hardly be taken in by his birth certificate; he would have to buttress his pretensions of being Lionel Lane by some other document. What? By God, he had it! Lionel Lane's draft card . . . ! The postman had said that Lane had died of consumption, and then it was highly likely that Lane had been classified in the draft as unfit for military duty . . .

He paid for his beer and went out into the nervously falling snow. There was a black cop standing at the corner and he accosted him, telling him that he had been six months in Arizona for his health, that he had lost his draft card, and that he had forgotten the address of his Draft Board . . . He gave the cop Lionel Lane's address and in turn the cop directed him to the Draft Board which was located in the basement of a church.

Cross was feeling better by the minute. When he found the church, which was located on West 134th Street, he saw a throng of young men hanging around the entrance. No; he'd not go in now; he'd wait until nearly closing time. He mingled with the boys and learned that the Draft Board did not close until nine o'clock that night. It was now a little after seven. He spent the hour and a half in a nearby movie and at ten minutes to nine approached the church, entered the basement and saw that a young Negro clerk was in charge; there were three or four other young men hanging about. When the clerk came to him, Cross recited his prepared lie:

"Look, I'm listed as unfit for military duty with this Board. I've been in Arizona for the past six months for my health and I'm sailing for France; I'm on my way to Switzerland . . . But I've lost my card. I've got to get a duplicate, or I won't be allowed aboard the ship—"

"What's your name and where do you live?"

"The name's Lionel Lane and I'm at 145 West 147th Street."

The clerk left. Cross was nervous. If Lane's death had already been reported, why, he'd simply bolt for it . . . The clerk returned with a folder.

"We've got your record here," the clerk began. "But how do I know you're Lionel Lane?"

"Here's my birth certificate," Cross said, presenting the duplicate he had gotten in Newark.

"Look," the clerk said, examining the certificate, "I'll fix up a duplicate card for you and I'll have the chairman sign it, but the secretary of the board is the man who gives the final okay and he's not here. You'll have to come back in the morning—"

"But I'm sailing in the morning. I've got my ticket. I'm packed to go—"

"Gosh," the clerk said. "This stumps me—"

"But I got to have that card," Cross insisted.

"But I don't have the authority to give it to you—"

"You're looking at my birth certificate," Cross pointed out.

"Look, anybody can have a birth certificate," the clerk said. "We do things here by routine. The chairman'll sign your card tonight. But the secretary's not in; he won't be in 'til tomorrow morning—"

"Okay," Cross assented to the fairness of the clerk's statement. "But, look, if I was trying to dodge the draft, do you think I'd come here and ask for a duplicate?"

"I guess not," the clerk grinned. "Say, what time do you sail?"

"I've got to be at the boat at ten—"

"Okay. I'll get the card ready, have the chairman sign it. You be here at nine sharp in the morning and the secretary'll give it to you."

"Is that all you can do?"

"That's all, buddy."

"Okay. Thanks."

The clerk turned to another young man and Cross walked into the corridor. When the office closed tonight, his draft card would be signed and on the desk of the chairman of the board. How could he get that card? If he waited till morning, the secretary might raise questions and cause trouble. He walked along the corridor, thinking frantically. He looked around; the lights in the inner offices had been turned off. He glanced over his shoulder and saw that the clerk was busy, bent over the files. Cross walked quickly to his left, not knowing where he was going. Could he hide in the office? No; that was too dangerous . . . How in God's name could he get back here tonight, after everyone had gone? He had it; yes, he'd open a latch on one of the windows near the ground . . . He advanced slowly and softly into the dark, his hand outstretched to prevent his colliding with unseen objects. He flicked on his lighter and shielded the flame with his hand. Yeah; there was a window . . . But could he reach it easily from the outside? He doused the light, pushed the latch on the window and lifted it slowly. Peering out, he could see that the window gave on to a fetid areaway. This was no good . . .

Footsteps in the corridor made him freeze; through the open doorway he saw that a light had been clicked on in the office next to him. He waited. Maybe he could hide in a clothes closet . . . ? The light went out and he heard footsteps retreating. The clerk had gone into that office for something and had returned to the front . . .

He sighed, crept into another office and at once saw the dim reflection of a street lamp. This was it . . . He unlatched the window and slid it up noiselessly. Fumbling in the dark, he took out his address book and tore off a page and inserted it beneath the sill, then stood debating. Maybe he ought to leave by this window . . . ? Naw; it was too risky. He closed the window; the piece of paper would help him to identify the window from the outside.

Reentering the corridor, he walked out boldly, feeling that it was better to give the impression that he was not afraid, that he knew where he was going. Outside, he ambled along in the drifting snow, scanning the street in both directions. There were not many passersby, but he saw lights shining through the stained glass windows of the church on the first floor. If a service was about to begin, all the better; it would mean that no one would be prying around in the basement. He walked on till he spied the bit of paper jutting from the window sill. Lights still blazed in the draft office. Sheltering himself in a doorway, he waited.

Ten minutes later the lights in the draft office winked out, one by one; finally, the clerk, flanked by two other men, emerged. Was it safe to enter now? Yes; he'd try it. He stood beneath the fluttering piece of paper and lingered till the street was empty; then, in one quick movement, he hoisted the window, climbed into the office and dropped to the floor amid a shower of heaped-up snow from the sill. He closed the window, pushed the lever of his lighter and peered about. The office was deserted. He went into the corridor and looked into all the rooms . . . Now, where was the desk of that Draft Board chairman . . . ? He approached a big, shiny desk that had a swivel chair and saw a neat pile of manila folders. He grabbed them, thumbed quickly through them. Yeah; goddammit, *here it was!* He detached his draft card; it was signed. He then read the items describing the physical appearance of Lionel Lane and grew thoughtful. Lionel Lane had weighed 158 pounds and he weighed only 148 . . . Well, he could always say that he had lost ten pounds, could he not? That's what tuberculosis did to you, didn't it . . . ? But this other item was more difficult; Lionel Lane was listed as being five feet six inches in height and he was five feet eight. It was a little thing, but it might cause him trouble . . . Oh, yes; he could fix that . . . He looked about for a typewriter; he would type an "8" over that "6"! He uncovered a machine; holding his lighter in his left hand, he inserted the card, jiggled it until the figure "8" coincided with the "6" and hit the key. There . . . He put the card into his billfold, doubled the folder, stuffed it into his inside coat pocket. Now, get out of here . . .

He stood, thinking. Soon the death of Lionel Lane would be reported to the board and the personnel would be wondering what had happened to the folder of Lionel Lane . . . There would be some sort of inquiry . . . A solution clicked in his mind. Yes, *all* the files should be destroyed. If *his* file alone was missing, questions would be raised; but if *all* the files were missing, then he had a chance . . . And he noticed that each manila folder was wrapped in cellophane and cellophane burned like hell . . . He opened a window so that a draft would feed the fire, then bent forward and ignited a folder; he watched the cellophane smoke, curl, leap into flame. He backed away, seeing the flames grow, spread from folder to folder; soon the top of the desk was one blazing, red sheet with thick, acrid smoke billowing ceilingward. He opened the door and hurried out, then stiffened in his tracks. Good God! His lips parted in stupefication. He heard the surging of a lusty hymn coming from above! He had forgotten that he was in a church! But there was no help for that now . . .

He left the door of the office open so that a current of air would sweep into the room; then he went down the dark corridor to a stairway and mounted to the street level. The singing came loud and sonorous:

> *Let the lower lights be burning!*
> *Send a gleam across the wave!*
> *Some poor fainting, struggling seaman*
> *You may rescue, you may save.*

He hurried into the street and looked back at the church, then up to the tall steeple which was faintly visible in the frantic flakes. He walked on slowly to the end of the block, wondering when the smoke or the flames would show. He saw a fire alarm box and paused. A man passed. Then a child. He waited until the street was empty, opened the box, pulled the lever, then walked briskly to a corner drugstore, entered, perched himself atop a stool where he could watch the front of the church. He ordered a cup of coffee, sipped it, waiting.

Suddenly he saw a man hurry from the church; then a small knot of men came out; soon a throng of people was pouring from the church door. A moment later he heard the sound of distant sirens.

"Looks like there's a fire somewhere," the clerk behind the counter said.

"I see some people running out of the church down the street," Cross said casually.

The clerk went to the window. "By God, you're right! Fire's coming out of the basement window of the church!"

He joined the clerk at the window. Yes, the draft office was blazing . . .

"How much is this cup of coffee?" he asked.

"Hunh?" the clerk grunted.

"How much is this coffee?"

"Ten cents."

Cross left a dime on the counter and walked calmly from the drugstore. He had a dinner engagement to meet some Communists.

A quarter of an hour later Cross climbed six flights and pushed the bell of Bob's flat. Bob himself opened the door and grabbed his arm.

"Man, give me your coat and hat— Sarah's here and raring to meet you," Bob said, guiding Cross straight to the kitchen where Sarah, a brown-skinned woman with a strong, hard face was cooking dinner. "Sarah, honey! C'mere! I want you to meet Mr. Lane!"

Sarah was bent over a table busily flattening dough with a rolling pin; she glanced up at Cross, then quickly back to her biscuit board.

"Just a sec," she answered placidly.

She was solidly built without being fat, yet her soft, pliable muscles seemed as strong as any man's. She had black hair, a well-shaped mouth and a firm chin. Her movements were deft as she cut the thin spread of dough into biscuits and placed them swiftly into tin pans and shoved them into an oven. She wiped her hands on a dish towel, turned and smiled. Then her face grew solemn as she came toward Cross and stared with eyes full of surprise. The memory of his recent attacks of dread returned and Cross's muscles grew rigid. Had Sarah seen him before? Maybe he had known her in Chicago? Because she was staring at him, he stared at her. Sarah advanced to within a few inches of Cross and broke into a wide grin.

"What's the matter, Sarah? Can't you say hello?" Bob exclaimed.

Sarah cupped her right palm under Cross's chin, cradling it gently. Then a wild roar of laughter spilled out of her; she bent double, unable to control herself. She sobered somewhat and, still holding Cross's face in her right palm, she said:

"Look at that face— *Lead Kindly Light* . . . And he's meeting some Communists tonight, hunh? Honest to Pete, man, you got the *sweetest* face I ever saw!"

She turned from Cross, ran to a chair, flopped in it, flung back her head and yelled at the top of her lungs. Bob joined in, but more sheepishly than Sarah. Their laughter filled the corridor. Maybe they were getting even with him for his having deceived Bob . . . ?

"Don't be mad, man! You got to get used to Sarah— She just blabs out what pops into her mind, that's all," Bob explained.

Cross had had the illusion of feeling at home with these outsiders, but now he felt himself being pushed more than ever into that position where he looked at others as though they were not human. He could have waved his hand and blotted them from existence with no more regret of taking human lives than if he had swatted a couple of insects. Why could he never make others realize how dangerous it was for them to make him feel like this? He lowered his eyes and stared at them, a tight smile hovering on his lips. He trembled to do something, but he clamped his teeth and reined himself in. He knew that he had the kind of face that would always look much younger than his age, but never in his life had another person grabbed hold of that face with their bare hands and made blatant fun of it. What kind of life had Sarah lived that made it possible for her to laugh so openly at him? Pity for her came into his mind, but he banished it, realizing that it was hard to hold pity for someone who most likely did not want it.

Sarah's breasts heaved and tears rolled down her cheeks; and Bob, more restrained—maybe because he had worked around whites and had learned more fear than Sarah— laughed a moment and, seeing that Cross was not angry enough to resort to action, started to laugh again, more uproariously than before, beating his palms against the walls of the hallway and stomping his feet on the floor.

"Okay," Cross said finally. "Maybe I look funny to you."

"Naw— You ain't funny!" Sarah spluttered. "You're just out of this world— And you want to be a Bolshevik! Why, child, they'll eat you for dessert!"

She could laugh no more; in fact, she had laughed so hard that her lips hung open and she breathed orgiastically. Bob stood before Cross, both of his hands resting lightly on Cross's shoulders to show that Cross must not be angry, and he laughed with such a wide mouth that Cross could see the back of his red throat.

"Sarah—stop it! You're *killing* me!" Bob moaned.

Cross sank into a chair and stared at a print of the Moscow Subway that hung on the wall. He had conquered his impulse to anger now; he did not respect them enough to be angry. In his eyes their value as human beings had gone; if they existed, all right; if they did not exist, that was all right too . . .

"Okay. Don't you think I deserve a drink for all that?" he asked them in tones of mild reproof.

"All right, honey," Sarah said at last. "I'm gonna show you my heart's in the right place. I'm gonna give you a *whole* glass of whiskey— You had whiskey before, ain't you?"

"You'd be surprised," Cross told her.

"Know one thing," Sarah said, pouring whiskey into a tumbler. "I'm laughing, but I wonder about you—"

"Why?" Cross asked.

"I see now how Bob made a mistake to trust you on that train," Sarah said soberly. "But I wouldn't've trusted you. No, sir! That man suit you got on, that nylon shirt, that woolen handmade tie—all that don't mean nothing to me. I'd trust that face of yours as far as I could throw an *elephant*,

and you know that ain't far! What you reckon the Communists gonna make out of you?"

"I don't know," Cross answered.

He understood now. Sarah and Bob felt that Communists
ought to look like Communists; that is, ragged, desperate,
with an air of something slightly crazy. Of course, there were
exceptions: white men of cold, sharp minds who sat in dim
offices and who ran things, the intellectuals. But Sarah and
Bob never expected to see a black intellectual and did not
know one when they saw one.

"When did you join the colored race?" Sarah asked, sniggling.

"I never joined," Cross said.

Sarah went off into the kitchen, shaking with laughter. Bob
stood near him and kept his right hand on Cross's shoulder.
Cross took a long swig from the tumbler; he needed it.

"Don't be mad, man," Bob said. "If we laugh at you, it's
'cause we like you, see?"

"I'm not angry," Cross said in a far-away voice that made
Bob sober quickly.

The doorbell rang and Cross was glad. If white guests were
arriving, Sarah and Bob would desist in their laughing at him.
Repressing his chuckles, Bob went to the door.

"Gil and Eva! Come in! I got somebody here I want you to
meet," Bob greeted his guests.

A stolid white man and a tall, blonde white girl came in.
Cross rose to meet them.

"I'm Gilbert Blount," the man said, extending his hand,
holding a fixed smile on his face. The man's eyes were hard,
watchful, grey, and bulbous.

"How are you, Mr. Blount?" Cross asked.

"I'm Gil to my friends," Blount said.

"I'm Lionel," Cross lied.

"And I'm Eva," the girl said and extended an incredibly
soft, white hand.

"Here's something in here to wet your throats!" Bob called
to them to come into the living room.

It was clear that Bob intended to leave them to talk together and Cross sensed that the meeting had been arranged.
What had Bob told Gil about him? Had he led Gil to believe

that he had done some great stroke of racial retaliation against whites? It would be like Bob to do such. All right, he'd let these Communists look him over and he would look them over.

But he did not like Gil; there was about the man, even before he had found more valid reasons for his aversion, a rigidity of bodily pose that irked him. Gil was thin without being wiry, tall without being big, aged without being old, and intellectual without partaking of the processes of thought. He spoke in a manner that seemed to indicate that he had difficulty getting the words out of his mouth. Life to Gil was a stubborn, humorless effort that revealed itself in the stiffness of his lips that barely moved as he spoke and a kind of mouthing of his huge teeth when he laughed, which was not often. And back of this was a kind of cold hunger in the man that Cross could not name, a waiting, calculating consciousness whose ends seemed remote.

Gil caught Cross's elbow in a firm grip and said: "Bob told me you were coming here tonight, and I'm glad you came. Whatever your background is, you can feel at home with us."

Cross smiled a smile that he hoped would be interpreted as gratitude. How quickly they work together, Cross thought with wonder. Gil had swallowed the lies he had palmed off on Bob and his reference to his background delighted him. What would Gil think if he really knew? Two strange backgrounds are meeting tonight, Cross told himself. I'm just as complicated as they are . . .

"I'd like to talk to you," Gil continued, guiding him into the living room. "Let's sit over here."

Yes, they've discussed me and they're losing no time. They feel that my being wanted by the police will make me rest my weary head on their red pillow . . . A slow tide of confidence and curiosity was seeping into Cross's consciousness.

"Sure. Whatever you like," Cross said, allowing himself to be led to a sofa in the corner of the room. Gil was going to try to recruit him, all right. But this baby doesn't know what he's got hold of tonight, Cross mused ironically. I've got as many fronts as he's got . . .

Gil sat opposite Cross and Eva pulled over a chair and sat

at the side of her husband. Bob came in and poured drinks, handed each of them a glass and left.

"What are you doing now?" Gil asked him bluntly.

Cross smiled and spread out his hands. "Frankly, nothing."

"How do you live?"

"From hand to mouth," he lied; he had almost seven hundred dollars in cash in his pocket.

"Where do you live?"

"On 116th Street in a rented room."

"Are you married?"

"Well, I was once—"

"That's all right. We're not prudes or moralists. That's your business. I just wanted to know if you are free—"

"I'm quite free," Cross said readily. He doesn't know how free I really am, Cross mused. If he knew how free I was, he'd jump out of his skin . . .

He was not a little shocked at Gil's colossal self-conceit. He acts like a God who is about to create a man . . . He has no conception of the privacy of other people's lives . . . He saw Gil's eyes regarding him steadily, coolly, as though Gil was already seeing to what use his life could be put.

"You don't mind my questioning you like this, do you?" Gil asked with a cold smile.

"No. Why should I?" Cross lied with friendly unctuousness.

"We Communists do not admit any subjectivity in human life," Gil said with a slow, even smile, as though proud that he could utter such a horrible statement with such light-mindedness.

"I see," Cross said, striving to keep his voice neutral.

He was seething with resentment at Gil's effrontery. Who in hell does he think he is? He had to brace himself to keep from taking issue not only with Gil's statement but with the whole attitude toward life implied in it. Cross felt himself slowly coming awake, feeling the real world about him. Here was a challenge the measure of which might meet his needs . . . Keep still, he told himself.

"Do you know anything about the revolutionary movement?"

"I know it sketchily in general outline, from 1917 onwards—"

"Where did you pick it up?"

"From books, of course. What do you think?" Cross had difficulty keeping irritation out of his voice.

"Accounts written by counter-revolutionary historians, no doubt," Gil pronounced placidly. He brought out his pipe and began to fill it leisurely with an aromatic tobacco.

Cross had come by his account of the Russian Revolution from the pens of Russian Bolsheviks themselves, but he did not bother to correct Gil's assumption. He sensed that accuracy was not the point here. Gil was trying to impress him, not with learning, but with some attitude of scorn so deep that argument was futile against it. Instead, he took advantage of Gil's silence to observe Eva who sat with her shapely nyloned knees close together and regarded him with wide, enigmatic eyes. When his gaze met hers, she smiled and looked off. She seemed tense, yet rigidly contained. She was a fragile girl of about twenty-four; her attitude was so distracted that one could feel that she would never speak frankly what was really on her mind. Despite this, she seemed kind, impulsive. Her eyes were a clear hazel; her nose small and straight; and her mouth, which was only slightly rouged, was almost severe in its sharpness. The overall aspect of her face, despite the shadow of a smile that flitted over it now and then, was one of tortured, organized concentration. Cross wondered how on earth had she come to be married to a coarse, inhuman character like Blount. Cross now shifted his gaze to Gil and was chagrined to find that Gil had been observing his observation of Eva. Gil smiled tolerantly and Cross found himself boiling with rage. *He thinks I've never met a white girl before . . .*

Something decisive was transpiring in him regarding Gil. He knew that Gil did not take his inner life into account and he felt compelled to do the same with Gil. *This damn thing's catching,* he told himself. *You have to descend to their level if you are to deal with them . . . There's no other way out . . .* But he really liked this; there was an absoluteness about it that appealed to him, excited him. To grapple with Gil would involve a total mobilization of all the resources of his personality, and the conflict would be religious in its intensity.

"What do you think of the position of the Communist Party on the Negro Question?" Gil asked him.

"I know nothing concrete about the Communist position on the Negro," Cross replied. "I know that you fight for Negro rights—"

"I'm surprised," Gil said rudely, ignoring what Cross had been about to say. "How can a man of your intelligence afford not to know the most important contribution on the Negro question that has yet been made?"

"Look, Gil," Cross said in spite of himself; he had not met this provocative kind of argument before and he felt a desire to plead extenuating circumstances. "I've not come across this question in a way that would make me want to go into it that deeply. I'm twenty-six years old and I've not paid much attention to politics."

"The whole of human life is politics, from the cradle to the grave," Gil said, sweeping Cross's explanation into a heap of dust. "For those who don't know this, so much the worse for them. In England and Germany the ruling classes start training their future rulers when they are mere boys. The Party does the same. That's why Communists have something to say about what happens on this earth. Men are not born masters; they are made into masters. We Communists understand that. And, my friend, it's time that you understood it too. History will not respect you nor forgive you for not knowing it. How can you sit there and be indifferent to the forces that shape and control your destiny? It's your job to find out how this world is run, Lionel. What do you know about dialectical materialism?"

Cross knew a little about the theory, but he knew that his scanty knowledge would never satisfy Gil, so he answered: "Nothing."

"Too bad for you," Gil said; there was no pity in his voice; he spoke as though a man as ignorant as Cross did not deserve to live.

Cross looked at Eva whose eyes flitted at once from his face. He clenched his teeth to keep down his anger. His feelings were bridling so that he found himself picking nervously at his lips with his fingernails. Goddamn this cool, brash man who, though in a different way, was treating him as Bob and

Sarah had. How easily he could kill Gil with no regret; Gil was making him feel that he was his enemy, not his personal enemy, but his enemy in general and in principle. And at the moment he could think of no words that he could ever muster that would convey to Gil the depth of his rejection of him. Cross recalled that he had once wished to be a rock that could feel nothing; well, he had met a man who had apparently tried to turn himself into one . . .

Bob passed the open door, poked his head in, grinned, and asked: "Everything's all right?"

"We're doing all right," Gil told Bob.

You conceited sonofabitch, Cross told Gil in his mind.

Gil leaned back and stared at the ceiling, puffing gently at his pipe. Yes, they are definitely trying to recruit me, Cross mused. But I need them, just as much as they need me . . . Then, why not? He could always leave them when he wanted to, couldn't he? And in the meanwhile he would have a chance to establish a new base, a new set of friends . . . As Cross waited on Gil to speak, he did not let his facial expression betray his acute consciousness of Gil's consciousness; through it all he sat listening with a soft, ambiguous smile. But could he, even for the sake of his own selfish ends, stomach this preposterous Gil?

"You must never be a victim," Eva said, stressing the word "victim".

Cross loved her for saying it so sweetly, but hated her assumption of superiority. Yet, in the end it was the soft light in Eva's eyes that made Cross say at last:

"Well, Gil, we're not all lucky enough to be able to keep abreast of events as well as you do."

"I'm not keeping abreast of events," Gil corrected him with imperturbable aloofness. "You learn revolutionary logic by working in the revolutionary movement. Yes, Lionel, you need to stop throwing your life away in individual protests against your exploiters. Pool your strength with your natural allies; get in the revolutionary movement and soak up the lessons of history."

"I'd never try to act before knowing what I was about," Cross told him.

"Look, guy," Gil took his pipe from his mouth and leaned

and pointed the stem at him. "I like you, see? I've seen you for about ten minutes and I'm willing to take a chance on you. If I made you a gift, would you accept it?"

Cross smiled and looked at him. These Communists mean business . . .

"My mother used to tell me: 'When somebody gives you something, take it; when somebody takes something away from you, cry'," Cross said.

Gil managed a wry smile, as though he did not approve of the folk-saying because it had not the sanction of Karl Marx; but Eva clapped her hands and laughed delightedly.

"I want to send you to the Workers' School," Gil said, "at my own expense. But there's only one catch to my offer . . ."

"What's that?"

"If I stake you to study, then you'll have to come and live with us."

"Why?" Cross asked, puzzled.

Did this man want him in the same house with a girl as beautiful as Eva? He was crazy . . .

"For many reasons," Gil explained. "First, I'd like to keep track of your progress. Second, I want you to help me in a fight against racism which I'm going to wage in the building in which I live. Third, I want to demonstrate to a certain man, my landlord, who needs to learn a lot, that a Negro is not afraid to live in his building. My landlord's a Fascist, an open Fascist! I want you to move into my apartment. We've a spare room."

Cross looked at Eva.

"We'd be happy to have you," she said; but she did not smile.

Cross sighed. He had not expected this. Well, why not? This man thinks he is cold; well, I'm just as cold as he is . . . Maybe more . . . He is trying to use me, but I'll make *use* of his trying to use me . . .

"I like to gamble sometimes," Cross said, rising. "I'm doing nothing with myself. I'll take you up on this and see where it leads. About the Fascist, lead me to him. I've been accused of many things in my life, but no one has yet said that I was afraid."

Gil rose; he beamed for the first time since he had been in the room and he clapped his hand on Cross's shoulder.

"You're a man in a million! That's the spirit I like to see, boy!" Gil said with stiff, jerky lips.

"The freedom of your people ought to be the most precious thing on earth to you," Eva said solemnly.

Smiling a smile that they thought was acquiescence but which was really irony, Cross stood to one side and watched them. As if at a signal, Bob and Sarah came into the room; there was no attempt to conceal the fact that all of them had discussed Cross previously and had decided to make the offer that Gil had tendered him. Bob was jubilant, slapping Cross on the back and telling him:

"You ain't got no worries now, boy. The Party'll take care of you . . . From now on, the Party's going to be your mother and your father."

Sarah whispered to him, grinning and struggling to repress her laughter: "You're something new, something special. You can go far with that face of yours. Nobody'll think you're up to anything."

Why do they have to crow so openly over me? Cross asked himself. Though he had agreed to give Gil's offer a try, he could not avoid feeling cheapened at the way they boasted of how they had been wise enough to know a "good man" when they saw one. I'll show 'em how good I am, Cross told himself.

Sarah turned and looked at the clock on the mantel; then she and Bob looked at each other.

"Where's Jack?" Bob asked.

"My dinner's being ruined," Sarah complained.

"I say let's eat," Bob said defiantly. "He knew what time we were eating."

"Ditto," said Sarah. "I don't like slaving over a hot stove cooking a good meal and letting it get cold. That Jack Hilton's always doing that. Who does he think he is?"

"He's held up at a meeting," Gil said.

"Come on, folks," Sarah called, beckoning. "Go into the dining room and sit down."

Cross detected in Bob a feeling of hostility toward the

absent Jack Hilton and he wondered about it. He joined the others at the dinner table, but even the deliciousness of Sarah's cooking could not banish his sense of their regarding him as a strange fish that they had hauled up out of the sea. Gil downed his food wordlessly, his attention far away. Eva gossiped with Sarah, and Bob ate lustily, now and again looking proudly at Cross. They were eating dessert when the doorbell rang.

"That's Jack," Sarah said with disgust.

"I'll let 'im in," Bob said, rising and going to the door.

Cross heard Bob greet the new guest: "Hey, Jack! You're late. We're eating dessert."

There was a low rumble of voices in the hallway and then Cross saw a slender man of about thirty enter the dining room with his overcoat still on. Flakes of melting snow clung to his hat, and a faint haze of vapor, precipitated by the warm air of the apartment, rose from his clothing. His eyes were dark brown, limpid, deep-set, and stared almost unblinkingly. The face was emaciated, the lips thin and hanging slightly open; the mouth was wide, a little loose. He had a shock of blond hair and his skin was sallow. Under his arm he carried a roll of papers which was slightly damp from the weather outside and he held both of his hands, which had no gloves, clasped tightly in front of him, as though his strained nerves had to have something to hold onto for sake of support. Cross had the impression that the man was under severe nervous strain, and that perhaps a slight emotional push would set him going.

No one save Bob had spoken to him and so far he had said nothing to anyone. All waited for him to speak. He glanced at Sarah and said dryly:

"I'm sorry I couldn't come in time to eat. But I was detained at the control commission."

Sarah forced a smile and mumbled: "That's all right, Jack."

"The Party comes first," Bob agreed.

"Sit down and have a drink, won't you?" Sarah asked him.

"I don't want a drink," he said. "I can stay but a minute. In fact, I've come on an important errand to speak to Bob."

"We can go into the bedroom," Bob suggested.

"No. I can say it right here," Jack Hilton said in hard, cold, precise tones.

He paused and Cross noticed that Hilton's shoes had cracks in them. The man's feet must be frozen . . .

"Bob Hunter," Jack Hilton began in a tone that sounded as though he was declaiming a prepared speech, "the Party has decided that you must not proceed any further in your attempt to organize any cells in the Dining Car Waiters' Union. The Party does not wish to see that task undertaken at this time. You must forthwith desist from all and any activities in that direction. For further instructions, you will report to your Fraction Cell. Is that clearly understood?"

The man's voice had gradually risen to a high pitch of oratory before he had finished; Cross felt that the importance of the message did not justify such a method of delivery, but he sensed behind the manner of speaking an attempt to impose a respect for higher authority.

"But, man," Bob protested, "what are you saying to me? I'm working at it night and day."

"Then stop it!" The words shot from Hilton's mouth.

"But, Jack," Bob yelled, "I already sent out the letters for a meeting—"

"Then send out letters and cancel the meeting!" Hilton said.

"But— Man, you don't know what you're doing! I declared myself to 'em in public as a Party member—"

Hilton took a step closer to Bob, and, taking the papers he had held under his arm, he doubled them in his right fist and slapped them against his leg to underscore each word he spoke.

"Hunter, when will you ever learn to respect a decision of the Party? You don't discuss decisions of the Party. You *obey* them!"

"But what am I gonna do?" Bob wailed. "I want to organize my union like the Party told me."

"The Party has altered its decision!" Hilton stated flatly.

"Jack," Cross spoke in a low, calm tone of voice, "listen, this is not as easy as you think. Bob has exposed himself as a member of the Party in order to recruit for the Party. Now, if he drops this work, what is he to do? He can't work for the union and he can't work for the company . . . And now you're telling him he mustn't go on working for the Party—"

"This has *nothing* to do with *you*," Hilton told Sarah. "This decision is between Hunter and the Party—"

Sarah leaped from the table and confronted Hilton. "It *has* something to do with me!" she blazed. "Bob's my husband, and what concerns *him* concerns *me!*"

"Not in the Party it doesn't," Hilton said.

"Then Bob's *not* going to obey any such damned decision!" Sarah shouted. "You wanted Bob to organize the waiters on the dining cars. Now, he's doing that. Then you say stop. Now, why, *why?*"

"The Party is not obliged to justify its decisions to you or anybody," Hilton said.

"I'm gonna keep on organizing," Bob said uncertainly to Hilton.

"Then you will be disciplined," Hilton said.

"What discipline? What can you do to me?" Bob asked, his eyes wide with wonder and anxiety.

"You can be expelled," Hilton told him. "And the Party will blacklist you throughout the labor movement. The Party will kill you. You can't *fight* the Party! *Understand* that?"

There was silence. Cross looked about the dining room. Gil leaned forward, listening, sucking contentedly at his pipe, his elbows resting on the table. There was a quiet twinkle in his eyes as he looked from Bob to Hilton and back again, following their dialogue. Eva was pale, stiff, and seemed not to be breathing; her eyes were full of a look that seemed to be protest. Sarah's eyes were blazing and her chest rose and fell rapidly; Cross could see the throbbing of a tiny vein in her neck. Bob stood bent forward a little, his lips hanging open, his eyes wide and glassy. His stance was a combination of subservience and aggression; it seemed that he was about to bow to Hilton's demands and yet at the same time he could have been ready to leap forward and grab Hilton's throat. Cross wondered if it occurred to Bob that he was trying to drag him into an inhuman machine like this . . . ? Maybe Bob's mind did not possess enough elasticity to bring such ideas to his consciousness . . . ?

"But what can I do?" Bob finally asked in a wail.

Gil rose and walked around the table to Bob and pointed the stem of his pipe into Bob's face.

"You're going to be a Bolshevik and obey the Party," Gil spoke with jerky authority.

"But my fellow workers'll think I'm crazy if I change my mind like that," Bob pointed out.

"That does not matter," Gil said. "You are an instrument of the Party. You exist to execute the Party's will. That's all there is to it."

"But I *feel*—" Bob began.

"Goddamn your damned feelings!" Gil spat. "Who cares about what you feel? Insofar as the Party is concerned, you've got no damned feelings!" Gil paused a moment; there was a look of wild exasperation in his bulbous eyes. "Bob, there's a hell of a lot you don't understand. What do you think men like Molotov do when they get a decision? They carry it *out*! Do you think the Party exists to provide an outlet for your personal feelings? Hell, no! What do you think the Party would be if such happened? We are not Socialists . . . We are *Communists*! And being a Communist is not easy. It means negating yourself, blotting out your personal life and listening only to the voice of the Party. The Party wants you to *obey*! The Party hopes that you can understand *why* you must obey; but even if you don't understand, you *must* obey. If you don't, then the Party will toss you aside, like a broken hammer, and seek another instrument that will obey. Don't think that you are indispensable because you're black and the Party needs you. Hell, no! The Party can find others to do what it wants! Is this asking too much? No. Why? Because the Party needs this obedience to carry out its aims. And what are those aims? The liberation of the working class and the defense of the Soviet Union. The Party, therefore, does not and cannot ask too much of any comrade. It's logical, is it not? The Party is conducting this fight on your behalf and you must fit into it. Is that clear?"

Bob nodded his head affirmatively and then Gil turned and stared at Cross. And Cross felt that a better demonstration of what he was in for could not have happened even if it had been arranged.

"Lane," Gil said, "you are looking at a Party problem. Do you understand it?"

"I understand it," Cross said.

"I must go," Hilton said; he turned and without another word walked out of the room. No one had moved to open the front door for him; Cross heard it slam shut. He looked at Gil and was astonished to see Gil watching him and smiling.

"Do you understand what I mean, Lane, when I say you can't learn this out of books?"

"Yes. But, listen, I see here two points of view. I see—"

His eyes caught sight of a gesture of Gil's hand, a motion that meant for him to remain silent; Cross knew that Gil did not want him to discuss Bob's Party problem in front of Bob.

"It's late," Gil exclaimed. "We must be going, Eva."

"Oh, dear, yes," Eva said. She turned to Sarah. "Darling, thank you for the wonderful dinner."

"It's nothing," Sarah said; she could not lift up her eyes.

Gil asked Cross, when he was close enough to him to talk in a whisper: "Can I give you a lift to 116th Street?"

"Sure," Cross said. He longed to talk to Bob, but felt that it would be better to do so out of the presence of Gil. He rose, burning with protest at what he had seen and heard.

Bob pretended to be brave; he grinned, wagged his head, and crooned: "Boy, the Party's tough, hunh? It's a great Party—"

"That's the spirit," Gil said, going for his overcoat.

"I don't like it," Sarah said, taking a pile of dirty dishes into the kitchen.

"She'll be all right," Bob sought to apologize for her.

"I *won't* be all right!" Sarah shouted at him, her face twisted with anger.

"Darling, let's go," Eva said.

Cross shook hands with Bob and went to the kitchen door to say good-bye to Sarah. The door was closed and when he pushed it open he saw Sarah sitting with her head bowed. Her shoulders were shaking; she was weeping. She had not heard him open the door, and Cross closed it softly and joined the others. He followed Gil and Eva silently down the stairs to the street. Not a word was spoken until they had all gotten into the car and were rolling over the lumpy drifts of snow. Cross was next to Eva and his nostrils were full of the delicate perfume that she wore. He stared straight ahead of him, feeling that his life had at last touched something that stirred him to his depths . . . He was not angry or outraged, just deeply thoughtful, full of wonder. He had witnessed a scene of naked force in which obedience had been exacted through fear and the intensity of the emotions involved shook him.

"Well, what are your impressions, Lionel?" Gil asked, smiling and looking ahead of him.

"It's interesting," Cross said; he did not want to talk now.

"Is that all?" Gil asked, chuckling.

"It's impressive," Cross conceded.

"I didn't expect you to see that tonight," Gil said soberly. "I'm just wondering if you understand it correctly. If you got the right interpretation?"

"I got the right one," Cross said tersely.

"You have a big future ahead of you," Eva said in a neutral, far-away tone that made Cross wonder what she meant.

"You'll be all right," Gil said.

"Here's 116th Street; you can drop me here," Cross said, relieved.

The car slowed and Gil and Eva looked solemnly at Cross.

"Well, Lionel, have you changed your mind?" Gil asked.

"Absolutely not!"

"Then we can expect you?"

"When do you want me?"

"Tonight. Now. Tomorrow. This week . . . Whenever you want to come," Gil said.

"Give me the address," Cross said.

"It's 13 Charles Street, second floor," Gil said.

"I'll be there about ten in the morning," Cross said. "I've one suitcase, that's all."

"Right," Gil said.

"Good night, Lionel," Eva said.

Gil waved his hand and the car moved off through the dim, snowy streets. Cross stood a moment, looking at its red taillight disappear. He mounted to his room, undressed, and lay on his bed. There was a smile on his face as he stared up into the darkness. They think I'm a little child, he told himself. I don't mind the way they act in organizing . . . I don't mind the wild way they give out their decisions . . . I don't even mind their self-righteousness . . . But that naked force . . . Why? At the mere recollection of Hilton's biting tones, he sucked in his breath. They didn't *have* to treat Bob that way . . . Bob'll follow *any* strong person . . . You can take his hand and lead 'im . . .

He sat on the side of the bed; sleep was far from him. "Once you get that kind of attitude structuralized in an organization that goes on from year to year, how can you ever get it removed . . . ?" he asked out loud.

Cross felt that he was at last awaking. The dream in which he had lived since he had fled Chicago was leaving him. The reality about him was beginning to vibrate: he was slowly becoming himself again, but it was a different self.

Finally, toward dawn, he turned over on his side and slept like a rock for the first time in many weeks.

BOOK THREE

DESCENT

For that which I do I allow not: for what I would, that I do
not; but what I hate, that I do.

—ST. PAUL

CROSS WAS AWARE of every echo of meaning surrounding
his decision to live with the Blounts. He had accepted
their invitation in bad faith which was now almost a congenital condition with him; but he realized that his adversaries
were also acting in bad faith, a bad faith of which they were
cynically proud. Bad faith, though reprehensible and regret-
table, was not unknown to Cross; not only had he been long
guilty of it in his personal relations, but he was convinced
that bad faith of some degree was an indigenous part of
living. The daily stifling of one's sense of terror in the face of
life, the far-flung conspiracy of pretending that life was tend-
ing toward a goal of redemption, the reasonless assumption
that one's dreams and desires were realizable—all of these
hourly, human feelings were bad faith. But when Cross saw
bad faith being practiced as a way of life, when he saw men
mobilizing the natural hopes and anxieties of other men for
their own selfish ends, he became all but hypnotized by the
spectacle.

He had no illusions regarding the complexity of the situation into which he was voluntarily entering. His past life had
prepared him for participating in such compounded duplicities. His temperament made him love to understand those
who thought that they were misleading him and it was fun to
use his position of being misled to, in his turn, mislead them
into a position where they thought that he was misunderstanding them. He knew, of course, that such complicated
games carried a risk of *his* misunderstanding those whom he
was supposed to understand, but he was willing to shoulder

such handicaps. Perhaps we might both misunderstand each other, he mused.

Need for money was not pulling him into this. He had no hankering for publicity, for to be known might mean the return of Cross Damon from the grave, and that would blast his life anew. Also his was not the itch to right wrongs done to others, though those wrongs did at times agitate him. And, above all, he possessed no notion of personal or social wrongs having been done to him; if any such wrongs had existed, he felt fully capable of righting them by his own lonely strength and effort.

It was an emotional compulsion, religious in its intensity, to feel and weigh the worth of himself that was pushing him into the arms of the one thing on earth that could transform his sense of dread, shape it, objectify it, and make it real and rational for him. Logic was guiding his sense of direction, but his emotional needs were dictating the kind of directions he chose.

His affinities with the turbulent instincts of Gil and Hilton were undeniable; he was, in a manner, their brother, just as Houston was his. His difference lay in his intractability being at bottom sharper and more recondite. Too full he was of personal pride to regard himself as an exploited victim; his was not the demand that he be given his share of a mythical heritage. His was a passion to recast, reforge himself anew, and he was certain that Gil and Hilton had once in their lives felt what he was now feeling, that his reaching out for another pitch of consciousness had haunted them just as now it plagued him. But they had resolved their tangled emotions in the rigid disciplines of Communist politics, thereby ejecting from their hearts the pathos of living, purging their consciousness of that perilous subjective tension that spells the humanity of man. And now they were warring to slay in others that same agony of life that had driven them to the wall.

What malevolently psychological advantages were theirs in the waging of their war! Who best could track down criminals than reformed criminals! Gil and Hilton were spiritual bloodhounds on the trail of men whose spirits had not yet been broken as theirs had been. Since they had been defeated, they had decreed that defeat be the lot of all . . .

It was not the objective reality of the revolutionary movement that was pulling so magnetically at Cross; it was something that that movement had and did not know it had that
was seducing his attention. It was its believing that it *knew*
life; its *conviction* that it had mastered the act of living; its *will*
that it could define the ends of existence that fascinated him
against his volition. Nowhere else save in these realms had he
encountered that brand of organized audacity directed toward
secular goals. He loathed their knowledge, their manners,
their ends; but he was almost persuaded that they had in a
wrong manner moved in a right direction for revealing the
content of human life on earth. He knew that their bristling
economic theories were simply but vastly clever fishing nets
which they dragged skillfully through muddy social waters to
snare the attention of shivering and hungry men; but many
men, the best of them, would not yield their allegiances on
purely economic grounds and he knew that the Party knew
this.

While packing his suitcase, he was struck by an idea. Suppose Gil was right in assuming that the Party was justified in
coercing obedience from others purely on the basis of its
strength? What was there, then, to keep an individual from
adopting the same policy? Apparently nothing save cunning
and ruthlessness . . .

"Gil'd want to kill me if he knew how I felt," he chuckled,
lumbering down the stairway with his suitcase.

A yellow sun was flooding the buildings with a pale light
that had no warmth. He headed for the subway and had gone
but ten yards when the image of Bob's face rose before his
eyes. Yes! How was Bob making out? Had he kept the Party's
decision? Instead of going to Gil's place, he rode uptown and
made his way to Bob's apartment. Bob answered the door.

"Speak of the devil!" Bob greeted him. "Come in, man. We
were just talking 'bout you. You got your suitcase— Going to
Gil's, hunh?"

"Yeah." Cross looked searchingly at Bob whose face wore a
mask of cheerfulness. "You seem all right after what happened
last night."

"Yeah, man," Bob boasted. "That ain't nothing—"

"The hell it ain't!" Sarah's voice boomed from the living room.

"Man, Sarah's mad," Bob said, becoming crestfallen at the sound of her voice. "Go on in."

Bob followed him and the moment Cross stepped into the living room he saw Sarah's angry face.

"Hey, Pretty," Sarah greeted him in cold tones.

"I thought you were going to laugh at me today," Cross said.

"I ain't laughing at no sonofabitch today," Sarah replied.

"She don't understand that the Party has to have discipline," Bob explained. "Women think we men can do as we like—"

"You joined the Party to organize, didn't you?" Sarah demanded.

"Yeah; sure, Sarah. But listen— Lemme explain—"

"You ain't explaining nothing!" Sarah overrode him. "A white man held out a stick to you and said, 'Jump!' And, by God, you jumped, just like any nigger—"

"Listen, woman! This is the *Party*! This—"

"But it's a *white* man's Party, ain't it?" Sarah demanded.

Bob turned to Cross and shook his head helplessly.

"Why don't they want you to go on with your work?" Cross asked Bob.

"He don't know," Sarah answered for Bob. "They walk in here and tell 'im what to do, and he hates it, but he *obeys*! They don't even tell 'im why, but he *obeys*!" She glared at Bob. "Even in the South when the white folks lynched you, they told you *why*! You didn't agree with 'em, but, by God, they told you *why*!"

"Sarah," Bob began, "the Party's an army—"

"Goddamn your Party!" Sarah blazed, leaping to her feet. "What in hell did I marry, a Marxist or a mouse? Listen, nigger, you're going to *organize*, you hear?"

"Baby," Bob whined. "Look, Lionel's new to the Party—"

"Let 'im hear it all!" Sarah yelled. "Let 'im know what he's getting into." Bitter tears filled her eyes; she turned to Cross. "All my life I've seen niggers knuckling down to white people. I saw my mama knuckling down when I was a child in the South. And nothing hurt me so much as when I saw a white man kick her one day . . . Know what I mean? *Kick* her! I said kick her with his *goddamn* foot. I was 'bout six; mama was serving in the white man's house; I was watching from the kitchen door. Mama tripped and fell with the tray and boiling soup splashed all over her. But the white man wasn't worried 'bout that. Hell, naw! He was mad 'cause his dinner was spoiled, so he *kicked* her. It'll stay in my mind till my dying day . . . And everywhere I've looked since I've seen nothing but white folks kicking niggers who are kneeling down . . . Know why I don't go to church, Lionel? 'Cause I have to *kneel* in front of that white priest, and I'll be god-damned if I'll do it. Now, we're in the revolution and the *same* goddamn white man comes along. But he's in the Party now."

"Baby, it's different," Bob wailed.

"Don't tell me it's different; it's the *same* damn thing!" Sarah sat heavily in a chair and her head dropped; she seemed ashamed of her outburst. "Maybe the Party wanted you to expose yourself that way," she began again in a reflective tone. "You're no good to the union, you're no good to the company, and, if you don't obey the Party, you're no good to them. They got you trapped —"

"Sarah," Bob spoke solemnly. "A good Bolshevik obeys. Lenin obeyed, didn't he? Molotov obeys —"

"Then, honey," Sarah sneered at him, "I want you to be one of them who tells the *others* to obey, see? Read your Marx and organize. Hunh? *That* scares you, don't it? They done put the fear of God in your soul!" She rose again, trembling with anger. "Listen, I'm working and helping to support you to *organize*! I'm feeding you to *organize*! Now, you either *orga- nize* or *go*!" She whirled to Cross. "The Party scared the pee out of him this morning. He went to the Control Commis- sion to find out why they didn't want him to go on with his work. When he got back here, he was sick —"

"I *wasn't* sick," Bob protested, ashamed that Cross should know.

"You looked *green*," Sarah said. "And when a man as dark as you looks *green*, he *sick*!"

Bob grabbed his head with his hands, sank into a seat; his

body began to tremble. He was suffering, a wet rag billowing between the blasts of Sarah and the Party. Cross was unable to look at him; he stared out of the window.

"What are you going to do, Bob?" Cross asked patiently.

"Hell, man. I don't know," Bob sighed.

"What do you *want* to do?" Cross asked.

Bob's eyes searched Cross's face as though seeking an answer there; he licked his lips and mumbled despairingly:

"I want to organize Negroes—"

"Well, why don't you?"

"You reckon I could do it? Reckon I ought to?" he asked sheepishly.

"You ought to do what you want to do," Cross told him.

Sarah watched Bob with the cold eyes that only a woman can have for her husband. Cross knew that Bob would never win. Bob was too scared to act alone; he had to have a master. The Party had sunk its hold deep in Bob's heart and, if Bob left the Party, he would have to find another . . .

"I'm gonna stick to my own people," he said heavily, his eyes glistening. He had run from one master to another: his race. "That's what I'm gonna do."

"Then, *do* it, Bob," Cross said. "I'll help you."

"You want to help organize Negroes?" Bob asked eagerly, jumping to his feet.

"No. I want to help *you*," Cross told him in clipped tones.

Bob was puzzled; he brushed the meaning in Cross's words aside. He paced nervously with eyes full of anxiety. "One thing's got me worried," he mumbled. "The Party knows I'm illegally in this country—"

"So what?" Sarah asked.

"Supposed they turn me in to the Immigration folks to get rid of me—?"

"The *Communists*?" Cross asked.

"Sure, man," Bob said. "When the Party fights, they fight with everything."

"They wouldn't dare," Sarah said.

Cross felt that Bob's worries were farfetched. After all, was Bob that important to the Party? He rose to leave and Bob grabbed his hand in gratitude. Sarah followed him to the door. As Cross descended the stairs he wondered why some men wanted to be free and some did not, why some needed freedom and others did not even feel its loss when they did not have it.

After witnessing Bob's turmoil, he had doubts about going to Gil's. Was not Gil but another Hilton? And why did the Party demand abject obedience? He recalled Bob's having told him that the Party was "now your mother and your father", which meant that if he obeyed, the Party would take care of him, but, if he disobeyed, the Party would destroy him. And he had not the right to know *why* he was obeying . . . Why blind obedience? Yet, upon reflection, he found some cynical merit in the Party's demand for it. If no reasons are assigned for a given command, then you cannot criticize, for you do not understand what you are doing. And if obedience without reasons is demanded for little things, it would hold, as a matter of ingrained habit, for bigger and more dangerous things . . . But why had the Party chosen that procedure? Had they found that men would *not* obey otherwise? That could hardly be true, for each day millions of southern Negroes obeyed southern whites; millions of South African natives obeyed the white powers above them; millions of Germans had obeyed Hitler; and in most cases these millions had been given some fantastic excuse to justify the command of obedience. The Nazis tried to win the loyalty of their subjects by conferring upon them ornate titles, noneconomic rewards of various sorts, and by devising schemes of sport and joy. But the only motive that Hilton had held out to Bob was fear. Did the Communists *prefer* fear? He sighed and glanced out of the subway window just in time to discover that the train was slowing for his stop. Well, the answer to his questions was in Gil's apartment . . .

The Blounts lived in a sparsely furnished, seven-room apartment on the second floor of a red brick building on Charles Street. Eva was not in and Gil received Cross with determined stolidity. The questions that had thronged Cross's mind were now informing his sensibilities. If there was something here to understand, then he, Cross, would get it.

"How are you?" Gil asked him emotionally.

"Fine."

"Follow me," Gil said, heading down a narrow hallway.

Gil showed him a small room overlooking a depressing stretch of straggling wooden fences separating backyards.

"Will this suit your needs?" Gil asked.

"Most certainly."

"Leave your suitcase and let's have some beer," Gil said and left.

Cross placed his suitcase in a corner and walked slowly down the hallway, passing first what was obviously Gil's bedroom, then Eva's bedroom, and next the dining room, the living room, and finally coming to the kitchen in which Gil stood pouring beer into two tall glasses.

"You get the layout of the place?" Gil asked without looking around.

"Yes; I see it." He knows I've looked the joint over . . .

"The bathroom is next door," Gil said. He pointed to a rear door in the kitchen. "That's Eva's studio. She paints, you know."

"Oh; I didn't know," Cross said.

"She's a good painter," Gil told him. "Now, follow me."

Gil took the glasses into the living room and sat one glass for Cross and another for himself on the end tables of two easy chairs. Cross noticed the slow precision with which Gil moved.

"You are observant," Gil observed.

"Just a habit," Cross said.

When they were seated, Gil studied Cross silently for some seconds, took a swallow of beer, lit his pipe and puffed the bowl to a glowing red. He held the burnt-out match delicately in his fingers, then laid it aside carefully in an ashtray. Why does he act like that? Cross asked himself. Or, maybe he was observing the man *too* closely? He acts like he wants to mesmerize me; if he does, he certainly picked the wrong subject . . .

"Did anyone see you come up?" Gil asked.

"Not a soul. Why?"

Gil did not answer; he acted as though he had not heard.

"I'd like for you to sit around a week, go to meetings, listen a bit before you start your lessons in the Workers' School," Gil said.

"Just as you say," Cross agreed.

Gil rose and went to his bookcase and took down a volume, parted the leaves to a certain page, and stood reading for some minutes, puffing slowly on his pipe. He finally sat and spoke while looking out of the window.

"We are going to launch a campaign against realtors who discriminate against Negroes here in Greenwich Village," Gil explained. "There is no law against Negroes living anywhere in this city they want to, but landlords have banded together and made codes against Negroes. One of the leading supporters of this code is the man who lives downstairs; he is my landlord."

Gil's attitude began to assume a pattern of meaning. Cross recalled that Gil had asked him if he had been observed by anyone on his entering the building, and when he had told Gil that no one had seen him and had asked Gil to explain why he had asked such a question, Gil had remained silent. It was clear that Gil was jealously reserving to himself the right to tell Cross the facts in his own way, to paint the entire picture, put in the shadings, the interpretations, the sense of direction. And the words Cross heard would constitute a law which he had to memorize carefully . . . But *why*? Cross asked himself. Let him come out and say what he wants . . .

"This'll be a tough fight," Gil went on. "We'll be attacking the most deeply entrenched money interests in this city. The man downstairs is called Langley Herndon; he's an ex-real estate broker; he's now retired. He's a dyed-in-the-wool Negro hater. He has told me that if he had his way, he'd kill every Negro he could lay his hands on . . .

"Now, here's our strategy. He's going to know soon enough that you're living in my apartment, and the moment he knows, trouble will start. Just enter and leave the building normally. Maintain a polite attitude toward everyone you meet. We mustn't let any side issues develop here; we mustn't give anybody a chance to say that you were rude or insulting to them; understand? Be reserved. If this Herndon should speak to you, and he will, just act as if you were not aware of trespassing his racial boundaries. Let him take the offensive in every instance, that is, up to the point of violence. Now, Lionel, I have a lease . . ." He paused and pulled a batch of papers out of his inside coat pocket. "It's drawn between you and me. The lease I hold with Herndon gives me the right to sublet in whole or in part. Now, the lease I want you to sign was drawn up by a Party lawyer. This whole plan has been most carefully mapped out. Your staying here is perfectly legal; not only human and decent, but *legal*.

"Now, armed with this lease, Herndon has no real recourse to law to throw you or me out. But, of course, he has his goons, his tough boys who may try to waylay you. The cops will be on his side; make no mistake about that.

"Now, let me tell you the kind of man this Herndon is. I mentioned last night that he was a Fascist. He is. I'm not understating it. Herndon began his life as a Texas oil man and he made piles of money. He has the old-fashioned American racist notions, all of them, right up to the hilt, including the so-called biological inferiority of the Negro. He even claims that he has found a philosophical basis and justification for his racial hatred. Understand? He hates not only Negroes, Jews, Chinese, but *all* non-Anglo-Saxons . . . And he is smart enough to give you a mile of specious arguments, gotten out of crackpot books, for his anti-Semitism, anti-Negroism, etc. All of his arguments boil down to this: God made him and his kind to rule over the lower breeds. And God was so kind and thoughtful as to arrange that he be paid handsomely for it. Of course, he has conceived this God of his in the image of a highly successful oil or real estate man, just a little more powerful and wonderful than he is. Herndon is quite anxious to collaborate with God by shouldering a rifle, if necessary, and helping God to defend what God has so generously given him. Herndon feels that God was absolutely right in giving him what he's got, but he does not completely trust God's judgment when it comes to his keeping it.

"As soon as he knows that you're in the building, the entire neighborhood will know it. That ought to happen within the next few hours. From that moment on, you'll have to watch out. Now, I'm getting you a gun and a permit to carry one . . ."

"I've got a gun," Cross told him. "But no permit."

Gil frowned and studied the floor. "How long have you carried a gun?"

"A few weeks. Especially when I travel—"

"You carry it on you?"

"Yes."

"May I see it?"

Cross tendered Gil his gun and Gil broke it, copied down the serial number and returned it.

"A Party contact will help get you a permit," Gil continued, but the tone of his voice had changed.

He's worried about the gun, Cross thought. Otherwise, I've acted in a way to make him trust me, to make him feel that he is the boss; but my having a gun makes him feel that I might have a will of my own . . .

"If and when Herndon moves against us," Gil resumed, "we'll break the case in the *Daily Worker*; we'll break it in England, in France, in China, and the Soviet Union—"

"You don't think a court would uphold your lease?" Cross asked.

Gil seemed annoyed. He gazed down at the figures in the carpet for a moment.

"Lionel, courts are instrumentalities of bourgeois law," he said slowly. "We are going to try this case in the public mind. Above all, this case must serve the Party's organizational interests."

Cross was worried. What would the publicity mean for him? Ought he tell Gil that he could not risk that? No; he would wait; he could always disappear if things went in the wrong direction . . .

"Are you in agreement with this plan?" Gil asked.

"Of course," Cross lied.

"Then tell me what would you think of anyone who tried to defeat this fight for Negroes to live where they wanted to?" Gil asked slowly.

"Why," Cross stammered, "he would be a sonofabitch, to say the least."

Gil did not react to this definition. He stared straight at Cross and then leaned back in his chair. His pipe had gone out and he relit it. Suddenly Gil's eyes seemed to become unseeing.

"He would be a counter-revolutionary," Gil pronounced at last. "And he would deserve to be destroyed by the Party."

Gil's words made Cross at last understand what had been bothering him all along. It came in the tone of Gil's words, in the chilled promise of cold vengeance that edged his voice. *Power!* This was power he saw in action. That was why Gil had evaded answering his questions; Gil had made him assume a position of disadvantage, of waiting to be told what to do. The meaning unfolded like the petals of a black flower in the depths of a swamp. That was why fear was used; that was why no rewards of a tangible nature were given. It worked like this: Gil could lord it over Cross; and, in turn, as his payment for his suffering Gil's domination, Cross could lord it over somebody else. It was odd that he had not sensed it before; it had been *too* simple, *too* elementary. His mind worked feverishly, analyzing the concept. Here was something more recondite than mere political strategy; it was a *life* strategy using political methods as its tools . . . Its essence was a voluptuousness, a deep-going sensuality that took cognizance of fundamental human needs and the answers to those needs. It related man to man in a fearfully organic way. To hold absolute power over others, to define what they should love or fear, to decide if they were to live or die and thereby to ravage the whole of their beings—that was a sensuality that made sexual passion look pale by comparison. It was a noneconomic conception of existence. The rewards for those followers who deserved them did not cost one penny; the only price attached to rewards was the abject suffering of some individual victim who was dominated by the recipient of the reward of power . . . No, they were not dumb, these Gils and Hiltons . . . They knew a thing or two about mankind. They had reached far back into history and had dredged up from its black waters the most ancient of all realities: man's desire to be a god . . . How far wrong were most people in their appraisal of dictators! The popular opinion was that these men were hankering for their pick of beautiful virgins, good food, fragrant cigars, aged whiskey, land, gold . . . But what these men wanted was something much harder to get and their mere getting of it was in itself a way of their keeping it. It was power, not just the exercise of bureaucratic control, but personal power to be wielded directly upon the lives and bodies of others. He recalled now how Hilton and Gil had looked at Bob when Bob had pled against the Party's decision. They had enjoyed it, loved it!

"Do you understand?" he heard Gil asking him.

Cross sighed, looked up and met Gil's eyes with a level stare. "Yes, I understand," he said.

He understood now why Gil had moved so slowly, why his manner was so studied. He had been giving Cross a chance to observe! And he remembered that Gil had been watching him to see that he was watching! The heart of Communism could not be taught; it had to be learned by living, by participation in its rituals.

He heard a key turning in the lock of the door.

"That's Eva," Gil said.

A moment later Eva, wind-blown and cherry-cheeked, with an armful of packages, rushed into the room. Her face held a bright, fixed expression of cheerfulness.

"Welcome," she sang out in her nervous, high-strung way.

Cross stood and smiled at her and wondered if her strained manner was covering her distaste at his presence in the apartment . . . There was something in her attitude that bothered him.

"Thank you," he told her. "I'm here and we're planning—"

"And you'll get action," Eva promised him self-consciously. "If Gil planned it, it's really planned. Hunh, darling?" She bent and kissed Gil lightly on the forehead. "I must get lunch ready now." She turned to Cross. "Just make yourself at home."

"Oh, Eva," Gil called. "I'm not eating lunch in. In fact, I must leave now. Why don't you eat with Lionel? I've got to make a speech at the Dyers' Union. I'll be in for dinner."

"Very well, Gil," Eva said; her face showed no expression.

Gil turned to Cross. "Keep your eyes open, boy." He laughed for the first time. "The fight is on!"

Eva walked slowly into the hallway and a moment later Cross heard her rattling pots and pans in the kitchen. Gil got into his overcoat and left. Cross went to his room and stretched out on his bed, thinking, mulling. His was the hungry type of mind that needed only a scrap of an idea to feed upon, to start his analytical processes rolling. This thing of power . . . Why had he overlooked it till now . . . ? Well, he had not been in those areas of life where power had held forth or reigned openly. Excitement grew in him; he felt that he was beginning to look at the emotional skeleton of man. He understood now the hard Communist insistence on strict obedience in things that had no direct relation to politics proper or to their keeping tight grasp of the reins of power. Once a thorough system of sensual power as a way of life had gotten hold of a man's heart to the extent that it ordered and defined all of his relations, it was bound to codify and arrange all of his life's activities into one organic unity. This systematizing of the sensual impulses of man to be a god must needs be jealous of all rival systems of sensuality, even those found in poetry and music. Cross, lying on his bed and staring at the ceiling, marveled at the astuteness of both Communist and Fascist politicians who had banned the demonic contagions of jazz. And now, too, he could understand why the Communists, instead of shooting the capitalists and bankers as they had so ardently sworn that they would do when they came to power, made instead with blood in their eyes straight for the school teachers, priests, writers, artists, poets, musicians, and the deposed bourgeois governmental rulers as the men who held for them the deadliest of threats to their keeping and extending their power . . .

He saw now that those who, in trying to rationalize their fears of Communism, had said that the practice of Communism was contrary to human nature were naïve or blind to awful facts which they had not the courage to admit; for, as Cross could see, there was not perhaps on earth a system of governing men which was more solidly built upon the sadly embarrassing cupidities of the human heart and its hunger to embrace the unembraceable. Of course, this system of sensualization of the concept of power did not prevail alone in the Communist or Fascist worlds; the Communists had merely rationalized it, brought it nakedly and unseemingly into the open. This systematization of the sensuality of power prevailed, though in a different form, in the so-called capitalistic bourgeois world; it was everywhere, in religion as well as in government, and in all art that was worthy of the name. And bourgeois rulers, along with the men of the church, had forged through time and tradition methods of concealing these systems of sensual power under thick layers of legal, institutionalized, ritualized, ideological, and religious trappings. But at the very heart of this system were the knowing and conscious men who wielded power, saying little or nothing of the real nature of the black art they practiced, the nameless religion by which they lived.

He knew instinctively that such subjects could not readily be explored in discussions with others, for its very victims— if, in strict sense it could be said that they were victims— would deny its reality perhaps more vociferously than those who held in their hands the reins of this system of power. Cross's insight into the functioning of the emotions of a Gil or a Hilton enabled him to isolate his own past actions and gain some measure of insight into them; it had been the blind coercions of a hungry sensuality that had made him try to hug delusions to his heart when he had suspected the malevolence of the innocent and had tried to posit upon the unknowing motives that they could not possibly have had. He rolled over and sat up in bed, his mouth open. He was seeing a vision, but at long last it was not an unreal one. This vision made reality more meaningful, made what his eyes saw take on coherence and depth. For the first time since that snowy evening in Chicago when he had decided to flee, when the waters of desire had drained off the world and had left it dry of interest, meaning began to trickle back again in drops, rivulets . . . He was, in his mind and feelings, isolating this central impulse of informing action by which he and other men lived. There was a hunger for power reaching out of the senses of man and trying to say something in symbols of action. What message, if any, was written in those hieroglyphics of energy? That these actions were far more basic than the mere arrangements of economic relations obtaining between rival social classes, he was convinced. Maybe . . .

A light knock came upon his door.

"Lionel!" It was Eva calling.

"You?"

"Lunch is waiting—"

"Coming."

He washed up and went into the dining room and sat at the table, facing Eva who now, though friendly, still seemed to avoid his eyes.

"I don't know what you like to eat," she said, smiling.

"Anything'll do me, Eva," he told her, seeing her now in the light of his ponderous reflections of a moment ago.

"I suppose you and Gil went over a lot today. You'll see that Gil has a grip on life," she said in a strained matter-of-fact tone devoid of any boasting.

"He has indeed," Cross agreed merely to keep the talk going.

As she served him he studied her and was amazed to find that she looked even younger without rouge on her lips and artificial coloring on her cheeks. How did this child—for there was an undeniable childishness about her—fit into his dark broodings and interpretations of Gil's politics? He longed to ask her how she had come to marry Gil, for every move she made and every word she uttered belied her being his wife.

"Are you a native New Yorker; that is, born here, I mean?" he asked.

"Yes; I'm one of those rare ones. I was born about three blocks from here," she said, laughing, keeping her eyes down.

"Did you grow up in the Communist Party?"

"Oh, God no. I was an orphan . . . I encountered the Party when I met Gil." She still did not look at him.

"Oh, I see."

"Do you like music?" she asked.

He had hoped that she would discuss politics; but either she did not want to or she evaded the subject because of its lack of interest for her.

"It's the one thing I know least about, I'm ashamed to admit," he confessed. "I've heard some classical music and liked it; but my level is jazz and folk songs, I'm afraid."

"Really?" She was surprised and thoughtful for a moment. "The reason I asked is that we have stacks of symphonic records over in the left-hand corner of the living room and you are free to play them if you like."

As the lunch progressed, she spoke in a quietly melodious voice of her love of music, painting, poetry, and the beauty of

France which she had seen last summer. Without seeming to, she avoided all mention of herself and made no political observations whatsoever. The simplicity of her manner made him doubt the validity of the theory he had hatched out a few minutes ago. Yet she lives in this communist world and she must know, he thought.

"Say, what was behind that little scene at Bob's last night?" he asked boldly.

"What scene?" She looked startled.

"I'm referring to Hilton's laying down the law to Bob—"

"Oh, *that* . . ." She frowned and murmured, "I'm afraid that Gil will have to explain that."

Either she did not know or she did not want to tell. He did not wish to create the impression that he was fishing for information and he quickly assumed an attitude of naïveté.

"There's so much to learn," he said wistfully. "I must be patient."

"I was *once* as bewildered as you are," she said meaningfully.

It was definite that she was evading him; he sensed reserves of emotion in her and he cast about for a way to make her open up.

"Look, don't think I'm nosey, but are you active in the Party?"

"Not exactly," she said. "I paint." She was frowning.

"Oh, really? Social subjects?" He encouraged her to talk.

A flicker of dismay darted across her face. She's afraid to talk, he thought. She bit her lips and her long eyelashes shadowed her cheeks. She took up a slice of bread, broke it nervously, then put it aside as a sudden impulse came to life in her.

"No. I'm a nonobjective painter," she said modestly.

Cross stared. The wife of a Communist leader painting nonobjectively?

"You don't like nonobjective painting, do you?" she asked, putting a soft challenge in her voice.

"But I do; absolutely," he answered honestly. "Say, I've a theory about it—"

". . . . . . . ?" she said, but she did not look at him. She was evidently struggling with herself. Then impulsively. "I'd like to hear it."

"Well, you see, maybe my notion is kind of far-fetched," he began, glad that they had at last found some common ground. "Nonobjective painting expresses the dominant consciousness of modern man . . . Sounds corny, hunh? But I mean it." He hesitated, wondering what approach would get beneath her reserve. "Modern consciousness is Godlessness and nonobjective painting reflects this negatively. There is really no nonobjective painting without either a strong assumption of atheism or an active expression of it, whether the nonobjective painter realizes it or not . . ."

"We agree so far," she said as though thinking of something else.

"I mean Godlessness in a strict sense," he argued. "There is nothing but *us, man,* and the world that *man* has made. Beyond that, there's nothing else. The natural world around us which cradles our existence and which we claim we know is just a huge, unknowable something or other . . . We may find out how it works, discover some of its so-called laws, but we don't know it and can't know it . . . Nature's not *us;* it's different. A part of us is nature, but that part of us that's human and free is opposed to nature. What there is of the natural world that seems human to us is what we have projected out upon it from our own hearts. We created cities, roads, factories, etc. Sunsets, waterfalls, and landscapes are but a few accidental aspects of nature that we happen to like, that somehow reflect moods of ours . . . So we are prone to forget all of the other phases of nature that are terrible, inhuman, alien to us . . . Now, my notion is that since this is true, that the world we see is the world we make by our manual or emotional projection, why not let us be honest and paint our own projections, our fantasies, our own moods, our own conceptions of what things are. Let's paint our feelings *directly.* Why let objects master us? Let's take forms, planes, surfaces, colors, volumes, space, etc., and make them express ourselves by our arrangement of them. It's an act of pure creation . . ."

"You've said it," she exclaimed looking fully at him for the first time. "I'm surprised."

"Why?"

"Not many people feel like that," she said. "I'd not have

thought that a colored person would like nonobjective art. Your people are so realistic and drenched in life, the world . . . Colored people are so robustly healthy."

"*Some* of us," he said.

"And you're not? How did that happen?"

"It's a long story," he said. "Some people are pushed deeper into their environment and some are pushed completely out of it."

"Do you feel *that* much aloneness?" she asked in surprise.

"Yes; and you?"

"Yes," she said simply and was silent.

"I'd like awfully to see your work."

"All right. But . . ."

"But what?"

"I'd rather you didn't tell Gil we talked about this," she said, reddening.

"I see," he said. What's she afraid of . . . ?

After lunch she took him into a cluttered, dusty room behind the kitchen; it reeked of oil and turpentine. She stood timidly behind him as he looked at walls covered with canvases; more were stacked in corners. The power of her work was immediately apparent; a bewildering array of seemingly disassociated forms—squares, cubes, spheres, triangles, rhombs, trapezes, planes, spirals, crystals, meteors, atomistic constructions, and strange micro-organisms—struggled in space lit sombrely by achromatic tints. Cross advanced to the canvas upon which she was evidently working and which rested upon a huge easel. Between irregular volumes and planes was a feeling of tremendous tension created by points of quiet and steady light, a light that seemed hardly there, yet tying all of her space into one organic whole. Out of a darkly brooding background surged broken forms swimming lyrically in mysterious light stemming from an unseen source. The magical fragility of this light, touching off surprising harmonies of tones, falling in space and bringing to sight half-sensed patterns of form, was Eva, her sense of herself . . . In her work she seemed to be straining to say something that possessed and gripped her life; she spoke tersely, almost cruelly through her forms. Her painting at bottom was the work of a poet trying to make color and form sing in an absolute and total manner. There was a blatant brutality about her volumes, some of which were smashed, cracked, and presented a tactile surface carrying an illusion of such roughness that one felt that the skin of the hand would be torn by touching it . . . He wondered what life experiences made her paint such images of latent danger . . . ?

"Have you exhibited?"

"Yes; last year. Just before I married—"

"You have enough for another exhibit now."

"I shan't exhibit again soon," she said.

"How was your work received?"

"Very well," she muttered.

"And why aren't you going to exhibit again soon?"

"Oh, Lionel, I must go," she said hurriedly, ignoring his question. "Stay and look at them as long as you like . . . Here are the keys to the apartment; one's for the downstairs and the other's for the front door up here. I'm off to do some shopping and then I'll do a concert." She flashed him a quick smile. "Come and go as you like. But watch out for Herndon downstairs . . ."

She left him and a few moments later he heard the front door open and close. She had not wanted to talk to him, but what she had seemed too shy to say in words shouted and pled for her in images. For two hours he looked at every canvas in the room, placing them in the light, examining them from far and near. He had the illusion, while studying them, of standing somehow at the center of Eva's ego and being captured by the private, subjective world that was hers, a world that was frightening in the stark quality of its aloneness; and he knew that it was out of a sense of aloneness that these bold, brutal images, nameless and timeless, had come with the force of compulsions. At least she's lucky to be able to say her terrors and agonies in form and color, he said a little enviously to himself.

With a cigarette glowing in his lips, he went back into the apartment and wandered aimlessly from room to room, probing and idly searching. He smiled, feeling the presence of Eva and Gil as he spied among their belongings. Why did they have two separate bedrooms? Twin beds were all right, but two bedrooms? He recalled the little, pecking kiss that Eva had given Gil when she had come in from her shopping and he was certain that there was something wrong between them.

He ended up in Eva's bedroom, prowling in drawers and desks. At the bottom of a pile of dusty sheets of music lying on the floor of a clothes closet he came across a stack of bound notebooks; he opened one. They were Eva's diaries . . . Ought he risk peeking a little into one? He glanced guiltily over his shoulder. When would she be back? To be surprised reading her intimate diary would be awful . . . He stepped into the hallway and saw that there was a safety night-chain on the door. Yes; he had it . . . He would put the night-chain in place and if Gil or Eva returned suddenly, he could always say that he had put it on in order to be on guard if Herndon came up . . . He chained the door and went back into Eva's bedroom and picked up a volume of the diary that dated back six months of that year. He began reading the small, clear, schoolgirlish handwriting:

"*June 10th*

"—I'm at last in Paris, city of my dreams! What a wedding gift from Gil! Poor dear, he's too busy with Party work to show me the beauty of this wonderful Paris; his assignments keep him going from morning 'til night . . . But I do manage to see it for myself. The art exhibits, the artists' studios, the sense of leisure, the love of beauty—will I ever be the same again after all this?

"Notre Dame! Rising nobly in the warm summer night like a floodlit dream— The tourist bus is crawling away, taking me from this vision of beauty, remote, fragile, infused with the mood of eternity. At the next stop I got off the bus and walked back to Notre Dame; I could not keep to the schedule of a tourist bus! I sat on a bench and gazed at Notre Dame 'til almost dawn . . . How quiet the city is . . . A lonely, shabby man is pushing a handcart through the city streets. Lines, space, harmony softened by dark mists . . . Dusk of dawn kissing the pavements with tenderness . . . I doubt if Gil would understand feelings like these, yet they mean so much to me, to my heart . . . Mine is the glory of those angels against the background of that pearly, infinite sky . . .

"*June 15th*

"I'm so numbed with shock that I can hardly think . . . Is this my honeymoon? Is it possible that Gil has betrayed me so cruelly, cynically? For days now I've pretended to be ill to avoid having it out with him, but in the end I must do it. It all began one afternoon when I went to see a Left Bank art exhibit. I stayed behind and got to talking to some of the younger artists, both American and French, all of whom were complete strangers to me. One young man, an American expatriate, obviously a Trotskyite, began a violent tirade against the Party, charging that membership in the Party was death to artists. I told him that I was a painter and did not think so. He then told me not to be naïve like that silly but gifted Eva Blount girl who had had such a stunningly successful exhibit in New York last spring . . . He did not know who I was, and I asked him what was so naïve about Eva Blount . . . He said that it was being whispered about that Gil Blount had been ordered by the Party to marry her, to get her into the Party for prestige purposes. He went on talking of other instances where such had happened . . . I was silent; I felt cold, dead . . . To stand in a crowd of people and hear them talk of you like that!!! He said that it was common knowledge in the labor movement that Gil Blount had been told to recruit Eva Blount . . . I asked him how did he know this, and what right had he to spread such foul gossip about people he did not know . . . He then went on to tell of facts which only someone close to the revolutionary movement could know . . . He said that Gil's secretary, Rose Lampkin, was his mistress and had been for years, and that at the same time she was spying on Gil . . . I could not contradict him . . . His words suddenly opened up a vast vista of understanding which I fought against desperately. Am I so naïve . . . ?

"To hear one's private life spoken about so brutally, in public! God, can this be true? Yet his words explain so much! Is that why Gil is away from home so much? Is that why he never comes to me except when he's drunk? Oh, God, I feel I've no ground under my feet anymore— I must confront Gil with this . . . But how? Ought I run off? But to where?

"And that Rose Lampkin woman, Gil's secretary . . . Is that his mistress? Is that why he insisted that she accompany us to Paris? The more I think, the sicker I get! I try to tell myself that this cannot be true, yet in my heart I know it and feel it . . .

"June 17th

"Gil has all but said that it's true! Which means that when I confronted him, he would not say anything!!! He raves at me, telling me that I'm trying to undermine his Party position! That I'm slandering him! I asked him to send Rose back to New York, and he said that it was the Party's decision that Rose remain with him . . . And Rose, when she came to the hotel this morning, had a cold smirk on her face. She knows that I know! According to Gil, I must accept this betrayal and be loyal to the Party; to be loyal to my feelings means betraying the Party! I don't know what to do— I feel that everybody's laughing at me, that everybody knows— *I could kill Gil!*

"*June 18th*

"I must be calm— I've only my work left; that's all. I tell myself all day long that I must give my life to my work. If I make a sudden, hysterical move and lose grip on myself, run off, the Party can always say that I deserted and degenerated! Gil has predicted as much! Can there be betrayals as intimately cynical as this? I'm a fool to wonder, for it is true, it stares me in the face . . . But I don't want to believe it. That's what makes it possible; no one *wants* to believe it . . . What coldness people are capable of! I walk the streets all day to keep thoughts of suicide from filling my head—

"*June 19th*

"Can I work now? My whole life seems tainted, unclean . . . I've asked Gil to take me back to New York; he says he will as soon as his duties with the French Party are over. I begged him to give me fare, and he says no . . . I'm alone again, just as I was in the orphan home. I didn't lose heart then and I mustn't now. I won't; I can't give up; I must work, work, work, paint . . . But can I paint again? The Party lifted me up in its hands and showed me to the world, and if I disown them, they'll disown me . . . What a trap!

"Gil warned me that I must not talk of this! He demanded to know who told me about the Party deciding that he was to marry me . . . He accuses me of having anti-Party friends!

"I'm afraid. If I stay with Gil, I'll loathe myself; if I run off, the Party will attack me publicly, branding me a renegade. All of my friends are Party people and they would no longer speak to me . . . Night and day Gil demands that I be loyal to the Party. But I owe myself some loyalty too. How can I face myself in the years to come, knowing that I have been bought, and in such a shameful way? Gil says that my personal feelings do not count . . . Doesn't he know he's killing me . . . ?

"*June 20th*

"I've been hurt; there's no doubt about it. I stand before my easel and cannot paint. I'm numb; my love of work is gone. When Gil comes into the hotel room, I begin to tremble with shame and rage . . . And he tells me that I must not, cannot talk to anybody . . . If I protest, the Party will destroy me . . . Last night he relented a tiny bit and said that I could be free only if I let the Party choose a husband for me . . . It seems that I'm now guilty not because of what I've done, but because of what I know . . . Goddamn this deception!

"June 21st

"I've begun to notice things that I've never noticed before. Is this because of what Gil and the Party have done to me? I feel like a victim and everywhere I look I think I can see other victims in the making . . . I've just come from a movie where I saw mothers with their young children. It was a horrible gangster film with a tense, melodramatic atmosphere. How can mothers take their children into such places? I should hate to have my children getting used to sights of violence, death, brutality . . . When for years a child has seen men hitting other men, killing or getting killed, he gets used to it. In time it does not impress him any more . . . He gets used to it, and death, betrayal, deception become just unimpressive facts of life, just 'one of those things' . . .

"June 23rd

"Gil came in at 2 A.M., drunk. He's ashamed to face me when he's sober. I understand it: drunk, he's still a free Communist; sober, he's still a slave of his boyhood upbringing in the Bronx and is ashamed of what he's done . . . To every argument I raise, he has one answer: 'You don't understand!' I've got a knife with which I cut canvases and I sleep with it under my pillow. Gil will *never* touch me again, drunk or sober . . .

"My eyes are red and raw from weeping and sleeplessness. Never did I dream that I'd be brought to this! Before this the world was a sad place, but now it's sad *and* dangerous . . . The worst part of all this is that I've no preparation for it; there was no warning. There's nothing I've ever read or heard that could have prepared me for this . . . After father died when I was six, I lived in that orphan home; but even there life seemed rational. Hunger, cold, study; making sacrifices to attend art school—all of that was rational. When I began to win scholarships, all the deprivations were redeemed. But this deliberate deception—? Where does it fit in?

"Gil is sullen, silent; a cold wall— He has his friends; I've none; I'm alone— I've no friends unless I consent to accept what has been done to me! I must be a partner to this crime in order to be forgiven! I see it now; there can be no crimes like this unless there is the consent of the victim! My fear to talk, my silence makes this possible! But dare I speak? Who would believe me? Who'd care? How can I go on like this . . . ?

"June 24th

"I'm afraid my loneliness and melancholy are making me morbid . . . Injustice has always been merely a word to me, now it's a reality. Gil and the Party have opened my eyes and I see . . . In the Paris Metro today I saw something that made me sad. In front of me, on one seat, sat a young mother, middle-class, her face well done-up and glowing with motherly pride; she was holding a little girl of about two years of age on her knees. And that sweet little baby girl, all dressed up in delicate, lacy things took a liking to a pale little boy of about nine or thereabouts. He was filthy, badly dressed; he seemed too mature for his age; he sat next to a huge, vulgar, toothless, harsh-voiced woman—no doubt his mother. Both the little children were at once keen on each other, but the big woman kept telling her son to stop looking and smiling at the baby. The little girl's hands tried to take hold of those of the boy and the boy was enjoying it. The young mother did not like it, but she was too well-bred to want to hurt the little boy's feelings. Maybe the big woman was afraid of what the smartly dressed young woman would say? Anyway, the two women got terribly nervous and finally the young mother pried the tiny, playful, rosy little fingers out of the boy's dirty hands . . . The baby cried and I wanted to cry too— I wonder if Gil realizes how awful people can feel when something happens to them that they cannot understand? I've sworn that Gil will never touch me again . . . I'll die first!

"July 10th

"We're back in New York. My friends are asking me about my honeymoon and I'm forced to smile . . . God, how can I keep up this deception any longer? I'm noticing other victims now. I've become aware of colored people. God, how they take it! Compared to their deception, mine is nothing . . . Yet they manage to go on living, even smiling. How do they do it? They must be strong, healthy, unspoiled by the lies of the white man's world.

"July 12th

"My world has failed me and everything in it . . . What Gil and his Party have done to me is ruining my life, making me possess fantastic notions. My loathing of Gil has gone so far that I cannot any longer abide the color pink. I no longer want to paint in reds and blues and greens . . . They now remind me of Gil's deception. That's why I'm beginning to adore colored people; I could live my life with sunburnt people; I wish I was a warm, rich, brown color—

"July 18th

"I've begged Gil for a little money to start out for myself and he says no; the Party says no; it's no everywhere . . .

"We're in a new apartment and the landlord is truly a Fascist! This morning I met him on the stoop and said good morning to him. For some reason I asked him if there were any black people in the neighborhood. He must have thought that I objected to them, for he said: 'Oh, no; nothing like that around here, lady. But there's a Chinese laundry down the street—' 'But Chinese are not black,' I said. 'Oh, lady, you don't know. They're *almost* black . . . These colored people are all the same . . . God's marked 'em all red, yellow, brown, and black so we could know 'em . . .' Good God, what a world we live in . . ."

Cross smiled and flipped the pages of the diary and began reading the last entry:

"March 3rd

"Bob Hunter, one of the Party organizers, came rushing in to see Gil. When I told him that Gil was out his face fell and he pouted like a child. I like him because he is so open about his desire to fight and free his people from oppression. Bob told me to tell Gil that we must be sure to come to his apartment for dinner tonight— Bob bubbles over with the news of his finding a new, wonderful recruit for the Party. He is a young Negro living under an assumed name, a fugitive from southern racists. He is, according to Bob, who swore me to secrecy, a bright young Negro intellectual who had some dire trouble with whites and committed some crime and is in hiding to save his life. Bob met the young man on a train and he is certain that he has killed a white man and that there is a price on his head . . . It sounds so exciting, terrible, pitiful . . . And they're bringing him into the *Party*! Another victim? I wish I could talk to him and tell him something . . . Colored people are so trusting and naïve . . . He's going to be misled by Gil, just as I have been . . ."

Cross closed the diary; now that he had learned something of Eva's life, he did not want to read any more. He knew enough to make a numbing sense of recognition go through him. Impulsively he wanted to run to her and talk to her, to tell her that she was not alone. But that was foolish. Secrecy was how the world was run. Millions felt alike, but were ashamed to admit it. Here was a lost, brave woman who had enough sensitivity and intelligence to understand what he had to say. She was a victim like he; the difference was that he was a willing victim and she was an involuntary one . . . She protested and he said yes. And a world yawned between his yes and her no . . .

But, Christ, how could she go on living that life? Her tense, artificial manner was now clear. She did not want to talk about politics; she was afraid of what she would say . . . She wanted to help him; and he wanted to help her . . .

And Gil was trusting him because of Bob's foolish stories! Yes; that was rich. Bob had led the Party to feel that it had found a real victim of race hate! Well . . .

He felt sluggish; he replaced the diary and decided to take a walk. He went out of the front door, listening to hear a harsh voice challenging him. But nothing happened. He walked to Washington Square and stood looking at the pigeons fluttering around the treetops, alighting in the snowy grass. He went past the bookshops on Fourth Avenue, browsing here and there. It was cold; he would go home.

He was entering the building when the door of the apartment of Langley Herndon opened. Cross saw a white face watching him from behind thick spectacles. He shut the door to the street, taking his time, then turned and started up the stairs.

"Hey, *you*! Wait a minute!"

It was the voice of a man who was used to issuing orders. Cross paused, turned his head, and registered a look of make-believe surprise.

"What do you want here?" the man asked, coming up to him.

"What do you mean?" Cross countered. "I'm going up to my room."

"Your *room*? Are you *living* here?" Herndon demanded.

"Of course. And who are you? Why are you asking me all this?"

"I just happen to own this goddamn building, that's all," Herndon said with rough irony. "I say who can and can't live here!"

"But I'm not going into *your* apartment," he pretended to misunderstand. "I live upstair "

"I don't give a good goddamn *where* you live!" Herndon snapped. "You can't stay in this building—"

"Now, wait a minute! I've signed a lease with Mr. Blount—"

"You can't talk to me that way!"

Herndon advanced and Cross doubled his fist.

"Watch out! You're old and I don't want to hurt you!" He saw Herndon pause and blink his eyes. "If you want to talk to me, all right. But don't touch me, see?"

Herndon was short, grey, flabby, with a wide mouth. His eyes were reddish and teary at the inflamed corners. His hair was black and slicked flat to the crown of a large, partly bald skull. He was violently agitated and seemed not to know what move to make. His face grew brick red.

"How long have you been in this building?" Herndon asked finally.

"For almost a week," Cross lied.

Herndon looked Cross over, his eyes traveling from Cross's necktie to his shoes.

"Say, come in here," Herndon said suddenly. "I want to talk to you."

Cross knew that the man had changed his tactics. He's going to try to scare me in another way now . . . He stepped into a nicely furnished room which had a large desk. A wood fire burned in the grate and shadows danced along the walls. Herndon studied Cross for some seconds.

"Listen," he began in a tone of voice that indicated that he was stooping to give advice to someone who he doubted had sense enough to profit by it. "You are being misled. For thirty years I've had a strict policy about renting, and nobody's going to make me change it. This lease you're talking about— It's nothing. Forget it. The quicker, the better for you. I'm going to see Blount tonight and give 'im hell. Get me straight. I don't give a good goddamn about what happens to you, see? I could crush you, if I wanted to. Now, go upstairs and pack your stuff and get the hell out of there! You're black and you don't belong there and you goddamn well know it."

"Thanks," Cross said in a low, clear voice. "I'm staying here as long as Mr. Blount says I can. It's your move."

"So, you're a Communist, hey?"

"No, I'm not."

"Oh, yes, you are, and you think you're being smart," Herndon's voice was rising. "I can take care of your kind. You Reds think you—"

"I told you that I'm not a Communist; I'm *anti*-Communist!" Cross said sternly.

"I don't give a good goddamn *what* kind of a Communist you are!" Herndon shouted.

"I didn't think you did," Cross said quietly. "That's why I insisted on telling you. I'm black and that's what's riling you. But I will not move from here."

Herndon, his lips quivering, yanked open a drawer of the desk.

"Be careful, man," Cross warned him, ramming his hand into his coat pocket. "I'm armed. If you pull out a gun, I'll shoot you!" Cross was bent forward, his entire body tense, his eyes not blinking.

Herndon slammed the drawer shut and came to the side of his desk.

"Get out of here, you black sonofabitch!" he shouted, his body trembling with rage. "Get out of this house! Get out of this building! Get out of my sight! If I see you again, I'll kill you, you hear?"

Cross did not move; he stood towering over Herndon whose mouth held flecks of foam at the corners.

"I'm going, but I never turn my back on a man who's yelling at me," he said slowly.

Herndon's lips moved soundlessly. Cross kept his eyes on Herndon and moved backwards to the door, still clutching his gun. With his left hand he groped for the knob, turned it, and pulled the door open.

"Mr. Herndon, whenever you're in my presence, be careful," Cross said. "You've threatened me and I won't forget it."

He went through the door and shut it. Things would happen fast now. He smiled as he went upstairs. The encounter with Herndon had given him a lift, had almost made the last shred of dreaminess leave him. This thing'll be decided tonight one way or the other, he told himself as he entered the apartment.

Eva returned an hour later. He had to be careful in her

presence; he must not let her feel that he had spied on her intimate life.

"Oh, Lionel!" she called.

He went into the hallway and saw Eva still wearing her coat; her cheeks were red and excitement was in her eyes.

"Yes?"

"Herndon says he wants to see Gil as soon as he comes in," Eva said breathlessly. "What happened? Did you have a run in with 'im?"

"We had it," Cross said.

"Did he get rough?"

"He wanted to pull a gun, but I told him I had one, too."

"Oh, Lord—" She leaned weakly against the wall. "Poor Lionel . . ."

Her eyes were full of pity, and Cross knew that she felt that he too was a victim of the Party, that the Party was using him for bait. I'm tougher than you think I am, he said to himself.

"It's nothing," he said. "I like his kind."

"Oh, dear! Where's Gil?" She was trembling.

"Now, Eva, don't worry," Cross tried to soothe her. "Nothing's going to happen for the moment, anyway. His next move will be to try to scare Gil, and I don't think Gil scares easily."

"Don't you want a drink or something?" she asked, looking at him as though she expected to see him collapse.

"I never refuse a drink," he said.

She brought out a bottle of cognac.

"I brought this from France last summer," she said, "feeling that I might need it sometime. And, now's the time."

Cross looked at her and smiled. Bless her; she's feeling good because she feels that she's of some use to me . . .

"Look," he said, pushing the glass she had filled to her. "I think you need this more than I do."

She drank from the glass and poured one for him.

"What do you think will happen, Lionel?" she asked in a whisper. "That Herndon's capable of anything— Oh, God, Lionel, do you think it's *worth* it?"

Cross could see that she was on the verge of telling him to ditch the Party, to get out, to save himself. At that moment he heard Gil's key turning in the lock of the door and a pall of anxiety came over Eva's face. Cross could see Gil hanging up his coat in the hallway. As Gil entered, Eva turned as though to speak to Cross, but checked herself.

"Hello, everybody," Gil said placidly.

"Tired, Gil?" Eva asked; she was trying to act natural.

"Not especially," he said, shrugging. He drew his wallet from his coat pocket and extracted a paper from it, saying: "Here's the permit for your gun, Lionel. The Party had a lawyer pull some strings . . . But be careful, guy."

"Thanks," Cross said. "I can tell you that this permit comes just in time. I met Herndon today."

"Really? And how was it?"

"Rugged."

Eva rushed forward and she caught hold of the lapels of Gil's coat. "You mustn't let Lionel get into this," she spoke hysterically. "Herndon said he wanted to see you the moment you came in . . . And he's already threatened Lionel with a gun—"

"Let Lionel tell me what happened," Gil said, gently pushing Eva to one side, struggling to master his annoyance.

"Well," Cross began. "I was returning from—"

"Just a moment," Gil said. He took out his pipe and began to fill it with tobacco; then he paused and looked intently at Eva. Eva stared; she seemed on the verge of speaking, but controlled herself.

"I must see about dinner," she mumbled, flushing red. She left the room and Gil lit his pipe, sucked at it.

"I'm listening," he said.

Cross related what had transpired, leaving out nothing. Gil made no comment; he rose and stood at a window looking out, smoking silently. Then he turned, sat at his desk and began writing upon a pad of paper. Eva came on tiptoe to the door, peered in apprehensively, then left. Cross lit a cigarette and waited. I'll make him guess at what I'm feeling just as I have to guess at what he's feeling, he told himself.

The doorbell pealed. Gil paused in his writing, lifted his hand from the page, then began writing again. Eva ran to the door, her eyes round with fear.

"Gil," she called timidly.

"Yes," Gil answered, but not turning or looking at her.

"Maybe it's Herndon— Shall I answer?" she asked in a whisper.

"You're always to answer the door," he said calmly.

As though seeking support, Eva looked at Cross.

"If it's Herndon, do be careful," she said.

"Eva!" Gil barked at her.

"I'll answer it," Cross said.

"No, Lionel. Eva will answer the door," Gil said in slow, heavy accents of authority.

Cross wanted to rise and take the man by the throat. Why does he act like that? Then he tried to dismiss it from his mind. After all, I'm no angel, he mused. It's really none of my business . . . He was now sorry that he had read Eva's diary; his knowing her as he did made it impossible for him to regard her with detachment. Eva lingered a moment longer at the door, then vanished.

"Oh!" Eva's frightened voice came from the hallway a moment later.

"I'm sorry, Eva— Did I scare you? Is Gil home? I got to see 'im quick— It's awfully important—"

"Come in, Bob— But what's the matter? You look sick or something— Did you have some trouble downstairs?"

"Trouble? Yes. But not downstairs . . . What do you mean? Is Gil here?"

"He's in the living room," Eva said.

Gil had stopped writing, his pen poised over the sheet of paper. His eyes hardened as Bob, his face twitching, his eyes bloodshot and staring, appeared in the doorway.

"Hey, Lane," Bob called to Cross; there was no heartiness in his voice.

Gil whirled in his seat and demanded: "What do you want here, Bob?"

Bob acted as if he had not heard; he sank weakly into a chair. He looked at Gil and forced a sick grin that faded quickly and his face went lifeless, his eyes staring at the floor in a kind of stupor. A large drop of mucus formed at the tip of his flat, brown nose, hovered there for a second, then dropped to his upper lip. He licked at it, unaware that he did so.

"Gil," he begged, "you've got to help me."

Eva stood in the doorway. Cross sat watching. Gil was looking at Bob with half-turned body. Bob turned to Cross.

"Lane, you got to talk to 'im for me—"

"Bob!" Gil shouted, his tone full of dangerous warning. "Lane has nothing to do with this, and you damn well know it! What are you trying to do? Disturb his faith in the Party? You've said enough already to be brought up on serious charges!"

"I just want to talk to 'im—"

"You're trying to influence Lane!" Gil shouted again, leaping to his feet. "You're organizing against the Party right *here* in my presence!"

"No, no, Gil—"

"You're trying to turn Lane against the Party right under my eyes!"

"Oh, God, no! No, Gil!"

"You are guilty right now of ideological factionalism!"

"What's that?" Bob asked incredulously.

"You are trying to get Lane to support your ideas," Gil accused Bob.

Bob sighed; he had come to plead innocent to one crime and now he found himself accused of still another crime. Cross felt certain that Gil did not want him to witness this.

"I'll go to my room," he offered.

"No; stay right here," Gil ordered.

And Cross suddenly realized that Gil wanted him to see what was happening. Gil's chastisement of Bob could either be a warning or an object lesson. How efficient this is, Cross marveled. Not a single word or gesture is wasted. By observing this, Cross, too, could learn how to break and ravage the spirits of others, or he could see what would happen to him if he disobeyed. Eva remained in the doorway, her eyes fixed upon Bob's face. Gil was looking at Eva with eyes full of warning, but Eva was not aware of his gaze. The moment, however, she saw it, she blushed and hurriedly left the room.

"Now, what's the matter with you, Bob?" Gil asked at last.

Bob had not taken off his hat or his coat. Dirty snow melted on his shoes and tiny rings of water were forming on the carpet. Bob spoke in a broken whimper:

"The Party voted to expel me, Gil—"

"I know that," Gil said calmly.

"But Gil, I don't wanna leave the Party— You got to help me— My life's in the Party— The Party's all I got in the world— I made a mistake—"

"Tell that to the Party," Gil said, turning and sitting again at his desk.

"Oh, please, Gil— You don't understand— I don't even want to say it, man— You *know* my problem—I'm British— Only the *Party* knows it!" Bob rose and went to the back of Gil and whispered despairingly: "Listen, an hour ago the Immigration men came to my flat, see? Lucky, I didn't go to the door—Sarah went. She told 'em in a loud voice that I was out— I heard 'em talking to Sarah and I slipped down the back stairs— I came here, to *you*, Gil— You're my friend— Gil, for God's sake, don't let 'em do this; don't let the Party do this to me—"

"How do you know it was the Party?" Gil asked.

"But *only* the Party knew!"

"But how do you *know* the Party did it?" Gil demanded.

"Listen, I once heard Hilton threaten another West Indian Negro like me— He said he could drop an unsigned note to the Immigration folks if he didn't behave—"

"But have you any *proof* that the Party told the Government?" Gil demanded.

Bob shook his head; his eyes were blank and empty. Cross saw the point; if Bob had no proof, what harm could Bob's accusation do?

"Naw; I ain't got no proof . . ."

Gil rose and stood over Bob.

"Are you accusing the Party of playing the role of a stool pigeon?" he thundered.

Bob winced as though he had been slapped.

"No, no, no!"

"Then what in hell *are* you saying?"

"Gil, listen to me. Ten years ago I had to run off from Trinidad to keep the British from putting me in jail for Party activity— If I go back, they'll snatch me off the boat and take me straight to jail for *ten* years— Ten years in jail in the tropics is death— I mean *death*, man— Don't you understand?"

"I understand," Gil said, nodding his head. "But that doesn't explain why you fought the Party."

"I didn't know I was *fighting* the Party . . . I don't want to fight the Party . . ."

"You took a position *against* the Party! That's counter-revolution! And for counter-revolutionists the Party has no mercy!" Gil told him.

"Gil, you got to tell 'em to give me another chance . . . The Party can *hide* me . . . Let me go to Mexico, any-where—"

"Who are you to *defy* the Party?"

"I ain't nobody, *nothing* . . ." Bob slid from his chair and lay prone on the floor. "This is *too* much, Gil— Please, please, don't let 'em do this to me! I was wrong! I confess! And I'll do anything you say, Gil! You're on the Central Committee and they'll listen to you. I been to Headquarters and they won't even talk to me—"

Cross was stunned. He wanted to rise and place his foot on Bob's neck and cut off the flow of whining words. Gil watched Bob with calm, placid eyes and Cross wondered how many men and women Gil had seen in such prostrate positions of penitent surrender to enable him to stare at Bob with so aloof and yet engrossed a passion.

"Did you meet anybody when you came up here?" Gil asked suddenly.

Bob blinked his eyes bewilderedly. "Meet anybody? No; I saw nobody . . . Gil, *please!*"

"All right, Bob. You can go now."

Bob's body galvanized itself to a sitting position on the floor; his hand went to his mouth in dismay.

"Where?"

"I don't care *where* you go—"

"But they'll *get* me, Gil! Look, I'll give my *life* to the Party!"

"The Party doesn't want your life." Gil smiled.

Cross closed his eyes. His anger was centered against Bob for his weakness. No wonder Gil would not give in! The more merciless Gil was the more Bob would yield. Eva came to the door, her eyes avoiding Bob. Cross could see her legs trembling.

"Gil, dinner's ready."

"Go ahead and eat, Lionel. I'll join you later," Gil said.

Cross rose and went out of the room, his eyes avoiding Bob who sobbed on the floor. He had no appetite, but he sat at the table and Eva served him. As he chewed his food, he heard Gil's voice rising in accusation, then Bob's voice falling in meek pleas. Then came a pause during which Bob coughed loudly. Finally there was a sound of footsteps in the hallway. Gil was saying something to Bob at the door, then the door closed. Cross looked at Eva; her eyes were full of fear, and her hand shook slightly as she ate. Gil came briskly to the table, sat, keeping his eyes in front of him. He volunteered no information and acted as though he knew that no one would dare ask for any.

"God, I'm hungry," Gil said pleasantly and reached for the platter of roast beef.

After he had served himself generously, Gil turned to Cross and asked: "Say, did you see who won the chess tournament in Moscow? I was too busy to buy a paper."

"No, I don't know who won," Cross said, slightly nonplussed.

"Do you play chess?" Gil asked.

"No."

"You ought to learn. It's wonderful for relaxation," Gil advised him.

As dinner proceeded in silence, Cross was aware that a feeling of tranquility had descended upon him. In his mind Gil had receded far off until he had become a tiny, little luminous figure upon which all of his attention was focussed. It was as if he was squinting his eye along the barrel of a rifle toward some distant and elusive target and at long last the center of the target had come within the hairline of the sight.

After he had drained his cup of coffee, Gil chuckled softly and asked: "What time is it?" He looked at his wrist watch. "Hummm . . . Ten past nine— I'd better get down and see Herr Herndon."

"Do you want me to come with you?" Cross asked.

"Why?" Gil asked, lifting his brows in surprise.

Cross said nothing. Eva sat stiff, staring with protesting eyes into her empty coffee cup. Then she lifted her eyes to Gil and Cross saw the light of protest die. God, she's scared, Cross thought. If she's that afraid of him, how she must hate him . . . !

Gil stood and went into the hallway, then out of the door. Eva rose suddenly, as though feeling that she had to drown her anxieties in activity, and began clearing the dishes from the table.

"I'll help you," Cross said, taking a stack of plates and starting for the kitchen.

"No, Lionel—"

"Why not?" he said, continuing to clear the table.

"You don't have to, you know," she said.

"I want to," he said. He wanted to be near her.

Then they both were still. Coming from downstairs were loud voices. Cross could distinguish the voice of Gil, then that of Herndon. They were at it strongly. The dishes slid from Eva's hands to the table with a clatter, then she clutched the back of the chair till her knuckles showed white.

"Do you think I ought to go down?" he asked Eva.

She shook her head.

"No. If he said no, then don't. He'd be awfully angry, and when he's angry he doesn't speak for weeks—" She caught herself; she had said more than she had intended. "Lionel, really, don't bother with the dishes. Do what you like . . ." Irritation was in her voice.

He knew that he was making her more nervous; she did not want him to see her state of mind.

"Okay."

He went to his room and the voices were clearer; he put his ear to the floor and heard shouts that carried sounds of hot anger, but no words were distinguishable. He lay on his bed, then jerked upright; there had come a sharp snapping as of wood breaking, then a dull thump, and all was silent. The door of his room flew open and Eva stood there, clasping her hands in front of her, staring at him with eyes filled with terror.

"What was that?"

Cross stood and went to her, she clutched his hand tightly.

"Don't you think I ought to go down?" he asked.

"Yes," she agreed impulsively. Then her body flinched and she shut her eyes in desperation. "No; no; he'd be angry. He'd think that you thought he couldn't handle it—" Tears leaped into her eyes and she turned from him. "If he gets hurt, he'll wonder why we didn't do something. He'll think I did it on purpose—"

"On *purpose?*" he asked.

Yes; she was fighting against a wish for something to happen to Gil; she was longing for someone to put him out of her life . . .

A hoarse scream came from downstairs.

"I'm going down," Cross said suddenly.

"Yes, Lionel," Eva breathed; she was pale, trembling.

He went quickly into the hallway. He realized as he went down the steps that he was acting more as a kind of proxy for the feelings of Eva than his own. *I* really don't care, he thought. When he reached the landing of the first floor, he paused. There came to his ears the sound of grunts, scuffling feet, and the thud of blows. He crept on tiptoe to the door and placed his ear to the panel. Yes, they were fighting . . . Was the door locked? He turned the knob; the door swung in and Cross looked at the two men grappling with each other. Gil lashed out with his right fist, bashing Herndon a crushing blow on the ear and sending him reeling backwards. Herndon collided with a table and when he turned Cross could see that he had the fire poker in his right hand. Cross looked quickly at Gil and saw what he had not seen when he had first looked into the room. Gil was bloody, his face covered with reddish streaks where the fire poker had ripped into his flesh.

Both men were oblivious of Cross who stood in the doorway with a bitter smile on his face. Cross could barely contain his bubbling glee as he watched the bloody battle. Which man did he hate more? Many times during the past twenty-four hours he had wished both of them dead and now he was looking at them batter each other's brains out . . . Let 'em fight it out, he said to himself.

He spun round at the sound of footsteps behind him on the stairs. Eva was descending with wild eyes, her hair flying behind her. He grabbed her shoulders and held her, wanting to keep her out of the room. Eva twisted loose and ran to the doorway. Cross followed and stood behind her. Eva grabbed hold of both jambs of the door and screamed as she saw Gil sinking to the floor under the blows of Herndon's fire poker.

Herndon turned and stared at Eva, still clutching the poker in his right hand. He had the look of a man struggling to awaken from a dream. Then Cross saw the muscles of Herndon's face twitch as he advanced menacingly toward them.

"Get out, or I'll kill you both!" Herndon growled.

Eva screamed again, backed violently into Cross, then turned and ran up the stairs. Before Cross could move, Herndon was upon him and he ducked in time to save his head a swishing blow from the poker which caught him on his right shoulder, leaving a searing line of fire in his flesh. He leaped aside and watched Herndon stumble toward the rear of the hall. Cross felt for his gun, then decided that he would run. It was not fear for Herndon that was making him abandon the fight; he was hoping that Herndon would reenter the room and battle again with Gil . . . He took the stairs four at a time and was halfway up when he heard another scuffling lunge behind him; he paused and glanced back. Gil had rushed out of the room and had grabbed Herndon; the two men now wrestled for possession of the fire poker, rolling, clawing, going from Cross's sight as they fell through the doorway back into the room. Cross caressed his bruised shoulder and looked upward; the door of Gil's apartment was open and he heard Eva's frantic voice.

"Don't you understand? I want the police! For God's sake—"

Cross entered the hallway. Eva thrust the telephone into his hands.

"Lionel, here; call the police . . . I can't make the operator understand anything."

"Okay," he breathed.

"Are you hurt?"

"Not much . . ."

He picked up the telephone, placed the receiver to his ear and heard the metallic hum of the line. He jiggled the hook, then paused, turning his head as another burst of sound came from downstairs. Eva sprang through the doorway, heading for downstairs.

"Eva!" he called after her.

Good Lord, what ought he do? She'll get hurt down there with that Fascist . . . Her sense of guilt's making her over-react to help Gil . . . He left the phone and ran after her, catching her on the landing and dragging her back into the apartment.

"No, no," he told her. "You can't go down there . . . *You* call the police—"

"I don't know what to do," she whimpered.

"I'll go down and help Gil," he said.

Eva stared at him helplessly, her body moving indecisively. He thrust the telephone into her hands and ran from the room, stumbling down the stairs. In the lower hallway, he stood, hearing the sound of the fight. He debated: yes; he *had* to help Gil . . . What would Gil say if he did not? His failure to go to Gil's aid would be something he could never explain . . .

Again he stood in the doorway of Herndon's apartment. They were still fighting. Herndon was rushing at Gil again, the poker raised to strike. Gil backed off, his hands lifted to protect his face and head. Herndon crashed the poker into Gil's hands which seemed to wilt under the blow. The poker flew from Herndon's fingers and clattered to the floor. Gil snatched it up quickly and, with it, charged into Herndon, his face livid with fury; he whacked two telling blows home to Herndon's head and face and Cross heard the tinkling of glass shards as Herndon's spectacles broke and showered from his eyes.

Cross watched, disdainful, detached. He saw that there was a broken table leg lying near the fireplace; someone had no doubt been sent crashing into the table and the heavy oaken leg had snapped in two near the top of the table. Teeth bared, Gil now lifted the poker once again to send another blow to Herndon; but, as his arm was about to descend, the tip of the poker caught in the glass chandelier swinging from the ceiling. There was a musical storm of falling crystal and the ceiling light went out, leaving the room lit only by the leaping shadows of the fire. The force that Gil had put behind that swooping blow now carried him headlong to the floor, the poker bounding free once more.

Catlike, Herndon was on it and before Gil could rise Herndon was raining deadly blows upon the head and face of Gil.

Suddenly a fullness of knowledge declared itself within Cross and he knew what he wanted to do. He was acting before he knew it. He reached down and seized hold of the heavy oaken leg of the table and turned and lifted it high in the air, feeling the solid weight of the wood in his hand, and then he sent it flying squarely into the bloody forehead of Herndon. The impact of the blow sent a tremor along the muscles of his arm. Herndon fell like an ox and lay still. He had no doubt crushed the man's skull. Tense, he stood looking down at Herndon, waiting to see if he would move again. He was concentrated, aware of nothing but Herndon's still, bloody form. Then he was startled; he whirled to see Gil struggling heavily to his feet, blood streaming from his face and neck, clotting his eyes. Cross stared for a moment. He was not through. The imperious feeling that had impelled him to action was not fulfilled. His eyes were unblinkingly on Gil's face. Yes, this other insect had to be crushed, blotted out of existence . . .

His fingers gradually tightened about the oaken table leg; his arm lifted slowly into the air. Gil was dabbing clumsily with his handkerchief at the blood on his neck and cheeks. Cross let go with the table leg, smashing it into the left side of Gil's head. Gil trembled for a split second, then fell headlong toward the fireplace where flames danced and cast wild red shadows over the walls. Cross's hand sank slowly to his side, the table leg resting lightly on the floor, its edges stained with blood. There was silence save for the slow ticking of an ornate clock on the desk.

He filled his lungs and sighed deeply. For perhaps a minute he did not move; his sense gradually assumed a tone of anxiety and he stared more intently at the two bloody forms stretched grotesquely on the smeared rug. Then he sucked in his breath and whirled toward the door. Oh, God, it was still open! Had anyone seen him? He rushed to it and closed it; then turned back to the room and the two inert forms over which red shadows of the fire flickered. Were they dead? He touched Herndon's shoulder; the man was still; the wide, thin lips hung open; blood oozed from one corner of the mouth.

Cross hesitated a second, then lifted the table leg and chopped again into the skull. The body rolled over from force of the blow.

Cross now turned to Gil whose head lay near the fire. He caught hold of one of Gil's legs and yanked the body from the fireplace into the center of the room where he could get a better chance to deliver another blow at the head. Again he lifted the table leg and whacked at Gil and he knew that Gil would never move again.

The universe seemed to be rushing at him with all the concreteness of its totality. He was anchored once again in life, in the flow of things; the world glowed with an interest so sharp that it made his body ache. He had had no plan when he had dealt those blows of death, but now he feared for himself, felt the need of a plan of defense. He knew exactly what he had done; he had done it deliberately, even though he had not planned it. He had not been blank of mind when he had done it, and he was resolved that he would never claim any such thing.

He took one last quick look about the room. One of the drawers of Herndon's desk was open and Cross could see the butt of Herndon's gun half-pulled out. He could almost reconstruct what had happened between the two men. Gil had no doubt grabbed Herndon just as Herndon had been about to seize the gun. And after that they had fought so desperately that neither of them had had a chance to get the gun, or they had forgotten it . . .

The plan sprang full and ripe in his imagination, his body, his senses; he took out his handkerchief and quickly wiped the table leg which he held in his hand, making sure that no trace of his fingerprints would remain. He went to Herndon, holding the table leg with the handkerchief so that his hand would not touch it, and forced the fingers of Herndon's right hand about it several times so that the man's prints would be found . . . He was breathing heavily. The winking shadows of the fire flicked warningly through the room. Still holding the leg with the handkerchief, he went to Gil and closed Gil's loose fingers about it, letting the wooden leg trail uncertainly about the lifeless hand. He took the fire poker, wiped it clean and inserted it in the fingers of Herndon's right hand . . .

No; he changed his mind; he'd let the fire poker rest a few inches from Herndon's hand . . . That was more natural . . . He looked swiftly around to make sure that he was leaving no marks of his having been in the room. He had to hurry . . . The door? Fingerprints on the knob . . . ? No; he would not bother about them. After all, if he made things *too* clean, the police would get suspicious . . . And he had been down here talking to Herndon earlier this afternoon . . . Sure . . . His prints had a right to be on the door. Go up to Eva . . . What would he tell her? There would be questions from the police, from Party leaders, from Eva, from everybody . . . The news- papers . . . ? What would they say? Well, he was just a Negro roomer who had gone down at the suggestion of Mrs. Blount to see what was happening and had seen them fighting . . .

He opened the door; the downstairs hallway was empty. He caught hold of the door handle and was about to shut it when an idea came to him. Suppose someone came to see Herndon and found both Herndon and Gil dead? Ah, yes; it was better to push the tiny lever on the lock and let the door lock itself. The door would be locked when the police and the Party leaders arrived. That was the trick. They would have to knock down the door. *And he, on his second trip down, had not been able to see what was happening; he had only heard sounds* . . . He adjusted the lock and pulled the door to, hearing it catch. He tried the handle; it was locked. Now, what motive on earth could he have had in killing the two of them? Let them figure that out . . .

He started up the stairs, then paused and looked down at himself. Was there any blood on him? He looked at his hands, his coat, his shoes. He could see nothing. Oh, yes; his hand- kerchief; it was bloody from where he had wiped the finger- prints from the fire poker and the table leg . . . He would have to burn it. Yes; he'd put it into the kitchen incinerator the first chance he got. And, to be absolutely sure, he would ditch the clothes he was wearing. The police had scientific ways of examining particles and arriving at damaging conclu- sions. He stood in front of Gil's apartment door and com- posed himself. Yes; he had to act hurriedly and frantically now. He grabbed hold of the doorknob and rattled it bru- tally. It was locked.

"Eva!" he yelled.

"Is that you, Lionel? Is Gil with you?"

"It's me; Lionel! Open the door quick!"

He heard the night-chain rattling; she had locked herself in. She opened the door and backed fearfully away from him.

"Did you call the police?" he asked her.

"No. I called Jack Hilton; he's calling the police— What happened?"

He searched her face; her eyes were bleak and frightened. Would she be glad that Gil was dead? Didn't she want him dead so that she could be free?

"The door down there is locked and I can't hear a thing," he told her. "Gil's still in there . . ."

"Oh, God," she whimpered.

He longed to know what was going on in her mind. Was she hoping that Gil was dead? And was she feeling guilty because she was hoping it? If so, then she'd act violently now; she'd try to ease her burden of guilt.

"The door's locked?" she repeated in a quiet voice.

"Yes."

"I'm liquid with fear . . . Look, Lionel, call Jack Hilton again and tell 'im— He thinks maybe Gil's all right now—"

Her voice died in her throat and she had spun around and was out of the door before Cross could grab her. He debated: he had a wound on his shoulder to prove that he had tried to help Gil and maybe it would be a good thing for Eva to see that the door was locked. Then, Eva, panting and whimpering, came rushing in again.

"He's there!" she gasped. "He's coming up here . . ."

"Who?"

"Herndon— I saw 'im on the stairs— He has his gun—"

Was she crazy? Herndon was dead. Eva ran past him into her bedroom. Cross approached the door and looked out; he heard footsteps mounting the stairs on the floor above him. Ah, Eva had thought she had seen Herndon, but she had mistaken another man for Herndon . . . He shut the door and put on the night-chain. Yes; that was something that could be used in his favor. Eva had thought that she had seen Herndon coming up the stairs! *That meant that her testimony would indicate that Herndon was still living after he had come up to the apartment for the second time . . . That could mean that Gil and Herndon killed each other!* By God, *that* was the plan! He would stick to that story . . .

"Eva!" he called to her. "Give me Hilton's phone number!"

When she did not answer, he went to her. She was lying on the floor of her bedroom; she had fainted. He lifted her to her bed, got a wet towel from the bathroom and patted her face with it. Her eyelids fluttered.

"Give me Hilton's phone number," he asked her.

"My purse," she murmured.

He got her purse and took it to her; she gave him an address book and whispered: "Find the number there, under H . . ."

Cross thumbed through the book, found the number, then walked slowly toward the telephone. His mind clearly grasped the entire situation and every muscle of his body was relaxed. Now, I'd like to see them figure that out, he told himself with a grim smile. I killed two little gods . . . He paused, frowning. But they would have killed me too if they had found me like that . . . Yet, he could not get it straight. Just a moment ago it had all seemed so simple. But now it was knotted and complicated. There was in him no regret for what he had done; no, none at all. But how *could* he have done it? He too had acted like a little god. He had stood amidst those red and flickering shadows, tense and consumed with cold rage, and had judged them and had found them guilty of insulting his sense of life and had carried out a sentence of death upon them. Like Hilton and Gil had acted toward Bob, so had he acted toward Gil and Herndon; he had assumed the role of policeman, judge, supreme court, and executioner,—all in one swift and terrible moment. But, if he resented their being little gods, how could he do the same? His self-assurance ebbed, his pride waned under the impact of his own reflections. Oh, Christ, their disease had reached out and claimed him too. He had been subverted by the contagion of the lawless; he had been defeated by that which he had sought to destroy. He sank listlessly into the chair by the side of the telephone. Yet, no matter what happened, he had to call Hilton; he had to phone that little god . . . ! He was limp. What was the matter with him? He was, yes, he was trapped in the

coils of his own doings. He had acted, had shattered the
dream that surrounded him, and now the world, including
himself in it, had turned mockingly into a concrete, waking
nightmare from which he could see no way of escaping. He
had become what he had tried to destroy, had taken on the
guise of the monster he had slain. Held to a point of attention
more by the logic of events than by his own reasoning, his
consciousness charged with a sense of meaninglessness, he
bent toward the telephone and dialed . . .

BOOK FOUR

DESPAIR

The wine of life is drawn; and the mere lees
Is left this vault to brag of.
— SHAKESPEARE'S *Macbeth*

THE SEDUCTIONS of vanity have lured countless men to
destinies that have confounded them, left them straitened
and undone. After an arduous journey of experience it is not
good to stare in dismay at a world that one was creating without being aware of it, and there is no chastening of the spirit
so severely sobering as that rankling sense of guilt that springs
from a knowledge of having been snared into the mire of
disillusionment when one thought that one was soaring on
wings of intellectual pride to a freedom remote from the
errors and frailties of the gullible. At times there comes into
the lives of men realizations so paralyzing that, for the first
time, their hands reach out fumblingly for the touch of another human being.

In Cross's despair it was upon Eva's trapped and deceived
heart — into whose depths he had stolen a criminal glimpse —
that he now instinctively leaned, his wounded pride groping
toward that one shelter where he hoped waited someone who
loathed cruelty and yearned to place a kiss of fraternity upon
the betrayed and victimized. And, as much for a dawning rev-
erence for her as for the protection of his own self-love, he
tried desperately to shield her from the shock of rough events
that he knew would be soon sweeping on tidal waves toward
the both of them. Many despairs and regrets later, via his
acutely developed habit of reflection, when he had reexam-
ined his behavior following his bloody snatching of the lives
of Gil and Herndon, he could find nothing remiss in how he
had deported himself. To an important extent the logic de-

rived from a mixing of his temperament and gratuitous opportunity had determined his attitude. To have fled immediately upon his gory acts would have been to confess his guilt
openly, and to have tried to explain either to the police or
to the Party the complex composition of the elementary
judgment-feeling that had spurred him to such acts of ethical
murder would have been to succumb to a gesture of sheer
naïveté of which he was far too intelligent to be capable. He
reasoned that it was much safer to lie, to dodge, to blend with
the changing hues of the foliage of the landscape for safety in
eluding his pursuers.

In talking to Hilton over the telephone, Cross was careful
to assume the role of a subordinate, a humble outsider, a man
speaking for a temporarily incapacitated woman.

"But Eva phoned and told me that you'd gone down to
help Gil," Hilton said in a baffled tone of voice.

"But the door was *locked* this time—"

"Did you try to get in?"

"Yeah. I banged and knocked and hollered—"

"And Herndon didn't answer?"

"No."

"And did you hear anything?"

"Fighting, like I told you—"

"Did you try to get help from anywhere?"

"Eva called you—"

"And the first time you went down, he hit you?"

"Yes, with the fire poker—"

"Where's Eva now?"

"She fainted. She's lying down."

"You hear any noise now?"

"Nothing; nothing at all."

"And Herndon ran Eva back into the apartment, hunh?"

"Yes; I was trying to phone you and she ran out—"

"He had a gun?"

"She said so. I didn't see him. I bolted the door when she
came running back in."

"Did Gil seem badly hurt?"

"Gosh, I don't know. I only got a glimpse of 'im," Cross
was purposefully vague. "Look, you ought to come over and

I could explain it all. I just moved in this morning, see? This Herndon jumped me at sight, told me to get the hell out, wanted to pull a gun on me, said he'd kill me—"

"Where was Gil when you first looked through the door?"

"He was lying on the floor."

"Herndon knocked him down?"

"Seems like it. Herndon had the fire poker in his hand—"

"Did you *see* him strike Gil?"

"Yes."

"Was Gil conscious?"

"I don't know—"

"And you're sure that Eva saw him on the stairs a few minutes ago?"

"Sure; she said so."

"Okay. Now, listen, don't let anybody into the apartment until I come, unless it's the police or somebody from the Party, see?"

"All right."

"That's all. I'll be right over." The line clicked.

Not once had any emotion entered Hilton's voice as he questioned Cross over the telephone, but Cross noticed that throughout Hilton's inquiries had run a theme that puzzled him. Ah, he knew now! Hilton was already trying to establish the fact that Herndon was the *aggressor*. Cross, knowing that Gil was dead, decided that his own defense could best served by his feeding the Party's hunger for a martyred hero, dead or alive. He marveled at how instinctively Hilton was reacting in terms of the Party's organizational needs. If, in describing what he had seen when he had looked into the doorway, he said that Gil had seemed to be getting the worst of it, that Herndon had been standing over Gil with the fire poker, then the Party would claim, when it found that Gil was dead, that Herndon, the fascist beast, had killed him, and had later died of wounds which Gil, in self-defense, had inflicted on him during the course of the struggle. And then there was that fantastic windfall of luck of Eva's thinking that she had seen Herndon after Herndon had been killed and after the door had been locked! Cross knew that he had to be careful in relating what he had seen, had always to keep sternly in mind that he must do no interpreting at all, that the

Party and the police had to weigh what had happened and place their own assessment and value upon it. His aim would be to establish in the minds of the police and Party leaders that Herndon had been alive when he had last looked into the room, that Gil had been hurt, unconscious, maybe dying, and after that the door had been locked . . .

And would not Eva be his unconscious ally? He was convinced that her actions had been determined by an awful sense of guilt toward Gil. Her fantasy of seeing Herndon with a gun on the stairs was but her own feeling that Herndon ought to kill her now that Herndon had done her secret bidding by killing Gil . . . And Eva no doubt felt that he was, like she, a victim of the Party's complicated duplicities . . . Yes, he had a chance to stand clear of suspicion as long as he could manipulate or count upon the guilt-feelings of others.

Cross took a deep breath and tried to keep the facts straight in his mind. This thing had come upon him so suddenly that its reality had not sunk home to him in all of its fullness. Had he killed them or was it a teasing fantasy? He was counting on their both being dead, or his whole plan was crazy. Or, if Gil lived, he was in trouble, both with the police and the Party. He longed to creep downstairs and make sure that they were both dead, but he feared complications would ensue if he broke open the door and looked in . . . And suppose someone saw him in the lower hallway now? But those men *must* be dead. God knows he had pounded them hard enough. Gil would have to be a superman to live after the many slashes that Herndon had rained down upon him and the heavy whacks he had showered upon his defenseless head at the end . . . Of Herndon he could be certain; that Fascist was dead . . .

"Lionel . . ." Eva's voice was calling.

"Yes?"

He went in to her; she was half leaning on her elbow in bed and she looked at him with eyes brimming with fear and guilt.

"Did Gil seem badly hurt?"

"I don't know," he answered her softly.

"What did Hilton say?"

"He said for us to stay here; he's on his way over now. He's phoned the police and the Party."

"But we should try to do something for Gil—"

"The door's *locked*, Eva—"

"Oh, God," she wailed, "I wish Hilton'd come. You hear anything down there now?"

"No," Cross said. "I was listening in the front hall, but I couldn't hear anything."

She broke down again and began weeping. "I can't stand this life— This deception— This everlasting violence— Is there no way to be human any more . . . ?"

Before he could stop her, she had sprung from the bed and was running on swift feet down the hall to the door.

"Gil! Gil!" she was screaming.

"Eva!" he yelled and started after her.

"He'll blame me if we don't help 'im," she sobbed hysterically. "And the Party'll want to know *why* we didn't help 'im . . ." She sobered quickly and stared at him, realizing that she was trying to explain something that he could not possibly understand.

Yes; she, like him, was wondering if Gil was really dead. A wounded Gil, a living Gil, would be a calamity for the both of them. He longed to put her at peace, to tell her that she was free. But he could not. He caught her on the landing, about to descend the stairs. He grabbed her shoulders.

"Herndon's dangerous," he argued. "And Hilton said for us to *keep* from down there—"

"Gil may be hurt," she whimpered. "We could help him—"

"The door's *locked*!" he insisted. Yes, he would stress that she must be loyal to the Party, something which she feared more than she feared Gil. "The Party will perhaps make a test case of this, see? We *can't* interfere . . ." A better idea leaped into his mind; she felt that he was a victim of the Party and he would try to exploit her delusion. That's it . . . "Look, Eva," he argued solemnly, "this is complicated. The reason that Hilton doesn't want me to go down there is that I'm *colored*, see? You know the police . . . They'd try to frame me . . ."

She wilted, turned, and buried her face on his shoulder. Hers was a world ruled by fear. He led her back into the apartment and bolted the door; sweat stood on his forehead.

He guided her steps to the bed and gently helped her upon it. They were silent; there came the sound of footsteps in the hallway. Eva strained, lifting herself almost to a sitting position. Could that be the police or Hilton? Cross heard the footsteps mount the stairway. No; it was somebody who lived upstairs.

"The Cushmans," Eva whispered. "They're anti-Party."

Cross stared at her in amazement. To her the world was either Party or anti-Party, and all in between did not count. He sat on a chair at the side of the bed. Eva was shaking; he could hear her teeth rattling. He longed to take hold of her and soothe her, but dared not.

"You think they'll blame us if Gil's badly hurt?" she asked in a whisper.

The Party ruled her not only positively but negatively. It was not only what she did that would make her guilty, but also what she did not do . . .

"We did what we could," he told her. "This was not our idea, Eva. They should have sent someone to help Gil . . . And he wouldn't let me go down with 'im . . ."

Her sense of guilt was a hot bed of coals and she was squirming on it. Cross rose and Eva reached impulsively and grabbed his hand and clung to it.

"Don't go," she begged.

"I was going to try to listen at the door—"

"Don't leave me here," she pled in a whisper of panic.

He sat again on the edge of the bed and felt nervous tremors going through her body. If only he could tell her that she was free! But, no . . . If he told her that he had killed, the horror she felt for the Party would be transferred to him . . .

He was aware of her slim, willowy figure on the bed, the legs that tapered with such a long, slow curve, the suggestively dramatic roundness of her hips, the small but firm breasts, the long and delicate neck, and the hazel pools of her eyes now dark and anxious with dread; and desire for desire rose in him for her for the first time. Oh, God, he must not think of that now . . . He felt the soft pressure from her thin, almost transparent fingers on his hand and she became woman as body of woman for his senses. The depths of him stirred as he realized that she was now alone in the world and did not know it; in a peculiar sense she was at his mercy. What he did or did not do, what he said or did not say would affect her more profoundly now than anything that would ever happen to her. Already she was his in a deeper sense than the sexual, in a sense that included the sexual. At this moment she was again an orphan; she had only him to depend upon and he could now, like Gil had done with Bob, ravage her entire being without any resistance from her. From the poignant pages of her diary and from the fact that Gil was dead and she did not know it, he possessed a comprehension of her existence that she had not the capacity to imagine. Would she suspect him? *Could* she suspect him? She believed that colored people were caught up in life, healthy, untouched and unspoiled by the cynical world of political deceptions . . . Had she not referred to "us" when she spoke of her fear of the Party?

For the first time since he had killed, he felt guilty. It was not a guilt for his having murdered; it was because he now saw that he held over the life of Eva a godlike power and knowledge that even Gil or the Party had not held. He had killed Gil and Herndon because they had wanted to play god to others, and their brutal strivings had struck him as being so utterly obscene that he had torn their lives from them in a moment of supreme conviction that he and he alone was right and that they were eternally wrong. And now Gil lay still and dead downstairs amid the trembling red shadows and he sat here holding Eva's hand, desiring her body. And the wall of deception which he had begun to erect to conceal the nature of her husband's death would throw her, perhaps, into his arms . . .

If the actions of Gil and Herndon were monstrously inhuman, then was not what he was doing also devoid of humanity? If there was a valid difference, just where did it lie? Was the innocence of Gil and Herndon the less because they had millions of supporters, because time and tradition, law and religion had mounted a shield of justification before them? And his guilt, was it the more because he was alone and had no counsel but his own? If Gil or Herndon had done what he had done, would it have worried them? Was not his worrying proof that he was wrong? Did he not need about him the sanctioning buttress of the faces of his brothers in crime to make him feel at home with his deed?

His sense of despair deepened and he yearned for the first time to be free of this circling, brooding that filled his skull, this elusive shadow of himself that tortured him. To go on killing would only sink him deeper into these quicksands of guilt which he wanted so much to avoid. What way was there out of this? The desperately naïve idea of confessing everything to Eva came to him. Might not she, being another victim, understand and help him? *No!* That was crazy . . . She believed him an *innocent* victim, not a *guilty* one! No; he could talk to no one now; he had to tread this guilty treadmill alone . . .

He recovered himself as the fingers of Eva's hand tightened about his own.

"Are you frightened, Lionel?"

"No."

"What can we tell them?"

"The truth. We'll tell them what happened . . ."

He knew that, childlike, she was already thinking that maybe a lie would be a better kind of truth to tell than to try to conceal the guilt that had so long smouldered in her heart. Why was he mulling and hesitating? Ride this thing out and take this lovely girl and live with her . . .

"What are you thinking, Lionel?"

"Nothing," he breathed.

"They'll say we acted wrongly, won't they?"

"How could they?" he asked. "We couldn't do any more than we did—"

"Oh, why did the Party push *you* into this?" she wailed.

"We're in it together," he told her.

"Gil may be wanting us to help him; maybe he's hurt," she began to weep again.

The doorbell rang.

"Go, Lionel!"

Cross ran and let in Jack Hilton and another man. They stared at one another for a moment in silence. Eva came running from the bedroom.

"He's still down there, Jack— Can't you do something?" she implored. "Maybe he's hurt . . ."

Hilton's face turned pale and he spun to Cross.

"But the police? Aren't they here *yet*?"

"No," Cross told him.

"And Gil's *still* down there?"

"Yes."

"And that door's still locked?"

"I guess so," Cross stammered.

"My God—" Hilton said, whirling and going through the door. He halted, turned, and beckoned to his companion. "Come *on*, Menti!"

They thundered down the stairs. Eva followed Menti; and Cross, lingeringly, followed Eva, watching Hilton's movements, wondering what his tactics would be. They paused momentarily in the downstairs hallway. Hilton advanced to the door of Herndon's apartment.

"Is this the door?"

"Yes," Cross told him.

Hilton grabbed the knob and rattled it.

"Gil! Are you there?" Hilton called loudly.

"Gil! Gil!" Eva yelled, hammering on the panels of the door with her fists.

"You'd better break it down," Cross said. "I've called and called—"

Hilton hesitated, then ran to the rear door and tried the handle. He walked back toward them with worried eyes.

"Put your shoulder to it, Menti," Hilton said.

"Okay," Menti agreed eagerly.

Menti, tall, black of hair, with a nervous, too-white face, backed off to the bottom of the stairs, quickly hunched his shoulders and sent himself toward the door and in the second of his body hitting the panels, the door burst in, banging loudly against a wall inside. Menti blocked Cross's vision and he could see nothing; he remembered the room lit by flames and dancing shadows, but the wood fire had died down and, though he had forgotten it, the light on the ceiling had gone out when Gil had accidentally struck the chandelier with the fire poker. Eva pushed past him, then stopped, her face gazing at the floor of Herndon's study.

"Gil! Oh, God, Gil!" she screamed and ran forward.

Cross could now see the dim outlines of Gil and Herndon lying outstretched on the rug. They were as he had left them, the table leg and the fire poker lying near their right hands, their faces darkened with splotches of blood.

"What's happened?" Hilton asked in singsong voice.

"Good Christ," Menti breathed.

"Gil! Gil!" Eva was still screaming, advancing slowly into the room.

Hilton stood without moving, his thin lips hanging open. Eva was now bent over Gil, her hands reaching out as though to touch him, then she closed her eyes and turned her body and leaned weakly against a wall, wailing and sobbing. Cross was observing closely and waiting for questions. Hilton was the first to master himself; he rushed forward, knelt at Gil's side and felt for his pulse. His eyes lifted to Eva's face; then he looked at Cross; he stood slowly, turning and looking at Menti. Only later did he glance at Herndon, then kneel and feel for his pulse.

"Help 'im," Eva begged, staring at Gil as though she expected him to rise and accuse her.

"We better call the police again," Menti said.

"Better call a doctor," Cross ventured.

"Naw; wait," Hilton said, speaking in a vague tone with bated breath, his eyes straying from face to face. "Look, don't touch anything here . . . Let's get upstairs!"

"Get a doctor," Eva begged. "He's bleeding . . . Somebody *do* something . . ." She knelt to touch Gil, but Hilton grabbed her arm.

"Gil's dead, Eva," Hilton told her softly. "Don't touch anything."

"No! No!" Eva screamed, cringed, jammed her fingers against her teeth and sank to the floor. Cross lifted her and held her by her shoulders, conscious that Hilton's eyes were upon him. As he held Eva he knew that now was beginning the time of his drastic test, a test he did not want, for, if he won it, what had he won? Eva? He had not killed to get her. Hilton was still staring at him; then Hilton turned and walked slowly to the hall door. Menti ran to Hilton and grabbed his arm.

"Hadn't I better call the Party again?" he asked.

"We haven't time," Hilton said. "The police'll be here any minute now."

Menti was nonplussed; his eyes narrowed and he stared at Hilton.

"I'm going to call the Party," he said.

"Take it easy, Menti," Hilton said with a slow, ironic smile. "This is more complicated than you think. I'm in charge here. I spoke to Blimin over the phone and he told me to take complete responsibility. *This* is political . . ."

"I see," Menti said, dropping his eyes.

Hilton was now staring at Cross with eyes round with astonishment. And Cross, as he watched Hilton, knew that this was the man he had to cope with, and a slow hatred for Hilton began to surge up in him. He still kept his arm about Eva who was trembling and sagging against him. Why was Hilton staring at him so? Was he already suspecting him? Hilton was a member of the upper circles of the Party and he was no fool. So free were the minds of these Communists that one could not predict what motives would prompt their actions. Cross held himself alert, every atom of him striving supremely to be aware of what was taking place.

"We've no time to lose," Hilton told them roughly. "Everybody get upstairs at once. Stay in the apartment 'til I come."

"No, no," Eva sobbed. "Help Gil—"

"Go upstairs, Eva," Hilton said. "It's too late."

Cross led Eva into the hallway and struggled with her up the steps; Menti helped him, but was looking over his shoulder to see what Hilton was doing. When inside the apartment, Eva clutched Menti and begged:

"Can't something be done, Menti? It's not too late, *is* it?"

"Take it easy, Eva," Menti said. "Hilton's doing everything . . ."

Cross eased Eva upon the sofa of the living room and Menti sat next to her, holding her shoulders. Hilton entered a moment later and Cross could see sweat standing on his forehead.

"He should've broken that door down," Menti told Hilton, nodding to Cross.

"No; he did right," Hilton said. "He's colored . . . This thing is complicated . . ."

"Oh," Menti breathed.

Hilton rushed out of the room and Cross could hear him putting the night-chain on the front door. Hilton returned and knelt at Eva's side.

"Eva," he began in a hurried but composed voice, "can you understand me? Are you fit to be questioned? We don't have much time—"

"But maybe he's not dead, Jack," Eva whimpered. "Try . . . Try to *do* something . . ."

"They're *both* dead, Eva," Hilton explained calmly.

"God in Heaven," Eva sobbed.

"Eva," Hilton spoke sternly. "We've no time for that . . . You must get hold of yourself. You're in the Party. You must rise above all display of personal feeling. There's something of decisive importance to the memory of Gil that I must discuss with you. You hear me?"

"Yes," Eva breathed, trying to still the shaking of her body; she turned wild eyes to Hilton and nodded her head.

"Gil's been killed by a Fascist," Hilton explained. "He was carrying out Party orders when he was killed; he fell in line of duty . . . That must be understood. This is a *Party* matter. The bourgeois press'll try to twist those facts downstairs, and we must see that they don't. I'm sure that Gil, if he were with us now, would agree emphatically to that."

"Yes," Eva said, nodding her head slowly; she glanced at Cross and buried her face in her hands.

Cross grasped the approach; it was as he had hoped it would be. But they had not questioned him yet; that was to come.

"Now, Eva," Hilton was saying, "tell me quickly what happened . . ."

"Ask Lionel . . . I only saw him beating Gil," she said.

"You were not in the room at all?" Hilton asked Eva.

"No . . ." Eva sighed.

Hilton rose and faced Cross.

"Were you in the room?"

"No," Cross said. "I was looking in through the door. He came at me, hit me with the poker— Right here—"

"Start from the beginning and tell me quickly," Hilton urged.

Cross sketched the story briefly, telling the facts just as they had happened, but omitting that he had been in the room.

"God, I'm sorry about Gil," he ended up.

"This is war," Hilton said. "We must expect casualties. Gil was brave." He studied Cross. "I saw you at Bob's last night, didn't I?"

"Yes."

"What's your name?"

"Lionel Lane."

"You've got to help us with this thing," Hilton said. "You were Gil's friend . . ."

"I'll do what I can."

"Listen to me carefully, all of you," Hilton began. "The important thing here is who died *first*. Get it?"

"What do you mean?" Menti asked.

"If it's proved that Herndon died first, then they'll want to brand Gil as a murderer," Hilton explained swiftly.

"But Eva saw Herndon alive with a gun . . . He was after her," Cross told him.

"Yes; I know that," Hilton said. "But when you looked into the door and saw Herndon beating Gil . . . Gil was not able to defend himself, was he? Herndon was killing him . . . Do you understand? It's important."

Menti approached Cross and caught hold of his arm.

"Look, guy, Gil was killed by that Fascist," Menti said. "Do you understand that?"

"Gil died fighting for your people, for *you*," Hilton reminded him.

"I know that," Cross said, simulating bafflement; he knew what they were driving at, but he did not want to seem to grasp it too quickly. He squinted his eyes and looked at the floor; he felt like laughing out loud. They were now begging *him* to believe something that he was praying that *they* would believe!

Cross looked at Eva. Though she had stopped sobbing, Cross could see that she could not quite follow what was being said. Cross felt that now was the time to cooperate with the Party, to demonstrate class consciousness, to cast his solidarity with the revolution. He nodded his head, looking slowly from Hilton to Menti.

"When I looked through the doorway, I saw Herndon with his foot on Gil's chest— He was hitting Gil— With the poker— I don't know how many times he hit 'im— Then Eva came down and Herndon saw us. He ran us back upstairs with the fire poker . . ."

"Yes," Eva sighed.

"And Gil couldn't move when you looked into that door?" Hilton demanded.

"No, he was out, unconscious, it seems to me . . ."

Hilton turned to Eva.

"And you saw Herndon *after* Lionel was up here? He was coming to get into the apartment, hunh? You ran back in and shut the door, didn't you, Eva? He had his gun?"

"Yes," she said.

"That is *proof*," Hilton said.

Cross wondered if Eva really believed that . . . Her sense of guilt was making her paint a picture that was helping him!

"Lionel, you just tell the cops what you saw; stick to your story," Menti said. "Cops are your enemies, boy. Look at what they have done to your people . . . Don't forget the lynchings . . . No matter *what* they do to you, say *nothing* but the truth; you hear? Gil gave his life for *you*. Herndon miscalculated; he thought he could scare Gil . . . When Herndon killed Gil, he was really killing *you*; you understand?"

"I understand," Cross answered.

"You better call those cops again," Menti said.

Hilton left and a moment later Cross heard him dialing the telephone. Menti stood looking at Cross and Eva, and Cross could guess what was going through the man's mind. Menti was hoping that Eva would be able to keep him in line, keep him loyal to the Party; and no doubt that same idea was in the back of Hilton's mind.

"Poor girl," Menti said to Cross, nodding toward Eva. "We owe it to her to protect the name of Gil."

"You can depend on me," Cross assured him; the corners of his mouth twitched, for he was wondering just what they would depend upon him for: to lie for the Party or to try to win Eva? And, back of it all, he was protecting his own wild despair of having surrendered to his pride to the point of having killed . . .

Hilton returned to the room absentmindedly puffing at a cigarette. His bony, ascetic face was tensely concentrated. Cross marveled at the self-possession of this man who, twenty-four hours ago, had mercilessly reduced Bob's enthusiasm for organizing to a quivering heap of whimpering flesh, and Cross was certain that no regretful memories or stings of remorse lingered on in Hilton's mind as he now coldly grappled with this new crisis. Men like Hilton did not spend their days scheming how to get hold of dollars; they worked at organizing and exploiting the raw stuff of human emotions. In their being close to the common impulses of men, in their cynical acceptance of the cupidities of the human heart, in their frank recognition of outlandish passions they were akin to priests. Now that he had killed Gil and had elected to remain near Eva, this man was his adversary, an adversary who played a game whose stakes held nothing less than life and death . . . Cross fought feebly against an intellectual pride that was rising in him and making him want to cope with Hilton, to show him that he and his kind did not possess a monopoly of knowledge about the emotional nature of man. And again Cross was dismayed at himself for contracting the ailment he hated. To fight Hilton meant fighting Hilton on Hilton's own ground, just as he had had to kill Gil and Herndon on their own ground, and that in itself was a defeat, a travesty of the impulse that had first moved him . . . Was all action doomed to this kind of degradation? How did one get around that? Or maybe you couldn't get around it? Perhaps he was staring right now at the focal point of modern history: if you fought men who tried to conquer you in terms of total power you too had to use total power and in the end you became what you tried to defeat . . .

Hilton was restless, chronically ill at ease, shifting from foot to foot, as if he feared that if he stood still he would commit some violent act. There was about his face and eyes that same impression of intolerable strain that had been so noticeable to Cross last night at Bob's. Here was a human instrument that had placed the total capacities of its life completely at the disposal of the Party . . . Cross could feel that Hilton, at this very moment, was pondering some question concerning him, for Hilton's wary eyes were fixed upon his face. Finally Hilton said to Cross:

"Come into the kitchen a moment."

"Sure."

Menti was talking to Eva now in low, consoling tones and Cross left her to trail behind Hilton. When they were inside the kitchen, Hilton shut the door and turned to Cross. He smiled and asked:

"How's she taking it?"

"As you see," Cross answered, on guard.

"You think we ought to get somebody to be with her?"

"Gosh, I don't know." He thought the question odd, for Hilton had shown no concern about Eva's state until now. "She can take care of herself. She shows little of what's going on in her."

"*That's* what I'm scared of," Hilton said in a tone of amused wonder. "She might even be glad that Gil is dead when she's over the shock. Gil was a first-class sonofabitch, if ever there was one. He was an absolutely cold fish whom I tried always to avoid, if I could . . ." He caught hold of Cross's arm and squeezed it. "You're not so bourgeois that speaking the truth about the dead bothers you . . ."

"Hell, no," Cross said; he was genuinely surprised. What was the man getting at?

"Gil was snobbish to the point of inciting murder, really," Hilton went on, smiling wryly. "Frankly, I've no sympathy for him. I'm a Communist and a dead man, so far as I'm concerned, is just so much cold meat." He chuckled uneasily. "He never liked me. I'm just an ex-school teacher, but Gil's father was a 1905'er . . . His real name was Bernstein. He grew up in the Bronx with the air of revolution in his home and it always made him feel that he was of the red elite. He hit at me several times politically, but I dodged him. He was widely hated in the Party."

"I didn't know that," Cross said. Why's he telling me this?

"And Eva's a cold one too," he went on in a tone of voice

that told Cross that he was now getting to his point. "There was no love lost between Gil and Eva . . . Don't kid yourself. In the Party, we know things."

Hilton looked at Cross curiously. He's worried about Eva and he's wondering how much I know . . . He decided not to tell Hilton that he knew Eva's marriage had been arranged by the Party, and that Eva had been in revolt, had been seething with hatred and despair.

"She knows a lot about the Party, but Gil was her only real link to us," Hilton pursued his theme. His lips moved without emitting words.

"Have you heard her say anything against the Party?" he asked finally.

Cross decided at once that he would defend Eva: their interests were identical.

"Never." He reflected that he was a newcomer and his word would not mean much. "She's never spoken an anti-Party word— In fact, I've asked her about political issues, but she'd never talk. Of course, you know that I'm not yet a member of the Party . . ."

"She likes colored people," Hilton said. He hastened to add: "I'm not saying that in a nasty way. She does. Tell me, do you think she trusts you?"

Cross understood at last. Hilton was asking him to watch over Eva! And he was longing to do just that, but not for Hilton's or the Party's sake. And, no doubt, in the living room Menti was hinting to Eva to keep an eye on Cross . . .

"I don't know," Cross said cautiously.

"From what I see of her reactions, I think she does," Hilton said with a sly smile.

He was angry, but he hid his feelings. He sensed that at some time in the past Hilton must have made advances to Eva and had been repulsed; and now, in the interests of the Party, he was giving her up. What a man . . . ! Cross thought.

"Why aren't you a member of the Party?"

"Well, I just met Gil and Eva last night."

"That's long enough. You are a Negro and you've an instinct for this sort of thing. I don't mean a racial instinct; it's a socially conditioned instinct for dissimulation which white

Americans have bred in you, and you've had to practice it in order to survive. Watching and coping with the racially charged behavior of white Americans are a part of your learning how to live in this country. Look, every day in this land some white man is cussing out some defenseless Negro. But that white bastard is too stupid in intelligence and deficient in imagination to realize that his actions are being duplicated a million times in a million other spots by other whites who feel hatred for Negroes just like he does; therefore, he is too blind to see that this daily wave of a million tiny assaults acts to build up a vast reservoir of resentment in Negroes. At night at home Negroes discuss this bitterly. But the next morning, smiling, they show up on their jobs, swearing that they love white people . . . Why? You know the answer. They have to live, eat, have a roof over their heads . . . So they collaborate with people who they feel are their sworn enemies . . . White America has built up something in you that can help the Party now. Defend yourself against these cops who are coming, and, if you do, you are defending the Party and your own interests at the same time. If you are honest in your heart, you cannot deny the Party. What about it, Lionel?"

How astute the man was! The average white American could never drag such simple truths past his lips, and here was a man confessing it with fluent passion. Did the average white American suspect that men like Hilton existed, men who could easily rise above their petty feelings of racial hatred and, instead of allowing the racial phobias of the mob to dominate their lives, could cynically make use of the racially defensive attitudes instilled in Negroes by the ill-treatment meted out by whites, could use such racial consciousnesses as weapons in their own bitterly determined struggle for power by exploiting this racial consciousness in their own behalf? This Hilton knew his country as only a man who had lived in it but not of it could know it. He was a man who, like Houston, like Gil, was an outsider and was free in what he apprehended. But I'm an outsider too, Cross thought musingly. I'll let him use me for what *I* want to be used for . . .

"I have no objections," Cross said softly.

What greater protection could he dream of than this? The Party he loathed was going to help defend him . . .

"Now, when the police questioning is over, I want to talk to you," Hilton said, giving Cross a card with his address upon it. "I don't live far from here—"

"Okay," Cross agreed, taking the card from him.

They shook hands.

"Just look after Eva," Hilton said. "If anything develops, get in touch with me. In fact, I think you'd better stay close to her."

Cross did not trust himself to answer. He simply nodded. Hilton looked nervously at his wrist watch.

"The police are slow in coming," he commented.

They returned to the living room. Eva was stretched out on the sofa. Cross went to her, bent down and asked:

"Can I get you something, Eva?"

She shook her head, forcing a wan smile to her lips. Menti looked at Hilton and winked. Hilton knelt at the knees of Eva and caught hold of her hand.

"Darling, Gil's gone, but the Party's still here. Your Party lives," he said softly, in solemn tones. "I've no doubt but that you're going to be able to do what you're called upon to do. Here's the situation. Herndon called Gil down to make him put Lionel out of the apartment. You heard noises and you and Lionel went down to see what was the matter. Herndon was beating Gil— He drove both of you upstairs, beating Lionel with the poker— You heard more noises— Eva, you tried to phone the police, but couldn't get through. So you phoned me and I phoned the cops; understand? Then you and Lionel heard more noises and screams. You sent Lionel down to help Gil . . . But the door was locked. Lionel came back up to phone the cops and, Eva, you started down again— But Herndon ran you back up with his gun— You saw 'im on the stairs with his gun— You both then locked yourselves in, see? You phoned me again— I came with Menti— We broke down the door—" Hilton gripped Eva's arm tightly. "Now, listen, we *didn't* tell you what we found down there, Eva . . . You hear? You *understand* that?"

"What do you mean?" Eva asked, baffled.

"I mean this," Hilton explained. "You and Lionel *did not* go down with us— You and Lionel remained *up here*; understand? You don't know that Gil's *dead*, see? When you hear that he's dead, you must *scream*! Your husband's been *murdered*. Herndon's guilty of *murder*; see? That's all. Herndon's the *murderer*. The rest of the burden's on us . . ."

Eva nodded her head, tears streaming again on her cheeks.

"You are a *Communist*, Eva," Hilton emphasized. "We Communists do what we *have* to do. It's our life."

Then the room was deathly still, for, in the distance, came the faintly rising wail of a siren.

"Are you all right, Eva?" Menti asked.

"I'm all right," Eva said, steeling herself.

The police are coming, Cross told himself. If Eva could face them, then, God knows, he ought to be able to. Buttressed by these two men whose profession was based on a defiance of the men of the law, he would have more than an equal chance. For a moment a nostalgic regret seized hold of him. Why was he not *with* them? Especially at times like this he welcomed their support. As an ally against racist white Americans, they had no peers. But he knew that that was not all. He recalled Bob's squirming on the floor, begging for a mercy that the Party would not grant. No; no, he would not swallow that happening to him . . . The sirens were near now, nearer, then nearer still. Suddenly he could hear them no more and he knew that the police were downstairs in the snow-choked streets in front of the house.

Cross knew that another world, Herndon's world, was coming; the police agents of that world were as much against him as the dead man Herndon had been. And Hilton and Menti were his allies and wanted to defend him, whatever their motives. He was black and, in the baleful eyes of the men who were coming, he had no right to be here in a white apartment building in a white neighborhood. He leaned against the wall, waiting, thinking. Why was it like this? As a Negro, he was not even free enough to choose his own allies.

What a cheap price Hilton was paying for his loyalty! And for men like Hilton, detached from impulses of racial hatred, what a trifling effort to expend to capture the allegiance of millions of people! Was not a world that left itself open to such easy attacks a stupid world, a doomed world, a rotten world not worth fighting for or saving? Since Herndon's world considered him only half-human, why did he not, out of spite and in defense of his own human dignity, turn on that world and, with the help of such base and dubious allies as Hilton and Menti, destroy it? But what would happen to him after that world was destroyed . . . ? Would he not be at the mercy of the Hiltons and Mentis . . . ? Hunh? What a black choice . . . !

He was now hearing the slow, heavy tramp of feet on the stairs. There came the sound of a brutal wrenching at the knob of the door, then the bell pealed impatiently. Cross moved to the center of the room, but Hilton waved him back.

"Stay put. I'll get this. I'll do the talking until they ask you something," Hilton said, going out.

Menti sat holding his arms about Eva and looking at Cross. Cross winked at Menti and Menti smiled. He had to give these men some assurance. He heard Hilton open the door.

"What's the trouble here?" The voice was rough and aggressive.

"There's been an awful fight downstairs," Cross heard Hilton explaining. "I think you'd better go down and see—"

"Whose apartment is this and *who* are you?"

"I'm a friend of one of the men downstairs, Mr. Gilbert Blount," Hilton's voice came clear and steady. "But, say, I think you ought to take a look quick—"

"I asked *you* your name?"

"Hilton, Jack Hilton . . ."

"And where do you live?"

"At the Albert Hotel on University Place."

"And what were these men fighting about?"

"Well, it seems that the landlord, Mr. Herndon, objected to a certain tenant—"

"We'll see about that," a flat, brutal voice sounded.

There was silence. Cross could hear voices but could not make out what was being said.

"What are you doing here now?"

"Mrs. Blount, the wife of one of the men downstairs, asked

me to come over," Hilton explained. "Look, don't you think you ought to take a look and see what's happened to the men down there—?"

"Where's Mrs. Blount now?"

"In the living room," Hilton answered. "But maybe a doctor could help those men—"

"Look, Mister, we know our job, so don't try to tell us what to do, see?"

"Well, I just thought—"

"We want to see Mrs. Blount," a hard voice insisted.

"Sure. Come in. That way— She's in the living room."

Cross heard feet coming down the hallway. Eva sat up, supported by Menti's arm. Two policemen, tall and seemingly of Irish extraction, came into the room and at once stopped dead in their tracks at the sight of the dark face of Cross. The older of the two policemen stared at Cross, Eva, Menti, then at Hilton, and finally his large, bold, grey eyes rested on Cross again.

"What's the matter with you people? Are you color blind?" he demanded with a faint sneer on his lips.

"Who are you?" Menti asked.

"Lieutenant Farrel. This is Officer Clark, my aide." He turned toward Eva. "Are you Mrs. Blount?"

"I am," Eva whispered.

"What seems to be the trouble, lady," Farrel asked.

"My husband— He's downstairs— I'm afraid he's hurt— He had an argument with the landlord, Mr. Herndon—"

"Who are these people?" Lieutenant Farrel asked, glancing at Menti and then Cross.

"My name's Herbert Menti, a friend of Mrs. Blount. And this is Lionel Lane, who lives here."

"*You* live here?" Farrel asked Cross, lifting his eyebrows.

"Yes," Cross answered.

"Why?"

"Why not?" Cross countered.

Farrel stared, then rocked back on his heels and looked over the people. "Are you *married* to anybody here?" Farrel demanded.

"No. I room here. I'm a student," Cross said.

"Uh huh," Farrel said.

"Is there anything illegal with Mr. Lane's being here?" Hilton asked pointedly.

"No," Farrel said, pulling down the corners of his mouth. "It's legal, just *legal*."

There was silence in the room as the pounding of feet on the stairs was heard. An officer stumbled through the door, panting, his face red and his eyes round with shock.

"Farrel, downstairs—" he gasped. "Quick, man— Wheeew! Looks like they bashed each other to death! It's a regular slaughterhouse, for real . . . You have to *see* it to believe it—"

"*Two?*" Farrel asked, his mouth dropping open.

"Yep. *Two*, no less."

Cross's eyes went quickly to Eva's face. Could she cope with this? He saw her hesitate a second, then rise, her eyes blazing with disbelief.

"No, *no* . . . ! *What* are you saying? Gil, Gil, *Gil!*" she screamed.

"Lady," Farrel called to her.

"Oh, my poor Gil!" Eva cried, running toward the door.

Farrel grabbed her. Eva struggled, trying to break loose.

"Let me go; let me go . . . Gil— Gil—"

She pulled from Farrel's arms and sank to the floor, sobbing convulsively.

"They've killed my poor husband— Oh, God, help poor Gil—"

"Is that his wife?" the new policeman asked.

"Yes," Menti answered.

"You'd better get her to lie down," Clark said.

"Eva, come with me," Menti said, lifting Eva from the floor. "Darling, take it easy— We don't know for sure yet—"

"I want to go to Gil," she cried.

"No, no; you must stay here," Menti insisted. "Lie here on the sofa—"

Cross was transfixed. She had done it. She had conquered her genuine grief and had replaced it with a pretended one, and somehow he felt that the pretended one was more real than the other. It rang with a sincerity that stemmed from a conscious act of creation.

". . . one used a table leg and the other a fire poker, it seems," the cop was explaining to Farrel.

Farrel's eyes widened in wonder.

"Is it too late to do anything for 'em?" Hilton asked, making sure to include Herndon in his question.

"Clark, stand guard here," Farrel said, ignoring Hilton. He beckoned the other policeman. "Come on. We'll have to get the Medical Examiner if what you say is true . . ."

Grim-lipped, Clark towered over Eva, Menti, Hilton and Cross. Sounds of voices and commotions could be heard downstairs now.

"He didn't seem to like you, Lane," Hilton said.

"Look," the policeman on guard held up his hand in a warning. "I must tell you that I can repeat anything I hear you say, see? So be careful."

"I don't give a damn what you do," Hilton shot at the cop. "I've nothing to hide here. None of us has. Now, I say that that damned Lieutenant Farrel made some nasty cracks here about Mr. Lane. He called us color-blind. He wanted to know if Lane was married to anybody here . . . Now, you can damn well repeat *that* to Headquarters, if you want to. If you don't, I will. Mr. Lane has more than a legal right to be here."

The cop reddened with embarrassment.

"I reckon you got something there, buddy," he said in tones of conciliation.

Cross assumed a relaxed, detached air to what was happening, but he managed to keep a furtive eye on Eva. He had enough insight into the psychological reactions of white Americans in racial matters to know that there were possible two main lines of development in the events under way: the average cop would either consider him fair game and concentrate upon him as a Negro, or he would seize upon the Communist political angle for purposes of public exploitation. I'm going to sit tight and see which way the cat jumps, Cross mused, feeling proud that he was conscious of their consciousness. It was, of course, possible, but not probable, that they might combine the two issues and whip up a lynch atmosphere. Barring some fantastic fact coming to light, he did not see how they could think of him in relation to the deaths of Gil and Herndon. And, even if they did, there were the machinating temperaments of both Hilton and Menti working to advance the organizational interests of the Party by placing the blame for Gil's death on Herndon, and thereby protecting him.

He noticed that Eva was now as calm as marble. Balling a handkerchief in her right fist, she sat looking bleakly in front of her. His eyes caught hers and he saw in them a glint of recognition. Yes, she's with me. She thinks I'm a victim too . . . Her sense of guilt was throwing her on his side; she had long been wanting to be free of Gil and now that she was free she wants to unburden her guilt on to someone else, on to Herndon . . .

Lieutenant Farrel came back into the room, puffing from climbing the stairs; his heavy brows were knitted in perplexity. Following him was another policeman with a notebook and pencil in hand. He demanded the names, ages, occupations, and identification of all present. Cross accounted for himself as a student and showed his birth certificate and draft card. Hilton was a free lance writer and Menti spoke of himself as an unemployed printer. The room was quiet; no one volunteered any further information. The burden of getting at what happened fell upon Farrel, and he was a more chastened man now that he had seen the charnel house in Herndon's living room.

"Well, who'll lead off and tell what happened?"

There was silence. Menti looked at Hilton and Hilton looked at Cross. Cross cleared his throat and spoke in low, polite tones:

"I'm afraid that you'll have to rely upon me for the details as to how this started."

Farrel was impressed at the manner in which Cross spoke.

"And what did you have to do with it?"

"Nothing, directly. But I saw Mr. Herndon striking Mr. Blount with a fire poker . . ."

Under questioning by Farrel, Cross related what had been agreed upon among him and Hilton and Menti. He kept his account terse, making no interpretations at all, leaving the cops to make their own inferences. Farrel frowned, looking from face to face. Briefly, Hilton related how he had received two phone calls, one from Eva and another from Lionel. He told of phoning the police, of picking up his friend Menti, and rushing over. He related how they had found Lionel and Eva huddled in fear in the apartment, how they had gone down and bashed in the door and found the men lying there, bloody, still . . .

"We didn't tell Mrs. Blount anything . . . We waited for you . . ." Hilton wound up.

"Madam, do you know of any reason why anyone would want to kill your husband?" Farrel asked Eva.

Eva rose magnificently to the question; she threw her hands to her mouth and screamed: "He killed my husband! He killed poor Gil!"

"You mean that *Herndon* killed him?" Hilton demanded, looking at Farrel. "Didn't he?"

"We don't know," Farrel said.

"But there are eyewitnesses who saw Herndon beating Blount . . ." said Menti.

"That's for the Medical Examiner to say," Farrel hedged.

"But where *were* you guys?" Hilton demanded. "I phoned you thirty minutes ago. I got here in ten minutes—"

"We're pretty busy these days," Farrel said sadly. "We got here as soon as we could— This may be a job for the D.A."

Cross was attention. *Ely Houston?* God . . . Would Houston recall his false name? He was certain that Houston had a vivid recollection of the talk they had had in his compartment on the train. Houston was capable of finding out the truth about him, could even *guess* the truth . . . Houston, a hunchback, an outsider, a man whose physical deformity had forced him to live in but not of the normal rounds of ritualized life, knew the demonic feelings of men who played god because he himself was of the demonic clan, having hidden his kinship with the rebellious by publicly upholding the laws and promises that men live by . . . And Cross knew that his crimes were of a nature that Houston would not only find engrossing but challenging. Houston understood those rare-judgment-feelings that made men kill for no motives defined or known in the realms of law. Cross had no real fear of Farrel, or Clark, or the other flatfoots who wandered blunderingly in and out of the apartment, but for Houston he had something akin to terror . . . The cops were baffled, half-scared men who hid their bewilderment by loud-mouthed blustering; but Houston was so placed psychologically in life that he would feel intuitively at home with his crimes, for he was akin to Gil, to Herndon, to Hilton, and to Cross in temperament and outlook; he had the kind of consciousness that could grasp the mercurial emotions of men whom society had never tamed or disciplined, men whose will had never been broken, men who were wild but sensitive, savage but civilized, intellectual but somehow intrinsically poetic in their inmost hearts.

Farrel left the room and made a lengthy telephone call in the hallway; at last he came in with his verdict.

"All of you must consider yourselves under house arrest," he began. "I'm posting an officer at the door of the apartment for tonight. There are a lot of questions that must be answered. In the morning all of you must face the District Attorney and give him your stories and account for yourselves. The Medical Examiner is downstairs working now—"

"But what is the meaning of this?" Hilton demanded.

"We must determine how those men died downstairs—" Farrel said.

"But it's all very simple," Menti said.

"Mr. Lane told you what happened," Hilton said.

"I'm only obeying orders," Farrel said.

"You mean we have to stay here all night—?" Menti asked.

"Absolutely," Farrel snapped.

"But my wife; she'll be upset," Menti objected.

"You got a phone at home?"

"Yes."

"Then call her," Farrel directed.

"And I'll have to stay too?" Hilton demanded.

"I'm afraid so, sir," Farrel said.

"But *why?*"

"Listen, I'm acting under the orders of the District Attorney. He is acting according to the reports he's getting from the Medical Examiner downstairs. If you want to, I can take you to see an Assistant D.A. Maybe you can arrange something with him . . ."

"The hell with it," Hilton said.

Eva was weeping now afresh.

"I want to see Gil," she sobbed. "Please, please—"

"I'm sorry, lady," Clark said. "They've taken his body to the Morgue."

" . . . and it looks like they killed each other," Farrel was saying in a low voice to another officer.

"It's the most freakish thing I ever saw," the other officer said.

Finally Cross, Eva, Hilton, and Menti were alone; the police had gone, stationing a young cop on guard in the hallway in front of the apartment door. For awhile there was silence among the four of them. Eva was weeping noiselessly but earnestly now, and Cross observed that her grief at this moment had none of that spontaneousness of emotion that had characterized the grief she had pretended for the cops. She was free now; her secret wish had come true . . . Was that why she was weeping?

Cross was frantically trying to weigh all the possibilities involved. Could the Party let Eva, with her guilty knowledge, go free? And the Party's attitude toward him? For the moment the Party was his ally, but Communists were not naïve enough to accept him merely on a basis of a declaration of solidarity. They wanted something more . . . And what could that be . . . ? For its own defense, the Party was trying to dump Eva into his arms, knowing that black and white love could find shelter nowhere else so readily as under its red aegis . . . Well, for the time being, he'd accept the situation as it was, but not for the Party's reasons . . .

Cross watched Hilton. Eva was resting on the sofa with her face buried in the crook of her elbow, her chest heaving. Menti patted her shoulder. Hilton paced the floor, puffing at the inevitable cigarette that protruded from his lips.

"It didn't go too badly," Hilton spoke as though wanting to share his thoughts. "But, of course, the real showdown will come in the morning with the D.A." He looked at Cross. "You did well. Maintain the same attitude tomorrow. We're behind you."

"I'll try," Cross mumbled; he wondered if he ought to tell Hilton that he had already met the District Attorney. He decided not to; there was no purpose in adding items that would inflame Hilton's already suspicious mind. I'll try to take care of it when it comes, he told himself. But Hilton worried him. The man was *too* calm, *too* collected, his face always a tense, blank mask. How *much* of his reactions was he concealing . . . ?

"I'm sleepy," Hilton said, stretching his arms above his head and giving a yawn that was *too* genuine.

"Why don't you and Menti sleep in Gil's room," Eva suggested in a whisper.

"Okay, I'm turning in," Hilton said. But even now he did not demonstrate any feeling of sympathy for Eva. "Good night," he said, and headed for the hallway.

"Is there anything I can do for you, Eva?" Cross asked.

"No. You should rest, Lionel," she said, looking pityingly at him. "We brought you into a mess, didn't we? I'm sorry . . ."

"Good night," Menti called to her.

An hour later Cross was in bed, turning sleeplessly from side to side, trying mentally to cope with the threat of Ely Houston. What would he think of these deaths? Would he not think it somewhat odd that both Gil and Herndon had been men of extreme ideas? Oh, God . . . Cross sat upright in bed with a wild jerk of his body. Jesus . . . *That bloody handkerchief . . . !* He had to get rid of it before the District Attorney showed up in the morning; it had been in the pocket of his pants until now . . . He got out of bed, pulled on his bathrobe, took the wadded handkerchief and put it into the pocket of the robe and quietly opened the door to the hallway. The apartment was quiet and dark. If anybody demanded where he was going, he could always say that he was on his way to the bathroom . . . He stole silently down the dark hallway to the door of the kitchen. He paused, listening for sounds, then turned the knob, pushed the door inward, and went inside. Faint blue light fell through a window, casting a ghostly radiance over the gas stove, the sink, and the refrigerator. Yes, there was the incinerator . . . He could see and would not have to turn on the light. He crossed the floor and lifted the lid and tossed the guilty handkerchief quickly down. He smelt a whiff of smoke; it would burn soon. His tension ebbed a bit. He turned to go to his room and, like thunder, the kitchen light blazed on. He caught his breath,

Hilton was sitting in a chair near the wall, the habitual cigarette hanging unlit from his lips.

"I didn't know you were there," Cross breathed, struggling to stifle his panic.

"What's the matter?" Hilton asked. "You can't sleep either?"

Cross thought rapidly. Had Hilton seen him throw the handkerchief away? He did not think so. Then his job now was to act naturally and not rouse Hilton's suspicions.

"I thought I'd get a glass of milk," Cross mumbled. "Haha— I threw my cigarette down the incinerator— I smoke too much." Ought he have said that? Good God, this sonofabitch Hilton . . .

Moving self-consciously, he took a tumbler from a cupboard and went to the refrigerator and poured some milk.

"Aren't you going to sleep?" Cross asked, taking a sip from the glass.

"I never sleep much," Hilton grumbled. "Just sitting, thinking . . ."

"That's a goddamn shame about Gil, isn't it?" Cross felt compelled to say.

"Yeah," Hilton drawled.

"I should've broken down that damned door," Cross accused himself.

"You did what he told you to, didn't you? You've nothing to worry about."

"Yes. But to die like that—"

"A Communist is a soldier, Lane. He's prepared to die."

"I'm so new at all of this—"

"You're not so new. You know what you're doing."

"But I don't understand—"

"You understand enough," Hilton cut him short.

What was Hilton thinking? The very manner in which he spoke bothered Cross. But what the hell! He was going to sleep . . . Hilton knew nothing yet.

"I'm tired; good night," Cross said.

"Good night, Lane," Hilton said, staring at the far wall.

Had Hilton seen anything? He went down the hallway, then paused, listening. There were no sounds. No, Hilton had seen nothing; if he had, he surely would have said something about it. Hilton was no bashful boy . . . Now that he felt out of danger, Cross's heart began to pound with excitement. If Hilton had caught him with that bloody handkerchief, he would have been in Hilton's power for the rest of his life. He would either have had to kill Hilton on the spot, or make a break for it through one of the windows of the apartment. To be in the power of a cold little god like Hilton was about the most awful thing that could happen to a man. He would have trampled on me night and day, Cross thought, shivering with relief. He entered his room and, fumbling in the dark, he pulled off his robe and got into bed.

"Lionel—"

It was Eva's voice coming from nearby; it was low and plaintive. Terror flooded him. Maybe they *all* knew what he had done!

"Eva?"

"Yes."

What was she doing here in his room in the dark? Did she know that he had just burned the handkerchief? He reached out to turn on the light and his hand knocked over a book.

"No," Eva whispered.

He felt her fingers seize hold of his hand.

"Don't turn on the light."

"What's the matter, Eva?"

He felt both of her hands now gripping his own, as though she was trying to hang on to him for life's sake.

"I didn't know you were out of your room," she began, her voice catching in her throat. "I knocked and when you didn't answer, I came in . . ."

Cross felt hot tears dropping on to his fingers.

"Lionel, forgive me— But I'm so *scared*— And I'm so much *alone*— You'll never know how alone I am— I'm bothering you, I know— But I can't stay in my room alone," she sobbed. "Oh, God, I'm no good— I'm *too* scared—" For a second she was silent. Then she spoke again in a changed tone of voice: "You're colored and you're strong. I'll never know how you manage to face those awful people and never flinch or quail . . . You're prepared for them and I'm not . . . Have pity on me and let me stay here near you . . ."

Her breathing filled the black darkness. Her soul was reaching gropingly toward him for protection, advice, solace. Cross smiled, feeling that he was listening to her words as perhaps God listened to prayers . . . A wave of hot pride flooded him. She was laying her life at his feet. With but a gesture of his hand he could own her, shield her from the Party, from fear, from her own sense of guilt . . .

"You'll be cold," he said softly.

"No, no . . . I'll be all right."

"Here; take my robe . . ."

"All right," she consented.

He heard her moving amid a rustling of garments in the dark, and then he felt her hands again, her fingers entwining themselves in his own.

"You don't mind, Lionel? Please, don't send me away . . ."

"No, Eva."

"I just can't stand fear, and I'm full of fear when I'm alone in times like these . . . And I've been scared so long . . ."

"Just rest easy. You'll be all right. Don't worry . . ."

"I thought you'd understand . . . Listen, don't tell the others I came in here," she begged convulsively. "I'm ashamed of being so scared."

"No one will ever know," he told her.

"I don't mind so much if I cry before *you*, but I could never cry before *them*," she whispered. "And I *need* to cry . . ."

Her weeping now was real, different from the pretended weeping for the Party and different from the weeping she had done in front of Hilton and Menti. In front of the universe of white skins, she was too frozen with fear to cry; but with people of color who she felt were victims and, hence, more understanding, she could weep without check. He wanted to lift her from the floor and take her into the bed, but he felt that such would violate her budding trust.

"Lionel," she called in a whisper.

"Yes?"

She controlled her sobbing and was silent for some moments.

"We could have saved Gil," she whimpered.

"But, Eva, how could we know that that would happen?" he asked her gently, trying to purge her of her sense of guilt.

"But the Party might think that we *let* him be killed," she whispered.

She was not confessing to him, but she was near it.

"But, *why?*" he asked in make-believe astonishment.

She wept afresh, resting her head on his shoulder, gripping his hands rigidly, convulsively.

"You don't understand," she said despairingly. "People are worse than you think . . . They treat you bad because you're colored, but me— People like me, they take our *lives* away . . ."

He was silent. He had given his life away. How could he ever tell her that he understood what had blasted her self-confidence?

"You'll be all right," he said gently.

"You shouldn't be in this. You've suffered enough—"

"I'm used to it, Eva."

"Why's there so much cruelty? I want to die; life's *too* much, *too* much . . ." Her breathing came loud and hoarse. "Is it wrong to feel like that, Lionel?"

"We all feel it. But we have to fight it," he told her.

"Did you ever want to kill yourself?"

"Yes."

"Oh, Lionel!"

Her fingers gripped his like bands of steel. Then he felt her fingers disengage themselves from his and a moment later they were touching his lips, eyes, his hair, tenderly, softly.

"Those cops were horrible to you tonight, weren't they?"

"It was nothing."

"I'm so sorry, Lionel," she sighed. "You have it hard enough, and then we drag you into this . . ."

He understood. She was pitying him for his being black and having to take the scoffs and insults of the white world; and, in doing so, she was pitying him for the wrong reasons. But he could not tell her that. Oh, God . . . If only he could find a way of begging her pity for his having killed Gil, for his having let his soul take on the shape of monstrousness, for his having forgotten his humanity. That was the pitying he needed . . . He knew that Eva, too, had been forced to live as an outsider; she, too, in a different sort of way, was on his side. Maybe, in the future, he could tell her, could unburden himself and feel free once before he died?

He felt her moving and then she was sliding into bed with him.

"Just hold me a little, Lionel," she whispered, shivering and clinging to him.

He held her, feeling her hot tears on his face.

"I'm so cold, so scared, so lost," she sobbed.

At last she grew quiet and later he could tell that she had gone to sleep. It was then that he knew he loved her, wanted to try to banish the dread that haunted her, wanted to tell her what he knew of terror and hopelessness. He held in his arms one woman who was willing to understand, whom life had so tempered that he could talk to her, but between them stood a wall not of race but of mutual guilt, blood, and mistaken identity . . .

Pale dawn crept into the room. Cross looked down at Eva's wan face; she slept as one exhausted. He shook her gently, calling softly to her:

"Eva . . ."

Her eyes fluttered open; when she saw him, she buried her face in his bosom.

"Darling, go to your room," he told her. "It's better that way with Hilton and Menti in the apartment."

"Yes; you're right, Lionel."

She kissed him lightly on his lips and whispered: "Thank you, darling."

And she was gone. The more he thought of her the more he began to care about what would happen to him. Could he fight his way through and have this girl? It seemed impossible, yet that was what he wanted. I mustn't think about it, he told himself. He closed his eyes, but he could still smell the faint odor of her hair, feel the delicate pressure of her fingers upon his face, her lips on his . . . He gritted his teeth and mumbled aloud: Oh, goddamn . . .

Hilton roused him at eight-thirty by rapping on the door.

"Lane, come and get some coffee," Hilton called.

Cross tumbled from bed. Oh, yes . . . He would change his suit . . . And at the first opportunity he would get rid of the clothes he had worn when he had struck down Gil and Herndon . . .

When he went into the kitchen, he found that Hilton had set up breakfast. Eva and Menti were already at the table. Cross sat and began sipping his coffee. What about that bloody handkerchief? Hilton was busy making toast and everything seemed normal. He saw Hilton go to the incinerator and dump some waste paper into it. Yes, he was safe for the time being . . .

Menti ate broodingly. Hilton moved quickly about the kitchen like a man who must either do something or become exasperated. Cross let his eyes rest on Eva; she was pale and tired, looking off into space; finally she did glance at him and there flitted into her eyes a sign that she was with him; he felt better.

The doorbell rang and Hilton started nervously.

"This is it, I think," Hilton said.

Hilton left and a moment later, before Cross could prepare himself, the hunched form of Ely Houston filled the doorway. Cross stared unblinkingly. Houston entered the kitchen and paused; his eyes traveled swiftly around the room and at last rested on Cross.

"Well," Houston exclaimed, "what in the world are you doing here?"

Cross stood, smiled, and reached out his hand to Houston who shook it warmly.

"How are you, Mr. Houston?" Cross said evenly. "I live here."

"At last I've tracked you down," Houston said.

Hilton, Menti, and Eva were thunderstruck. Hilton was staring at Cross with an open mouth and Cross could tell that he was thinking that maybe he was a police spy.

"How is it that you know the District Attorney?" Hilton asked softly.

"Mr. Houston and I have met before," Cross explained lightly.

Houston advanced into the kitchen, followed by Farrel and a tall, lean, grey-haired man on whose chest Cross could see a police badge. Farrel too stared at Cross and said:

"Why didn't you tell me you were a big-shot, boy?"

"I'm not," Cross said.

Everyone was standing now except Eva; tension and distrust hung in the air. The tall, lean man stood in one corner and surveyed the faces of Cross, Menti, and Hilton.

"I've asked about you," Houston began, addressing himself to Cross, "but I couldn't get a line on you . . . I'll never forget that talk we had. Know one thing? I made notes on your ideas." Houston seemed to have forgotten that he had come to investigate the deaths of two men; he was excited and seemed in a holiday mood. "Now, what was it you said . . . ?" Houston paused, ran his hand into his pocket and pulled out a notebook. "I've got it right here, you see." As he thumbed the leaves, the tall man stared in bewilderment at Houston, saying nothing. "Ha— Here it is: 'Man is nothing in particular . . .' You see? I don't forget."

"I see you don't," Cross said.

Hilton was so nervous that he could not control the shaking of his hands. Menti stared, but there was a sardonic smile on his thin lips. Only Eva was listening to Houston.

"Well, what is this all about?" Houston asked of Cross, rubbing his hands together. "We can talk about special problems later— Oh, yes— What was the name you gave me?"

"The name is Lane, Lionel Lane," Cross said.

"Lionel Lane," Houston repeated, paused; then went on. "Mr. Lane, this is the Medical Examiner, Dr. Stockton . . ."

Cross nodded to Dr. Stockton and the doctor nodded to him.

"Farrel," Houston demanded. "What have we got here?"

As Farrel outlined to Houston what he had found downstairs, Houston moved with vacant eyes about the kitchen, his lips pursed, his hat in his hand, his hump seeming to follow him. He walked softly, flat-footedly, as if he feared that he would disturb some delicate process of thought by jarring his brain. He began to frown as Farrel described details of the scene of blood and death.

"And these two men, what were their backgrounds?" Houston asked at last.

"That's a damned strange thing, Mr. D.A.," Farrel said. "Gilbert Blount was a member of the Central Committee of the Communist Party of the United States—"

"You're kidding," Houston protested with wide eyes.

"No, sir," Farrel insisted. "It's a fact—"

"And who's the other one?"

"His twin. A Fascist, they say—"

"What's his name?"

"Langley Herndon—"

Houston snapped his finger, as though trying to recall something.

"Langley Herndon . . . ! Ah! I remember him— He used to write for the *Crusader* sometimes," Houston said. "Hunh! A violent baby— Bloodthirsty— Welcomed Hitler and publicly lauded his extermination of the Jews. Said that America should use the Negro as a scapegoat around which to unify the nation—" He looked at Cross and smiled. "Herndon was perfectly cynical. He argued that anything could be done for any reason . . . He had the Negro singled out as a target, a menace, a danger . . . The Negro was America's ace in the hole if the nation ever experienced any real internal stress. You could say that the nigger was the cause of it and get the rest of the nation to forget its problems and unite to get rid of the niggers . . . Ingenious, hunh?" Houston chuckled and turned to Dr. Stockton. "Well, Doc, how does it look to you? What's your verdict?"

Dr. Stockton cleared his throat, advanced to the kitchen table and rested his briefcase upon it. He took out a sheaf of papers and leafed through them. He lifted his eyes at last to Houston.

"Mr. District Attorney, this is either very simple or very complicated . . ."

"Make it simple," Houston said.

"I'll let you decide that," Dr. Stockton said.

"Oh, wait a minute," Houston interrupted him. He turned and faced Eva, Hilton, Menti, and Cross. "Who are these people? Is anybody here related to either Blount or Herndon?"

"This is Mrs. Blount," Cross told Houston.

"Oh, Madam, I beg your pardon," Houston apologized. "If I'd known it was you, I'd not have spoken as I have. I'm awfully sorry . . ."

"It's nothing," Eva mumbled.

"These things are unpleasant, but we have to get these facts straight— Oh, yes; and the other two gentlemen?"

Farrel introduced Hilton and Menti as friends of Eva.

"All right, Dr. Stockton, you may proceed—"

"Well, Mr. District Attorney, I've all the reports right here. What we can make of these reports is quite another matter. Our Pathological Chemist, Dr. Reddick, has submitted a mass of details. I'll begin first with Blount . . ." He began reading from the report: " 'Multiple incised wounds of scalp; congestion and oedema of brain . . .' "

"Dr. Stockton," Houston interrupted him. "Forgive me— Suppose we save all that for the formal hearing, eh? Right now I just want to know if I'm to look for a murderer or not. Give me this wrapped up in a nutshell . . ."

"Right," Dr. Stockton replied, putting his papers aside. "To all intents and purposes, Mr. District Attorney, these two blokes battered each other to death. All concrete evidence points toward that . . . Let's take that aspect of it first . . . And, mind you, I'm leaving out all question of motive for the time being . . . The definite ascertaining of a different motive could alter the entire picture of our findings . . . Now, due to the great disorder of the room downstairs, we've not yet been able to reconstruct exactly what happened. Yet, the concrete evidence we possess points to the fact of an argument that led to a fist fight . . . There's evidence that Herndon attempted strangulation upon Blount . . . Blount must have freed himself, for the next stage of the fight was with the fire poker. Who grabbed the fire poker first, we do not know. Now, here's the strange thing. *Both* men bear evidence of having been hit with the poker, which means that during the course of the fight the poker must have been lost from the possession of one or the other of the men. In other words, they took turns in lamming each other . . . Follow me?"

"You're saying," Houston paraphrased, "that one man could have dropped the fire poker and the other could have grabbed it?"

"Or," Dr. Stockton added, "one could have wrested the poker from the hands of the other. That happens quite frequently in brawls. A man is pounding another man's brains out with a pop bottle. The other takes the bottle away from him and starts in with the bottle upon the aggressor with the aggressor's own weapon . . . Well, that seems to have happened at the beginning of this fight.

"Now, a third stage of the fight comes. The table leg is now used as the weapon. Just how they got hold of it, we do not know. It seems utterly unlikely that either of the two men had time enough to stop the fight and break that leg off the table. We surmise that one of them crashed against the table in falling and broke the table, the leg coming off, breaking in two . . . The first man who saw that table leg dived for it and took it as his weapon.

"At the present moment, with what we've got to go on, we surmise that Blount got hold of the leg first—"

"How do you figure that?"

"It's a guess," Dr. Stockton said. "The most single powerful blow dealt with that table leg was against the forehead of Herndon . . . That blow could have caused death, not at once, but certainly Herndon would have died of it eventually. Most certainly he was stunned by it and we further surmise that he kept on his feet and continued the fight . . . Now, here's another strange fact in a strange case. *Both* men bear marks of that table leg on their heads . . . That can only be accounted for, too, on the basis that the table leg, like the fire poker, changed hands during the course of the fight, which is highly likely . . . *But,* and this puzzles me, was Herndon *able,* physically *able* to deliver such death-dealing blows upon Blount's head *after* he had received that crushing blow to his own forehead . . . ? Yet the facts point to such. It's possible . . . Men have been known to possess remarkable strength just before dying; men have been known to aim and fire a gun with sharp accuracy and then die straightaway . . . *If* Herndon was able to deal a death-dealing blow to Blount, after having received such a blow himself, then the case is simple."

"Is there any way of telling, Dr. Stockton, how much *time* intervened between these blows?" Houston asked.

"That's impossible," Dr. Stockton said. "Our impression is that those blows were all delivered at approximately the same time. At the most, a half hour could have intervened, but we think the whole fracas took place in about fifteen minutes."

"In other words, you don't think that one man could have been knocked out, could have come to, and resumed the fight . . . ?" Houston asked.

"That's highly speculative," the doctor said. "It *would* explain how Herndon was able to deal such hard blows after he had been mortally wounded. There are some 'ifs' here . . . But these 'ifs' only make the whole picture more complicated." Dr. Stockton paused and pulled forth a batch of photographs from his briefcase. "This is how they looked when the officers arrived . . ." He handed the photographs to Houston.

Rocking on his heels, Houston looked at the photographs and his eyes bulged with suppressed horror. Cross could see a slanting glimpse of the pictures and at once there leaped into his mind the image of that red room with its flickering flames and the two still, bloody forms stretched out on the carpet, drenched in their own blood . . .

"Lovely," Houston commented softly, returning the photographs to Dr. Stockton. He turned to look at Eva. "Would the lady mind excusing herself?" Houston asked.

"Not at all," Eva said; she rose and left the kitchen.

Cross's eyes followed her with anxiety as her wan, tight face went from view.

"There's no use in her hearing this sordid mess," Houston mumbled. He rubbed his hands together, glanced about the room, and then spoke in a loud, sonorous voice:

"Perfect setup. Two extremes meet. A plus and a minus— And they cancel each other out . . . And who could hate each other more than two men like that? It's the Russian-German war all over again, eh? Could be . . . Sounds like it. It fits, doesn't it? Motives? Dr. Stockton, you spoke of leaving out motives . . . Why? You have all the motives on earth here, my dear doctor. These two men were totally opposed to each other in all aspects of life. You might call such motives *natural life* motives . . . Oh, I know that there is no such thing in law as that. But there will be one day . . . I'm sure of it. We might call such motives jealousy. But it's total jealousy. The kind of jealousy the Bible speaks of when it refers to God's being a jealous God, hunh?" Houston looked around the room and smiled.

Cross was trembling; he felt that maybe Houston knew that he was guilty and was mocking him. Was Houston teasing him by speaking his *own* ideas out loud, testing them on the people present? Whose ideas belonged to whom? What crazy luck he had in having this hunchback, the one man he had ever met who understood him, to track him down? Did Houston know how maddeningly close he stood to the truth?

"There's another possibility," Dr. Stockton's voice sounded patiently.

"There are millions of possibilities," Houston said, waving his hand. He looked at Cross. "Of course, there's this problem of Herndon hating to have Negroes in his building, but I take it that that was simply a tiny aspect of his total jealousy toward Blount—"

Hilton and Menti were silent, tight-lipped, staring first at Houston and then at Cross. Cross waited, wondering what other versions of the crime did the Medical Examiner have in mind.

"So they killed each other," Houston went on. He turned to Farrel. "According to you, Herndon killed Blount, hunh? Yes, he was seen standing over Blount with the fire poker . . . He was strong enough to chase Mrs. Blount up the steps with a gun . . . That fits. He later dies of wounds that Blount had inflicted on him. A double murder, or double manslaughter, whatever you want to call it." Houston faced Dr. Stockton. "Is that more or less your opinion?"

A trace of hesitancy showed in Dr. Stockton's eyes; then he shrugged and said:

"More or less."

"More or less?" Houston was astonished. "What's your reservation?"

"Somebody could have come upon them while they were fighting and killed them both," Dr. Stockton said somewhat sheepishly; he was obviously embarrassed at the farfetched nature of his theory.

Cross felt suspended over a bottomless void. He had thought that Houston would have arrived at that solution first; but, no, it was Dr. Stockton who had put his finger on the truth.

"Good Lord!" Houston exclaimed. "Why can't you fellows take facts just as you find them? Why do you want to make life more complicated than it is, and it's damn well complicated, if you ask me. Now, Dr. Stockton, what motive on earth could anybody have in coming upon those two men fighting and then killing the both of them?"

"I don't know." Dr. Stockton shrugged his shoulders.

"I don't know either," Houston said. "The damned thing's simple. Two hotheads met and had a fight over their total views of life. They fought. One died and then the other died. And for my money, there's something of poetic justice in the whole damn thing."

"Is that the official interpretation, Mr. District Attorney?" Dr. Stockton asked.

"Oh, Dr. Stockton, I'm not trying to encroach upon your duties," Houston said, smiling blandly. "If not this interpretation, then what have you to offer?"

"I don't know," Dr. Stockton said. He turned to Cross and stared at him for several seconds. "You're the young man who saw them fighting?"

"Yes, sir," Cross answered.

"What time did Blount go down to see Herndon?" Dr. Stockton asked.

"It was about ten past nine o'clock," Cross answered.

"How do you know that?" the doctor asked.

"Just before leaving the dinner table, Mr. Blount looked at his watch and told the time to us, and said he had to leave."

Houston came forward and stood in front of Cross. Cross felt that his feet were resting on air, that he could sink right down through the floor.

"How long was Blount gone from the apartment before you went down there?" Houston asked.

Cross frowned, thinking. He felt that it was not really a matter of time; either they found a motive, *his* motive, and accused him or they did not. So he could tell the truth.

"That's really hard to say . . . It's better to tell you what happened. Mrs. Blount was worried. I was too. I offered to go down with Blount, to help him, defend him if anything happened . . . But he wouldn't hear of it. He was a proud man . . . And Mrs. Blount warned me not to interfere. She said he'd be angry, wildly angry if I did . . . I was helping Mrs. Blount clear away the things from the table. Then we began hearing loud voices. We knew that they were quarreling. I offered to go down and Mrs. Blount said no, that he'd be angry. I went to my room and was lying on my bed . . . It was then that I heard that loud noise, like something breaking, a big piece of wood . . . That was the table, maybe . . ."

"No doubt," Dr. Stockton said. "Go on . . ."

"Mrs. Blount came running to me. She was terribly upset. It seems—"

"How long were you in the room before Mrs. Blount came running to you?" Dr. Stockton asked.

"I don't know," Cross said truthfully. "Maybe five minutes; maybe longer . . ."

"And Mrs. Blount asked you to go down?"

"Well, not exactly . . . She didn't seem to know what to do . . . So I offered to go down. But she said no. Then we heard a scream—"

"Could you tell who it was that screamed?"

"No," Cross said honestly. "This time I said I'd go down, and she agreed . . . But she was still afraid. You see, really, she was more afraid of Blount himself than of anything happening to him. The moment I got downstairs in the hallway, I knew a fight was going on . . . I ran to the door, opened it, and saw Herndon beating Blount with the fire poker . . . Blount was on the floor and Herndon had his foot on his chest and was lamming away. I didn't hear Mrs. Blount come down, but all at once I felt her hand touching my back. She started screaming and Herndon saw us . . . He came at us with the fire poker . . . I blocked him just long enough for Mrs. Blount to run upstairs, and Herndon swiped me across the shoulder with the poker . . ." Cross paused, pulled off his coat, opened his shirt and showed his shoulder.

"Why didn't you call the police?" Houston wanted to know.

"When I got upstairs, Mrs. Blount was calling the police . . . She didn't seem able to get connections . . . She asked me to call, then she ran out of the room to go downstairs again . . . I was scared she'd get hurt, so I ran after her, caught her on the landing and brought her back to the apartment. We kept hearing the fighting; there were shouts, screams . . . Mrs. Blount asked me to phone the police—"

"And didn't you phone?" Houston asked.

"No; I wanted to try to help Mr. Blount . . . I told her to phone and I ran downstairs. But I found the door locked this time. I rattled the knob— I called, yelled— I could hear 'em fighting—"

"Whose name did you call?" Dr. Stockton asked.

"Mr. Blount's name. I didn't know what to do. I went back upstairs and—"

"How long were you downstairs the second time?"

"I don't know. Maybe five minutes, maybe longer . . . When I went back to tell Mrs. Blount, she told me that she'd phoned Mr. Hilton and that Mr. Hilton was phoning the police. You see, she thought surely that Mr. Blount was coming up with me. And when I told her that he was still down there, she went really wild . . . I was trying to call the police when she ran out of the door again. This time she came flying back. She said Herndon had his gun and was on his way up . . ."

"Did you see 'im?" Houston asked.

"No. I barred the door. Mrs. Blount fainted and I put water on her face . . ."

Dr. Stockton turned to Farrel, frowning.

"Where was Herndon's gun, Lieutenant?" Dr. Stockton asked.

"In the drawer of his desk," Farrel explained. "The drawer was half-pulled out. Seems like somebody had just tossed it in there. Might have been the last thing Herndon did before he died."

"Perhaps," Dr. Stockton said slowly.

Cross was still as stone. He could feel that they were not satisfied with this interpretation, but they could find no other that would explain the facts. Houston seemed inclined to accept the picture that Cross had painted. Good. Let the doctor and his scientists discover something else, if they could. Things were not going so badly. But he had to be careful of this man Houston; after all, he may be stalling just to see how he would react. The doctor had hit upon the right solution, but he had no background of ideas to make it stick, no understanding or grasp of the range of motives that could explain it all. And Houston had that, but he seemed not to care to bother with it. Was Houston playing a game?

Dr. Stockton began putting his papers and photographs back into his briefcase.

"Well, I'll have to leave the motives to you, Mr. District Attorney," he said. "My findings are as follows: double murder or double manslaughter . . . The two men died so close together that I'd not like to say who died first, so—"

"Mr. District Attorney," Hilton spoke up for the first time. "There's more to this than you gentlemen are admitting. A man has been murdered. That man was Gilbert Blount. The murderer was Langley Herndon. Now, allow me to identify myself a little more before I continue. I'm a member of the editorial board of the *Daily Worker*. I was a colleague of Gilbert Blount. I want to protest against the light-handed manner in which this case is being handled. The issues here are basically social, and you gentlemen are playing around with probabilities and psychological facts. I'm insisting that some measure of responsibility be shown here. This case has a background of politics, sir. I said *politics*, and I mean it. And you do not want to look into that phase of it, yet the only real motives can be found there. We have *proof* that Herndon killed Blount. Mr. Lane here is an eyewitness . . . He saw Herndon striking Blount with a poker about the head . . . Herndon later struck Mr. Lane with that same fire poker. I'm speaking of the moral side of this case . . . You saw that frightened little woman who just left this room. Herndon chased that poor woman with a gun, terrorized her! Now, I maintain that it's unfair to leave the impression in the public mind that her husband was a murderer—"

Dr. Stockton had his briefcase in his hand.

"Mr. District Attorney, I must be off . . . The rest is up to you. There is no possibility of my giving you an opinion as to who died first. From a clinical point of view, we've nothing to go on. Good morning, gentlemen."

Dr. Stockton walked briskly out of the room. Hilton's thin face turned livid; he whirled to Houston and began to shout:

"Mr. District Attorney, it's but fair to warn you that the *Daily Worker* and the labor movement will fight you about any interpretation of this case that points to Blount as a murderer. He was defending his life against a fascist attack! He was defending his home, his wife, his friend against a man who has publicly advocated the extermination of all racial minorities. Herndon *sent* for Blount to come and see him. Mrs. Blount will testify to that. And Herndon was wildly angry when he did it . . . He later pulled a gun on Mrs. Blount herself . . . There was but one issue in this thing: Could Mr. Lane, a Negro, remain in this apartment? Now, you know that that is true, and so do I. We all know it. Only yesterday morning Herndon threatened the life of Mr. Lane here . . ."

"Look, Mr.— What's your name?"

"Hilton. John Hilton."

"I see your point, Mr. Hilton," Houston said. "In this particular investigation our aim is to determine *who* died first. And that is something for the Medical Examiner to find out. I asked him who died first, and he says he doesn't know. He has thrown in the sponge. He says that they died so close together in terms of time that it's anybody's guess—"

"But there's another angle to this," Hilton was persistent. "Look, Mr. District Attorney, this Herndon has threatened Mr. Blount many times. He threatened Mr. Lane here. He had the *intent*. Now, there is a *real* difference."

"But no proof," Houston said.

"Yes, there is proof," Hilton overrode Houston. "This man's writings are fascistic. He has advocated the extermination of non-Anglo-Saxon minorities—"

"Oh, Christ, man!" Houston exploded. "That's farfetched. If you're going to bring that up, why not cite all the Communist arguments and threats against the bourgeoisie? That would make Blount the guilty one, wouldn't it?"

"No," Hilton said.

"Why not? If you're going to be fair, you'll have to admit it," Houston insisted. "Now, look, here is how things stand. We don't know which man died first. We are not going to call this case an instance of double murder. What right has anybody to make Blount a murderer in the eyes of his wife? And, by the same token, what right has anybody to make Herndon a murderer in the eyes of his relatives even if they are not here to protect his name? All right, in the light of what the

Medical Examiner has said, I'm going to call this double man-slaughter . . ."

"And we'll call it just plain murder!" Hilton's voice rose in shrill denunciation. "You're taking the side of property in this investigation—"

Cross listened with amazement. Yes, sane men did misread reality. Just as he had once had fantasies, so now he was looking at men who were passionately arguing about their own fantasies, trying to decide which fantasy was to be taken for reality. No one in the room knew the truth of what had happened but he, and yet they were ready to fight and kill, if need be, for what they thought was the truth.

"I beg your pardon, sir," Houston said.

"This is an issue of property versus the individual and his freedom!" Hilton shouted.

"I'm taking no such stand," Houston maintained.

"You're giving the benefit of the doubt to capital!" Hilton charged.

"I'm abiding by the decision of the Medical Examiner," Houston corrected him. "I'll deal with facts and facts alone . . . You're trying to read your class conscious ideas into this investigation, and the law will not accept it."

"We will charge *murder*," Hilton hissed.

Cross had his fists doubled. He wanted to scream at Hilton to stop agitating. Let sleeping dogs lie . . . The more Hilton pressed his case for a class conscious interpretation of the facts, the more dangerous it was for him. Damn Hilton . . . He was trying to prove something false anyhow. And so was Houston. Cross could see that Hilton's attack, though rejected, had somewhat disturbed Houston who was staring thoughtfully off into space. So far Houston had accepted what seemed like a straightforward and normal account of the facts, but if Hilton kept on plugging away in that dogged manner of his, why, Houston might really start thinking; and if he started thinking, there was but one other real direction for his mind to travel. And that damned Houston, if he had the will, could find out the truth . . .

"Patrol, ask Mrs. Blount to come here a moment, will you?" Houston asked.

"Yes, sir."

Farrel left the room and a moment later Eva appeared in the doorway.

"Mrs. Blount, I'm sorry this has to happen in your home," Houston began. "I must question each person here separately. I'd like the use of your living room, if I may."

"Of course," Eva answered in a lifeless manner.

"Now, Farrel, in about ten minutes, send me these people one by one," Houston instructed. "Begin with Mrs. Blount— You are well enough to answer questions, aren't you?"

"Yes," Eva whispered.

Houston went out of the kitchen.

Hilton sidled up to Cross and forced a smile.

"You are some fellow, Lane." Hilton pulled down the corners of his lips in a scowl.

"What do you mean?"

"How did you get to know *him*?"

"So you think I'm in the pay of the police, hunh?" Cross asked, laughing. "I met him once on a train. That's all." A look of doubt was still in Hilton's eyes. "If you don't believe it, then I can't help it. You can check my statements, if you like. After all, how did I know that I'd ever meet him again?"

His words seemed to have some effect, for Hilton was now a little easier in attitude.

"Just the same, I'd like to know more about that," Hilton said.

"Sure," Cross said. "Whenever you like. I've no secrets."

The hell with him, Cross thought. Only one thing worried him about Hilton. Would the man try to poison his relations with Eva? Anger rose slowly in him. He would fight for Eva. He tried to catch her eye, but she was sunk in deep thought, staring blankly before her. He longed to be at her side when she was with Houston, but he knew that that was impossible. What was to be his relationship to her now that Gil was dead? Did it mean that he would have to move from the apartment? After the police had gone, he would talk to her about it. He would tell her, openly and frankly, that he did not ever want to leave her.

Farrel came to the door.

"Mrs. Blount," he called.

Eva rose and followed Farrel into the hallway. Hilton at once closed the kitchen door and turned to Cross.

"What are your plans, Lane?"

"I have no plans," Cross told him.

"Do you intend to stay here?"

"I don't know."

"If you don't, who does?"

"I'm going to speak to Eva about it," Cross said.

"When?"

"Look, I can't very well bother her *now*," Cross protested.

Hilton paced the floor. This man is after me, but why
. . . ? He thought of Bob's squirming on the floor, weeping;
he thought of Bob's dodging the Immigration authorities and
again he was drifting into that state of danger where he was
judging others with supreme and final contempt. What right
had Hilton to say who could live and who could not live?
Damn him . . . Hilton must have sensed his mood, for he
came close to Cross and clapped him on the shoulder.

"You're okay, Lane," he said. "We just have to be careful,
that's all. But I must see you sometime, *soon*. As *soon* as this is
over."

"Sure," Cross said.

At some time in the future, he had a score to settle with
this little god and it filled him with anger to think of it; then
he was angry with himself for getting angry. I must keep
cool, he told himself. Farrel came to the door and beckoned
to Hilton who strode out with defiance in his eyes and manner. A moment later Cross could hear Hilton's strident voice
rising in vehement argument with Houston. Why didn't the
damn fool let well enough alone? If he kept hammering at
Houston, Houston would, in the end, start wondering about
the case, start trying to find new theories he could make fit
into it. He strained to hear what was being said in the living
room, but could not make out any words. He looked at
Menti and Menti smiled.

"He's tough, that Hilton," Menti said, nodding approvingly.

"Yes," Cross agreed.

"Eva likes you," Menti said.

"She's a wonderful person," Cross said.

Cross thought that Menti was a weak man who followed
Hilton's lead. Could he placate Hilton a little through Menti?
He would try.

"Hilton seems suspicious of me," Cross said. "Is it because I know Houston?"

"Well," Menti drawled, pulling at his ear and smiling with embarrassment, "knowing cops is not exactly in our line, you know."

"But I've no relations with this man," Cross defended himself. "I met him simply and honestly in the dining car of a train some weeks ago." He recalled that Bob had witnessed their meeting and he added: "Look, I remember now . . . Bob saw it happen—"

"Bob? Bob Hunter?"

"Yes. You know Bob?"

"Let me give you a tip," Menti said, jerking down the corners of his mouth. "From now on, it's not wise to give the name of Bob Hunter as a reference in the Party."

"Why?"

"He's a counter-revolutionary," Menti said simply.

Cross blinked. He had blundered. He felt that he had become entangled in moving shadows.

"You're new to all this," Menti told him kindly. "I believe you're solid. But Hilton trusts nothing and nobody but the Party."

Cross decided to beg and wheedle a bit; he wanted to remain near Eva and the Party had the power to take her from him.

"Look, I've been in connection with the Party for only twenty-four hours," he argued. "I've worked for Hilton, so far . . . I'd like to set his mind straight. What does he think I'm after?"

"What *are* you after?" Menti demanded.

That shot caught Cross squarely unawares. "You distrust me too?"

"We distrust everybody," Menti said.

"Why do you distrust me?"

"We don't know you."

"All right," Cross said, feeling trapped. "Tell me what I should do in order to be trusted by the Party—"

"You have to belong to the Party," Menti said.

"I'm going to join—"

"I don't mean that."

"What *do* you mean, then?"

Menti chuckled cynically, scratched his chin, and looked quizzically at Cross.

"You have to *belong* to the Party," Menti said.

Then Cross understood. The Party would have to have some hold on him before it could trust him; the Party would have to own him morally. And Menti had spoken of it as casually as if he had been reciting the number of inches in a foot . . .

"Do you *belong* to the Party?" Cross asked softly.

"Yes. I've no life except that of the Party. I have no wish, no dream, no will except that of the Party," Menti confessed.

Cross stared in disbelief. Menti had willingly submitted himself to be ravaged and violated by others. And Cross felt that he could never surrender that completely to anybody or anything.

"I don't understand," Cross murmured.

"I know you don't," Menti said indulgently.

"But suppose the Party told you to do something you didn't want to do?"

"That's unthinkable," Menti said stoutly.

"Even unto death?"

"Even unto death and beyond," Menti maintained.

"Beyond?" Cross echoed. "Do you believe in a beyond?"

"In a sense, yes," Menti answered. "If, after I'm dead, the Party wanted to make use of me, wanted to place some interpretation upon my life or death, upon any of my actions for organizational or propaganda purposes, it has the right."

"But, Menti, don't you feel that you've got some value that's yours and yours alone?"

"In the eyes of the Party, no."

They both started at the vicious slamming of a door down the hallway. Hilton stomped into the kitchen, his face distorted with anger.

"That goddamn sonofabitch," he railed.

Farrel came into the door, beckoned to Menti and said: "You're next."

Hilton took hold of Menti's arm and hissed: "Tell him to go to hell for me!"

"Take it easy, guy," Farrel warned.

Alone with Cross, Hilton changed his attitude quickly.

"When you go in there, stick to your story, see?"

"You can depend on me," Cross assured him.

"We'll see."

"Look," Cross could no longer hold himself in, "you make me feel that I'm guilty of something. You don't trust me. Okay. Distrust breeds distrust. Now that I feel that you don't trust me, I wonder if I ought to trust you—"

"You want to change your story to the D.A.?" Hilton asked.

"Hell, no! Why should I? My talking to the D.A. has nothing to do with it. But, hell, man, don't make me feel I'm dirt under your feet. I don't like it."

Hilton grinned and relented.

"Lane, there's only one thing I want to ask of you—"

"What's that?"

"Take care of Eva."

"I'll do my best."

"I *know* you will," Hilton said and went abruptly out of the kitchen and out of the apartment.

What had he meant? Cross's hands twitched. I'd like to ram that bastard's head against a wall, he muttered to himself.

A few moments later Farrel tapped him on the shoulder.

"You're the last."

When Cross entered the living room, Houston was sitting smoking a cigarette.

"There you are," he greeted Cross. "Sit down."

As Cross sat Houston rose and began to pace the floor, chuckling, now and then tossing a glance at Cross. Had Houston changed his mind? Was he about to spring a trap?

"Tell me, Lane, what do you make out of all this?"

"I hardly know, really, Mr. Houston."

"I wonder how many men in this land refuse to acknowledge the laws of our society?" Houston mused out loud.

"That would be hard to find out, wouldn't it?" Cross asked.

"Yes. And that's just why I'm asking," Houston continued. "Farrel, like the Medical Examiner, keeps mumbling about how somebody could have come upon those two men while they were fighting and killed both of them. That's possible, but highly improbable. What kind of motive could such a killer have? That's what's puzzling me."

Cross was silent. Houston had returned to this dangerous ground. Why? He had to watch himself now. If he disputed such a theory, Houston might think that he was afraid of it. But if he acted casually, nonchalantly about it, would not that make Houston think that he was disinterested, had no emotional connections with it?

"I thought you had accepted the idea of their having killed each other," Cross said, simulating surprise.

"Maybe yes, maybe no," Houston mused. "I'm just playing with this idea. Now, such a killer could not be either a Communist or a Fascist, could he?"

"Why not?" Cross asked.

"Why would a Communist want to kill another Communist in the presence of a Fascist?"

"I draw a blank there," Cross answered.

"And, the other way around, why would a Fascist want to kill a brother Fascist in the presence of a Communist?"

"I couldn't think of a motive."

Cross thought he saw a way of confusing the issue and he put in quickly: "Suppose a Communist came upon two men fighting . . . Suppose Blount was killing Herndon and his brother Communist helped Blount finish him off and then killed Blount too?"

"Why?" Houston asked, stopping and staring.

"I don't know," Cross said. "I'm just exploring possibilities. Now, suppose a friend of Herndon showed up under the opposite circumstances? Suppose he helped to finish off Blount and then killed Herndon—?"

"Why?" Houston demanded again.

"I don't know."

"I don't know either," Houston said. "But while we're on this theory of a third man, suppose either Blount or Herndon killed one another and a third man came upon the victor and killed him. Why? No, your theory is wrong. If there's anything in a third man showing up, after you left, and joining in this fight—and I doubt this—he'd have to be somebody psychologically akin to either Blount or Herndon and yet somehow outside of them, I can't see either a Communist or a Fascist acting in that way."

"Come to think of it, I'm inclined to agree with you,"

Cross said, trembling at how close to danger he was; only a shadow of a thought separated him from being considered guilty in Houston's eyes.

Houston paced the floor again, sucking at his cigarette.

"Such a killer, if he existed, would have to, for psychological reasons, be akin to both of them, wouldn't he? At least he'd have to *understand* them . . ."

"Why?" Cross asked, smiling.

"Only a brother absolutist would have any motives for killing them on purely ideological grounds," Houston went on. "Let us suppose a normal person came upon those two men fighting . . . What would he do? He would do what you did when you looked into the room. You called the police, or you had Hilton call the police. Now, we've checked the time. It *is* possible that after you left the door, somebody did go into the room and find them fighting. But, in order to kill the two of them on ideological grounds, this killer would have to have the support of a *third* set of ideas . . . We've checked Herndon's apartment; nothing has been stolen. He had plenty of enemies, but they were nowhere near that apartment last night. Now, who is that *third* man with the *third* set of ideas?"

"And what is that *third* set of ideas?" Cross asked.

"That no ideas are necessary to justify his acts," Houston stated without hesitation.

Cross felt a spasm go through his body. Yes, at last Houston was on the right track. But such a track did not lead to proof. He gave a gentle laugh to cover his terror.

Houston continued: "Now, let's see. Just for the sake of argument let us say that Blount, a Communist, hence an outlaw like you and me at heart, has his gang, that is, the Party on his side . . . Now, this Herndon is an outlaw too, but an *old* one. Tradition backs him . . . When he needs it, he has the law on his side, certain sections of society, money, the owners of property . . . Now, both of these men feel that it is beneath their dignity to obey the rules and laws made by what they would choose to call 'others', see? Now, this strange, dream-killer that lives on neither land nor sea, must be somehow akin to these two men, or he would not suspect that they are laws unto themselves. Only this outside killer who does not as yet exist knows that force and force alone guarantees the safety of these two tyrants. This mythical killer partakes of both their notions of lawlessness. That's what makes it possible for him to kill them . . ."

"Two questions I'd like to ask," Cross interposed. "First, why would he partake of their lawlessness? And why do you think that Communist and Fascist ideas are alike?"

"When did I mention *ideas?*" Houston asked scornfully. "Ideas are just so much froth on the top of a mug of beer, my dear boy. Men are inventing ideas every day to justify for themselves and others their actions and needs. What makes these *three* men akin is the identity of the impulses in their hearts—"

It was not lost upon Cross that they were now discussing *three* men instead of two, and all three of these men were psychologically akin.

"Mr. Houston, that's a rather fantastic assumption," Cross said; he hoped that Houston would not suspect how deeply he agreed with him. "How can you *prove* that the same impulse actuates all three men?"

Houston paused in his pacing, turned, looked at Cross and then slowly tapped his broad chest with his right thumb.

"I have proof right *here*, Lane," he said quietly.

"What do you mean?" Cross asked, trying to keep anxiety out of his voice.

Houston did not answer at once; he resumed his pacing, his eyes deep with reflection.

"The proof is easy to see, but it is rather a daring kind of proof. Of course, this kind of proof cannot be introduced into court. It has a psychological basis," Houston explained. "It's an 'as if' proof . . . Know what I mean? It's an intuition; it must first come from your own heart, see? How do I know that all three men feel alike? I know because *I* feel that way . . ." Houston sized Cross up. "And I think you feel that way too; that is, if I recall correctly your attitude on the train. The only difference is this: you and I have not acted upon this impulse of ours. The moment we act 'as if' it's true, then it's truly got it? But we've both *got* it The proof of that is that we both understand it; that's the proof.

"A lawless man has to rein himself in. A man of lawless impulses living amidst a society which seeks to restrain instincts for the common good must be a kind of subjective prison. How such a man must live and sweat behind the bars of himself! God, the millions of prisons in this world! Men simply copied the realities of their hearts when they built prisons. They simply extended into objective reality what was already a subjective reality. Only jailors really believe in jails . . . Only men full of criminal feelings can create a criminal code. Only an enemy of Christianity, like Saint Paul, could establish Christianity. Men who fear drink want laws passed against drinking. Men who cannot manage their sexual appetites launch crusades against vice . . . Lane, we're outsiders and we can understand these new Twentieth Century outlaws, for in our hearts we are outlaws too.

"Here are the psychological origins of tyranny. Don't kid yourself, boy. Napoleon, Mussolini, Stalin, and Hitler knew what they were doing when they cast their beady eyes upon their subjects . . . When a man stood accused, objective evidence was of no avail. The dictator had but to glance into his own heart, and he knew at once that the prisoner at the bar was guilty! For, he reasoned, had he stood in the prisoner's place, he would have been guilty . . . How in hell did he become dictator without becoming guilty? Without breaking all the laws in sight . . . ?

"Now, let's get back to our *third* man who's realized all of this without acting upon it . . . Two tyrants are fighting in a room and our *third* man shows up. He feels towards those two men as those two men feel towards the masses of people . . . He's playing the same game, but on a much smaller scale. Who knows, maybe he's been hurt by both sides? He kills 'em, and with no more compunction than if he were killing flies . . . That man who kills like that is a bleak and tragic man. He is the Twentieth Century writ small . . . Do you get what I'm driving at, Lane?"

Was Houston teasing him? Or was he only talking? Cross laughed again to still his nervous dread. He told himself that he should keep quiet, that he was a damn fool to talk, yet he felt an overpowering desire to help Houston develop his theory.

"The man you are describing," Cross said slowly, listening with numbed dread at the sound of his own voice, "is one for whom all ethical laws are suspended. He acts like a god."

"Like a god!" Houston almost shouted. "That's the word I've been groping for. That's it exactly. But how can you tell when a man feels like that? You walk along the street and all faces look more or less alike. There's no clue to what each man feels or thinks. Indeed, such a man would be hard to detect, for in normal behavior he would act like all other men, maybe a little more subdued than others. But, above all, this man must feel that he *knows* what's right. Then, all at once, he sees something that violates that sense of right and he strikes out to set it as it ought to be. Then he resumes his cool and correct manner of living. But that, of course, is purely external. What must go on in a man like that? He must be something of an inferno, hunh? Something like the original chaos out of which life and order is supposed to have come." Houston paused and stared again off into space, and when he spoke there was a note of wonder in his voice: "I wonder if such men have any value? Might not they be the *real* lawgivers . . . Maybe . . . Who knows?"

Houston stood in front of Cross and laughed. Cross joined him in laughter, feeling something creeping over the surface of the skin of his body.

"Some idea, hunh?" Houston asked.

"Yes," Cross said.

Cross waited to be challenged, to be accused. Houston turned and went to the door.

"Farrel," he called.

Cross held his breath. Had he called Farrel to arrest him?

"We'll wash this thing up," Houston said over his shoulder to Cross.

Farrel came to the door.

"Make it manslaughter," he told Farrel. "Double manslaughter. Any other theory is too fantastic."

"Just as you say, Mr. D.A.," Farrel said.

"Now," Houston began, "let's talk about us. When can I see you sometime?"

"Any time you like."

"What are you doing now?"

"I'm planning to attend some classes at the university . . ."

Cross was conscious as he talked that he was speaking as out of a dream. A moment ago he had been positive that he was about to be arrested, and now he sat here free. The room seemed to sway slowly around him.

"Will you have dinner with me some evening?"

"With pleasure."

"What about Sunday evening at Frank's in Harlem?"

"Sure. What time?"

"Eight. Right?"

"Right."

"And forget this mess about Blount and Herndon," Houston said, winking. "Good riddance, I think."

They shook hands and Houston strode to the door, then turned and said casually: "You'll have to testify, maybe, at a hearing of the Medical Examiner, you know."

"Oh, all right," Cross murmured.

Houston left. Cross sat alone and closed his eyes; he wanted to keep them closed and not look any more upon the sight of the world. He recalled Houston's saying that most lawbreakers longed to be punished and he wondered if such was smouldering in him . . . Why did not this thing rest easily on his heart? Or was he only deluding himself in thinking that he was free? He was suddenly tired. Was it worthwhile going on? Eva . . . Yes! There was a hope that one day he could talk to her. She would understand. She too was a victim. But—suppose she knew what he had done? How would she feel about him then? He leaned his forehead on the palm of his hand and the only answer he could find was no answer . . .

Half an hour later he pulled to his feet and went in search of Eva. The door of her room was open and he saw her lying fully dressed across her bed. He should leave; his staying was no good for her . . . He pictured himself getting his suitcase, hat, and coat and going in search of a hiding place . . . A slight nervousness went through him and he was about to act when he heard her voice.

"Lionel?"

"Yes."

"Come in, Lionel," she said.

He went to the bed and bent to her.

"Are you all right?" he asked.

"I'm numb. Are they gone?"

"Yes."

"What did they decide?"

"It's double manslaughter."

"Poor Gil . . ."

"Listen, Eva—"

"Yes."

"You know that Gil asked me to come and stay here. He wanted to send me to the Workers' School. Now, Gil's gone. I don't know what to do."

She lifted her head and her hazel eyes looked at him.

"Do you want to leave, Lionel?"

"No. I never want to leave you, Eva."

Her eyes fell; he could see her chest heaving with effort. She finally looked at him, reached out her hand and touched him, and said in a low, clear voice:

"If you leave, I shall kill myself—"

"God, no," he said. "I'm here. I want to be here near you—Listen, tell me; have you any money?"

"Money?" she repeated with a bitter laugh. "I've nothing. I've not worked at my painting in six months. All Gil and I had was his salary from the Party. I've not sold a picture in over a year . . . I don't know what the Party thinks of me."

Her voice died and her eyes assumed a scared, haunted look. Cross knew that she was wondering if they would let her wander free with her guilty knowledge.

"Look, I have a few hundred dollars," he said.

"Oh, no, Lionel," she protested. "That's impossible! I can't touch that."

"Why?"

"It isn't right. I must work—"

"Eventually, yes. But right now, you need not worry. Look, after this is over, let's go away somewhere together. The Gatineau Mountains in Canada. It'll be safe there, quiet, far from all this—"

Her eyes shone, then tears clouded them.

"I'm sorry about Gil, but Lionel, I'm glad that you are out of that trap," she spoke softly.

"Trap?" he asked; he could not let her know that he knew.

"There's so much I have to tell you—" She gazed off. "Gil told you he wanted to fight for you. It's true; he wanted to. But he was fighting for something else too. His idea of the world—"

"But aren't the two things one thing?" he asked to get her notion of it. "He's fighting for Russia; Russia needs men like me; so when he fights for me he's hitting at the rotten basis that holds up the world that's against Russia. Isn't that it?"

Eva sighed and shook her head.

"You were only a means," she said. "Lionel, the Party sees facts in motion . . . God, what language! But there's no other way to say it. *Facts in motion* . . . You are a fact to them, not a person. You're oppressed, so, to gain your help, they claim they'll fight for you but only in so far as your fight helps them." She looked fearfully about the dim room, as though afraid that someone was listening. "You must break away from this . . ."

He agreed with her, but where could he go? She thought him a helpless victim; but, rather, he was what she hated. He had been using the Party in the same manner that the Party had been using him.

"I understand," he lied softly to her.

"I'm free now," she breathed. "But for how long? What will they say to me now that Gil's gone? Will they let me go? Will I be able to work again? Can I find new friends?" A twisted smile was on her lips. "Don't mind me, Lionel. I'll tell you what's worrying me later."

"Tell me now, Eva," he urged her. "It's better for you."

She hesitated; she was struggling with herself. Her life was in crisis.

"Lionel, I've been deceived in a way that you'll never know," she whimpered, trying to keep her lips from trembling. "You're colored and maybe you can understand . . . Perhaps you've lived all of your life with something that I've met only recently . . . When you were a child, you studied the same books I studied in school, yet you knew that what you read in those books did not apply to you; you knew you

were colored and that the white world made an exception
. . . You could prepare yourself against disillusionment. With
me, I believed in the Party, all they told me . . . Then I found
that it was make-believe . . . I can't even now tell you what
they did to me . . . They've blighted me, my life, my work
. . . I'm filled with shame and I want to hide . . . Where can
I hide, Lionel?"

"Eva, I'd feel happier than I ever dreamed if I could win
your trust. You can believe again in life . . . You *can*! You
must . . . I shall trust you, and if my trust helps you, then
you'll trust me in the end. I know it. You've never really been
trusted; you've been told what to do, what to think and what
to feel, and when it failed you, betrayed you, you hated yourself and the world. I shall trust you—"

"Oh, God, Lionel, I do so much want to try," she gasped,
reaching out her arms and pressing him convulsively to her
bosom.

He held her tightly, full of a sense of hot despair. What was
he doing? Did he, as lost as he was, have the right to talk to
her like this? How could he make promises to her? How
could he believe in her when he did not believe in himself?
Could he tell her of how he had abandoned his mother,
Gladys, his three sons, how he had killed Joe Thomas, Gil,
Herndon . . . ? Could he tell her that his life was steeped
in deception, that he was the essence of the world that she
hated and feared? Yet he felt that the cure of his nameless
malady lay in winning her trust and love . . .

But could this shrinking and delicate Eva bear the mere
hearing of his story? Would she not turn from him in loathing? He felt her tiny, cool hands on his face; he looked into
her giving, pleading eyes.

"I want your people to be my people," she said, surrendering her life to him. "I want to feel all the hurt and shame of
being black— Let me bear some of it, then I'll feel that I'm
worth something. I wish I was black. I do, I *do*— Let me
share the fear, the humiliation—"

She was wanting to love him for his being black, and he
wanted her love to help him to redeem himself in his own
eyes for his crimes! How could this ever be! Could he allow
her to love him for his Negritude when being a Negro was

the least important thing in his life? He wanted her for reasons which he doubted he could ever tell her, and she loved him for reasons which he did not have. He closed his eyes and rested his head on her shoulder. Yet he wanted that sensitive heart of hers to be his monitor, to check him from sinking into brutality, from succumbing to cruelty, and she wanted to love him for his being black because she thought he was an innocent victim.

"What's the matter, darling?" she asked.

"Nothing," he whispered. "Just tired."

"Poor Lionel . . ."

He was not Lionel Lane. He was nothing, nobody . . . He had tossed his humanity to the winds, and now he wanted it back. He would shatter this poor girl's heart if he took what she was offering. He pulled away from her and walked aimlessly about the room, his eyes unseeing. He needed her if he was to go on living, but would his taking of her kill her?

"Don't worry, Lionel," she smiled at him. "In the future when white men strike at you, they'll see me there at your side."

He buried his face in his hands, closed his eyes and groaned: "God . . ."

She rose and ran to him.

"What's the matter? Don't you want me to be with you?"

"Yes," he whispered despairingly.

"Then why are you so wrought up?"

He must not heap his troubles upon her. He should fly from this room, this girl, this hope of love . . . He seized her face tenderly in his palms and forced a smile to his lips.

"I'll be all right," he said.

"I only want to help you," she said. "For the first time in my life I am beginning to feel I can help somebody —"

Gently Cross crushed her face to his chest to keep her from seeing the bleak look on his face.

"Bless you, Eva," he whispered.

"We'll be together," she pledged herself.

"Together," he repeated wonderingly; but his eyes were gazing toward a distant shore which he was certain he would never reach.

The doorbell rang. Eva broke from him, smiled, kissed him

and turned and ran to the door. It was Sarah, grim, gaunt of face, her eyes dark and full of anger.

"Is Hilton here?" she asked without ceremony.

"No; he's gone," Eva told her.

Cross went to Sarah.

"What's the matter? Where's Bob?" Cross asked her.

"I want to see Hilton," Sarah said, ignoring his question. "I'm going to kill him—"

"Oh, darling," Eva wailed. "What's wrong?"

Sarah doubled her fists, lifted them toward the ceiling and bared her teeth in a rage of bitter hate.

"The Party told on Bob— The Immigration men caught him this morning when he came to the apartment for his clothes— Bob's dead— He can't live out those years in that prison in Trinidad— And I'm going to pay off whoever did it— Bob said that Hilton threatened to do it, and only Hilton and the Party knew about Bob's being illegally in the country . . ."

She sank into a chair and sobbed.

"But how could that be possible?" Eva demanded, turning to Cross.

Cross was witnessing the birth of a new Eva. He knew that when she had been with Gil, she would never have been able openly to question or challenge a decision of the Party. And now she was demanding answers.

"It's all my fault," Sarah wept. "I pushed him to disobey the decision . . . He did what I asked and now they got 'im . . . He was screaming when they took him away." She clenched her teeth. "How they fooled 'im. Last night he phoned me and said that Gil had told him that everything would be fixed. He was to go to Mexico—"

"Sarah," Cross took hold of her shoulder. "I have something to tell you. Gil is dead. He was killed last night."

Sarah stared, her lips hanging open.

"What did you say?" she gasped.

"Gil's dead. He was killed last night— He was in an argument with his landlord downstairs . . ."

Sarah rose and stood as though she herself had been condemned. Then impulsively she threw her arms about Eva.

"God, have mercy," she cried.

Cross watched the two women, both of whom had lost their husbands, weep. One husband had died suddenly; the other would die slowly over the years behind the bars of a prison on a hot island.

"I could kill the one who did that to Bob," Eva cried.

Cross's lips parted. That was what he had been wanting to do to Hilton, kill him; but he had fought down the notion. Now Eva was planting it again in his mind. No, no; he would not kill again. Then what did one do when confronted with the Hiltons of this world? Let them trample freely over whom they liked? Never . . . But then what? To kill Hilton was a way of redeeming what Hilton had done to Bob; and also it was a way of lending multiplicity to Hilton's acts, of making them right somehow. To kill him was a way, really, of exonerating him, of justifying him. Yet, what other course was there? To make an appeal to the heart of a man like Hilton was out of the question, for he was beyond any such sentimental considerations. This was a problem the full implications of which only men akin to Hilton and Gil could really see and understand, for they alone knew how far cut off from life one was when one assumed the role of the godlike. Was there no turning back? Once the tie had snapped, was it forever? Cross knew that the only difference between him and Hilton was that his demonism was not buttressed by ideas, a goal. So why should he care? But he did. And he hated Hilton as only one can hate something which is a part of one's own heart.

"Lionel, can't we do something?" Eva asked, oblivious of the gravity of her question. "Let's start *now*! Let's redeem ourselves and help Bob some way, hunh?"

"But what can we do? Bob's gone now—" Cross explained gently.

"It's too late to help Bob," Sarah said. "They've got 'im."

"This has got to stop," Eva cried. "Isn't there some way, Lionel? There must be . . . Men like that should be *killed*!"

She embraced Sarah again and the two women wept for the men they had lost.

He walked slowly from the women and went into the living room and sat down, wrestling with contradictions he could not resolve. Was killing the kind of punishment that Hilton needed? If he killed Hilton, would not someone try to kill him for killing Hilton . . . ? Where did it end? Forgiving the man was out of the question, for a Gil or a Herndon would look upon it as weakness and would use it to establish a crushing defeat upon him who offered forgiveness. Was there not a kind of punishment that could make Hilton repent . . . ? Was that the word: *repent*? Renounce one's aims and go over to the side of the adversary . . . ? But suppose the lawbreaker felt that the adversary had no rights, was so absolutely wrong that he would rather die than submit . . . ?

The pathos of Bob's fate was that Bob had been so weak, so easily persuaded, so needful of a master that the Party simply had no real need of his liquidation. Cross's broodings suddenly became organized and he went back to Sarah and Eva.

"Sarah, tell me, what Party plans did Bob hurt when he continued to organize?" Cross asked her.

"They were planning to launch a campaign for peace, and if Bob's union had been known as Red—and it was bound to be if Bob had kept on—everybody would have balked at signing any peace appeals. That's all . . . Bob got in their way and they kicked 'im to death." Sarah's eyes narrowed. "The police give you the third degree but the Party gave Bob the fourth degree . . ."

"This must not *be*," Eva said in tones of horror.

Cross wandered restlessly back into the living room. He searched in his pockets and found Hilton's card, then stood staring, holding his wallet in his hand. Yes; if he went to see Hilton, it would be better to leave his money behind. God only knows what might happen . . . He secreted his wad of greenbacks in his suitcase and again stood brooding. Suddenly he moved with purpose; he strode into the hallway and put on his overcoat.

"I'm going down for a bit," he told Eva. He studied Sarah for a moment. "Sarah, why don't you stay with Eva awhile?"

"Sure. I hate being by myself in that empty flat now . . ."

When Cross went down into the snowy street, his gun was nestling close to his hip as he walked. He reached the corner, paused, staring thoughtfully. He should go back and remain with Eva. He was safe then, safe from himself. To mull over Hilton's crimes would unhinge his impulses and make him want to act in that wild, crazy fashion again. But he kept on walking. He reached University Place and saw the dark red brick bulk of the Albert Hotel where Hilton lived. Was he in? And what would he say to Hilton when he found him? He did not know. Yet he was in the throes of an irrational compulsion to see Hilton . . . He entered the hotel lobby and walked to the desk.

"Is Mr. John Hilton in?" he asked the clerk on duty.

"Mr. Hilton, Mr. Hilton—" The clerk turned and studied the board on which hung the keys of the rooms. "Room 342 . . . I'm sorry, sir. But he's out."

"Do you know when he'll be back?"

"I'm sorry. I don't know. He left no message."

"Thank you."

Cross went out into the streets again, walking at random. It was afternoon and he had not eaten. The day was grey, sunless; the air was damp, cold. He passed men and women whose faces expressed the intensity of their personal concerns. His eyes drifted distractedly over drugstore windows, the facades of stone and brick houses, the long green buses pulling through icy streets, and now and then idly up at some tall, apartment hotel building. He longed suddenly to be near Eva; but that, too, was a dubious thing. Why not flee now and start afresh? But he had once done that and it had led to nothing, to the nowhere in which he now lived. Running off was no solution, for he would simply take his problems with him. In any new place he would be worse off, for Eva would not be there.

He entered a drugstore and ate a ham sandwich and drank a hot cup of coffee, neither of which he tasted. Was it that he had gotten himself into such an emotional state that nothing meant anything anymore, or was it that *too* much meaning had now entered his life, more meaning than he could handle? When on the streets again he came to a tavern and went in and drank a glass of beer. He saw a pinball machine in a corner; he dropped a coin into the slot, thumped the tiny little shining balls with a lever and watched them veer and jump and bounce amid the flickering lights; he heard the excited clatter of machinery as the scores flashed in yellow numbers on a glass screen in front of him and there was a girl in a scanty red bathing suit and she danced and leaped and romped on a gleaming and curving sandy beach under tall palm trees . . . He played twice and did not win. What the hell was he doing? Was he so lost that he had to resort to this for distraction? Disgust drove him at last out into the streets again.

Hilton lay like a coiled threat deep in his mind. He had condemned Bob to ten years of suffering and Cross was now trying to find some way of getting at him . . . His anger kept rising. Only the presence of Eva could evoke in him the drive to forget himself. Yes, he would make of that girl his life's project, his life's aim; he would take her hand and lead her and, in leading her, he would be leading himself out of despair toward some kind of hope . . . Suppose Hilton tried to take Eva from him; Hilton had the authority of the Party and could make endless trouble . . . Hell, he had to have it out with that man, *now* — He could not go on with Hilton looming like a black storm cloud over his head.

He turned and made his way back to the Albert Hotel and entered. "But why ask for Hilton?" he asked himself in a low voice. Just go up and knock on the door of his room. Sure . . . He crossed the lobby and stood in front of the elevator, waiting. Naw; walk up . . . He turned and saw that no one was observing him and he took the stairs to the right. Yes; room 342 would be on the third floor . . . When he reached the third floor corridor, he looked for the number. He came to the door of Hilton's room and paused; the door stood open and he could hear the whirr of a vacuum cleaner. He stepped to one side and waited. Was Hilton married? Or living with some girl? Strangely, he had not taken into consideration that Hilton might not be alone . . . He peered into the doorway and saw the white uniform and the bare, dark brown arm of a Negro maid, then he stiffened as he heard footsteps and he walked quickly away, looking over his shoulder. The Negro maid came out with a pile of dirty linen over her arm and headed down the hallway, leaving the door open. She was, no doubt, going to dump the soiled linen into some receptacle. Cross thought quickly; there might be a bare chance of his hiding in the room . . . The maid went out of sight and he ducked through the door and looked about frantically. Yes; the clothes closet. He opened it, slid in, and crouched in a corner, smelling the sweetishly sour odor of stale sweat. He pulled the door shut. Footsteps sounded again and he heard the maid humming a spiritual. Then the low whine of the vacuum cleaner came to his ears, and when it stopped there was the musical flow of water in the bathroom. More footsteps, silence. Had she gone? He heard the door slam and all was quiet. A moment later he emerged and looked about; the room was empty, untidy. Books were piled helter-skelter; soiled shirts and socks lay about. A greyish light seeped in through half-closed Venetian blinds. He looked in the bathroom to make sure that he was alone, then turned to the cluttered top of the dresser and studied the comb, brush, and a tube of shaving soap. He began pulling out dresser drawers. Clothing, pamphlets, a scrapbook, a flashlight . . . His breath caught in his throat. *What!* Good God in Heaven! What was this? That *Hilton*! What a tricky man . . . On top of a pair of pyjamas lay the balled and bloody handkerchief which he thought he had burnt by dropping it into the incinerator. The crumpled handkerchief showed burnt spots where it had lain on a pile of hot ashes; in fact, one corner was charred black . . . He stood without moving a muscle, unable to believe what his eyes saw so plainly. So Hilton had known all along! But why had he not said anything? Why had Hilton defended him so ardently before the police? Then he understood . . . Hilton was saving this handkerchief as his trump card; he was trying to *own* him morally . . . Hilton had seen him drop that handkerchief into the incinerator and had pretended that he had noticed nothing; and when he had gone back to his room, Hilton had gone downstairs and had gotten hold of it . . . Had bribed the cop at the door, perhaps . . . Or he had gone down to the basement this morning on leaving the apartment and had raked it out of the ashes. The fact was: Hilton had proof of his guilt! Eva had been in his room last night and maybe Hilton had eavesdropped at his door . . . ? Of course! That was the meaning of that last crack that Hilton had made just before he had left the apartment. Hilton had asked him to look after Eva and when he had said that he would do so, Hilton had said, "I *know* you will."

Gingerly, he stuffed the handkerchief into his pocket, then paused. No; it was not safe to put the handkerchief in his pocket like that. He withdrew the spotted handkerchief and then pulled forth his clean, freshly-laundered one. Yes, he would wrap the spotted handkerchief in the clean one; in that way, if he happened to pull out his handkerchief, he would not run the risk of dangling the bloody one carelessly in the face of some stranger. He tightly balled the bloody handkerchief and then wrapped the clean one around it, squeezing and crumpling the clean one so that it would look used and natural, so that no one would think that anything was wrong . . .

He rummaged further in the dresser drawers. Ah— A gun! A .32 and fully loaded . . . He took it and broke it and emptied the bullets into his palm and pocketed them. Now, he was ready to face Hilton. Where was he? Had he gone to the headquarters of the Communist Party? If he had, why had he not taken the handkerchief with him? Or did he have some other devious idea in mind? Anyway, it seemed that Hilton had not acted against him yet. Well, Hilton had had his chance; he would not act, not *now*. What a fool he had been! These Communists were so intelligently tricky that it was hard to cope with them. When Hilton came, he would have to be on his guard each second, for the man was dangerous. How calm he had acted this morning! A disciplined man, cold, precise, farseeing, ruthless. Hilton was free of such infantile stupidities as racial hatred; he was no frightened, white American dope worried about a white girl who slept with a colored boy . . . Hilton was after power and his keeping his mouth shut about Cross's guilt was but one more step along the road to getting hold of a bright young man whose life he would own and whose talents would serve him in his struggle for power . . .

Cross looked further in the room and found nothing of interest. He saw a little radio on the night table at the bedside. He looked at his wrist watch; it was nearing five o'clock. Where was Hilton? Had he gone to the police? No; if he had, he certainly would have taken the handkerchief with him as evidence . . . He sat in a chair near the bed and turned on the radio, softly, and listened to the low, surging beat of jazz music. He kept his hand in his pocket on his gun and waited . . .

Half an hour later he jerked alert. A key turned with a click in the lock of the door. Cross quickly twirled the knob on the radio, leaving the radio still turned on, going in a soft hum. His hand was on his gun and the gun was jammed deep in his overcoat pocket. The door swung in and Hilton, with a toothpick slanting downward from one corner of his thin lips, came into the room and stopped short, blinking his eyes at the sight of Cross. Hilton's body twitched as from an electric shock; he rushed to the dresser and yanked open the drawer that had held his .32 . . . How quick the man was, Cross thought. He smiled at Hilton, stepped past him and shut the door to the corridor. Hilton was pawing frantically in the dresser drawer, then he was still for a second. He spun around and faced Cross, his eyes bulging, his hands empty and trembling.

"I've got your gun, Hilton," Cross told him matter-of-factly.

Cross pulled out the .32 with his left hand and at the same time he drew his own .38 with his right.

"Say," Hilton began in a whisper. "What's wrong?"

"Are you asking me?" Cross mocked him.

Hilton's face was grey, his eyes like brown, flat discs of metal. He moved nervously, backing away from Cross one moment and advancing the next, his mouth working spasmodically. Cross could see that he was about to give vent to some sound.

"If you shout, Hilton, I'll just have to shoot you," Cross told him, accenting the gravity of his words. "Anything you do to attract attention of other people to this room, will be a sign for me to kill you. Now, man, have some sense. I'm in danger, and I'd not hesitate to shoot, see? I was a fool to underestimate you once, but I'll not do it twice. You're clever, intelligent, and I shall treat you as such."

Cross could almost see the rapid calculations spinning around in Hilton's brain. He had backed off to a wall now and stared at Cross with parted lips; sweat began to gleam on his forehead.

"What do you want, Lane?" Hilton asked.

"Why didn't you tell me you knew what I'd done?" Cross asked.

"What you'd done?" Hilton pretended amazement. "What are you talking about?"

"Quit stalling, Hilton," Cross said. "Look, I found the handkerchief . . . You got it out of the incinerator—"

"Oh," Hilton said, turning pale.

"You knew what I'd done. Why didn't you tell the cops?"

"Because I was glad that you'd done it," Hilton said promptly, simply. "It solved a multitude of problems for me. Gil stood between me and one of the most important assignments on the Central Committee. Gil is gone and I've already got the job. I've wanted Eva for a long time; you freed her . . . Gil's death was like a gift dropped from the sky."

Ah, Cross recalled how Hilton had spoken of Gil last night . . . But he had not thought that that much hate and cupidity had been behind those casual words!

"And when did you know I'd done it?"

"Your coolness made me suspect you right off," Hilton explained without a trace of emotion. "I'm not so stupid a white man that I cannot tell the difference between fear and self-possession in a Negro. You were self-possessed. The cops thought you were just another scared darky. Okay, Lane. You got the handkerchief. Let's make a deal. Let's be reasonable. You wanted Eva. Well, you got her . . . Okay. Take off and let's call it quits—"

"So you think it was to get Eva that I did it?"

"Hell, yes. She's nuts about you and you're in love with her," Hilton said.

"It wasn't because of Eva," Cross told him.

"Then what was it?"

"You'll never know."

"Another revolutionary group?"

"No."

"You're with the police, then?"

"Hell, no."

"Then why did you do it?"

Cross laughed. Just as every man, perhaps, has his price, so every man, it seems, has a limit to his intelligence. Hilton knew that Cross was sincere and it bewildered him.

"I'll trade with you," Hilton urged him. "I don't know what your angle is, but shooting's not going to help anybody . . ."

"It's not that easy, boy," Cross told him. "You and your crowd are smart. I trust *nobody* now."

"I'll not tell 'em, neither the Party or the police," Hilton swore. "Look, I just left Party headquarters. I'm taking Gil's place, in addition to my other assignment. So everything's settled. I was after getting my hands on a quick boy like you, but, hell, you got away. Okay. No hard feelings. You go your way and I'll go mine. To hell with Gil. I don't care. I know you'll never speak of it, and God knows I won't. After all, I helped you with the D.A., didn't I? I kept making a racket about how Herndon was the murderer, didn't I? And Eva worships you . . . You got what you want, hunh? Things went your way."

Hilton's voice had come in a low, urgent stream of words, all precise and straight to the point.

"What about Bob?"

"Bob?" Hilton blinked. "What the hell do you care?" Hilton's eyes were round with surprise. "Was he your brother or something?"

"No. You sent Bob to Trinidad, to his death—"

"So what? There are a million Bob Hunters. What do they mean? They don't count . . ."

Cross smiled bitterly. How those quiet words riled him! He had to deal with this man in a way that would make him feel what he felt.

"Sit down, Hilton."

Hilton hesitated; he did not know what was coming; his eyes darted and glittered. He licked his lips.

"Make no mistake, Hilton," Cross warned him. "I'd kill you in a minute. If you've got any tricks in mind, forget 'em."

"I've no tricks, Lane. I want to live . . ."

"So did Bob," Cross said. "Now, sit down . . . In that chair there, where I can see you."

Hilton sat and Cross sat on the edge of the bed and held his gun on Hilton.

"I want to know some things, Hilton," he began.

"Let's be reasonable," Hilton said. "Let's not be foolish about this. There's no sense in being drastic . . ."

The man had begun to plead for his life.

"How is it that you care so much for your life and nothing for Bob's?" Cross demanded.

"And what in hell do *you* care for life?" Hilton shot at him.

Cross smiled bitterly. It was a fair question.

"Who do you think *you* are to kill as *you* did?" Hilton demanded. "Herndon's no loss. But Gil was helping you, wasn't he? He took you into his home, trusted you, didn't he? And I shielded you from the cops, didn't I? What are you kicking about, Lane? Let's call it quits."

"No," Cross said thoughtfully. "There's something here I want to understand . . . I'm caught in these quicksands of compulsive actions, just like you are. But, Hilton, I'm reluctantly in it. I don't like it. I want to get out of it . . ."

"But killing me isn't going to get you out of it," Hilton reminded him eagerly, seizing upon every angle to save himself. "The only way out is to *stop*."

"I won't stop; I can't stop as long as men like you keep playing your dirty, tricky games," Cross said; and there was a genuine despair in his voice. "I won't ever feel free as long as you exist, even if you are not hunting me down. You and men like you are my enemies. Bob Hunters will go on being shipped to their deaths as long as you live . . . And don't give me this goddamn argument about your helping me. You help others when it *suits* you, and when it doesn't, you *don't*!"

"That's the law of life," Hilton stated simply.

"It isn't," Cross contradicted him in a frenzy that made Hilton's face turn still whiter. "Maybe you're trying to *make* it into a law—"

"It's what I've found, Lane; and it's what you'll find too."

"I don't believe it," Cross said, realizing that what Hilton had said was true from the past nature of his own experience. "And even if it's true now, we can change it. We can make it different, it must be different . . ."

"Why?" Hilton asked mockingly.

"Because— Because—"

"You're looking for paradise on earth," Hilton told him, managing a soft smile. "You're confused, Lane. You're seeking for something that doesn't exist. You want to redeem life on this earth with so-called meaning— But what you see before your eyes is all there is. Get all that idealistic rot out of your head, boy—"

"I'm *not* idealistic," Cross insisted.

"You are!" Hilton swore. "You're an inverted idealist. You're groping for some overall concept with which to tie all life together. There is none, Lane." Hilton was struggling to master his fear; he was trying to get at Cross's feelings, trying to make him feel that he was his older brother, that they shared basically the same views of life, and that Cross should accept his guidance. "Living in this world, Lane, is what we make it, and we make what there is of it. Beyond that there's nothing, nothing whatsoever, nothing at all . . . To think that there's something is to be foolish; to act as if there is something is to be mad . . . Now, let's do business like rational men. Let's make a deal. You do what you want to do, and I'll do what I want. We'll leave each other alone. I don't give a *damn* what you do . . ."

But Cross was not moved. He still held the gun on Hilton, smiling a little, appreciating Hilton's tactics. Then he shook his head; he could not accept what he had heard. There was an anchorage somewhere to be found. The logic of Hilton reduced all actions of life to a kind of trading in death. And that was not his sense of it; he had killed, but not to exalt that. He had been trying to find a way out, to test himself, to see, to know; but not killing just to live . . .

"You don't feel that there is any real justification for anything, hunh, Hilton?"

"Hell, no! I am here, alive, real. That's all the justification there is and will ever be, Lane," Hilton spoke earnestly, advancing arguments to save his life. "Let's start from that. I let you live and you let me live . . ."

"Why should I, if there's no justification? And suppose we break our contract?"

"Then one of us dies, that's all. What the hell is there so important about men dying? Tell me. We're not like the goddamn bourgeois, Lane. We don't make deals in shoes, cotton,

iron, and wool . . . We make deals in human lives. Those are
the good deals, the important deals, the history-making deals
when they are made in a big way. Sweep your illusions aside,
Lane. Get down to what is left, and that is: life, life; bare,
naked, unjustifiable life; just life existing there and for no reason and no end. The end and the reason are for us to say, to
project. That's all. My wanting to live even in this reasonless
way is the only check and guarantee you have that I'll keep
my promise."

"That's not *enough!*" Cross shouted.

"You're a romantic fool!" Hilton shouted in turn. "You're a
kid! An idiot! You're just going about spilling blood for no
reason at all, looking for what doesn't exist!"

"And what do *you* kill for?" Cross asked tauntingly.

"Practical reasons."

"And Bob was betrayed to death for practical reasons?"

"Yes. For practical reasons."

"But they were such trivially practical reasons," Cross protested, remembering the agony on Bob's face. "Couldn't there
be—?"

"A pretense? Why? Look at it simply, Lane. Why fool yourself? I'm speaking to you now out of the depths of my heart.
You know and understand too much to go about looking for
rainbows. Let's trade. I've no proof against you. If anything
ever happens to you, I'll help you; I'll remember and will
stand by you. After all, Lane, no matter what plan I had in
mind, I wasn't going to kill you—"

"That's just it!" Cross burst out. "I might forgive you if
you had been going to kill me. But, no; you were going to
make me a slave. I would never have been able to draw a free
breath as long as I lived if you had had your way. I'd have
suffered, night and day. You would have dominated my consciousness. No, no, Hilton, there's more here than you say.
Goddammit, there *is!* If not, then why all this meaningless
suffering? If you had killed me, that would have been a simple
act. Killing Bob might have been in a way merciful. He
wasn't happy. But to make him suffer ten long years! Hell, *no!*
Your ... life is just life, a simple act of accidental possession in
the hands of him who happens to have it. But what's *suffering?* That rests in the senses . . . You might argue that you

could snatch a life, blot out a consciousness and get away with it because you're strong and free enough to do it; but why turn a consciousness into a flame of suffering and let it lie, squirming . . . ? No!" Cross's eyes were unblinking, seeing not Hilton sitting there staring at him, but Eva's diary, those pages telling of deception, of shame, of fear; and, too, he was remembering his own agonies in Chicago. He rose from the bed and looked wildly about the room.

"No, Lane," Hilton was saying. "What are you going to do?"

Yes, he would turn up the radio, good and loud; it would help drown out the pistol shot. He turned the knob up and a leaping flood of jazz music filled the room. Hilton rose slowly, sensing that Cross was preparing to act. Cross kept the gun on him, then he saw the bed. Yes, make him get down there between those mattresses, and the sound of the bullet would not be heard.

"Lane, Lane, you're crazy!" Hilton was saying, his head shaking.

Cross saw that the man was losing his grip, was going to pieces.

"Take it easy, Hilton," Cross told him.

"You can't get away with it, Lane!" Hilton begged. His hands lifted themselves in a plea. "They'll hear the shot— Somebody will know— They'll catch you— Listen, you want money? I got a few thousand— I'll give you anything— But *don't* do this . . ."

Cross was possessed. He was crouching a little in the knees and his finger was conscious of the trigger. No, not yet; load the .32 and use it . . . That was better . . . He backed off from Hilton, pulled out the .32, and, holding his own gun on Hilton, he took one bullet from his pocket. He took his handkerchief and quickly wiped the bullet clean of his fingerprints and slipped it into a chamber of Hilton's gun, his eyes hard on Hilton's face. His fingers fumbled as he worked, for he expected Hilton to make an effort to overpower him while he was nervously busy breaking the .32 and putting the cartridge in . . .

Trusting, hoping for luck, Hilton rushed at him and Cross met the attack with a sharp blow from the butt of his gun across Hilton's forehead. The man slumped to the floor, still conscious, his eyes filmed with fear.

"No, Lane; no, no!"

Hilton was weeping now, suffering. Cross knew that he had to do it quickly or he could not do it at all. The sight of that tortured face was unnerving him. He stopped, grabbed Hilton by the collar, and yanked him toward the bed. He was surprised at how light the man was; and Hilton, in his craven fear, offered little resistance, as though he thought that being pliable might placate Cross and make him compassionate enough to spare his life.

"No, no, no . . . For God's sake, Lane, don't *kill* me!"

He put his gun in his pocket and now held the .32 in his right hand. He kicked Hilton and muttered:

"Get on the bed!"

He had to act quickly, or this man's wild face would make him stop. Hilton, with glazed eyes, scrambled obediently upon the bed, his hand still held shakingly before his eyes.

"Lane, Lane, listen— *Please!*" he sobbed.

Cross paused. Never in his life had he seen a man so undone by fear. He grabbed Hilton's head and, pulling one corner of the mattress up, he forced it over Hilton's head. Quick, quick, or he could not do it. Hilton's fingers were now clawing at Cross's hand that held his head to the bed. Cross placed the .32 at Hilton's temple and squeezed the trigger; there was a click. Oh, God, four of the chambers were empty; only one chamber was filled. Hilton's mouth was moving, but fear robbed him of the capacity of speech. Cross squeezed his finger on the trigger again and another empty click sounded, then again and there was a spurt of blue flame and a gaping hole showed in Hilton's temple and Cross was aware of the dancing waves of jazz music that swirled around the room. He saw that circling the bloody bullet hole in Hilton's temple were black powder burns.

He dropped the corner of the mattress and lowered the volume of the radio. Hilton's hands still moved; a labored breathing went in and out of the thin lips; there was a groan and the form on the bed was quiet. Cross strained, listening. There were no sounds in the corridor. He had to get out of here . . . The .32 . . . Yes . . . He wiped it clean of fingerprints on the sheet of the bed and tossed it beside Hilton's hand. He paused, then forced the gun into Hilton's fingers.

He looked about. His fingerprints— Suddenly he did not want to try to save himself. What was the use? But he had to. He took a dirty shirt of Hilton's and wiped wherever he thought he had touched. He had to go, had to get out of this room. He was more concerned with getting away from the sight of that grotesquely grey face with its gaping mouth than with saving himself. He went to the door, opened it slowly and looked into the corridor. He saw the retreating back of a man. He waited until the man had turned a corner, then he went out of the room, drawing the door to, and walked toward the elevator. He seemed to be floating along without effort; he was never able to remember afterwards making any attempt to run or hide. But when he got to the elevator, he pushed a button and then seemed to realize that he ought not be seen by the elevator boy. The shadow of the car heaved into view through the glass door of the elevator and he ducked away. He saw a flight of steps leading down; he took them, running, then slowed and walked on down to the lobby. Act natural, he told himself. He walked across the lobby, passing one or two people who glanced casually at him. He came to the newsstand and stopped.

"A *Daily News*," he said.

He paid for the paper and, as he turned to walk to the door, there flitted through his head an idea of a way to establish something resembling a partial alibi for himself . . . Ought he try it? Why not? Holding the paper before his eyes and pretending to scan the headlines, he glanced quickly about. No one seemed to be aware of him. Yes, he would do it. He went casually to the desk and asked the clerk:

"Is Mr. Hilton in?"

"Oh, yes; I think he's in now, sir," the clerk replied; he seemed to remember that Cross had asked for Hilton before. Turning, he examined the board holding the keys, then spoke to a brunette girl who sat facing a switchboard to his left. "Will you ring Mr. Hilton, please . . . ? Room 342."

"Okay," the girl said.

"Who shall we tell him is calling?" the clerk asked.

"Lionel Lane."

"Tell 'im Mr. Lane is calling," the clerk told the girl.

Cross watched the girl plug in on room 342 and jiggle a tiny lever. A young woman with a suitcase came to the desk and Cross stepped to one side and listened as she inquired for a room . . .

"There's no answer from Mr. Hilton," the girl at the switchboard told the clerk.

"No answer?" the clerk asked. "But I saw him go up a few minutes ago."

"I'll try again," the girl said.

"Won't you wait a second?" the clerk asked Cross. "We're trying to locate Mr. Hilton."

"Certainly."

"Did you have an appointment with 'im?"

"Well, yes. He asked me to come and see him as soon as possible. No time was specified," Cross explained.

"She's ringing him again," the clerk said, giving the woman with the suitcase the hotel register to sign. "Won't you sit down?"

"Thanks," Cross said.

He sat. He hoped that his present actions would indicate in any future inquiry that he had not been upstairs. Would a murderer act as calmly and politely as he was acting now?

"There's no response at all from Mr. Hilton's room," Cross heard the girl speaking.

"I'm sorry, sir," the clerk said, "but we don't seem to be able to locate Mr. Hilton for the moment."

"That'll be all right," Cross said, rising.

"Would you care to wait awhile?"

"Well . . ."

"Would you like to leave a message?"

Before Cross could answer the elevator door opened and several people came out into the lobby.

"Just a minute," the clerk said, turning to the elevator boy. "Say, Sam, did Mr. Hilton go up?"

Sam looked blank and shook his head.

"I don't know."

"What's the matter with your eyes?"

"I can't remember everybody who rides in this elevator," the boy complained.

"Maybe he's in the dining room," the clerk said.

"Maybe," Sam said, getting into his elevator to ride another load of passengers up.

"Look," Cross said. "I'll just leave a note."

"Right, sir."

On a pad of paper supplied by the clerk, Cross wrote:

Dear Hilton: I was by to see you twice this afternoon. I'll try again tomorrow morning. Everything's fine. Hope you got some sleep after that session last night.

                                                              Lane.

P.S. Don't worry about anything. Eva's doing wonderfully well.

P.P.S. Since you're so busy, why don't you phone me instead and let's fix a time?

He folded the note and handed it to the clerk who pushed it into the letter slot, numbered 342, of the keyboard behind him.

"Thank you," Cross said.

"You're welcome, sir."

It was not until Cross had gone out into the cold streets that the full reaction to what he had done began to set in. He trembled as he walked. Had he acted normal enough? Could it not now be argued in favor of his innocence that he had asked for Jack Hilton *twice*? As his mind grasped more fully the folly of his having killed Hilton, a sense of nauseous depression seized him. He had killed Jack Hilton for many reasons: to redeem Bob's betrayal, for the sake of Sarah's indignation, for Eva's deceived heart; but mainly it had been to rid himself of that sense of outrage that Hilton's attitude had evoked in him, Hilton's assumption that he could have made a slave of him. He was mired deeper now than ever in the bog of consequences flowing from his compelling acts. He would be caught . . . Surely they would come at him now. To be found on the fringes of *two* crimes would certainly make the police think that something was wrong . . . All right; so what? Was he not already lost anyway . . . ?

But was it as bad as all that? Did he not have an ironical array of invisible allies on his side? Would not the police have a rather difficult job of proving his guilt in terms of motives? What motives could they impute to him? The police would first have to prove that he had killed Gil and Herndon before they could get near his motive for having killed Hilton . . . Lacking concrete evidence, the police would have to fall back upon psychological motives. And in that realm he was certain that even Houston, that old outlaw who had trapped himself with the law, that outsider who was privy to the secrets of the moon's dark side, would find it well-nigh impossible to bring himself to the point of believing him guilty . . . Even if Houston should actually believe him guilty, would he dare express his theories about it publicly? Houston had a passion for toying with daring ideas, but juggling with possibilities and realistically putting one's self in a position to say definitely that a man committed a particular crime because of those possibilities were two wholly different things. And especially when the crime stemmed from such a ghostly set of reasons . . .

Were not the queer motives of his crimes in themselves a kind of ally? Would not Houston, precisely because of his position of public trust, instinctively hesitate to expound an idea that went contrary to the basic tenets of normal and even abnormal actions? (For abnormal actions carried with them an aura of irresponsibility, and Cross considered himself *responsible*!) Would not his accuser have to place himself, in branding him guilty, in a *psychological* attitude that would spell the same kind of guilt that resided in the heart of the criminal? There was an inescapable element of contagion here . . . Who could possibly suspect him of being guilty on the basis of his *real* motives unless he himself had wrestled fatally with the same serpentine motives in his own heart? And if one had so wrestled, might he not, on finding Cross guilty, feel inclined to cross the line of law and arraign himself on Cross's side? Was that not the secret of all the revolutionary "front" groups? You flaunted a program that would appeal to a part of the forces of the enemy; you induced a section of the enemy forces to work with you and, while your enemies were standing at your side and seeing the world as you saw it, experiencing life as you lived it, they could decide that yours was as right as the side to which they belonged . . . Until now Cross had been lucky enough to leave no tangible clues behind, and the only clues open to anybody's inspection so far were only his motives . . .

His crimes constituted so decisive a divergence from the plane of ordinary moral considerations, stemmed from so weird an angle of perspective that he who would find him guilty must needs go so far as to place himself at that same point of vision that he had had while committing his crimes; and that person, his accuser, would automatically and of necessity have to become entangled in the very guilt he would denounce! He who would judge him would have to be as much outside of the canons of normal living as he before his guilt would become evident to that judge!

These were the intangible factors that made Cross, deep in his heart, rely upon Houston, the defender of the law, to condone and protect his breaking of the law. That Houston would track him down in time he was certain, but was Houston psychologically free to act upon what he found? Had not Houston admitted that maybe some men had the right to become lawgivers? Was there not, maybe, in Houston's heart the capacity to *respect* some forms of forceful crime? Had not men respected the crimes of Napoleon, Stalin, Mussolini, and Hitler . . . ?

There was no confusion in Cross's mind about this. He knew well that laws, on threat of dire punishment, enjoined men against certain specific acts; but did not those laws, by their very act of being laws, by describing the crimes they prohibited, represent negative projections of man's consciousness to check his own compulsive urge to commit the very crimes which the laws inveighed against? Was not the secret force of law itself really much deeper than the mere negative injunction against certain acts? Did not the positive aspects of law imply a conspiratorial understanding on the part of vast numbers of men to prevent, in terms of action, certain areas of consciousness from *thoughtlessly* assuming the upper hand in their lives? Was not law a struggle of man against man within man? Men who made and executed laws knew that the specific laws they framed or enforced would be violated, and it was not only to brook these specific violations of the law that they intended when they made and enforced those laws.

The real aim of law was to *inhibit* in the consciousness of man
certain kinds of consciousnesses which the law had to *evoke*
clearly and sharply in man's consciousness, for the law pos-
sesses the strange capacity of creating vividly in man's consciousness a sense of the reality of the crime it seeks to
suppress . . .

Law, then, by inhibiting man's actions, posits a sense of
crime in man; law makes the criminal consciousness of man;
law makes crime a sensual object, but it casts about that sen-
sually forbidden object a dark halo of dread . . . Implied in
law is a free choice to each man living under the law; indeed,
one could almost say a free challenge is embedded in the law:
if you are *strong* enough, you can do so . . . But you must
know what you are doing . . .

Cross shrewdly suspected that Houston, a self-confessed
outlaw, knew this, felt it; and it was what had made him become an active defender of the law; he *had* to represent the
law in order to protect himself against his own weakness and
fear . . .

He turned off Eighth Street and walked toward home. As
he neared Herndon's apartment building he became aware
that a police car was pulling slowly into Charles Street at the
opposite end of the block. Did they know already? Tension
waxed in him. Yes, he would act natural, keep his wits about
him. A confrontation regarding the death of Hilton would be
far more serious than the questions he had answered regarding the deaths of Gil and Herndon. The police would now
wonder at the coincidence of his being disquietingly near the
scenes of *two* murders in twenty-four hours . . .

Yes, the occupants of the police car had evidently spotted
him, for the car slowed and he arrived at the entrance of
Herndon's building at the same time that the car did. He
feigned to pay no attention to the car and turned to mount
the steps of the stoop. The door of the car flew open and a
cop leaped to the sidewalk, ran, grabbed his arm, and spun
him around.

"Just a minute!"

Cross gaped at the cop a moment in simulated surprise.

"What's the matter? What do you want?"

"We want to talk to you!"

Two more policemen came running from the car and the three of them surrounded him in the growing darkness of the street. Several people paused and stared. One of the cops barked roughly:

"Get going— This is none of your business!"

The passersby moved reluctantly on.

"What do you want?" Cross asked.

"You're Lionel Lane?"

"That's right."

"You'd better come with us."

"I'll come willingly, but why?"

"You'll know why soon enough."

He allowed himself to be led, looking in alarm from one face to the other. He would pretend to be stunned; he would not talk. As they pushed him into the car, he glanced up at the lighted windows of Eva's apartment and wondered if she knew. He was sitting jammed between the policemen when the car jerked into motion and the siren rose to a wail as the car picked up speed. Then his breath was knocked out of him as the cops seized him from both left and right and patted his pockets. They found his gun and snatched it.

"Ah, a Colt .38 . . . So you carry a gun, hunh?"

"Of course . . ."

"What the hell do you mean by 'Of course'?"

The cop broke the gun and extracted the bullets.

"I've a permit to carry a gun," he told them gently.

There was a moment's silence. Cross took his wallet from his inside coat pocket and tendered the permit.

"Jesus! It was issued yesterday," a cop exclaimed.

"Has the gun been fired?"

"Doesn't look or smell like it . . ."

Three minutes later the siren died and the car pulled to a screeching stop and the doors were yanked open. Cross was pushed out and hustled into the interior of a police station and made to sit facing a tough, wide-mouthed, grey-haired policeman who stood behind a desk. Cross noticed that a plaque on the desk identified the man as: Captain Ross.

"We picked 'im up in front of where he lives," a cop reported to the captain. "We grabbed him about two minutes after we got the call. He had this . . ." The cop put Cross's gun on the desk. "Here's his permit."

The captain quickly examined the gun, then eyed Cross intently. He rose and stood over Cross.

"Frisk 'im," the captain ordered.

One policeman held him while another swiftly emptied his pockets and piled his package of cigarettes, his ring of keys, his wallet, his lighter, his loose coins, and his folded newspaper upon the desk. He had a moment of wild panic when the policeman pulled the balled handkerchief from his pocket . . . But the policeman handled it gingerly, as though he was afraid of germs. He had been lucky to have thought of wrapping the bloody handkerchief inside the clean one.

"Okay," the captain said. "Take your stuff. Where do you live?"

"13 Charles Street."

"What do you do for a living?"

"I'm a student."

"Where?"

"Well, I haven't enrolled yet—"

"Where were you going when the officer met you?"

"Home. I was in front of the house where I live."

"Why do you carry a gun?"

"My life has been threatened."

"By whom?"

"My landlord who was—"

"When was this?"

"Yesterday. You see—"

"Have you used this gun recently?"

"No. I haven't fired that gun in over five years."

"Do you know John Hilton?"

"Of course. I just left his hotel—"

"You had an appointment with him?"

"That's right. But why are you asking me all this—?"

"We'll do the questioning. Now, what was the purpose of your visit to Mr. Hilton?"

"He invited me to see him."

"What did you say to 'im?"

The police had not mentioned that Hilton was dead, and Cross knew that they were trying to trap him into some inadvertent admission that he knew that Hilton was dead or that he had recently seen him.

"Nothing. He wasn't in."

"But you *saw* him?"

"No, I didn't . . . What's wrong?"

"Did you have a quarrel with 'im?"

"No. I've never quarreled with him."

"You were good friends?"

"I wouldn't quite say that."

"Why?"

"I just met the man two nights ago—"

"And when you saw him just a few minutes ago—"

"I haven't seen Mr. Hilton since ten o'clock this morning."

"Did he give you an appointment to see him another time?"

"What do you mean?" Cross knew that the captain was still trying to trick him into admitting that he had seen Hilton.

"I mean, when you left him this afternoon, when did he tell you that you could see him?"

"But I didn't *see* him this afternoon, I tell you."

"What did he want to see you about?"

"Well," Cross allowed himself to relax a little. "He wanted to talk politics— Look, you know as well as I that Hilton's a Communist. But I thought it was legal to talk to him."

The captain sat down and pulled from the desk drawer the note which he had given to the clerk in the hotel.

"Did you write this?"

Cross affected to be astonished as he examined the note.

"Yes. I wrote this this afternoon, about forty-five minutes ago; or maybe half an hour . . . But how did you get this? I thought I left it for Mr. Hilton . . ."

"Did you push it under the door of his room?"

"No. I left it at the desk. But where did you get it?"

"We found it," the captain said vaguely.

The police were trying in every way possible to drag him into an area where he would make a damaging admission.

"Then Hilton must have dropped it out of his pocket, or something like that. Or maybe the hotel clerk dropped it, lost it . . . But I could swear I left it at the desk with the clerk," Cross allowed himself to be confused, bewildered. He looked nonplussed from one face to another. The policemen were puzzled. "What's this all about? What do you want with me? Did Mr. Hilton say something to you?"

"Mr. Hilton had an accident—"

"Oh," Cross said in surprise. "Not serious, I hope— An automobile accident?"

"You tried to see Hilton earlier today?" the captain asked, ignoring his question.

"Yes."

"And he wasn't in?"

"That's right."

"Did you see Hilton at any time today?"

"Yes. It was this morning when he left the apartment where I live. But what's this all about? What has that got to do with his being hurt? If you told me what you wanted, maybe I could help you," Cross said.

"When did you see Hilton *after* he left you this morning?" the captain continued to ignore his request for more information. "You saw him?"

"No."

"Did Hilton ever threaten you?"

"No; why should he? Look, let me explain . . . Hilton came last night—"

"We're doing the questioning. You just answer!" the captain reminded him. "Do you know of anyone who'd want to harm Hilton?"

Cross gaped and let his eyes assume a roundness of understanding. This is the closest the captain had come to saying that some *person* had hurt Hilton. Now, ought he try to confuse them by telling them about Bob and Sarah? Bob and Sarah had real, ordinary motives for wanting to kill Hilton and the both of them had airtight alibis . . . So what harm would it do to tell of the row that Bob had had with Gil and Hilton? It would give their literal minds something to chew upon for a few minutes.

"Well, look now . . . Let me think . . ."

"Don't think! Talk! Tell what you know. This is serious."

"Well, it's kind of complicated and I'm rather a stranger to all of them, you see. These people, you know, are Communists, all of them. They had a hot argument the other night about Party matters . . ."

"What people and where was the argument?"

"Bob Hunter and Hilton— It was at Bob's place—"

"Go on; get to the point!"

His eyes roved from face to face. Yes, they were eager to hear the story. He could turn their minds away from him. Bob was on Ellis Island and had the best of all possible alibis. And no doubt Sarah could prove that she had been with Eva at the time that Hilton was killed. He related to them the tale of Bob's illegal entry into the country, of how Hilton had—according to Bob's way of explaining it—threatened to have him deported to Trinidad if he did not obey the Party . . .

"You see, according to Bob, Hilton was going to tip off the Immigration authorities and have him picked up," Cross said.

"Where's this Bob Hunter now?" the captain demanded.

"He was at Ellis Island the last I heard," Cross said gently. "They picked him up for deportation."

The faces of the policemen showed keen disappointment.

"And his wife, Sarah? Where's she now?"

"At my house, maybe. That is, if she's not gone to her own home by now—"

"Where does she live?"

He gave them the information. He was sure that Sarah could readily account for herself. He was using Sarah to fill out his story, to put his recital in a frame of reference that would make his attitude seem normal and cooperative.

"Lane, did you go up to Hilton's room?" the captain asked suddenly, softly.

"No; I told you he wasn't in."

"Did you ever fire a .32?"

"No. I own a .38. You see my gun—"

"Aren't you associated with Hilton in some way?"

"No. But why do you ask me that?"

"You could have walked up the stairs, you know," the captain suggested.

"What stairs?" Cross asked.

"The hotel stairs. Didn't you walk up to Hilton's room?"

"Good God, no! I told you I didn't *see* Hilton!"

There was silence. The captain turned to his desk and wrote something hurriedly upon a pad, tore off the sheet and handed it to a policeman.

"Check at Ellis Island about this Bob Hunter. Make sure he's still there and hasn't been out . . . And send out a radio call for this Sarah, his wife—"

"Say!" Cross exclaimed. "Look, here—" He pretended to be overcome with contrition. "I didn't mean to get Sarah in trouble . . . She's all upset about her husband. I'm sure that she hasn't done anything to anybody. She'll hate me for making people think that she's done something . . ."

"We'll take good care and keep what you've told us strictly confidential, Mr. Lane," the captain said. "Now, let me tell you that Hilton was found dead a few minutes ago in his hotel room . . ."

Cross lifted his head with a jerk and stared at the captain.

"Dead?" he echoed.

"Yeah."

He kept his eyes intently upon the captain's face, then took a deep breath; he looked disbelievingly around the room at the faces and leaned weakly forward and rested his hands on the edge of the captain's desk, as though for support.

"God," he sighed. "And I was trying to see him all afternoon."

"You did not go to his room?"

"Of course not. He wasn't in . . ." He paused. "God, he might've been dead when I was asking for him."

"That's possible," the captain said.

"And only last night his friend, Mr. Blount was killed— What's happening—?"

"Blount? Gilbert Blount?" the captain asked, his mouth hanging open.

"Yes. That was Hilton's friend. I'm living in Mr. Blount's apartment. I just spoke to the District Attorney this morning about all of this"

The policemen were astonished. He knew that their minds were wandering far from him now.

"Get the District Attorney's office on the telephone," the captain ordered. "We'll see what this is all about."

"Yes, sir," a policeman answered and left the room.

Cross sat and waited.

"How deep are you in this Communist business?" the captain asked.

Cross relaxed a bit; their minds were now working normally, leading them into paths where they could find nothing against him.

"I'm not in it at all," he answered. "I belong to no political organizations whatsoever."

"How long have you known Blount?"

"Two days."

"How did you come to meet him?"

"At Bob Hunter's place."

"How did you meet Bob Hunter?"

"On a train."

"And Hilton? How long have you known him?"

"Two days. I met them both the same night."

"Did you ever hear anybody threaten either of them?"

"No."

"Did Bob Hunter or his wife ever threaten them?"

"They had a hot argument, but nobody threatened anybody."

"By the way, let me see your draft card."

Cross tendered his draft card; the captain examined it, copied down some information from it and handed it back to him.

"Where were you born?"

"In Newark, New Jersey."

"Where did you go to school?"

"In Newark."

"This Hilton, what kind of a man was he?"

"What do you mean?"

"His behavior . . . ?"

"Well, he struck me as being very intelligent. He never said much. He's an ex-school teacher."

"Where did he teach school?"

"I don't know. Look, I hardly know the man. I spoke to him for the first time this morning and for only a few minutes—"

"But he wanted to discuss politics with you, didn't he?"

"Sure; I'll talk and have a drink with anybody. Why not? I'd take a drink with you even . . ."

"No thanks," the captain said, smiling suddenly. "Did Hilton owe you any money?"

The captain's manner made Cross feel that he had given up any hope of linking him with the killing of Hilton.

"No. Not a cent."

"Did you *owe* him something?"

"Nothing."

"Did he have a girl friend?"

"I don't know."

"Any men friends?"

"Yes. He was with a guy called Menti—"

"Menti what?"

"I don't remember his first name. He was just called Menti—"

"Spell it."

Cross spelled out Menti's name.

"Where does he live?"

"I don't know."

"Had he quarreled with Hilton?"

"Not in my presence."

"Now, Lane, account for your movements during the afternoon."

Cross sighed, looked at the ceiling, then at the faces around him. He laughed and said:

"You'll have to let me think a minute—"

"Take your time," the captain said.

He told them of his movements in complete detail, leaving out only the half hour he had been in Hilton's room. He was deliberately shrewd enough to get the sequence of his actions twisted and several times he had to interrupt himself and re-order the chronology of events. He told them of his visit to the drugstore, the bar, of his two visits to the hotel, the newspaper he had bought. He told of waiting in the lobby while the girl at the switchboard tried to ring Hilton; of how the clerk had questioned the elevator boy about Hilton's having gone up to his room. When he was pressed to give a description of how much time he had spent in each place, he grew vague in a helpless sort of way and would not commit himself. Instead he tried to recall in concrete detail all the many tiny things he had done or seen. He even told them of his playing the pinball machine and he extended the number of times he had tried to win . . .

"We'll check on all of this," the captain told him. "Lane, you can go now. But don't change your address. And say nothing about this to no one."

"Just as you say, Captain. And if I can help you in any way, I'd be glad to do so. I didn't know Hilton very well, but I'd do what I could—"

The telephone rang and the captain picked up the receiver and listened.

"Okay," he said, hanging up. "Lane, I'm afraid that you'll have to stick by. The D.A.'s coming over."

"You mean Mr. Houston?"

"Yes."

"Sure. He's a swell guy. I've got a date to have dinner with him Sunday evening . . ."

The policemen looked at one another. All of his words had been designed to lure their thoughts away from him, but not too definitely; he was assuming that a mild doubt in their minds was better than a certainty. His strategy was not to account for himself so cleverly that they would suspect that he was giving them a carefully doctored story. It was a sounder policy to make them wonder a little, search, check, and find nothing . . .

He sat alone in an anteroom waiting for the arrival of Houston. What would the old hunchback think now? Even if he *thought* him guilty, what could he do? Would Houston want to hold him for investigation? But would he not need the justification of some iota of evidence to do that? Houston could, of course, put him in the Tombs and then carry on his investigation. But would he? Would he not think that these two crimes were of a political nature? That some Communist had become disgruntled and had killed Gil and, having killed him, had to kill Herndon to silence him? Would he not think that maybe the same disgruntled Communist had had to kill Hilton to silence him also? While he waited, one of the cops came to him and gave him his gun and the permit.

"The D.A.'s on his way over," the cop said.

"Thanks," Cross said, pocketing his gun.

Cross saw Houston arrive; a policeman escorted him into the captain's office. They're giving me a going-over in there, Cross thought. Half an hour later Cross was taken into the captain's office to confront Houston. They were alone. Houston was grim, tense. He moved lightly and nervously about the room, more stooped and humped than ever, throwing a darting glance at Cross from time to time. Finally he stopped in front of Cross and said:

"You seem to be getting to know the police pretty well."

"Looks like it, doesn't it?" Cross said.

"Is there anything you want to add to what you've told the captain?" Houston asked.

"No; not that I can think of."

"You were *not* in Hilton's room today?"

"Absolutely not."

"And you are *not* in the Party?" Houston asked.

"No. I'm not a member of the Party nor have I ever been."

"Had they asked you to join?"

"Of course."

"And what did you say?"

"I stalled. I talked with them about general subjects—"

"And you did *not* see Hilton?"

"I did not."

"When did you last see him?"

"When he left Blount's apartment this morning."

"Were you in communication with him by phone or in any other way since then?"

"No. There'd be no reason for me to be."

Houston paused and brought his fist down on the edge of the captain's desk.

"I wonder what are these damned totalitarians killing each other about!"

"That would be hard to tell," Cross said softly.

"Lane, you know something about how men's minds work. Now, do you think that what we were discussing this morning could have any relation or bearing on these killings?"

Cross felt dread enter him. Houston was again sniffing around on that highly dangerous ground.

"Gosh, I don't know, Mr. Houston," he heaved a mumbling sigh. "It's all fantastic."

"And nothing like it *could* happen," Houston spoke as though he was protesting against something in his own mind. "It's these Communists . . . They're involved in something. Maybe Blount and Hilton were mixed up in spying . . ."

"And Herndon?" Cross felt compelled to ask.

"Goddammit, it doesn't make sense," Houston spluttered, planting himself in front of Cross. "There *must* be a *third* man involved in this."

"It's beginning to appear like it," Cross said, looking Houston straight in the eyes.

Again Houston was wading in his direction. But could Houston permit himself to accept what he was undoubtedly thinking? Could he bring himself to admit that he was standing and looking at a man who acknowledged no laws? Did not the very thought create a dizzy kind of guilt? He saw the hunchback blink his eyes and shake his head . . . Yes; he's backing off from it; he's scared . . .

"There's absolutely nothing concrete to go on in all of this," Houston said as though he was talking of Cross directly for the first time. "I have to keep fighting myself to reject the one and only theory that could tie all of this together . . ."

"What theory is that?"

Cross held his body so tense that he feared that Houston would notice it.

"Could there be a man in whose mind and consciousness all the hopes and inhibitions of the last two thousand years have died? A man whose consciousness has not been conditioned by our culture? A man speaking our language, dressing and behaving like we do, and yet living on a completely different plane? A man who would be the return of ancient man, pre-Christian man? Do you know what I mean?"

Cross felt his body grow hot. His judgment told him to keep quiet, to pretend ignorance; but his emotions clamored to enter this discussion, to tell what he knew. He drew his breath, pushed his personal feelings aside and, when he spoke, he was discussing himself in terms that were displaced and projected.

"He's a man living in our modern industrial cities, but he is devoid of all the moral influences of Christianity. He has all the unique advantages of being privy to our knowledge, but he has either rejected it or had somehow escaped its influence. That he's an atheist goes without saying, but he'd be something more than an atheist. He'd be something like a pagan, but a pagan who feels no need to worship . . . And, by the nature of things, such a man sooner or later is bound to appear. Since we are speculating about this, why can't we say, in theory, that maybe he is appearing already? Modern man sleeps in the myths of the Greeks and the Jews. Those myths are now dying in his head and in his heart. They can no longer serve him. When they are really gone, those myths, *man* returns. Ancient man . . . And what's there to guide him? Nothing at all but his own desires, which would be his only values."

Cross confessed his crime as much as he dared. Houston stood looking moodily out of a dingy window.

"I don't believe it," Houston muttered at last. "It's the Communists. They know something of this. I'm sure of that." But there was no conviction in his voice. He turned to Cross and spoke without looking at him. "All right, Lane. That's all."

"I'll be seeing you Sunday night at Frank's, hunh?"

"What?" Houston asked; he seemed preoccupied. "Oh, yes. Of course. And keep away from those Communists, boy."

"I shall."

Houston's eyes still avoided him. He was rigid a moment, then he turned and strode out of the captain's office, leaving the door ajar. Cross watched his humped back disappear down a dim corridor. He didn't dare . . . The hunchback had looked right at it and had turned his face away! The captain entered.

"That's all, Lane."

"Good evening, sir."

He went out into the street. Yes, he was going to Eva . . . Out of the corner of his eyes he was vaguely conscious of a man leaning against the wall of a building and reading a newspaper. *My, I wonder if they are trailing me . . . ?* He'd see. He was spent; he needed a drink. He headed toward Sixth Avenue, saw a bar; he paused and looked over his shoulder. Yes; the man was following him . . . He went into the bar and had a whiskey. God, how could he get out of this? He wanted to rise and yell for help. Would it not be better to see Houston and tell him that he had gotten in too deep, that he was afraid of himself? His head felt hot; his fingers were trembling. He yearned for the sight of Eva. If only he could talk to somebody! To wander always alone in this desert was too much . . . Once again he had killed and he feared that this time he would be caught. Maybe I *want* to be caught, he told himself. Is that it . . . ? He didn't care . . . He had done what he had wanted to do, hadn't he? Then why worry . . . He paid for his drink and went out into the streets again. The man with the newspaper fell in slowly behind him. He had to see Eva, yet he feared seeing her. He knew that he had to tell her everything now; he *had* to tell . . .

He walked aimlessly, turning corners. He glanced over his shoulder; the man was still trailing him. The street lamps came on, gleaming through the misty winter night. The traffic was heavy. Eva would be worrying, wondering what had happened to him . . . Yes; go to her, get it over with, tell her . . . He'd throw himself upon her mercy.

He turned toward Charles Street and as he neared the apartment he knew that the man was still following him. To hell with him . . . His hands felt like ice, but his body and his face were burning. God, I must have fever . . . He shivered. He came to the building and stared at the windows of Herndon's apartment. That fool! How much of the world's suffering had been inflicted on men by Herndon and his kind? He was not sorry that he had killed him. He would do it again, if need be . . . He shook his head, realizing that Herndon had felt the same about him. How bewilderingly tangled it all was . . .

He went up the steps and entered the downstairs hallway; he paused, full of contrition at the thought of Eva. Could he face her? He had to, to keep alive he had to face her. He pulled up the stairs and stood uncertainly before the door. He pushed the bell; the door swung open and Eva was looking at him.

"Lionel, where on earth have you been?" she asked him.

He did not answer; he pushed past her and went stumbling into the living room. She followed him and he did not want to look into her face. He glared about nervously, then turned and went into the hallway again, heading for his room.

"Lionel, what's the matter?"

He flopped on his bed and closed his eyes. He felt her fingers on his face.

"You have a fever," she said in alarm. "You silly boy; why did you tramp about so long in the cold? Listen, the police came here asking for Sarah . . . They wouldn't tell me why. What do you suppose they want with her? Do you hear me? Darling, what's the matter? Sarah fixed some food for us. Are you hungry? Oh, God, you must be ill . . . Open your eyes and look at me! Oh, Lionel, you're *really* ill! Here, let me help get you out of your clothes. You must rest. You're under too great a strain. Lord, what have we done to you— Poor boy— I'll get you some hot tea, hunh?"

He felt he wanted to die. What was he worth in the presence of this girl? He was ill, but not with the kind of illness she thought. He felt her pulling off his shoes, then when she tried to get his coat off, he opened his eyes and looked at her.

"Eva," he whispered.

"Darling, you're exhausted," she said. "Where were you and what were you doing?"

"I don't know," he answered her truthfully.

"Did someone bother you?"

He did not answer. She helped him to undress and he lay under the covers quietly, keeping his eyes closed. Eva pulled down the shades and he could feel that the room had grown dark. She cradled his head in her arms and whispered to him:

"Can I get you something?"

"No."

He was fighting the fight of his life. His lips were tightly clamped, his eyes closed. He knew that he wanted to spill it all out, everything. Yet he held still, hoping that it would not come. It no longer now depended upon his debating if he should tell or not, but upon how much strength he had. He opened his eyes and looked at her. Oh, God, such trust in that face . . . How could he tell her? He pulled himself free and stood up in the darkness of the room, his back to her.

"Lionel, get back in bed! You have a temperature," she wailed.

She caught his arm and led him back to the bed; he allowed himself to be guided by her, his eyes glazed and unseeing. She placed her cool palm on his forehead.

"You're burning with fever . . ."

"Naw," he groaned.

"You haven't eaten—"

"I don't care."

"You've got to take care of yourself— You're worried, that's all. Listen, tramping about the streets in the cold and brooding, what's the good of it? You must take care of yourself. You hear? You stood up to those cops fine, you talked wonderfully . . . Then afterwards you start fretting and you break down . . . You mustn't let them get you like that, Lionel. Now, more than ever, you've got to be strong. We have no gang with us now. No Party . . . We're alone, and that means we've got to fight, fight, and be careful . . ."

He stiffened. He'd scream if she kept expressing her faith and belief in him. He tried to pull away from the tug of her hand.

"Lionel, look at me— Look at me— I love you," she whispered.

He shot from the bed and stood up in the darkness of the room, trembling; his body was hot yet he felt cold.

"Lionel, what's wrong?"

"Everything," he breathed.

"Can't you tell me? Did somebody bother you?"

"No."

"Then what is it?"

He was still, his body rigid. Then he felt his lips forming sounds, heard words issuing from his mouth.

"Eva, I killed Hilton—"

"What?"

"I killed Hilton . . ."

"Lionel, get to bed," she said sternly. "You've got a fever."

"No; listen—" He still did not turn around. "My name's not Lionel Lane. It's Cross Damon. Oh, God, what have I done? I've killed and killed and killed . . . Eva, save me; help to save me—"

He felt her arms about him, tugging at him.

"Get in bed, darling," she begged. "You're sick."

She pushed him back to the bed and held him again in her arms.

"Eva, you must hear—"

"No; don't think, don't talk," she cautioned. "Lie still! Be quiet, honey."

"I *must* talk," he said. "I must tell you— Darling, I killed your husband— It was I who struck both Gil and Herndon down—"

"Oh, *God*, Lionel," she cried. "You're delirious!"

"No, no; I'm not," he cried to her. "I killed Gil—I, I killed him, Eva. And Herndon, too. And Hilton— Just now, I did. And in Chicago, I killed a man— Oh, God—Eva, don't leave me now. I need you, I need somebody—"

He clutched at her arms and she held him tightly, like one holding a child.

"Don't leave me, Eva— Never leave me— Promise me you won't— Promise me," he begged.

"I promise," she whispered.

"If you leave me, it's all over,"

"I'll never leave you, Lionel."

What was this? She was not listening to what he was telling her. She thought him delirious. Mad. Wild.

"Eva, don't you realize what I've been telling you? I, *I* killed Gil, Herndon, Hilton, and another man . . . My hands are wet with blood . . ."

She stopped his mouth with her hand, and then he felt tears, hot and copious, falling on to his face.

"Hush, darling," she said. "You're sick."

She pulled away from him and he lay there, his eyes closed, trying to realize that she did not believe him. He heard her moving softly about behind him, and then he was paralyzed with surprise when he felt her soft, naked body coming into bed and nestling close to him. Her warm arms went about his neck and she pulled his face to hers and he felt her lips clinging to his. Good God, he had told her his horror and had expected to hear her scream and run from him, and now she was surrendering herself, giving her gift to the man she loved, hoping to cure the distraction of his mind by placing a benediction upon his senses. For a moment he was rigid, not knowing what to do. Then the warmth of her reached him, stole into his blood; and he was still, tasting the sweet pull of her clinging lips on his. He sighed, lay still for a moment, then caught her face in his hands and kissed her while there whirled above his head a knowledge of what was happening. She had thought his confession was an eruption of delirium; she had been moved to pity by his state of wild anxiousness. What he had tried to tell her had sounded so fantastic that she had with swift instinct rejected it as unreal, as a figment of a fevered imagination, the irresponsible babblings of a sick man. She would never be able to comprehend that he was a lost soul, spinning like a stray atom far beyond the ken of her mind to conceive. The extremity of his state had unveiled Eva, had made hope and trust rise in her for the first time since her deception. She was with him, close to him, mingling the warmth of her flesh with his, but she did not understand who or what he was or what he had done, could not believe it when she heard it. Yet he needed her. And then he turned to her and took her in his arms and had her so slowly and so intensely and with such a mounting frenzy of sensual greed that they both died the little death together and he lay staring into the dark with wide, vacant eyes, afraid even to think. And then, quietly, as his sense of reality returned, as he felt himself again in the room on the bed with her, something close to a prayer rose up from his heart . . . Show me a way not to hurt her . . . Not to let her know . . . I don't want to kill this sweet girl clinging to me . . . I should not have let it happen . . . And his despair seeped from his hot and tired eyes in large, salty tears . . .

Cross now groped his way through uneasy hours under the protection of the fragile shadow of Eva's colossal illusion. This girl was loving him not for his crimes but for virtues that he did not and could not possess. His happiness was now a kind of terror and he strove in vain to banish from his consciousness the realization that he epitomized the quintessence of all that which Eva most deeply loathed and would flee to avoid. He would clamp his teeth in sterile fury when he saw that though Eva was his kind of woman, he was not her kind of man nor would he ever be. But he begged the grace of nameless powers to let him linger with her for yet awhile before he went to grapple with the dark tides of his destiny. During the next few hours they moved around each other with slow and muted tenderness. He knew that she was unaware that he was cringing in anxiety lest she ask the meaning of those horrible syllables that had been on his confessionally loosened tongue, and he knew that when she did ask him, he would have to push his words past a choking throat and tell her. He ached with anxiety as he watched the flame of love and trust glowing in her eyes, for it was he who had lit that fire with his unintentional deception, and he knew that when she finally gained a knowledge of what he was, it would be snuffed out; and his heart shuddered in fear of her going back into her feminine house and slamming the door on life forever.

Early that evening a bailiff showed up with a summons demanding their presence the following morning at the hearing to be held over the bodies of Gil and Herndon at the office of the Chief Medical Examiner.

"Will it be awful, Lionel?" she asked.

"I'm afraid so, darling. But you must brace yourself for it."

"Lionel," she called.

Tenderly she caught hold of his hand, turned his face to her, smiled faintly, then let her lashes rest upon her wan cheeks.

"Yes, Eva," he prompted her; yet quailing for fear that she would ask him about his confessional eruption.

"Tell me, darling," she inquired in a whisper, "is it wrong to love so soon like this?"

Dismay made his lips tremble. "Trust is the heart of life," he whispered and felt he wanted something to strike him dead. "How can one's trusting another be bad?"

She opened her hazel eyes full on him. "I trust you," she said simply. "I wanted to help you and I saw a way to do it . . ."

"Bless you, Eva," he said, averting his face, feeling a con-striction in his throat.

"Sarah'll be here in the morning to help me. I must find a black dress—"

"Will you need to buy any clothes?"

"No, honey. I've plenty. Look, you must rest. I'll handle this," she smiled.

How wrapped up she was in her love! How demurely happy! He wandered into the living room, his hands trembling. Could he let her go on like that? But how could he undo it? He sat, his mind roving back over the deaths of Gil and Herndon and Hilton, his feelings protesting against the whole, wild nightmare; but he could think of no concrete move to make. He recalled having bought a newspaper. Had there been anything in it about the deaths of Gil and Herndon? He found the folded copy of the newspaper jammed into his overcoat pocket. When he had bought it in the lobby of the Hotel Albert right after leaving Hilton sprawled and bloody on the bed, he had been too harassed and frightened to read it. He opened it and was amazed to see an artist's pen-and-ink drawing covering the entire front page under a tall, black headline:

DOUBLE TOTALITARIAN MURDER

The picture showed two tall, popeyed, hawk-faced young men in their shirt sleeves — in truth, both men had worn coats and Herndon had been fifty-eight years of age and Gil had been thirty-six — lamming each other in a savage rage; one was flaying a fire poker and the other was wielding a huge table leg which he held high in the air and was about to crash it down upon the head of the other. Cross's lips twitched in a smile at the expressions of exaggerated hatred which the artist had injected into the facial features of both men; their long, unruly hair was matted and falling almost into their eyes; they were unshaven and their skins were pimply; their teeth were bared, long, and pointed, resembling the fangs of wolves or dogs; and the fingers of their hands were gnarled, lumpy, with long, curving nails suggestive of animal claws. The background depicted by the artist was not the fascist Herndon's chastely furnished study, but a filthy den whose ceiling was cracking and peeling, showing the laths. The corners of the room revealed dense spiderwebs; several empty whiskey bottles lay on the floor. Tacked to the torn wallpaper were several photographs of nude women in various erotic postures, each

carrying at the bottom legends such as: FREE LOVE—JOY
AND MADNESS—NIGHT OF ABANDON, etc.

Cross blinked in disbelief, not knowing whether to laugh
or curse. He lowered the paper and sat in deep reflection.
Then he muttered out loud:

"But this is a kind of inverted pro-communist and pro-nazi
propaganda. They've so distorted these men that no one
could ever recognize their psychological types . . . A Gil or a
Herndon might be working at the City Desk of the *Daily
News* this very moment . . . What kind of people make up
these papers? There couldn't be a better way of disguising
totalitarian aims than this."

He lifted the paper again and read the long caption running beneath the drawing:

> Hardened Metropolitan police circles were rocked
> and stunned late yesterday by the Greenwich Village
> sensationally freakish double murder of a Communist
> by a Fascist and of a Fascist by a Communist. Though
> the Medical Examiner has technically dubbed the
> double crime as double manslaughter, it was learned
> through unusually reliable sources that these men's dis-
> eased brains had been poisoned by the dangerously eso-
> teric doctrines of communal property advocated in the
> decadent writings of the notorious German author Karl
> Marx, and the Superman ideas sponsored by the
> syphilis-infected German philosopher Friedrich Nietz-
> sche who died in an insane asylum. These two rowdy
> agitators, Gilbert Blount and Langley Herndon, clashed
> bloodily in a quarrel regarding racial amalgamation the-
> ories and both died of their mutually inflicted wounds.
> (See page 3 for further details.)

Cross tossed the paper aside in disgust; then he remembered that Eva might get hold of it and become upset. He
took it into the kitchen and dropped it into the incinerator.
He paused; oh, God, that goddamned handkerchief that had
brought so much trouble! It was still in his pocket! He looked
around; he was alone in the kitchen. He took the balled,
reddish handkerchief from his pocket and stared at the burns,

then once again he dropped it into the incinerator, hoping that this would be the last time he had to get rid of it.

Still brooding over the garbled newspaper story, he went back into the living room. What protection did men have against the Blounts and the Herndons of this world if newspapers could give no better interpretation of what they were after than what he had read? Was it that you could not understand the totalitarians unless you partook of their malady? He understood them; but, of course, he was akin to them, differing from them only in that he did not have a party, the sanction of ideas, a gang to aid him and to abet his actions by the threat of force. Both Gil and Herndon were so much more intelligent than the men who had written the news story that it was pathetic. Did that mean that the future was in the hands of men suffering from this terrible sickness? And that the shape of that future would be determined by which of these monsters would be triumphant . . . ? Did the arrogant confidence of these two monsters stem from their secret knowledge that they knew that those who sought to defeat them would have to become like them, have to turn into the very kind of monsters they wanted to destroy? Was it that the totalitarians *knew* that, historically, no matter if they won or lost battles, that the war against individuality and for the subjugation of freedom was bound to be won by their side? Cross shook his head in wonder.

Could they eventually trace Hilton's death to him? Now that he longed to plot out a future with Eva, he could not let his mind stray too far into the realms of hope; he might be accused at any time . . .

He sighed, rose, strode restlessly about. Eva came in and looked anxiously at him.

"How are you, darling?"

"I'm fine," he lied.

She sat at Gil's desk and began sorting papers.

"You have no more fever?"

"None at all. I'm all right."

She rose and went to him; he knew that she had not come into the room to look for papers, but to be near him, to see that he was not fretting.

"Why don't you relax. It's better for you."

"I'll try, Eva," he said and stretched out on the sofa.

He lay with closed eyes, but relaxation was impossible. Eva knelt at the side of the sofa.

"Come to bed, darling. You need sleep . . ."

"Let me just lie here and think a little—"

"You're not worrying? Tell me the truth."

"I'm not worrying, Eva," he lied despairingly.

She kissed him, gazed long into his dark, brooding eyes.

"Everything'll be all right," she said cheerfully. "You'll see."

"As long as you are there, I'll be all right," he told her.

"I'm all in; I'm going to bed."

"Do that, Eva. I'll be along in a little while—"

"And don't go out into that cold again. We'll soon be free from all this terror . . . We'll be where a big, blue sky stretches over our heads, with the wind blowing through the high pine trees . . . They tell me that the lakes in the Gatineau are blue and deep and clear . . ."

"Yes."

"And all this deception'll be at an end," she murmured hopefully. "Things'll be as clear, as sharp as mountains on the horizon . . ." She sighed. "I want to paint again . . . This time I want to create images common to everybody, symbols that can link men together . . . Rest now, Lionel."

She was gone. He closed his eyes. Despair was in him so sharply that he was not aware of the room's four walls about him. What could he do for Eva . . . ? His obsession was with him again. How much time did he have before his foolish world caved in?

Oh, yes; the radio . . . What time did the evening news come on? He turned the dial on the radio, keeping the tone barely audible, and listened to the impish notes of blue-jazz leap and cavort in freedom . . . At ten-thirty there was a pause in the outpouring of jazz and a sonorously masculine voice recited a medley of political news items, and then:

The second Communist leader in twenty-four hours has been found shot to death by a .32 calibre revolver under baffling circumstances in a Greenwich Village hotel room late today. The body, that of John Hilton, 32, an school teacher, a million Communist leader and a recently elected member of the powerful Central

Committee of the Communist Party, was discovered by a colored cleaning maid as she was making her rounds early this evening.

John Hilton died as a result of a fatal bullet wound in his left temple. Death, according to the Medical Examiner, was instantaneous. The death scene showed no signs of violence or physical struggle save for a slight abrasion on the forehead of Hilton.

Though all present indications point to suicide, police are continuing their investigation. Murder has not been ruled out.

Hilton's death comes a few hours after that of Gilbert Blount, another member of the Central Committee of the Communist Party, whose place on the Central Committee had already been taken by John Hilton. In labor circles speculation is rife as to whether Hilton was killed by some recently expelled member of the Communist Party.

That was all; Cross switched off the radio and stood up. He had not been mentioned, and whether the police would find some trail leading to him was problematical. He went to the window and stared into the winter night; traces of snow and ice showed on the pavements and sidewalks. A heavy mist hung over the city and the houses on the opposite side of the street were dim and ghostly. Occasionally a man or a woman hurried past.

Now that the news of Hilton's death was public, what would Eva think when she heard it? Would she still believe that he had been babbling senselessly when he had come in earlier that evening? Or would the news of Hilton's death plant a tiny seed of doubt in her mind, a doubt that would grow until she regarded him with fearfully questioning eyes? Though Eva was sleeping, he felt driven to know what she would say; it was much better to learn her reaction now than later. The anxious tension of waiting to see if she would suspect him without his telling her was greater than the dread of what she would say when she knew that at least some part of his incoherent outpourings was true.

As though being guided by some imperious influence, he walked slowly toward Eva's bedroom and stood hesitantly in the partially opened doorway, listening to her quiet, regular breathing in the dark. Would it not be better for her to die now and be spared the pain and shock which he knew he had

to bring yet to her? Had he not told Hilton that death was
better than prolonged and inflamed suffering? Did he not
owe it to her to kill her and thereby guard her from the
monstrousness of himself? He advanced to the bed and his
right hand lifted itself above her head and hovered there.
God, no; no more of this killing whose logic led on and on
into the grey, deadening reaches of inhuman meaning . . . !
His damned habit of relentless thinking was mangling the
very tendons and nerves of the flesh of life! Eva stirred
uneasily on the bed and gave forth a profound sigh, a sigh
that told him that the destiny of the soul from which it
came could not be encompassed by his churning mental
processes alone. As he stood there in the dark straining at a
decision, he could see that the grinding mechanisms of
man's thought could destroy all of life on earth and leave this
watery globe bare of the human beings who had produced
the thinking . . .

Living thus tensely in his thoughts, Cross knew that this
executing of the sentences of thought on life was a kind of
continuous madness whose logical end was suicide. No matter how hot and furious the degree of his thinking, he could
not convince himself that to kill Eva to ward off the suffering
that the future would bring into the world for her was right.
By snatching her life he could stave off the suffering, the
pain that *he* thought would be hers, but did *his* insight into
what the future held justify his killing her on that basis? The
answer to that question was beyond his reach. To slay Gil and
Herndon and Hilton in a fit of cold rage because they had
outraged his sense of existence was one thing; but only if he
were *outside* of life itself, beyond existence, could he make
such a judgment about Eva whom he loved. How could he
ever be able to tell, after killing Eva, that his judgment had
been a correct one? Hate yearned to destroy and sought to
forget, but love could not. Love strove creatively toward days
that had yet to come. If he killed himself, his processes of
thought stopped. Or did they? How could he ever tell after
having killed himself that his judgment-act had been the right

His hand was still trembling in the air; he was not feeling,

just thinking . . . Logic sustained by love could lift future
suffering from her, but love informed by hope could keep her
with him to live out the unpredictable chances of life. For
life's sake, he would spare Eva. For Eva's sake, he would spare
her life. Time alone made this teeming world gush and roar
like a Niagara with its richness of unforeseeable events; it was
only by plunging rashly onward that one could see at all. And
even if a god could exist he would have to be bound to some
extent by that . . .

Cross grasped the foot of the bed with his hand to steady
his trembling legs. Eva turned over and mumbled something
in her sleep and he could see the faint, crystalline sheen of her
soft white cheeks glowing like a half-perceived image in the
dark. His breath went from his lungs in a long, despairing
suspire; he reached out his hand, the fingers still shaking from
the throes of indecision, touched her shoulder tenderly, and
whispered:

"Eva, darling . . ."

He felt her warm body give a slight start, and then her face
turned toward him.

"Yes, Lionel."

"Listen, darling. I've something to tell you . . ."

"Yes?"

"I was listening to the radio and some news about Hilton
just came over."

"What is it?"

"He's been killed, shot in his hotel room," he said quietly.

Eva was still as stone for a moment, then she stared at him
with a look of wildness in her eyes. Was she considering him
guilty? He held his breath and waited. Was she linking up his
gibberish with what he was now telling her? She gasped and
her hand went to her mouth.

"Oh, God . . . *Why?* Who did it?"

"I don't know," he whispered.

She was silent. Did she know? Why didn't she speak? What
was the meaning of that fixed, bleak stare? Yes; her hand was
moving now; he could hear the whispering rustle of the bed-
covers. Then he felt as though he would fall to the floor as
her fingers touched his hand.

"I feel awful," she whispered in horror. "*Only* today I said he should be killed . . ." Her wide eyes glistened in the shadows. Her lips hung speechless; she looked at the faint outlines of the walls of the room, then turned again to him. "Do you think it's the Party? Has he disobeyed them?"

His forehead rested on the edge of the bed and he knelt to her, as though mutely appealing against her judgment.

"I don't know," he breathed.

Couldn't she tell? He heard her breath catching in her throat, then the sound of soft crying came to him.

"Why, why, Lionel, is life like this?" she begged of him. "I feel darkness closing in all around me . . . I'm afraid . . . Hold me . . ."

Her trembling arms groped for him and he held her.

"I'm sorry," he mumbled.

"Hilton always frightened me," Eva whispered. "I never liked him. Why, I don't know. And he had just turned poor Bob over to the authorities . . . It's *wrong* to kill like that, Lionel . . ."

Cross bowed his head; he knew that those words, though she did not know it, were really directed at him . . .

"I'm sorry I had to tell you like this. But try to sleep now," he said. "Try and forget it . . ."

He still held her. Her sobs grew less and finally, as though overwhelmed by too much horror, she slept once more. Cross rose and went into the living room and stood at the front window. Eva's own sense of guilt had protected her from suspecting him; she had recoiled because she too had had the impulse to kill Hilton. Eva was *too* good, believed *too* strongly in life. Maybe this belief in goodness was her life, and once it was gone, what then?

Ought he vanish into the winter night and leave her forever? He had a chance to make a clean run for it before suspicion pointed in his direction. In his deserting her like this she would not know what he had done; there would be a hurt in her heart for awhile, but in the end she would get over it and there would always remain a spot of tenderness in her memory for him. And if he stayed, he would surely have to face the shock of her learning of his monstrous deeds. Was there the remotest hope of her still loving him after she had discovered the reaches and depths of his problem? Again the pages of her diary stood before his eyes and his question answered itself. But where could he run to? And what was he running from? He knew that in any hiding place, under whatever guise he chose to conceal himself, he would be alone with himself to meditate in dismay upon the ungovernable compulsiveness of himself and the loss of his sense of direction in life.

No . . . He had to remain. And if he ran off, would not Houston then be certain of his guilt? He cocked his head, listening; from far off came the wail of a siren so faint that it seemed that he was imagining it. Would those sirens sound for him soon? And if they caught him, what would he do? Questions like that agitated him more than the recollection of his crimes. The shame of having to tell, to explain to strangers was overpowering. That could not happen; he would make use of his gun on himself first . . .

It was only in relation to Eva that his thoughts could shape themselves with any meaning. Was not there some way of telling her and stealing the horror from it as he did so? Nervously, he rubbed his forehead. He was only fretting himself into a state of jitters by forever juggling farfetched possibilities like this. He would go to bed. Half an hour later he lay down by the sleeping form of Eva, but he did not close his eyes. He knew her hurt, but could she ever know his? Was there really no direct bridge between the subjective worlds of people? Was the possibility of communication only a kind of pretense, an arrangement assumed to exist but which really did not? Was the core of the subjective life of each person sealed off absolutely from that of another and one could tell what transpired in another heart only when the contents of that heart were projected outwardly in some objective form? He recalled that Eva had not responded to him as he really was; his life had somehow represented for her something which she had yearned to embrace; and he lay here now knowing from having stolen a lawless glimpse into her diary what she felt, her deception, her shame, but unable really to touch her heart, feeling that she was forever beyond his reach. A dizzy terror came over him. Were we really that much alone in this life? Were all human hearts encased in this irredeem-

able isolation and we only had the satisfaction of fooling ourselves that we were together? He groaned softly and did not
close his eyes in sleep until dawn crept into the room.

A little after eight o'clock he was awakened by the ringing
of the doorbell. Eva was still sleeping. He put on his robe and
went to the door. It was Sarah, ashen of face and shaking
with fear.

"Good morning, Sarah," Cross said casually, braced to hear
her tell of what experience she had had with the police.

"God, Lionel, did you know that Hilton's dead?"

"Yes; I heard about it on the radio."

"Do you know where I slept last night?"

"No. What do you mean?"

"In the police station," Sarah explained with indignation.
"I've been in jail, you hear? When I got home last night, the
cops were waiting for me at the door of my apartment . . .
They hauled me to jail and grilled me for four hours . . . I'm
so glad Bob's in Ellis Island, or they'd have him now, for
sure."

"But why did they take you to jail?" Cross asked.

"They had the idea that I killed Hilton because Hilton told
on Bob—"

"But how did they find out about that?"

"I don't know. Lionel, what's *happening?*"

"God only knows, Sarah."

Sarah was hanging up her overcoat in the hallway.

"You think it was the Party?" she asked in a whisper.

"Who knows—" Cross knew now that she did not suspect
him. "When I came in last night, Eva told me the cops had
been here asking for you."

"Here?" Sarah echoed.

"Yes."

"How's Eva?"

"She's sleeping," Cross told her.

He told Sarah to wait while he dressed, and then he
brewed a pot of coffee.

"I know it's wrong," Sarah began, drinking her coffee, "but
I can't say I'm sorry about Hilton . . . But that can't help
poor Bob now. He's gone." She sat down her cup and wept.

"Lionel, I still hate Hilton. He's dead and I still hate 'im . . ." She shook her head. "There was something cold about Hilton."

"I daresay Hilton would have agreed with you," Cross said.

"Lionel, what do you suppose Hilton got out of sending Bob to his death?"

"Nothing."

"Then why did he take such drastic action for Bob's little offense against the Party?"

"Hilton was obeying orders, and he believed in the orders."

"But Bob's *human*," Sarah protested.

"To Hilton, Bob was only something to be sacrificed in the interests of a vast design," Cross explained.

"To make a better world?" Sarah asked; her voice was strangely hopeful.

Cross knew that she was now seeking for something to redeem the suffering and death that Bob would inherit.

"No, Sarah. To Hilton and men like him the world is perfect just like it is. They just want a chance to rule that world."

"I don't understand," Sarah sighed.

"It's better maybe not to understand," Cross told her.

They fell silent. An idea came to Cross. Eva was deeply attached to Sarah, and would not his case be stronger if he threw the two women together? His position was so weak that he felt he needed the strength and help of a woman whose reactions were as straightforward as those of Sarah.

"What are you going to do now, Sarah?" he asked her. "Bob's gone and you're alone."

"I don't know," she mumbled.

"Look, after the hearing with the Medical Examiner, suppose Eva and I moved up to Harlem with you for awhile?"

Sarah's eyes brightened.

"Oh, I'd like that— I'm so alone up there . . . But what would Eva think of it?"

"I don't know. I haven't asked her yet, but I will."

Sarah's feminine instinct for matchmaking came to the fore in her.

"Eva likes you," she said in a tone of voice that indicated that she approved. "What's she going to do now that Gil's dead?"

"She wants to be with me—"

"Oh!" Sarah pondered a moment, then she smiled. "Old Funny Face—" She was moody again, thinking of her own lonely life. "Some people have all the luck."

The official aspects of the Medical Examiner's hearing, which was a kind of inquest, did not prove to be as much of an ordeal as either Cross or Eva had feared. It fell to Cross to bear the burden of giving the longest and most detailed testimony of all the witnesses, for the Communist Party's able and noisy lawyer strove tenaciously to obtain a verdict branding Langley Herndon as the murderer of Gil. Cross, knowing that the Party, in its own interests, would leap to protect him if the police turned on him, answered repeatedly and emphatically that he had seen Herndon beating Gil with the fire poker and he even went so far in his lies as to testify that Gil had not seemed to be in a condition to defend himself.

Eva testified of having seen Herndon with his gun on the stairs; she told of her running back into the apartment and of Lionel Lane's bolting the door against him. But Eva's and Cross's testimony was not strong enough to influence the studied, scientific opinion of the cool Medical Examiner who contended that both men died in point of time so close together that he could not honorably or justifiably entertain any verdict save that of double manslaughter. In so far as Cross was personally concerned, the hearing was a success; he had managed to deflect all thoughts of guilt from himself.

The most frightening phase of the hearing came after the verdict had been rendered, for newsmen crowded around to get photographs of Eva. Cross was glad that he was forgotten, for he dreaded having his face appear in the press under the false name of Lionel Lane. Sarah hurried Eva to a waiting car provided by the Party and they managed to get away with but a few flashbulbs exploding in Eva's anxious, drawn, and veiled face. Menti had been assigned by the Party to accompany them, and he drove the car. Back in Charles Street, in the lower hallway of the building, they had run into another battery of newsmen and Cross's admiration for Menti rose as he watched him tersely and ruthlessly dispatch the reporters and photographers. At last they were in the shelter of the apartment and Cross fastened the night-chain on the door. Sarah took Eva to her room and Cross paced to and fro, preoccupied, conscious of Menti hanging on for no apparent reason. Menti's presence irked Cross; he had nothing in common with this lackey and wished that he would make himself absent. Menti was a hireling, an errand boy, a white-collar by-product of the American industrial world who had offered his meaningless, self-despised existence to the Party to be used, ravaged, dominated, and filled with a purpose, any purpose as long as the burden of the responsibility of his own life was lifted from his quaking shoulders.

"You seem nervous, Lane," Menti commented, smiling and sucking at his cigarette. "What's the matter?"

"Just restless," Cross answered.

"You know, the Party's interested in you," Menti said in a voice that carried a multiplicity of meanings: ironical, teasing, threatening, warning . . .

Cross paused and studied the servile mask of geniality that always served to hide Menti's real motives. Was Menti spying on him for the Party? Cross felt that it was safe to assume that he was . . .

"Why?" Cross asked.

"The Party's interested in intelligent men, and you are intelligent," Menti said in tones of flattery, as though bound to give even Cross, an outsider, his due.

"But I know so little about these matters, Menti," Cross protested, knowing that he knew more than Menti would believe.

"Too bad Gil couldn't've lived to coach you until you were seasoned," Menti said in a tone of wistful regret. "Gil told Hilton before he died that you had the makings of a real Bolshevik: outlook, temperament, and all . . . You liked Gil, didn't you?"

"Of course, Menti," Cross lied in a full-bodied tone. "Gil was my friend."

"And I reckon you liked Hilton too, didn't you?" Menti asked slowly, watching Cross's face.

"Of course," Cross lied. "But I didn't know poor Hilton very well . . ."

"Too bad. He was a brilliant guy. He could have been a damn good friend of yours if they hadn't killed 'im . . ."

"Has the Party got any line on who did it?" Cross asked.

"No," Menti said. "But they'll find out. The Party never sleeps, boy. Once they get an idea into their heads, they *never* give up."

"What idea have they got?"

"How do I know?" Menti said, smiling and studying Cross.

Cross restrained a chuckle, then resumed his striding to and fro. He could handle this Menti. He was certain that Hilton had not taken Menti into his confidence. But did Menti himself suspect him? Cross grew irritable. It was wearying to give the attention and strain necessary to keep track of the motives of Party people. The hell with Menti . . . But in his heart he hoped fervently that no other fool would pop up to threaten him; he was sick of the thought of murder.

"Say, Menti, have the police found any clues as to who killed Hilton?" he asked.

"Nothing. But we know he didn't kill himself," Menti said.

"Really? How do you know?"

"We just know. He didn't have any reason. Say, Lane, could I ask you a question?"

Cross turned and stood in front of Menti, his hands deep in his pockets. Just try to figure me out, boy, Cross mused.

"Sure. What is it?"

"What school did you say you came from?"

"I didn't say," Cross told him; yes, Menti was digging at him now.

"But you told the D.A. that you came from Fisk . . ."

So this clown was not so dumb after all. The Party had checked with Houston and Menti had been informed. Cross's eyes narrowed.

"Why are you asking me this, Menti?" Cross countered softly. He was determined not to let this man see him in any way rattled.

"To find out the truth, of course," Menti said.

"Did the Party ask you to?"

"Yes," Menti answered honestly, looking boldly at Cross.

For the first time the reality of Menti broke through to Cross. There was a shy fanaticism in the man's deep, brown eyes, an apologetic inferiority in his demeanor, an ingratiating humility even in the way he talked—all of which hid something that Cross could not fathom. What was this man up to? That the Party trusted Menti was obvious. But how far would Menti go? Cross blamed himself for having not gotten to know Menti better.

"You knew Hilton well, didn't you?" Cross asked him.

"Better than he knew himself," Menti smiled and hung his head, a sheepish look coming into his eyes.

Then Cross knew. Menti had been spying on Hilton! And Hilton had suspected it, but had not been certain of it. That was why Hilton had not told Menti about his finding of the bloody handkerchief! How complicated it was! What a system of life! Spies spying upon spies who were being spied upon! Imagine a society like that! It would be an elaborate kind of transparent ant heap in which the most intimate feelings of all the men and women in it would be known, a glass jailhouse in which the subjective existence of each man and woman would be public each living moment . . . And if an alien happened to show up in that ant heap, it would at once become evident because that alien would be at once opaque and, hence, known as alien. And for his spying in this ant heap, each spy would derive, as his reward, a satisfaction from the godlike position which he could assume in relation to his neighbor. This spy would not be a complete god, of course; being a complete god would be reserved for the distant dictator. But being a little god was better than being no god at all . . . It was perfect, giving each spy something for his pains and hopes, and supplying each with an explanation for his suffering should he fail . . .

Cross admitted that he had made a psychological mistake; he should have observed Menti closer. Intuitively he sensed an almost organic servility that would make this man lend himself to any use by those whom he respected and loved. He had now to try to get to this man, for he felt that the influence of the Party on Menti's mind now caused Menti to regard him as an opaque object that had to be accounted for. He studied Menti's too-white, sensitive face, almost a woman's face; he looked wonderingly at the deep, brooding eyes that never let you hold their gaze for long; at the bluish tint that always showed just beneath his dead-white, close-shaven skin; at those long and tapering fingers that were sensitive without being in any way delicate . . . The man seemed like an empty, waiting vessel that could be easily filled with either a frightened acquiescence or a strident brutality; or, if necessary, a combination of both.

Cross sat next to Menti and asked him:

"Menti, what have you got against me?"

"Personally, nothing." Menti's voice was affable.

"What do you think I'm up to?"

"I don't know."

"Have you seen me do anything that would make you suspicious of me?"

"No."

"Then why are you prying into me?"

"We don't know you," Menti said without anger.

"What do you want to know about me?"

"Everything."

"What do you call 'knowing' somebody, Menti?"

Menti smiled, crushed out a cigarette, and lit another one.

"It's possible to know enough about a man to know when he would or wouldn't do certain things," Menti said.

"You talk about people as if they were machines, something *made*," Cross protested. "How can you predict behavior?"

"By a man's convictions," Menti said. "By where he stands in the context of a concrete situation."

"So the Party can tell in *advance* if a man will be guilty or not in any given instance?" Cross asked. "You mean to say that?"

"Just that," Menti said. "The logic of a position will make a man act in a certain way. Given a man with a given set of convictions, and given a situation, the Party can tell what that man would do."

"And you could condemn him in advance of his deed?"

"Certainly. It's logical, isn't it?" Menti asked earnestly.

Cross knew that Menti was reflecting the attitude of the Party.

"What are you trying to find out about me?"

"Who you are and what you are doing."

Menti was fluent in his answers and Cross knew that the Party would soon know that he had asked these questions. He would try to send back a human answer.

"I'm a Negro, Menti; I'm trying to learn," Cross lied.

"Learn *what*?"

"How to live."

"Hunh. You mean how the *Party* lives?"

"Hell, no. Have I ever asked you anything about the Party?"

"No. But you got Eva—"

"But Eva's not a political person, Menti. You know that."

"She was Gil's wife."

"So what? Are you moral?"

"The Party is not moral," Menti answered, declining to assert his personal opinion. "You love Eva, don't you?"

"Yes, I do."

"Why?"

"She's a woman, one I've been seeking all my life."

"And she happened to be a wife of a member of the Central Committee—"

"She knows nothing of politics," Cross protested.

"You found that out, didn't you?" Menti demanded.

"Yes."

"Why?" Menti demanded in insolent tones.

It was hopeless. Goddamn this dirty spoon in the hands of the Party! Cross rose. This man would not, could not believe that there existed men who could, at some moments of their lives, be honest as Cross was now honest with him about Eva. Indeed, Cross could feel that his love of Eva would assume baffling guises in the Party's mind. The simpler and more human a thing was, the more the Party feared it . . .

"Listen, Menti, if the Party wants to know anything about me, let 'em come and ask me," Cross said. "They don't have to go licking around the District Attorney . . ."

"They'll come to you; don't worry," Menti assured him. "They went to the D.A. because you know 'im."

And what would Houston think of their asking? Cross felt that he was in danger, but it was not acute yet. Yes, he would move Eva out of this apartment tonight. His real hope was that he could get Eva to trust him and run off somewhere with her. But what explanations could he give her for such a drastic move? The only reasons he could give her would be of a nature that would guarantee her not coming . . . Menti stood and put on his overcoat; he paused, a cigarette smouldering in his lips.

"The Party's checked at Fisk University and has found that you never went to school there," Menti came to the point at last.

"So?"

"Then why did you tell the D.A. that you went there?"

"Must I tell the D.A. the truth?" Cross hedged.

"Tell me, what do you plan to do now?"

"Nothing."

"You got any money?"

"Not much."

"You're staying with Eva here?"

"If she lets me," he said.

"She'll let you," Menti said.

Cross was angry, but he knew that he had invited that crack. He held his peace. But it was clear that the crux of the Party's attitude was his relationship with Eva.

"I'm blowing, guy," Menti said and left.

Cross sat and brooded. If the Party checked up on him, they would run into a blank wall, and then what would they do? Just because his life was not transparent, would they get suspicious? The secret side of him was a handicap in the Party's eyes . . . The more they probed into his background to uncover his identity, the more inflamed would their suspicions become. But what would they be suspicious of? And suspicion was not proof of murder. They would have to peel off layer after layer of pretense, uncover front after front of make-believe and where would it lead them in the end?

Eventually, of course, the police could trace him by his fingerprints back to his Post Office identity in Chicago. But what would that really prove? They would run into a truly bewildering set of facts . . .

Sarah came out of Eva's room.

"She wants to see you, Funny Face," Sarah said.

Sarah looked lost, piqued; he could see that she was losing weight. And Eva's happiness was exciting her jealousy.

"I'm going to ask Eva to come to your place," he told her. "We'll all chip in together on the expenses, hunh?"

"I could use some money," Sarah told him flatly. "I've no work now. I got to look for something."

"Don't worry," Cross told her.

He went in to Eva who lay pale and limp on the bed. She summoned a smile for him. He took her hand and they were silent for a long time.

"Eva, I've an idea . . . Until Gil is buried, let us go and live with Sarah in Harlem. It'll take you away from this apartment, those reporters, and you'll be in different surroundings," he explained.

She was thoughtful for a moment, then nodded her head in assent.

"That would be nice. I've always wanted to live there. Is it all right with Sarah?"

"She loves it."

"And we can be alone there, Lionel," Eva said with a sense of relief.

Life in Sarah's sixth-floor walk-up apartment eased the sense of strain in Cross, but it did not free him from the probing presence of Menti who came the next morning, expressing great astonishment at the fact that they had moved. He had gone to the Charles Street apartment, he said, and rang and rang and no one had answered the door.

"Then I knew that if anyone would know where Eva was, it would be Sarah," Menti explained.

He had come, he told them unctuously, to bring Eva news of the Party's elaborate arrangements for Gil's funeral. All Sunday morning Gil's body would lie in state in a union hall, guarded by Communist militants, and in the afternoon it would be shipped to Gil's family in the Bronx for burial. As Menti described the reaction of the Party to Gil's death, Cross could see that Gil's dying was being used to excite admiration for Party leaders in general. Gil had already, in Party circles, been deified as a kind of god who had laid down his only life as a sacrifice on the altar of freedom. Menti then, with measured movements which were supposed to be consonant with death and grief, hauled from his pockets a huge batch of messages of condolence which had come from as far away as Moscow. But Cross observed that Communists were not good when it came to paying respects to the dead; there was something embarrassingly self-conscious about Menti's manner as he sought to convince Eva of the touching solicitude of the Party for her in her bereavement. It's hard to pretend something about death that you really don't feel, Cross thought.

"Now, Eva," Menti went on, smiling slightly. "Don't think the Party has forgotten you. The Party never forgets its own." He drew forth from an inner coat pocket a big envelope and handed it to Eva.

"What's this?" she asked.

"It's for you. Look at it and see," Menti urged.

Cross was standing behind Eva when she tore open the envelope; it was filled with greenbacks.

"But why?" Eva asked, her eyes round with surprise.

"It's yours," Menti said. "You're Gil's widow. The Party will look after you . . ."

"But I can work," Eva's voice faltered. "I'm an artist—"

"Do you spurn the sympathy of the Party?" Menti asked.

"Oh, no . . . It's not that, Menti," Eva said. "But I've never worked for the Party. I was only Gil's wife . . ."

"You helped Gil, you comforted him; you enabled him to keep up his hard pace of work for the Party . . ."

Eva's eyes filled with a look of terror and she sank to the floor and sobbed, shaking her head. Cross knew what was going through her mind. All that Menti had just said about Eva's relationship to Gil was blatantly untrue; Eva had not helped him because she felt she had been deceived and turned into an object, a thing, a means . . . Then what was the meaning of this gesture of the Party? It was a threat wrapped in kindness . . . They were seeking a way to keep a hold over Eva, trying to buy her loyalty, laying the basis for future demands. Cross could feel that the Party was delicately making its first moves against him. He felt alarm, but he knew that he had some time yet before things would become serious enough to warrant his taking action.

"But why are you crying so, my dear?" Menti asked. "Are you surprised?"

"But I shouldn't take it," Eva evaded his question. "I've no right to it."

"The Party is loyal to you," Menti pointed out.

"Yes," Eva gulped.

"And don't you want to be loyal to the Party?"

Eva did not reply; she turned her fear-filled eyes questioningly upon Cross's face, seeking his guidance. And Cross noticed that Eva's appeal for his advice was not lost upon Menti's smilingly observant eyes, eyes that traveled cryptically from Eva's face to Cross's, and then back to Eva's again . . .

Cross found himself paraphrasing a Biblical passage:

"Thou shalt not depend upon others, nor trust them: for this your Party is a jealous Party, visiting the suspicions of the leaders upon the members unto the third and fourth friends of the friends around the Party . . ."

He was now sure that Menti was reporting back to the Party every nuance which he could observe between him and Eva. He hated the money that the Party was offering, but he could not afford to tell Eva not to accept it. He must make them guess at what he knew and felt.

"Why not, honey? It's for you . . ."

"But I don't *want* it, Lionel," she whispered; she was still afraid that the Party would try to dictate her life.

Cross cursed himself. Each step he took carried him deeper into a morass of lies and deceit.

"The Party feels an obligation," Cross said, trying to make his lie sound genuine. "If you refuse, they'll wonder what reasons you could have."

"Exactly," Menti said.

Cross did not believe what Menti had said, and he knew that Menti knew that he did not believe it.

"Oh, all right," Eva sighed. "But I'm young and I have my painting!"

"As soon as you're rested and settled, the Party wants you to paint," Menti told her hurriedly. "Now, tomorrow's Sunday. I'll pick you up in the morning at nine and take you to the union hall, hunh?"

Eva nodded her head. Menti shook hands with her and left. Sarah, who had overheard it all from the back of the room, came forward with a tight and angry face.

"Well, I'll be goddamned," Sarah swore.

"What's the matter?" Eva asked.

"They pay you, but *me* . . . ? I lost Bob, but do they give me one red cent? They took Bob from me, but do they *care?*" Bitter tears welled in her eyes.

"Oh, Sarah," Eva protested guiltily. "Here, you take this money. You need it." She held out the envelope with a gesture of childish generosity.

"I don't want it!" Sarah shouted.

"But, Sarah," Eva wept, "I didn't *ask* the Party for it . . ."

"I ain't mad at you," Sarah stormed. "I'm mad at them! I'm convinced that there's something fishy behind this. They don't give a good goddamn about what happens to you. They're trying to buy your loyalty for some reason." Sarah turned to Cross. "What do you think, Lionel?"

"I don't know, Sarah," he lied helplessly; he agreed with Sarah, but he could not tell her so, at least not yet.

Cross wondered if he was underestimating the Party. Though the Party was not an official adjunct to the police department, it did have wide powers of an effective and peculiar nature; it had its own underground apparatus and special methods of investigation. But what could they do with their findings? And he was convinced that he would have more than ample warning of their movements before they got too close to him.

Late that evening, immediately following dinner, Cross knew that the Party was adamantly on his trail, for Menti showed up accompanied by a short, dark Negro who hovered silently behind him, keeping on his hat and overcoat. This man, known as Hank, had a black, blank mask for a face, a greyish scar that went diagonally across his lips and chin, eyes that held a look of chronic hate whose origin seemed to go back to some inaccessible past. Cross knew that the Party had given Menti assistance in the form of this thug to help in spying upon him and Eva. This meant that the Party had not acted because it had not quite made up its mind. But what were the leaders thinking? Did they regard him as a spy? If so, for whom? And would they ever be able to fathom his motive in killing Gil? Or would they in the end just create some imaginary crime and try to brand him with its guilt? He knew that they were fully capable of that . . .

Menti pretended that the Party had asked for papers of an urgent political nature that Gil had left behind in his desk. Eva willingly surrendered to Menti the keys of the apartment on Charles Street. Cross had no fear of the Party finding anything incriminating in Eva's apartment, for he had brought his only suitcase with him. Before leaving, Menti lingered at the door, smiling, looking thoughtfully off into space. Hank stood behind Menti, morose, his eyes darting about.

"How are you getting on, Lane?" Menti asked.

"Oh, so-so," Cross said.

"Only so-so?" Menti asked. "You need money?"

"No."

Hank was listening so intently that his eyes glittered.

"The Party's curious about you," Menti said.

"You've told me I'm under suspicion," Cross said. "But you haven't told me what I'm suspected of."

"Say, where were you born?" Menti asked suddenly. "I want to know."

"You mean the Party wants to know— Tell the Party folks to come and ask me what they want to hear—"

"I'm the Party; I'm asking—"

"You think I'm with the police, don't you?" Cross evaded him.

Menti laughed, then playfully slapped Cross on the shoulder.

"Hell, Lane, we're not children," Menti said. "You've no connections with the police; we've investigated and we know . . . Say, tell me, when did you last see Hilton?"

"I tried to see him yesterday afternoon. But he wasn't in."

"What time was that?"

"Gosh, I don't know," Cross smiled. "Is it important?"

"Could be." Menti was baffled at Cross's casual manner. "Can you *prove* you didn't see 'im?"

"I haven't bothered to think about that," Cross said.

"The hotel clerk said a guy of your description asked for Hilton around four o'clock," Menti told him. "That must have been you, hunh?"

"Maybe. There are many Negroes who look like me," Cross said; he knew that they were trying clumsily to link him with Hilton's death.

"Not likely," Menti said. "At least they don't act like you. The hotel clerk remembers you because you acted self-assured, like a man who knows his way around."

"I know my way around," Cross laughed.

"Good-bye," Menti said suddenly.

They left. Cross shut the door and at once Sarah came out of the living room and Cross could see that she had overheard the conversation.

"What are they after you for?" she asked.

"They are crazy," Cross told her, laughing. "You know, they are trying to build up a case . . . They want to accuse me of killing Hilton . . ."

"Good God!" Sarah looked stunned. "Could it be because you're living with Eva? But the Party isn't interested in things like that. They're trying to put their finger on you for something and they're going about it slow and easy. They know you're here with Eva and won't run off—"

"You think so?" Cross asked to test her intuitions.

"I *know* it; I *can* feel it . . ."

Cross forced a laugh and shrugged his shoulders.

Just before going to bed that night, when they were alone together, Eva came demurely to him with a package wrapped up in heavy brown paper. He saw a look of devotion and trust in her tranquil, hazel eyes. She knelt at his feet and caught hold of his hand.

"Lionel," she whispered.

"Yes, darling."

In her attitude was a mute giving of her life to him that sprang from a sense of her newly gained freedom.

"Lionel," she began, "I'm going to let you know something that I once swore that I'd never divulge to anyone on earth. I want you to know the Party you're dealing with . . . They deceived me with Gil. Darling, here in this package are my diaries. They contain my hope and my despair . . . You must not let them make you a victim, too . . . They're clever. Menti's hounding you for something . . . Read these diaries and know the world in which I once lived . . ."

Cross's eyes fell; he tried to keep his sense of shame from showing.

"You must know the kind of woman with whom you've

elected to go through life," Eva continued bravely, her eyes full upon his face. "Life has made me akin to you. The world has treated me as it has treated you. You'll see that when you read this . . ."

Cross was a riot of impulses; he wanted to tell her that he had already read them; that he was not worthy of what she was doing; that he too had a past to tell of; that it was to her that he ought to kneel and not she to him . . . One impulse canceled the other and he said nothing; then he seized her and crushed her to him in an outburst of despair that was so deep and sharp that it seemed to stop his breath.

"Until death, Lionel," she whispered.

"Yes; until death," he sighed and bit his lips. He clung to her and hid his face; he did not want her to see the tears that stood stingingly in his eyes. When she pulled herself free, she laughed and wiped his eyes with the tips of her fingers.

"You silly-billy," she said.

"You make me feel that way," he told her truthfully.

"Look, let's go to a midnight movie," she suggested. "I'm tired of being cooped up."

"Okay."

No sooner was he upon the street with Eva than he saw Menti and Hank lurking in a shadowy doorway near a corner. And he knew that Menti had seen him, for the man lowered his head and walked off quickly, pulling Hank after him. He did not call Eva's attention to Menti, feeling that it would only worry her. With Eva clinging to his arm, he moved on over patches of snow and ice, wondering what the Party knew and when it planned to act.

He was now under twenty-four-hour surveillance. Did they think he was going to run off? Were they working with the District Attorney? He felt that he could handle the Party, but Houston was another matter. He damned the day he had met the man who knew so well the spiritual malady that had plagued and undone him—the dilemma of the ethical criminal, the millions of men who lived in the tiny crevices of industrial society completely cut off from humanity, the teeming multitudes of little gods who ruled their own private worlds and acknowledged no outside authority. Hating that part of himself that he could not manage, Cross must perforce fear and hate Houston who knew how close to crime men of his kind had by necessity to live.

After the movie they returned to the apartment to find that Sarah was not in. Eva was worried; it was past two o'clock in the morning and she lamented that they had not had the foresight to invite Sarah along with them, and Cross agreed with her, but for reasons of his own. He suspected that Sarah was with Menti . . .

Sarah arrived around three o'clock accompanied by Menti, Hank, and another elderly, portly, white-haired, well-dressed man. Sarah, slightly tipsy from drink, came straight to Cross with a knowing look in her eyes. They've been pumping her, Cross thought.

"Lionel, I want you to meet Menti's friend, Mr. Blimin," Sarah said.

"How are you?" Cross said.

"I'm glad to meet you, Lane," Blimin said.

They shook hands. Menti at once went to Blimin and Hank and took both of them by their arms.

"Say, you two wanted to find that little room, didn't you?"

"Oh, yes," Blimin said, looking around the room at Cross, Eva, and Sarah. "Will you excuse me?"

Menti herded the two of them into the hallway. It did not look natural. Cross knew that Menti had gotten Blimin and Hank out of the room in order to say something to them of a confidential nature. The moment Menti's footsteps had ceased to sound in the hallway, Sarah rushed to Cross and Eva and burst out in a loud whisper:

"You should have heard what they were asking me about you—"

"Yes? Tell me," Cross urged her.

"Blimin wanted to know your age, your background, how you spoke, who your mother was, who your father was, what school you came from, what organizations you belonged to . . ."

"Good God!" Cross forced himself to laugh.

"But, *why?*" Eva stood and indignation blazed in her eyes.

"I don't know," Sarah said.

Eva turned to Cross and said: "What do they mean? You've got to tell them off, Lionel."

"I'll do that," he said.

"If you don't tell them, I will," Eva swore with anger.

"But this just started today, honey," he reminded her. He had to keep this thing to normal proportions in her mind. "I'll see them as soon as the ceremony for Gil's over."

"And tell them to keep out of our life," Eva demanded.

"But, wait— I haven't told you everything yet," Sarah said. "That Blimin wanted to know what kind of books you read, what kind of mail you received, if you spoke any foreign languages, if you had any secret appointments, if a lot of telephone calls came for you, how large were the bills you spent, what kind of people came to see you, if I could hear you typing late at night, if you mailed any big envelopes . . . Lord, he was like a lawyer."

"Don't worry, Sarah," Cross told her. "They're worried about Gil and Hilton and they're trying to find out who killed them."

"But why are they snooping around *us*?" Eva demanded.

"Listen, Lionel," Sarah said with deep care. "I hope to God that you're not like Bob. Don't have a past for them to dig into. This is exactly how they were acting before they turned Bob over to the Immigration authorities . . . Oh, God, I hate those people, I *hate* 'em!" Tears of rage blinded Sarah.

"But there are others who are worse than Communists," Cross told Sarah. "The Communists are kittens; but there are tigers in the jungle."

"What do you mean?" Sarah asked.

"Communists are trained and organized; but there are men, their equals, who have never been broken. *They* are more dangerous than Communists!"

"Well, I hate 'em, *hate* 'em *all*!" Sarah hissed.

"If you hate them, then you'll never understand them," Cross explained.

"Why in hell would I want to understand them?" Sarah demanded.

The doorknob turned and Menti, Blimin, and Hank re-entered the room. Blimin came straight to Cross and went to work.

"Say, they tell me you were a friend of Gil," Blimin said.

"That's right," Cross answered.

"And you knew Hilton?"

"Not as well as I knew Gil."

"Is this your first time to become acquainted with the Party?"

"That's it."

"What do you think of our Party?"

"Well, I doubt if I know it well enough to form a worthwhile opinion," Cross hedged.

"Could I ask you a direct question?"

"Of course."

"Lane, are you now, directly or indirectly, verbally or organizationally, by proxy or on your own behalf engaged in anti-Party activity?" Blimin let the words roll neatly off the tip of his tongue.

Cross rose from the side of Eva and faced Blimin. How could he tell this man something that would set his mind at rest, and yet not leave in him the impression that he was evading anything.

"You don't have to answer unless you want to, Lane," Blimin said.

"I'm hesitating in order to give full weight to what you've asked me," Cross said.

The Communists were at last boldly leaping into an area where the police had feared to tread. His relation to the Party was the reverse of his relation to Houston. The essence of the Party was an open lawlessness and it could smell lawlessness in others even when it could not identify it correctly. What tactic could he use here? His first move should be to find out how much they suspected and the degree and intensity of their seriousness.

"Mr. Blimin, I suppose this is as good a time as any for us to have a showdown," Cross began. "What are you suspecting me of? Why are you posing all these vague and roundabout questions?"

"Blimin's not a man to play with," Menti reminded Cross.

"We're careful in the Party, Lane," Blimin said. "And we don't know who you are. You are a close friend of Eva. Eva is close to us, and so you are close to us, but we don't know you. I'd like to see you account for yourself, to put it frankly. We've been trying to get a line on you, and the more we try, the less we find. You don't add up. What do you think of things? How do you feel? To our Party, these questions are of paramount importance. Our Party is under attack from many quarters. You show up suddenly on the scene, and two of our best leaders die under questionable circumstances and you are nearby . . . Naturally, the question arises: *Who is Lionel Lane?* What organization does he belong to? What are his interests? Who are his friends? What ideas does he hold? Now, Lane, I'm here to listen to you. I'm an old man and I'm a pretty good judge of men. If you're honest and on the up and up, I'll be able to tell it, feel it. If you're hiding something, I can tell that too. Is what I'm asking fair?"

"It's fair," Cross conceded.

"Are you willing to talk?"

"Of course," Cross laughed. He knew that Blimin could not drag his secret from him; his past was safe; his past was himself. "I know nothing of the ideology of the Party."

Blimin's face changed; he stood; his eyes grew hard; when he spoke his words were strident and underlined with a tinge of viciousness.

"I'm not talking about ideology. You're a man with the ability to grasp situations. I know that . . . You know goddamn well what I'm wondering about you."

"Well," Cross drawled, "I know you know I'm a stranger—"

"No; no!" Blimin slapped his hand through the air with a gesture of disdain. "I mean this— Your appearance in our midst coincides with death and violence! I'm talking to the point now . . . In the eyes of the Party you are under *suspicion*."

"You suspect me of what?" Cross asked boldly.

"Of almost anything and everything," Blimin stated his case.

"And what do you expect me to do about that?" Cross egged him on.

"Clear yourself of suspicion, or we will take measures to see that you do not remain longer in our midst," Blimin said.

"This is vague," Cross argued. "I'm guilty, you say; but you don't say what I'm supposed to be guilty of—"

"You're dodging, Lane! Right now you're guilty of evading my questions— Look, you can't play 'possum with us. You're dealing with experienced men. You are supposed to have a background that would make you acceptable to us, but you've not revealed it. We don't understand you, and we don't like to be with people we don't understand. The world in which we live is much too dangerous for us to tolerate you a moment longer."

"Look, for Christ's sake," Cross begged. "I've not had a chance to say anything to anybody yet . . . Gil died suddenly; he was the only high-ranking member of the Party I'd talked to."

"Lane, stop trying to make me believe that you are naïve!" Blimin shouted. "I'm *serious!*"

Eva rose; anger shone in her eyes.

"Comrade Blimin—"

"You keep quiet!" Blimin ordered. "This is no time for you to speak!"

"But—" Eva protested.

"You'll get your chance to speak to the Party later about all this," Blimin said, waving a fat forefinger at her.

"Mr. Blimin, what do you want to know?" Cross demanded of him. "You must tell me, for I refuse to relate my entire life to you and let you pick out what part of my life you want and then brand me with it."

"I don't understand all this," Sarah mumbled uneasily.

"This is no concern of yours!" Blimin snapped at Sarah. His anger fully roused, he whirled on Cross. "Lane, what the hell ghastly joke is this you're pulling on the knowingest people on earth, the Communists? Who the goddamn hell do you think you *are?* What are you *doing* here? When we try to check on you, we run into a maze that leads nowhere. That's no *accident*. Are you a spy? Frankly, we doubt it; we thought so at first, but you've not been close enough to us to get hold of any information. Don't you think, now, that we are scared of you? If we were, you'd not be breathing now . . . But we want to know . . ."

"Know *what*?"

"Are you a *killer*?"

"No!" Eva screamed.

"God in Heaven," Sarah gasped.

The room was silent. He had at last been accused. Now, he had to act. First, he'd let the Party know that he knew what the score was in the world. He'd make them feel that maybe they could use him despite all the vague clouds of suspicion around him. He would make use of Blimin's urging him to talk to make a bid to them.

"We've no evidence, you might say," Blimin went on with his charge. "That's right; we haven't. But *you* are evidence. You come—death! *Why?* Lane, I'm accusing you of EVERY-THING! Now, *talk* for your *life*!" Blimin pronounced a provisional death sentence.

Cross laughed softly, went to the sofa and sat down, lit a cigarette, lifted smiling eyes to Blimin as he drew smoke deep into his lungs.

"Do you think I'm crazy enough to try to defend myself against a charge about which I know nothing? You say you don't understand me. Well, I'm going to talk, and *you're* going to listen. I'm not the kind of fool who'd let you push him into a position of defending himself against a charge of something he's never even dreamed of doing— If you make me do that, why, I'd really be somehow guilty—"

Cross rose, went to the center table and poured out a glass of water; he acted slowly, methodically, taking his time. I'm acting like Gil acted when he was trying to impress me, he told himself. He drained the glass, turned to Blimin, and he confessed not as Blimin wanted him to, but as he felt it. It was as though he was not only speaking to Blimin, but to and for himself, trying to clarify his predicament in his own eyes.

"Now, Mr. Blimin, I take it for granted that you are a member of the Central Committee of the Communist Party, or you would not be here talking to me tonight, or rather this morning. It's half past three . . . Oh, no; you needn't bother to affirm or deny it. I assume you are here for your Party. Let's let it go at that. I'd like for you to take back a straight message to them. They may not like my answer, and I'm not going to try to couch it in terms that will please them. My answer is just simply my way of looking at things, my slant, if you want to call it that.

"One way, among a variety of others, of looking at what is happening in this world today is to view all modern history as being tied together by one overall meaning. And that meaning is this: to a greater or less degree, all human life on this earth today *can* be described as moving away from traditional, agrarian, simple handicraft ways of life toward modern industrialization. Some nations, owing mainly to their historical backgrounds, have already made this journey, have already, so to speak, exhausted their industrial potentials of development and are industrially overripe. I'm referring to nations like England, Japan, Germany, etc. In these nations the problem of the future structure of society and the question of what kind of faith will sustain the individual in his daily life constitute a kind of chronic spiritual terror."

"Lane," Blimin accused him, "you're evading my question—"

"You asked me what I thought and felt about things," Cross shot at him. "Do you want to hear it or not?"

"But get to the point," Blimin insisted.

"Are you in a hurry?" Cross asked. "If so, I'll talk to you some other time—"

"Get to the point, Lane," Blimin said.

"This *is* my point," Cross said. "Now, Mr. Blimin, as I said, other nations, such as China, India, and the vast stretches of Africa have hardly begun this journey toward industrialization. The human and physical resources of these huge nations, comprising as they do more than one half of the human race and more than one half of the territory of the earth, have been stimulated as much as retarded by the impact of Western imperialism; they were retarded inasmuch as they were captive peoples in the hands of the industrialists of the West who needed their physical labor and the natural riches of their soil to keep the giant industrial machines of the West going . . . They were stimulated to leave their tribal ancestral anchorages of living by being sucked into the orbit of industrial enterprises operating under the management of whites in their homelands under their own eyes . . . The hands of the West reached out greedily for the natural resources of these quaint peoples, but, in reaching, they awakened black, red, brown, and yellow men from their long slumber and sent them, willy-nilly, hurtling down the road of industrialization . . .

"During the past seventy years, America, under the ideological banner of free enterprise, fought a bloody civil war and defeated its agrarian provinces and launched itself, with no pre-history and practically no traditions to check it, upon a program of industrialization the equal of which, in terms of speed and magnitude, the world has never seen. From my point of view, this industrial program could have been accomplished under any dozen different ideological banners. The ideas were not as important as people thought they were; the important thing was the fact of industrialization. Of course, and it is understandable, the defenders of this industrial program justified their dazzling progress by claiming that an organic relationship obtained between their ideas and industrialization. But, really, there was none . . .

"Now, during the past thirty-five years, under the ideological banner of Dialectical Materialism, a small group of ruthless men in Russia seized political power and the entire state apparatus and established a dictatorship. Rationalizing human life to the last degree, they launched a vast, well-disciplined program of industrialization which now rivals that of the United States of America in pretentiousness and power . . . Again I say that what happened in Russia, just as with what happened in America, could have happened under a dozen different ideological banners . . . If you lived in Russia and made such a statement, they'd shoot you; and if you lived in America and made such a statement, they'd blacklist you and starve you to death . . . Modern man still believes in magic; he lives in a rational world but insists on interpreting the events of that world in terms of mystical forces. The simple fact is, the social cat can be skinned in many different ways. The coming history of the many new nations now launching their industrial programs will prove this to be true . . ."

"So!" Blimin exploded, "you sneer at our ideology? You

ignore the role of the working class, hunh? You see no difference between Russia and the rest of the imperialist powers?"

"Mr. Blimin," Cross said patiently, "I'm talking to you as
one man to another. I'm propaganda-proof. Communism has
two truths, two faces. The face you're talking about now is
for the workers, for the public, not for me. I look at facts,
processes—"

"You're slandering—"

"Don't impute motives to me," Cross insisted. "Am I condemning you and men like you for what you've done? You
did what you did because you had to! Anybody who launches
himself on the road to naked power is caught in a trap . . .
You use idealistic words as your smoke-screen, but behind
that screen you *rule* . . . It's a question of *power*!"

"I'll not tolerate your reducing the noble aims of Lenin to a
power-hungry man," Blimin raged.

"But Lenin admitted it," Cross told him. "Lenin repeatedly
chided his comrades for lacking the will-to-power . . . Again,
Mr. Blimin, if you want to talk to me, please understand that
I'm not naïve. Your propaganda is *not* for me . . . Do you get
that? Now, let me get back to my point . . .

"You may like industrialization or you may hate it. You
may think that the process of industrialization ought to be
stopped, that it has done great harm to mankind. Or you may
feel that it is best to flee from this industrial machine and find
haven in some tropical island. (Those little islands, too, are
being caught up in the global tide of industrialization and
soon there will be no hideaways.) Neither attitude really has
anything to do with the basic reality of industrialization itself,
which is a neutral process. Industrialization is simply an efficient way of making and doing things, labor-saving, a life-
saving way of living. Industrialization is simply a hammer or a
saw which has grown infinitely complex and, in itself, is not
evil and cannot be evil . . . We can either find ways of controlling this complex hammer or saw and make it serve us, or
we can simply drift, let industrial life bog us down, as we
have already done. In any case, the sweep of industrialization
has gone on far, its spirit has entered so deep in the hearts and
habits of men, that we cannot stop it now even if we wanted
to. It is a part of us and we are a part of it; if we go on, it

goes on, so organically is it a part of our living . . . It cannot be stopped unless we all die or revert to a manner of living which would reduce our lives to a kind of Old Testament simplicity, which is highly unlikely.

"Quickening the process of industrialization was the marriage of scientific knowledge and industry. The interaction between the two progressed like a game of leapfrog. The more society became industrialized, the more men learned about the nature of the world in which they lived, and the more knowledge they gained from that world, the more skill they had in applying their knowledge to the methods of industry . . .

"Now, had this global tide of industrialization consisted only of this, we'd have no problem at all. Indeed, the world would be piled high with products and this earth would be the long-dreamed-of goal of mankind.

"What I've described becomes interesting only in the light of one question: What kind of a queer animal is this being called man who embarked—and without quite knowing it!—upon this program of industrialization? Well, his most dominant characteristic is an enormous propensity toward fear. He is the most scared and trembling of all the animals, and I'm not forgetting those wild ones who live in jungles . . . Learned men have long declaimed upon the thinking and loving capacities of man, but we have yet to hear of man's fears. It might well be that the most important part of human existence is fear itself . . .

"Primitive man, naked and afraid, found that only *one* thing could really quiet his terrors: that is, *Untruth*. He stuffed his head full of myths, and if he had not, he might well have died from fear itself. How many people on this earth die from fear is something we've yet to find out; but that is another story . . .

"The degree and quality of man's fears can be gauged by the scope and density of his myths, that is, by the ingenious manner in which he disguised the world about him. Man was afraid of the clamoring world of storms, volcanoes, and heaving waves and he wanted to change that world. His myths sought to recast that world, tame it, make it more humanly meaningful and endurable. The more abjectly frightened the nation or race of men, the more their myths and religions projected out upon the world another world in *front* of the real world, or, in another way of speaking, they projected another world *behind* the real world they saw, lived, suffered, and died in. Until today almost all of man's worlds have been either pre-worlds or back-worlds, *never* the *real* world . . . (The ancient nations today we call great are the ones who left behind them those towering monuments of fear in the forms of their so-called cultures!)

"That real world man did not want; he was not stout-hearted enough to endure its dangers and uncertainties . . . In making his pre-worlds, he always saw reality as a wonderful drama enacted for his special benefit; there were gods and counter-gods locked in deadly conflict the outcome of which spelled good or evil for him, all shaping his destiny. In making his back-worlds man was vain enough to believe that this real world could not be all, that there was another world into which he could somehow escape when he died. Entrance into that back-world depended upon how faithfully he observed certain compulsive rituals which he, in his fear and anxiety, had created over eons of time to placate his sense of dread.

"Man cringed even before the ordinary workings of his own mind; he would not even dare admit the authorship of his own fantasies. He found himself so complex that he fled from himself. That which transpired in his heart he projected out into the skies, or else he would not have been able to sleep at night . . .

"War, famines, earthquakes, epidemics, and social upheavals made no impact upon man's myth-worlds; indeed, calamities served but to strengthen them, for man felt that he was somehow guilty when he was overwhelmed with disaster, had somehow failed to pronounce the magic talisman correctly when catastrophe descended upon him. One thing, however, did get at those myth-worlds, did gnaw at them until they fell from man's eyes and left him staring in dismay at the real, natural, workaday world from which he had for millions of years shied in fright . . .

"The ravaging scourge that tore away the veil of myth-worlds was science and industry; science slowly painting another world, the real one; and industry uprooting man from his ancestral, ritualized existence and casting him into rational schemes of living in vast, impersonal cities. A split took place in man's consciousness; he began living in the real world by the totems and taboos that had guided him in the world of myths . . . But that could not last for long. Today we are in the midst of that crisis . . . The real world stands at last before our eyes and we don't want to look at it, don't know how to live in it; it terrifies us. All of the vast dramas which man once thought took place in the skies now transpire in our hearts and we quake and are moved compulsively to do what we know not . . ."

"You deliberately and consistently omit to mention the role of the working class," Blimin pointed out, smiling. "It was oppression that awakened man from his slumber . . ."

"Oppression was simply an added irritant," Cross said. "Even if man had not been oppressed, this crisis would have taken place, and you know it. Oppression was a part of the process of industrialization—"

"And wars? You omit war altogether," Blimin said.

"When used as it was used," Cross told him, "industrialization was a kind of war against mankind. That same war might be going on in Russia today, for all I know . . . But let me get on.

"Now, this real world in which we live today has a strange tone and aspect. We Twentieth Century Westerners have outlived the faith of our fathers; our minds have grown so skeptical that we cannot accept the old scheme of moral precepts which once guided man's life. In our modern industrial society we try to steer our hearts by improvised, pragmatic rules which are, in the end, no rules at all. If there are people who tell you that they live by traditional values and precepts— such as the English sometimes pretend—then they are either lying to you or to themselves; maybe they are lying both ways . . . There is no modern industrial nation on earth today that makes decisions based upon anything remotely resembling the injunctions of the Old or New Testament; this holds true in their domestic as well as in their foreign policies.

"Of course, the historical transition from the unreal myth-worlds of yesterday to the bleak, terrifying world of today was not sudden, did not take place all at once. Acting as a brake upon the hot winds of scientific knowledge and the tidal waves of industrial erosion was a group of wonderful people, unhappily now extinct, called liberals. Full of the juices of human kindness, these people decided that they were going to be good, honest Christians without believing in Christianity which their logical minds found offensive. Let reason prevail, they declared. But these kindhearted atheists got scared. They went so far down the godless road that they could see a black nothingness looming as its final end. They retreated in fear. They helped to undermine the old world, but they discovered that the building of a new world was much harder than they had suspected. They called for new systems of ideas, and when no valid ones were forthcoming, they demanded new myths that would not insult the intelligence of man. For their pains they got programs for wars and revolutions . . .

"But one must not overlook the fact that, had it not been for these liberals, the full flood of a senseless existence would have long since broken through the myths of progress which have sustained modern man so far. They did an impossible job with great skill, those liberals. Future history will regard the liberals as the last great defenders of that which really could not be defended, as the last spokesmen of historical man as we've known him for the past two thousand years.

"All of this brings us to one central, decisive fact: the consequences of the atheistic position of modern man, for most men today are atheists, even though they don't know it or won't admit it. They live, dream, and plan on the assumption that there is no God. The full implications of this are enormous. It means that God no longer really concerns us as a reality beyond life, but simply as something projected compulsively from men's minds in answer to their chronic need to be rid of fear, something to meet the obscure needs of daily lives lived amidst strange and threatening facts."

"At least we agree on *something*," Blimin muttered, eyeing Cross askance. "You see the central fact, so why don't you admit the rest? Only the Party can save this world, give it guidance, direction—"

"Mr. Blimin," Cross overrode him, "since religion is dead, religion is everywhere . . . Religion was once an affair of the church; it is now in the streets in each man's heart. Once there were priests; now every man's a priest. Religion's a compulsion, and a compulsion seems to spring from something total in us, catching up in its mighty grip all the other forces of life—sex, intellect, will, physical strength, and carrying them forward toward—what goals? We wish we knew . . . Compulsions exist as much in the individual as in society. Lucky is the man who can share his neighbor's religion! Damned is the man who must invent his own god! Shun that man, for he is a part of the vast cosmos; he is akin to it and he can no more know himself than he can know the world of which he is in some mysterious way a part . . . Blessed is the artificial man, the determined man, the social man . . .

"Mr. Blimin, I'm not even an atheist. To me it's just too bad that some people must lean on imagined gods, that's all. Yet I'd not have it otherwise. They need religion. All right; let them have it. What harm does it do? And it does make for a greater measure of social stability. But I object if somebody grabs me when I'm a defenseless child and injects into me a sedative—the power of which lasts for a lifetime!—which no one would ever be able to tell if I'll ever need or not!

"Now, what does this mean,—that I don't believe in God? It means that I, and you too, can do what we damn well please on this earth. Many men have been doing just that, of course, for a long time, but they didn't have the courage to admit it. They pretended that they were following higher laws, practicing virtue, etc. But such clumsy games exposed themselves before long. Naïve governments allowed historical records to be kept! Imagine the British, past masters of exploitation and duplicity, allowing a Karl Marx into their British Museum to pore over and unravel the pretensions and self-deceptions of British banditry! Such records of blatant chicanery served thoughtful and astute men as guides in the building of new, scientific, and more efficient methods of deception!

"Today governments, democratic or totalitarian, are much wiser. It is better, they feel, for mankind to be unconscious —or ignorant, which is the same thing—than knowing.

They regard the writing of history as the most supremely important of all tasks. Modern governments today watch their history and since men seem to have developed a habit of wanting to know what has happened, they doctor up events, rewrite the past, improvise limited myths and give those myths to the masses of men. But this history is a simple, inspected history, fumigated, purged, and sterilized of all contagious ideas that might lead to the illnesses of independence, freedom, and individuality. Mankind is coming of age . . .

"Those few strong men who do not want to be duped, and who are stout enough in their hearts to accept a godless world, are quite willing, aye, anxious to let the masses of men rest comfortably in their warm cocoons of traditional illusions. Men are more easily and cheaply governed when they fear ghosts more than guns! The real slaves of the Twentieth Century are not those sharecroppers who wince at the stinging swish of a riding boss's whip; the slaves of today are those who are congenitally afraid of the new and the untried, who fall on their knees and break into a deep sweat when confronted with the horrible truth of the uncertain and enigmatic nature of life . . .

"It is the strong at the top, however, who represent modern man. Beyond themselves, their dreams, their hopes, their plans, they know that there is nothing . . .

"Now, the next point, Mr. Blimin— Most of the decisive historic events that happen in this world are not known until *after* they have happened. Few are the people who know the meaning of what they are living through, who even have an inkling of what is happening to them. That's the big trouble with history . . .

"Now, Mr. Blimin, keep that point in mind while I remind you of what is happening in the great cities of the earth today—Chicago, Detroit, Pittsburg, London, Manchester, Paris, Tokyo, Hong Kong, and the rest. These cities are, for the most part, vast pools of human misery, networks of raw human nerves exposed without benefit of illusion or hope to the new, godless world wrought by industrial man. Industrial life plus a rampant capitalism have blasted the lives of men in these cities; those who are lucky enough not to be hungry are ridden with exquisite psychological sufferings. The people of these cities are lost; some of them are so lost that they no longer even know it, and they are the real lost ones. They haunt the movies for distraction; they gamble; they depress their sensibilities with alcohol; or they seek strong sensations to dull their sense of a meaningless existence . . .

"Now, Mr. Blimin, above these so-called toiling masses, for whom I have some sympathy but not as much as you'd expect, are the few industrialists and politicians who yell night and day about freedom, democracy, high wages, etc. These are the exploiters of the millions of rats caught in the industrial trap. That they make great profits out of the exercise of their lordship is perhaps the least of their crimes—"

"Oh, you're showing your true colors," Blimin snorted. "Are you defending *exploitation* now? Next you're going to tell me what wonderful philanthropists these capitalists are—"

"Not at all. It just so happens, Mr. Blimin," Cross explained, "that I think that their crime is a blacker one than mere exploitation. The end-results of their rule is that they keep the lives of their rats pitched to a mean, sordid level of consciousness. It's right here where you and I disagree deeply. Your wonderful trade unions for a quarter of a century have been fighting for so-called standards of living for workers, fighting for higher wages . . . Had I had anything to say about the goals of those trade unions, I'd have insisted that their fight be to escape completely the domination of the capitalists . . . Not that the workers become richer, but that they become more human, freer . . . You don't want that, Mr. Blimin, and the capitalists don't want it. Why? Because you cannot dupe free men who can think and know . . .

"Now back to my theme . . . The point is not so much that these capitalists despise their rats, but that they despise themselves and all mankind. To keep their rats contented, they strive to convince them that their rats' lives are more glorious, better, richer than at any time in history, and, in the end, they come to believe in their own lies. Consequently today the content of human life on earth is what these cheap-minded men say it is. They are jealous and uneasy, these men, of anyone who tries to lure their rats away. They preach to their rats that their nation is the best of any of the nations, and that as rats they are the very best of all possible rats. They even have I-Am-A-Rat days . . . As long as this works, it's wonderful. The only real enemies of this system are not the rats themselves, but those outsiders who are conscious of what is happening and who seek to change the consciousness of the rats who are being controlled. In situations like this, public consciousness is the key to political power . . . The essence of life today is psychological; men may take power with arms, but their keeping of it is by other means . . . Get me so far, Mr. Blimin?

"Now, rising up from time to time from the pools of restless millions in these vast cities are men who seek to head new movements. Their appearance is much rarer than is popularly supposed, just as genuine revolutions on this earth are rare, few and far between . . . These men who rise to challenge the rulers are jealous men. They feel that they are just as good as the men who rule; indeed, they suspect that they are better . . . They see the countless mistakes that are being made by the men who rule and they think that they could do a more honest, a much cleaner job, a more efficient job. For simplicity's sake, let's call them the Jealous Rebels—"

"Lane!" Blimin thundered, rising in anger. "You *are* cynical, that's all! How can you say Lenin was jealous? He had the fate of mankind close to his heart! We love people—"

Cross was tempted to tell of what Hilton had told him just before he had shot him; but no, he couldn't do that.

"Mr. Blimin, *please*, be honest," Cross begged. "You must assume that I know what this is all about. Don't tell me about the nobility of labor, the glorious future . . . *You* don't believe in that. That's for others, and you damn well know it. You and men of your type are convinced that you know how the game goes and you've thrown down the gauntlet to the capitalists, conservatives, socialists, etc. You Jealous Rebels are intellectuals who know your history and you are anxious not to make the mistakes of your predecessors in rebellious undertakings. You feel that life has become crummy and meaningless and you feel you can give it more meaning than the clumsy men who now rule.

"The thinking of the revolutionary is a cold kind of

thinking; he has a realistic insight into history; he has, above all, a sense of what power is, what it's for, both as a means of governing other men and as a means of personal expression. That absolute power is corrupting, à la Lord Acton, is something revolutionaries laugh at. These Jealous Rebels would much rather be corrupted with absolute power than live under the heels of men whom they despise.

"In order to test themselves, to make life a meaningful game, these Jealous Rebels proceed to organize political parties, communist parties, nazi parties, fascist parties, all kinds of parties—"

"No!" Blimin roared. "You cannot equate or confound Communism with Fascism! They are *different!*"

"I admit they are different," Cross conceded. "But the degree of the difference is not worth arguing about. Fascists operate from a narrow, limited basis; they preach nationality, race, soil, blood, folk-feeling and other rot to capture men's hearts. What makes one man a Fascist and another a Communist might be found in the degree in which they are integrated with their culture. The more alienated a man is, the more he'd lean toward Communism . . ."

"Toward rationality," Blimin stated.

"No," Cross corrected him. "Communists *use* rationality. I admit that the Communists are more intelligent, more general in their approach, but the same power-hungry heart beats behind the desire to rule! I'm on pre-political ground here, Mr. Blimin. And you know I'm speaking the truth.

"Now, where do these Jealous Rebels get their programs . . . ? Out of books? From Plato's *Republic*? No! Their programs are but the crude translations of the daydreams of the man in the street, daydreams in which the Jealous Rebels do not believe!

"In order to catch their prey, they deliberately spin vast spiderwebs of ideology, the glittering strands of which are designed to appeal to the hopes of hopeful men. Yes, there are men who think that ideas will lead them to freedom and a fuller life, and these are the men who are the natural victims of the Jealous Rebels who do not feel that to dupe others in this way is immoral; it is their conviction that this is the way life is and only the naïve think to the contrary . . .

"Their aims? Direct and naked power! They know as few others that there is no valid, functioning religion to take the place of the values and creeds of yesterday; and they know that political power, if it is to perform in the minds and emotions of men the role and efficacy that the idea of God once performed, must be total and absolute. These Jealous Rebels are sustained by a sense of the total meaning—or lack of meaning!—of human life on this earth. Their courage is derived from the fact that, win or lose, they are making history, that what they do is decisive for mankind. Caught up passionately in such a realistic myth, what will not an ardent man do . . . ?

"These men are free from petty prejudices. They have to be free from such, for it is precisely the prejudices of *others* that they seek to manipulate for their own uses. They will commit any crime, but never in passion. They work slowly, deliberately, with refinement even. And whatever natural terrors of life there are in the hearts of men, whatever stupid prejudices they harbor in their damp souls, they know how to rouse and sustain those terrors and prejudices and mobilize them for *their* ends. The mere act of hoping, believing, of being alive makes you a prospective victim for these knowing men! Modern life is a kind of confidence game; if you dream, you can be defeated unless you are careful that you do not dream a dream that has been set up for you!

"I'm not so naïve as to believe that these men want to *change* the world! Why, they love human nature just as it is! They simply want their chance to show what they can do with that world and the people in it. To their minds human life on this earth is a process that is transparently *known*! They are out to grab the entire body of mankind and they will replace faith and habit with organization and discipline . . . *And they feel that they have a chance to do it!*

"Since God as functioning reality in men's minds and hearts has gone, since the death of the gallant liberal, every event of the modern world feeds the growing movement toward the total and absolute, making the Jealous Rebels believe that they have allies everywhere . . . Wars, by mobilizing men into vast armies to fight and die for ideals that are transparently fraudulent, justify this drift toward the total and absolute in modern life. Industrial capitalism, whether it operates for profit or not, herds men around assembly lines to perform senseless tasks—all of which conditions men toward the acceptance of the total and absolute in modern life. Implicit in all political and speculative thought are the germs of ideas that prefigure the triumph of the total and absolute attitudes in modern life. Communication, inventions, radio, television, movies, atomic energy, by annihilating distance and space and the atmosphere of mystery and romance, create the conditions for the creation of organizations reflecting the total and absolute in modern life. Commercial advertising, cheapening and devaluing our notions of human personality, develops and perfects techniques which can be used by political leaders who want to enthrone the total and absolute in modern life. Even anti-communists and anti-fascists must, by fighting the totalitarian threat by using the methods of the totalitarians—and there are no other methods, it seems, to use—guarantee and make inevitable this surge toward the total and absolute in modern life.

"There is no escaping what the future holds. We are going back, *back* to something earlier, maybe better, maybe worse, maybe something more terrifyingly human! These few hundred years of freedom, empire building, voting, liberty, democracy—these will be regarded as the *romantic* centuries in human history. There will be in that future no trial by jury, no writs of habeas corpus, no freedom of speech, of religion—all of this is being buried and not by Communists or Fascists alone, but by their opponents as well. All hands are shoveling clay on to the body of freedom before it even dies, while it lies breathing its last . . .

"There are some people today who sincerely but mistakenly believe that by going to war against a totalitarian nation that they can save the past of which they are so deeply fond. Unwilling or unable to believe that the crisis is as serious and deep as it really is, these people want to launch vast armies and smash the evildoers and reestablish a reign of peace and goodwill—the right to exploit others without interference! —on earth. What these sincere people do not realize is that Communism and Fascism are but the political expressions of the Twentieth Century's atheistic way of life, and that the future will reveal many, many more of these absolutistic systems whose brutality and rigor will make the present-day systems seem like summer outings. The most ludicrous and tragic spectacle on earth is to see a powerful nation bleeding itself white to build up vast heaps of armaments to put down a menace that cannot be put down by military means at all . . . Wars will but tear away the last shreds of belief, leaving man's heart more naked and compulsive than ever before. Can atom bombs correct a man's sense of life? Can ultimatums alter the basic beliefs or nonbeliefs of millions of men? Can you shoot attitudes?

"Mr. Blimin, if you believe that I believe what I've told you, how do you think I'm a menace to your Party? True, I may not believe your Party's aims, but I know enough about politics to know that I could not change your Party, or, as an individual, fight it. So what are you scared of in me? I give you my word that I do not belong to any political party on this earth, and I don't think I will ever join one.

"Now, you asked me what am I doing? Knowing and seeing what is happening in the world today, I don't think that there is much of anything that one can do about it. But there is one little thing, it seems to me, that a man owes to himself. He can look bravely at this horrible totalitarian reptile and, while doing so, discipline his dread, his fear and study it coolly, observe every slither and convolution of its sensuous movements and note down with calmness the pertinent facts. In the face of the totalitarian danger, these facts can help a man to save himself; and he may then be able to call the attention of others around him to the presence and meaning of this reptile and its multitudinous writhings . . .

"That's all, Mr. Blimin. I'm not really anti anything."

There was a long silence. Blimin sat looking at the floor, lifting his eyes now and then to Cross's face. Blimin's eyes were serious; he seemed not to know if he should believe Cross or not; or, if he did believe Cross, then in what way . . . ? Finally Blimin rose, laughed, stared at Cross and said:

"You've answered my question, but I'm afraid that you've raised more questions than you've answered. Frankly, Lane, it's dangerous for a man knowing and feeling what you know and feel to hang around loosely on the peripheries of our Party . . ."

"I came in contact with the Party in quite a natural manner, Mr. Blimin," Cross told him. "I was eating in a dining car one morning and met the late Mr. Bob Hunter . . ."

Blimin reddened. Bob was enroute to Trinidad and the Party had helped to speed him on his way. Blimin covered his embarrassment by shrugging and laughing.

"Well, I won't bother you any more tonight, Lane," he said.

"It's no bother," Cross said.

Hank still stood in the background of the room, his hat and coat still on, his eyes intent upon the face of Cross. Menti had been impressed by what Cross had said; he stared, grinned, winked, and said:

"With a gift of gab like that, you ought to be on the Central Committee."

"No," Cross said. "You don't want men in your Party who can think."

"It all depends," Blimin mumbled; he was leaving the door open.

Yet, Blimin was worried. Cross had tempted him, made him feel that maybe he would work with them, that maybe he could be persuaded . . . *Maybe* . . . Blimin and Menti left with cryptic smiles, but Hank was not moved; his face still held that blank, stolid expression as he went from sight.

"Lionel, I'm worried," Eva confessed. "How could they think that you, knowing what you know, would stoop to killing . . . ?"

"They can't find who killed Gil and Hilton, so they've got to get a scapegoat," Cross said in a cool, level tone.

"Oh, God," Eva moaned.

Cross watched her closely, wondering if she remembered his confessional babblings. For a moment her stare was full on him, then she looked at the floor. Suddenly she reached for his hand and squeezed it tightly.

"These Communists are mad!" Sarah exclaimed. "I think some spy with a grudge against the Party killed Gil and Hilton."

"If they really knew Lionel, they'd never think he would do anything like that," Eva said.

Cross was numb in his heart. Couldn't they tell he was guilty? Yes, it was their own innocence that kept them from seeing his guilt; they identified themselves with what they hoped he was, and, since they were innocent, he *must* be innocent.

"Now, don't go worrying about foolishness like this," he gently chided the two women, forcing a smile.

Back in the bedroom, he pondered and weighed his chances. Had he spoken too much to Blimin? But how else could he have behaved? He had given vent to his feelings in a way that he hoped would take some of the pressure of the Party off him. Would a normally guilty man have spoken like that? No. The Party knew now that he was not with the police; they knew also that he was not spying for another political party. What motive, then, could he have had, from their point of view, for killing . . . ? They'll think I did it because of Eva! No; Communists were not unintelligent; they could not seriously think that. There was one thing of which he was certain: They would never credit him with as much freedom to act as they had. A certain psychological blindness seemed to be the hallmark of all men who had to create their own worlds . . . All other men were mere material for them; they could admit no rivals, no equals; other men were either above them or below them.

Long after Eva had gone to sleep in his arms, he lay awake wondering if he could ride out this trouble and keep her with him. He was suffering this torturing surveillance of the Party only to keep near her. It was dawn before he managed to close his eyes in sleep.

The next morning Cross eagerly searched the Sunday papers in vain for further mention of Hilton. Nor was there any news on the radio. Maybe things would quiet down for awhile? But he knew that the Party and the police were still hunting, probing, observing. Dread was still with him; he lived in the anticipation of another sudden confrontation that would send him hurtling down the path of blood again . . .

After breakfast Menti and Hank came with a car and took them to the union hall. Long queues of workers were entering the doors and filing slowly past the dark, shining coffin in which Gil lay with ashen and upturned face. Huge wreaths of flowers were banked about the coffin which was surrounded by Communist militants standing stiffly at attention. Cross was impressed by the soberness of the shabby men and women who had come to pay their tribute to Gil. It's better than spending their time playing pinball machines, seeing movies or drinking in bars, he admitted musingly to himself.

Eva was sobbing quietly as he led her by the arm to the coffin. Why's she weeping? he wondered. Was it for grief over Gil? That could hardly be, for she had hated him. Was it because her life had been blasted? Or was it because she was on the verge of freedom? Maybe it was simply because she was overwhelmed . . .

Cross stood looking at Gil's cold and tired face which seemed now somewhat shrunken, but still retaining its lines of rigidity of character. There lies a modern man, Cross said to himself sadly. He lived as reasonlessly as he died . . . Life, to him, was a game devoid of all significance except that which he put into it. Life was a game and he played it with all of his skill to the bitter end. Cross was convinced that Gil, in an abstract sense, could not have disagreed with the manner in which he had met his death. Gil just experienced a sudden transitional leap in the dialectical materialistic development of life, that's all . . . Cross repressed a wry smile as he gently led Eva from the side of the coffin.

After the Party had had its last say over the body of Gil, Gil's sister, Blanche, a greying woman of forty-odd from the Bronx, deeply religious and sharply color-conscious, took charge and began to make arrangements for the shipment of Gil's remains for proper religious ceremonies and burial. Cross kept discreetly in the background while Eva and Blanche, who were strained, cold, and distant toward each other, discussed the disposition of Gil's books, furniture, and other personal belongings.

Blimin accosted Cross cordially at the back of the union hall.

"I've been thinking over your analysis of last night," Blimin said. "With a little discipline, we could do something with you."

"And?" Cross prompted him to talk.

"Why do you shun us when you understand so much?"

"I'm not shunning anybody," Cross told him.

"I can see why Gil wanted to train you," Blimin said. "Why have you changed your mind? You accepted Gil's offer—"

"I've been so busy coping with suspicions that I've had no chance to think of anything," Cross said.

"Lane, is there anything you *want*?" Blimin asked.

"What do you mean?"

"For a man of your ability, the Party can make exceptions," Blimin explained. "Or maybe you've *got* what you want already?"

Cross stared. This was the nearest the Party had come to hinting that he had perhaps killed Gil to get Eva! And Blimin had implied that if he would surrender, the Party would consider forgiving him for even that! But that meant giving up Eva . . . !

"Blimin, I don't like talk like this," Cross said.

"It's easier and simpler when we know what a man wants," Blimin went relentlessly on. "But with you, we don't know what you want. Well, good-bye." Blimin turned and walked off briskly.

Menti, still accompanied by the sullen Hank, was restrained, cordial, and noncommittal as he drove them back to Harlem. The nervous tension of the ceremony had given Eva a headache for which she took some aspirins and went to bed. Cross loitered in the living room, mulling over his dinner engagement with Houston. What had the Party said to him? And how much weight would Houston give to what the Party had said? He knew that the best proof of Houston's suspiciousness would be for Houston to begin straightaway prying into his past. And it was too late now for him to fabricate a new past for himself. Every lie he told now would only increase his difficulties. Ought he to slip out of the apartment and vanish? Such an act would declare his guilt, and it would mean losing Eva forever.

He left the apartment early to keep his dinner appointment with Houston, he wanted a chance to breathe some fresh air and organize his thoughts prior to confronting a man whose mind he feared. Houston knew what power was and loved it, or else he would not have stood to be elected to a public office. Would he, if he had Cross dead-to-rights, ravage him as he had seen Gil ravage Bob and Eva? Such was possible . . . Cross knew in his heart that the first man, from the police or from the Party, who could sense intuitively what his psychological state was would know that he was guilty. But in order to know that they would have to have courage enough to admit the character of the world in which he and they both lived; and he seriously doubted if Houston really had that much courage.

Reluctantly he made his way toward Frank's Restaurant on 125th Street through the cold wintry air. About him neon lights shimmered in red and blue and green and rose. For the first time in months Cross could see the sky stretching above the tenement roofs. A few clusters of brittle stars winked in a blue-black luminosity. Cars whirred over the icy asphalt pavement with sticky whines. He tramped grimly past towering Negro churches from whose doorways rolled softly, almost apologetically, the plaintive spirituals of his people. How lucky they were, those black worshippers, to be able to feel lonely together! What fantastic blessings were theirs to be able to express their sense of abandonment in a manner that bound them in unison! But with whom could he join in howling his loneliness?

When he came in view of Frank's Restaurant, he paused, dropped his cigarette and stomped out its glow with his heel. Then his body jerked; out of a corner of his eyes he saw two white men approaching. He lifted his head and looked at them. There was a light of intentionality in their eyes that gripped him and his lips parted slowly.

"Are you Lionel Lane?" one of the men asked.

"That's right," he answered.

One of the men pulled his right hand from his coat pocket and pushed his outstretched palm under Cross's nose; in that palm gleamed a police badge.

"I'm Detective Hornsby, attached to the District Attorney's office," he said.

"Yes?" he said and waited.

"You had an appointment, I believe, with the District Attorney here at eight o'clock?"

"That's right."

"The District Attorney cannot make it. We tried to see you at your apartment, but you had gone," Hornsby said.

"I'm sorry," Cross mumbled and waited; there was something else he knew that these men had to tell him.

"The District Attorney asked us to bring you to him," Hornsby said.

Cross noticed that the other detective had his hands jammed into his overcoat pockets and he had not spoken a word or moved.

"Am I being arrested?" Cross asked softly.

"We cannot answer any questions, I'm afraid. Will you come along with us?" Hornsby asked.

So this was it at last. The dinner engagement was resolving itself into an official confrontation. What did they know? Ought he make a dash for it? No; he could not get away; they might have other armed, plain-clothes men nearby. He did not move and they had not moved. He was suddenly tired. The face of Eva flashed through his mind; he would lose her. And if he lost her, what else mattered? He sighed, nodded his head.

"All right," he said quietly.

"Are you armed?" Hornsby asked.

He hesitated, then smiled. "Yes."

"Where's the gun? Don't move. Just tell us and we'll take it from you."

"It's on my right hip," he said.

They were efficient; they relieved him of his gun without attracting the attention of a single passerby.

"The car is that black sedan at the curb. Walk toward it between us and get in," Hornsby said.

Cross did as he was told; when seated in the car he leaned back and sighed. His despair drained off him in one second and he felt that he wanted to sleep. And in the next instant he knew exactly what he had to do. He would do nothing, say nothing; there was nothing that he could really say. Let them make their case; he would not help or hinder them. He would bear it as though it was not he himself who was undergoing it. The car moved off into the night, heading downtown, and he lay back, his heart locked against the world. I'll see what they can make out of me, he said to himself.

BOOK FIVE

DECISION

. . . Man is the only being who makes promises.
—FRIEDRICH NIETZSCHE

CROSS FOUND HIMSELF in the uniquely ironic position of comprehending far more keenly than his captors the nature and meaning of the situation confronting him. Even while the car in which he sat huddled between the two detectives bore him toward the office of the District Attorney, he could anticipate the general methods and approach of the police. They had first to prove who he was. Well, let them; that was their business, not his . . . He wondered how much of his path of blood and deception had they uncovered; but his wonderment was devoid of any desire to erect a strategy of legal defense for himself. That did not concern him at all; his preoccupations were more basic and recondite.

He knew that he had cynically scorned, wantonly violated every commitment that civilized men owe, in terms of common honesty and sacred honor, to those with whom they live. That, in essence, was his crime. The rest of his brutal and bloody thrashings about were the mere offshoots of that one central, cardinal fact. And for the crime of his contemptuous repudiation of all the fundamental promises that men live by he intended to make no legal defense for the good and ample reason that he well knew that no such defense was possible. And he was staunchly resolved to face his would-be judgers with a tight mouth from which not one word to help clarify his emotions or motives would issue. He would compel them, by a challenging silence, to identify his attitude.

And Houston . . . ? Was he still juggling ideas or had he found the courage to put two and two together? Houston, of all the officers of the law, could put the "finger" on him; could brand him guilty in a psychological sense. But had he dug up enough proof to make a legal charge stick? And would Houston dare explain his conception of this guilt to his colleagues? Would not a man in so responsible a position run the risk of losing public confidence by merely putting such notions into words . . . ? Cross barely suppressed a smile as he glanced furtively at the stolid faces of the two detectives who sat to either side of him.

The moment he entered the police car he knew that his search was over. There were to be no more of those torrid promptings of his heart to make him confess his horrible deeds and then wrestle and sweat to restrain his urge to kill the recipient of his confession. The burden of what was to be proved would fall upon those who had brought him to heel. His crimes had carried a stamp of the absolute and if they wanted to nail him down, their actions and attitudes would have to carry a stamp of the absolute against him. Let them haul up all of his bloody doings and turn them this way and that and see what conclusions they could come to . . .

There were two immediate dangers threatening him. The District Attorney could, if he were so minded, remand him for psychological observation at Bellevue; all right, he was confident of being declared sane. The other danger was more indirect, more difficult. Suppose the police had unraveled all that he had done and suppose the general public felt so revolted that they would want to drag him into some dirty alley and take his life and be done with it. He understood that reaction and feared it; it was the same cold fury he had felt against Herndon and Gil and Hilton . . . Should such now fall to him, he would be watching his own compulsions in reverse! If he could avoid those two pitfalls, he was prepared, willing even, to undergo whatever inquisitions they could serve up.

At some point in his past life, while living the normal ritual of days allotted to us all, he had come to a consciousness of having somehow fallen into a vast web of pledges and promises which he had not intended to make and whose implied obligations had been slowly smothering his spirit; and, by a stroke of freakish good luck, he had been able to rip the viscous strands of that web and fling them behind him. As always he was honest with himself; he knew, of course, that his commitments had been no more galling or burdensome than those which other millions of men and women about him shouldered so uncomplainingly every day; yet he knew that deep in the hearts of many of those millions was the same desire—shamefaced, inarticulate, and impotent—to have done with them as he had. It was not because he was a Negro that he had found his obligations intolerable; it was because there resided in his heart a sharp sense of freedom that had somehow escaped being dulled by intimidating conditions. Cross had never really been tamed . . .

He felt that at the time of his making his promises,—it had started in his childhood, before he had even been able to talk!—that his true and free consent had not been asked or given and that he had not been in a condition to understand the far-reaching nature of what he had been asked to pledge.

What was the question with which he, in his silence, would confront them? It was this: If he was to be loyal, to love, to show pity, mercy, forgiveness; if he was to abstain from cruelty, to be mindful of the rights of others, to live and let live, to believe in such resounding words as glory, culture, civilization, and progress, then let them demonstrate how it was to be done so that the carrying out of these duties and the practicing of these virtues in the modern world would not reduce a healthy, hungry man to a creature of nervous dread and paint that man's look of the world in the black hues of meaninglessness.

To be sure, accident had made possible his decision to dishonor those unwritten vows that he had been circumstantially made to promise, but his eagerness in embracing the opportunities presented by that subway accident had robbed that accident of its element of contingency, and the rest had flowed naturally and inevitably.

The assumptive promises he had welched on were not materially anchored, yet they were indubitably the things of this world, comprising as they did the veritable axis of daily existence. He, like Gil and Hilton, but for radically divergent reasons, had not been concerned with the buying and selling of corn, bonds, machinery, paper, or steel. It had been the naked, irreducible facts of sentient life itself that he had tried to grapple with in his snapping asunder the ties that bound him. It was the restrictions of marriage, the duties to children, obligations to friends, to sweethearts, and blood kin that he had struck at so blindly and—gallantly? For Cross had had no party, no myths, no tradition, no race, no soil, no culture, and no ideas—except perhaps the idea that ideas in themselves were, at best, dubious!

What made him wonder so anxiously about how much they knew of his past was that he was desirous of being put at once in the center of what was about to happen to him. He detested surprises. To be confronted continuously with the unforeseen when his movements were restricted would deprive his attitude of coherence and balance, and it was an evenness of deportment that he wanted to cling to now above all. For Cross was proud and was proud of his pride and knew it.

And Eva—? His memory of her made a dart of wincing pain go through him. He had at last found a recollection which he could not reduce to some impulse projected out of his hungry heart, for Eva's loneliness as expressed in her life and in her painting had become identified with the deepest regions of his being. He could have shared so much with her; they could have walked together through life; he could have been an anchor to her and she to him. But all chance of that was now gone . . .

The police car pulled to a stop and Cross looked curiously at the entrance of a huge building.

"Is this the District Attorney's office?" he asked.

"Yep," Hornsby said.

The detectives guided Cross out and escorted him through a wide door, across a deserted, spacious lobby, and stood to either side of him as they were lifted up in an elevator to the tenth floor. He was marched down a white-tiled corridor and into the anteroom of an ornately furnished office in which two uniformed policemen stood guard. Hornsby pushed open a door and Cross was ushered into the presence of Houston who, flanked by two other men, sat behind a large desk staring solemnly at him.

"Here's your man, sir," Hornsby said, saluting, turning, and leaving with the other officer.

Cross stared at the three men wordlessly. He was not going to say anything. Theirs was the burden. Houston, leaning back in a swivel chair, both watchful and relaxed, stroked his chin. Cross knew that he was in the presence of men sworn to punish those who did not obey the mandates formulated to protect lives and property, and toward them he felt no bitterness, no hate; he did not regard them as his enemies. He understood the origin of their power and authority and the scope of their duties, and he did not look upon his being hauled here as an act of injustice. Had the situation been different, he would not have hesitated to have sat down and talked with them, tried to show them that really his so-called crime was derived basically from the fact that he saw and felt the world differently than they did; he would have even tried, had he had the chance, to make them see and feel it as he did. But he knew that was useless now; it was too late . . . But he would not help or hinder them; theirs was the power, theirs the initiative.

Houston finally pulled himself erect and came from behind his desk on those softly padded feet of his, his body moving slowly and stiffly, his hump seemingly more prominent than Cross could ever remember having seen it. Houston's face was tensely concentrated, his eyes deeply absorbed with inner considerations. His long, dangling arms and his pointed, strong fingers swung grotesquely at his sides. He turned and studied a pile of papers on his desk for a moment, then whirled to Cross and said:

"I hardly know where to begin with you. I wish to God I hadn't met you on that train, or hadn't talked to you. It would make my task easier . . ."

"I'm sorry if I'm embarrassing you, Mr. Houston," Cross smiled as he spoke.

Houston stared, then glanced at his two aides and again at Cross.

"Do you know what this is all about?" Houston asked; he acted as though he was puzzled as to what line to take.

"I know nothing whatsoever," Cross replied affably.

"I'd been looking forward to having dinner with you, then these reports began to flood in here," Houston sighed.

The other two men, both standing, were youngish. One, the younger, was lawyerish in appearance. The other was tall, grey at the temples, and had the air of being a high-ranking police official, though he was dressed in plain clothes.

"Is there anything you want to say before we begin questioning you, Lane or Damon or what the hell your name is?"

So they had found out who he was! Well, good . . . But what else did they know?

"I have nothing whatever to say," Cross answered.

"Do you acknowledge the name of Cross Damon to be your real, your own, your true name?" Houston asked.

"I acknowledge nothing," Cross replied.

The three men looked at one another.

"Listen, you're intelligent enough, of course, to realize that I cannot force you to answer my questions. You also know that you have the right to counsel. You know too that what you tell me I can use against you in court. I can't force you to incriminate yourself. But whatever it is you're hiding, it would be better if you told me; it would be easier for you in the long run."

Cross smiled. He would at once set Houston straight about that.

"You may question me, sir," he said, hoping that Houston would question him, for that was the only way in which he could tell how much Houston knew, "but I reserve the right to answer what questions of yours I please. I might as well tell you that I'm not concerned with incriminating myself. I'm a perfectly free agent and if I elect to remain silent to some of your questions, it is for reasons of my own."

"Right," Houston said, staring thoughtfully at Cross. He then went back to his desk and sat. "Sit down."

"I prefer standing for awhile, if you don't mind," Cross said; he felt better on his feet to face what was coming. He was alert, tense, but free of all dread and compulsions. He was focussed to a point of supreme self-defense.

"If you like," Houston muttered. "Now, let's start at the beginning. You worked until about a month and a half ago as a clerk in the Post Office in Chicago, did you not?"

"I don't affirm it or deny it," Cross said.

"But, Damon, we've *proof* of who you are," Houston said.

"We got your fingerprints out of Mrs. Blount's apartment and the FBI has at last identified you."

Cross did not answer; his facial expression did not change.

"Do you now persist in denying your identity?"

"I affirm or deny nothing," Cross repeated.

Houston frowned, then he turned to the elder of his two aides. "Bring in that secretary of the Postal Union, Neil," Houston ordered.

"Right, sir," Neil answered, going to a door and beckoning.

Finch, with whom Cross had negotiated his eight-hundred-dollar loan, walked slowly into the room. He stopped and stared at Cross; Cross returned Finch's gaze with level eyes.

"Is this man known to you as Cross Damon?" Houston asked.

"Yes, sir. That's him, all right. I'd know him in a million," Finch said eagerly. "Hello, Damon."

Cross kept his eyes steadily on Finch's face and did not answer.

"Are you in trouble, boy?" Finch asked cordially.

Cross was silent, but his lips twitched in a slight smile.

"You'd swear to this identification in court?" Houston asked.

"Of course, I would," Finch said.

"Well, that's all, Mr. Finch. Thanks for your cooperation."

"Not at all. Are you through with me, sir?" Finch asked.

"Yes; for the time being."

Finch started out, turning and straining his neck, his baffled eyes remaining on Cross's face until he collided with the edge of the opened door. Neil had to grab Finch's arm to keep him from falling. Cross's face broke into a wide grin; he watched Finch vanish down the hallway, holding his hand to his forehead where he had bumped it against the door.

"Are you crazy?" Houston's voice came to him.

"I'm sorry, sir," Cross said.

"What are you laughing at?"

"Finch was so amazed that he did not see the door," Cross explained soberly.

"You may be the damned world's fool. I'm through with you," Houston snapped. "You are presumed to be dead, you know that?"

"I know nothing," Cross said.

"You were in a subway accident. Do you acknowledge that?"

"I acknowledge nothing, sir."

"Good God, man!" Houston exploded. "Maybe you're an amnesia victim. Do you recall being injured in the subway accident?"

"I've nothing to say."

"You say you *don't* remember?"

"I say *nothing*, sir."

"If you say you don't remember, it simplifies things—"

"I say nothing," he repeated.

He doubted now if Houston knew of the hotel in which he had met Jenny and had killed Joe Thomas. So far nothing of a damaging nature had come to light. Some of his past was known. So what?

"We'll see about that," Houston said; he was plainly annoyed. "It's just possible you're telling the truth. You may have been injured and don't recall anything . . ."

Cross knew that Houston was now toying with the idea that he *was* perhaps an amnesia victim; but no one knew for sure that he had been in the subway accident and he loathed anybody's thinking that his conduct had been influenced by any injury.

"May I state quite clearly and plainly, Mr. Houston, that I've never at any time in my life sustained any injuries of whatever nature that would cause me any lapse of memory," Cross said.

Houston was momentarily rattled and his mouth gaped: the two men behind him blinked their eyes. Yeah; they'd been planning to bait me with that amnesia approach, he told himself.

"What is this, a game?" Houston demanded.

"That depends upon your interpretation, sir."

"What are you hiding, Damon?"

"I affirm or deny nothing."

"You know of that accident," Houston spoke in a puzzled tone of voice. "You admitted it by implication. But you don't want to take advantage of that accident to justify anything you've done." Houston had spoken in a tone of voice that showed that he was thinking out loud, trying to find a way to get at Cross. He rose and walked close to Cross and stared into his face and said in a low, charged voice: "Damon, I've some very bad news for you."

"Yes," Cross said, holding tense and ready for surprises.

"Damon, your mother died in Chicago yesterday. She was astonished that you were still alive. It is believed that she died of shock, the shock of what you had done to her . . ."

He held still. Was this true? Or was Houston lying, trying to break him down? He was aware that Houston was watching every flicker of his eyelids. His mother was over sixty; she had been in frail health for a long time, and he was inclined to believe that what Houston had said was true . . . And the shock of what he had done had killed her? A churning wave went through his stomach, but he steeled himself against emotion. Well, he had already grieved over her once, and so it made no real difference now. A slow sigh went from him. He saw again his mother as he had seen her that last time, walking with faltering steps over the snow in front of the church, going to get into the car that was to bear his supposed body to the cemetery for burial . . . How bent and frail she had looked! How lost, uncomprehending, and weak . . . But not a facial muscle moved as he gazed into the eyes of Houston. Houston turned and walked slowly back to his desk, glancing at his aides as he did so. He sat and resumed his watching of Cross's face. He's waiting for the news to sink in, Cross thought. He felt that he ought to be sorry, but he could not summon the necessary degree of emotion. Had she suffered much? Then the truth of it dawned upon him; his mother had been dead for him for years, and that was why he had been able to reflect upon her so coldly and analytically while she had still been living . . . To him his mother's reality was that she had taught him to feel what he was now feeling. He was at this moment living out the sense of life that she had conferred upon him, a sense of life which, in the end, he had accepted as his own. It had been her moral strictures that had made him a criminal in a deeper sense than Houston's ques-tions so far would claim.

"Did you hear what I said, Damon?" Houston asked softly.

"Certainly."

"And what's your reaction?"

"Nothing."

"You're not even curious as to how she died?"

Cross struggled with himself; yes, Houston was using the tactics of Gil and Hilton. Houston was attempting to bring him repentantly to his knees, trying to rule him through the deep conditioning that all men felt in common for their parents.

"No," he said, the words coming softly from his lips.

Houston shook his head in disbelief.

"Damon, do you deny meeting me in the dining car of a train on the 8th of February last?"

"I affirm or deny nothing."

"Do you belong to any organizations whatsoever?"

"I belong to nothing."

"Do you subscribe to any political philosophy?"

"I subscribe to nothing."

"Are you working for any foreign government?"

"No."

"Have you ever made any public speeches?"

"No."

"Did you ever write under your own or an assumed name in any periodical or newspaper?"

"No."

"Have you ever been in jail?"

"I've nothing to say."

"Did you ever commit a felony?"

"I admit nothing."

Houston leaped to his feet and walked with long strides toward Cross.

"Damon, did you kill Gilbert Blount?" Houston thundered.

"I've nothing to say."

"Did you kill Langley Herndon?"

"I affirm or deny nothing."

"Did you kill Jack Hilton?"

"I affirm or deny nothing."

Houston had reached the important questions, but he had not mentioned Joe Thomas yet. Did that mean that he did not have to worry about Joe? Surely, Houston would have thrown it at him if he had known . . . He was not absolutely certain about Joe Thomas, but he was reasonably sure . . . What could have happened there? Perhaps the Chicago police had marked it "Unsolved"? Now, what evidence did they have against him in relation to Gil and Herndon and Hilton . . . ? Houston's eyes were wide and intent as they stared at his face, but Cross knew that those eyes were reflecting processes of thought far removed from the questions that Houston had asked so far.

"Do you hate Communism, Damon?" Houston asked softly, suddenly.

Now, Houston had gotten to the point. This is where I must be careful . . . Houston had now entered territory known well to both of them.

"What a strange question to ask me," Cross stalled.

"I'm asking you do you hate Communism?" Houston insisted.

"How can one *hate* Communism?" he asked, smiling.

"Then you love Communism?"

"No."

"Are you a member of any so-called revolutionary party?"

"No."

"Were you *ever* a member of the Communist Party?"

"No. And I've never been a Fascist either."

"I know that—"

"How *could* you know that?" Cross asked.

Houston blinked, pulled down the corners of his mouth. "You're a Negro—"

"Negroes can be Fascists too," Cross told him.

"Are you a Fascist then?"

"No."

"The Fascist angle is not important; they wouldn't take you in anyhow," Houston said with a tinge of satisfaction.

"Fundamentally, Fascism has nothing to do with race," Cross told him.

"Are you bragging about that?"

"I'm stating facts to you, sir."

"Do you believe in Communism?"

"How can one believe in Communism?" Cross countered again.

He saw that Houston resented his question; he knew that Houston was seeking for a motive for the deaths of Gil and Hilton, and Houston knew that he knew it.

"Isn't Communism something that one believes in?" Houston asked.

Cross drew a deep breath. Ought he wade out into this? Why not? If he did, he would isolate himself so sharply in a psychological sense that Houston would be bound to get a faint clue, but a psychological clue only. And there was a vast distance between psychological clues and concrete proof.

"It's true that there are some people who do believe in the ideology of Communism," Cross explained. "But real Communist leaders do not believe in its ideology as an article of faith. Such an ideology is simply in their hands and minds an instrument for organizing people. A real Communist would have a certain degree of contempt for you if you passionately believed in his ideology. He would accept you as a follower, but not as an equal. The real heart of Communism, Mr. Houston, is the will to power. And you know that, sir, as well as I do."

"Would you use such an instrument in organizing people?"

"I wouldn't touch such an instrument with a ten-foot pole," Cross said earnestly.

"Why?"

"I think such an instrument is an insult to human life and intelligence," Cross said.

"Well, what kind of instrument would you use in organizing people?"

"I don't know, sir."

"But you agree that people ought to be organized?"

"Certainly, sir."

"Why?"

"Human life on this earth must proceed on some rational basis, sir."

"Then, what organizational instrument would you advocate?"

"None. I've not discovered any to my liking, sir."

"And still you feel that human society needs organization? That it stands in urgent need of such, in your opinion?"

"Yes; of course. It's self-evident."

"You feel that the inability of men to form stable governments in the nations of the world proves that, don't you?"

"It's self-evident, sir."

"You know that if America pulled its support from Europe, Europe would collapse?"

"Yes."

"Are you willing to see that support pulled out?"

"No."

"You agree with that support?"

"No."

"You think it's bad?"

"Yes; it is very bad."

"But you do not advocate its being pulled out?"

"No."

"Why?"

"It's better than nothing, sir."

"But it's bad?"

"Yes."

"Why?"

"It doesn't answer their needs, sir. It's a stopgap."

"Would Communism answer their needs?"

"No. Of course not."

"What, then, would answer their needs, in your opinion?"

"Really, Mr. Houston— You are aware as well as I am of the complex nature of human needs, especially the needs of modern man . . . We've been over this ground once. Maybe there's no answer to their needs—"

"Do you support the Red Chinese?"

"I don't support 'em or fight 'em; they're just Red Chinese, sir. It's the way they've organized themselves."

"Don't you think they could have organized themselves our way?"

"Why should they?"

"I'm asking you do you think they ought to have done it our way?"

"I could not say yes to that unless, first, I felt that ours was the system that they should have, sir. Second, I'm the kind of man who simply cannot feel that kind of godlike imperiousness to impose my will on others."

"But you feel that all of this unrest on earth today is because man is seeking for an organization of his social life?"

"He urgently needs one," Cross said stoutly. "I'm guilty of
thinking and believing that, sir."

Houston blinked, sighed. His eyes roved restlessly about
the room.

"Yes, you told me that on the train when I first met you.
But I'm not accusing you of any such—"

"I know it, sir," Cross said jovially. "I was just making a
little confession to you."

"It's no crime under our laws to believe that something or
other ought to be done in society—"

"I beg your pardon, sir. In my opinion, it is right *there*
where the real crime is," Cross maintained. "A man today
who believes that he cannot live by the articles of faith of his
society is a criminal and you know it, even though Congress
has not gotten around to making such into law. You know
that as well as I do, sir. We've talked about that."

Houston threw up his hands. Cross was amused. Houston
was looking right at his guilt, and would not admit it. Houston stared at him with wide, startled eyes, then, glancing
guiltily at his aides, sat again at his desk, poring over his stack
of papers. Cross wanted to laugh. What did papers have to do
with this? Houston looked at Neil, nodded to him, and Neil
hurriedly left the room. He's executing something previously
agreed upon, Cross said to himself. He waited. Houston
looked up suddenly.

"Damon, suppose you come upon a man attempting to
organize human society in a way that was supremely offensive
to you, what would you do?" Houston asked in a slow, loud
tone.

He was asking indirectly if he had killed Gil and Herndon
and Hilton.

"I decline to say."

"You don't like Communists, do you?"

"No."

"Which do you hate more? Communists or Fascists?"

"Well, I'm afraid I hate the Fascists more, sir."

"Why?"

"Well, they've more real support. Of course, this is a debatable question. Maybe I feel like that because I'm a Negro and Fascists are dead against us."

"If you saw an opportunity to send two of them to their graves in one blow, would you do it?"

Cross looked at Houston and laughed.

"Would *you*?" he countered.

"Will you answer the question?" Houston demanded.

"I decline to answer, sir," Cross said.

"Why?"

"Because you know the answer."

"You would kill them, wouldn't you?"

"I decline to answer."

"Goddammit, I'll break your spirit yet!" Houston raged.

The next face that showed in the doorway made Cross feel that he should have been sitting down, because, for a moment, he felt like falling. It was Gladys. She was smartly dressed. Her face was pale with apprehension and her movements stiff with shock. She was clutching a pocketbook and staring at Cross. Houston looked quickly from Gladys to Cross. Gladys reached out a trembling hand and caught hold of the edge of the desk for support. Cross was furious; he gritted his teeth. What point was there in Houston's dragging Gladys into this? Yes; Houston, too, liked to play at being a little god, liked to ravage the souls of others. That was why he was District Attorney . . . And Cross vowed that Houston would never see him humbled, unnerved, or weeping. Houston had thought that the sight of Gladys would make him break down and talk. Well, he would not react. He would show Houston that he had miscalculated. Then Cross sucked in his breath sharply; from the open door behind Gladys, being led by Neil, came his three sons, Cross, Jr., Robert, and Peter. He whirled to Houston and saw an expression of sensual excitement upon the hunchback's lean face. That sonofabitch . . . Cross, Jr., his eyes wide and his lips parted, stared at his father, then clutched his mother's hand, whimpering:

"Mummy, is he *Daddy* for real?"

Cross felt the muscles in his calves aching. Robert and Peter stood close to Gladys, staring; they, too, began weeping, the flow of their tears being caused more by fear and uneasiness than any understanding.

"Why did Daddy come back, Mummy?" Peter asked.

"It's *not* Daddy," Robert said emphatically, indignantly, still crying.

Keep still, Cross told himself. His body was rigid. He had often imagined many kinds of confrontations, but he had never dreamed of this. To let his sons see him standing mute, stony . . . ! He could *kill* Houston! His anger was so hot that he could not permit himself to look into Houston's face.

Gladys, blinded by tears, her mouth distorted with silent weeping, groped for her children and huddled them clumsily about her, trying to keep her face averted. Cross returned the stares of everyone in the room without allowing his face to betray any expression whatever. Then he could hold it in no longer.

"Why are you doing this?" the words broke from him in a spasm of rage.

"At last I got a rise out of you, hunh?" Houston asked, wetting his lips with his tongue, reveling in deep satisfaction. "I had your wife and children flown here this morning from Chicago . . ."

Cross could tell that Houston was trying to justify his actions.

"I didn't want to make any mistake about identifying you, Damon," Houston said.

But Cross was not be be fooled; he knew that Houston loved this, just as he too sometimes loved lording it over others. But that look of sensual triumph on Houston's face had already sent Cross scuttling back to his shell of iron reserve, to his stance of defense. All right, suppose they were his sons? He had given them up, hadn't he? He would make a supreme effort and remain cold, hard. Sentiment must not subvert him now. He was lost, that much was true; but he must not let human claims drag him into a position where Houston could crow over him . . . Nothing could so undo him so easily now as Houston's gloating or bragging. Those frightened, little brown-faced boys were his sons, flesh of his flesh; they were the future of himself and he had rejected that self.

"Damon, I realize that you and your wife did not get along

together," Houston said. "She told me that. But, man, here are your children . . . They need you. Go to them."

Cross made his face a mask.

"Damon, can you stand there and look at the bewildered faces of those children and say nothing?" Houston demanded.

Cross shut out the sight of the world and tried not to hear.

"You can redeem yourself with them, Damon," Houston was saying. "Are you going to let them remember you all of their lives like *this*? Boys love to think of their fathers as strong, wise men," Houston went implacably on. "To many a son the image of his father is what lifts him up in life. A father can make a boy feel that he has a sure foundation under him, can give him confidence . . ."

Cross summoned all his control and pushed Houston's words away; he would not react; he would not be human; he was shunt of these claims and he would die shunt of them . . .

Houston turned and looked at Gladys whose face was hidden by her crumpled handkerchief; the woman's body seemed so rigid that if one touched her ever so lightly she would fall prone.

"Mrs. Damon," Houston began in a loud, clear voice, "do you recognize this man standing there?" Houston pointed at Cross.

Gladys slowly turned her face and stared at Cross with wet, red eyes. Then she quickly bowed her head; both of her hands convulsively covered her face in one shuddering motion and her chest heaved as she wept in dry gulps. Houston gently grasped her shoulder and led her to a chair.

"I'm asking you: Do you recognize this man as your husband, Mrs. Damon?" Houston demanded.

Gladys was still, then she shook her head with a slow, dreamy movement, shook it negatively and at once Cross knew that Gladys was not shaking her head in answer to Houston's question, but was asserting her right to reject him as he had once rejected her! Gladys was protesting his presence on earth. Houston's face showed astonishment; he did not understand what was transpiring in the woman. He had thought that a storm of words would have poured out of

Gladys, and that he, Cross, would have been moved to pity. Cross knew that Gladys would rather have had him dead.

"Mrs. Damon, I *asked* you if that is your *husband*?"

Her cheeks wet with tears as far down as her chin, Gladys finally nodded her head affirmatively. Houston blinked in bewilderment.

"Now, *which* answer is it, Mrs. Damon," Houston demanded. "Is he your *husband*, or is he *not*?"

Cross burst into a gale of laughter that made the bodies of everyone in the room jerk. Houston gaped at Cross, then his face settled into a mold of anger. Cross knew that there was a conflict in Gladys. Her first reaction had been to say that she did not know him; then she had wanted to be honest with the District Attorney and had said yes. And now she was more confused than ever and she shook her head again, negatively. It was an identity deeper than that which Houston was asking for that Gladys was denying.

"Mrs. Damon, again I ask you, is this your husband, Cross Damon?"

Gladys rose, turned her back on Cross, nodded affirmatively to Houston and murmured brokenly: "Yes; it's he—"

She ran to the door, turned, snatched wildly at her children, grabbing them by their clothes and pulling them into the other room.

"But, Mrs. Damon, you—" Houston was trying to speak.

"No, no, no!" Gladys screamed and wept and the little boys joined her in crying, crying because they saw their mother unnerved and bitterly hysterical.

"Help her, Neil," Houston said; comprehension was now in his eyes.

The two men assisted Gladys into the next room and finally the door closed. Cross still stood, his face impassive.

"You are the lowest sonofabitch I've ever seen in all of my life," Houston said savagely.

"I return the compliment," Cross said. "What on earth did you gain by dragging her in here?"

Houston did not answer and Cross knew that he could not. Houston ran his spread fingers through his hair and sat again behind his desk, glaring at Cross.

"Damon, I'll get to the point. The Communists have been badgering me night and day to take action against you. They are charging that you killed Blount, Hilton, and Herndon," Houston told him.

"And what are *you* charging me with?" Cross asked.

Houston did not reply.

"How can you charge me merely on the insistence of Communists who are suspicious and frightened of me?" Cross demanded.

"*Why* are they frightened of you?"

"Ask them."

"Are you a member of any anti-Communist group?"

"I'm not a member of *anything*, Mr. Houston."

"Are you anti-Communist even as an individual?"

"I'll tell you as I told them: I'm not anti anything."

"But you don't support them, do you?"

"Hell, no. And millions of other men don't either—"

"But you are like them in your reactions. That much I know," Houston said. "And the motive is right here."

"You think so?"

"The strongest motive on earth—"

"There are millions of men with the same motives—"

"I've no evidence against you, Damon, or Lane; if I had, I'd tell you so. I'm straight in this office. But I had a right to find out who you are," Houston explained in a tired voice. "There's another motive you could have had—"

"Yes?"

"You wanted Mrs. Blount. Men have killed for women before—"

"Mr. Houston, I don't believe that you really believe that," Cross told him. "Before Gil died, I never touched his wife, never so much as looked at her with desire in my eyes. Now, for the rest of this mess, you will have to prove your case against me."

"You started living with Mrs. Blount right off, before her husband was even buried," Houston charged.

"What law did I violate in doing that?" Cross countered. "And don't forget that I was living in the apartment when he died."

"You took her to Harlem—"

"That was to get her away from the press."

Cross was now convinced that Houston had no evidence; he had thought that Cross would have collapsed at the sight of Gladys and his sons and would have made some fatal mistake, some slip that would have helped him to build his case.

"The Communist case against you is as follows," Houston told him. "They claim that you went downstairs that night to see if Blount was all right. You saw him wounded. You finished him off. Then Herndon came upon you and you had to kill him. Hilton found out about it in some way, and you had to kill him to keep him silent."

"I've no comment to make on that."

Houston stood again and Neil and the other assistant reentered the room.

"I was thinking of remanding you for a psychiatric examination," Houston said.

"What purpose would that serve?" asked the youngish man who had stood silent through all of this.

"Sending me for psychiatric observation would be as good an excuse as any to hold me on," Cross told him placidly.

Houston sat down heavily in his chair.

"Hell, *no!*" He turned and stared exasperatedly at the youngish man who had spoken. "I'm not going to play games with this man. I've run this office straight so far, and I'll continue. If the police and the Medical Examiner cannot dig up enough evidence, I'll be damned if I'll hold him 'til they cook up something."

Cross realized that the youngish man was no doubt a psychiatrist.

"No opinion that we could give you from the hospital would be of any legal use in relation to what I've heard so far. The man seems to be orientated and is defending himself," the young man said.

Houston stood and smiled shyly at Cross.

"That's all for tonight, Lane," he said.

"You mean you are through with me for the time being?" Cross asked.

"For the time being, yes. You may go."

Neil held open the door for him and Cross slowly walked

toward it; then he paused, his mind filled with an impish notion. He turned to Houston.

"The best way to get a victim is to find an innocent man," he told the District Attorney. "An *absolutely* innocent man. Such a man is *free* to be charged with anything. An innocent man is overwhelmed when he is falsely accused and he is at a loss for words. He doesn't know how to defend himself," Cross went on, teasing the District Attorney. "You don't really need much evidence at all to charge an innocent man. The bigger the charge, the more likely people are to think that that man *must* have done something, or else no one would have charged him. The way to make a man guilty is to attack him without cause, without reason. The logic there is: if he was not guilty, no one would have dared to charge him. I was innocent to the extent that I didn't have a good name that would stand up under investigation. I had a secret name and you found it, ergo, I'm guilty of something. Good night, sir."

He walked down the corridor to the elevator and dropped to the street, thinking, I've got to see Eva . . . He grabbed a taxi and shot uptown. He knew that Houston was not through with him yet. But I *dare* him to admit what he knows . . . He already knows, but of what use is his knowledge . . . ? But the Party . . . ? That was another thing. They did not have to be certain to brand you guilty. If they could not *understand* you, then you were guilty! Yes; he'd have to take Eva away at once, take her out of New York. He'd ask her to come away tonight . . .

He paid the taxi and looked up at the windows of Sarah's apartment. Lights were blazing through the curtains. Were Menti and Hank up there? He grew hot with hate. He'd send them packing, those fools! He'd take Eva with him right now . . .

He bounded up the steps and pushed the bell of the door. Sarah opened it almost at once. Her face was tense with fear and curiosity.

"Did the police find you?"

"Yes. Where's Eva?"

"But what have you done, Lionel? What did they want?"

"Nothing. But where's Eva?"

"She's gone. With Menti and Blimin— But what are the cops after you for?"

"It's nothing— Where did Menti and Blimin take Eva?"

"I don't know. They just asked her to come with them. But are you in some kind of trouble?"

He sighed. Then whirled as the doorbell rang.

"Maybe that's Eva now," Sarah said, hurrying.

It was Eva. She came quickly and excitedly into the hallway. She was a little stooped, as though bent with dread; she stopped at the sight of Cross. Her face went white and her eyes held a wild, scared look. She knows something . . . The Party had told her; he could feel it. He ran toward her.

"God, Eva, what's the matter?"

She backed away from him, stumbling against a wall, her eyes transfixed with terror.

"Eva, let me tell you everything!" he cried.

She looked at him with an opened mouth and shook her head.

"Darling, listen. I've been wanting to tell you—"

"Your name's not Lionel . . . You're married, aren't you?"

"Yes," he sighed.

"Why didn't you tell me?" she demanded in helpless despair.

"I'll explain everything . . ."

"Oh, God, the Party's accusing you of *everything*— All night I've battled and fought and wept and screamed to save you— To protect you— And they say I'm wrong; they say you're guilty of something— Why didn't you tell me this . . . ? Where's your wife?"

"She's here in the city somewhere; but you and I are together—"

"Does she love you?"

How like a woman to think of those little things first!

"No."

"Do you love her?"

"No."

"You have three small sons—?"

"Yes."

"You deserted them?"

"Yes, Eva."

"And you know that your mother died yesterday?"

"Yes."

"Then you're really the man who ran off from Chicago, leaving his family—?"

"Yes."

"You don't love your family?"

"No."

His answers had come automatically; he was staring at the floor, waiting for her to question him further. Eva covered her eyes with her hands and leaned against the wall. She sighed in despair.

"What kind of a man are you?" she asked in a whisper.

He had confessed a part of it; now he had to tell her all. She had to believe in him, help him, understand him . . .

"Eva, come into the room," he begged her. "I must talk to you—"

"I feel dead," Eva whimpered. "*Why* did you fool me?" She choked and wept for a moment. "Nothing you ever told me was true . . . And Lionel's not your name! Oh, God!"

Sarah was staring from one to the other with an open mouth.

"What's happened?" she asked.

"His name's not Lionel Lane," Eva sobbed.

Sarah backed away from Cross as though he had become a leper.

"You mean you gave us *another* false name?" she demanded indignantly. "You gave Bob a false name the first time you met him . . ."

"I must talk to you, Eva," he said. "Come into the room. I love you. This *can't* break us up. It *mustn't*. I'll explain everything. You'll see."

Sarah stepped between him and Eva.

"What are you doing to her? Leave her alone— She's scared to death—"

"I've *got* to talk to her, Sarah. I'll explain everything to you later," he said, taking Sarah's arm and pushing her to one side.

He was clinging to a thread of hope. He knew that in spite of all, she still believed in him. But what was he to tell her? Her staunch confidence in him had helped her to weather the storm she had met at the Party headquarters, and now she had come meekly to him for confirmation of what she had fought for, and he could not give it to her. He took her gently by the arm and led her down the hallway and into their bedroom. He could feel the tension in her body as she moved, pulling jerkily but feebly against his hand. He wanted more than anything on earth to keep her, and yet he did not know how; he had no notion of what to say. He closed the bedroom door and turned to her.

"*What's* your name?" she asked him softly.

"Cross Damon," he answered, but he could not look her in the eye.

"*Why* didn't you tell me this before?"

"I was afraid to, and I was ashamed," he told her truthfully.

He glanced at her now and what he saw filled him with frenzy. There were other and bigger questions looming behind those clear, hazel eyes, and those questions condemned him more crushingly than anything that Houston could have said to him. He saw her lips move several times, but no words came from her. She turned from him and leaned against the wall, sobbing softly.

"I gave you my diary to read," she whimpered. "I thought you'd be honest with me . . . *You've* deceived me too!"

"I was frightened of telling you everything, of telling you the truth," he said. "I was afraid that you'd run off from me."

"Lionel—" She paused and cried afresh. "I don't even know what to call you now . . ." She went to the bed and sank upon it, staring in bleak dismay before her.

Yes, she wants to ask me about Gil . . . She wants to know . . . Oh, God! He went to his knees and clutched his arms about her legs. He would beg and plead for his life. He waited in agony for her to ask, and he felt that he could scarcely draw his breath into his lungs.

"Eva," he begged. "It's not too late. If you love me, it's never too late. Remember that. You told me you loved me, and I need you now. If you turn from me, the world collapses . . ."

"So— S-s-so it w-was *true* . . . What you told me that night? When you came in?"

He hung his head and could not answer.

"You were trying to tell me something— You were all mixed up and you spoke of killing men— Oh, God—! I thought you were delirious, ill. I thought you were talking out of your mind because of fever and worry . . ."

She had asked him directly at last! And he could not lift his eyes to look her in the face. He tightened his arms about her legs, afraid to let go of her.

"Eva, I love you; I love you," he mumbled frantically. "You must remember that. I'm crazed with fear and worry now. Don't leave me . . ."

"You *did* it, then? What the Party said?"

"What did they say?"

"They said you killed Gil to get me . . ."

He was tempted. Ought he tell her a lie and let her think that? Would it not touch her heart and make the look of the world seem less strange and hostile to her? Would it not make her love him the more? But would he not be locking himself up again behind the wall of himself if he lied to her again? What would lying solve now? Nothing . . . And what made it so hellishly difficult was that when he lifted his eyes he could see in her face that she was expecting to hear him say that he had killed Gil for her, to get her, out of his love for her.

"Nooooo," he breathed. "I killed Gil . . . But it was not for you—"

"Oh, God in Heaven! Why *did* you kill him, Lionel?"

"I don't know," he whispered.

"*Why?* There must be some *reason* . . ."

He shook his head; his body was trembling all over.

"You *must* know; you *say* you did it," she said.

Could he ever tell her? He had to try. He had to talk or he could not go on living. He had to try to get for once in his life from behind himself, to walk out of his house as she had once walked out of her house to meet him.

"Eva," he whispered hoarsely, still clutching her legs. "It goes way back . . . God, help me to explain . . . I *want* to explain . . ." He felt hot tears rolling down his cheeks. "You see, Eva, I don't *believe in anything* . . ." He spoke in a tone of voice that he knew sounded unreal, not convincing. But how could he make it sound otherwise? How did one *tell* these things?

"What had Gil done to you?" she asked in a whisper that carried an overtone of hope.

"Nothing," he sighed and felt that he would choke. "Oh, God, he did nothing to me . . . Eva, I'm praying to you to try to understand me . . . *Somebody* must understand me . . . I'll die if you don't understand . . . Look, when you can't believe in anything, when you're just here on this earth and there's nothing, *nothing* else . . . Oh, Christ, I can't explain it! You have to *feel* it! You have to *live* it! It has to be in your blood before it can become real to you . . . I feel like I'm talking to you from another world . . . Trying to talk to you through a glass wall . . . I know you can't understand . . . But, Eva, you must love me and trust me!" He shook his head in bewilderment. "If you understood, you'd suffer too like I did . . . Oh, no; you'll never understand this . . ." Despair was full in him. "I didn't ever want to tell you like this . . ." All of his hope had gone and he was talking to her out of a sense of futility.

"When did you kill him?"

"When I went down to see what had happened . . . They were fighting . . . God, I can't explain how I felt . . . When I looked at them, I suddenly hated them both . . . They'd done nothing to me . . . They weren't even paying any attention to me; they were fighting so hard that they didn't even know that I was in the room . . ." He knew that what he was saying did not sound convincing to her. And the knowledge of it maddened him; he stood and began shouting: "Don't you *understand*? You've been scared, haven't you? You know what it means to live senselessly? When every day is a foolish day? And when I stood in that room I saw more senselessness and foolishness right before my eyes and I felt a way to stop it! I hated what I saw! And I hated myself because all my life I was unable to do anything about it . . . I tell you, I *hated* it. It insulted me . . . I wanted to blot it out, wipe it from the face of the earth . . ." It seemed that he had forgotten that he was speaking to her; his hands and arms made gestures as he stood in the dim room before her and reenacted his crime. "I

took the table leg and battered Herndon down, killed him
. . . I did it; yes . . . I wasn't angry with him personally; not
then . . . I'd been angry with him before, but I felt no anger
then . . . I killed 'im because I didn't think he had a right to
live . . . Did you ever feel like that about anybody? No; you
couldn't feel that . . ." He paused and rubbed his eyes; then
he seemed to remember that he was telling her about what
had happened. "Then I hit Gil . . . He wasn't expecting it
. . . I was mad with them . . . No; not personally mad.
Don't you know what I mean . . . ? I can't say it right, goddammit, I *can't* . . . I wanted to live so badly; I wanted a
good life so terribly much that what I saw made me mad, *mad*
. . . And I killed them . . . Eva, *believe me* . . . It was that
that made me kill them . . ." He looked at her and there was
no light of comprehension in her eyes. "Oh, God, you don't
believe me . . . You *can't* believe me . . . But you *must*, Eva;
you *can*; you of all the people in the world can understand
. . . I *know* it . . ." His voice died away in a whisper. Then
he resumed, reciting his words as though he was reliving the
scene of the murder and blood again. "I kept hitting them
until they were dead . . . I wasn't sorry . . . I knew I was
right . . . Then I wiped off all the fingerprints . . . I didn't
want to be caught; I didn't want to be punished . . . Then I
came up to you . . . That's what I did, Eva. Now, can you
understand that?"

She was white as a sheet; she seemed not to breathe.

"And Hilton *too*?" she asked in a whisper.

"Yes," he sighed.

"Because he knew?"

"No; not exactly. No."

"Then *why*?"

"Mainly because of what he did to Bob . . . And because
of what he wanted to do to me," he said, speaking mechanically.

She was still as a block of ice. Her eyes stared unseeingly
into the shadows of the room. Then he saw her body jerk as
some idea came into her mind.

"That night when you were trying to tell me," she began in
a whisper. "You spoke of Chicago . . . She shook her head

helplessly, then bit her pale lips. "You said you killed some-body else . . ."

"Eva, Eva . . . Please, I need help . . . If ever a man needed your love, I need it . . . I've killed and killed . . . Have mercy on me . . . Pity me, but not for what has been done to me, but for what I've done to others and myself . . . You be my judge; you tell me if I'm to live now . . . Can you tell me . . . ?"

She was edging away from him; her eyes reflected horror.

"But I thought you were against brutality— I thought you were going to tell me what Gil had done to you— I thought you hated suffering—"

"I do!" he shouted. "That's why I did it! I couldn't stand the thought of it, the sight of it . . . !"

She did not believe him; she could not believe him. She was a reluctant victim and he was a willing one . . . He stared fully at her and reached out his hand to touch her. She leaped away from him, gasping, and scrambled to her feet.

"Eva," he pleaded.

She ran from him, to the door. He started after her, frantic, his bloodshot eyes glistening.

"Eva, please try to understand . . . It's hard . . . I know . . . But try, *try* . . . I can redeem myself . . . Let me be with you . . ." He was praying to her.

She gave a short scream and ran out of the room. He fol-lowed her out of the door. Sarah came rushing down the hall.

"What's the matter?"

"Sarah, Sarah, help me," Eva wailed.

"Lionel, leave her alone," Sarah yelled.

Eva clutched Sarah and clung to her, her body shaking.

"Lionel, what have you done to her?"

Then abruptly, Eva twisted around in the arms of Sarah and looked at Cross and while she was looking he saw the light go out of her eyes. She seemed stricken, not knowing where she was; she pulled away from Sarah and ran on down the hall until she came to the door of the living room. She paused, looked wildly about her, then ran into the living room and slammed the door. He rushed to the door and heard the lock click.

"Eva, for God's sake, listen . . ."

"What did you do to her?" Sarah wailed.

"Leave me alone, will you!" he told her savagely.

"But, Lionel, you're driving her crazy . . ."

The front doorbell pealed and Cross stood wondering who it was. The hell with whoever was coming . . . He pounded on the door of the living room with his fists as Sarah went down the hall to the front door.

"Eva, let me come in and talk to you," he begged her, but deep in him he felt that she never would.

Menti came through the front door; Sarah was holding the door open for him. Behind Menti was Hank, sullen, his hands thrust deep in his overcoat pockets. Menti paused, sensing that something was happening.

"What's the matter here?" he asked.

"Eva's locked herself inside and won't come out," Sarah said.

"What are *you* doing here?" Menti asked Cross.

"The hell with you," Cross snapped at him. "I've a right to be here."

"I thought the D.A. had grabbed you," Menti said.

"He did, but I'm free now," Cross told him. "Your Party's trick didn't work, Menti."

"Be careful of what you say about the Party—"

"Oh, God, don't fight in here," Sarah begged.

"Eva," Cross called through the door. "Open the door, honey!"

Cross felt his legs trembling. What could he do? If he could only talk to her, quiet her down, he might make her see what had happened to him.

"Eva!" he called again.

Cross turned and looked appealingly at Sarah.

"Don't you have a key to this door?"

"No," she said, shaking her head.

Cross put his ear to the panel of the door; he could hear no sounds. God, what could she be doing?

"Eva! Eva!" He took hold of the doorknob and rattled it furiously.

He was conscious that Menti was looking at him with a

sardonic smile. That sonofabitch . . . ! But maybe Menti could help make Eva open the door.

"Menti, call her. Tell her to open the door."

"Why? Leave her alone . . . What can I do if she runs away from you?" Menti said, chuckling.

"Damn you!" Cross growled. He saw Hank staring at him with tense hatred. "And you too!" Cross spat at him. He turned to the door again. "Eva!"

There came a loud, heavy pounding upon the front hall door. Sarah started toward it, then paused, looking at Cross. The pounding came again. Then a hoarse voice yelled:

"Say, open up in there!"

Sarah opened the door and backed away as a tall, black man rushed into the hallway, his eyes wide with excitement.

"Say, wasn't it from this apartment that a woman jumped from a window . . . ?" he asked, looking from one to the other of them.

Sarah, Hank, Menti, and Cross—all of them were silent, standing open-mouthed, staring at the black man's face. Cross, for a moment, could not think; his feelings froze; he was not even aware of his surroundings. Then a realization of what the man had said came to him in the form of a flashing image of Eva's frail body hurtling through the icy air of the night outside. The words clanged in his mind as though someone was shouting in his ears: Oh, God, it's Eva . . . ! For a split second the world was blotted out; then he was running and stumbling through the doorway, falling and sliding down the dark, winding flights of rickety stairs. He reached the street panting and aching from where he had knocked himself against the walls and bannisters on his way down. He leaped clear of the steps of the stoop and saw that a crowd of Negroes had already begun to gather in a knot near the edge of the sidewalk. He sprinted to them, plowing them aside. Yes . . . There was Eva . . . She was lying half on her stomach with her face to the pavement, her body twisted so that the toes of her shoes were pointing upwards and her face was hidden in the snow. Already blobs of blood had seeped from her head and Cross could see where someone had stepped on a loosened lock of her blonde hair, crunching and burying it in the dirty snow. *Eva!* The word rang so loud in his mind that he was not conscious of what went on about him. He had lost. She had fled from him forever; she had taken one swift look into the black depths of his heart, into the churning horror of his deeds and had been so revolted that she had chosen this way out, had slammed her door on life.

He knelt, turned her gently over, stared at the bruised and shattered face, the gaping, defenseless mouth, the flattened nostrils from which blood streaked and stained his trembling hands.

"Eva, Eva," he whimpered and cradled her head in his arms.

He looked up at the looming circle of dark faces for the first time, his eyes pleading for help.

"Get a doctor," he begged.

"Better get the police," someone said roughly.

"Did he *kill* her?"

"Maybe a car ran over her . . ."

"Naw; somebody pushed her out of a window—"

"I heard her hit the sidewalk; it was like a pistol shot!"

"Look, she's a *white* gal!"

"What *she* doing up here in Harlem?"

"Get some help, please," Cross pleaded. "Somebody— Somebody *do* something— She's hurt!"

An elderly Negro with white hair bent to him and whispered: "I sent in an alarm for the police."

"Did she jump outta a window?"

"It was from up there— One, two, three, four— Lord, she fell *six* floors— She's dead or she'll die—"

Cross held his breath and stared directly in front of him, holding Eva against his chest; he was afraid to look down at her broken face and her half-opened eyes . . . He knew that he had to look and a sigh went from him as he saw those hazel eyes now filmed and unseeing. She was limp in his arms and her body felt terribly light, as though her substance was dwindling as he held her. He bent closer and saw that under the waving, tumbling coils of her blonde hair the top of her skull had been bashed in bloodily. His lips trembled as he realized that it was hopeless. Gently, he eased her body back to the snow-packed pavement and felt for her pulse; she had none. He hardly knew what happened after that. He kept kneeling, staring at her, repeating softly:

"Eva, Eva . . ."

At last Menti was at his side, and there was the dark form of Hank looming menacingly in the background. Sarah, her eyes bulging, her fingers twisting nervously, stood whimpering. And then there came to his ears the distant sound of sirens, the sirens he had so long feared, sirens that rose to a hysterical scream on the winter air. They were not sounding for him, those sirens, but for the only woman he had ever loved. He was now locked in loneliness.

"Why did she do it?" Menti asked.

Cross glanced at him and did not answer. He saw that Menti's face was calm, composed, alert, devoid of grief or shock, his eyes glowing with the intense, detached curiosity of a man long schooled in disaster. To those hard, disciplined eyes the sight of Eva's crumpled body was a thing to be expected, was something that fitted inevitably into life's dark design.

"Did somebody push her out?" a man's voice asked.

"No, no," Sarah said. "She jumped. I was there . . ."

"*Why* did she do it, Lane?" Menti asked again, softly, insistently into Cross's ear.

Cross looked into Menti's eyes without making any sign that he had heard him. The sirens were wailing closer now; then he saw the police cars turn the corner with screeching brakes; there was a swish of tires on ice and snow as the cars skidded to a stop. Blue-coated officers leaped out and ran forward. Cross saw Menti rise, detach himself stealthily from the crowd, walk down the sidewalk and slink into a candy store. Yes, Menti was going to call the Party and report. Cross envied the strength and self-possession which Menti derived from his total submissiveness to the Party; it was the Mentis of this earth that made power possible, that made leadership possible; silent Menti was, enduring, uncomplaining, obscure, humble, dutiful . . . Without the Mentis of this world, men could not move in concerted action, whether they wished to move to left or right, toward slavery or freedom, toward war or peace . . . The millions of obedient Mentis were the foundation of human life, society, mankind . . . What was the meaning of Menti? What did he want? What could buy his loyalty? What did he need? One thing was certain, no government on earth today was really offering Menti what he really wanted . . . Maybe no government could . . . ? Cross sighed.

"My God," a young white cop said as he bent forward, "what's she doing in Harlem?"

Another cop felt for Eva's pulse.

"Call for an ambulance, *quick!*" he said.

"Now, what happened?" another cop demanded.

"She jumped from the window of my apartment," Sarah managed to say.

"*Who* are *you?*"

"Sarah Hunter. I live up there on the sixth floor— Where you see the lights in the window," Sarah explained in halting tones, pointing. "I don't know what made her do it . . . Her husband was killed two days ago . . . Maybe that's why— But she didn't seem worried or anything— It was sudden-like—"

"What's her name?"

"Mrs. Eva Blount."

"Where did she live?"

"At 13 Charles Street, but she was staying with me . . ."

"Hunh?" the cop grunted, looking at Cross, then at Menti who had come back. He turned and addressed a young cop. "You better get hold of the Medical Examiner's office . . ." The young cop rushed off to the police car.

Cross stood up. He could feel Menti's elbow touching him. The cops were now asking the names and addresses of those who had seen Eva fall, what time she had fallen, and who had seen her in the neighborhood before. Cross gave his name and address, so did Menti and Sarah.

"You three," the cop said, indicating Cross, Menti, and Sarah, "will have to come to the station with us."

Cross did not care; it was over for him. Eva was gone; she had slipped through his clutching, clumsy fingers . . . He had botched it and Eva's crushed and mute face told him that this was hell: this swooping sense of meaninglessness, this having done what could never be undone . . . He had in him to the full the feeling that had sent him on this long, bloody, twisting road: self-loathing . . .

"She's gone," he heard a cop say.

"Really?"

"Yep."

From the throat of the night another siren screamed. That must be the ambulance . . . Eva was dead and now in recollection he knew her for what she had meant to him; already he was feeling what he had been grasping for in his loving her. That capacity in him to suffer had seized upon this lovely, frail girl as the representation and appearance in life of what he felt had to be protected and defended. To that frightened heart he had made, out of his compulsive need for companionship, out of his hunger for solace, a promise that he had not been able to keep, that he had *known* he could not keep, and, as the intensity of his lying promise had swollen, so had her distance from him widened until at last she was forever beyond his reach. Self-love as well as self-hate had dogged him to the end and he had not been able to outwit the predetermined molds of his destiny. And his too-keen habit of self-reflection would not permit him to hide from himself what he had done. Between him and Eva a mutual selfishness had entwined itself, each feeding greedily on the other and on itself, and, in that reciprocally devouring passion his falsely pledged promise had been the single element that had broken the unity, smashing it beyond all mending, all recall, for eternity.

Two internes pushed past Cross. An ague seized him as he saw them lift Eva's limp body and place it upon a stretcher and march with it to the ambulance and shove it into the rear door. The motor roared; the ambulance started off and the siren rose to a screaming pitch . . . Eva . . . Eva . . . He was alone.

"All right, folks— Break it up, now— Move along— Get going—" the police were saying.

Cross, Sarah, and Menti were jammed into the back seat of a police car and driven to a nearby police station where they had to wait in a dirty anteroom for hours. It was the Party again that tried unwittingly to come to Cross's assistance, for Menti, bending to him and whispering, said:

"Tell 'em nothing. Just say she jumped, but nobody saw her, see? But nothing else. We don't talk to cops."

Cross and Sarah nodded. He saw a look of wonder in Sarah's eyes as she stared at him. Yes, Sarah was silently asking what it was that he had said to Eva that had made her so wildly hysterical, had made her lock herself in the room and jump . . . And Cross was aware that Menti now regarded him with mounting hatred; his eyes were harder than agate as they rested on Cross's face. I'm glad that Sarah was there when Eva jumped, he told himself. Menti would like to accuse me of pushing her out of the window . . . The Party would be more suspicious of him now than ever. The hour was approaching when he would have to flee New York and try his luckless fortune elsewhere; that is, if Houston did not first place a fatal finger upon him.

They were questioned in relays, and when Cross's turn came, he obeyed Menti's injunction to the extent that he told a simple story of a girl whose husband had just been killed; he said that grief, maybe, had made her jump out of the window. But he thought better of Menti's advice and felt that he ought to tell the impersonal captain who was questioning him that he had just been interviewed by the District Attorney, for they would most surely discover it after he had gone and they would come rushing to question him again, thinking that he had for some reason tried to conceal it.

Complications arose at once; the puzzled captain telephoned Houston and Cross was instructed to go back home and remain there until further notice, and he was informed that a police guard would be placed at the front and back doors of the apartment.

When he emerged from the police station, Sarah and Menti had gone. He walked back to the apartment alone, climbed the steps and found a cop on guard in the hallway.

"You live here?" the cop asked.

"Yeah."

"If you go in, you can't come out 'til the D.A. says so," the cop informed him.

"I know that," Cross said.

The cop let him pass. He let himself in and went straight to the room he had shared with Eva and stood staring at her comb and lipstick on the cluttered top of the dresser. A few strands of her blonde hair still clung curlingly to the bristles of the hairbrush. There was her purse, an ashtray of cigarette stubs whose tips showed the rouge she had worn, a delicately scented handkerchief, a crumpled wad of face tissue . . . His throat ached and he fell upon the bed, burying his face in the pillow and lay as still as death, longing for oblivion, for the world to close in on him and swallow him forever.

He started when the door opened. It was Menti; he had not bothered to knock. Resentment flooded Cross and he did not care to rise to receive him. Menti left the door ajar and came to the bed and sat upon it, a few inches from Cross. These sonofabitches! They presumed they owned him, that they could come upon him when they liked, that he had no inviolate, private world of his own into which they could not penetrate at will. He clenched his teeth and kept his eyes averted and waited for Menti to speak. Then he was forced to look at Menti, for Menti gave forth a series of low, contented chuckles.

"You *are* an important man," Menti said.

"What the hell are you talking about?" Cross demanded.

"The whole Central Committee is meeting just about you," Menti informed him. "You sure bring trouble. You've been in this city just a few days, but wherever you show your face, death's not far behind . . ." Menti rubbed his chin meditatively and continued: "Why did Eva jump?"

"You ought to be telling me," Cross hedged; he wanted to know what had been said when the Party questioned Eva. "She was terribly upset when she came in. She said she'd been to a Party meeting—"

"Did she tell *you* that?" Menti asked.

"Sure. Why not?"

"She was instructed *not* to."

"By whom?"

"The Party—"

"But why?"

"Well," Menti said, ignoring Cross's question, "she was

never really a Bolshevik, you know." Menti shook his head in wonder. "She was a self-centered bourgeois artist . . . Say, do you know that the Party estimates that only about thirteen percent of all artists and intellectuals ever make the grade with us?" Menti smiled, indicating that Eva was no great loss. He continued: "Eva broke a decision when she talked to you. But what did she say . . . ?"

Cross saw an opportunity to sow confusion in Menti's mind by interpreting Eva's words to his advantage.

"She was horrified," he said. "She said that the Party was trying to convince her that I'd killed Gil to get her— But she knew that that wasn't true. I'd never said a word to Eva until after Herndon had killed Gil— It was Eva who made the advances. She came to my room that very night—"

Menti was impressed; he nodded his head.

"Hilton told the Party that," he admitted. "I don't get this."

"I didn't kill Gil to get Eva," Cross went on. "Anybody who thinks that is crazy. You and your Party are looking for the wrong *motives*, Menti . . . I ought to be hopping mad at you and your comrades for putting the D.A. on me. But he's no fool. Do you think a guy walks into a man's apartment and that very night kills him to take his wife? Good Lord, Menti, *think* a little. Do you think I'd risk my neck doing a thing like that? All right, maybe someone *did* go in there and kill the two of them. But how do you know they did it just to get Eva? Think of the many people the Party has wronged . . . They might have had a motive . . . A woman could have done it . . ."

"What woman?" Menti asked slyly.

"Look, Menti," Cross said shrewdly, "don't think everybody's naïve. Eva was a victim . . ."

"How do you know that?" Menti demanded. "What kind of a victim?"

"The Party tricked her into marrying Gil—"

"Who told you *that*?"

"Eva did," Cross lied readily. "Even Eva had a motive for killing Gil . . . But, of course, she was with me when Herndon killed Gil—"

"And you were with her when Hilton was killed!" Menti asked, fishing.

"No."

"Where were you then?" Menti tried to tie him down.

"In a bar. I've accounted for myself with the police," Cross maintained. "Look, I'm just as worried about the motive that could have made anybody go in there and kill Gil and Herndon as you are . . . But to say that getting Eva was the motive . . . Why, that's underestimating people, Menti . . ." Cross could barely repress a smile as he argued gently. "Maybe Gil had enemies with strange motives, motives which only the Party could understand . . . Did you ever think of that?"

Before Menti could answer, Cross saw the form of Blimin come through the door and head for the bed. He understood why Menti had left the door ajar; it was to give Blimin a chance to eavesdrop on their conversation.

"I see I won't have to repeat what I've said," Cross said to Blimin.

Blimin smiled coldly, planted himself in front of Cross and studied him for some time. Cross met the stare calmly, waiting.

"Well, at last we know *who* you are, Damon," Blimin said.

"So?"

"What are you up to? What's your game?"

"I'm trying to live, Mr. Blimin—"

"Do you want to join our Party?"

"Frankly, no."

"Menti says you promised Hilton that you would."

"That was before I'd met you, sir," Cross said.

"What did you tell Mrs. Blount?"

"Nothing," Cross said, looking Blimin straight in the eyes.

"Tell me, have you ever been outside of the continental boundaries of the United States?" Blimin asked.

"No. I've not been to Russia, Italy, Germany, Mexico, Argentina, or Spain . . ."

"Now that Mrs. Blount's dead, what do you intend to do?"

"I don't know."

"May I ask what arrangements did you make with the District Attorney?"

"None. He put me through the paces, but he had no evidence to hold me on," Cross explained good-naturedly.

"Don't you consider it an honor to be asked to join the Party?" Blimin was smiling now.

Cross had watched Blimin's mood change; the man had assumed a debonair attitude, as though all of his previous questions had not been as important as he had pretended. But Cross was not to be taken in by this belated pretense of cordiality; he knew that it meant simply that the Party was more baffled about him and his motives than ever; and they were trying to get closer to him in order to learn more about him. How free these men were! How they could turn, change; how they played make-believe with human emotions! They sensed, as Houston had, that in some as yet unknown and oblique way he was related to them and, being of their moods and temperament, he could too sense this in them. One had to be sensitive here; one had to realize that one was to some extent understood, and one had to act in a way that would not completely kill their trust; yet, at the same time, one had to be in a position not to let them make one pledge more than one was willing to yield. If he refused to promise to join the Party now they might suspect that his finality and abruptness had back of it something fatally serious; yes, he would make his attitude more equivocal . . .

"If you're not anti-Party, then why do you so flatly refuse to consider the Party's invitation to become a member?" Blimin asked.

"Look, man," Cross protested. "I've just undergone a prolonged grilling at the hands of the District Attorney . . . And it was you and your friends who egged the D.A. to pin something on me . . . Now, I ask you: don't you think I'm right when I hesitate to embrace you? Haven't you a sense of balance?"

"Come now, Lane or Damon," Blimin chided him unctuously. "We admit we put you through the paces. But we were trying to protect ourselves. Can you really blame us for that?"

Cross bowed his head in thought. He wondered why Menti and Blimin had been allowed to enter the apartment and talk to him? They must be trying to get information from me for the police, he reasoned. He could not trust anyone now . . .

"I can't give you an answer now," he hedged, leaving the

door open. "I'm just too tired and upset. I've got to get my bearings— Look, as soon as I hit this city and touched the Party, my life's turned upside down—"

"I understand," Blimin said softly.

Cross did not believe that Blimin understood, and he knew that Blimin knew that he did not believe it; they had reached that point where mutual lies made further communication impossible. But at least they had arrived at a truce. Cross smiled and said:

"Can't we talk about this later?"

"Of course," Blimin agreed readily, his mind busy elsewhere. "You're staying here?"

"Yes."

"Then we'll see you, hunh?"

"Of course."

Menti and Blimin left. They've gone straight to the police to report, he assured himself. They had been gone barely two minutes before Sarah came to him.

"I know there ain't no use asking you what it's all about, 'cause you ain't gonna tell me," she protested tearfully.

"Sarah, I'm tired; sit down, though," he said, lying back on the bed.

"What happened to Eva? And what is your name? You make me scared . . ." She let her voice trail off in confusion. Then, as though she did not expect him to answer, she said: "I'm sick of all this. I'm alone. I'm thirty-five years old. And what have I got? Nothing. Bob's gone; they took 'im from me. The Party? The hell with it. I'll never work with them again. Listen, Lionel, you know what I'm gonna do? I'm gonna do what my mother told me to do when I was sick and tired and didn't know where I was going—"

"What are you going to do?"

"I'm going to confession."

"Are you Catholic?"

"Yes," she said. "I ditched the church 'cause I felt they were doping me . . . But, now—I give up . . . I'm lost; I don't know if I'm going or coming . . . Bob and Gil and Hilton and now Eva . . . Why? It scares me . . . Only God can answer all this . . . Don't you think so?"

She was completely rattled. Her eyes had that restless, desperate look of one tired and confused and unable to support the feeling of it any longer.

"What are you talking about, Sarah? Only God can answer what?"

"These killings . . ." She groped for words. "Life doesn't make sense any more; it's crazy . . . People getting killed and nobody even sorry about it . . . It ain't *right* . . . I can't understand it. You know, Menti really laughed about Eva?" she stated in a half-questioning tone.

Poor Sarah . . . She was crushed and scared. She had to rest, to find support, a master; she was yearning to submit.

"What are you going to do, Lionel . . . ?" She paused, shook her head and looked at him with wonder. "Your name's Cross; that's what Menti said. I don't like it; I like Lionel better . . ."

She was reacting to him now as woman; she knew that he was alone and she was wondering if she, maybe, could somehow team up with him. How movingly simple this woman was! She, like Eva, would recoil in horror (or maybe laughter; who knows?) if she knew the kind of man she was letting her dreams mull over.

"Forget me, Sarah," he told her directly.

"But what must I do?"

"What do you want to do?" he asked her.

"Oh, no," she murmured, shaking her head in fear. "You asked Bob that question just before they took him away. You told him to do what he wanted . . . No; no; I don't want to do that. Look what it brings!"

She did not want the responsibility of her life any longer. Why was life given to man if man could not handle it?

"Sarah, what I'm trying to ask you is this: What helps you most? What makes you feel better, good, 'sent' as you call it?" he asked her gently.

She brooded a bit, her face soft with memory.

"When I was a child I was happy," she mused. "At least, I thought I was . . ."

Cross wanted hotly to dispute that; he was convinced that there were no happy childhoods, that the myth of the happy childhood had been invented by middle class people to show that their parents had had money when they were children, or by people whose memories of unpleasant days were so defective that they could delude themselves into believing that they had come into this world "trailing clouds of glory". Anthropologists, sociologists, psychologists, and the best accounts of childhood in all the serious and responsible literature of mankind depicted the child as coming into the world as a nasty, stinking little criminal savage (charming because it was harmless!) wholly intent upon the gratification of its own egoistic pleasures and satisfactions. Its criminality became subjective in relation to the checking of its unbridled impulses, and it was not until its imperious will had been subdued that it became civilized in some sense. And enough of the child-criminal had survived in Cross to make him know that criminal-consciousness, which is another name for childhood, could never be happy.

But why argue with Sarah about all of this? Her case was urgent and truths of this nature would serve but to make her more unhappy.

"And what do you think made you happy when you were a child, Sarah?"

"I don't know for sure," Sarah sighed. "But I didn't keep wondering about things like this . . . I believed in God . . . I went to Mass . . . Everything was simple . . ."

"And you want it to be simple again," he said. "I know . . . Well, do what you were doing when you were a child and see if it makes life simple again. Now, what do you really want to do? Look at me and tell me . . ."

"I want to find a man . . ."

"Can you? Be honest."

"I'm pretty old for that," she sighed, bit her lips. "I'm fat now. And I've no confidence in myself anymore," she let her voice die in her throat and tears began to well into her eyes. She bent forward and cried: "I'm going to Confession . . ."

Well, why not? All the church had to do was predict that life was terrible, that man would become overwhelmed with contradictory experiences. They could drill this simple, elementary truth of life into the hearts of impressionable children. Then the Fathers of the church could sit back and watch the generations of the sons and daughters of men grow up and go forth on their little voyages of proud, vain desire, could watch them with soft, ironic smiles, for they knew that sooner or later they would come crawling back to the faith of their childhood, seeking solace, whimpering for mercy, for forgiveness. Cross rose and paced the room, looking at Sarah now and then, smiling compassionately at her. Sarah leaped to her feet, her face wet with tears and her eyes hard with outrage.

"Are you laughing at me?" she demanded. "Then you *must* be crazy, like Menti said . . ."

"So, Menti said that, hunh?"

"And, by God, now I'm beginning to believe he's right!"

Cross went to her and placed his hand tenderly on top of her head.

"It might be better for you if you did believe that," he said.

She stopped crying and stared at him, not understanding. "Why do you say that?"

"You need rest, Sarah," he said. "Take your burden to God and lay it down . . . Remember, He said: *'Come unto me all ye that labor and are heavy laden, and I will give you rest . . .'?"*

"But you don't *believe* that," she protested, baffled, half-scared. "I know you don't. *Do* you?"

"No," he could not resist telling her the truth.

"Then why do you tell *me* that?"

"Perhaps God uses the Devil to guide people home," he told her impishly.

Sarah blinked, then she ran to him, her lips curling with hate and scorn; she began hitting him with her doubled fists. Cross ducked his head and burst into prolonged laughter.

"Don't, Sarah," he protested good-naturedly.

"You *bastard*! You're making *fun* of me! I could kill you, kill you . . . I swear, I could! You hear, I could kill you . . ." She paused, thinking, blinked her eyes. "Maybe you *did* kill them like Menti said . . ."

"It's you who're talking about killing me," he reminded her. "When did I ever say I wanted to kill somebody?"

"You're laughing, but you can't fool me," she said, her eyes lit with Intuition. "I saw something crazy in you the first time . . ."

"Oh, no!" Cross protested, chuckling. "You laughed at me. Remember how you laughed?"

"I didn't know you then—"

"My dear, you don't know me now," Cross told her. "But look, in all seriousness, I tell you that you ought to go back to your church. You *need* it."

She did not know what to think. She saw that Cross was both serious and amused. The expression on her face told him that thoughts were clashing violently in her mind. Her mouth hung open, then her lips became compressed.

"You are a *devil!*" she burst out bitterly. "You're making fun of me and it ain't *right!* It ain't *good* to laugh at people for things like *that* . . . You like to see suffering . . ."

"I do not," he said.

"You do; I see it in you—"

"Sarah, what I feel does not concern you; forget it," he told her. "You asked my advice; I say you ought to go back to God."

"And what are you going to do?"

"Nothing," he said simply, quietly, looking at her with eyes that twinkled for the first time in many weeks.

She gazed at him, then looked away. She went to the door, pivoted; her mind was made up.

"*I don't like you!*" she shouted in a sudden rage and went out, slamming the door.

Yes, Sarah was going back to the church. What did it matter that the church had no answer for the ills of this earth? The priests could at least tell her to stop hoping for anything in this life, to curb and deny her desires, to forget her humiliating color consciousness, her poverty, that all of that was as nothing in the eyes of an eternal God. And for those who were weak, was that not right, fitting, necessary? Was it such a bad world, after all? The only trouble was that he and his kind were restlessly envious of the priests, the churches, the Communists, the Fascists, the men of power . . . That was it. He would have to live without that green foam of jealousy welling into his eyes and blinding him to how weak he was in relation to their organized strength. Render unto church that which is the church's, and render unto the Party that which is the Party's . . . But where would *he* stand? Was there no neutral ground?

He sat on the bed, looking at his suitcase. He ought to pack his things. Yes . . . He moved about listlessly, absent-minded, slowly filling the suitcase without conviction that he would ever have the right to move about again in freedom. Oh, yes; there was something he really wanted to do; he would take Eva's diaries with him, keep them as a memento . . . He pulled out the dresser drawer and saw that they were not there. He looked through all the drawers, under the bed, in the clothes closet. Now, where had he put them? Maybe Eva had taken them back when she had heard the Party's suspicions? But he did not believe that she would have done that without first telling him; it was not like Eva's transparent honesty. Then where *were* they? *The Party!* He would bet his life that Menti had taken them . . . Goddamn him! He had wanted those diaries . . . Well, if Menti had stolen them, they were gone. To argue with the Party about them was useless.

Through the closed door of his room came the faint tinkling of the front doorbell. He stood still, waiting, wondering whom it could be. Was it Menti again with his everlasting Hank? He placed his ear to the door panel and listened.

"Is Lane or Damon in?"

It was Houston's voice. Had he dug up any new evidence against him? Was he coming finally to arrest him?

Sarah's voice sounded cold and clipped: "He's in his room . . . There . . ."

Houston's footsteps echoed down the hallway and died in front of his door. Cross sank upon the bed. He would let Houston take the initiative. Eva was dead and there was no fight in him. A series of sharp knocks sounded on the door.

"Come in," he called.

The door swung open and there was Houston and behind him loomed a tall, blue-coated officer. Under Houston's arm was a bulky package wrapped in brown paper. Houston turned to the officer and said: "Wait down the hall."

"Yes, sir."

The officer left and Houston came in and closed the door

softly behind him. He approached Cross, smiling vaguely. Houston had a relaxed, confident air and Cross felt that his time had come. He *knows* now . . . All right; if this was the end, then he did not care . . . Houston looked around, found a chair, dragged it to the bed and eased his deformed body on to it, some two feet from Cross. Cross felt sweat breaking out over his chest and he cursed himself for being unable to control his physical reactions. Well, why didn't the hunchback sonofabitch speak? Why did he sit there with that goddamn gloating smirk on his face? He longed for his gun; if he had it in his hands he would shoot the hell out of that little triumphant god even if he burned for it . . . All right; he had lost, but Houston would see that he could take his defeat without flinching.

"Damon, I've solved it. You're guilty. You killed Blount, Herndon, and Hilton . . ."

Houston's voice rang with finality. Cross waited; his role was to say nothing. Let Houston carry the ball. Slowly Houston unwrapped the brown package and there lay the set of thin angular notebooks: the diaries of Eva . . .

"You're a lucky, blundering fool," Houston spat at him. "The only witness I could have put in the box against you was Eva Blount, and she's dead. If she hadn't leaped from that window, you'd be on your way to the electric chair . . . If she had lived, she would have told me what you told her, and what you *told* her made her kill herself. I've found out that much, Damon." Houston rubbed his hands nervously across his eyes. "Goddammit, I was your unwitting accomplice for seventy-two hours! I just couldn't bring myself to admit what I knew in my heart to be true! And no doubt you were banking on just that. What made that girl kill herself was what made me unable to admit that you were guilty. I wonder if you planned it like that? No; I don't think you did. It was too perfect to be planned. You depended upon the human heart rejecting a horror of that magnitude and you were almost right, almost successful . . ."

"How did you get those diaries?" Cross asked him. "From the Party?"

"No. An officer took them from this room when you and

the others were in the police station," Houston said. "I've read them and I understand it *all* now."

"Did she mention me in there?" he asked, feeling that he had to know at once.

"Only a little, toward the end— What she said did not matter. It was what she *was* that mattered," Houston told him. "She said that she loved you, but that was all. But what a victim was that Eva Blount!"

Houston carelessly tossed the notebooks upon the bed, at Cross's side. Cross was surprised, wondering why Houston was returning the books to him.

"It was all very simple when at last I'd found the key," Houston began in a slow, measured tone. "And the key was this deceived woman, Eva Blount . . . Look Damon, I'm an honest man; I'm not going to brag or lie to you. Right off I want to confess that I was haywire in the beginning. That damned Communist Party pushed me off on the wrong track. That paranoiac Blimin was at my office day and night, demanding action, yelling that you had killed Blount and Herndon because of Eva . . . The Party claimed at first that you were a Trotskyite, then they swore that you were a government spy. In the end they screamed that you saw an opportunity to kill Blount and take his wife and you took it . . . Funny, isn't it, how they misread things? Every man, it seems, interprets the world in the light of his habits and desires. The Party shouted at me: 'He sold out to get the girl!' Their own slogans blinded them. They argued that you had to kill Herndon because Herndon had seen you kill Blount; further, they claimed that Hilton had found out somehow and that you then had to kill him . . . Despite the fact that they could not offer any evidence in support of this, I, at first, felt that it did sound rather plausible. But deep down I was worried; it was *too* pat; it did not suit your character, did not fit what you told me that morning on the train. Remember? 'Man's nothing in particular . . .'

"What a baffling chase you gave us! In the first place, you seemed so innocent, *too* innocent; we made only the most perfunctory investigations . . . When we began to feel that you *must* know something, we checked your draft card and, lo and behold, a fire had destroyed the records! I wonder if you could have had anything to do with that? You won't answer? All right; it isn't important . . . Then, for twenty-four hours, we made no new moves against you. But Hilton's death told us that we were up against something sinister. We decided to track down every lead, no matter how trivial . . .

"It was not until we, almost as an afterthought, tried to verify your birth certificate that we began to think of you seriously as a possible murderer. What a joke that certificate was! In Newark the clerks in the Bureau of Vital Statistics remembered you, but we thought that we were surely on the wrong track when we heard their description of you! Boy, what an actor you are! You should have been on the stage . . . When at last we were certain that you were Lionel Lane and that Lionel Lane was dead, we were back where we started from. It was decided that you had assumed this man's name, and we swung then toward thinking that you were in some Communist opposition group. But that fizzled. No political group in America had ever heard of you . . .

"Then we began checking your fingerprints and we ran into another stone wall. For the second time we discovered that you were dead . . . Cross Damon, Negro postal clerk of Chicago: *dead* . . . Killed in a subway accident. The FBI flew to Chicago to make sure. They reported to me that you were no more . . . They even exhumed the other Negro's body, but that didn't tell us anything. Then the police started checking with the Missing Persons Bureau. We found that a man of your height and description had been reported missing the day after you were *supposed* to have been killed . . . Who was this man? He was a cleaner and dresser of chickens in a meat market . . .

"Finally we had to rely on comparing descriptions of you that we got from Chicago with what we could observe of you here in New York, then we knew that we had the right man. We knew you were Cross Damon, no matter how many dead men you were hiding behind . . .

"But was it possible that Cross Damon was doing all of this killing. But why? That was the most baffling aspect of all. You'll never know how I struggled against accepting your guilt. *I didn't want to believe it.* After having isolated you, identified you, we faced a riddle. Nothing in your entire background had touched politics. Then I had a brainstorm. I wired Chicago to send me a list of the titles of the books you'd left behind in your room and when they wired back a long list I was delighted . . . That was the first real clue. Your Nietzsche, your Hegel, your Jaspers, your Heidegger, your Husserl, your Kierkegaard, and your Dostoevsky were the clues . . . I said to myself that we are dealing with a man who has wallowed in guilty thought. But the more I pondered this thing, the sorrier I felt for you. I began to feel as though I'd killed Blount, Herndon, and Hilton myself . . .

"And when I read those diaries and saw into the deceived heart of this little Eva, I knew damn well that you did not kill to get her. She was hysterically waiting for some man to ask her to run off from that impossible Blount and his Party . . . I visited her studio and looked at those powerful projections of nonobjective horror she had painted; then I read her diaries and I knew you'd love her, understand her; she was a sensitive artist and represented in her life and work a quality of suffering that would move a heart like yours. In spirit, Eva was your sister. Both of you were abandoned, fearful, without a form or discipline for living; and, therefore, you were both a prey to compulsions. In the face of life, she shrank, but you advanced. But here, attack or retreat, is a form of fear. No; you didn't kill to get her; you didn't have to. You'd want to lead her, remake her, save her, and at bottom you'd be wanting, in doing this, to save yourself . . . And she was ripe to respond on the same basis; she wanted to *help* you . . .

"Damon, last night you said something that hurt me. When I had the cops pick you up and bring you to my office, when I was putting the heat on you, you told me— Well, you implied that I was a kind of monster for confronting you with your wife and children— No, Damon, I'm not that kind of a man. If I were a sadist, I could have had you locked up in the Tombs days ago for investigation, but I didn't." Houston smiled ironically. "I wouldn't deliberately torture anything or anybody on this earth. But, of course, I do so live that I find myself in situations where people are suffering. After all, why did I become a District Attorney? But, hell, that's another story.

"No; I wasn't torturing you last night. I was trying to identify you; I had to be absolutely certain that you were Cross Damon, postal clerk of Chicago, supposedly dead, married, etc. But there was another thing I wanted to know. I had to see how you would react when I told you of your mother's death, how you would react when you saw your sons . . . I'm a District Attorney, Damon; I was tracking down emotional clues; I was doing my police work . . .

"You were so inhuman that I would not have believed it unless I'd seen it. Today many sociologists say that the American Negro, having been stripped of his African tribal culture, has not had time to become completely adjusted to our mores, that the life of the family of the Western World has not had time to sink in, etc. But with you, you are adjusted and more . . . You've grown up and gone beyond our rituals. I knew that you were beyond organized religion, but I didn't suspect that you were already beyond the family. Last night you stood there in my office and committed the greatest and last crime of all. You did not bat your eye when I told you that your mother was dead. It hurt you, yes; I could see it, but you rode it out. Boy, you had killed your mother long, long ago . . . You must have known your mother well, understood her both emotionally and intellectually; and when one can see and weigh one's mother like that, well, she's dead to one . . . And when you saw those three fine sons of yours! They tugged at your heart and memory and you were wildly angry and ashamed; but you rode out that too; you overcame it . . . And I said to myself: 'This man *could* have killed Blount, Herndon, and Hilton . . . Only *he* could have done it. He has the emotional capacity—or *lack* of it!—to do it.'

"Then I sat down and thought. After all, Damon, as I told you on the train that morning, I'm close enough to you, being a hunchback, being an outsider, to know how some of your feelings and thought processes *must* go. In a sense, I'm your brother . . . We men are not complete strangers on this earth. The world changes, but men are always the same. And especially the various basic types of men—and you are an ancient, fundamental type—run the same.

"When I first talked to you in the Blount apartment, how you must have laughed at me! I walked all around you and could not see you! And then Hilton started his crazy, class-conscious pressure. Strange, the Communists had access to this insight as well as I and they didn't want to see . . ."

Cross was still. Yes; he was caught. But where was the *proof*? Eva could not witness against him. Had Houston, then, some hidden evidence? If this was the best that Houston could do, why, he would simply walk into court and keep his damned mouth shut and let him see if he could convict him.

"Damon, you are an atheist," Houston resumed, "and that is the heart of this matter. You know what convinced me that you were guilty? No; I didn't find any clues you'd left behind . . . It was in a realm far afield that I found conclusive proof. Where?" Houston lifted his arm toward the window. "Right out there in those teeming streets . . . Damon, you act individually just like modern man lives in the mass each day.

"You see, hopeful men seize upon every tiny incident and read the dreams of their hearts into them. Each hour of the day men are asking: 'Do you think we'll have peace? Don't you think what General So-and-So said means we'll have war? Don't you think that the White House pronouncement means that prices will be lower?' Or maybe he observes that his neighbor is reading a radical book and comes to the conclusion that he is a spy and ought to be killed? And, Damon, that was the way you were living. The only difference was that your compulsions were negative, had no direction . . .

"In the old days we were concerned with mobs, with thousands of men running amuck in the streets. The mob has conquered completely. When the mob has grown so vast that you cannot see it, then it is everywhere. Today the compulsive acts of the lynching mobs have become enthroned in each individual heart . . . Every man now acts as a criminal, a policeman, a judge, and an executioner . . .

"But to come back to this individual mob-you who is called Cross Damon. What an atheist you are! You know, real atheists are rare, really. A genuine atheist is a real Christian turned upside down; God descends from the sky and takes up abode, so to speak, behind the fleshy bars of his heart! Men argue about their not believing in God and the mere act of doing so makes them believers. It is only when they do not

feel the need to deny Him that they really do not believe in
Him." Houston rose in his excitement and paced the floor, as
though he had forgotten the existence of Cross. "*You went all
the way!* You have drawn all the conclusions and deductions
that could be drawn from the atheistic position and you have
inherited the feelings that only real atheists can have. At first I
didn't believe it, but when you stared so unfeelingly at your
sons, when you laughed when your poor wife could not summon enough strength to identify you, I knew that you were
beyond the pale of all the *little* feelings, the *humble* feelings,
the *human* feelings . . . *I knew that you could do anything!*
Not in a towering rage, not to save falling mankind, not to
establish social justice, not for glory . . . But just because
you happen to feel like that one day . . .

"You are a free man. Ideas do not knock you off your
feet, make you dizzy, make you fall down and serve others.
You always suspect that ideas are in the service of other
people . . . Oh, I *know* you, boy! Blimin told me about your
ideas."

Cross hovered over a vast void. Was this man making fun of
him or was he sympathizing with him? What he had feared
most had come; there was nothing he could hide from
Houston. He kept his eyes on the floor, afraid to look up at
Houston's passion-inflamed face.

"You felt that you were right, but not in the sense that you
had to insist upon it. No! Does one explain when he says
he wants three teaspoons of sugar in his coffee instead of
two? You don't have to justify that, do you? You had risen—
or sunk!—to that attitude toward the lives of those about
you . . .

"But, Damon, you made one fatal mistake. You saw
through all the ideologies, pretenses, frauds, but you did not
see through *yourself.* How magnificently you tossed away this
God who plagues and helps man so much! But you did not
and could not toss out of your heart that part of you from
which the God notion had come. And what part of a man is
that? It is desire . . . Don't you know it? Why didn't you just
live a quiet life like all other men? That's the correct way of
being godless. Why be restless? Why let desire plague you?
Why not conquer it too?"

Houston was questioning Cross in a kind manner, like a brother would question him.

"Desire? Why does man desire? It's crazy, for it's almost certain that he'll never get what he desires . . . Is desire not a kind of warning in man to let him know that he is limited? Is desire in man not a kind of danger signal of man to himself? Desire is the mad thing, the irrational thing. Damon, you peeled off layer after layer of illusion and make-believe and stripped yourself down to just simply naked desire and you thought that you had gotten hold of the core of reality. And, in a sense, you had. But what does one *do* with desire? Man desires ultimately to be a god . . . Man desires *everything* . . . Why not? Desire is a restless, floating demon . . . Desire tries to seize itself and never can . . . It's an illusion, but the most solid one! Desire is what snared you, my boy. You felt that what brooked desire could be killed; what annoyed, could be gotten rid of . . .

"Only a man feeling like that could have gone down into that room and seen those two men fighting it out, and then killed the *both* of them! Not taking sides . . . Not preferring the lesser evil . . . Just a sweeping and supreme gesture of disdain and disgust with the both of them! And only a man akin to them could have hated them that much, and you know it, Damon! You slew them just because they offended you . . . It was just like taking a cinder out of your eye because it stings a bit . . ."

Houston paused in front of Cross and chuckled, his eyes bright and mischievous. Cross looked at him and said to himself: That must have been how I looked when Sarah saw me laughing at her! Sarah had gotten angry, had leaped to her feet and had tried to beat him with her doubled fists, had shouted and cursed him; but he could not afford to act that way with Houston. Pride held him still. To show resentment would give the game away. No; he would sit and take it all.

"How you must have felt in that awful room! I wish you'd tell me! Did you calculate every movement? Or did you act without knowing it? Did you realize what you were doing? Or did you invent the idea of it afterwards? How did those two men look to you? And which one did you kill first? I'll bet a million dollars that, even though you're a free man, you killed Herndon first, eh? You're a Negro and you know what Fascism means to you and your people. Even a man like you cannot be as indifferent as he would like . . . Your feet, Damon, I'll bet, were of earthy clay and you killed Herndon first . . . Won't you tell me? No? All right . . . I'll not press you; these are unimportant details . . .

"Ha-ha-ha! Of course, I don't believe that Eva Blount saw Herndon on those stairs. I can't *prove* that she didn't, but I don't believe it. She was wrought up; she wished Blount out of her life, wanted him dead . . . She imagined she saw Herndon. And I'll bet you you seized upon her fantasy and tried to fool us all with it . . .

"I know that Blount would not have touched you. He thought he had snared you into his ideological spiderweb and that you were his slave, his moral slave, the slave who believes in the ideas that are given to him . . . But, if you killed Blount first, Herndon would have killed you the next instant, wouldn't he? I'm right, hunh? Ha-ha-ha! I'm clever, boy, when I get my sights at last leveled on the right target. And you must certainly have gotten a rich, deep satisfaction out of killing that nigger-hater, Herndon. And Blount's face must have been a study in amazement when you suddenly turned on him . . .

"Then you wiped off all the fingerprints; there was none of yours in the room except on the door. And they had a right to be there, for you had been in the room talking to Herndon that afternoon, hadn't you?

"All right . . . Now comes a gap that I can't fill— I don't know how Hilton found out that you had killed the two of them . . . Did you tell him? Hunh? No; you don't want to answer? All right. You can tell me . . . No; you must not. Then I'd be bound by my oath of office and I'd have to use it against you . . . Ha-ha . . . Get the point, Damon?

"But I don't think you told Hilton anything. You're much too clever for that. Anyhow, he found out someway . . . These Communists eat and breathe suspicion. He had his eyes on you from the beginning, according to the Party, but not for any reason, just in general . . . And he caught you in your little godly game . . .

"You went to see him. You must have known that he

knew. I must admit that I'm a bit foggy about this part of it. He had asked you to come and talk to him about joining the Party . . . But I can't believe that you went there for that. *That* might have been your excuse . . . But that was not your purpose. After all, Damon, I'm only human. I can't know all. I'm not a god and do not claim to be one, or want to be one. Ha-ha-ha . . . I curb my desires, you see?

"But, if I know the Hilton type, and I do to some extent, I'd expect a deal to be made. Damon, why wasn't there a deal, an understanding arrived at between you and Hilton? Maybe the reality of this beautiful Eva had begun to enter the picture to some extent then? Maybe you two just hated each other naturally because you were so much alike? You little gods who traffic in human life, who buy and sell the souls of men, why couldn't you have not made a trade?

"Well, I guess that maybe you couldn't trust each other, hunh? That's the big trouble with gods when they get together. Gods cannot share power; each god must have all the power or he's no god. Logical, hunh? For, what's a god if he has a rival? So damn much jealousy enters, hunh? Look at Hitler and Stalin . . . Boy, if they could have been reasonable, they could have divided this whole earth up between them. But, no; each felt that he and he alone had to have the whole earth. So they chewed each other up. When gods fall out, little worms can live . . .

"But, joking aside . . . You killed Hilton with his own gun and you didn't leave a clue. How did you get into the hotel? You were at the hotel desk early that afternoon, but no one remembers seeing you there after that, either entering or leaving. Of course, they have a rather racially liberal policy at the Albert Hotel and Negroes leaving or entering would not be the occasion for anybody's noticing, would it? And sometimes I suppose all things work together for the loves and desires of little gods?"

Cross felt dead. How could this man lay open his life with such decisive strokes? With such mocking cynicism? Goddamn him to hell!

"Now, these diaries . . . This girl deceived by the Party

. . . This naïve child made the mistake of thinking that she had found in you something clean, pure, something her heart had dreamed of. In *you*, of all the men on earth! She looked upon you and your people as her brothers and sisters in suffering . . . What irony! Hurt, deceived, she projected out upon you her desires! Afraid of deception, she embraced a fount of deception! Full of timid, feminine desire, she flings her arms about a furnace of desire and is consumed in it . . . Then you, in your desert of loneliness, must have told her what you had done. She'd fought the Party for you, told them upon her life that you were an innocent man . . . And, in a sense, she was right; you were innocent of what the Party was charging. But, for a reason I do not know, you told her and she leaped . . . That's how I figure it. What you told her was too much for her. You made her feel that she could no longer trust any person on this earth. She leaped from that window to escape the kind of world you showed her! You *drove* her out of life. What you told her was the crowning horror of all the horrors! The apex of deception . . . And you *had* to tell her; you wanted her help. But did you tell her that Gil had not done anything to you? Did you tell her that you killed Gil for *nothing*? Boy, did you, could you go that far? I wonder . . .

"Damon, those diaries told me that you were guilty, and that girl's leaping from that window was proof of it. Will you admit it? No? Your silence is a confession! Your inability to challenge me is proof! I'm waiting . . . *Speak!* Tell me I'm wrong . . . You *can't!*"

Houston turned, opened the door of the room and went out. Cross lay watching the door swing a little to and fro on a squeaky hinge. Well, Houston was going to get the cops and they were going to take him to the station now . . . This was the end. But what evidence did Houston have? What facts to buttress all of this? So far he had cited nothing but psychological facts. Come to think of it, they were not even psychological facts. They were feelings, lightninglike intuitions which only a man who had lived long on that lower (or was it a higher?) level of life could know. He heard Houston's footsteps coming back. He braced himself.

Houston entered the room with a glass of water in his right hand. He stood looking at Cross a solemn moment, then he lifted the glass to his lips and drained it thirstily, his humped body resembling that of a huge, waiting spider.

"I was thirsty," Houston confessed in the voice of a man who had satisfied a physical need. He sighed. "I haven't spoken so much since I was last facing a jury a month ago."

Cross could bear it no longer; his lips trembled.

"Get it over with! If you think you'll drag one word from me, you're crazy!" he shouted.

"Now," Houston spoke in a soothing tone, "don't spoil it all. You were playing your role so well . . ."

"You're gloating over me! Okay, start your damned wheels turning to punish me . . . !"

"Hold on, my friend. I'm not through yet," Houston said with a feeling of deep relish in his voice. "You'll be punished, but not in the way *you* think. Ah, I know . . . You have visions of lashes, third degree sessions, blinding spotlights in your eyes, questions popping at you for hours on end. You may even think of mobs, for all I know . . . And all of this because the cops want you to confess. But, Damon, you've confessed already . . ."

Hot tension leaped in Cross. Had he overlooked something silly that would send him to the chair? Had he left some foolish thing undone that would make him look like an adolescent boy stealing apples from a neighbor's orchard?

"Confession?" he stammered. "What do you mean?"

Houston threw back his head and laughed. "You confessed to *me*, just to *me*, to *me* alone. See? I've no concrete evidence to use in court against you . . ."

Was the man crazy? What was he getting at?

"Listen, Damon, you made your own law," Houston pronounced. "And, by God, I, for one, am going to let you live by it. I'm pretty certain you're finished with this killing phase . . . So, I'm going to let you go. See? Yes; just go! *You're free!* Just like that." Houston snapped his fingers in Cross's face. "I'm going to let you keep this in your heart 'til the end of your days. Sleep with it, eat with it, brood over it, make love with it . . . You are going to punish yourself, see? You are your own law, so you'll be your own judge . . . I wouldn't

help you by taking you to jail . . . I've very little concrete
evidence to haul you into court on anyhow; it's likely I
couldn't convict you . . . And I'll not give you the satisfaction of sitting in a court of law with those tight lips of yours
and gloating at me or any jury while we tried to prove the
impossible. What the hell could a jury of housewives, like the
simple-minded Sarah Hunter, make out of a guy like you? I'll
not give you the chance to make that kind of a fool out of me,
Damon! No, sir! I'm much too smart for that.

"These killings will be marked unsolved. And, in a sense,
they are. Even now I cannot say why you killed in a rational
manner, in a manner that would persuade others . . . I've not
told anyone of what I've found about you." Houston tapped
his head. "It's all right here. And it'll stay there. You're trembling . . . Oh, yes; I understand now. You thought that I was
going to get the cop to arrest you when I went out for that
glass of water . . . ? Ha-ha-ha! Oh, you're sweating, hunh?
Boy, you'll sweat tears of terror, night and day. That's the lot
of a little god. Didn't you know that gods were lonely? When
you eat, a part of you will stand back, shy and embarrassed.
When you make love, a part of you will turn away in shame.
From now on, there will be a dead hand holding life back
from you . . . Will you find your way back? I doubt it. To
whom could you tell your story, Damon? Who will listen? A
psychoanalyst? You have no respect for them, and what the
hell could they do for you? They'd be frightened of you;
they'd rush out of their consulting rooms, their hair standing
on end, screaming with terror. No; they are not for you, my
boy. It's between *you* and *you*, you and yourself."

Houston stood looking down with musing eyes at Cross.
And Cross felt sweat running down his face; it was on his
chest, seeping down his arms. Even his legs were wet. Suddenly he wanted to beg this man not to leave him. He could
not believe that it was like this that it was to end . . . But he
could make no move.

"That's all," Houston said. "Whatever nameless powers
that be, may they have something like mercy on your tor-
mented soul."

He turned and strode out of the room. Cross could hear
him speaking in low tones to Sarah, then there came the echo

of his footsteps along the hallway; then he heard the front door open and close. He was alone. He felt like screaming for Houston to come back, to talk to him, to tell him what to do. But he clamped his teeth and held still. I'm alone, he said to himself. He felt dizzy. Terror wrapped him around in a sheet of flame and his body wept tears . . . The prop had gone; Houston had gone; the world against which he had pitched his rebellion had pitied him, almost forgiven him . . . The thing he had been fighting had turned its face from him as though he was no longer worthy of having an opponent and this rejection was a judgment so inhuman that he could not bear to think of it.

He had broken all of his promises to the world and the people in it, but he had never reckoned on that world turning on him and breaking its promise to him too! He was not to be punished! Men would not give meaning to what he had done! Society would not even look at it, recognize it! That was not fair, wasn't right, just . . . The ludicrous nature of his protest came to him and he smiled wryly at his own self-deception. Always back deep in his mind, he had counted on their railing at him, storming, cursing, condemning . . . Instead, nothing, silence, the silence that roars like an indifferent cataract, the silence that reaches like a casual clap of thunder to the end of space and time . . .

He had to talk to somebody! But to whom? No; he had to keep this crime choked in his throat. He, like others, had to pretend that nothing like this could ever happen; he had to collaborate and help keep the secret. He had to go forward into the future and pretend that the world was as tradition said it was . . .

His head dropped senselessly to the bedcover and he drifted off into that state of bleak relaxation that comes after an exhausting strain. He was not sleeping, not fully awake; he was existing with an alien world looming implacably over and against him. But all of his compulsions were gone, leaving him empty of even desire . . .

He did not stir from his room until late the next morning, and when he did emerge, it was to go into the kitchen with

Eva's diary. Since Houston had laid his self-hate and his self-love so mockingly naked, he felt that he no longer had any right to keep the diary and he was resolved to burn it. He opened one of the notebooks and tore out a sheet; just before touching the page to the flame of his lighter, he let his eyes stray listlessly over the lines, reading:

"March 3rd
"Last night was in Harlem and had dinner with Bob and Sarah Hunter. A tall, sensitive young Negro, Lionel Lane, was there; he was tense and seemed to be seeking for something in life. He struck me as one who would leave no stone unturned to find his destiny. Gil was taken with him and asked him to come and live with us awhile . . . Will he too be 'used' as I have been? How can I warn him? I dreamed of him after going to bed— I thought he asked me to come and see him and I was afraid because he lived in Harlem— Then I became so ashamed of my fear that I decided to go anyhow. I dreamed that when I got to Harlem there was, for some reason, a huge crowd of people waiting to see me and I felt quite embarrassed and lost . . . I was trembling, fearing to be asked to explain why I was in Harlem. Lionel came and rescued me; he was so magnificently himself, so self-assured among his own people who loved and respected him. The moment he arrived the crowd changed its attitude toward me . . . Then he took my arm and led me down the street; he was smiling as we passed in front of the masses of strange people. A wave of happiness flooded me and I fainted . . . Is not all virtue with the oppressed who are not corrupted? I must find some way of saving this boy from the muck in which my life has become bogged . . . But how can I do it?

"March 4th
"Lionel is now in the apartment and I'm filled with a sense of dread. I'd planned to remain in all day, but since he is here, I've decided to go out. I'll go to a concert in the afternoon. That is as good an excuse as any to get away . . . But I must try to save him from his own naïveté . . . He is so quiet, trusting, sensitive . . . What is he thinking all the time? I see him sitting and brooding and his eyes hold the most self-absorbing look I've ever seen in a human being . . . God, he must be suffering . . . ? Is he mulling over the past wrongs done to him and his people? I wish I could help someone like that."

Cross crumpled the sheet, held it to the flame, and watched it burn. Once he turned his head sharply, feeling that Eva was standing near, watching him . . . Slowly he burnt the pages, dropped the charred remains in the sink, ran water over them and flushed them down the drain. When he finished he lifted his eyes and looked out of the window.

Bright sunshine was flooding the world with warm, yellow light and he became aware that he could hear the soft, faint sounds of water dripping. Yes, a thaw had set in. The ice was melting; the snow was dissolving and flowing from the roofs . . .

He heard the front door of the apartment open and close; a moment later Sarah came into the kitchen. She had been out into the streets and was still wearing her overcoat.

"I knew you were tired and I didn't want to awaken you," she began without ceremony. "But now you are up and I can talk to you."

"Yes, Sarah. What is it?"

"I want you to move." She did not look at him as she spoke.

"Of course. What do I owe you for our staying here . . ."

"Nothing." Her voice was bitter.

"I can pay my way." He wanted to help her, but he did not know how.

"I don't want your money," she said. "I'm starting a new life . . . I went to confession this morning." Her voice was metallic, cold.

"I'm glad for you," Cross said. He was suddenly resentful of the fact that Sarah had failed to see that he, of his own accord, was about to move. "Is your telling me to move so bluntly your first act of Christian charity?"

Sarah's eyes hardened.

"This is *my* apartment—" she began.

"I don't dispute that," Cross told her. "But I thought your practicing religion again would make you a little kind . . . I'm all packed to go. I've enough money to take care of myself for a bit . . . And for that, I'm damned lucky. I'm glad that I'm not in your hurry . . ."

"I don't want to argue with you—"

"You won't. I'll get out in five minutes."

There was no communication between them. Couldn't they part as friends who had a little sympathy for each other? Cross looked at her and knew at once that there was no way. Sarah desired too much. Only a great promise could lift her up and help her to live again. Promises . . . ? Could he ever make promises again? And he could not promise anything to Sarah; she had already received from her church a promise covering the whole of her life on this earth and the life to come . . . He turned from her, entered his room, picked up his suitcase, and went into the hall. Sarah stood in the kitchen doorway, looking at him.

"Good-bye, Sarah."

She did not answer; he saw her face reflect a struggle. He started toward her and she burst into tears, whirled, turned into the kitchen and slammed the door. He pivoted on his heels and walked on down the hall, opened the door and went out.

The streets were wet under the glare of a bright sun. He paused on the stoop; he had no notion where he was going. He heard water gurgling in the gutters, running toward the conduits of the sewers. He walked toward Seventh Avenue, thinking: Was it possible that all he had learned in the last few weeks would remain locked forever in his heart? Would he ever be able to say anything about it? And Eva . . . ?

He became aware of someone following him and he turned. It was Menti and behind Menti was that sullen, inexpressive Hank whose hands were jammed as always in his overcoat pockets, his eyes staring hard at Cross from beneath the brim of a dirty hat.

Cross stopped and waited for Menti to catch up with him. "Are you following me, Menti?"

"Where are you going?" Menti asked, grinning.

"I don't know. Tell the Party that I said I didn't know."

"Leaving town?"

"I don't know."

"How can one get in touch with you?"

"You can't."

"You won't have an address?"

"Maybe not."

"Well, I'll be seeing you," Menti said. "Don't forget the Party."

"How could I ever forget the Party?" Cross asked him.

Menti grinned and turned away. Cross kept on to the end of the block. He was moving again among people. But how could he ever make a bridge from him to them? To live with them again would mean making promises, commitments. But he had strayed so far that little commitments were now of no avail. He would have to start all over again. And it was impossible to do that *alone* . . .

He checked his suitcase and went into a cinema and sat looking at the moving shadows on the screen without understanding their import. Two hours later he came out and had lunch. Once again he stood upon the sidewalk, will-less, aimless. Then he was agitated. There was Menti down at the far end of the block, and Hank was behind him. They were watching him. Goddamn them . . .

He came to Lenox Avenue and headed toward downtown. He saw another movie house. He looked over his shoulder; Menti and Hank were moving toward him . . . Quickly he paid his admission and ducked into the sheltering darkness of the cinema, looking now and then to see if Menti or his man was near . . . He could not find them.

When he emerged three hours later, stiff and thirsty, Menti and Hank were not to be seen. Had he ditched them? Maybe . . . Dusk was falling upon Harlem. Neon lights gleamed in the deepening mists. He went into a bar and sat in the rear, facing the door, keeping watch. He downed several whiskies which he could not feel or taste. What was he going to do? Find another room or leave town . . . ?

Once more on the sidewalk, he looked for Menti. Suddenly he longed for the shelter of a well-lighted place, something like a huge hotel lobby with throngs of people and hard, glaring electric bulbs shedding clarity and safety upon everything . . . He found himself facing Central Park. He paused at a street corner till the red traffic light turned green, then he moved out and walked alongside Central Park, heading toward downtown.

He glanced over his shoulder, feeling that he was being

followed; but there was no one to be seen on the night streets behind him. An occasional car whizzed past, its headlights illuminating the foggy night about him for a moment, then leaving him alone in the dark once more. Ahead he saw a young couple coming toward him, engrossed in each other . . . A sense of Eva flashed through him and he knew that the bleakness he was now feeling came from the desire he had had of having her with him . . . This homelessness would not have been so difficult to bear if he had not based his hopes on being with her.

Again he paused and glanced over his shoulder. Yes; there were two dark forms lurking in the shadows about a block away. Menti and Hank were after him . . . And he was in a bad spot here next to Central Park. He was in danger; he looked around him in panic. He had to hide somewhere, quickly . . . If he could dodge them tonight, he would leave the city first thing tomorrow morning . . . A taxi? But there was none in sight. If only he had the shelter of the home of a friend in which to hide . . . Who? Oh, God, yes . . . *Hattie!* He'd quite forgotten her. He had run off from her and left her to fend for herself with her confidence men. How had she made out? He would call her now, and if she was in, he'd go right over . . .

Ahead of him, across the street, were the lights of a drugstore. He looked again over his shoulder and saw the dark forms of Menti and Hank standing, watching. He crossed the street and entered the drugstore, breathing easier amidst the neon lights, the rows of colored bottles, the gleaming mirrors . . . He thumbed through a telephone directory, found Hattie's number, dropped a coin in the box, and dialed. He heard the faint sound of her phone ringing. Maybe she had already lost her home and had moved . . . ?

"Hello." It was Hattie's voice; it sounded tired.

"Hattie?"

"Yes. Who's this?"

"Hattie, this is Jordan. Addison Jordan. Remember?"

There was a pause and he heard her gasp.

"Oh, God! What *happened* to you?" Her voice was cold and distant.

"Look, I want to see you. I'll tell you everything . . ."

"Where are you?"

"In a drugstore, near Central Park."

"Why did you run off like that?"

"Oh, God, Hattie. I know I acted badly . . ."

"What do you want now?"

"I want to see you. Now. Tonight."

"Listen, I'm in a mess. Maybe I can see you next week—Look, you see, I'm in trouble. I'm losing my home . . . You understand?"

He heard her sobbing quietly.

"Did the police ever catch White and Mills?" he asked.

"No," she heaved over the line. "There was no trace of 'em. And today I was supposed to pay $250 to straighten out the mortgage. I didn't have it. I must get out in the morning; the bank is taking over the house . . ."

"You say you need $250?"

"Yes."

"Hattie, I'll let you have it. I've got it with me. Can I see you now?"

There was a moment's silence.

"You mean that really?" she asked, a note of scared hope was in her voice.

"Yes; I tell you I got it with me, in cash."

"Oh, God . . ."

"I'll take a taxi over right now, hear?"

"Oh, God in Heaven," she cried. "But, don't fool me, please . . ."

"I'll see you in ten minutes, Hattie."

"Okay. But don't fool me—"

He hung up. He would hide with her until he made up his mind where he wanted to go. He left the phone booth and looked through the drugstore window. Menti and Hank were not in sight. Central Park lay black and silent across the street. He went out and looked for a taxi. There was none . . . Well, he'd walk until he saw one. He swung along the pavement, full of desperate hope . . . He'd give Hattie the $250; it would be worth it to hide himself, and he owed it to her for what he had done by running off . . . How quiet the night was! Had Menti and Hank given him up? There's a taxi . . .

"Taxi!" he bellowed.

The taxi slowed and pulled to a curb half a block away alongside the park. He broke into a wild run, waving his hand to assure the driver that he was coming. He crossed the street and walked with the park flanking him. He was lucky after all . . .

A second later he heard a snapping sound, as of a twig being broken, and then a faint footfall; there was a shower of something like loose gravel and in the same instant he felt tearing through his chest a searing streak of fire and a loud, sharp report smote his ears as his body jerked forward. The next moment he was sprawled flat on his back, having pitched headlong over his suitcase. He was staring toward a sky he could not see. Pain ripped at his chest. He had been shot. Somewhere in the region of his heart was a jumping, pulsing pain. He heard footsteps running. The Party . . . Then his inner world began to turn as dark as that world around him. He heard vague voices.

"You hurt, Mister?"

He felt someone tugging at his arm and pain rose from his chest in one huge red wave and engulfed him.

When Cross opened his eyes again he was aware of a dim light in a partially darkened room. He was cold and tired. As some measure of consciousness returned, he struggled to lift himself upon his elbow, but he felt an alien hand softly restraining him.

"You must be still."

It was the voice of a woman. He struggled to focus his eyes and mumbled: "What happened?"

"You're hurt. Lie still."

The nurse was a foggy blur of white. Yes, he was in a hospital and then he felt again that awful ball of fire in his chest and he was aware that he was laboring in his breathing. He tried to lift his right hand, but it was too, too heavy. They got me, he thought. He felt no wonder, hate, or surprise. He had been going to the taxi and they had shot him . . . A fit of un controllable coughing seized him and shadows closed in again.

A long time later, his eyes fluttered weakly open and he saw daylight. The dim figure of a nurse in white leaned over him and beyond her he was vaguely conscious of other people whose presence seemed remote and unimportant.

"Damon," a familiar voice came into his ear. "Can you hear me?"

He heard the question, but it seemed foolish to try to answer. He attempted again to focus his eyes, but could not.

"Damon, this is Houston, the District Attorney. Can you talk a little . . . ?"

A fleeting smile passed through him, making his lips twitch slightly. Houston! His pal! The old hunchback! The wise old scared outlaw who had found a way of embracing his fear so that he could live and act without being too scared! He longed to see Houston; once more he sought to focus his eyes, but the face looming over him remained a blob of pink.

"Who shot you, Damon? Did you see him?"

How foolish and unessential it was to ask him that now! What did it matter?

"Was it the Party? Can you hear me? Was it the Party folks who shot you?" The voice was insistent.

Yes; he'd try to answer; he struggled to move his tongue and shape his lips and he whispered:

"I don't know. I think so . . ."

"Don't try to talk too much, Damon. Just listen and answer briefly. Save your strength . . . Did the Party find out you had killed Gil and Hilton?"

"No," he whispered.

"Then why do you think they shot you?"

"They guessed . . ."

"You didn't confess, didn't tell 'em?"

"No."

"Did they have any proof? How did they know?"

"They didn't know . . . They didn't understand me . . . And they shoot what they don't understand . . ."

"Listen, if you can give me anything to go on, I'll prosecute them."

Cross sighed. His lips were dry, burning. What silliness was Houston talking? He had been living by a law and that law had turned on him. That was all.

"Forget it," he whispered.

"But if you know anything—"

"Skip it."

Pain seized him again and he felt someone holding his arm; they were injecting a sedative into him to quiet the pain.

"Damon, this is Houston still . . . Look, is there anything you want to tell me? These killings, were there more of them?"

Oh, God, that poor clown of a Joe Thomas . . . !

"Yes . . ."

"Where?"

"One other man . . . In Chicago. His name was Joe Thomas . . . I killed him in a hotel room to keep him from . . . betraying me . . ."

"Is that all?"

"That's all . . . Isn't that . . . *enough?*"

He felt suddenly sleepy and he had to fight against it. He had nestling blackly deep in him a knowledge of his pending end that made him know that he had but a short time in which to say anything.

"Damon, can you hear me?"

"Yes," he managed to whisper.

Houston's voice seemed to be closer now and the tone had changed; it was the voice of a brother asking an urgent, confidential question.

"Damon, listen to me, just listen and think about what I'm asking and then try to answer . . . This is Houston still talking to you . . . Damon, you were an outsider . . . You know what I mean, don't you? You lived apart . . . Damon, tell me, why did you choose to live that way?"

The damned old curious outlaw! He never forgot anything. He was still on his trail . . . Still hunting him down . . . Sure; he'd tell 'im . . .

"I wanted to be free . . . To feel what I was worth . . . What living meant to me . . . I loved life too . . . much . . ."

"And what did you find?"

"Nothing . . ." He lay very still and summoned all of his strength. "The search can't be done alone," he let his voice issue from a dry throat in which he felt death lurking. "Never alone . . . Alone a man is nothing . . . Man is a promise that he must never break . . ."

"Is there anything, Damon, you want me to tell anybody?"

His mind reeled at the question. There was so much and yet it was so little . . .

"I wish I had some way to give the meaning of my life to others . . . To make a bridge from man to man . . . Starting from scratch every time is . . . is no good. Tell them not to come down this road . . . Men hate themselves and it makes them hate others . . . We must find some way of being good to ourselves . . . Man is all we've got . . . I wish I could ask men to meet themselves . . . We're different from what we seem . . . Maybe worse, maybe better . . . But certainly different . . . We're strangers to ourselves." He was silent for a moment, then he continued, whispering: "Don't think I'm so odd and strange . . . I'm not . . . I'm legion . . . I've lived alone, but I'm everywhere . . . Man is returning to the earth . . . For a long time he has been sleeping, wrapped in a dream . . . He is awakening now, awakening from his dreams and finding himself in a waking nightmare . . . The myth-men are going . . . The real men, the last men are coming . . . Somebody must prepare the way for them . . . Tell the world what they are like . . . We are here already, if others but had the courage to see us . . ."

He felt a weak impulse to laugh. His strength was flowing rapidly from him. His eyes would not focus. The world that was visible was a grey, translucent screen that had begun to shimmer and waver. He closed his eyes and struggled with his tongue and lips to try to shape words.

"Do you understand what I mean, Damon?" Houston asked softly. "I'm talking about *you*, your life . . . How was it with *you*, Damon?"

His eyes stared bleakly. His effort was supreme; his lips parted; his tongue moved; he cursed that damned ball of seething fire that raged in his chest and managed to get his reluctant breath past it to make words:

"It . . . It was . . . horrible . . ."

There was a short silence, then Houston's voice came again: "What do you mean? What was horrible?"

The effort to keep his heavy eyes open was too much and it was not worth trying. He stopped fighting and let his lids droop and darkness soothed him for a moment; once more he struggled grimly to control his lips and tongue, to still that exploding ball of fire that leaped white hot in his chest; then he said in a softly falling, dying whisper:

"All of it . . ."

"But why? *Why?* Try and tell me . . ."

"Because in my heart . . . I'm . . . I felt . . . I'm *innocent* . . . That's what made the horror . . ."

He felt his dull head falling helplessly to one side. Huge black shadows were descending softly down upon him. He took a chest full of air and sighed . . .

He was dead.

London–Paris, 1952

Chronology

1908   Born Richard Nathaniel Wright, September 4, on Rucker's Plantation, a farm near Roxie, Mississippi, 22 miles east of Natchez, first child of Nathan Wright, an illiterate sharecropper, and Ella Wilson Wright, a schoolteacher. (All four grandparents had been born in slavery. Father was born shortly before 1880, the son of Nathaniel Wright, a freed slave who farmed a plot of land he had been given at the end of the Civil War. Maternal grandfather, Richard Wilson, born March 21, 1847, served in the United States Navy in 1865, then became disillusioned because of a bureaucratic error that deprived him of his pension. Maternal grandmother, Margaret Bolton Wilson, of Irish, Scottish, American Indian, and African descent, was virtually white in appearance. A house slave before the Emancipation, she later became a midwife nurse, a devoted Seventh-day Adventist, and the strict head of her Natchez household, which included eight surviving children. Mother, born 1883, married Nathan Wright in 1907 despite her parents' disapproval, and then gave up school teaching to work on the farm.)

1910   Brother Leon Alan, called Alan, born September 24.

1911–12   Unable to care for her children while working on the farm, mother takes Wright and his brother to live with Wilson family in Natchez. Father rejoins family and finds work in a sawmill. Wright accidentally sets fire to grandparents' house.

1913–14   Family moves to Memphis, Tennessee, by steamboat. Father deserts family to live with another woman, leaving them impoverished. Mother finds work as a cook.

1915–16   Wright enters school at Howe Institute, Memphis, in September 1915. Mother falls seriously ill in early 1916. Grandmother comes to care for family. After grandmother returns home, mother puts Wright and his brother in the Settlement House, Methodist orphanage in Memphis, where they stay for over a month. Spends relatively pleasant summer at 1107 Lynch Street in Jackson, Mississippi, where maternal grandparents now live, before going with mother and brother to Elaine, Arkansas, to live with his favorite aunt, Maggie (his mother's younger sister), and her husband, Silas Hoskins, a saloon-keeper.

1917–18   After Hoskins is murdered by whites who want his prosperous liquor business, terrified family flees to West Helena, Arkansas, then returns to Jackson with Aunt Maggie to live with the Wilsons. After several months they go back to West Helena, where mother and aunt find work cooking and cleaning for whites. Aunt Maggie leaves with her lover, "Professor" Matthews, a fugitive from the law (they eventually settle in Detroit).

1918–19   Wright enters local school in fall 1918. Mother's health deteriorates early in 1919 and Wright is forced to leave school to earn money. Delivers wood and laundry and carries lunches to railroad workers. Family moves frequently because of lack of rent money; Wright gathers stray pieces of coal along railroad tracks to heat their home. Mother suffers paralyzing stroke, and grandmother comes to bring the family back to Jackson. Aunt Maggie helps care for mother, then takes Leon Alan back to Detriot with her; other aunts and uncles help pay for mother's treatment.

1919–20   Wright moves into home of aunt and uncle, Clark and Jody Wilson, in nearby Greenwood, Mississippi, where he is able to attend school. Finds household calm and orderly but his aunt and uncle cold and unsympathetic, and is terrified by episodes of sleepwalking. Returns to grandparents' home in Jackson. Mother begins to show signs of recovery from paralysis, then has relapse caused by a cerebral blood clot that leaves her virtually crippled. Her illness impoverishes the family, already hurt by the rheumatism that makes Grandfather Wilson unable to work.

1920–21   Enters Seventh-day Adventist school taught by his youngest aunt, Addie. Only nine years older than Wright, she is a rigid disciplinarian often at odds with him. Wright rebels against the rules and practices of the religion, including its diet, which forbids eating pork. Finds himself opposed to his family in general, except for his mother, who is too sick to help him.

1921–22   Enters the fifth grade of the Jim Hill School in Jackson, two years behind his age group. Does well, quickly gains in confidence, and is soon promoted to the sixth grade. Begins friendships, some of them lasting into his adulthood, with a number of other students, including Dick Jordan, Joe Brown, Perry Booker, D. C. Blackburn, Lewis Anderson, Sarah McNeamer, and Essie Lee Ward. Takes job as a newsboy, which gives him the chance to read material forbidden at home because of religious prohibitions. Family life continues to be difficult, although his mother's health improves slightly. Travels briefly during summer in the Mississippi Delta region as "secretary-accountant" to an insurance agent, W. Mance. The trip allows him to know better the rural South, but he is dismayed by the illiteracy and lack of education he encounters among blacks.

1922–23   Enters the seventh grade. Grandfather Wilson dies November 8. After many arguments, grandmother reluctantly lets Wright take jobs after school and on Saturday (the Seventh-day Adventist sabbath). Runs errands and performs small chores, mainly for whites. For the first time has enough money to buy school books, food to combat his chronic hunger, and clothing. Baptized in the Methodist Church, mainly to please his mother. Avidly reads pulp magazines, dime novels, and books and magazines discarded by others. Uncle Thomas Wilson, his wife, and their two daughters come to live with the family in spring 1923. Mother's health worsens. Wright works during the summer at a brickyard and as a caddy at a golf course.

1923–24   Enters eighth grade at the Smith Robertson Junior High School, Jackson (a former slave, Smith Robertson had become a successful local barber and a community leader; the school, built in 1894, was the first black institution of its kind in Jackson). Until he can afford a bicycle, Wright walks several miles daily to and from the school. Makes new friends at school, including Wade Griffin, Varnie Reed, Arthur Leaner, and Minnie Farish. Begins working for the Walls, a white family he finds kindly (will serve them for two years). Later remembers writing his first short story, "The Voodoo of Hell's Half-Acre," in late winter (story is reported to have been published in the spring as "Hell's Half-Acre" in the Jackson *Southern Register*, a black weekly newspaper; no copies are known to be extant). Brother Leon Alan returns from Detroit. Wright is initially pleased, but their relationship soon disappoints him. Works for the American Optical Company, cleaning workshop and making deliveries.

1924–25 Enters ninth grade at Smith Robertson Junior High School, and graduates on May 29, 1925, as valedictorian. Rejects graduation speech prepared for him by the principal and instead delivers his own, "The Attributes of Life." Works as a delivery boy, sales clerk, hotel hallboy and bellboy, and in a movie theater. Begins classes in fall at newly founded Lanier High School, but quits a few weeks later to earn money. Leaves Jackson for Memphis, Tennessee, where he boards with a family at 570 Beale Street.

1926 Works for low pay as a dishwasher and delivery boy and at the Merry Optical Company. Reads widely in *Harper's*, *Atlantic Monthly*, *The American Mercury*, and other magazines. Moves to 875 Griffith Place.

1927 Joined by mother, who is still in poor health, and brother; they take an apartment together at 370 Washington Street. After reading an editorial highly critical of H. L. Mencken, long noted as a critic of the white South, Wright seeks out Mencken's *Prejudices* and *A Book of Prefaces* and is particularly impressed by Mencken's iconoclasm and use of "words as weapons." These books serve as guides to further reading, including works by Theodore Dreiser, Sinclair Lewis, Sherwood Anderson, the elder Alexandre Dumas, Frank Harris, and O. Henry. Aunt Maggie, who has been deserted by "Professor" Matthews, joins family in the fall. In December, Wright and Maggie, who hopes to open a beauty salon, move to the South Side of Chicago, while mother and Leon Alan return to Jackson. Sees his aunt Cleopatra ("Sissy"), but is disappointed to find that she lives in a rooming house, not an apartment, and moves into a rooming house with Aunt Maggie.

1928 Works as delivery boy in a delicatessen, then as a dishwasher. Wright finds Chicago stimulating and less racially oppressive than the South, but is often dismayed by the pace and disarray of urban life. Passes written examination for the postal service in the spring, then begins work in the summer as a temporary employee at 65 cents an hour. Rents an apartment with Aunt Maggie and is joined by mother and brother. In the fall Wright fails the postal service medical examination required for a permanent position because of chronic undernourishment and returns to dishwashing. Disputes over money and his reading cause tension with Aunt Maggie. Wright takes another apartment for family and invites his aunt Cleopatra to move in with them.

1929   After undertaking a crash diet to increase his weight, Wright passes the physical examination and is hired by the central post office at Clark Street and Jackson Boulevard as a substitute clerk and mail sorter. Moves with family to four rooms at 4831 Vincennes Avenue, which allows him to read and write in relative comfort. Dislikes the post office bureaucracy, but becomes friendly with many fellow workers, both black and white. Among his friends are schoolmates from the South, including Essie Lee Ward, Arthur Leaner, and Joe Brown. Writes steadily and attends meetings of a local black literary group, but feels distant from its middle-class members. Attracted by the Universal Negro Improvement Association, a group inspired by Marcus Garvey, but does not join it.

1930   Volume of mail drops in decline following the 1929 Wall Street crash; Wright has his working hours cut back before losing his job altogether. South Side sinks into economic depression. Works temporarily for post office in the summer. Mother suffers a relapse, aunt Cleopatra has a heart attack, and brother develops stomach ulcers. Begins work on "Cesspool," novel about black life in Chicago. Enrolls in tenth grade at Hyde Park Public School, but soon drops out.

1931   Reads books recommended by friend William Harper (who will later own a bookstore on the South Side). Wright is particularly impressed by Dreiser and Joseph Conrad, and continues to write. Short story "Superstition" is published in April *Abbott's Monthly Magazine*, a black journal (magazine fails before Wright is paid). Through a distant relative, finds job as a funeral insurance agent for several burial societies. Also works as an assistant to a black Republican precinct captain during the mayoral campaign, and at the post office in December. Becomes interested in views of Communist orators and organizers, especially those in the League of Struggle for Negro Rights.

1932   Sells insurance policies door-to-door and works briefly as an assistant to a Democratic precinct captain. Family moves to slum apartment as Wright is increasingly unable to sell policies to blacks impoverished by the Depression. Asks for and receives relief assistance from the Cook County Bureau of Public Welfare, which finds him a temporary job as a street cleaner. Works at the post office during the Christmas season.

1933   Digs ditches in the Cook County Forest Preserves, then works at Michael Reese Hospital, caring for animals used in medical research. Recruited by fellow post office worker Abraham Aaron to join the newly formed Chicago branch of the John Reed Club, a national literary organization sponsored by the Communist party. Welcomed and encouraged by the almost entirely white membership of the club, Wright begins to read and study *New Masses* and *International Literature*, the organ of the International League of Revolutionary Writers. Writes and submits revolutionary poems ("I Have Seen Black Hands," "A Red Love Note") to *Left Front*, the magazine of the midwestern John Reed Clubs. Elected executive secretary of the Chicago John Reed Club and organizes a successful lecture series which allows him to meet a variety of intellectuals. Gives lecture at open forum on "The Literature of the Negro."

1934   Hoping to consolidate his position in the John Reed Club, Wright joins the Communist party; is also impressed by the party's opposition to racial discrimination. Publishes poetry in *Left Front*, *Anvil*, and *New Masses*. Becomes a member of the editorial board of *Left Front*. Enjoys literary and social friendships with Bill Jordan, Abraham Chapman, Howard Nutt, Laurence Lipton, Nelson Algren, Joyce Gourfain, and Jane Newton. Grandmother Wilson comes to Chicago to join the family; they move to apartment at 4804 St. Lawrence Avenue, near the railroad tracks. Mother's paralysis returns after attack of encephalitis. Wright is laid off by the hospital in the summer, and again works as a street sweeper and ditch digger before being hired to supervise a youth club organized to counter juvenile delinquency among blacks on the South Side. Attends Middle West Writers' Congress in August and the national congress of John Reed Clubs in September. Dismayed by party decision to cease publication of *Left Front* and to dissolve the John Reed Clubs in 1935 as part of its Popular Front strategy. Meets Jack Conroy, editor of *Anvil*. Reading in Chicago by this time includes Henry James (especially the Prefaces to the New York Edition), Gertrude Stein (notably her *Three Lives*, with its portrait of a black character, Melanctha Herbert), Faulkner, T. S. Eliot, Sherwood Anderson, Dos Passos, O'Neill, Stephen Crane, Dreiser, Whitman, Poe, D. H. Lawrence, Conrad, Galsworthy, Hardy, Dickens, George Moore, Carlyle, Swift, Shakespeare, Tolstoy, Dostoevsky, Turgenev, Chekhov, Proust, Dumas, and Balzac. Lectures on the career of Langston Hughes to the Indianapolis John Reed Club in November and contributes fee to new publication *Midland Left*.

1935   Publishes leftist poetry in *Midland Left*, a short-lived journal, *New Masses* ("Red Leaves of Red Books" and "Spread Your Sunshine"), and *International Literature* ("A Red Slogan"). Family moves to 2636 Grove Avenue. Begins submitting novel "Cesspool" to publishers (later retitled *Lawd Today!* by Wright; it is rejected repeatedly over the next two years, then published posthumously as *Lawd Today* in 1963 by Walker and Company). Wright attends the first American Writers' Congress, held in New York in April. Speaks on "The Isolation of the Negro Writer," meets Chicago novelist James T. Farrell, and becomes one of fifty members of the national council of the newly formed League of American Writers. Works on story "Big Boy Leaves Home." Publishes "Between the World and Me," poem about lynching, in July–August *Partisan Review*. Falls seriously ill with attack of pneumonia during the summer. Article "Avant-Garde Writing" wins second prize in contest sponsored by two literary magazines but is never published. First piece of journalism, "Joe Louis

Uncovers Dynamite," describing the reaction of Chicago blacks to the Louis–Max Baer fight, published in *New Masses*. Grandmother Wilson dies. Family, with Wright still virtually its sole support, moves to 3743 Indiana Avenue. Wright is hired by the Federal Writers' Project (part of the Works Progress Administration) to help research the history of Illinois and of the Negro in Chicago for the Illinois volume in the American Guide Series. Discusses influence of Hemingway with fellow writers in federal project.

1936   Publishes "Transcontinental," a six-page radical poem influenced by Whitman and Louis Aragon, in January *International Literature*. Becomes a principal organizer of the Communist party–sponsored National Negro Congress (successor to the League of Struggle for Negro Rights), held in Chicago in February, and reports on it for *New Masses*. Transferred in spring to the Federal Theatre Project, where he serves as literary adviser and press agent for the Negro Federal Theatre of Chicago and becomes involved in dramatic productions. Finishes two one-act plays based in part on a section of his unpublished novel. In April, Wright takes a leading role in the new South Side Writers' Group (members will include Arna Bontemps, Frank Marshall Davis, Theodore Ward, Fenton Johnson, Horace Cayton, and Margaret Walker). Takes an active role in the Middle West Writers' Congress, held in Chicago June 14–15. Because of what he later describes as a Communist plot against him on the Federal Theatre Project assignment, Wright returns to the Writers' Project, where he becomes a group coordinator. Story "Big Boy Leaves Home" appears in anthology *The New Caravan* in November and receives critical attention and praise in mainstream newspapers and journals.

1937   Publishes poem "We of the Streets" in April *New Masses* and story "Silt" in the August number. Breaks with the Communist party in Chicago, basically over the question of his freedom as a writer. Brother finds job with the Works Progress Administration and assumes some responsibility for support of the family. Wright ranks first in postal service examination in Chicago, but turns down offer in May of permanent position at approximately $2,000 a year in order to move to New York City to pursue career as a writer. Stays briefly with artist acquaintances in Greenwich Village, then moves to Harlem; by mid-June he has a furnished room in the Douglass Hotel at 809 St. Nicholas Avenue. Attends Second American Writers' Congress as a delegate and serves as a session president; stresses the need for writers to think of themselves as writers first and not as laborers. Becomes Harlem editor of the Communist newspaper *Daily Worker* and writes over 200 articles for it during the year, including pieces on blues singer Leadbelly and the continuing Scottsboro Boys controversy. With Dorothy West and Marian Minus, helps launch magazine *New Challenge*, designed to present black life "in relationship to the struggle against war and Fascism." Wright publishes "The Ethics of Living Jim Crow—An Autobiographical Sketch" in *American Stuff: WPA Writers' Anthology* (essay is later included in the second edition of *Uncle Tom's Children* and incorporated into *Black Boy*). In November, publishes influential essay "Blueprint for Negro Writing" in *New Challenge*, criticizing past black literature and urging a Marxist-influenced approach that would transcend nationalism. Lacking party support, *New Challenge* fails after one number. Befriends 23-year-old Ralph Ellison. Wright's second novel, "Tarbaby's Dawn," about a black adolescent in the South, is rejected by publishers (it remains unpublished). Learns that story "Fire and Cloud" has won first prize ($500) among 600 entries in *Story Magazine* contest. Wright joins the New York Federal Writers' Project (will write the Harlem section for *New York Panorama* and work on "The Harlems" in *The New York City Guide*).

1938   Rents furnished room at 139 West 143rd Street. Engages Paul Reynolds, Jr., as literary agent. Reynolds makes arrangements to place *Uncle Tom's Children: Four Novellas* ("Big Boy Leaves Home," "Down by the Riverside," "Long Black Song," and "Fire and Cloud") with editor Edward Aswell at Harper and Brothers, beginning Wright's long association with Aswell and Harper; book is published in March and is widely praised. Sends Aswell outline of novel about a black youth in Chicago. Announces plans to marry daughter of his Harlem landlady in May, but then cancels wedding, telling friends that a medical examination had revealed that the young woman has congenital syphilis. Moves into home of friends from

Chicago, Jane and Herbert Newton, at 175 Carleton Ave-
nue in Brooklyn. Story "Bright and Morning Star"
appears in May *New Masses*. Writes about the second Joe
Louis – Max Schmeling fight in the June *Daily Worker* and
July *New Masses*. In June, replaces Horace Gregory on the
editorial board of the literature section of *New Masses*.
Works steadily on new novel; often writes in Fort Greene
Park in the mornings, and discusses his progress with Jane
Newton. Asks Margaret Walker to send him newspaper
accounts of the case of Robert Nixon, a young Chicago
black man accused of murder (executed in August 1939).
Moves in the fall with the Newtons to 522 Gates Avenue.
Congressman Martin Dies, chairman of the House Special
Committee on Un-American Activities, denounces "The
Ethics of Living Jim Crow" during an investigation of the
Federal Writers' Project. Finishes first draft of novel, now
titled *Native Son*, in October and receives $400 advance
from Harper in November. "Fire and Cloud" wins the
O. Henry Memorial Award ($200). Travels to Chicago in
November to research settings and events used in *Native
Son*. Moves with Newtons to 87 Lefferts Place.

1939   Meets Ellen Poplar (b. 1912), daughter of Polish Jewish im-
migrants and a Communist party organizer in Brooklyn.
Completes revised version of novel in February and shows
it to Reynolds. Awarded Guggenheim Fellowship ($2,500)
in March and resigns from the Federal Writers' Project in
May. Discusses black American writing with Langston
Hughes, Alain Locke, Countee Cullen, and Warren
Cochrane during meeting of Harlem Cultural Congress.
After Newtons' landlord evicts them, Wright moves to
Douglass Hotel at 809 St. Nicholas Avenue in May, rent-
ing room next to Theodore Ward, a friend from Chicago.
Becomes close to Ellen Poplar and considers marrying her,
but also sees Dhima Rose Meadman, a modern-dance
teacher of Russian Jewish ancestry. Plays active role at
Third American Writers' Congress. Finishes *Native Son* on
June 10. Ward dramatizes "Bright and Morning Star." The
story is included in Edward O'Brien's *Best American Short
Stories, 1939* and *Fifty Best American Short Stories (1914–1939)*.
Begins work on new novel, "Little Sister." Marries Dhima
Rose Meadman in August in Episcopal church on Con-
vent Avenue, with Ralph Ellison serving as best man.
Lives with his wife, her two-year-old son by an earlier

marriage, and his mother-in-law in large apartment on fashionable Hamilton Terrace in Harlem. Attends Festival of Negro Culture held in Chicago in September. Moves to Crompond, New York, to work on "Little Sister" (it is never completed).

1940   Visits Chicago in February and buys house for his family on Vincennes Avenue. Has lunch in Chicago with W.E.B. Du Bois, Langston Hughes, and Arna Bontemps. *Native Son* published by Harper and Brothers March 1 and is offered by the Book-of-the-Month Club as one of its two main selections. In three weeks it sells 215,000 copies. Wright delivers talk "How 'Bigger' Was Born" at Columbia University on March 12 (later published as a pamphlet by Harper, then added to future printings of *Native Son*). *Native Son* is banned in Birmingham, Alabama, libraries. Takes his first airplane flight when he accompanies *Life* magazine photographers to Chicago for an article on the South Side; tours the area with sociologist Horace Cayton, beginning long friendship (article is later canceled). Sails in April for Veracruz, Mexico, with wife, her son, mother-in-law, and wife's pianist. Rents ten-room villa in the Miraval Colony in Cuernevaca. Takes lessons in Spanish and studies the guitar. Reunited with Herbert Kline, friend from the Chicago John Reed Club, who is filming documentary *The Forgotten Village* with John Steinbeck; Wright travels with them through the countryside and takes an interest in the filming. Signs contract with John Houseman and Orson Welles for stage production of *Native Son*. Marriage becomes strained. Wright leaves Mexico in June and travels through the South alone. Visits his father, a poor and broken farm laborer, in Natchez, but is unable to make anything other than a token reconciliation with him. Goes to Chapel Hill, North Carolina, to begin collaboration with Paul Green on stage adaptation of *Native Son*. Meets producer John Houseman and drives to New York with him. Travels to Chicago to do research for book on black American life featuring photographs selected by Edwin Rosskam. Wright and Langston Hughes are guests of honor at reception given by Jack Conroy and Nelson Algren to launch magazine *New Anvil*. Returns to Chapel Hill in July to continue work with Paul Green. Elected vice-president of the League of American Writers. Harper reissues story collection as *Uncle Tom's Children:*

Five Long Stories with "Bright and Morning Star" added and "The Ethics of Living Jim Crow" as an introduction. Starts divorce proceedings. Moves in with the Newtons, now at 343 Grand Avenue in Brooklyn; in the autumn Ellen Poplar moves into the Newton house. In September Wright is elected a vice-president of American Peace Mobilization, a Communist-sponsored group opposed to American involvement in World War II. Works with Houseman on revising stage version of *Native Son* (both Wright and Houseman think that Green has diverged too much from the novel); Houseman agrees that Orson Welles, who is finishing *Citizen Kane*, should direct. Story "Almos' a Man" appears in *O. Henry Award Prize Stories of 1940*.

1941   In January the National Association for the Advancement of Colored People awards Wright the Spingarn Medal, given annually to the black American judged to have made the most notable achievement in the preceding year. Rehearsals for *Native Son* begin in February. Marries Ellen Poplar in Coytesville, New Jersey, on March 12. They move to 473 West 140th Street. *Native Son*, starring Canada Lee, opens at St. James Theatre on March 24 after a benefit performance for the NAACP. Reviews are generally favorable, though the play is attacked in the Hearst papers, which are hostile to Welles following *Citizen Kane*. Production runs in New York until June 15. Welles' striking but costly staging causes production to lose some money, but it recovers during successful tour of Pittsburgh, Boston, Chicago, Milwaukee, Detroit, St. Louis, and Baltimore. Wright asks the governor of New Jersey to parole Clinton Brewer, a black man imprisoned since 1923 for murdering a young woman, arguing that Brewer, who had taught himself music composition, has rehabilitated himself (Brewer is released July 8; Wright had previously sent one of his pieces to his friend, record producer and talent scout John Hammond, who arranged for Count Basie to record it). Begins novel "Black Hope" (never completed). Introduces Ellen to his family in Chicago during visit in April. Signs appeal of forty members of the League of American Writers against American intervention in the war that appears in *New Masses* May 27, and publishes "Not My People's War" in *New Masses* June 17. After Germany invades the Soviet Union, June 22, American Peace Mobilization changes its name to American

People's Mobilization. Wright travels to Houston with Horace Cayton and John Hammond to accept Spingarn award from NAACP convention on June 27. Delivers enthusiastically received speech, in which his criticism of Roosevelt administration racial policies is muted in response to Communist party pressure. Lectures at Writers' Schools sponsored by the League of American Writers. Wrights move to 11 Revere Place, Brooklyn, in July. At John Hammond's request, Wright writes "Note on Jim Crow Blues" as a preface to the blues singer Josh White's *Southern Exposure,* an album of three recordings attacking segregation. Hammond then produces recording of Paul Robeson singing Wright's blues song "King Joe," accompanied by the Count Basie orchestra. *12 Million Black Voices: A Folk History of the Negro in the United States*, with photographs selected by Edwin Rosskam (one taken by Wright), published by Viking Press in October to enthusiastic reviews. Wright reads *Dark Legend*, a psychoanalytic study of matricide by psychiatrist Frederic Wertham, then writes to Wertham about Clinton Brewer, who had murdered another young woman within months of his release. Wertham intervenes in the case and helps save Brewer from execution (Wright and Wertham begin close friendship, and Wright becomes increasingly interested in psychoanalysis). Finishes draft of novel "The Man Who Lived Underground." Signs petition "Communication to All American Writers" in December 16 *New Masses*, supporting America's entry into the war after the December 7 Japanese attack on Pearl Harbor.

1942   Mother and Aunt Maggie rejoin Addie in Jackson, Mississippi (brother remains in Chicago, though house on Vincennes Avenue is sold two years later). Daughter Julia, Wright's first child, born April 15. Wrights move in summer to 7 Middagh Street, a 19th-century house near the Brooklyn Bridge shared by George Davis, Carson McCullers, and other writers and artists. Excerpts from "The Man Who Lived Underground" appear in *Accent*. As the sole support of his family, Wright is classified 3-A and not drafted. Unsuccessfully tries to secure a special commission in the psychological warfare or propaganda services of the army. *Native Son* returns to Broadway in October (runs until January 1943). Publishes "What You Don't Know Won't Hurt You," article describing some of his experiences as a hospital janitor in Chicago, in December *Harper's Magazine*. Breaks quietly with the Communist party over its unwillingness to confront wartime racial discrimination and its continuing attempts to control his writing.

1943   Accompanied by Horace Cayton, Wright goes to Fisk University, Nashville, in April to deliver talk on his experiences with racism. Strong reaction from the audience leads Wright to begin autobiography *American Hunger*. Neighbors and associates are interviewed by the Federal Bureau of Investigation. (Files obtained under the Freedom of Information Act in the 1970s show that the FBI began an investigation in December 1942 to determine if *12 Million Black Voices* was prosecutable under the sedition statutes. Although the sedition investigation is concluded in 1943, the FBI will continue to monitor Wright's activities, chiefly through the use of informers, for the remainder of his life.) Wrights move in August to 89 Lefferts Place in Brooklyn Heights. Helps organize the Citizens' Emergency Conference for Interracial Unity in response to widespread riots in Harlem following the wounding of a black soldier by white police in August. Finishes *American Hunger* in December.

1944   Writes film scenario "Melody Limited," about group of black singers during Reconstruction (scenario is never produced). Becomes friends with C.L.R. James, a Trinidad-born historian and Trotskyist, with whom he plans a book, "The Negro Speaks," and a journal, "American Pages" (neither of these projects appear), and his wife, Constance Webb. Writes series of radio programs on the life of a black family for producer Leston Huntley and is frustrated when Huntley is unable to place the series, in part because of criticism by middle-class blacks. Attends party held in honor of Theodore Dreiser on June 2, where Wright and Dreiser discuss the influence of life in Chicago on their attitudes. Deepens friendship with Dorothy Norman, New York *Post* editorial writer and editor of *Twice a Year*, who introduces him to existentialist philosophy and literature. Book-of-the-Month Club tells Harper that it will accept only the first section of *American Hunger*, describing Wright's experiences in the South; Wright agrees to this arrangement. Changes title to *Black Boy*. (Second section, telling of Wright's life in Chicago, is published as *American Hunger* by Harper & Row in 1977.) Wrights vacation in August outside Ottawa and in the nearby Gatineau country in Quebec. Excerpts from second section of autobiography appear as "I Tried to Be a Communist" in *Atlantic Monthly*, August–September, making public Wright's break with the Communist party. He is denounced by various party organs, including *New Masses* and the *Daily Worker*. Helps the Chicago poet Gwendolyn Brooks to place her first book, *A Street in Bronzeville*. Expanded version of "The Man Who Lived Underground" is published as a novella in *Cross Section*.

1945   To circumvent racial discrimination, Wrights form the "Richelieu Realty Co." and use their lawyer as an intermediary in buying a house at 13 Charles Street in Greenwich Village. (Residence is delayed by their waiting for a Communist tenant hostile to Wright to leave and by redecorating.) Reviews books for *P.M.* newspaper; his highly favorable review of Gertrude Stein's *Wars I Have Seen* leads to correspondence with her. *Black Boy: A Record of Childhood and Youth* published by Harper and Brothers in March to enthusiastic reviews. The book is number one on the bestseller list from April 29 to June 6 and stirs controversy when it is denounced as obscene in the U.S. Senate by Democrat Theodore Bilbo of Mississippi. Takes part in several radio programs, including the nationally influential "Town Meeting," where he argues the negative on the question "Are We Solving America's Race Problem?" In the summer, Wrights vacation on island off Quebec City, and Wright lectures at the Bread Loaf writers' school in Middlebury, Vermont. Writes long introduction to *Black Metropolis*, a sociological study of black Chicago by Horace Cayton and St. Clair Drake. Befriending a number of younger writers, white and black, Wright helps the 20-year-old James Baldwin win a Eugene F. Saxton Foundation Fellowship. Publishes a favorable review of Chester Himes's first novel, *If He Hollers Let Him Go*, and lends Himes $1,000. In the fall, Wrights move to an apartment at 82 Washington Place in Greenwich Village to be closer to a school for Julia. Wright undertakes four-month lecture tour but stops after six weeks because of exhaustion.

1946   Serves as honorary pallbearer at funeral on January 12
              of poet Countee Cullen, attending service at Salem Meth-
              odist Church in Harlem and burial at Woodlawn Ceme-
              tery in the Bronx. By January 19, *Black Boy* has sold 195,000
              copies in the Harper trade edition and 351,000 through the
              Book-of-the-Month Club, making it the fourth best-
              selling non-fiction title of 1945. Wright, his psychiatrist
              friend Dr. Frederic Wertham, and others found the La-
              fargue Clinic, a free psychiatric clinic in Harlem. Meets
              Jean-Paul Sartre in New York. Receives invitation to visit
              France, but requests for a passport meet with opposition.
              Wright goes to Washington for an interview and enlists
              the aid of Dorothy Norman (who appoints him co-editor
              of *Twice a Year*), Gertrude Stein, and French cultural atta-
              ché, anthropologist Claude Lévi-Strauss, who sends him
              an official invitation from the French government to visit
              Paris for a month. Wright leaves New York on May 1. In
              Paris, welcomed by Gertrude Stein and by almost all the
              important French literary societies and circles. (Stein dies
              on July 27 after operation for cancer.) Meets Simone de
              Beauvoir and André Gide, whose *Travels in the Congo*
              has impressed Wright, as well as Léopold Sédar Senghor
              of Senegal, Aimé Césaire of Martinique, and others in
              the *Négritude* movement. Assists Senghor, Césaire, and
              Alioune Diop of Senegal in founding the magazine *Pré-
              sence Africaine* and attends its first board meeting at the
              Brasserie Lipp. Donates a manuscript to an auction for
              benefit of experimental dramatist Antonin Artaud. "The
              Man Who Killed a Shadow" published in French in *Les
              Lettres Françaises* (first appears in English in 1949 in mag-
              azine *Zero*). Leaves Paris in late December and travels to
              London.

1947   Meets the Trinidad-born intellectual George Padmore
              and dines with members of the Coloured Writers' Associ-
              ation, including its president, Cedric Dover, author of
              Half Caste, and the colored South African journalist
              and novelist Peter Abrahams. Returns to New York in
              January. Moves with family into their Charles Street house
              in Greenwich Village. Helps to welcome Simone de Beau-
              voir to New York in the spring. Refuses offer from
              Hollywood producer to film *Native Son* with character
              Bigger Thomas changed to a white man. Wright's works
              are being translated into French, Italian, German, Dutch,

and Czech. Decides to return to Europe permanently with his family, partially in response to the racial hostility they are encountering in New York. Sells Greenwich Village house in June. Vacations at a cottage at Wading River, Long Island, owned by a friend. Buys an Oldsmobile sedan to take to Europe. Wright, his wife, and daughter reach Paris in August. They rent rooms from a friend, Odette Lieutier, in her apartment on the rue de Lille, then move into an apartment at 166 Avenue de Neuilly. Albin Michel publishes French translation of *Native Son* in autumn.

1948   Begins to read more deeply in existentialism, including Heidegger and Husserl. Sees much of Sartre and Simone de Beauvoir. Wright is particularly impressed by Camus' *The Stranger*, and begins work on an existentialist novel, eventually titled *The Outsider*. Gallimard translation of *Black Boy* wins French Critics' Award. Wright establishes friendships with the Reverend Clayton Williams, pastor of the American Church, and with Harry Goldberg of the American Library. Becomes unofficial spokesman for African-American colony in Paris, which includes James Baldwin. Visits Italy for the publication there of *Native Son*. Meets with Carlo Levi and Ignazio Silone, who later introduces him to Arthur Koestler in Paris. Interviewed by his Italian translator, Fernanda Pivano, Wright says he likes to read *Metamorphosis*, *Moby-Dick*, *Ulysses*, and *The Sound and the Fury*. Travels through Belgium to London, where he sees a performance of *Native Son* and renews friendship with George Padmore, who stirs Wright's interest in the question of colonialism in Africa. Moves with family to 14 rue Monsieur le Prince in the Latin Quarter in May. Ellen returns to New York in June to select furniture and other possessions for their new life in France. Wright is beset by recurring sinus problems and influenza. His tonsils are removed. Aids Sartre and Camus in the leadership of the Rassemblement Démocratique Révolutionnaire (RDR), an organization of intellectuals critical of both the Soviet Union and the United States. Wright plays prominent role in its writers' congress, held in Paris on December 13, delivering lengthy speech (translated by Simone de Beauvoir). Spends $6,000 to buy Paul Green's share of film rights to *Native Son* in hopes of making screen version with French director Pierre Chenal.

1949   Daughter Rachel born January 17 at the American Hospi-
           tal. Wright travels again to Rome and to Switzerland, for
           the publication of *Black Boy*. In April, James T. Farrell and
           Nelson Algren visit him in Paris. Suspects socialist David
           Rousset of trying to shift the RDR toward a more pro-
           American, anti-Soviet stance. Refuses to attend large
           RDR rally held on April 30 (organization soon splits and
           dissolves). In May, visits London to consult with Richard
           Crossman, who is including "I Tried to Be a Communist"
           with similar essays by Koestler, Gide, Silone, Stephen
           Spender, and Louis Fischer in collection *The God That
           Failed* (published later in year, book is widely reviewed).
           Continues work on his existentialist novel. Assists George
           Plimpton and others in launching of *Paris Review*. James
           Baldwin's essay "Everybody's Protest Novel," attacking
           Stowe's *Uncle Tom's Cabin* but including criticism of *Na-
           tive Son*, sours relationship between Wright and Baldwin.
           Wright writes screenplay for *Native Son*, adding several
           dream sequences to the story, then revises it with Chenal.
           After Canada Lee withdraws from project because of new
           commitments and worsening health, Wright undertakes to
           play the main role of Bigger Thomas. Sails for the United
           States in August, briefly visiting New York before going
           to Chicago for filming of exteriors for *Native Son*. Sees
           old friends Horace Cayton, St. Clair Drake, and others.
           Leaves New York in September for Argentina, where film
           is being made (Chenal had worked there during World
           War II, and political pressure had blocked access to French
           studios). Makes brief stops in Trinidad, Brazil, and Uru-
           guay before arriving in Buenos Aires in October. Loses 35
           pounds in preparation for the role by following strict diet
           and exercise program. Continues working on screenplay
           with Chenal.

1950   Production is delayed by financial problems. Wright finds
           atmosphere of Argentine life under the Perón dictatorship
           oppressive. Filming ends in June. Wright leaves Buenos
           Aires in July. Stops briefly in Brazil and Trinidad, spends
           two weeks in Haiti, then returns to Paris by way of New
           York, where he visits Frederic Wertham and the Lafargue
           Clinic. In Paris, begins work on screenplay about Tous-
           saint L'Ouverture of Haiti. Works with James Ivory on
           "Revelation of Negro Art," an exhibition that includes
           works from the Musée de l'Homme and song and dance

performances at the Cité Universitaire. Vacations in the fall in the Swiss and French Alps, visiting Basel, Zurich, and the Aoste Valley, where he is a jury member with Paul Eluard, Louis Bromfield, and others for international San Vicente literary prize. Founds and becomes president of the Franco-American Fellowship, intended to protest official American policies and oppose racial discrimination by American companies and organizations active in France. Fellowship members take precautions when meeting in anticipation of surveillance by the American government (files released in the 1970s show that the Fellowship was monitored by informers employed by the Central Intelligence Agency and the FBI).

1951   Lectures in Turin, Genoa, and Rome in January. *Sangre Negra* (the film version of *Native Son*) opens to acclaim in Buenos Aires on March 30. American distributor cuts almost 30 minutes from film under pressure from New York state censors (original length was approximately 105 minutes); shortened version opens in New York on June 16 to unfavorable reviews. (Several states ban the film, but it is shown in Beverly Hills and, in spring 1952, in Mississippi, where members of Wright's family see it.) A partially restored print is warmly received at the Venice Film Festival in August. The Milan press praises Wright's acting; in general, his performance is deemed sincere but awkward, especially by American critics who compare it with Canada Lee's stage version. Wright visits the sociologist Gunnar Myrdal in Geneva, beginning a long friendship. With Jean Cocteau, inaugurates the Cercle International du Théâtre et du Cinéma. *New Story Magazine* accepts excerpts from Jean Genet's *Our Lady of the Flowers* on Wright's recommendation. Baldwin's essay "Many Thousands Gone," an explicit attack on Wright in *Partisan Review* (November–December), leads to painful break between the writers. Submits screenplay about refugees forced to choose between sides in the Cold War to the French Association of Film Writers.

1952   Travels to England in February. Spends several months in London and Catford, Surrey, completing the first full version of *The Outsider*. Vacations with his family in Corrèze at the end of August and continues to revise and cut novel. Refuses suggestion by John Fischer, his new Harper editor, that he come to the United States for the publication of his book, citing the risk that he would be subpoenaed by an anti-Communist congressional investigating committee. Begins work in December on a novel about a white psychopathic murderer, based in part on his experience with Clinton Brewer.

1953 Begins correspondence with Frantz Fanon. *The Outsider* published by Harper and Brothers in March. Reviews are mixed; sales are initially brisk but eventually disappointing in comparison to *Native Son* and *Black Boy*. Wright composes an introduction to *In the Castle of My Skin*, first novel by the young Barbados writer George Lamming. Friendship with Sartre cools as Sartre moves closer to Communism. Wright's circle of friends remains wide, including Americans such as Chester Himes and William Gardner Smith, but he begins to withdraw from official organizations and to avoid formal gatherings. He is a regular at favorite cafés such as the Monaco and Tournon, where he entertains a steady stream of visitors from America, including Elmer Carter, Dorothy Norman, Nelson Algren, E. Franklin Frazier, and Louis Wirth. Discusses treatment of Algerians in France with Ben Burns, editor of *Ebony* magazine, during his visit. Wright tells Burns that he avoids criticizing French policies for fear of being deported. Ellen Wright begins work as a literary agent with Hélène Bokanowski, a prolific translator of Wright's work. From June to August, Wright travels in the Gold Coast (then a British colony with limited self-government, after 1957 the independent country of Ghana) to collect material for a book on Africa. Boat stops briefly in Freetown, Sierra Leone, en route to Takoradi; from there travels by road 170 miles to Accra, his main stop. Meets Prime Minister Kwame Nkrumah and other members of the pro-independence Convention People's Party, as well as Osei Agyeman Prempeh II, king of the Ashanti, and other traditional leaders. Excursions take him from Accra to Cape Coast, Christianborg, and Prampram; visits slave-trading fortresses and dungeons. Travels almost 3,000 miles in a chauffeur-driven car, touring the interior through Koforidua to Mampong, and the seventh Takoradi to Kumasi regions. In general, Wright is fascinated by Africans but is reinforced in his sense of self as a

Western intellectual. Visits England to discuss his impressions with George and Dorothy Padmore before returning to Paris in September to begin work on book about his trip. Undergoes surgery for hernia.

1954   Revises book on Africa. Decides to write an account of Spanish life and culture. Drives his Citroen almost 4,000 miles between August 15 and September 9 on a route that includes Barcelona, Valencia, Saragossa, Guadalajara, Madrid, Córdoba, Seville, Granada, and Málaga. On September 16 State Department and FBI officials interview Wright in Paris about his relationship to the Communist party when he goes to renew his passport. *Black Power: A Record of Reactions in a Land of Pathos*, about his African trip, published by Harper and Brothers September 22. Receives mixed reviews in America, but is widely praised in France. *Savage Holiday*, novel about psychopathic murderer, is published as a paperback original by Avon after having been rejected by Harper. Book attracts little attention in the United States but is well received as *Le Dieu de Mascarade* in France. Visits Geneva with Gunnar Myrdal for further research on Spain at the United Nations library. Lectures on Africa in Amsterdam in October, where he meets Margrit de Sablonière, his Dutch translator, and begins an important friendship with her. Returns to Spain on November 8. Hires a driver and travels through Irun and on to Madrid, where he stays before returning to Paris in mid-December.

1955   An old Chicago friend, the cartoonist Ollie "Bootsie" Harrington, arrives to live in France. Wright secures funding for his attendance at forthcoming conference of non-aligned nations in Bandung, Indonesia, from the Paris office of the Congress for Cultural Freedom, an international alliance of anti-Communist intellectuals. Returns to Spain February 20, and spends several weeks there, including Holy Week in Granada and Seville. Leaves Spain on April 10 for Indonesia. At Bandung, Wright shares room with missionary Winburn T. Thomas. Leaders attending conference include Nehru (with whom Wright speaks), Sukarno, Sihanouk, Nasser, and Zhou Enlai. Remains in Indonesia at home of Thomas until May 5, working on notes of his impressions, then returns to Europe via

Ceylon and Kenya. Begins writing an account of the conference. Spends July to October with family at their new country home, a small farm in village of Ailly in eastern Normandy. Plans series of novels dealing with the conflicts between individuals and society (including one set in Aztec Mexico), but abandons the project on the advice of Reynolds and Aswell (now with McGraw-Hill). Returns to Paris when daughter Rachel falls ill with scarlet fever, then goes back to Ailly when her continued quarantine makes work at home difficult. *Bandoeng: 1.500.000.000 hommes*, French translation of book on non-aligned conference, published in December.

1956   Prepares manuscript of book on Spain in February and March, often living alone at Ailly, where he enjoys hours of gardening. Fearing deportation, remains silent on Algerian war of independence while in France (will offer guarded criticism of war when in other European countries). *The Color Curtain: A Report on the Bandung Conference*, with an introduction by Gunnar Myrdal, published March 19 by World Publishers in America and receives favorable reviews. Revises and cuts book on Spain. Adapts Louis Sapin's play *Papa Bon Dieu* as *Daddy Goodness* but is unable to have it produced. First Congress of Negro Artists and Writers, sponsored by *Présence Africaine* and which Wright had helped plan, meets in Paris in September, attended by delegates from Africa, the United States, and the Caribbean. Wright speaks on "Tradition and Industrialization: The Tragic Plight of the African Elites" and participates in several sessions. Suspects that *Présence Africaine* is being secretly taken over by the French government through anti-nationalist Africans and considers withdrawing from its activities. Lectures in Hamburg on "The Psychological Reactions of Oppressed Peoples" and tours the city with Ellen. Attends a meeting in London of the Congress for Cultural Freedom, organized by Arthur Koestler. Travels alone to Stockholm in late November for the Swedish publication of *The Outsider*; it sells 35,000 copies in four days (*Native Son* had sold 75,000 copies and *Black Boy* 65,000). Lectures in Sweden, Norway, and Denmark before returning to Paris in early December. Agrees to help found the American Society for African Culture, inspired by the French Société Africaine de Culture.

Returning to native material, Wright begins work on novel set in Mississippi.

1957   Aunt Maggie dies January 20 in Jackson, Mississippi, where she had been taking care of Wright's mother (Wright has continued to help support them through the years). Mother moves in with a niece, then goes to Chicago at the end of June to live with Leon Alan. *Pagan Spain* published by Harper in February to good reviews but weak sales. Works at Ailly on new novel. Travels throughout Italy with Ellen during the spring. Visits West Germany in July to interview black American servicemen stationed there. *White Man, Listen!*, a collection of essays drawn from Wright's lectures, published October 15 by Doubleday (where Edward Aswell is now an editor). The book is especially well-received by the black press in the United States.

1958   Finishes *The Long Dream*, Mississippi novel, and begins "Island of Hallucinations," sequel set in France. Seeking to renew his passport, he is again compelled to report to the American embassy in February and sign a statement admitting his past membership in the Communist party. Becomes increasingly alienated from the black community in Paris, which is torn by suspicion and dissension; finds himself the object of resentment, including rumors that he is an agent of the FBI or the CIA. Depressed and isolated from other blacks, Wright suspects that he is being persecuted by agents of the U.S. government. Takes part in a session of the Congress for Cultural Freedom, and in seminars on American literature sponsored by the American Cultural Center in Paris. Supports Sartre and Simone de Beauvoir in their opposition to the new regime of General de Gaulle. Works on new novel at Ailly during summer. *The Long Dream* published by Doubleday in October to often hostile reviews and flat sales. When Leon Alan telegraphs that their mother is seriously ill, Wright is forced to borrow extra money from Reynolds to send to his brother. Edward Aswell, his long-time editor, dies November 5. Considers moving to England and enlists aid of Labour member of Parliament John Strachey, who obtains assurances from the Home Secretary that Wright's application for residence will be fairly considered. Wright distances himself from various organizations he had previously supported, including *Présence Africaine* and the Société Africaine de Culture.

1959   Mother dies January 14. Wright sends the manuscript of "Island of Hallucinations" to Reynolds in February. Later in the month, he spends a day with Martin Luther King, Jr., who is passing through Paris en route to India. Timothy Seldes (Aswell's successor at Doubleday) asks for major revisions in "Island of Hallucinations"; Wright puts book aside (it is never completed). Discouraged by financial worries, weak reviews, poor health, and frustrating state of his novel, Wright continues to curtail his public activities. Declines to attend the second Congress of Black Writers and Artists in Rome. Plans a study of French Africa. After Doubleday promises a $2,500 advance, Wright asks the American Society for African Culture for an additional $7,500, but is turned down; believes CIA infiltration of the organization is responsible for his rejection. Tired of what he considers to be growing American political and cultural influence in French life and in the wake of increased attacks by other expatriate black writers, Wright prepares to leave France and live in England. Sells farm at Ailly. His play *Daddy Goodness* is produced in Paris in the spring. Wright falls ill in June with attack of amoebic dysentery, probably picked up in Africa. Illness persists despite treatment at American Hospital. Vacations at the Moulin d'Andé near Saint-Pierre du Vauvray in Normandy. With daughter Julia now at the University of Cambridge, his wife Ellen and daughter Rachel establish themselves in London. Ellen works there as a literary agent and looks for a permanent home for the family. Wright begins writing haiku (eventually completes some 4,000 pieces). Harassed by British passport officials during visit to England in September. Sees George Padmore, who dies not long after Wright's visit. Wright returns to England for the funeral. Tries to obtain resident visa from the Home Office, but is denied one without explanation. Alone in Paris, he sells home on rue Monsieur le Prince and moves to a two-room apartment on rue Régis. Recovers from dysentery but continues to have intestinal problems. Among his close friends at this time are Michel and Hélène Bokanowski, Colette and Rémi Dreyfus, Simone de Beauvoir, Ollie Harrington, and the Reverend Clayton Williams. "Big Black Good Man" is included in *Best American Stories of 1958*.

1960   *The Long Dream*, adapted by Ketti Frings, opens on Broadway February 17 to poor reviews and closes within a week. Translation of *The Long Dream* well-received in France, but earnings are not enough to quell Wright's deepening anxiety about money. In April, driving his own Peugeot, Wright accompanies his gastroenterologist, Victor Schwartzmann, and Dr. Schwartzmann's father to medical conference in Leiden, Holland, where he visits Magrit de Sablonière. Selects and arranges 811 haiku for possible publication. Declines offers from Congress for Cultural Freedom to attend conferences on Tolstoy in Venice and New Delhi, believing that the organization is controlled by the American government (the Congress is later shown to have received substantial covert funding from the CIA). Records series of interviews concerning his work in June for French radio. Spends much of summer at Moulin d'Andé, where he begins new novel, "A Father's Law." Falls ill on return to Paris in September. Julia Wright decides to study at the Sorbonne and visits her father before returning to England to pack her belongings. In September, Dorothy Padmore comes to visit. Later, old Chicago friend Arna Bontemps makes his first visit to Paris. Wright delivers lecture on November 8 at the American Church on the situation of black artists and intellectuals. Accuses the American government of creating and manipulating dissension among them through spies and provocateurs. Continues to suffer from intestinal difficulties and dizzy spells. Finishes complete proofreading of collection of stories, *Eight Men* (published by World Publishers in 1961). Welcomes Langston Hughes to his home for a brief but enjoyable visit on the morning of November 26, then enters the Eugene Gibez Clinic for diagnostic examinations and convalescence. Dies there of a heart attack shortly before 11:00 P.M., November 28. Cremated, along with a copy of *Black Boy*, at the Père Lachaise cemetery December 3, where his ashes are interred.

Note on the Texts

This volume presents the text of Richard Wright's autobiography *Black Boy* (*American Hunger*) from a complete set of page proofs dating from the spring of 1944. It presents the text of *The Outsider* from Wright's final typescript of the novel, submitted to his publishers in October 1952. These are the last versions of the texts that Wright prepared without external intervention—by the Book-of-the-Month Club in the case of *Black Boy*, and by his publisher in the case of *The Outsider*. A great deal of material pertaining to the publication of these works, including typescripts, proofs, and correspondence between Wright and his publishers, is in the James Weldon Johnson Collection of the Beinecke Library at Yale University and in the Harper and Brothers archive in the Firestone Library at Princeton University.

Wright began intensive work on his autobiography, initially entitled "Black Confession," in 1943. On December 17, 1943, he delivered the manuscript, now titled *American Hunger*, to his friend and agent, Paul Reynolds. It was divided into two sections: "Southern Night," treating his life in the South before he moved to Chicago in 1927, and "The Horror and the Glory," continuing his story in Chicago into the 1930s. The work was accepted by Edward Aswell of Harper and Brothers in January 1944. By early May 1944 the book was in page proofs and scheduled for fall publication.

Aswell sent bound sets of page proofs to other authors for promotional statements in May. Around this time a copy was also sent to the Book-of-the-Month Club for consideration. Aswell had earlier gotten Wright's agreement to revise one scene in the book he thought might be considered obscene. By late June the club's judges had expressed interest, but they asked Aswell if Wright would agree to publish only the first section of the work. Wright sent Aswell the altered version of the scene (see note to p. 180.25–34 in this volume) and agreed to shorten the book if the club decided to adopt it. (The title page in a sheaf of page proofs of *American Hunger* now held at Beinecke Library, bears written instructions, under the heading "If the Book Club Takes It," for the replacement of the objectionable passage and the elimination of the second section, with the proviso "Hold till Book of the Month decides.")

The book jacket had already been designed when Wright wrote to Aswell on August 10 to suggest changing the title to *Black Boy*: "Now, this is not very original, but I think it covers the book. It is honest. Straight. And many people say it to themselves when they see a Negro and wonder how he lives. Black Boy seems to me to be not only a title, but also a kind of heading of the whole general theme."

Late in August 1944 the work was formally accepted by the book club and re-scheduled for release the following spring under its new title. Wright supplied several pages of new concluding material, working with Dorothy Canfield Fisher of the Book-of-the-Month Club (see note to p. 246.5 in this volume). Though Wright was pleased with the book's selection by the club and the income it generated, he wrote in his journal that pressure from Communists had led the book club to ask him to drop the second section, which dealt with his involvement with the Communist party in Chicago. Although "The Horror and the Glory" remained unpublished, selections from it appeared in magazines at the time: "I Tried to Be a Communist" in *Atlantic Monthly* (August–September 1944), "American Hunger" in *Mademoiselle* (September 1945), and "Early Days in Chicago" in *Cross Section* (1945). These articles were reprinted numerous times during the 1940s and 1950s. The entire text of the second section was first published by Harper and Row in 1977 from the surviving page proofs, under the title *American Hunger*, which Wright had originally applied to the work as a whole. The present volume for the first time brings together the complete text of Wright's autobiography, using the page proofs set before the intervention of the Book-of-the-Month Club.

Wright began making notes for the novel that became *The Outsider* in 1948 while living in Paris. In February 1952 he went to England to do intensive work on the manuscript, and by April or May he had finished a first draft and sent it to his agent, Paul Reynolds, who suggested some revisions. Wright sent him a second typescript in July (now in the Johnson Collection at the Beinecke Library, catalogued as JWJ Wright

#854). Reynolds then had the revised typescript delivered to Jack Fischer, who had replaced Edward Aswell as Wright's editor at Harper and Brothers when Aswell left the firm. Both Reynolds and Fischer sent Wright lists of suggested revisions, but the kinds of changes they asked for were very different. Paul Reynolds sent Wright specific factual questions and raised issues of plausibility and continuity. Jack Fischer, on the other hand, relying on a reading by a consultant who remains unidentified, asked Wright to cut the novel by one-third (from 220,000 to 150,000 words), to eliminate the beginning through the subway wreck, to drop the Joe and Jenny sequence, to cut the entire Hattie episode, and to shorten or eliminate passages involving stream-of-consciousness and philosophical monologue. If followed, these revisions would have produced a very different novel from the one Wright had written. Fischer was interested in scheduling the novel for publication the following March, and he asked Wright to supply the final manuscript by October 1. Fischer also proposed to make the cuts and revisions at Harper, with Wright to see and approve the changes, but Wright declined the offer, preferring to make the revisions himself.

Wright worked on the novel through August and September, making revisions in three stages. He used the typescript returned from Fischer (JWJ Wright #854) to mark his revisions, then incorporated them onto a re-typed master-copy (JWJ Wright #856) that showed the old page numbers from the previous version; and finally he prepared a clean copy (JWJ Wright #858) incorporating some further revisions. This typescript was submitted to Harper and Brothers early in October. Wright did shorten the novel from its original length of 741 typescript pages to 620 pages by compressing certain passages, but he resisted Fischer's suggestions to eliminate entire sections of the novel. (Letters and typescripts now in the Johnson Collection at the Beinecke Library and in the Harper and Brothers archive in the Firestone Library of Princeton University reveal that Wright had a less than ideal working relationship with Fischer.) Wright incorporated, on the other hand, many of the revisions suggested by Paul Reynolds, whose advice he appreciated.

Wright submitted his final manuscript within days of when

Harper and Brothers had requested it in order to meet the scheduled March 1953 publication date. However, in November 1952, after another reading by the unidentified consultant, Fischer again requested that Wright cut out the Hattie sequence. Wright had already shortened it to some extent and now reluctantly shortened it further. He was forced to use his master-copy (JWJ Wright #856) as a guide, since he had sent both the ribbon and carbon copies of the final typescript (JWJ Wright #858) to New York for the publisher's use. Wright prepared unnumbered pages of copy to show how the cutting should be done and sent these to Fischer. These pages were inserted by Harper and Brothers into the final typescript (JWJ Wright #858), replacing the pages that had previously contained the scene. In addition, two other pages and many whole passages and words were removed by a copy-editor for the publisher without Wright's knowledge (the pages that were removed are not known to be extant). Wright was later informed that some minor cutting had been done in house, but that he would be able to restore the cut material, if he wished, when correcting galleys. (For examples of the larger cuts made by the publisher, see the notes to this volume.) Because of the rush to produce books for March publication, however, he was allowed only 48 hours to read the galleys that incorporated the changes made by the publisher. Wright received galleys on December 20 and returned the first portion on December 21 and the remainder by December 23. These galleys are not known to survive, but there are some variants between the published book and the copy-edited typescript. A few of them seem to be instances where Wright attempted to restore his original meaning, but the time allotted was too short to allow him to do very much. In order to meet the schedule for publication, Wright had agreed that further reading of proofs be done by the publisher.

The Outsider was published by Harper and Brothers on March 18, 1953. Wright received advance copies in late February, and on March 17 he sent Fischer a list of 12 typographical errors, followed by another list of four errors several weeks later. Though Fischer included 13 of these corrections in a list of changes he sent to the printer, there is no evidence that any of these corrections were ever made in later printings or subsequent editions. Of the 16 corrections requested by Wright, only five apply to the text printed in this volume; these have been incorporated at the following places: at 429.35, "on to her" has been changed to "onto her"; at 454.25, "come in" has been changed to "come out"; at 565.25, "hold on to" has been changed to "hold onto"; at 737.39, "condolences" has been changed to "condolence"; and at 823.19, a sentence has been added: ". . . Blimin told me about your ideas.'"

In order to eliminate the effects of the unauthorized copy-editing done by the publisher, this volume prints the text of the final typescript of *The Outsider*, submitted by Wright in October 1952 (JWJ Wright #858), ignoring the editorial markings, and uses Wright's master-copy (JWJ Wright #856) for those pages removed by the publisher from the final typescript at the following places: pp. 488.6–28, 513.18–524.22, 618.6–28, and 835.12–836.28.

This volume presents the proof and typescript texts chosen for inclusion without change, except for the correction of typographical errors. Spelling, punctuation, and capitalization often are expressive features and they are not altered, even when inconsistent or irregular. The following is a list of the typographical errors corrected, cited by page and line number: 30.25, asker; 158.4, *now*."; 252.5, Dont'; 252.21, too; 261.23, mixed,; 261.25, thing; 296.34, talk; 299.39, value; 300.14, artist; 350.7, enemy, "I; 359.37, but not; 374.20, "Say; 380.12, walking; 380.23, walking; 382.20, Moreoever; 389.15, whom; 391.30, quiet,; 394.39, what're they; 394.40, what they're; 395.34, scarda; 398.11, harrassed; 398.27, wore; 399.34, identing; 402.20, damned; 405.5, said; 407.6, beserk; 407.13, there was; 407.25, said; 409.15, halldoor; 409.27, proceded; 418.11, tussel; 418.22, scene of; 423.10, penicillen; 430.16, existence; 431.31, musn't; 432.22, six years; 433.15, than; 433.16, childrens'; 434.6, divising; 435.15, "Hello,"; 438.2, said,; 440.16, eight-hundred dollar; 440.24, everyday; 441.29, would'nt; 442.4, Assistand; 444.22, mightly; 448.5, Absolutely; 451.12, *occured*; 451.26, *26 year-old*; 452.38, rammified; 454.6, very day; 458.18, to a; 459.17, accroutrements; 459.40, starting; 465.19, Be; 469.34, ir-resistably, 470.2, Gladys, his, 470.8, Joes, 485.38, accomoda-tions; 488.14, it; 488.21, non-exsitent; 491.38, that saw; 493.25, priest;; 499.13, raising of; 507.29, particular'",; 508.30, simple;

514.24, an an; 516.14, $100,000-apartment; 517.3, $100,000-apartment; 517.7, subtly; 519.14, "I; 521.15, white; 521.37, "She; 522.1, feling; 522.4, grapsed; 522.37, him; 522.39, Crosd; 523.25, back; 527.5, emminent; 527.7, facist; 533.2, decollete; 533.31, everyday; 534.13, twelve years; 536.8–9, realtives; 537.21, heared; 540.18, was not; 541.33, worse; 542.14, worse; 546.35, Jordon; 559.24, unctiousness; 560.28, obervation; 561.13, want to make me; 564.12, tended; 564.27, mantle; 564.34, let; 566.8, precede; 567.4, had; 567.34, agression; 568.28, indispensible; 569.1, said.; 570.1, was rolling; 578.32, five-room; 581.9, made; 583.34, virgins;; 586.31, were written; 588.32, wife a; 593.35, get?; 595.15, becomes; 597.20, told him; 599.26, whom; 599.27, mislead; 603.37, mucous; 608.1, saw that the; 608.32, sharp,; 610.7, advance; 611.26, tingling; 616.20, yes,; 616.37, destory; 618.13, dissillusionment; 620.40, interpretating; 622.13, down to; 624.3, effect; 624.33, lay; 625.12, trod; 626.36, chandalier; 631.35, in back; 635.16, whom; 638.25, Who's; 638.40, downstairs; 645.12, spontanenousness; 645.13, her grief; 649.30, whom; 658.5, his; 660.20, Corss; 660.23, moment,; 660.29, Blount saw; 661.31, Cross as; 664.39, Housten; 666.21, sometime; 667.32, We; 671.37, "others"; 674.4, that's; 674.14–15, external; 680.36, in a; 683.32, any more; 684.10, would; 684.38, receptable; 685.5, whines; 692.15, reason; 693.6, shame of; 695.5, Hilton; 695.16, ralize; 695.39, Whom; 699.30, enveighed; 699.37, know; 700.24, wit; 702.12, this; 702.34, Or; 703.30, effected; 704.26, We're; 707.26, tended; 709.12, telepone; 717.13, keen; 720.25, Supermen; 720.26, syphillis; 724.29, but it was; 727.40–728.1, irredeemible; 734.17, "knowing"; 737.26, unctiously; 742.15, your; 743.30, four hour; 743.35, —dilemma; 745.11, dollar bills; 749.14, you; 753.15, the products; 753.16, long dreamed; 755.10, out; 758.7, sterlized; 759.15, philanthrophists; 759.33, capitalist; 760.3, its; 760.11, Blimen; 761.20, alieniated; 762.27, naïve to; 764.30, to others; 767.4, Communists; 769.3, dead to; 772.4, NEITZSCHE; 773.9, was to; 774.1, committments; 774.3, everyday; 774.16, question which; 774.18, it he; 774.32, flowed as; 774.39, sentinent; 775.8, desirious; 775.32, a ornately; 776.26, wished; 778.10–11, eight hundred dollar-loan; 778.15, known; 786.30, sucked his; 789.28, and and; 792.8, Attorny; 796.7, legs afraid,; 799.18, gasping; 799.34, strickened; 800.6, whomever; 802.2, words; 802.18, Someone; 804.22,

What; 809.19, sometime; 809.35, Now,; 809.40, on me; 810.32–33, unctiously; 811.30, I'm; 812.32, "sent"; 816.8, momento; 816.20–21, tingling; 817.9, sonofabtich; 817.30, backing; 817.33, I was; 821.9, believe; 821.30, it.; 831.13, "used"; 835.36, Addision; 836.36, Hatte; 839.28, anything?; 841.3, softly,.

Notes

In the notes below, the reference numbers denote page and line of this volume (the line count includes chapter headings). No note is made for information available in standard desk-reference books such as *Webster's Collegiate* and *Webster's Biographical* dictionaries. Footnotes in the text are Wright's own. For more biographical background than is included in the Chronology, see: Michel Fabre, *The Unfinished Quest of Richard Wright*, translated from the French by Isabel Barzun, (New York: William Morrow & Company, Inc., 1973); Addison Gayle, *Richard Wright: Ordeal of a Native Son* (Garden City, New York: Anchor Books/Doubleday, 1980); Constance Webb, *Richard Wright: A Biography* (New York: G. P. Putnam's Sons, 1968). For references to works by Wright and to other studies, see: Charles T. Davis and Michael Fabre, *Richard Wright: a primary bibliography* (Boston: G. K. Hall & Co., 1982); and Keneth Kinnamon, *A Richard Wright Bibliography: Fifty Years of Criticism and Commentary, 1933–1982* (Westport, Connecticut: Greenwood Press, 1988).

BLACK BOY

3.1–5 *Part . . . —JOB*] Omitted for the 1945 and all later editions set from that text.

38.29–30 *Bluebeard . . . Wives*] Traditional story; the classic version, *Blue Beard*, is by the French poet and author of fairy tales, Charles Perrault (1628–1703).

55.24 war . . . declared?"] The United States declared war on Germany April 6, 1917, and entered World War I, which had begun in 1914.

74.11 "The war is over,"] The armistice was signed November 11, 1918.

79.17 *Amazing . . . sounds*] Cf. *Amazing Grace*, line 1. Sometimes represented as a Negro spiritual, the hymn was composed by John Newton (1725–1807) and published in *Olney Hymns* (1779) by Newton and William Cowper. Newton, who from 1745 to 1754 had been a sailor on slave ships and the captain of a slaving vessel, underwent a religious conversion during a storm at sea in 1748. Later ordained, he devoted his life to the ministry and became an important influence on the life of perhaps the greatest English abolitionist, William Wilberforce (1759–1833).

98.2–3 Seventh-Day Adventist Church] The observance of the seventh day as the Sabbath derives from the commandment: "Six days shalt thou labor . . . but the seventh day is the sabbath of the Lord thy God." The sect originated as the largest branch of Millerism, an interchurch movement led by William Miller who in 1831 began preaching that the Second Coming of Christ was imminent, and might occur in 1843 or 1844. A branch of the Millerites, or Adventists, that was later to adopt the name Seventh-day Adventists, came to believe that the 1843–44 date related to the beginning of an "investigative judgment" in heaven, which would end with Christ's return and the final judgment at an indefinite time. The church was formally organized in 1863. Among the main tenets of this fundamentally evangelic Protestant creed are the divine and supreme authority of the Bible; the comprehensive authority of the Ten Commandments; and the divine example of Jesus Christ's life. The gift of prophecy is a significant part of church teaching. The literal, premillenial Second Coming of Christ is insisted on, starting with Jerusalem and extending to all nations; Israel will be specially favored and restored. The dead will rise at the resurrection, at which time the earthly acknowledgement of the righteous and the eternal punishment through final death of the wicked will come to pass. Members must accept the doctrine of the church, repent their sins, and accept baptism by immersion. The church is supported through not only tithing but also the expected additional material generosity of its members.

112.8–9   how Jacob . . . angel] Jacob hears an angel in a dream in Genesis 31:11–13, wrestles an angel in 32:24–31, and sees angels in 28:12 and 32:2.

120.32–37   *But the . . . as thou . . .*] Deuteronomy 5:13.

127.37–38   *Flynn's . . . Magazine*] Magazines first published by Frank Munsey (1854–1925): *Flynn's Weekly Detective Fiction* (1924–42), and *Argosy All-Story Weekly* (1920–29), so-named after a merger of the fiction magazines *The Argosy* (1888) and *All-Story* (1889). (After another merger, it became *All-Story Combined with Munsey's* in 1929.)

135.12–15   elections . . . power] Under the first Reconstruction Act, passed on March 2, 1867, former Confederate states seeking to regain their congressional representation were required to adopt new constitutions enfranchising black males. Mississippi voters approved a new constitution meeting this requirement on November 30, 1869, and the state regained its representation in Congress on February 23, 1870. The Republicans won the state elections in 1869, and the legislature subsequently elected two black men, Hiram Revels (served 1870–71) and Blanche K. Bruce (served 1875–81), to the U.S. Senate. In 1875 white supremacists organized a campaign of violence and intimidation intended to win the state elections for the Democrats. After dozens of blacks were murdered in Yazoo City and Clinton in September, Republican governor Adelbert Ames asked President Ulysses S. Grant to deploy federal troops against the "White Liners." The appeal for intervention was unsuccessful, and the Democrats won an overwhelming victory in the

November 1875 election. Their control of the state government effectively disenfranchised blacks in elections thereafter.

146.22 *This . . . know . . .*] From "This May Be the Last Time," a traditional spiritual.

146.32–33 *It ain't . . . prayer . . .*] From "Standing In the Need of Prayer," a gospel song.

149.8 "right hand of fellowship."] See Galatians 2:9.

159.15 *Southern Register*] The weekly, one of the first attempts to establish a black newspaper in Jackson, began in the autumn of 1923 and was edited and printed by Malcolm Rogers; Wright's story (no copies are known to be extant) is said to have appeared in the spring of 1924.

161.19 Get-Rich-Quick Wallingford series] Get-Rich-Quick Wallingford was the name of the character, and the title of the first book, in the series (1908–13) by George Randolph Chester in which Wallingford and his partner "Blackie" Daw, a pair of likable rascals, set about making a fortune. The first book was subtitled "A Cheerful Account of the Rise and Fall of an American Business Buccaneer."

180.25–34 "Richard . . . did it."] Revised in 1944 for the book club review to read:

> "Nigger, you think you'll ever amount to anything?" he asked in a slow, sadistic voice.
> "I don't know, sir," I answered, turning my head away.
> "What do niggers think about?" he asked.
> "I don't know, sir," I said, my head still averted.
> "If I was a nigger, I'd kill myself," he said.
> I said nothing. I was angry.
> "You don't know why?" he asked.
> I still said nothing.
> "But I don't reckon niggers mind being niggers," he said suddenly and laughed.

233.4–6 *Commercial . . .* article] "Another Mencken Absurdity" (May 28, 1927).

233.7–8 editor . . . *Mercury*] Mencken founded the literary magazine *American Mercury* with George Nathan in 1924, and was its editor until 1933. In it he attacked, among other targets, Puritanism, conservatism, religion, and what he called the American "booboisie." Contributors included Theodore Dreiser, Eugene O'Neill, Sherwood Anderson, Carl Sandburg, Edgar Lee Masters, and Carl Van Vechten.

236.27–31 *A Book . . . Prejudices.*] *A Book of Prefaces* (1917) comprises four chapters: "Joseph Conrad," "Theodore Dreiser," "James Huneker," and

"Puritanism as a Literary Force." Mencken published six collections of essays called *Prejudices* (1919–27). Perhaps his best-known essay and his liveliest attack on the white South, "The Sahara of the Bozart," appeared in *Prejudices: Second Series* (1920).

246.5   I fled.]   Added to the 1945 edition as a conclusion after the second part was cut from the work:

The next day when I was already in full flight—aboard a northward bound train—I could not have accounted, if it had been demanded of me, for all the varied forces that were making me reject the culture that had molded and shaped me. I was leaving without a qualm, without a single backward glance. The face of the South that I had known was hostile and forbidding, and yet out of all the conflicts and the curses, the blows and the anger, the tension and the terror, I had somehow gotten the idea that life could be different, could be lived in a fuller and richer manner. As had happened when I had fled the orphan home, I was now running more away from something than toward something. But that did not matter to me. My mood was: I've got to get away; I can't stay here.

But what was it that always made me feel that way? What was it that made me conscious of possibilities? From where in this southern darkness had I caught a sense of freedom? Why was it that I was able to act upon vaguely felt notions? What was it that made me feel things deeply enough for me to try to order my life by my feelings? The external world of whites and blacks, which was the only world that I had ever known, surely had not evoked in me any belief in myself. The people I had met had advised and demanded submission. What, then, was I after? How dare I consider my feelings superior to the gross environment that sought to claim me?

It had been only through books—at best, no more than vicarious cultural transfusions—that I had managed to keep myself alive in a negatively vital way. Whenever my environment had failed to support or nourish me, I had clutched at books; consequently, my belief in books had risen more out of a sense of desperation than from any abiding conviction of their ultimate value. In a peculiar sense, life had trapped me in a realm of emotional rejection; I had not embraced insurgency through open choice. Existing emotionally on the sheer, thin margin of southern culture, I had felt that nothing short of life itself hung upon each of my actions and decisions; and I had grown used to change, to movement, to making many adjustments.

In the main, my hope was merely a kind of self-defence, a conviction that if I did not leave I would perish, either because of possible violence of others against me, or because of my possible violence against them. The substance of my hope was formless and devoid of any real sense of direction, for in my southern living I had seen no looming landmark by which I could, in a positive sense, guide my daily actions. The shocks of southern living had rendered my personality tender and swollen, tense and volatile, and my flight was more a shunning of external and internal dangers than an attempt to embrace what I felt I wanted.

It had been my accidental reading of fiction and literary criticism that had evoked in me vague glimpses of life's possibilities. Of course, I had never seen or met the men who wrote the books I read, and the kind of world in which they lived was as alien to me as the moon. But what had enabled me to overcome my chronic distrust was that these books—written by men like Dreiser, Masters, Mencken, Anderson, and Lewis—seemed defensively critical of the straitened American environment. These writers seemed to feel that America could be shaped nearer to the hearts of those who lived in it. And it was out of these novels and stories and articles, out of the emotional impact of imaginative constructions of heroic or tragic deeds, that I felt touching my face a tinge of warmth from an unseen light; and in my leaving I was groping toward that invisible light, always trying to keep my face so set and turned that I would not lose the hope of its faint promise, using it as my justification for action.

The white South said that it knew "niggers," and I was what the white South called a "nigger." Well, the white South had never known me—never known what I thought, what I felt. The white South said that I had a "place" in life. Well, I had never felt my "place"; or, rather, my deepest instincts had always made me reject the "place" to which the white South had assigned me. It had never occurred to me that I was in any way an inferior being. And no word that I had ever heard fall from the lips of southern white men had ever made me really doubt the worth of my own humanity. True, I had lied. I had stolen. I had struggled to contain my seething anger. I had fought. And it was perhaps a mere accident that I had never killed . . . But in what other ways had the South allowed me to be natural, to be real, to be myself, except in rejection, rebellion, and aggression?

Not only had the southern whites not known me, but, more important still, as I had lived in the South I had not had the chance to learn who I was. The pressure of southern living kept me from being the kind of person that I might have been. I had been what my surroundings had demanded, what my family—conforming to the dictates of the whites above them—had exacted of me, and what the whites had said that I must be. Never being fully able to be myself, I had slowly learned that the South could recognize but a part of a man, could accept but a fragment of his personality, and all the rest—the best and deepest things of heart and mind—were tossed away in blind ignorance and hate.

I was leaving the South to fling myself into the unknown, to meet other situations that would perhaps elicit from me other responses. And if I could meet enough of a different life, then, perhaps, gradually and slowly I might learn who I was, what I might be. I was not leaving the South to forget the South, but so that some day I might understand it, might come to know what its rigors had done to me, to its children. I fled so that the numbness of my defensive living might thaw out and let me feel the pain—years later and far away—of what living in the South had meant.

Yet, deep down, I knew that I could never really leave the South, for my feelings had already been formed by the South, for there had been slowly instilled into my personality and consciousness, black though I was, the culture of the South. So, in leaving, I was taking a part of the South to transplant in alien soil, to see if it could grow differently, if it could drink of new and cool rains, bend in strange winds, respond to the warmth of other suns, and, perhaps, to bloom . . . And if that miracle ever happened, then I would know that there was yet hope in that southern swamp of despair and violence, that light could emerge even out of the blackest of the southern night. I would know that the South too could overcome its fear, its hate, its cowardice, its heritage of guilt and blood, its burden of anxiety and compulsive cruelty.

With ever watchful eyes and bearing scars, visible and invisible, I headed North, full of a hazy notion that life could be lived with dignity, that the personalities of others should not be violated, that men should be able to confront men without fear or shame, that if men were lucky in their living on earth they might win some redeeming meaning for their having struggled and suffered here beneath the stars.

265.19   While . . . stomach] "At night . . ." This and the following two notes show penciled revisions made by Wright on a copy of page proofs some time after the book club had decided to take only Part One.

265.25   my family.] "my people."

269.16   I spent . . . reading] "I read . . ."

282.18   Hoover . . . marchers] Between 15,000 and 20,000 unemployed World War I veterans gathered in Washington, D.C., in late May and early June 1932, camping on open ground by the Anacostia River and in vacant public buildings near the Capitol. The veterans sought to pressure Congress into passing an appropriation that would allow veterans of World War I to cash in at full value bonus certificates granted them in 1924; the certificates were scheduled to mature in 1945. A bill meeting their demands was passed by the House of Representatives on June 15, but was defeated in the Senate several days later. Several thousand men left Washington after Congress adjourned on July 16, but the remainder vowed to stay. President Herbert Hoover adamantly opposed the cash redemption scheme and accused the leadership of the "Bonus Army" of being Communists and radicals rather than patriotic ex-servicemen, as they claimed. On Hoover's orders, troops led by General Douglas MacArthur used tanks, bayonets, and tear gas to rout the remaining marchers from their camps and shelters on July 28, 1932.

284.35   "Big . . . Thompson] William Hale "Big Bill" Thompson (1869–1944) was mayor of Chicago from 1915 to 1923 and from 1927 to 1931. In 1931 he defeated Judge John H. Lyle in the Republican primary, but lost his bid for re-election to Democrat Anton J. Cermak.

290.20   Aschheim-Zondek tests] Selmor Aschheim (1878–1965) and Bernhardt Zondek (1891–1961) were German gynecologists and obstetricians who developed a test for pregnancy in which urine from women was injected into immature mice. Urine from pregnant women caused enlarged ovaries in the mice, as well as other noticeable effects. Rabbits were later used instead of mice.

290.21   Wassermann tests] August-Paul von Wassermann (1866–1925) was a German bacteriologist noted for developing the Wassermann test for syphilis, which he announced in 1906.

300.13   Anvil, . . . Conroy,] Anvil magazine (1932–1935), a journal of fiction and poetry edited by Jack Conroy (1899–1980) and actively supported by the Communist party. Its motto was "We Prefer Crude Vigor to Polished Banality." In 1935, it merged with Partisan Review (begun as a John Reed Club magazine), but dissatisfaction with this arrangement led to the birth in 1939 of New Anvil, which lasted only six issues. In addition to Wright, the two Anvil magazines also published work by James T. Farrell, Langston Hughes, Nelson Algren, William Carlos Williams, and Meridel Le Sueur, among other notable writers. Conroy, a novelist with a particular interest in folklore, started out as a self-educated labor leader in his native Moberly, Missouri, before turning to a literary career.

300.15   John Reed Club] The John Reed Club was started in 1929 by the editorial board of New Masses in accordance with the principles of agitation, education, and propaganda enunciated the previous year by the Comintern (Communist International). It was named in honor of the poet and journalist John Reed (1887–1920), author of Ten Days That Shook the World, and the only American buried at the foot of the Kremlin wall with other heroes of the Russian Revolution. The club had as its major aim the broadening of the cultural appeal of radical socialism. By 1934, there were some thirty clubs in cities and towns across the United States. They attracted many of the leading progressive writers, especially among the young, including black Americans such as Wright and Langston Hughes.

301.18–19   Left Front,] A magazine of the John Reed Club, begun in 1933. It was one of several magazines of the 1930s specializing in proletarian literature.

301.27   Masses] New Masses, so-named after the radical socialist journal of art and literature The Masses, which was edited by Max Eastman from 1913 to

1918, and suppressed during World War I as seditious. *New Masses* commenced monthly publication in 1927 as a radical journal of art and literature. In 1934, after it became a weekly, *New Masses* emerged as perhaps the major journal of its kind in the United States throughout the 1930s. In 1948, following a marked decline in its influence, it was subsumed by the newly formed *Masses & Mainstream*.

301.31–32   *International Literature*]   Published in various languages and strongly supported by the Soviet government, *International Literature* was perhaps the leading literary journal of the international Communist movement in the 1930s.

301.34–39   introduced . . . Czechoslovakia]   Among those Wright met in Chicago were the artist Morris Topchevky, author Nelson Algren, and filmmaker Herbert Kline, who made the political documentary *Crisis: A Film of the Nazi Way* (1938), which ended with the German entry into the Sudetenland, annexed from Czechoslovakia after the signing of the Munich Pact.

318.7–17   Trotsky . . . activity]   In April 1926 Leon Trotsky joined his former rivals Grigori Zinoviev and Lev Kamenev in forming a "United Opposition" to the leadership of Nikolai Bukharin and Joseph Stalin. Trotsky and his allies accused Bukharin and Stalin of failing to support revolutionary Communist movements outside the Soviet Union and demanded the curtailment of the party and government bureaucracy, an end to conciliatory policies toward prosperous landowning peasants, and the beginning of planned industrial development. Their views were rejected by a majority of the Communist Party Central Committee, and in October 1926 all three publicly abjured further opposition activity. They resumed their criticism of the leadership in May 1927 and in September defied the party Politburo by printing their political platform and attempting to circulate it among delegates to the forthcoming Fifteenth Party Congress. After the secret police seized their printing press, the opposition organized protest demonstrations in Moscow and Leningrad on November 7, 1927, the tenth anniversary of the Bolshevik Revolution. Trotsky and Zinoviev were expelled from the Communist party on November 14 for violating the ban against factions within the party, instituted by Lenin in 1921. In January 1928 Trotsky was exiled to Soviet Central Asia, and in January 1929 he was deported from the Soviet Union to Turkey. Zinoviev and Kamenev were shot in 1936 after confessing to counterrevolutionary conspiracy at a public show trial. Trotsky was assassinated in Mexico by a Soviet agent in 1940.

318.35   Stalin's . . . *Question*]   *Marxism and the National and Colonial Question* (1934), a revised edition of *Marxism and the National Question*, first published in 1913.

327.7   People's Front]   In the summer of 1934 the executive committee of the Communist International (Comintern) instructed Communist parties to begin forming alliances with non-Communist movements as part of the struggle against fascism. These instructions reversed a 1928 decision of the Comintern to abandon alliances with Western socialists and denounce social democratic parties as "social fascists." The new "people's front" strategy, also known as the "united front" or "popular front," became the official policy of the Comintern at its Seventh Congress, held in the summer of 1935, and remained in effect until the signing of the German-Soviet nonaggression pact on August 23, 1939.

333.7–8   Negro . . . Association] The Harlem branch of the Young Men's Christian Association, located on 135th Street near Lenox Avenue, was a focal point of cultural activity during and after the Harlem Renaissance of the 1920s, as well as the residence of many newcomers to Harlem during the same period.

336.13–14   article . . . Louis] In his first piece of journalism, "Joe Louis Uncovers Dynamite" (October 8, 1935), Wright described the reaction of Chicago blacks to the fight in New York, September 24, 1935, in which Louis defeated former world heavyweight champion Max Baer.

340.33–34   Communist International] The Third International, also known as the Communist International (Comintern), was founded by Lenin in 1919 to provide revolutionary Communist leadership to the worldwide socialist movement. It was dissolved in 1943.

346.18   Federal Negro Theater] A unit of the Federal Theatre Project (funded by Congress as a Depression measure, and headed nationally by Hallie Flanagan). The unit was designed to serve the perceived interests of blacks. Although most of the plays staged by the Theatre came from the traditional repertoire, the Chicago unit produced the premiere of Theodore Ward's *Big White Fog* in April 1937.

347.2   Works Progress Administration] A federal agency established by President Franklin D. Roosevelt in 1935 to combat unemployment as part of his New Deal policy. The WPA administered several cultural programs, including the Federal Art Project, the Federal Writers' Project, and the Federal Theatre Project, as well as a vast program of public road, bridge, and building construction. Its activities were curtailed by Congress in 1939 and the agency was abolished in 1943.

347.9   Charles DeSheim] DeSheim, an actor and director in repertory and stock company productions, was later associated with the Old Globe Theatre Shakespearean productions at the New York World's Fair (1939–40), and in 1940 appeared in *Journey to Jerusalem* at the National Theater in Washington, D.C. He died in 1941.

349.11   white . . . company] The Federal Experimental Theatre was a unit of the Federal Theatre Project that emphasized avant garde plays. Although the FTP had as one of its central goals the encouragement of uncensored adult theater, more plays by Shakespeare were produced than works by any other author, with works by Eugene O'Neill and George Bernard Shaw following closely in frequency. Because many controversial political dramas were also produced, opposition to the FTP grew among conservatives and resulted in its abolition by Congress in 1939.

363.20–29   *Arise, . . . earth!*]   Verses 1–2 of "The International." Written in 1871 by Eugène Pottier, a member of the Paris Commune, it became the anthem of the international socialist movement, and was later adopted by the Communists. Adolphe Degeyter composed the music.

364.16   *A better . . . birth . . .*]   "The International," Verse 4.

THE OUTSIDER

367.2–6   *Cruelty . . .* BLAKE]   "The Divine Image," stanza 1.

368.1–2   *For Rachel . . . soil*]   Added by Wright in proof stages.

369.3–6   Dread . . . —KIERKEGAARD]   From an 1842 entry in *Journals.* The translation is by William Lowrie and appears in his introduction to Kierkegaard's *The Concept of Dread* (1944). Wright condensed the last part of Lowrie's translation, which reads: " . . . for one fears, but what one fears one desires."

370.22–25   *If the . . . come up*]   A common refrain, variations of which appear in several blues songs.

371.29–32   Tiny . . . snow.]   Cut for the book edition. This note and others like it give some examples of cuts and revisions made by Harper editors without Wright's knowledge.

371.34–36   Joe sobered . . . chuckled.]   Cut for the book edition.

390.1–5   He shuddered . . . depress him.]   Cut for the book edition.

391.10–20   "Son, . . . Cross?"]   Cut for the book edition.

397.5   5743 Indiana]   In 1935, Wright lived with his family at 3743 Indiana Avenue.

400.29–35   It was . . . first time.]   Cut for the book edition.

411.10–12   He felt . . . attacks.]   Cut for the book edition.

411.13–15   He would . . . overcome.]   Cut for the book edition.

411.23–26   They knew . . . as man.]   Cut for the book edition.

415.4–10   "Did . . . role.]   Cut for the book edition.

425.31   Cross.]   In the book, a sentence was inserted here: "Until now he had managed to keep up his classes at the University, but he lost heart for study and dropped out of school."

442.11   Tribune Tower] Ambitiously planned by the owners of the wealthy Chicago *Tribune* newspaper, and built finally as a Gothic tower directly influenced by medieval European cathedrals, the tower was formally opened on July 6, 1925, on Michigan Avenue in downtown Chicago.

466.34   faces] During preparation of the book edition, "faces" was changed to "thought" by an editor at Harper. In the proof stages it was changed again and appears in the book edition as "image."

470.25–30   "What . . . cynically.] Cut for the book edition.

485.13–16   spilled . . . phlegm;] In the book edition, cut to read: "spilled over a flattened grapefruit hull; . . ."

486.18–21   When Joe's . . . Jenny.] Cut for the book edition.

488.3–5   As silent . . . CRANE] From "Legend." Written in 1924, the poem was first published in 1930.

488.6–30   CROSS'S . . . sustain himself.] Cut for the book edition.

500.32–39   "After . . . conscious of it.] Cut for the book edition.

501.3–4   For those . . . drama . . ."] Cut for the book edition.

505.10–11   The American . . . coward.] Cut for the book edition.

511.23–26   His morbid . . . reality.] Cut for the book edition.

513.18–524.17   What stalled . . . out of the room.] Cut for the book edition.

526.21–527.14   Because Cross . . . man Cross] Cut and revised for the book edition to read: "Cross's heart was full of a longing to search for himself and create a future . . ."

527.37–528.4   Another sign . . . asterisks.] Cut for the book edition.

536.3–5   "Looks . . . mumbled.] Cut for the book edition.

543.10   "They . . . Lionel,"] In the book edition, changed to: "'They call me Lionel Lane,' . . ."

543.11–31   "Lionel what?" . . . at whom.] Cut for the book edition.

553.27–30   *Let . . . save.*]   From the hymn composed by the Pennsylvania-born religious singer and composer Philip Paul Bliss (1838–76).

555.10–12   Then a wild . . . right palm,]   In the book edition, revised to read: "Then she began to laugh, still holding Cross's face."

555.13   *Lead, Kindly Light*]   Hymn (1835), words by John Henry Newman, then a minister in the Church of England (later a Roman Catholic cardinal).

555.16–17   flopped . . . lungs.]   In the book edition, revised to read: " . . . laughing even louder."

556.3–9   Sarah's . . . floor.]   Cut for the book edition.

556.14–20   She could . . . Bob moaned.]   Cut for the book edition.

570.32   13 Charles Street]   The address of a house in Greenwich Village that Wright and his wife bought in 1945.

572.3–5   For that . . . PAUL]   Romans 7:15.

582.14   *Daily Worker*]   The newspaper, based in New York City, was first published in 1924 by the Communist party and served for some time as its official organ. Chronically plagued by financial problems as well as editorial and political pressures, the newspaper officially closed in 1957.

588.36–589.39   "Say, . . . "Why?"]   Cut for the book edition.

590.24–25   atomistic . . . micro-organisms]   Cut for the book edition.

590.28–31   Between . . . organic whole.]   Cut for the book edition.

590.38–591.6   she spoke tersely . . . danger . . . ?]   Cut for the book edition.

591.31   bold, brutal]   In the book edition, revised to read: "haunted . . ."

593.10–11   silly but gifted]   Cut for the book edition.

593.24–26   His words . . . naïve . . . ?]   Cut for the book edition.

593.31–32   But how? . . . to where?]   Cut for the book edition.

594.8–9   run off . . . degenerated!]   Cut for the book edition.

594.22–23   The Party . . . trap!]   Cut for the book edition.

595.2–3   Goddamn this deception!]   Cut for the book edition.

611.1–4   he called . . . help Gil . . .]   Cut for the book edition.

618.6–619.11   The seductions . . . pursuers.]   Cut for the book edition.

632.38–40   There was . . . Bob's.]   Cut for the book edition.

642.8–11   . . . Her sense . . . Herndon . . .]   Cut for the book edition.

655.34–656.3   "You're saying," . . . this fight.]   Cut and revised for the book edition to: " 'Right,' Houston said."

664.13–37   "I beg . . . truth . . .]   Cut for the book edition.

668.12–30   Cross stared . . . Party, no."]   Cut for the book edition.

671.29–672.16   Houston continued . . . psychologically akin.]   Cut for the book edition.

681.38–682.14   He walked . . . and Eva.]   Cut for the book edition.

696.32–697.3   Before . . . passengers up.]   Cut for the book edition.

698.19–700.19   Were not . . . fear . . .]   Cut for the book edition.

707.33–708.5   "This Hilton, . . . money?"]   Cut for the book edition.

708.8–23   "No. . . . presence."]   Cut for the book edition.

709.20–27   All of . . . nothing . . .]   Cut for the book edition.

720.4–12   He lowered . . . this."]   Cut for the book edition.

739.9   Biblical passage:]   Cf. Exodus 20:5 and Deuteronomy 5:9.

761.4   That absolute . . . Acton,]   "Power tends to corrupt and absolute power corrupts absolutely," from a letter to Bishop Mandell Creighton, April 5, 1887. John Emerich Edward Dalberg (1834–1902), first Baron Acton, was a leader of liberal Roman Catholics in England who questioned the doctrine of papal infallibility enunciated in 1870 by the First Vatican Council.

772.3–4   . . . Man . . . NIETZSCHE]   Cf. *The Genealogy of Morals* (1887), "Second Essay, 'Guilt,' 'Bad Conscience,' and the Like," parts 1–2.

803.33–804.7   Cross envied . . . sighed.]   Cut for the book edition.

813.3   "trailing . . . glory"]   From stanza 5, line 7, "Ode: Intimations of Immortality from Recollections of Early Childhood" (1807), by William Wordsworth: "But trailing clouds of glory do we come / From God, who is our home."

813.3–15   Anthropologists, . . . happy.]   Cut for the book edition.

814.19–20   'Come . . . rest . . .']   Matthew 11:28.

835.19–836.39   Who? . . . him up?]   Cut for the book edition.

CATALOGING INFORMATION

Wright, Richard, 1908–1960.
    Later Works: Black Boy (American Hunger), The Outsider.
    Edited by Arnold Rampersad

    (The Library of America ; 56)
    1. Afro-Americans—Literary Collections. I. Title: Black boy
(American hunger). II. Title: The outsider. III. Series: The
Library of America.

PS3545.R815   1991   813'.52—dc20   91–60540
ISBN 0–940450–67–4 (alk. paper)

This book is set in 10 point Linotron Galliard,
a face designed for photocomposition by Matthew Carter
and based on the sixteenth-century face Granjon. The paper
is acid-free Ecusta Nyalite and meets the requirements for perma-
nence of the American National Standards Institute. The binding
material is Brillianta, a 100% woven rayon cloth made by
Van Heek-Scholco Textielfabrieken, Holland. The com-
position is by Haddon Craftsmen, Inc., and The
Clarinda Company. Printing and binding
by R. R. Donnelley & Sons Company.
Designed by Bruce Campbell.

THE LIBRARY OF AMERICA SERIES